The Witch's Box

KIM J COWIE

Kim J Cowie

To Carol with best wishes.

ISBN: 9781678485092

Independently Published by Bain Books.

Design by KJC

Author website: http:// kimjcowie.com

DEDICATION

To my late parents, with love.

Other books by Kim J Cowie:

The Plain Girl's Earrings
Deadly Journey

ACKNOWLEDGMENTS

With special thanks to Gil Harris and Chris Kershaw, whose comments and suggestions helped to greatly improve this novel.

Thanks also to beta readers Ashby Bailey, Sue Beasley, Tahnee Campbell, John Gosling, Chris S and L M deWit for their useful, encouraging and enthusiastic comments.

And to the many CC forum critiquers who suffered through earlier versions of this story.

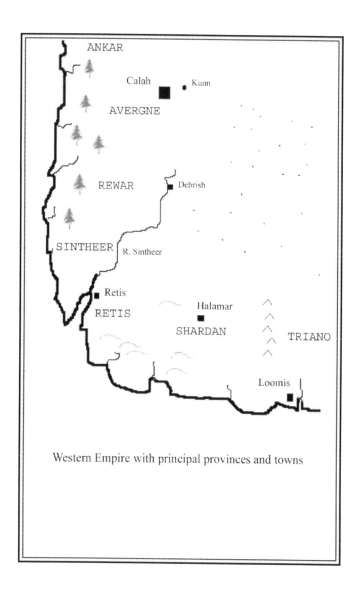

Western Empire with principal provinces and towns

-1-

With excited hands, Maihara tore the layers of coloured paper wrapping that hid her birthday present. The paper was printed with bright patterns enticing to a child's eyes. The other presents sent to her room had been labelled as gifts from her father, younger brother and sister. This one bore no label to indicate the sender, yet it had found its way to her room, a fussy place of drapes, bulky padded furniture and worn red carpets, high up in the juvenile wing of the Imperial Palace at Calah.

From the inner layer of wrapping she extracted a small black box fashioned from cunningly jointed ironwood, an exotic and dense material. It had no visible lid or catch or hinge, but when she pressed at where a catch might lie it sprang open at her touch.

Inside was a slip of paper sealed with a blob of red wax, and below that several rolled and flattened scrolls. Below the scrolls a bright mirror lay in a nesting of red velveteen.

She made a face and pushed the box aside. The box was weird, and she'd hoped for some jewelled ornament she could wear now that she was fourteen.

She broke the seal on the note and peered at the crabbed black handwriting.

'*You are a descendant of the Vimrashan witch-queens. Guard this box with care, and learn your words of power.*'

"What?" Maihara stared at the note, and at the items she had taken out of the box. Besides the mirror lay a shiny black stone and seven scrolls marked with difficult old lettering, two of them inscribed in a language she couldn't read. One of the vellum scrolls had come undone. She unrolled it and read words written in faded old-fashioned

1

script, words that said something about the spirit of a magician.

Was this a joke? But the objects looked old and worn, not a suitable present for a princess.

People whispered that her mother had been of Vimrashan blood, and even a witch. Remarks she overheard made it clear that being a witch was disreputable, shameful, even feared. She had loved her mother. Tears dampened her eyes. This was not funny at all.

A footfall sounded in the corridor. The maids would be coming soon to fit her into her new party dress. *Guard this box with care,* the note said. With a shiver of fear she jerked open a dressing-table drawer and hid the dark box and scrolls under coloured silk scarves.

The door of her room flung open and her sister Sihrima bustled in. Two years younger than herself, Sihrima was skinny with freckled cheeks and with dark hair like Maihara's but less curly. Most people thought Sihrima had a prettier face.

"What's that?" Sihrima asked. "Another present?"

"Some weird thing," Maihara said, caught off guard. She folded the sheet of note-paper to discourage Sihrima from reading it.

Sihrima snatched it and frowned as she tried to read the faded script. "Vimrashan witch-queens? Maihara's a witch!"

"No I'm not." Maihara made a lunge and retrieved the note. "It's somebody's idea of a mean joke. Now clear off."

Sihrima smirked and stuck out her tongue. "Witch."

Maihara grabbed her sister, hugged her for a moment and bundled her out of the door. "Out! I have to change."

In the darkest curtained recess of her bedroom lurked a metal-bound chest where stored her most personal things, asides from her shelf of precious books. She crammed the scrolls back into the ironwood box and shut it, the lid seam once more invisible. Pulling out some items to make room, she thrust the box into the bottom of the chest, under discarded toys and dressing-up clothes.

The torn wrapping paper and outer box lay beside a small, battered doll she could not bring herself to throw out. It was carved from wood, painted in natural colours, with glued-on hair and tiny garments. She was a little old to play with dolls, now strange and embarrassing things were happening to her body. It was changing and filling out from that of a child to that of a young woman. She missed her mother, who would come to her bedside during her childhood illnesses and reassure her that she would recover.

The maids arrived and dressed her in a new red dress, a creation of layers, ruffs and flounces in lace and velvet, embroidered and sewn with pearls, that hid her puppy-fat. She descended to the floor below where her teenage ladies-in-waiting ooed and aahed over the dress. The ladies took over from her maids and escorted the birthday princess along corridors with moulded ceilings, hung paintings and woven carpets into the next wing, where they descended a grand double-bow staircase, crossed a marble floor and finally entered the Great Hall, lit by daylight from above. The hall had originally been a courtyard, but Maihara's great-grandfather had covered it with a part-glazed roof. By night it was lit by a score of chandeliers. A noise of hundreds of voices greeted her as she entered a space decorated with ribbons, the walls a riot of gilded carving. Long tables were set with white cloths, patterned crockery and silvered cutlery, and servants bustled to and fro with platters of cake and confectionery, and bottles of wine.

As she made her entrance, announced at the double doors by a herald, guests and family applauded. Nobles in elaborate, brightly coloured robes and gowns, sparkling with jewels, lined the two long sides of the room. Her father, the Emperor Cordan, fourth of the Zircon dynasty, sat on the raised dais at the far end. He was almost bald, with a brown forked beard and long moustache, now sprinkled with grey. He wore layers of robes of sober colours, all embroidered with significant designs and trimmed at the edges with silver braid. On his head he wore a simple circlet of gold with a few jewels in it, as if to show that he did not need the kind of overstated crown that mere kings wore.

The noble guests stepped aside, smiling and applauding as she made her way through the hall past the tables laden with party delicacies. At the top was a polished table with gilded legs. Maihara was to stand by it and receive gifts from nobles seeking favour with the Imperial Family. Young princesses didn't get to sit in the Imperial presence.

Soon, she stood by the table, graciously receiving wrapped gifts as guests brought them up. The first sycophant in line was announced as the Count of Debrish, and handed over a package wrapped in red glittery paper. Maihara thanked him courteously and handed over the present to a servant who opened it and displayed the contents to the crowd. It was a blue dress covered in spangly ornament, and she suspected it would not fit her. She complimented the giver, before liveried servants folded the dress and took it away. The next gift was a fine doll in court costume, followed by a live and brilliantly plumaged bird in a silvered cage, a brooch that glittered enough to make her eyes hurt, and a small keyboard instrument with an inlaid case. She would rather have been given some rare books.

Her father leaned forward in his throne-like seat and spoke to her in a voice tinged with formality rather than warmth. "Are you pleased with your gifts, daughter?" His tone toward her had been a bit cooler of late.

Maihara looked up, catching a glimpse of a triumphalist allegorical ceiling painting over the Emperor's throne. "Yes, Your Grace, very pleased." She made a curtsy.

Sihrima, now in a more formal dress, chose this moment to run up to the throne. The Emperor gave an indulgent smile. Encouraged, Sihrima announced, "Father, Maihara got a weird present delivered to her room. A witchy present. The note says she's a Vim-rashan."

Maihara was all too aware that her sister's clear voice was carrying to the nearer part of the glittering crowd. She already knew what the court thought of Vimrashans. It struck a raw nerve.

"I am not!" she shouted back.

The sound of chatter in the hall hushed as her voice echoed from the roof. Her father's head jerked around and he glared at her. The guests made nervous titters. Everyone in the hall must have heard her shouting in a most un-demure and unladylike manner. A heat of embarrassment warmed her body.

"Who has been filling your head with this vile nonsense?" Cordan demanded in a harsh voice that frightened her. She had never before heard him speak to members of his family in this tone. She recoiled, unsure which princess was being addressed.

"We don't have any such foul creatures in our house," her father said, in a low voice. "Go to your room at once."

"But -" Sihrima bowed her head. The servants hustled her out of a side door.

Maihara took a breath, and called for the next present, anxious to restart the proceedings before her father banished her as well. Cordan glared, but did not intervene as another noble advanced with a fixed smile, holding out a fancily wrapped package. Instead, her father beckoned to one of his courtiers, and when the man approached the throne, gave him brief instructions Maihara could not hear.

Her heart beat fast with the shock. Everything had been fine till Sihrima mentioned the Vimrashan witch-queens, when her father had turned in an instant from indulgent father to angry Emperor.

With the present-giving completed, Maihara circulated with her ladies-in-waiting among the guests, accepting birthday wishes and compliments on her red dress. The guests were helping themselves to finger-foods from the tables and accepting glasses of pale wine from servants. Maihara caught several nobles staring at her in an odd way.

Young Lady Amarin, one of Maihara's teenage ladies-in-waiting and companions, leant over and whispered in Maihara's ear. "What was your sister talking about?"

"She was just being annoying, as usual," Maihara whispered back.

"What a pest she is, Your Grace."

With a heavy heart, Maihara returned to her room, where the maids took off the party dress, changing it for a plainer everyday outfit. She wiped away a tear. As soon as she finished changing, a firm knock came at the door of her dressing room.

One of the maids answered, admitting a thin-faced man clad in a hooded jacket stitched with the number 5, and dark trousers.

The newcomer faced her. "Your Grace, the Emperor has charged the Imperial Fifth Bureau to investigate. You have received a note?"

"Yes," Maihara managed.

"May I see it, please?"

In her haste, she had forgotten to put the note back in the box. She picked it up and saw only a blank sheet of thick, pink-tinted paper with a crease across it. She turned it over. Still blank. This was very odd. The writing had disappeared. That made it more likely the self-sealing box was magic, and so were its odd contents.

Wordlessly, she handed the unsealed note to the agent.

"This is blank."

"It is now. It faded."

The agent seemed to accept this. "Anything else come with it?"

"With it?" *Guard this box with care*, the note had said. If that box had any connection to her mother, witchy or otherwise, she had no intention of giving it up. But they'd assume the note came in some package. Her eyes shifted to the left, where the wrapping and doll lay.

With a swift movement, the agent picked up the doll and turned it over in his hands. "Did this come with it?"

"Yes," she said in a low voice. The lie came easily.

"Wrapped in what?"

"That wrapping."

The agent gathered up the wrapping in which the box

had come. "Cheap," he said as if to himself. "We'll deal with this."

He turned back to her. "Did you see who delivered this?"

"No, I didn't."

"When did you discover it?"

She had to think. It would be safer to approximate the truth. "Around the eleventh hour of the morning."

"And at what earlier time was it definitely not here?"

She glanced at his ill-favoured face. "When I got up, I suppose."

"So how did it arrive unseen by you?"

"I went to bathe and be dressed."

"And it was here on your return?"

"I assume so."

"What do you mean, Your Grace? Either it was or it wasn't."

"Several presents had arrived while I was out of the room."

The agent persisted with more questions to Maihara and the maids before he gave up and left.

"What a nasty man," the youngest maid said after the door closed.

"Hush," the second maid said. "He's only doing his job."

Soon, Maihara found herself escorted along corridors, past guest chambers, past function rooms adjoining the Great Hall, and through a metal-bound door into the so-called Fort, a castle-like tower attached to one end of the palace. Nowadays the Fort was used as a guardhouse. She was escorted into a distinctly utilitarian room, with a stone floor, walls of green-painted brick, and lit by a slit window with a metal bar across it. A set of partitioned shelves filled with papers occupied one wall.

Two men in tight-fitting, dark Fifth Bureau uniforms sat at a scuffed wooden table. They had cropped hair and hard-looking faces. They questioned her further about her magical Vimrashan present. Their manner, respectful but serious, confirmed her impression that Vimrashans and magic were discouraged as dangerous and anti-Imperial.

To Maihara's relief, nobody mentioned a box, as if her sister had not read that far or had only seen the rough outer pinewood box. It seemed they had not found out how the mystery package got among the other presents.

"You may be wondering why we're investigating this, Your Grace?" said one. "A law was enacted after the fall of the last of the Vimrashan witch-queens, barring any female of the Imperial line from practising the dark arts."

A chill shivered down her spine.

She deduced that they had already questioned Sihrima. "Your sister confirmed that the vellum had writing on it," one of the agents said. "But it's blank now. That suggests magic."

"Or light-sensitive ink," said the other agent.

"And there's that nasty-looking doll," said the first agent. "You have no idea who could have sent this?"

Maihara shook her head. This might have something to do with her dead mother, who had died in childbirth when Maihara was seven, but she dared not ask.

"Please tell his Grace or ourselves if you receive anything else," said the first agent. "We'll dispose of these evil things."

A small fire burned in a grate at one side of the room. The agent turned and thrust the wrappings, the vellum and the doll into the flames. The doll's dress and painted face smoked and darkened before flaring into flame.

Maihara allowed herself a moment of sadness. Animosity against the agents stirred in her. She had liked that doll, however grown-up she felt herself to be. It had come to her while her mother was alive.

Maihara later had the satisfaction of learning that Sihrima had received a scolding for unseemly behaviour at a grand function.

Next day, Maihara was summoned to her father's private study, a room furnished with masculine restraint, lined with bookshelves and decorated with several ornate brass-faced clocks. Odd mechanisms littered a side table. Her father regarded her with a cold eye and rebuked her for unladylike shouting. "You're starting to look and sound like your mother."

Why was it bad to be like her mother? Surprise and indignation stirred in her, but she lowered her head. This was the Emperor Cordan speaking.

"I'm sorry, Father, I'll try to do better in future."

"An Imperial Princess should always behave with dignity."

"Yes, Father." *Anything to appease him and get me out of here.*

Back in her room, Maihara reflected that her father must have been angry with her mother, over the rumours of her being a witch. If she looked like her mother, maybe that was why her father treated her with little warmth. But Maihara had no reason to think that she herself was a witch. It was so unfair. It made her all the more determined to keep the box hidden and investigate its magical contents further when it was safe.

-2-

Three years later:

Imperial Princess Maihara was not pleased with her tutor. "Why do we have to study this dusty dead language?" She thrust a thick book across the scarred desk-top with an irritated gesture, knocking a pen to the floor. "There's a war going on out there."

Maihara's chaperone, a young woman dressed in sober dark colours, looked up from her stitching.

Outside the schoolroom window, beyond the descending rows of tiled roof-tops, beyond the city wall, troops were digging in on fields of green crops. The flat Calah plain stretched to a hazy horizon. Beyond that horizon were more plains, and beyond them lay hills, small cities, rivers and the forested north. She had never been there, and now that war had swept over them they were unreachable. Instead she was confined to this dull palace.

Maihara eyed Tutor Demophon across the schoolroom table. An ill-favoured young man with freckles and sandy hair, wrapped in a scholar's thin grey cloak. From what her servants said, Demophon was the third son of a minor noble who must have had connections to get his son appointed as her tutor.

"The Army will take care of the war, Your Grace. But my instructions are to teach you languages, literature, poetry and courtly protocol. You may find them useful someday."

Lit by one ornate window, the room was plainly finished, with scarred furniture and scribbled-on walls, a contrast to the dazzling splendour of the public parts of the Palace. A bookcase filled with used books stood against one wall, and on the other side shelves bearing seed trays, plant pots, rock samples, brass mechanisms. The walls bore pinned on drawings and diagrams, and an oil portrait of the Emperor. From a hooked stand hung a complete replica of a human skeleton, carved from wood and painted a scabby white.

"Learning how to wage war might be more useful, since it's going on directly outside." She jabbed a finger toward the window.

"Your Grace, it's not a suitable subject for young ladies."

"Let me be the judge of that." The humid summer heat increased her irritation. She swept across the room with a flounce of skirts, and slid up the opening section of the window.

A murmur of sound wafted in from the city below, along with a sound of distant banging. The schoolroom was high up and afforded a safe view over the unsettling activity beyond the defences.

"Who's that down there, beyond the city wall?" Lines of men were digging a ditch and bank parallel with the city defences, dark figures swarmed like ants, and a mass of tents blocked the northern road. Among them, wooden towers and timber frames were being erected. The brothers of her lady companions opined that these were siege engines. She turned away from the swarm of warriors on the plain and gestured at her tutor. "That's the rebel army, isn't it? The enemy? Why are they there? Nobody will tell me anything."

Demophon formed a nervous smile. "May I speak frankly, Your Grace?"

Maihara gave a nod.

"It's true that the rebels have advanced to within sight of the walls, but to express anxiety is to show a regrettable lack of confidence in your father and the Imperial armies. Nor need you trouble yourself with the rebel demands."

Maihara faced her tutor across the room. "What demands?" It was common knowledge that the rebels had allied with the Dhikr invaders who ravaged the Imperial lands from the north. "Everyone else said they're just bad people who want to overthrow my father."

"Oh, they are. Their general Tarchon is demanding that slavery be abolished, and that people not be sold into bondage for failure to pay debts. They want the rich to pay taxes."

"And that's bad?" Maihara asked.

"Very bad. It would disrupt the way things are done in the Empire." Demophon's tone bore a whisper of sarcasm.

The door opened. An imposing man in dark garments entered and stood frowning at them. His jacket was braided with lace, his waistcoat jewelled.

"Lord Farnak." Maihara did not curtsy to the hard-faced and greying Lord Chancellor, but waited while he lowered his head in greeting. As Imperial Princess, the eldest of the Emperor's three children, she outranked him.

Demophon's face paled. He cut off what he had begun to say in mid-syllable and bowed low.

"Why aren't you teaching the Princess her lessons, Tutor? That's what you're paid to do, you idler."

Demophon flinched. He bowed again. "The Princess was asking about the war, Milord."

"I can see it from here," Maihara said. She pointed out of the window at the tents and lines of armed troops. "Isn't it time you did something to drive them away, Lord Farnak?"

Lord Farnak sighed. He directed a severe look at the tutor and pointed toward the door.

When the door closed behind Demophon, Lord Farnak turned to Maihara, ignoring the dark-haired chaperone who sat in a corner, head bent over her sampler work. "Please don't worry, Your Grace. The Emperor and his generals will soon defeat these Monist scum."

"So why not send out soldiers to destroy them?" Maihara asked.

"Well, it's more complicated than that," Farnak said, with a forced smile. "But don't worry your pretty head about it."

Maihara bristled. "Aren't you trying to gloss over inconvenient facts, Farnak?" She aimed a finger at the mass of besiegers visible beyond the walls, who were bringing forward lengths of timber. "They're outside the gates, rather than being a hundred leagues away. That makes me worry."

"I understand, Your Grace. But you are in no immediate danger."

Maihara was not convinced. "Suppose my father and my brother are killed in an enemy attack. Who will be in charge of the Empire then?"

Her little brother Prince Persis had a ceremonial position as a Marshal of the armed forces. The previous month, he had been reviewing troops outside the city in an event meant to demonstrate the Imperial Army's might in the face of the gathering revolt, when a noise and a glare of sunlight on armour had startled his horse. He fell off, scraping and bruising himself.

Farnak smiled thinly and nodded. "You will, Your Grace. But there would be a council of regents to make the decisions for you."

A flash of annoyance sparked. They meant to prevent her having any power, just because she was a girl. "So?" She paced across the room. "My father and his father before him fought to keep power in the Imperial family and not hand it to a cabal of nobles. That's what this war's about too, isn't it? But you want to take power away from your Empress and hand it to a council of nobles. If that's the kind of thing you want, why not talk terms with the rebels?"

Farnak's jaw dropped.

Had she gone too far in challenging Farnak? As Chancellor, he had control of the Empire's finances. He had the swagger of a powerful man, who could seize estates or even have people beheaded. Recently she had heard rumours that ruthless intrigue against those who stood in his way had aided his rise to power. Would he drop his mask, or pretend to be cross, telling her not to be a silly girl? She folded her arms and fixed him with a stare.

Farnak eyed her, as though he was making up his mind on some point. "I can assure you, Your Grace, in that event we would not attempt to remove your Imperial powers, merely advise."

"I'm glad to hear it, Farnak. Then perhaps you could spare a few moments to tell me what is really happening?"

Farnak lowered his head in assent. "I have business to attend to, before reporting to the Emperor at a Council meeting. I don't know what nonsense the servants have filled your head with. But in essence, we have ignored the insolent demands of this rebel, Tarchon, for some time. Then the Dhikr suddenly invaded from the north-east, and Tarchon allied himself with them. We sent out most of our army, a large force, to crush them."

Maihara listened in silence. Why had this powerful noble sought her out like this? He had more important things to do than talk to schoolgirls. Something dramatic must be afoot.

She glanced at the window. "And did they crush them? Doesn't look like it."

Farnak's gaze slid to the scene outside, where a further group of men was advancing from the north toward the rebel lines. A faint sound of hammering drifted in at the window. "Unfortunately, our troops had little experience of war, and when they met the Dhikr, who are all hardened warriors, the result was not as we would have wished."

"You mean, they got beaten and fled." Her unease grew. "And now what?"

Farnak looked away. "We are not in any immediate danger. The city wall makes a stout defensive position. So long as our troops man it, we can keep the enemy out."

She could see the top of the high wall, with its walkway and outer parapet. Only a handful of soldiers atop it faced the rebel army. "But if we venture outside the walls, even if we can get the men to go...?" Maihara drew a finger across her throat.

Farnak smiled, a smile that affected only his mouth. "Please do not worry, Your Grace." He lowered his voice. "The Emperor informs us that his workshops in the south-eastern sector of the Empire are producing an army of mechanical soldiers, which will soon march to our aid, and exterminate the scum outside."

Why was he telling her this? It sounded like another of her father's mad ideas. She had never seen anything more mechanical than a clock or gilded automaton.

"Oh really? Mechanical soldiers? How soon?" She tried to keep disbelief out of her voice.

"We don't doubt the Emperor's word for a moment, but we are concerned about the timescale." Farnak's tone and expression were giving nothing away.

Maihara nodded. Unless she heard more, she'd assume that Farnak was no more convinced than herself. "Any other concerns, Lord Farnak?"

"There is less food in the city than we supposed. Soon we will have to give priority to feeding the soldiers. And the enemy has been shooting their catapults into the city. It's starting to provoke unrest."

"They've what?" That was something else they had not told her.

"You can't see it from this side of the city, Your Grace."

She looked away from Farnak, and out of the window. "So, the siege? Are we going to wait till the food runs out? You need to do something."

"We are, Your Grace, but it's proving difficult."

"You mean you can't drive the enemy away, or give them what they're asking for?"

"Neither of these things are really possible, Your Grace."

Lord Farnak was powerful, but today he looked old, tired, and wrinkled. His beard and moustache needed a trim and a few brown crumbs clung to his dark cloak.

"You don't think they'll get in, do you?" She sensed that the Chancellor was as worried and unsure as herself, and she regretted now not having made more progress in investigating the magical box she had been given three years ago. It might have some relevance in the present crisis.

"We're hoping it won't come to that, Your Grace. Don't worry."

"Thank you, Farnak," Maihara said. "I hope they're not going to involve my brother in any of this."

"We might want him to appear and hearten the troops."

Maihara sighed. "He's in a funk and refusing to get on a horse again. They should never have tried to make a soldier of him."

Farnak's shoulders slumped. "I suppose we could put him on a podium."

His eyes were directed downward, over her dress. It was a new one, richly brocaded, more tightly fitted and with a lower neckline than she usually wore. She felt warm, and not because of the summer heat. Farnak was not looking at her as if she was furniture, as her tutor did. He eyed her as if she was a woman.

"You remind me of your mother, Princess."

"Surely not," Maihara murmured. Maihara's dark-haired mother was long dead. Thoughts flitted across her mind. The war. Old Farnak was being creepy. Maybe he had admired her mother too? She was seventeen now, almost an adult.

Lord Farnak shook himself. "My apologies."

"No need to apologise, Farnak." She took a step back. "What of the province of Shardan? Don't they have troops?" Her geography lessons had recently touched on the prosperous wine-growing region of Shardan, which lay some distance south-east of Calah, near the southern ocean coast and south of the central desert.

"Principality. They do, and they are not too far away, but the Emperor will not entertain their use."

"He won't? Better them than the Dhikr," Maihara said.

"Some ministers privately agree, but it's not wise to express such sentiments in your father's hearing." Farnak met her eyes, as if issuing a warning.

She nodded. "Quite." The Shardan resided in a country to the south. They had armies, and were loyal, but had supported a losing faction in a previous dynastic struggle that failed to unseat the Zircon family. Old history, to most people other than her father.

Lord Farnak gripped the lapels of his coat. "It's been interesting to speak to Your Grace. Perhaps it's time to broaden your political education. Have you ever thought of attending the Grand Council meetings?"

It surprised Maihara. "Oh, what? I'd be interested, but they won't let me, will they?"

"Who knows, Your Grace?" Farnak made a small bow. "I'll make your wishes known. Now excuse me, I really must go. I'll have a word with your tutor."

Farnak turned and made a brisk exit. The sound of his voice calling for Demophon and giving orders filtered from the passageway.

The lanky tutor re-entered the schoolroom, and bowed. "Your Grace, Lord Farnak has suggested that I should educate you further in the functioning of the Empire. I'm afraid it will be dull for you, but a suggestion from the Lord Chancellor is not one I can lightly ignore."

"No, please carry on," Maihara said. Her initial show of firmness seemed to have impressed Farnak. He had not been explicit about the reason for his visit, but he clearly had some idea in mind. Did he see her as a successor to her increasingly deranged father and ineffectual brother? Maihara had always believed she was clever.

This was an exciting development.

Maihara took notes with pen and ink as Demophon launched into his new subject. He lounged on an unused desk while fingering the edge of his thin cloak.

"The Inner Council meets frequently to advise your father on matters of state, and it includes officials with real power and whoever his favourite is at the time." Demophon gave the smirk she had seen many times before. "Then the

Varlord Order of Knights - they're not a state institution, but their members fill many major and minor posts of State."

Maihara's pen scratched busily. Demophon's mood had lightened in the absence of the Chancellor, and for a third son, her tutor appeared better informed than most on the subject of the levers of power.

"You seem to know a lot about this, Tutor."

He smiled, as though flattered. "I like to keep up with current affairs, Your Grace."

She sensed that he found her interest amusing. *What an irritating little man.*

Two servants brought in platters of bread, cheese and sliced meats for lunch. The tutor started to eat then excused himself and went out.

The chaperone lowered her stitching. "Lord Farnak appeared to appreciate the sight of Your Grace in this new dress."

Maihara shot her a look. Kafnis was tall and lithe, with wavy black hair pulled back in a bun from an unremarkable face. She spoke in a marked low-class accent and though not much older than Maihara was wont to offer her opinion when no people of authority were in earshot.

Maihara had been wondering what Farnak saw, other than a pudgy girl with a mass of dark curling hair. Farnak did appear to appreciate her dress, but it was none of the maid's damned business. Kafnis was in the habit of saying things that were not quite insolent, but which came within a hair's breadth of being so.

"Who can say, Kafnis? Perhaps."

"I have noticed that Tutor Demophon never remarks on your appearance, Your Grace."

Maihara had been thinking the same thought. She might as well be a statue, for all the effect she had on the young man. "Yes, indeed."

"There's talk that he prefers boys, Your Grace." Kafnis gave a brief grin.

The maid's directness startled Maihara. "Excuse me?" She was dimly aware that such preferences existed. "Isn't that rather unnatural? What does he want to do with them?"

"I couldn't say, Your Grace." The maid looked down at her needlework.

Maihara did not press the point. She knew there were topics the servants were not permitted to discuss with her, and they could be punished by having body parts painfully removed. She had seen a servant's face freeze in a rictus of fear when questioned too closely by an Imperial child, as when Sihrima had asked what two of her father's dogs were doing.

"At least, we don't have to worry about him mooning over you, or looking down your, er - bodice."

Maihara felt her face reddening. "You shouldn't be talking to me about that sort of thing. If the Emperor found out—" She didn't want the tutor staring down her cleavage, but Kafnis' bluntness was disturbing.

Kafnis frowned and looked away.

"Forget we mentioned this," Maihara said, stiffly.

"I'm sorry, Your Grace." Kafnis's burr had the barest hint of mockery.

It irked Maihara that it had never occurred to her to have the same suspicions concerning her tutor. It gave her an uneasy feeling. Kafnis should be more discreet. But she enjoyed having someone of a different class to talk to, even if the stuffier palace officials disapproved. Not that she knew much about Kafnis, whether she had family or where in the Palace she slept at night when not sleeping in Maihara's anteroom.

After lunch, as Demophon made diagrams with skritchy scratchy chalk on a blackboard, explaining the organisation of the army to her, a mild spirit of rebellion seized Maihara. Behind him and below, she could see the rebel army continuing its work. It would be interesting to hint that she was not satisfied by the conduct of the war, or the imperial policies, and see what further information her tutor would volunteer. Demophon took the bait, and explained to his apparently avid student that there were groups in the provinces who loathed her father's rule and wanted to make terms with the rebel Tarchon and his Dhikr allies. Many of the rebels were adherents to the new Monist or One God religion. Soon the fellow was explaining the demands of the rebels with more even-handedness than was proper.

"You're so wise, Tutor. Indeed, these injustices are distressing," Maihara had said in a low voice. "So is there rebel sentiment inside the city? Is there any danger of an uprising?"

"I couldn't say, Your Grace." Demophon steepled his fingers. "There may be sentiment in some quarters in favour of the rebels, just as there clearly is elsewhere." He glanced at the door and appeared to be choosing his words with care. "There's no group that could hope to hold out against the soldiers. They're afraid of what the Varlords would do to them and their families if they failed." Maihara was well aware of the Varlords, an elitist military order who held many army and government offices. She had seen them at various ceremonial functions and receptions, wearing gaudy armour or expensively tailored uniforms and looking pleased with themselves.

"You've told me that there were popular riots of protest in the northern cities. And that there is a large militia here, drawn from the small traders and artisans who are heavily taxed? Can we rely on them? What if they were all to make trouble at once, and try opening the gates, or something?"

Demophon nodded. A smile hovered over his thin lips. "Your analysis is very perceptive, Your Grace. But the city has garrisons, including the Palace Guard. They would be sent out to quell any dangerous disorder."

"Do you have a map?" Maihara asked. Unknown to her tutor, she had made a study of various books on warfare, including Gar Harth's classic military manual 'On War.'

"Of the city?" Demophon scrabbled under a pile of books and papers.

The maid looked up, while Maihara tapped her fingers.

Demophon slid a printed map of the city of Calah in front of her. It showed the principal gates, state buildings and streets. He gave Maihara an expectant look.

She tapped the map with a manicured finger. "Where are the garrisons?" She'd show him that a woman could understand military tactics too.

"At the Magunian Barracks, here, and at the Palace." Demophon pointed to a large hatched block near the centre of the map.

"And where are the rebel armies?"

"Here, and here. All round."

Maihara frowned. "And this is a gate, here?"

"Yes, Your Grace. The Semean Gate."

Maihara placed her finger next to the gate. "If I was a clever and treacherous rebel, I'd arrange a disturbance on the wall around here, to draw defenders away from the gate. Then I'd have my best fighters attempt to storm this gate from the inside and get it opened. To stop the garrison responding, I'd have another disturbance start in the low city here." She tapped at the opposite side of the map. "And this big street here?" She pointed to a wide street near the Semean Gate.

"Gorran Avenue."

"I'd have rioters block this with carts, burning things, to stop the garrison soldiers marching or riding down it."

Demophon stared at her open-mouthed. "By the One God, let's hope that our secret services are vigilant," he said at last.

The memory of her own encounter with the Fifth Bureau three years ago put her in a disagreeable mood. "Smaller towns and cities fell, I'm told. There's something wrong with this country."

Demophon smiled. "I'm sure all will be well, Your Grace. This is the Western capital. We've just been frightening ourselves."

She had enjoyed showing off with Gar Harth's military lore, and it did not occur to her that Demophon might take note of her plan or pass it on.

By the end of the afternoon, Maihara had word from Lord Farnak that he had secured permission for her to observe at the Inner Council meeting which was to be held that evening. Her father, Farnak and other grand nobles would be present.

Accompanied by her maid, Kafnis, Maihara returned to her own room to change into a more formal outfit. The comfortably furnished bedroom had patterned carpets, a plain white ceiling, a dado rail and, rather scuffed by young nobles, wood panelling on the lower part of the walls. A stuffed toy still sat on top of the chest of drawers. No splendour here.

Maihara left her rooms for the distant council room in a state of excitement. They were taking her seriously at last, admitting her to an adult council. They descended stairs, along a corridor overlooking a courtyard, turned a corner and nearing the centres of power followed another corridor lined with paintings, showy furniture and vases, descending again to reach the council chamber next to the Great Hall.

The Inner Council met in a room of modest size, with two arcs of velvet-padded seats facing a dais with a throne on it. The ceiling had fussy gilded plaster mouldings, the walls were hung with a russet velvety wall covering, and the door and window surrounds were of dark carved wood. Lords, some of whose faces Maihara already knew from public functions, were entering and taking up seats. They came in ones and twos, men with hunched shoulders, mean faces, grey or balding heads, and russet cloaks, like an assembly of giant red moles. Chancellor Farnak greeted her with a polite nod and a discreetly raised hand. Gratified, she returned the gesture. An aide of the Chancellor showed Maihara to a seat at one side of the rear row, and soon a flunky gestured for everyone to rise. Her father, robed and wearing the chain of Empire, entered and seated himself on the throne. He greeted her with a frown.

With a dozen nobles gathered, the meeting got under

way after a brief prayer to the Nine Gods.

"These half-educated rascals and agitators in the Freedom conspiracy have no loyalty to the Emperor," a fat, greying lord complained. "Hang the lot of them."

"This military collapse is a disgrace," a sour-faced lord said. "Many of us have lost valuable estates in the provinces overrun by this rebellion."

"Our generals are incompetent," another chimed in. "Half of them bought their commissions." A fourth started to describe atrocities committed by the Dhikr hordes, till his neighbour pointed out that a lady was present.

She was not hearing much in the way of constructive advice to solve the crisis. Her father tapped on the arm of his throne.

"Have any of you gentlemen any proposals on how to proceed?"

A couple of Lords made suggestions in harsh resentful tones. The generals should be sacked, and the army sent into battle. The rebel leader should be assassinated.

Her father's forked beard wagged from side to side. "Anyone else?"

Maihara raised a hand.

Her father looked at her but said nothing.

Maihara had been invited to this adult gathering, so she saw no reason why she shouldn't speak up. "My Lords, what exactly do these rebels want? Is there any concession we can make that will pry them away from the Dhikr?"

Her father scowled and slapped the arm of his throne. "No concessions to traitors! You be quiet, girl."

She looked away, silenced, heart thumping, and resentful of this response to her sensible question. Lord Farnak caught her eye and shook his head.

Her father went on to make the same claims that Farnak had alluded to, but at greater length, hinting at distant Imperial workshops, secret processes and skilled artificers.

"Regiments of artificial soldiers will soon join battle to crush and terrorise these invaders," he promised.

Maybe this project was really going on, but Farnak,

who ought to know, had appeared unconvinced. She doubted that any mechanical army would appear anytime soon.

The Lords likewise nodded and glanced at each other, applauded politely but refrained from further comment. As her father adjourned the meeting, she caught his purple eyes on her.

"I'll speak with the Imperial Princess later," he said, giving her a cold look.

Maihara's heart jumped.

Sihrima was not in her room, but Prince Persis sat on the floor of his dayroom, with an array of model soldiers, painted bright green, arrayed on the floor before him. He looked up as she entered, and she ruffled his long, dark hair. "What's all this? Model soldiers?"

"Father had them sent to me last year. He said they were a suitable toy for a prince."

"Did he now?" Maihara glanced at the shiny green ranks. "What are you doing with them?"

"They're in review formation. A prince should know how to review a body of troops, and order them to march off. Lord Farnak said so."

"He did?" Maihara's curiosity was aroused. Why should Farnak care, and why would he take an interest in Persis? "And do you enjoy drilling with these?" She gestured to the models. "I thought dressing up and playing pretend games were your thing?"

"It's all right," Persis said in a voice that lacked enthusiasm. "Father said that dressing up was unmanly."

"You're not a man; you're a boy." Since that awkward conversation with Kafnis, Maihara had began to wonder about her brother and how soon her illiberal father would turn a judgemental eye on his only son, who showed little aptitude or inclination for manly pursuits and was happy to play with his sisters. Cordan seemed to like small children well enough, but she felt that she herself had been judged and found wanting - a whiff of witchcraft, too mouthy and too like her mother.

Persis looked at her in surprise.

"Are you still sore from falling off that horse?"

"It's not too bad now," Persis said in a low voice.

Maihara had never been encouraged to ride, but she felt some empathy. "You should insist on a better behaved horse. Unless you want to refuse the horseback thing altogether. You could have a worse accident next time."

-3-

Maihara ate a breakfast she scarcely tasted, and headed for the schoolroom in resentful mood, accompanied by her maid, Kafnis. Directly after her silencing at the Inner Council had come a chilly interview, and a message from her father restricting her movements to the nursery section of the Palace, supposedly for her own safety. It was accompanied by an instruction that she learn to behave as a young lady should. Maihara fumed with resentment. Her father was treating her like a child. If she was in danger, so were her siblings. It seemed more of a punishment for daring to voice unpopular opinions. Feminine common sense was not welcome.

A note inked on heavy white paper was pinned to the schoolroom door. The script looked to her like Demophon's handwriting.

"My apologies to Her Grace Imperial Princess Maihara Cordana and my noble employers, but I am obliged to leave my post without notice and attend to urgent personal business. I doubt that I shall be able to return. Ars Demophon."

"The tutor's gone," Maihara said. "Bother." There'd be no more useful lessons on how the state worked. She had an unpleasant feeling that the tutor's disappearance had some connection with the fiasco of the previous evening, or with his Monist beliefs. No doubt her father had wondered where her well-articulated curiosity about the rebel ideology came from. Demophon had only been in post for two months. Could it be that Farnak had managed it all knowing how she might react, that he saw her as someone who might ultimately challenge him and had placed her in a position where she would annoy her father and fall out of favour? Or was she over-thinking this? She shivered. She'd be more careful in future.

Not sure what to do with the note, she handed it to Kafnis, who turned it, glanced at it and slipped it inside her dress.

"Should I tell the senior staff, Your Grace? Or would you like some free time?" Kafnis emphasised the last few words.

"Better tell them," Maihara said. She did not want to give the impression she had in any way connived at Demophon's departure.

Without lessons, an unfilled morning loomed. Maihara contemplated various options: trying to study in the schoolroom by herself, filing her nails, reading in her room, or seeking the company of her ladies-in-waiting. A rebellious urge itched, prompting a more diverting option.

"Kafnis," Maihara said. "Let's go visit the library."

"With respect, Princess, are you allowed to?"

"I don't see why I can't still. We can say that Lord Farnak authorised it. He should, anyway. It's educational."

"Yes, Your Grace."

The Palace Library lay directly below Maihara's rooms. It extended through many small rooms and was known to some as the 'Infinite Library' because a visitor could walk forever, turning corners and going up and down stairs without ever reaching an end of the miles of shelving. In fact, as her previous tutor had explained, it ran around all four sides of an inner courtyard and was raised on the south side to clear the height of two airy reception salons. The rooms were all furnished in the same style and formed a complete circuit. Demophon had added an interesting appendix - the reason the library was so big was that it was supposed to house a deposited copy of every book published in the Empire, and this was not done for altruistic reasons, but to check on seditious books and enable the Fifth Bureau to harass their authors.

"Isn't there a back way to it through this?" Maihara asked. In the corridor that connected her rooms and the schoolroom was an inconspicuous door, set into the panelling and made of the same wood. Maihara pointed at it and waited as Kafnis tried to open it.

"It's locked, Your Grace."

Maihara bit her lip in indecision. If she couldn't take the shortcut, she'd have to take the long way round, through the double doors and down the main stair. It was much more likely that she'd be intercepted.

Kafnis jingled metal inside her dress and gave Maihara an expectant look.

"Can you unlock that?"

"Yes, Your Grace." Kafnis produced a bunch of keys and unlocked the door within moments. A cramped and dark service stair curled downward in a brick-lined shaft.

The library corridor, more ornate than the one above, was deserted. Maihara tried the double library doors. They were unyielding. The crisis could have caused the able-bodied library staff to be assigned to more essential duties, and the aged senior custodian who glowered at her if she so much looked at anything outside the juvenile section would be having an extended breakfast at this hour.

"Can you unlock this?" Maihara asked.

Kafnis stood so that Maihara could not see the lock, glanced up and down the corridor and worked for long moments. The right-hand door yielded with a click.

Maihara let the double doors close behind her and looked around. All was quiet. There was no sign of the staff, only the smell of old paper and furniture polish. She rejoiced at the opportunity to explore the adult sections of the library, without the staff watching her every move. She'd had enough of books containing fairy tales and mild romances, or adventures of courtly knights of old, the kind of fluff judged suitable for young ladies.

In the long room, shelves of polished hardwood lined the walls, filled with leather-bound books. Two projecting double-sided bays had the ends richly carved to suggest various arts such as agriculture and architecture. Sun streamed in through tall windows. A fly buzzed.

"Kafnis, please report Demophon missing, and then come back here".

"Yes, Your Grace." Kafnis, beside her, made a slight bow.

There might be books on Imperial governance if she could find nothing more interesting. Maihara hurried past the romance section to look at the forbidden books.

First, she found the room dealing with natural sciences, biology and human reproduction. An illustrated text with colour plates showed her just how humans produced babies. Her mother had died before Maihara was able to ask her about this, and it was a forbidden subject her servants dared not mention to her. *So that is how it works.* Ridiculous, but strangely exciting. Unfamiliar feelings warmed her.

In a shelf of books about sex, she found the answer to her question about the tutor and boys. Red-faced, she scanned the pages avidly. Bizarre, but just like men to have two ways of having sex. Did they enjoy this sort of thing?

Men increasingly found her own body of interest. Or said she resembled her mother. Hadn't her own father been the first to say that? He didn't seem to like her much. Because she looked like her mother, who was suspected of being a witch? So far as she knew, she herself wasn't a witch, even though she had worked a few processes with the aid of that box. Holding the mirror that came with it and looking into it let her see a grid of symbols, which when pointed at launched a few childish and amusing spells that lit a light, played tunes in her head or made brightly coloured little animals appear. It should have done more, but her fourteen-year-old self had been unable to make sense of the scrolls. With luck, a book would help her explore further. Somebody who thought she was a witch had sent her that box on her fourteenth birthday, and her father had certainly reacted as if he feared someone had tried to awaken her latent magical powers.

She should have tried harder at the beginning to learn

the secrets of that box, instead of playing with it, but a terrifying incident had discouraged her. She had dozed off while exploring the box and contents under her bedclothes, falling into a dream in which she had explored through successive grids of magical symbols, which began to flash red. Her fingers hurt, and she had awoken to feel the box nipping her fingers between its base and lid. Worse, something alive had been in the room with her. She had smelled its sulphurous breath and seen its gleaming red eyes. Something the size of a dog. Claws clicked across the floor. Heart beating frantically, she had pulled her hand out of the box, and the lid had shut with a clunk. The beast had reacted and stepped back. She had waited, holding her breath till she was dizzy. The beast faded, till she sensed it no more. A nightmare? The next morning, there had been chatter that a red-eyed dog roaming the Palace had menaced staff. After that shock, the box stayed hidden at the bottom of her chest.

With the rebels outside and the Empire in crisis, it might be wise to find out if that Box held useful magical powers that she could bend to her control, regardless of what her father or anyone else thought. This library was the place to seek further knowledge.

With thumping heart and swift feet she searched now for books on magic. Men were allowed to study occult arts, so there should be books here. But after passing through several rooms, all lined from floor to ceiling with a dizzying number of leather-bound books, she had found nothing. Given her father's dislike of magic this should not have been a surprise. A wall blocked her onward progress, but a narrow stair went up to the right. Below the stair a half-height door was set in the panelling. On it was a yellowed paper label that said 'restricted'. This was crossed out and 'withdrawn' written below. The door was locked.

She scowled at it, before taking out her nail file and attacking the lock. If Kafnis had done this, couldn't she? Apparently not, but in her pocket were the keys to her bureau drawer and jewel box that she could try. Within a couple of minutes she had turned the simple lock and pried open the door. Inside was a cupboard with a sloping ceiling and three shelves. Dusty leather-bound books lay in a heap. She pulled out one and wiped off the dust. *'Heresies of the Nine Gods'*. Boring.

She set aside 'Sexual Perversions of the Xingui Southern Aborigines' and 'Autobiography of the Whore Baraxa'. Near the bottom she found a book on magic, then another. With trembling hands she stacked them on the top shelf and examined them one by one. They were all by male authors and, judging by the pronouns, written for male magicians. Some of them looked like fanciful tales, but others had listings of spells. She picked up a musty-smelling volume with obscure green and gold symbols embossed on the cover. This looked more like the real thing. She flicked through the pages. The prologue was headed *'The mark of a true magician.'*

'Very few people are able to truly perform magick. A true magician must be descended from the line of magick ancestors, of the ancient and only empowered tribe in the kingdom of Sar. These are known latterly as Vimrashans. Those lucky to have inherited this skill, can incant a simple spell and be instantly connected to the occult dimension. They can then perform all manner of marvellous things.'

She quivered with a sense of revelation. Vimrashans? With shaking hands, she picked up the book and wrapped it in her shawl.

And what was the spell? It had to be in this book somewhere, a book written in old-fashioned dialect no longer written or spoken. The rest of the books looked less promising than this musty volume. She sighed and placed them aside. The last book to catch her eye was a slim tome on Monism, a religion of which she knew little, save that it seemed to be popular with the lower orders of society - and rebels.

With the books wrapped in her shawl, a large rectangular outline was still visible, pushing out the fabric.

She thought of exploring onwards, up the stair, and returning to her entry point that way, but the deserted and silent library, with its musty smell of old books, suddenly smelt creepy. Maybe it really did go on for ever? She shut the cupboard, retraced her steps to where Kafnis waited, and let the doors close behind her.

"Are you borrowing a book, Your Grace?" the maid asked, with a slight smile. "Something grown-up?"

Maihara looked the maid right in the eyes, but spoiled the effect by being unable to resist a grin. "No, Kafnis, I am not borrowing a book." There were times when having the irreverent Kafnis around was definitely fun.

The maid took her cue and dropped her gaze. "Of course not, Your Grace." Kafnis fell into step behind her. "Princess, should I carry that book you're not borrowing for you?"

"No thank you," Maihara replied, unable to keep the levity out of her voice.

"It's not about knights-errant or fairy tales, then, Princess?"

"No."

Maihara did not elaborate as she climbed the spiral stair. Her maid was being helpful, but the thought of Kafnis becoming aware of her illicit magical studies filled her with sudden alarm. Kafnis was fun but too sharp, and not very respectful or discreet. She might continue asking about the illicit books, or even try to look at them. It was time to have her moved on.

Alone in her room, Maihara laid the borrowed books on the table. From the bottom of the metal-bound chest that lay in the darkest recess of her dressing room, she took out the small black ironwood box.

It was locked and had no catch or fastener, but it opened at her touch, just as it had on various occasions during the past years. Inside it, the bright mirror lay in a nesting of red velveteen. As she lifted it out, she recalled her earlier failures.

Now, with the newly found magic book and renewed

purpose, she would try again.
***

In the cellar of an old house, Kafnis, her clothes now dusty and hung with the remains of cobwebs, used a wooden pole to prise up a stone trapdoor in the floor. With a lighted oil-lantern in one hand, she descended into the darkness. She had followed this way before, but she did not like going down here. The lantern's flickering yellow flame lit the grimy walls of old cellars and forgotten corridors as she passed.

The city mound of Calah was built up solely from the remains of earlier constructions on the site. Often, the old buildings had been roofed over instead of demolished, so that a warren of subterranean halls, rooms, and alleys underlay the present-day streets. The palace stood at the highest point of the mound, and secret ways snaked under its walls, to many parts of the city.

Kafnis followed the curve of the mound downhill, through a succession of cellars and passages. After crossing under the massive curtain walls of the old fort, she went along a buried alley lined with bricked-up doors and windows, noisome with the odour of sewage. She came to an ancient stairway, slimy green and encrusted with salts, that led upwards, and listened before climbing it. One could never be sure which refuges remained safe.

At the top was new masonry and a freshly planed wooden door. She knocked, set down the lantern and waited.

The door opened inch by inch until a slice of a male face appeared behind the gap.

"Kafnis!" he said. "What brings you here?"

She knew him. "Something's happened. There's something I need to ask. May I come in?"

The door scraped open, and the man behind it, balding and clad in a workman's smock, stepped aside. This was Citizen Nurgis, a rebel sympathiser. Behind him, four crudely made pikes leaned against a stone wall. A familiar lanky figure, dressed in the fashionable breeches and cloak that denoted some sort of clerk, stood by a table as if he were about to address the balding man.

Kafnis directed a finger at the dandy. "He's the one I wanted to ask you about. What's he doing here?"

"You two know each other?" Nurgis asked.

"That's the older princess's tutor, Ars Demophon. Or rather, ex-tutor." Kafnis said. "He's left his job at the Palace. Don't trust him."

"And this is one of the princess's maids," Demophon said. "I find her presence a cause for concern." The dandy glanced toward a wooden stair in one corner.

"Don't be alarmed. Miss Kafnis is sympathetic to our cause," the balding man said.

Kafnis jerked a thumb toward the tutor. "What's he got to say?"

"I heard that the Crown Princess attended the Inner Council and uttered some opinions rather related to my teachings that the Emperor didn't like. A servant overheard him giving the princess a tongue-lashing. I didn't like the way Lord Farnak took note of me, so I felt it wise to decamp."

Kafnis remained uneasy. "Our network's not been uncovered, then?"

The tutor drew himself upright. "Not to my knowledge."

"Tutor Demophon says he has a plan," Nurgis said.

Kafnis was unimpressed. She doubted that any plan hatched by this prancing fool would have merit.

Demophon cleared his throat. "Now is the time we should act, comrades. While the foreign armies of Tarchon and the Dhikr stand outside our walls, the forces of the oppressors won't dare withdraw from the defences to put down internal revolt." He raised a fist. "This is the time to take up our weapons."

Citizen Nurgis lowered his chin and stared at the floor. "Is this a good time, Tutor? I mean, I don't fault your argument. But if our small band rises alone, the soldiers'll kill us all."

"You may die in any case when the foreigners storm and sack the city," said Demophon, in an exasperated tone. "What have you to lose? We should arise in glorious brotherhood and unite with Tarchon's radical movement to defeat the rich oppressors and usher in an era of rule by the people for the people."

Irritated by his manner, Kafnis interrupted. "You're not addressing a public meeting here, Tutor. Get to the point."

Demophon harrumphed and cleared his throat. "The popular militia are already armed and ready to strike. They plan to rise tomorrow, and wait on you for word of a two-pronged attack."

Kafnis rolled her eyes upward. She was aware of Nurgis' group of radicals, poorly armed but organised and enthusiastic, engaged in infiltration. The militia were the town watch, now finding themselves reduced in status, replaced on patrols and mocked by the regular soldiers who had retreated inside the city and reinforced the garrison. She doubted that many were radicals. Nurgis raised his head, and a faint smile animated his sallow features. "What is the plan? Can we distract the garrison while the rebels attack? If we seize the city, we could join hands with the rebel army."

"The plan is this: Radical forces will create disorder in the Low Town near the Semean Gate," said Demophon. "Then the militia will assault the guard-posts near the wall and the Semean Gate itself." He paused for effect. "The garrison will respond by sending out men from the barracks. But radical forces will block the Govian Avenue with carts and burning barricades, to delay the troops. If they try to go around, they'll be ambushed in the alleys." He chopped his right hand into the palm of the left.

Kafnis was sure she had heard details of this plan before.

"What about the loyalists?" Nurgis objected. "There was a fellow called Sett hanging around, going on about traitors."

"Nobody's seen him lately," Kafnis said.

Nurgis nodded. "Your basic plan's not bad. But what about the details? We need times, numbers, communications. I suppose there'll be meetings? I'll pass the word on."

"I will speak to the militia," said Demophon. "We need to sort out details and times, and a channel for co-ordinating with the rebels outside."

"And what about me?" Kafnis asked. "Is it safe for me to stay in the palace? People are asking why Demophon skipped off."

"That depends on how discreet you have been," Demophon said. "You could leave, if you're anxious."

Nurgis nodded assent.

"I see. Maihara's certainly not like her father. I should stay there and speak up for her if the palace is captured. She doesn't deserve to be executed."

Demophon smirked. "You like her, don't you?"

Kafnis shrugged. She did like Maihara, sensing a rebellious kindred spirit, but she was not admitting her feelings to these two.

Demophon crossed to the door that led into the buried way. Kafnis followed, after excusing herself.

Outside, she caught the tutor's sleeve. "I'm watching you, Tutor. Did you think up this scheme by yourself?"

Demophon scowled. "The proposal came from my good self. Some may think it obvious, but they didn't propose it, and I'm the comrade making it happen."

"Really?" Kafnis said. "I'm sure I heard someone else describing the same scheme, quite recently."

Demophon winced and avoided her gaze.

They emerged further along the surface streets, coming up a steep, winding stairway inside a disused watchtower. Squeezing out of a half-blocked doorway, they came out into a familiar narrow alley. A few paces away was a door with flaking paint. With disquiet, Kafnis saw they had arrived outside the place where she had been lodging. Did the dodgy tutor know everything?

Demophon knocked and waited, glancing up and down the crumbling, rubbish-strewn passage.

A snaggle-haired young woman dragged open the door, dressed in a grease-stained smock that had once been blue. She passed a hand over her lined forehead and stared at Demophon and Kafnis in surprise.

"Citizen, may I speak to Citizen Shardin?" Demophon whispered. Kafnis caught the woman's eye and shrugged.

"Shardin is out, comrade," the citizen said with a glance up the alley.

Demophon, already looking nervous, seemed discomfited. "Do you know where?"

"At his workshop, trying to earn a little money to pay the new defence tax, and support us," the young woman said. "It's hard."

The wood-crafting workshop was not far away. Demophon opened a sagging door, and they entered a space heady with the smell of fresh wood. A couple of workbenches took up much of the space, and piles of raw stacked timbers and boards occupied the remainder. Dust sparkled in a single ray of sunlight.

They found Shardin working at his bench. Shardin, a thickset man, greying, and wearing a brown smock, left off his chiselling and, with a nod to Kafnis, came to speak to Demophon in a low voice while a journeyman sawed at the other end of the room. Demophon outlined his proposal for what the armed citizen militia should do when rioting broke out. Kafnis glanced around the workshop, half-listening. Hadn't he told Nurgis the militia were ready for this plot? Yet here he was trying to persuade a militia leader to take part. He was running between them with lies.

Just because Demophon had radical ideas, that wasn't enough reason to trust him. And she did not trust him at all.

"What if we're the only ones who rise up?" Shardin frowned, and his tone indicated doubt.

"You won't be. Groups of apprentices and street

fighters have agreed to stir up disorder. When rioting starts, instead of aiding the oppressors, attack the garrison."

The carpenter clenched a fist. "I'm with you, comrade. But I'll have to sound out those who may be with us. There are plenty Empire loyalists and faint-hearts among the ranks. I'll get back to you when I've spoken."

Demophon nodded.

-4-

The day after getting her hands on the magic book from the library, Maihara pored over it with the contents of the box spread on her reading table. The book was set in a blocky typescript and the ink faded, with parts annotated in coloured inks which had survived the ravages of time less well.

A knock came at the door, and the ornate handle rattled. Maihara froze, then opened another book on top of the magic volume.

Lord Farnak entered and made a slight bow. He glanced at the books, scrolls and mirror lying on her table.

Her hands shook and a quiver of fear transfixed her. Farnak had tidied himself up since his last visit, which suggested he had recovered his composure over the crisis. What if he realised what she was doing?

"Your Grace, how are your constitutional studies progressing?"

She composed herself and took a breath. "Well enough, considering, Chancellor. You startled me. I got notes from Demophon and a few books." Apparently Farnak still meant to educate her for a leading role.

"That rogue. We are seeking a suitable replacement." Farnak paused. "Do you have concerns about any of the other servants?"

"I don't think so. I asked for that Kafnis to be transferred."

"That's in hand. The Fifth Bureau suspect the young woman has rebel sympathies." Farnak's expression was bland.

"Like Demophon," Maihara said. She wouldn't be surprised if Kafnis identified with the rebels, but after her initial panic she was having regrets about requesting Kafnis' removal.

"Quite so. I hope you have not been influenced by these people, Your Grace."

Maihara tilted her head and looked him in the face. She was no rebel. "Meaning?"

"Your remarks at the Inner Council seemed more sympathetic to the rebel point of view than one might have expected."

"Common sense."

Farnak folded his arms. "Some might find the remarks sensible, but uttering them in the hearing of the Emperor at your first Council meeting was not. He won't hear any word of concession or compromise."

"Have you met anyone from Shardan?"

"I have met a few of them in the course of State business. Councillor Nardone, for instance, was a helpful person. But this does not seem a good time to pursue these contacts."

Maihara nodded. Farnak was a much more experienced politician than herself, and after her chastening experience she had to admit he was right. "I've been confined to my rooms."

"So I heard. Even if your confinement is rescinded, you shouldn't attempt to leave the Palace. There's been unrest in the city, complaints about food prices and a small pro-rebel demonstration. The militia are unreliable, and we had to send out Imperial troops."

When Lord Farnak had gone, Maihara took a deep breath. Sweat dampened her armpits, not entirely because of the summer heat. Farnak had not reacted as if seeing anything unusual, but she would have to be more careful. His visit still implied he had a scheme in mind that might involve her. It was flattering that he held her in regard, in contrast to her father's cold attitude. She closed the constitutional volume and uncovered her magical book. It was a day of rest in the city, but not for princesses with guilty secrets.

Since receiving the box, she had not been able to do more than a child's magic with it. Holding the mirror let her see a grid of symbols floating as if just behind the glass. Trying to touch them, resting a fingertip on the glass, would instantly change the grid to a diagram or picture and often launch a childish and amusing spell, like a comic animal that danced in mid-air, its growls audible only to her. It ought to do more, but she could not figure out how. With luck, the book would help her.

The problem was where to start. She had the old scrolls from the box, and the volume from the library. The scrolls were in more than one hand, in an old-fashioned spidery script, difficult to read and faded in places. They had been folded in the past, damaging the tops or middles of lines of script. Then there was the book, bulky and as thick as three of her fingers. It had a musty odour and looked much more comprehensive than the scrolls. And its pages bore printed text. The book looked like the place to start. She had already spotted the 'key-word' *Arisa* handwritten onto an opening page.

Her heart sank as she examined the pages, set in an ornate old-fashioned font. The wording was archaic, differing so much from current usage that it was almost another language. She couldn't read this at sight, but it resembled Old Sarish, a language she had studied with Demophon, and he had provided her with a bilingual dictionary. With effort, she made out the sense of the opening pages. It was introductory waffle, thanking other scholars and making tantalising references to 'the secret power of the ancients'.

She flipped open the book near the end. Here the text said spell elements could be connected into sub-units that acted on the world, and these could be assembled into chains of command thousands of elements long, that could be stored and assembled into new spells. Loops, warehouses, grids...? Was her translation accurate? She held her head in her hands. If doing magic meant mental effort and intellectual power on this scale, it was all over. But she'd prided herself on being clever. She should be able to work around this, do something simpler.

Frustrated, she shut the book and sought a window in the northern corridor, part of the section to which she was confined, and looking out over rooftops and down to the city wall and the plain beyond. The besieging army still sprawled there, and the dark mass of men and equipment looked denser.

With a sigh, she returned to the scrolls. They spoke of nebulous ideas, of feelings and powers, of energy and purification, but she was not finding any instruction on how to do magic. The last one however spoke of the gateway that opened the way to the secrets of the ancients. It described the gateway as a ghostly grid with symbols and writing on it.

Wasn't that the same grid that appeared when she touched the mirror? She read on. "To invoke the gateway, the Vimrashan has to project the word *'Arisa'*". She knew now that *'Arisa'* meant 'Connect' in the long-dead language. Her fourteen-year-old self had skimmed over this and read of the invoking, without getting it to work.

What did it mean by 'project', anyway? She took *'Arisa'*, and imagined herself pushing the word outward. Nothing happened. So that wasn't it, or she wasn't doing it right. Again, straining her mental muscles and clenching her hands. Still nothing.

What, then? *Arisa* as spoken word? She thought her pronunciation was not too far off. *Arisa* as curly font lettering? Still nothing. Yet this had to be the right track.

If this was about connecting, what was she connecting to? The mirror? Maybe, or maybe not. Connecting. The Palace fort had a speaking tube running from the dining hall to the kitchen. It sounded funny when she put her ear to it. She sensed an unfamiliar presence. What to do with the key-word? A rectangle of dots appeared in her mind's eye. She imagined writing *Arisa* there. What now? Push.

Go. Do. In a blink, the ghostly grid appeared.

She gasped aloud. It worked. She did not need to be touching the mirror. This was a breakthrough. The grid of symbols floated in the air before her. But wait - this was not quite the same. She recognised the coloured light spell and a few others. But no funny animals. And a couple of symbols like closed doors.

She scrabbled through the pile of scrolls. What was she supposed to do next? Ah, here: 'Mentally touch the upper symbol and invoke your personal key-word.'

That had to mean a key-word like the one in the book. Surely a key-word was written in the scrolls as well, but she had not found it. The scrolls did not say a lot more that looked useful concerning the gateway. Here was the thing: grasping the mirror was an easy route in, suitable for a fourteen-year-old novice, but using key-words was another method she could use anywhere, once mastered.

The grid persisted. Formerly it had gone away when she turned the mirror over or hidden it in its box. If she could not banish it, that would be troublesome. A quiver of unease gripped her. There had to be a logical way to banish it. '*Zarisa*', maybe? That must be it. The word meant 'break' or 'disconnect', the reverse of '*Arisa*'. At this probing thought, the grid of icons vanished. What a relief. She was making progress. She invoked and banished the grid a few more times, and started and shut off the coloured lighting spell.

The closed door symbols remained obstinately shut. She guessed that they gave access to other functions. But where were the key-words she needed? There were none in the scrolls, unless they were subtly hidden in the texts.

If only she had an adept to guide her. Without a teacher, she'd have to go over the book and scrolls word by word. And without delay, before the city fell. Judging by the jumpy way her father had reacted at the mere mention of magic, if he found her doing this the reaction would not be pretty.

First, she'd thumb through the first part of the book to

see if the earlier chapters looked easier. She opened the book at random and started to read and translate the description of a spell. 'Allow the spell to sense the object. Set the search zone on the spell's map to search for a similar object. Note that if the search area is province-wide, it may take several hours. Specify map or Zorian co-ordinate readout.'

She stared at the text open-mouthed. This was nothing like what she had expected. An icy chill ran down her spine. Province-wide! Who knew what would happen if she went fooling with something like this? If it didn't kill her, angry men might tie her to a pile of wood and set fire to it. And yet, what potential power.

Hunger gnawed at her stomach, and nobody had brought her any lunch. She put the book away in her battered chest and pulled the bell-cord for service.

While waiting, she took out the slim book on the Monist religion she had taken from the library, and thumbed through it. The state religion, the worship of the Nine Gods, had always seemed to her a cold and fear-filled affair, in which one prayed and made sacrifices to remote gods represented by graven images, in an effort to appease them lest bad things happen. She could never remember the names of all the nine gods. The Monist faith as set out in the book was radically different. It was more of a philosophy of life, exhorting people to behave, do good and help their neighbours. There was some promise of happiness in an afterlife, and punishment after death for evildoers. She had heard that Monism was favoured by the poor, and by radicals and rebels, and now its appeal to them was clear. There was only one god, who had no images, and they had a pair of prophets, one male and one female. This religion interested her more than the worship of the Nine Gods, which she only took part in because everyone at Court did.

Half an hour later, two of her ladies-in-waiting arrived in a swirl of embroidered skirts, flushed and with agitated faces. Amarin, the taller, had straight blonde hair, smooth pale skin, good teeth, pretty features and a pleasant personality. Berna, dark and shorter with a curvaceous figure, had equally good full-lipped features, a beauty spot and a quieter personality. They carried baskets containing Maihara's lunch. Amarin and Berna were daughters of obscure noble households, sent from their country estates to serve at court, and usually as frivolous as one would expect of girls with no responsibilities except to be agreeable company and eventually marry some nobleman. Her heart lifted at the appearance of her friends, and their visit filled Maihara with a momentary hope that life was going on as normal.

The duo dropped the baskets on the table and made apologies for the delay.

"What's going on?" Maihara demanded, responding to their agitation with a sudden unease.

"You wouldn't know, not being allowed out of these rooms," Berna said. She wrung her hands together. "Half the kitchen staff have been sent away. The ones left were slow. They said no fresh produce had come in."

"There are rumours of bread riots, Your Grace," said Amarin. She had a smudge of flour on her smart court dress. Amarin set out a wine-glass, then caught it with her sleeve. It fell with a clatter and rolled on the table-top. Maihara caught it, but said nothing. Amarin's family home, a small manor north of the city, had already been over-run by the rebel advance. They'd had to console Amarin for the loss of her estate after her parents and siblings fled to Calah. This latest news was not good. Flustered, Amarin grappled with the decanter.

"Mobs are shouting pro-rebel slogans." Berna set out the plates of fancy bread and meats of Maihara's lunch with shaking hands. "They say the rebels have female fighters. Can you imagine?"

Maihara could not.

"The Emperor sent the Palace Guard into the Low City to help restore order," Amarin said.

"That's nonsense; it was the garrison troops," said Berna.

"There are fires in the Low City," Amarin said. "The whole city might burn down."

Maihara tried not to be infected by their panic. She grabbed two slices of bread and slipped spiced meat and sauce between them. "Is it still going on?" she asked, gripping the food with greasy fingers.

"We saw distant flames and a lot of smoke while we were on our way here, Your Grace," Berna said.

She ought to reassure them. They were her friends and companions after all, though they were far from soulmates. They weren't as sharp as the disrespectful Kafnis.

"It sounds troubling. But Lord Farnak assured me days ago that the city walls are strong enough to keep the rebels out, and the Palace wall is another line of defence, so we shouldn't panic."

They stared at her, round-eyed. "You think so, Your Grace?" Amarin said.

Maihara nodded. She ate quickly with sauce-smeared fingers. "Wine, please."

Decanter rattled on glass as Amarin poured watered wine, spilling a splash of red. "Sorry, Your Grace."

Maihara gulped down the weak wine. "Have you seen my sister or brother anywhere?"

"No, but I'm sure they're safe, Your Grace," Amarin said.

Maihara wiped her fingers, and saw her companions eyeing the half-cleared plates.

"Have you eaten?" They should be getting fed elsewhere.

The girls hesitated, and Maihara pointed to the plates. "Please help yourselves."

She stepped to her window and pushed aside the curtain. Smoke drifted across rooftops. The window gave onto a courtyard and showed her little of the outside world, but the room caught the morning light each day, and a warming sun when the sky was clear.

She was tired of being confined to these quiet rooms, and now they felt too isolated, less safe. She did not want to complain to these two excitable young women of her confinement here. They wanted reassurance, but she knew no more about the situation than they did.

She glanced behind. The girls had eaten most of the remaining food.

"Let's go up on the roof," Maihara said.

"Are you sure, Your Grace? Aren't you supposed to be, er—?" Amarin said.

"It's not far, and is anyone going to find out? Did you see any servants?"

"Not up here, Your Grace," Berna said.

Maihara led the way out of the room and up two flights of narrow stairs. She let Amarin unbolt a plain door and pull it back. Light streamed in, along with a breeze and a smell of smoke. They climbed out onto a flat roof. Close around them lay parapets, chimney stacks and sloping tiled roofs. In one corner stood a slim turret with slots in its rounded sides, used for housing messenger-birds. Below lay an inner courtyard on each side, and around the whole palace the high Palace wall enclosing an outer yard with various low out-buildings. Beyond the Palace walls lay the lesser buildings of the city. The streets ran downward toward the city wall, part hidden now by smoke. The sound from below rumbled louder than usual, more ominously.

A breeze tugged at Maihara's dress. "I can't see much down there. What did they tell you about this rioting?"

Amarin leaned on a stone parapet. "They say there was rioting in the Low City, and a protest in the mid-town around the garrison in Kass Street."

A distant clattering reached Maihara's ears. "Has anyone said what started this riot?"

"Complaints about lack of bread," Amarin said.

"The cooks say the protesters wanted the Emperor to talk to the rebels," said Berna.

"Idiots," Amarin said.

Maihara's stomach tightened. "Rioters won't get in.

That's why we have Palace guards. And a wall around the Palace." She pointed downward at the stone wall, three feet thick with a walkway behind the top.

A smell of wood smoke mixed with other burnt odours drifted across the roof. Berna coughed. "The guards say it's the work of Dhikr agents and Tarchon's spies."

"What if the Dhikr attack now, Your Grace?" asked Amarin.

Berna looked at her, large-eyed.

If the enemy had any sense, this would be the best time for them to attack, when the defenders were distracted. It would not help to share this thought with the nervous young ladies. "Lord Farnak says the city walls are a strong line of defence, and the enemy can't get in so long as our soldiers man the walls."

She clenched her fists in frustration. She deserved better information on the developing crisis than this. And, as well as trying magic, she should be laying plans to hide or escape if the worst happened.

As they returned to the lower floor and settled in Maihara's room, the door was flung open with a bang. The intruder, her younger sister Sihrima, wore a white dress that already had a smear of grime and a section of torn lace. Sihrima shared Maihara's dark curling hair, but remained slimmer with an oval face that some people found appealing, now lit up with a childish energy.

Maihara embraced her. "Where have you been, you pest? I was worried." She fingered the damage on her sister's dress. The two ladies curtsied. Sihrima ignored them.

Sihrima pouted. "The other wing. I was at Lady Saramisa's."

"They're letting you run around freely, despite the crisis?"

Sihrima gave her a blank look.

"We've been up on the roof," Lady Amarin said.

"Some trouble's going on in Calah," Maihara said.

"I hear there's been fighting in the city," Sihrima said in a loud voice. "Exciting, isn't it?" She paused to look at her sister. "Why, what's the matter with you?"

"Have you seen our brother?"

"No." Sihrima twirled around and came to rest against Berna's armchair.

"It's awful," Maihara said. "The city's burning. People killed in the streets."

Her sister skipped across the room and sat next to her. "Cheer up, Sis, they're all rabble anyway."

"Sihrima!" Maihara was shocked. "You shouldn't speak of the Emperor's subjects that way. They were probably misled by agitators from the rebels."

The ladies-in-waiting collected up the used dishes and prepared to leave.

"I'm bored," Sihrima said. "Isn't there anything to do?"

Maihara stared at her sister in disbelief. Sihrima did not seem to have grasped the seriousness of the situation. Two years younger than Maihara, Sihrima had no interest in learning, and was only interested in fun. Was there any point in trying to set her right?

"You realise this is real? We could be defeated by the rebels and these Dhikr? Even killed?"

Sihrima stared. She was beginning to get it.

"But we have soldiers?"

"Not enough. The Dhikr killed most of them up north."

"Who are the Dhikr?"

Maihara was speechless, but Lady Amarin filled the gap. "They're animals in scale armour. They've devastated the far north, killing, raping and burning."

Berna nodded.

Sihrima's lip trembled.

Maihara took her hands. "But we're not giving up hope yet, Sis. The city walls are strong."

With Sihrima departed, Maihara managed to work on her magic for only a short time before the ladies-in-waiting reappeared to divert her.

***

Kafnis helped a man she didn't know drag an old cupboard out from a tenement house. She had the lighter end as it bumped down three stone steps onto the cobbles.

"Over there," he said.

They dropped the cupboard alongside a pile of barrels, firewood and old furniture that blocked the wide avenue. An uprising was under way, and despite her misgivings she had to support the comrades.

"You think this will stop soldiers?" she asked, imagining armed and violent soldiery clambering over it, provoked further by the obstruction.

The man shrugged. "We'll find out soon."

Further up the avenue, insurgents had hauled a line of carts across it and lashed them together. A milling crowd jostled in the road, gripping stout sticks, sharp stakes and other improvised weapons. Angry men were digging up the roadway to provide stones for throwing. A sullen roar filled the air.

A cart emerged from a side street with more firewood. Kafnis helped unload it, tossing scrap wood onto the growing pile.

She caught sight of the portly Citizen Nurgis in the crowd and hurried over to him.

"Comrade Kafnis?" Nurgis said. "What are you doing here? I thought you were a maid at the palace?"

Kafnis's anger and resentment boiled over. She threw down the piece of wood she was holding. "Ex-maid. They threw me out on the street without my pay and without even being allowed to collect my things. They said the stuck-up little cow made some complaint about me."

The balding man gave a shrug as though he heard such tales of woe every day. "We'll find you a bed."

"No need." If the carpenter Shardin hadn't taken her off the street, she didn't know what she'd have done. "What's happening at the Semean Gate?" she asked. "Have they stormed it?"

"I didn't see. But our diversion near the Semean Gate to draw away the guards has started and I saw the militia forming up."

"And what are the rebels outside the walls doing?" Kafnis asked.

Nurgis footed a loose brick. "I couldn't see."

"We've contacted them?" Kafnis felt a clutch of fear.

"Demophon talked big about sending them a message, or sneaking an agent out, but I don't know if he was successful."

"Typical." She did not have much faith in Demophon's planning.

Nurgis hurried on. Kafnis waited in the crowd. Time passed. Surely the city magistrates would react to the blockage of the street soon and order its removal. An outbreak of shouting made her turn. A mounted trooper galloped up the avenue, took in the mob and the barricades, and dragged his horse to a halt, with sparks striking from its hooves. He made an about-turn, pursued by stones and catcalls, and disappeared into a side street.

The mob was packed more densely now. Still no ranks of troopers had appeared. Yells erupted from the cart barricade. Kafnis turned to look. She glimpsed a line of shiny helmets with plumes advancing. Cavalry.

The cavalry halted and dismounted. Shouting erupted, followed by cries of pain. Kafnis climbed the furniture barricade. The green-uniformed troopers were attacking the defenders on the carts and wagons and driving them off. Rocks flew forward, and one hit a cavalryman in the face.

Furniture and wood toppled as the troopers dragged a cart away, making a gap in the barricade. Kafnis's guts clenched in fear. If she stayed, she could be hurt here.

The cavalry, at least twenty in number, remounted and cantered through the gap in single file, lances forward. A hail of stones greeted them, as the crowd howled their rage. Cavalrymen slumped in their saddles or fell, and men ran among the horses, clubbing and stabbing. Three men pulled a cavalryman off his horse, and he disappeared under a mass of assailants.

A horn blew, and the cavalry retreated through the gap.

The mob, Kafnis among them, cheered wildly. A girl in plain, patched working jacket and skirt, hair untidily loose, clung to the barricade alongside Kafnis with an ecstatic expression, waving a green rebel flag.

Minutes later, the sound of tramping feet grew louder. A mass of Imperial soldiers advanced along the avenue at a jog. They paused at the line of carts, a few yards away, their hard and resolute faces half-hidden by helmets. A stentorian voice demanded that the barricades be removed otherwise they would kill the defenders. Kafnis flinched. She did not want to be the first to turn and run.

For answer, somebody thrust a burning torch into the barricade. She smelt hot oil and scrambled down the barricade into the street as flames took hold. Defiant cheering erupted around her.

The barricade burned. Heat from the flames warmed her face and woodsmoke made her cough and her eyes water. A section wobbled as though pulled or poked by the soldiers behind. Kafnis had not heard the town bells and sounding horns that would signal a general attack by the besiegers outside the walls. This wasn't good. She had no intention of being killed in Demophon's heroic last stand.

She turned to the girl beside her, who held the green flag. "Let's go." She slipped away with the girl, passing through a narrow footway into the next street that ran parallel to the avenue. It was much narrower, lined with tenements and cheap shops, and blocked by a cart and a pile of firewood. A small mob waited behind it.

Further on, they had to halt as a crowd surged toward them in a hurry to escape. From beyond them came the sound of fighting.

She pulled her companion into a building, where a woman and four children huddled in a shabby room. Sounds of fighting, cries and curses, came from outside. Inside, Kafnis' heart was hammering. The children wailed in fear.

A smell of smoke wafted in from elsewhere. It grew denser, but Kafnis ignored it till heat brushed her cheek.

The building in which she sheltered was on fire.

"We have to get out."

Her companion from the barricade looked at her wide-eyed. The family ignored her. They seemed more afraid of what was outside.

Kafnis grabbed the flag-girl's hand and stumbled outside. She glimpsed smoke, and armed men. She had to run.

"Halt!" a loud voice shouted. Kafnis jumped, and instead of halting, she ran on. A lance clattered at her feet. Bodies lay in the street, troopers and townspeople, some of them women.

A faint *whump* sounded close to her, followed by a cry, and her companion's hand pulled out of Kafnis's grasp. Kafnis turned. The girl lay face down across some rubbish of rags and spoiled fruit, with a fletched shaft sticking out of her back. The thugs had shot her with a crossbow. Behind her, another trooper levelled his weapon. Sick, furious and afraid, Kafnis ran on, weaving across the street. She darted into a narrow alley, and skidded to a halt shaking and gasping for breath, seeing the shiny figure of an Imperial trooper lounging against a window. After a couple of seconds she hurried on past. The man looked dead, lassoed against a broken, dirty window and stabbed in the neck or back. Bastard.

She burst out into another street. The main body of troopers must have passed here, for bodies littered the ground. Most were townspeople, but several were uniformed troopers, savagely hacked and bloodied where they fell. A building burned next to a charred barricade. Further uphill, where the street turned, troopers or rioters had smashed a building through from front to back, and bodies lay among the broken panels. Kafnis looked closer. There were a woman and children, killed by slash wounds. She looked away with a sickness of revulsion and nausea, wiping tears from her eyes. The nobles and their lackeys would pay for this.

-5-

Maihara awoke in the night and lay for a while with churning thoughts of magic, Demophon and her siblings. Wakeful, she looked from her window. Nothing to be seen in the gloom. The city lay in darkness, save in one sector where the clouds reflected a red glow. The sour tang of smoke and distant sound of shouting persisted.

When she woke again, morning light flooded the room, and the clock hands pointed well past her normal hour of rising. She tugged the bell-cord and called out, but nobody came. The corridor lay empty and silent. Her maids were not within earshot. She waited, then in frustration struggled to dress herself in a plain skirt and blouse.

She flung open the north-facing window in the passage, to see better than through its rippled glass. From outside came a confused clatter and roaring. Rooftops sparkled with dew in the morning light. The enemy formations had moved and occupied ground nearer the wall. They had raised a wooden tower-like construction near the city's battlements, and tiny figures crawled over it. Her heart beat quicker. What if the confident reassurances that she was safe inside the city were ill-founded? She regretted Kafnis' removal, wanting someone sharp-witted and sensible around her now. If that siege tower moved closer and allowed the rebels to scale the wall, they would all be in great danger. If she was ever to master the magic, with the enemy massing outside, the sooner she got on with it the better.

She thought of seeking company, but the prospect of being cooped up with excitable young ladies did not appeal. They would be concerned about their families and the servants on their estates. There'd be no salvation there. She took out the magic book, the mirror and the old scrolls from the chest and spread them on her table.

After an hour by the ever-ticking brass clock, she raised her head from the musty-smelling book and rubbed her eyes. Matters made more sense now. The book talked of the spell world having successive walls of closure, the first being accessed with the plain word *Arisa*, the second by a password, and likewise for more arcane levels beyond. This was a concept she understood, for the Imperial Palace was organised like this, with anyone allowed access the outer courtyard, and as one progressed along an enfilade of rooms toward the Emperor's private suite, ever greater levels of privilege were required.

It still did not explain the mirror or the references to energy, purification and so forth in the scrolls. But time was ticking by. Soon she would have to stop translating, try the password and hope she could control what happened.

She stood up and stretched. Somebody had to have delivered the magical box to her room on her fourteenth birthday. Someone who had access to her rooms, which suggested a servant or a lady-in-waiting. She had few memories of her mother's people. It had been so long ago.

She hauled on the bell-cord again, longing for a warm stimulating drink of *koosh*. What was Kafnis doing now, with the Palace staff re-deployed? It had been mean to move her on without a word of explanation, just because she had been anxious about keeping her magical investigations secret, and she felt a twinge of regret that she had not spared a thought for Kafnis' feelings.

With a sigh, she turned to the pile of creased and dog-eared scrolls. One of the scrolls contained passwords embedded in the handwritten text - on previous cursory reading she had taken them for fancy adjectives. She cursed her own carelessness. What a clueless little fool she'd been.

She took a breath. She'd figured out the *Arisa-Zarisa* pair the previous day. Now to try going further.

Arisa. The ghostly grid appeared. She offered it the first password, *Zargutal,* and at the second try the grid changed to another, that contained a small portrait of a woman with an elaborate unfamiliar hairstyle, and some lines of informal text. This was somebody's personal magic space that she was borrowing, someone almost certainly long dead, and the sense of intrusion made her pause. But what could Maihara the apprentice witch do in here? The grid comprised small framed images, with labels in the language of the book.

She translated swiftly, with the book as a guide, finding doors to letters, pictures and the like. This was akin to rifling through someone's private desk, but the owner was probably too long gone to mind. What was *Tools*? Her poised finger accidentally touched it in mid-air. A little frame asked for another password. She offered up the second available password, *mertitis*, and the ghostly view switched to several rows of little images, without the woman's picture.

So these were *Tools*. But what did they do? The symbols looked guessable, but she didn't want to do something alarming to a whole province. Her finger hovered, while her heart beat faster. Thumbing through the dictionary, she translated. That one was Light. She poked the symbol, and jumped back with a squeal as the room flooded with light. The illumination came diffusely from above. She turned it off, and, with heart thumping, examined the next symbol. She had no idea what *Tracer* could be for and it appeared to do nothing.

She got up and listened at the door. Silence. She looked along the corridor. Nobody about.

Back at the desk, *Spy* drew her finger to stab the ghostly button. A solid picture screen snapped into view in front of her, showing the wall of her room. She flinched, and let out a breath. A finger in the floating picture sent it careering around. It reacted to any touch and gesture, but was that the way to control it?

She reached for her magic book and dictionary. Some minutes of study later, she had the spy out in the north corridor, and looking at the double doors, beyond which lay the main stairs that went down to the great hall and staterooms. Farnak had stationed his guards at the head of the stairs to intercept any intruders. Whatever people whispered about Farnak, he was well-organised and dependable. Faint sound from the same point murmured into her ears.

A mumble of voices arose, and then the doors cracked open. In alarm, she snatched the spy back. Pulses racing, she hastened to close the spells before the incomers discovered her.

Zarisa. She breathed a sigh of relief as the ghostly frames snapped out of existence, and leant back in the chair. She was making progress and she'd got as far as commanding a useful spell. A good time to catch her breath before trying something else.

A knock sounded at the door. She slammed shut the books and put them and the scrolls out of sight in the desk drawer. Her heart hammered.

"Come in."

A maid entered carrying a meal on a tray.

Maihara breathed again. So it was lunchtime and this, miraculously, was lunch. A small fly flew in behind and buzzed around the tray. Maihara watched in horror. An orange train of glowing chevrons trailed the fly, tracking its every movement. Maihara stared, paralysed. It had to be one of the spells she had fiddled with, and it hadn't gone when she banished the rest. She'd be denounced as a witch.

"Are you all right, Your Grace?" the maid asked, with an expression of polite concern. She seemed oblivious of the circling fly and its orange tracer.

"The war," Maihara managed. "Is there any news?"

"It's the same as yesterday, Your Grace." The maid put down the tray and set out the cutlery. She swatted the fly aside, and left.

Stunned, Maihara sighed in relief. The magic was only visible to herself.

Maihara picked at her lunch. The meat was scorched, the vegetables under-cooked and nearly cold and the grapes wrinkly. The war had to be having a dire effect in the kitchens. This tasted like siege food already, but she finished it all.

As she ate, she checked the spells which she had tried out. At the personal space were the images for the spells, and under one was a label that translated as 'Used Not Long Ago.' That looked useful. Her heart rate slowed to normal as she turned the **Tracer** off. What a relief.

In reaction, a mood of elation crept over her. She had worked a second useful spell, and it appeared that ordinary people sensed nothing of her magical tinkering. She set herself to studying the crabbed and faded scrolls again.

At the north end of the corridor, Maihara held the heavy brocaded window curtain aside and looked out over the city rooftops and the distant wall below. The siege tower had moved forward and was almost at the Calah city wall. Distant figures swarmed atop the city defences. She drew a breath.

She still had not spoken to anyone about hiding or escaping should the city fall. This part of the palace was ominously quiet and time was running short. She put on a hooded outdoor cloak and hurried along the passage to the double doors at the west end of the wing, and down the second main staircase. Lady Amarin was talking to a pair of guards on a lower landing. That was a sign of normality, at least. They looked up.

"What's going on?"

Amarin's delicate features looked strained. "I'm not sure, Your Grace."

"Please go back to your rooms, Your Grace," a guard said. "You'll be safer there."

Not this again. Maihara took a step downward, hoping that the guards were not intent on following her father's orders to confine her even as the rebels broke in and the palace burnt down. "I'm going downstairs. I want to find your commanding Colonel and ask what's happening."

"But Your Grace—" The man frowned and extended a

restraining hand.

"One of you can come with me, if you like." She stepped past them, beckoning to Amarin and cutting off the impending argument.

The guards conferred in whispers and followed her. Few staff or servants were about as she made her way downstairs. She had never been to the stair foot before, not having had any prior reason to concern herself with the service workings of the palace, but the kitchens and, she hoped, the cellar access were in this direction. Access to the Fort which housed the palace garrison at the east end was also at ground floor level. Three floors down she smelled the stale odour of cooking. They were in a plain, grey-painted passage with scuffed walls, and several sets of doors.

Maihara wrinkled her nose. "It smells." The odour reminded her she was hungry again.

"It's the kitchens, Your Grace," Amarin said.

She faced the two guards. "Can one of you go find the Colonel? And I want to find out where my brother and sister are."

The shorter guard saluted. "Yes, Your Grace."

The taller and better-looking guard held open a double door for her and Amarin. A waft of hot air enveloped her, laden with cooking smells. In the arched kitchen passage, servants were talking rather than working.

"Ask them what's happening here," she told the guard in a low voice.

"What's happening, you people?" the guard asked. "Is there any news?"

"My brother says our soldiers beat off the attack on the walls," said a man wearing an apron.

"Why aren't you working?" the guard persisted. "And where are the staff?"

"The palace steward sent men to work out in the city and moved others around to cover. So, nobody knows what they're supposed to be doing," a tired-looking woman said.

Maihara looked through an open doorway, seeing a

great double-height room with black ovens at the back, an open fire for roasting carcases on a spit, tables piled with pots and baskets and chopping boards, and racks of shiny pots, jugs and moulds of all sizes. Little was happening in here.

"When are you sending up evening meals?" Lady Amarin asked.

The woman answered with a shrug.

"People are hungry," the guard said.

"Help yourself before the Dhikr do," said a youth with a cook's cap, pointing to the storerooms. "We're not looking."

For a moment the suggestion filled Maihara with outrage. Didn't they know who she was? Order was breaking down. Realisation seeped in that they didn't recognise her, as she was wrapped in a plain hooded cloak and accompanied by only one guard.

Her stomach growled and needed no further bidding. She looked in a couple of the cool, stone-shelved storerooms and helped herself to a pie and a fresh-smelling crusty loaf. While the guard talked to the servants, she swiped a bottle of wine from a rack and put it under her cloak. It all belonged to her father, anyway.

A grey-haired soldier stood in the passage. The tabs on his uniformed shoulders marked him as an officer, and a member of the military Varlord Order. His uniform smelt of smoke, and splashes of blood stained one of his sleeves.

"Your Grace? I'm Colonel Mattick, of the Palace Guard." He saluted. "How can I serve you?"

Her stomach lurched at the sight of the blood on Mattick's uniform. Lady Amarin stared at him in alarm. Something was happening, something not good. "You've been fighting, Colonel?"

"I was on detachment, Your Grace, helping put down the riots, and I have just returned. I assume you want to know what's going on?"

"I do." Maihara's heart thumped.

"Lord Farnak said you were to be properly briefed."

She hesitated. It would not be proper to have the servants listening. "A moment." She stepped into a storeroom. Amarin and the guard moved closer to hear what the man had to say.

Mattick appeared quite old, possibly even a father with a daughter her age. He cleared his throat. "Your Grace, during the night barrels of flaming tar fell on the east wall and some buildings inside, and on the breastworks outside. We presume it was a catapult attack over the marsh, the work of the enemy."

Amarin's mouth hung open.

"At noon, elements of the town militia revolted and attacked the defenders at the Semean Gate without warning. At the same time, riots broke out in several parts of the city, and when troops marched out to relieve the Semean Gate and restore order, their route was blocked by rioters and barricades in the Govran Avenue area, then they were ambushed and attacked."

Maihara listened in shock. This was the revolt plan, the one she had outlined with Demophon.

Mattick appeared to read her silence as rapt attention, and continued. "The attack on the gate failed when our troops spread along the city wall. In the Low Town, rioters seized the streets, but our forces went in to drive them back.

"We went right in and tore down barricades, cleared the main streets. Half of it was alight, buildings too. It was tough, and we lost a lot of men. They knew we wouldn't take prisoners, you see."

A horrible realisation swept over her. The casualties must have included women and children, killed by men who were protecting her and the Empire.

"It's over?"

"Still going on, Your Grace."

"Oh, no!"

She leaned on the wall with a thump and covered her face with her hands. Large numbers of people had died, and it was her fault. It couldn't be coincidence. That rascal

Demophon must have run off to put her plan into effect, and sparked a serious riot at a time when the Imperial soldiers needed to concentrate on defending the city walls against the armies of the rebels and Dhikr. To her fury and dismay, she started to cry.

A shadow loomed before her, and a large hand patted her on the shoulder.

"Stop that!" Lady Amarin cried. "How dare you touch Her Grace! You can be imprisoned for that."

Maihara lowered her hands and scowled at her lady-in-waiting. "Be quiet! Leave the man alone."

Amarin stared at her in shock.

The officer withdrew his hand. "I'm sorry, Princess. You're safe here. They're bad people, but we'll deal with them."

Amarin glared at Colonel Mattick.

Maihara stemmed her tears. The officer had misinterpreted her distress, but it would be unwise to enlighten him. She waved him back. "Thank you. I'm just a little overwrought."

The officer straightened up, looking at her as if she was the most amazing person he had ever met. "I'm sorry for acting disrespectfully, Your Grace."

"No need to apologise," Maihara said, meeting the man's eyes. "These are unusual times. The besiegers -" she sniffed. "The besiegers, did they do anything?"

"Some movement, Your Grace. They're still hoping we'll surrender."

"Where's Lord Farnak?"

"I'm not certain, Your Grace. There was a rumour - no, never mind."

The guard said something to Mattick in a low voice.

"Your Grace, you should be remaining on the upper east floor," Mattick said.

Resentment flared in her. "I hope I won't be trapped up there while the palace falls to the rebels, just because you are following the Emperor's orders. Is there any secret way out of this ornate prison, Colonel?"

Mattick made a hasty bow. "You mean the lower cellars, Your Grace. They're a labyrinth. Is that your wish?"

"It is."

Lady Amarın gasped. The officer apologised again and departed with long strides.

"You should report that man," Amarin said. Her tied-back blonde hair quivered.

"Leave it, Amarin," Maihara said, with a snap. "There's a war outside."

"Yes, Your Grace." Amarin ducked her head.

Upstairs she found from servants that her siblings were in the eastern wing on the fourth floor with guards nearby. She took herself and Amarin to the apartment of her ladies-in-waiting, on the floor below her room. They had three rooms including a sitting-room, all on the north side of the palace, and furnished with brown wood estate furniture, padded chairs and rainbow-coloured draperies and a couple of large indoor plants in pots.

Lady Berna greeted her mistress with enthusiasm. The dark-haired girl was flushed and giddier than usual.

Maihara's eye fell on an opened bottle and two glasses on their table. "You don't mind if I join your party? I've brought my own supplies."

The two ladies giggled. "Your Grace, we'd be honoured." Berna produced a third glass.

Maihara sat in a winged chair and attacked her meat pie, eating it without cutlery.

Colonel Mattick tapped at the door a while later. Maihara, making an effort to conduct herself in a sober manner, went to speak with him.

"The situation at the walls is becoming critical," he admitted. "Our orders are to defend the Palace and the Imperial family with our lives."

"I don't want to be defended to the last man," Maihara told him. She did not like what she was hearing. Either her father did not believe the city would fall, or he did not intend his family to attempt escape. "I want out, along with my brother and sister, if it comes to that."

"The cellars?"

She gave a nod. "Enough people are dying already."

Mattick nodded and made a salute. It appeared they understood each other.

"What did he want?" Amarin asked, stumbling across the rug.

"He was updating me on the situation," Maihara told her. There was no point in spreading alarm.

Between the three of them, they had finished the first bottle of wine. After a struggle, she got her wine opened and refilled her glass.

More young ladies-in-waiting came in with cakes and another bottle of wine. Berna fell asleep. Some of the other ladies left.

Maihara cradled her bottle. The wine had a strong flavour and took away the taste of pie. It also dulled her anxiety about her own safety, and her fear that her influence on Demophon's plan would be exposed. Her imprudent analysis for Demophon had led to her soldiers and hundreds of other people being killed. She took another swig of the wine.

The sex books in the library had been educational and also unsettling. That handsome guard who had escorted her here - what was he like under the nether part of his uniform? She giggled drunkenly at the thought. After reading those books she had taught herself more about how her own body responded. They couldn't call her an innocent little princess now. She topped up her glass and took another swig.

The wine warmed her insides and flushed her with pleasure. She wondered if the sensation of having s.e.x. was anything like this. But something else troubled her. She could not quite recall what it was, her mind wasn't working so well. Another sip of wine. She dabbled in illicit magic, and if anyone found out, she'd be in trouble. Across the room, the girls were chattering and shrieking with laughter, but Maihara felt disinclined to move. She glanced down and saw she had finished the bottle.

After a while, she felt sick. Her stomach rumbled, and she made it to the blue-patterned basin in Amarin and Bernas' wash-room before throwing up. She rinsed her mouth to get rid of the burning taste and then tottered back to the sitting-room to lie down. The room spun around her.

Maihara awoke the next morning, stiff and chilled, with a throbbing inside her wool-stuffed brain. Her mouth tasted foul; as though filled with bile.

She found the bell-cord for this suite, tugged on it and this time a servant came. With slurred and furry tongue, Maihara ordered that extra strong *koosh* be brought. Apparently the crisis had not yet come.

The sitting room smelt stale, and the floor was littered with garments, scraps of food and other remains of her debauch. She kicked an empty bottle into a corner, ignored its clatter and tinkling, then sat and waited with disinterest for the reviver that would make her feel human again. The bedroom door remained closed.

A maid brought in a cup and a steaming jug of the mild stimulant on an ebony tray and set it near her. The drink's humid, spiced aroma revived her spirits a little. She poured herself a cupful of the dark brown brew and let it restore energy to her stiff, weakened body. She drank another restorative cup. The throbbing of her temples and the foul taste in her mouth diminished, but she had no desire to eat the breakfast pastry.

Two old maids, wearing grey cotton dresses and white floppy caps, burst into the room. The grey-haired one sniffed the air and frowned.

They looked around, taking in the empty pie dish, bread crusts and used glass littering the floor.

Maihara stirred with unease as they stared at her round-eyed. Why these two? Maybe the regular servants had been redeployed and these aged nursemaids sent instead. This wasn't good.

"Monstrous!" the whiter-haired one cried. "It is

forbidden for the children of the Imperial court to touch alcohol. You must tell us how you got it. You must not drink, for it enslaves the mind and leads to all kinds of vice. You are such a naughty girl!"

Maihara hoped they were not going to tell the whole Palace. Was it really that obvious she'd got drunk on stolen wine? "What are you doing here?"

"The steward sent us to see if you girls were all right or needed anything," the old nursemaid quavered.

On the whole, Maihara was pleased that her regular servants had not turned up to see her in this state.

The second maid started pawing at Maihara's dress.

"What are you doing?" She pushed the hand away in outrage.

"Bad girl!" the grey-haired nursemaid exclaimed.

Maihara realised she had pie crumbs on her dress, and lost her temper. "Stop that, you old bag!" She grabbed the old woman's arm. The nurse was no match for a princess grown nearly to adult height and weight, and soon Maihara held her at arm's length.

"Cruel, unnatural girl!" The wizened old nurse whimpered as Maihara's fingers gripped her arm.

This wasn't good. Maihara let go. She drew herself up to her full height and glared at them. "You don't need to do that. I'm not a child. And I'm the Imperial Princess; show some respect."

The two old women stared at her, open-mouthed and wide-eyed with fright. "Your Grace!" They curtsied and whimpered apologies.

"What's going on outside? Has the enemy broken into the city yet?" Maihara asked.

"No, Your Grace, it seems their attack failed," said the white-haired one.

"You've made a mess, Princess," said the grey-haired nursemaid.

"Well, I've got a headache. Clear all this up." She took a step back.

"You shouldn't be drinking," the whiter-haired one

mumbled.

"That's my problem. You're here to serve me."

The nursemaids curtsied, looking sullen. "Yes, Your Grace."

They worked slowly, shooting her resentful looks, kneeling to pick up scraps from the carpet.

Maihara was relieved at having regained control of the situation, but a sensation of behaving meanly nagged her. The grey-haired one had minded her as a small child while the other looked ancient and confused enough to have nursed her parents' generation.

While the nursemaids cleaned up, she poured herself a third cup of koosh. She took it to the window, where she looked out at the city wall and formations of the enemy beyond. Out on the marshy plain, banners flapped above conical tents. Fighters had grouped in a mass as though they were about to try something. Men and horses dragged the siege tower up to the wall while others filled in a watery ditch. An imminent assault? A quiver of unease gripped her.

What was her father doing? She thumped the window-sill in frustration and resentment. Throughout this invasion crisis he had not once shown any sign of remembering she existed. And where was Lord Farnak? He had shown signs of taking her seriously, but he was also ignoring her now. Damn him.

"If you gossip about me, you'll be in trouble," she said to the nursemaids before exiting the suite. The nursemaids bowed repeatedly.

Maihara called a maid to her own suite. Before long, her dense, wavy hair had been washed and fastened up with pins behind her head, and she wore a new short-sleeved dress of blue satin. She sat, thinking. The temptation to stay in these comfortable rooms was strong, but should she wait, or was it time to get out?

-6-

Lord Farnak had warned Maihara not to speak of asking help from the Shardan, but aid from the Shardan, or someone, would be much better than pillage, arson and murder by the Dhikr horde, however much it offended the pride of her autocratic father. The Shardan resided in a country to the south. They fielded armies, and were loyal, but had supported a losing faction in a previous dynastic struggle. Old history, to most people other than Emperor Cordan. Somebody ought to summon their help. Maybe she could use the scrolls and mirror to make magic to do it quickly. Soon it would be too late. The enemy were readying their siege towers for an assault on the walls.

She read through the faded handwritten texts again, looking for a clue on how to begin this. She had worked hard on understanding the magic texts the previous afternoon. But what was the mirror for? She picked it up and noticed at once that something had changed. She now perceived two magical grids, or arrays of spells, one overlapping the other, the first being the mirror's and the second, the one that she had explored most recently. So *that* was what the mirror did. It bypassed the passwords, and if she learnt more levels, she would have a shortcut to them too.

She took a sip of water and contemplated what she had learnt so far. The book she had found in the library was the user's instructions. This magic would only work for Vimrashan descendants like herself who sensed the magical aura and had a working knowledge of an obsolete language. The mirror was a powerful aid, but not essential once she accessed the magic herself. The scrolls were additional notes, intended to help her learn the magic without a human mentor.

But why was it a mirror? To fool those not in on its secret, or was it more?

There were stories of magic mirrors, that one could enter, or which summoned dire things. The mirror's surface was hazy, as if she looked into it beyond her own reflection. She did not recall mention of the mirror in the scrolls, so looked through them again. 'The mirror is your portal,' one said. Well, yes, she'd discovered that. And an ominous line, 'The box contains dangerous power. Do not go there in ignorance.' And that was all.

There had been nothing dangerous so far, beyond the hazard of being found out. She turned to the book, skimming through chapters. One chapter described dire magics that did unpleasant or deadly things, but seemed to have nothing to do with what she had learnt so far. In the old folk stories, the magic world was but a heartbeat away in time, a hair's-breadth away in space, yet to attain it and tap its power was immensely difficult, and the sorcerer had to create the correct vibrations by chanting the spell. The voice of a young woman was thought to be particularly effective.

In a chapter on magical objects, she found a strong hint that the box itself could be a magical object. That was a revelation. Hadn't she had a fright three years ago after falling asleep with her hand in the box? She picked it up and examined it with minute attention. It was heavy, heavier than it ought to be, unless that was a property of the black wood, and it had a rectangular mirror, now heavily tarnished, set in the inside of the lid.

In the chapter on magical mirrors, she found a paragraph on summoning. Here was written a series of keywords for summoning entities. This was too tempting for her not to try it.

She put her hand to the mirror in the lid, and as her light fingers touched the ancient glass, it sang faintly in a rising trill. Yet she hesitated, and looked in the book again. What if this summoning went awry? On the next page she found a spell for de-summoning or banishing what one had summoned. "*Ephrai yai blagoth.*" She wrote it down and memorised it. The next paragraph was about commanding entities that one had summoned. On the same bit of paper she started drafting a message to the Shardan principality, seeking their help, begging them to send troops, and addressed to the Councillor Nardone whom Lord Farnak had mentioned.

Well, she would speak the line of summoning while looking in the mirror and see if it did anything.

By the window she held the box aloft in the sunlight, and as the luminary's yellow rays struck the glass it glowed, reflecting the many colours of the rainbow. Lowering the box, she stared into its luminous depths, and sensing the connection to the magic, pronounced the keywords of summoning. *Belial, atrogitz, Shardyn, ketaminic, zarapfostra, suminic, xaveniferic.* At each word, the grid of symbols changed to a fresh one, and with the last three, red words of warning appeared below the rows of symbols, seeming to ask 'Are you sure?'. The book had not said this was dangerous, so she pressed on.

The sequence stopped with an array of symbols that showed various creatures including one of a bird of prey carrying a cylinder in its claws. The Old Sarian label seemed to confirm it was a messenger. Perfect.

She balanced the lid against her arm while making a fair copy of her message and sealing it with a blob of wax and her personal seal. This done, she glanced into the mirror again. To her dismay, the array of symbols was overlaid by a flickering orange hourglass whose sand had almost run out, save for a few grains. The meaning was obvious. She jabbed for the messenger symbol, and with a chiming sound and flash of green the grid reverted to the previous one, then the one before that, and the one before that.

So, she had done the summoning, but where was the bird? She had assumed it would appear before her. She rested her head on her hands, calming her thoughts, strangely weary of the mental effort. She glanced at the closed window. No bird beating at the panes. The windswept roof?

With brisk fingers she locked the mirror away in its velvet coffin, along with the scrolls and book, and put the box back in the chest. She took an uneaten pastry, and pulled pins from her raven hair, letting it tumble about her shoulders.

She hastened up the narrow stairs till she reached the open roofs. A large flat roof, edged by a brick parapet and chimney stacks, gave a sweeping view of the rooftops of the city and the flat plains beyond. Nobody else was up here, not even the snooping Fifth Bureau. Below, enemy troops crawled like bugs against the walls. A conical brick turret stood on the edge of the roof. The turret, which she had seen on her previous visit to the roofs, was pierced by rows of bird-holes. Every vital point in the Empire had one of these messenger bird aviaries for sending and receiving urgent messages.

As she looked around, she saw a large bird with blue-grey feathers swoop down and shuffle on clawed feet into the turret. A sense of foolishness shot through her like a dart as the cooler air cleared her brain. This was what came of trying to plan after drinking too much wine.

She did not need any magic. All she had to do was use an outgoing bird to send a message begging for help. If matters became worse, the birds would be of no further use anyway. She could send the message tucked in her sleeve, then run back to her rooms and write more.

In the base of the structure were rows of cages, labelled. Several were empty, but the cage for SHAR had a large grey plumaged bird with darker wing feathers in it. The feathered creature, as big as a hunting hawk, regarded her with a round orange eye as she stuffed her note into one of the messenger-tubes from the basket below. She opened the cage and grabbed the bird by a leg. It objected strongly, squawking and flapping and pecking as she tried one-handed to clip the tube over its red-scaled leg.

"Ow!" The nasty creature had drawn blood with its free

foot, but if she let go, it would escape. She shifted her grip and got the tube on at last, and stepped back. The bird flapped its wings, rose a few feet and forced its way into a brick hole, with frantic movements, squawking. That was not what she wanted it to do, at all.

She looked up as a shadow passed over her, and her guts chilled with fear. The winged monstrosity was enormous, longer than a pair of inline carriage horses, and its appearance was evil. It flew on membranous wings stretched on ribs of bone, supporting a body armoured by blue and green scales, balanced by a papery kite-shaped tail. As it passed over her, its long toothy jaws opened and it emitted a blood-curdling caw.

She knew its name, for she had read it and seen its small image next to the messenger bird she had meant to summon. *Pterostrophe.*

She crouched behind the parapet, shaking. She sensed more magic in the sky above. A patch of the sky was a vile yellow, streaked with black. Screams and cries rose from the streets. She risked a look over the roof parapet, and saw small figures below, pointing upward. So she was not the only person who could see it. This was bad.

The pterostrophe swooped in a turn, passing low over the city's outer defensive wall. Soldiers scattered in panic, running and leaping down to safety. The creature defecated, dropping a black mess that sizzled on the wall top, and perched on a wall turret, where the stone crumbled and blackened as though even the touch of its claws was destructive.

She did not want this brute, shutting the box had not banished it, and she had no idea of how to control it. She had to get rid of the monster before it did worse things.

Trembling, she leant forward. "***Ephyai blagoth***!" The long bony beak yawned wide, displaying a row of raked teeth as the head turned to eye her. "Go away, you brute!" It was still there, shuffling to take off in her direction. She glanced at the paper and cried the command of dismissal, flinging up her pale, bare arms. "***Ephrai yai blagoth***!"

At once, the monster rose up, not flying, but more as though it was being sucked skyward. High above the roof, it croaked a shrill and nauseating cry. A black hole opened in the yellow patch and the monster ascended into it and was gone. With an inaudible snap, the black hole closed and vanished, leaving nothing but blue sky.

With a whimper of relief, she sank to the roof walkway. It was over.

A strong, heavy hand gripped her shoulder. "What witchery are you doing here?" grated a man's voice. Two men, one a guardsman, the other a civilian in a hooded cloak, had approached behind her.

She shook off the grasping hand. "How dare you touch me? Do you know who I am?"

The guardsman took a step back. The hooded one stood his ground. "You're one of several people we've been watching. You should be more careful who you associate with, Your Grace."

Maihara drew herself up and looked him in the eyes. "I'm the Imperial Princess, and if I want to come up here and feed birds, then I will."

The hooded one stared back. "And I'm an officer of the Fifth Bureau with a warrant to pursue traitors, whoever they are." He flashed an enamel badge.

"I'm not a traitor," she said with heat.

"Your contacts are traitors. And now we find you engaged in witchcraft."

She glanced around, looking for a way to get past them and gain the stairs. In the corner of her eye she saw the messenger bird stick a head out of its roost.

The hooded one crooked a finger. "Please come with us, Your Grace. We can get permission to compel you, soon enough."

She stood her ground. "My father will hear of this."

"Oh, he already has." His voice held a hint of mockery.

"I was just feeding the birds, and that horrible thing appeared," she said. Her ears were buzzing.

"Feeding a witch-creature," the hooded man said, and

crooked his finger again.

She was tempted to refuse, but they would lay hands on her, and the result would be the same.

It was as though she watched herself, and her two captors, through a window of thick glass. The magnitude of the disaster did not penetrate. They should not handle her so roughly, for she was Imperial Princess Maihara Zircona Cordana, Duchess of Avergne, of the ruling family of Sar, and they were common men. They led her away.

In a brick-built, whitewashed room of the fort that adjoined the palace, they threw her into a chair with straps on the arms. Brown wooden pigeonholes with papers in them lined one wall. Metal handcuffs, a notebook and a whip lay on a table. She sat within her bubble of shock while two Bureau agents, muscular and clad in dark, close-fitting trousers and jerkins, assailed her with questions. One had a hard, stubbly face, and a hood shadowed the scarred face of the other.

"Do you admit summoning the reptile?"

"Answer!" The hooded one dangled a whip.

She shook her head. "It just appeared. I didn't have anything to do with it."

"Do you admit sending it away?"

"I didn't do that either."

"Did you attract the reptile by your witchcraft?"

Frightened, she shook her head. "That's nonsense."

"We don't like witches here."

She refused to speak of any magic. Questioned about Demophon, Farnak and Kafnis, she denied any knowledge of their activities. They suspected Kafnis? She'd give no substance to their suspicions. Lord Farnak had not promised her anything. Surely, sooner or later word would reach someone more sympathetic, and these men would have to release her.

The agents kept their distance from her. The hard-faced one's eyes were wide as he shouted and threatened, but she knew too little of such men to tell if he most feared her and what she could do, or his masters, or the enemy at the gates.

The door of the dank room opened and a black-hooded man, the agent who had arrested her, looked in. He spoke to the two interrogators in a low voice. She caught only the word 'note' and her heart thumped.

The lead interrogator spoke. "Princess, we know what you were trying to do. The Emperor has been informed of your case and has given us the widest discretion. I suggest that you co-operate."

She shuddered, remembering her father's rage at the mere suggestion that she had witch-blood. There'd be no succour there.

Her mental barrier crumbled. She glanced around the room, with its whitewashed brick walls that smelled of damp, and the men's unwashed sweat. She heard their voices and felt their hate. They hated her because they were afraid of her. They hated her because of her crimes, and because she would not answer them. They hated her because they dared not mark her body, on pain of death. She was an Imperial Princess, so what could they really do?

If her father had disowned her, she would not admit to anything. Exasperated, they took her down two floors to a dank lower level and locked her in a bare cell.

"Who do you think you are, you fugging tart?" the hooded one shouted. "The enemy are storming the wall where that creature crapped. You think the Imperial family likes witches?"

They slammed and bolted the metal bars that closed the cell. Quivering with shock and outrage, she crouched on the gritty floor in the dim light that came through the bars from a skylight in the passage. They left, taking their light. She stretched her arms above her head and turned around in circles, touching chill masonry and feeling the confines of the space. In the darkness beyond her cell, a human voice moaned.

Surely they were just trying to frighten her? What could they do to her? She was the Emperor's daughter. Treason?

That was not what she had tried to do.

-7-

Maihara shifted on her lumpy straw mattress. In the perpetual gloom, it was hard to tell the time of day or night, and the rough blanket they had given her barely kept out the cold. Her dress was light, and the stones sucked warmth from her. She scratched at another itchy spot.

She'd endured a nasty dream in which metallic man-like creatures pursued her through tunnels, their gleaming talons extended to rend her flesh. The details dissolved with her waking. She'd seen an unpleasant clawed hand among a clutter of models and mechanisms when she'd peeked into her father's workshop a couple of months back. Maybe he knew that she had looked, contrary to his strict orders, and that was why he'd abandoned her down here.

A warder approached and thrust a bowl of greasy broth and a worn metal spoon under the iron bars. Maihara sampled the bowl's over-boiled and gristly contents, and gagged. Scraps of over-cooked vegetable and lumps of unidentifiable tough meat, rubbery things and gristle floated in a warm oily liquid. It was the most disgusting food she had ever tasted. She left most of it to congeal.

As the cold of the dank cell seeped into her bones, defiance had ebbed and fear took its place. Her demand that her father be told had borne no visible result, and she'd been here for what seemed like a day and night. Possibly only the agents knew where she lay. In any case, what person of influence could she rely on? Sensible people merely thought sorcery exotic, but those agents loathed 'witches'. Even she was alarmed by her new powers. The monster she summoned had attacked the city's defences. Sooner or later the agents would let hate and fear overcome their caution and apply tortures that left no mark.

Footsteps rang in the stone passage, and male voices murmured. The yellow glow of an approaching lamp brightened the walls. Maihara scrambled to her feet, heart thumping. They might be here to brutalise her. Or it might be a friend come to fetch her out. If nothing else, more palatable food and water would be welcome. They could not mean to keep her here for ever. Her hopes trembled.

A figure appeared on the other side of the bars. Behind him lurked a warder in black. She backed against a cold wall. The first man's face was indistinct, but he wore a courtier's cap and a cloak trimmed with silver braid. Unseen, another prisoner called out in a hoarse voice and rattled metal bars, but the warder ordered him to be quiet

Hope leapt in her. Here was a person of rank who would help her. "Lord Farnak?"

"Your Grace."

The voice was not Farnak's. Lord Susanon, whom she had seen with Farnak, wore a jacket and breeches of velvet under his dark blue cloak, but he looked as if he had slept in them. By the light of the lamp the warder carried, his face was unshaven, grey and drawn. Susanon appeared to be one of Farnak's allies and held some fancily titled position at Court that gave him an income without making much demand on his time.

Maihara sighed with muted relief. "Have you come to take me out of here?"

Lord Susanon shuffled his feet. "What exactly were you doing, to get yourself locked up like this? They accuse you of summoning a flying monster, by witchcraft. I didn't know you were a sorceress." His face was lined, and besides the neat grey beard and small moustache his thin cheeks bore a grey stubble.

"I just went up to the roof. Why shouldn't I?"

"And they accuse you of writing a note to the enemy."

Maihara gave an involuntary start.

"To whom, then? Who suggested it?" Susanon's eyes glinted.

Maihara bit her lip. "I drafted a note to the Shardan. Our

allies."

Lord Susanon frowned. "You disappoint me. We thought you were smart, but you're just as idiotic as your sister and brother. The Emperor will never consent to being rescued by them. And they're a long way away."

Stung, Maihara looked away. "I thought it would help. Can you get me out of here?"

Susanon shook his head. "Not yet. Not with those accusations against you. The Emperor himself approved your continued detention. You can't hear it down here, but there's a major attack in progress. Elements of the enemy have gotten into the city, possibly aided by that monster. If we win, we can see about getting you out and hushing up talk of witchcraft."

"If?" Maihara asked with sinking heart. "Where's Lord Farnak?" She had seen nothing of him for days.

"He's been put under house arrest, on suspicion of conspiring against the Emperor."

Her hopes shrivelled. Farnak arrested? Perhaps a scheme to advance her had been uncovered, and that was another reason to hold her here.

"Did the Bureau question you about Lord Farnak?" Susanon asked.

"Not much."

Susanon looked relieved. She supposed he had taken a risk in coming to visit her.

"What of the Shardan?" So far as she knew, that principality remained loyal.

"It's my understanding that they maintain their independence. The Army staff have requested a clarification. If we lose, you are probably as safe from harm down here as anywhere else."

"How are my brother and sister?"

"Safe and well in the Palace, for now."

The contrast with her own situation made her heartsick. So Mattick had not taken it upon himself to rescue her brother and sister in her absence. That was understandable. She had expected him to contact her again should the situation become critical.

"How's the food here?" Susanon asked.

"Awful." The mere memory aroused nausea.

"You should have been held in rooms more befitting your status. Perhaps they were afraid you could escape if not confined by metal. I'll speak to the guards." Susanon turned away.

If we lose. How would she be safer trapped in here?

"Wait!" She shook the bars.

Susanon did not respond and retreated out of sight with the warder.

Maihara sank onto her lumpy bed. Probably the Bureau told her father she had written a message to the Shardan. He would be furious. She murmured a prayer to the Nine Gods, but it was just a reflex. She didn't really believe in a collection of dusty images and her prayers to them had never worked before.

She tried again to find the magic aura she had sensed from her rooms. Down here, it was absent, screened by the stones or lost to her splintered thoughts. This was a heavy blow. With other options failing her, turning to the magic had been a last resort. But now nothing worked, and the deprivation was crushing. Perhaps there was some truth in what Susanon had said about the reason for putting her in this cell. She hit the stones with her fist, and tears came to her eyes.

She listened for sounds of fighting but heard nothing except the distant cries and rattling of chains from other prisoners. Time crawled like a snail. She prayed to the One God for the defeat of the invaders and that Susanon would exert himself to release her.

The next meal was better, with lean meat and crisp vegetables in a sauce. The warder left a large jug of water. After that, nothing came, for a very long time, save for distant thumps she felt through the stonework, cries and faint clashing of metal. Not knowing what was happening racked her with fear and despair. If the city was safe, why did no warders come? Would she perish here of hunger and thirst, forgotten? She pressed her cheek to the bars and looked up the dark passage, stomach growling, hoping someone would come, hoping they wouldn't. At each distant sound she stirred, thinking of food, imagining bestial invaders exploring the prison levels.

The palace maids had circulated alarming rumours about what happened in the territories overrun by the rebels. If she was to believe them, all women in these territories were likely to be raped repeatedly, and young women became the sex slaves of their conquerors. The tales about the rebels could be exaggeration, though her lady companions had spoken in horrified tones of the atrocities committed by the subhuman Dhikr, who might be outside the walls now. She crouched in a corner with her knees drawn up to her chest and her arms wrapped about her shins. The thought of brutish invaders tearing off her clothes and forcing her legs apart made her want to vomit with fear and revulsion.

Two men appeared at the bars, with a lantern. They stared in at her.

She didn't recognise their uniforms, which seemed a mixture of Imperial green jackets and scruffy civilian shirts and trews, or the stripe markings on their shoulders. Maihara quivered. This might mean release, food, or the horror of abuse. She half-rose to a crouch. This wasn't good. They could be rebels.

"A girl!" said one. "It's our lucky day."

Maihara backed from the bars to the cold rear wall, heart thumping. She felt a shameful trickle down her leg.

The taller thin-faced soldier had a bunch of keys and tried them one by one in the lock. Maihara, pressing her back into stone, prayed that none of them would fit.

"If you do anything to me, your leader will not be pleased." Her voice shook, but she straightened up and glared at them.

The shorter wider-faced soldier laughed. "Why would

that be, girl? Oo's gonna tell him?"

She thought quickly. "I am the Emperor's daughter. If you take me to your leaders, I am sure they will reward you." She made herself look the nearer man in the eyes.

The shorter soldier laughed, but the other said, "She talks posh, not like an ordinary girl. Dressed posh, too."

"Let's 'ave fun with her first."

Her throat was tight, and her armpits trickled with sweat.

"If you harm me, and what I say is true, you will be hanged. If you kill me, you will get nothing. If you capture one of the Imperial family, think how you will be rewarded. Your best option is to take me to your leader, unharmed." Her voice came out faint, with a final squeak.

The second soldier was silent while the first continued to fiddle with the keys and lock. "She's right," the taller man said. "We should take 'er to Lewtenant Grabisch."

"That sly fugger? He'll screw us. He'll bang her 'imsel, and we'll get nuffink," said the shorter soldier. "Lewtenant Harayam, he's new."

"All right, Harayam." The lock clicked, and the iron gate swung open.

The shorter soldier reached in. Maihara shrank back in alarm. The tall one lunged at the other and the soldiers scuffled. Maihara squealed.

"Don't maul her, you clown."

"Didn't mean nothing." The short one stopped struggling.

"Come out, girl, unless you wants to stay down 'ere and rot," said the taller soldier.

With trepidation Maihara came forward and edged past them toward the outer passage. A couple of unshaven and ragged prisoners rattled their bars and called out, feebly.

"Later, mateys," the taller soldier told them. They followed as she went along the arched stone passage and up the steps, her shadow creeping along the dank walls before her. Her heart hammered.

"Tasty arse," the shorter soldier said behind her, and

sniggered. Her fear about their intentions spiked.

They reached the main floor of the fort where the daylight half dazzled her, and crossed a vaulted hall. The soldiers walked on either side of her. There were bloodstains on the flagstones and smears where bodies had been dragged away. Pieces of wrecked furniture obstructed the floor. They detoured near a slit window which let in light and a stream of fresh air with a taint of smoke, and she made an eyes-left. One of her captors prodded her onward. She shuddered. Had she *really* seen that? - the pile of bloody corpses and the man dangling on a rope?

What had happened to her siblings? She'd heard talk of what the rebels did to nobles in the provinces they'd overrun. Dread crawled up her spine.

The duo took her to a whitewashed ground-floor room. A young officer, olive-skinned, wearing ill-fitting uniform trews and jacket and a green cap sat at a table, interviewing a thickset young man in civilian clothes whose muscles bulged out of the short sleeves of his shirt.

"I served in the Avergnian militia, sorr," the young man was saying, "and now the city is taken I thought me to join the regular rebel army." A sword in a plain scabbard hung from his belt.

The officer drummed his fingers on the desk as if made impatient by the youth's slow-paced and rustic-sounding speech. "What's your name, fellow?"

"Fofur, sorr."

"Well, Fofur, I commend your enthusiasm, but you've come to the wrong place. You need to find the 1st Regiment headquarters. It's in some street near here." He spoke with a more educated accent, but his face was flushed and he had a harassed air about him.

"Very good, sorr." Fofur sketched an approximate salute.

The officer leaned to one side, to see past the hulking young man. "Next," he shouted.

The soldiers holding Maihara saluted and dragged her forward. The officer, who had short curly dark hair, poked at the papers on his table in an effort to organise them.

"Found this prisoner in the cells, sir, says she's the Emperor's daughter."

"Really?" The officer, who wore what she took for lieutenant's stripes on his shoulders, scowled. "What would the Emperor's daughter be doing in the cells, you fools?"

"I was accused of a serious crime," Maihara said.

The officer jerked around and looked at her. "What crime?"

"Since you're the enemy, why would you care?"

The officer hesitated, slack-mouthed, showing a missing upper tooth. "We might. What's your name?"

She straightened her back and fixed the young officer with a look. "I am the Imperial Princess Maihara Zircona Cordana, Duchess of Avergne."

The young man seemed at a loss. He pointed to a wooden chair. "Please sit down, miss."

Maihara sat. Perhaps they weren't going to assault her. Her knees felt weak. "I'm usually addressed as Your Grace."

The officer shuffled his papers as though hoping to find instruction there on what to do with captured princesses. "Not any more, I think." He turned to the two soldiers. "You, find the commandant, and tell him we think we have the Emperor's daughter."

"Yes, sir," said the first soldier.

"Boss, what about some tink? We found this bint," said the second soldier.

The officer fumbled in his pocket and pulled out a couple of coins. "The commandant might give you more. Now, go!"

The soldiers took the coins and sloped off with a disappointed air. Maihara waited. The fort was alive with rebels, and a sense of horror oppressed her as she imagined what amount of killing had happened in the city.

The officer gave directions to a stream of soldiers who came with requests and reports. One, though clad in green jacket and trousers, had nape-length hair and a feminine figure. Maihara stared. What kind of people put women in military uniform?

"How long were you in the cells?" the officer asked, during a pause in the stream of enquirers.

"Several days. I lost count," Maihara said. She looked down. Her dress was grimy, and she smelt her armpits despite the odour of other unwashed bodies.

"Can I get you anything, miss?"

"Something to eat," Maihara said.

The curly-haired officer, who did not look much older than she was, stared at Maihara. "Why were you imprisoned, girl?"

She had a story prepared now. "I knew a noble whom I hear was accused of treason, and a weird flying creature came while I was on the roof, so they imagined all sorts of things."

The young man's eyes widened. "Magic?"

"It was nothing to do with me."

He stroked his chin. "You could be an impostor, not that I'd blame you for claiming to be more than you are, under the circumstances. Let's see if I can find someone to identify you."

He gave orders, and Maihara fidgeted in her chair. He could have paid mind to that earlier, she thought. Many people in the palace would be able to identify her, if they lived. But if the witness got the wrong idea, and denied her, it might end in disaster, with her handed over to brutes.

Soldiers brought in a dark-haired man in palace guard uniform.

"Do you know this girl?" the officer asked.

The captive stared at her blankly. "Sorry," he said at last.

The lieutenant glanced between Maihara and the captive, and gestured for the prisoner to be taken away.

Maihara's fear spiked. "I didn't know him either. Get someone else, a noble."

The lieutenant sighed. "You'd better not be wasting our time."

Within minutes, rebel soldiers dragged in another prisoner; a blond man, his shirt and fine trousers rumpled and grimy.

The soldiers held him before the young officer.

"I want you to identify this girl," the officer said.

The noble's eyes shifted to Maihara. She gave him a slight nod, heart pounding.

"That's Her Grace Maihara Zircona, Duchess of Avergne. The Emperor's eldest daughter."

The officer nodded in satisfaction and ordered that the man be taken back to his cell. Maihara sighed in relief.

The young officer turned to soldiers who stood idling nearby. Maihara sensed he was about to have her taken away and secured somewhere. "Wait! What has happened to my father, and my sister and brother?"

He turned back to stare at her. "You don't know? We have your brother and sister in custody, but we have not yet located the Emperor. Do you know where he might be?"

"No, I don't."

He narrowed his eyes. "You'll be punished if we find you're withholding information."

Maihara was not impressed. "Where have you looked?" she asked, in a pert tone.

"We ask the questions here. We searched the palace."

"All of it?"

"I told you, no questions." Her tone appeared to irritate the youth. "All of it."

"Then he could be anywhere." She made a sweeping gesture.

"Anywhere in the city, you mean."

Maihara shook her head. It was unlikely that her father had waited around to be plucked. Despite their difficult relations, the revelation pleased her.

"You know something, don't you, girl?"

"You got in, so why couldn't he get out?" People said the city mound was riddled with tunnels and old cellars, extending under the palace walls and maybe the city wall.

"Oh." The red-faced youth scowled. He gestured to the

idling soldiers. "You, lock her up and you, tell the General we've found the eldest Imperial daughter."

As the door slammed shut behind her, she glanced around the small room. The walls were whitewashed brick, and the glazed window was barred. The only furniture was a wooden bench, and a pile of jars and boxes lay in a corner. This place was part of the fort, the tower where the palace guard had been housed. At least there was light and air; it was an improvement on a subterranean cell.

A soldier brought in bread and cold meat on a plain white plate, but she had barely finished wolfing it down when rebel troopers led her upstairs. They took her into a stateroom, ornately panelled with carved wood, that she had visited for some ceremonial function the previous year. A coffered and painted ceiling soared above, and a great table occupied the centre of the room, with padded chairs ranked around it. Officers of the rebel force stood by holding papers and paying attention to a man who stood at the end of the table.

This man, dressed in a green jacket with gold general's epaulettes, pointed with a small cane to a boldly inked map of the city that lay on the table. He was of medium height, brown-haired, and his uniform resembled that of the regular army save for red cuff-bands. She took in an oval face, with deep-set eyes and a strong chin, and a stubbly beard and sideburns that half-hid a duelling scar. It was the face of a man who expected to be obeyed. As he asked questions, listened and gave orders, he reminded Maihara of men like Lord Farnak. Square-shouldered and deep chested, he stood straight and had the manner of a man who would be threatening in a fight. He had to be the leader here.

***

General Tarchon sensed a small disturbance at the doorway as two guards led the girl in. He glanced over to her then returned his attention to the staff officer who was presenting a schedule of supplies. "Just a moment."

He turned to inspect the girl as she was brought

forward. She wore a dress that had once been of plain design and good quality but was now grubby and had a dropped hem. Her hair was untidy, dark and wavy and a thick strand hung partly over her face, which was flushed and grimy. She wasn't slim, but stood straight-backed, looking around her with quick glances.

He had little doubt that the identification was correct. The costume and bearing suggested at least a minor noble, and with her prominent nose she had a look of some official portraits he had seen in the main palace. Princess Maihara, if this was she, arrived beside the head of the table, and his officers turned unbidden to examine her. She visibly tensed.

"This is her? The princess?"

"Yes, General," said one of the guards.

He stared into her face, guarding his expression. Her oddly coloured violet eyes flickered as she seemed to fight an impulse to look away. Attractive eyes.

"What's your name?"

"I am the Imperial Princess Maihara Zircona Cordana, Duchess of Avergne." Her voice was clear and aristocratic, with barely a tremor.

He made a frown. "That's a mouthful. What's your given name? Maihara?"

She nodded.

"I am General Tarchon, commander of the revolutionary army of Sar."

Maihara looked at him in surprise, her eyes widening.

"You?" She seemed to have expected someone older, or more diabolic.

Tarchon nodded. "Indeed." He swung the cane to point at her. "You can help us with something, Maihara. Where is your father hiding?"

She glared back at him. He knew that to use her given name was extremely rude, but he didn't care. He hated the nobility. Some of the high nobles his people had detained had been so arrogant they could hardly bear to address a commoner. He found that a punch in the face from one of his soldiers usually adjusted their attitude.

"You can address me as 'Your Grace'," she said.

"So where is he, Your Grace?" He gave her rank a sarcastic emphasis.

"I have no idea." She answered with an upward tilt of her head no doubt meant to tell him that even if she knew, there was no way she'd tell.

"If we find you've been lying to us..."

Maihara met his gaze and pressed her lips together.

Tarchon stared back, evaluating her. A spirited girl, not easily intimidated. He exhaled, and shook his head.

"So, what are we going to do with you, Maihara? What use are you?"

"I can think of a use for her," said one of the officers, and laughed. She flinched.

"Be silent, Kaugufan," said Tarchon, in a voice intended to cow the hilarity into silence. "When I want your boorish wit, I'll ask for it."

Men who had been about to laugh composed their faces. The girl's jaw dropped a fraction and the officer, cowed, took a half step back. "I apologise, General."

Tarchon returned his attention to Maihara, with an enquiring look.

"I can speak three languages, and I'm educated in arithmetic, geography, drawing, music and literature," she said.

"Useful, but hardly unique. Yet an advance on the other one."

She straightened her back. "My sister?" Her urgent tone radiated concern.

Tarchon did not care to discuss the sister, and brushed aside the question. "Have you ever seen life outside the Palace? Apart from going to balls, or looking down on the populace at processions?"

"Not much," Maihara admitted. She lowered her head and frowned, clearly not liking his tone.

"Many of my men want all the Imperials executed. What do you say to that?"

Maihara flinched but met his eye. "I'd rather stay alive." Perhaps she had already confronted such terrors on being arrested, imprisoned and detained by rough men.

He leaned forward. "So, what can you offer, to justify your existence?"

She stilled and her jaw dropped slightly as the question sank in. The officers in the room remained silent.

"As I said, I'm educated. And I'm the oldest sibling." That was little, to justify her life. She froze, apparently unable to speak.

"Ah." He turned to his closest officers, acting the part. "What's the oldest good for? Any experts here?"

The nearest officer leaned forward. "The snivelling boy is the Crown Prince, and first in succession. Under the Imperial law that is. But this one acts like a Crown Princess."

"Wasn't she accused of something?" Tarchon swept his gaze around the gathered officers. "Prisoner's escort, what can you tell us?"

"Sir, she was found in a cell below, sir. Apparently imprisoned for some crime, sir."

"If you please, General," said one of the officers, "according to the lieutenant's report, she was accused of sorcery."

Tarchon frowned. "Nobody welcomes a sorceress. What have you to say for yourself, girl?"

Maihara let her hands drop and stood straight. From her tense expression, it looked as though she was calculating what words would reduce her danger. She took a breath. "The accusations are false. I happened to be on the roof when a flying reptile came down and caused a panic. The accusers jumped to false conclusions."

"Is that so? Can you prove you're not a sorceress?" Tarchon asked.

"It's hard to prove a negative," Maihara said, looking him in the eye. He could sense the tension in her.

"That's true." Tarchon stroked his chin. She was speaking to him as if he was her equal. He didn't mind that;

it was better than looking down her nose or cringing for mercy like the others. She was little more than a child, not one of the major criminals, and she had a rounded, generous, rather kindly looking face. His interrogators could question her later, to discover if she knew anything of interest. He turned to his officers with a slight upturn of the corners of his mouth. "Colonel Impar, find out what she knows, and then put her in a decent room somewhere and arrange that she gets food, a change of clothes, a maid; that sort of thing."

Maihara let out her breath. She turned her head to look at them all, evidently distrusting their intentions, but relaxed. No trial or execution was imminent.

Impar's round eye-glasses glinted. "Yes, sir. Shall I let her associate with the other two afterwards?"

"Not yet. Not till we've investigated those Imperial accusations."

Guards in the ill-matched armour and uniforms of his rebels hustled Maihara away and down the stone stairs followed by the thin, silver-haired Impar. As she was taken down, another noble prisoner was being escorted up. Tarchon reached for the list of supplies and initialled it.

-8-

At first, Maihara was anxious as the carriage left the palace and rolled through streets littered with the debris of fighting and looting, passing tall buildings scarred by fire and broken windows, but she relaxed on noting the polite but relaxed demeanour of her guards.

They placed Maihara in a small suite of rooms in a white mansion, just outside the Palace walls. It was a compact, easily guarded building that had been the home of a noble or at least wealthy family. The mansion was distinguished by a coat of arms painted on doors and embossed in plaster, but she could not put a name to it. The owners were absent, either fled or taken away by the invaders, and their furniture and possessions pillaged. Her bedroom was carpeted and had been furnished with satinwood furniture of good quality and the walls washed with pink. Intruders had dragged furniture about, and strewn drawers and contents on the floor.

"We'll clear this up," said her thin-faced minder, Colonel Impar, with a glance at the escort soldiers. "Is there anything you want?"

"My clothes, from my room in the children's wing of the Palace," Maihara said.

The officer shrugged. He had a prominent nose and round-lensed spectacles, and she thought him rather rat-faced, and looking a little old to be a soldier.

"And my books," she added in a low voice.

"Anything else?" Impar asked in a sarcastic tone. She sensed that he disliked her.

"Your General would like me to have these things."

Impar gave her a look. "I'll see about it. Where's the room?"

She gave him directions. She wanted to ask for her wooden chest, but caution made her silent. If she asked for it, the inquisitive rat-faced one would be sure to look inside it and find her box. Better to lose it than draw attention to its incriminating contents. Much as she wanted it back, she dared not risk the rebels finding evidence that linked her to the terrifying pterostrophe.

She slumped in a chair while two women, recruited from who knew where, undid the disorder created when the house had been ransacked. They wore red arm-bands, which Maihara deduced meant that they had come with the rebels or were sympathisers. They piled garments and trinkets back into opened drawers, straightened pictures hanging on the walls and removed a slashed painting. Working together, they re-made the stripped four-poster bed and replaced the box-stool at its foot.

One of the women stood in the middle of the room, hands on hips. "Looks better now." She turned to Maihara. "You needing anything?"

Maihara picked up a hand-mirror from the dressing table and looked in it. Her forehead bore a smear of grime. Without that other mirror, her chances of raising any useful magic to get her out of here were crippled.

"I need to wash." She rubbed, but some of the dirt on her image remained. And a grey cobweb clung to her unruly hair.

"She needs a bath," the first woman said. The second woman sniffed.

"Do you want a bath?" the first woman said loudly to Maihara, as if she were deaf.

Maihara nodded. "Please see to it." She felt weary, and there seemed little prospect of making these women show proper respect. It was enough to be alive.

Not long afterwards, a portable bathtub of wood and metal arrived, followed by several pails of steaming water. The women dragged them into a smaller room that opened off the bedroom.

They ushered Maihara into the wash-room and

indicated that she should undress. After hesitating, Maihara complied. It appeared that they did not intend to assist her. She got in the tub and gave them an enquiring look.

"What?" said the second one in an unfriendly tone.

The duo clearly did not think it was their job to help Maihara bathe. She waved them out and reached for the flannel and the hunk of malodorous soap. After she washed, rinsed and dried herself, her skin glowed with cleanliness.

The women found her fresh clothes. The garments had obviously belonged to the previous adult occupant of the room but were too tight for Maihara's figure.

She asked to be taken to her rooms in the Palace, to collect various items. Her request was denied. Not giving up hope, she prevailed on the servants to go there and check on what remained.

The women left, leaving her to sit in the bedroom. It was disagreeable to be wearing someone else's ill-fitting clothes, but at least they were clean. The many objects in the room were a poignant reminder of another family's loss.

Alone at last, she sought the remains of her magic. The city's magical aura extended here, and in a moment she had accessed the first set of spells. And the second array? With a stab of dismay, she realised that, with the papers in front of her, she had never needed to memorise the passwords properly. What was it - *z-something*?

A desperate half-hour later she recollected them and breathed a huge sigh of relief. She wouldn't make that mistake again. Now she could send out the spy spell. Using magic gave her a headache, and the encounter with the pterostrophe had been a disaster, but she did not intend to use the dangerous deep levels of magic again, not that she could without the book.

Where were her sister and brother? She hoped that, like her, they were being decently treated. No doubt the rebels had mansions to spare. And her father? There was no word of his capture and the streets outside were quiet with no sound of rebel celebrations, so he could have got away. For the sake of the Empire, she wished it so.

And what of her companions Amarin and Berna? With a pang of guilt, she realised that she had barely thought of their fate.

She started the spy spell and embarked on a systematic search of the mansion, starting with this floor, sweeping the view around each room and listening. The glazed windows defined the limits of the building. She moved the view up a floor. Within minutes, the spy spell showed her that her brother and sister were in a room higher up in the same building, and apparently unhurt.

She banged on the door till a cross-looking soldier opened it.

"I want to see my brother and sister," she demanded. "Where are they?"

"I can't tell you." His face showed indifference. "Orders."

"Whose orders?"

"General orders. We don't go telling prisoners that sort of information."

"That's just an excuse. I want to speak to your superior officer."

The lanky Colonel Impar came some time later, with two soldiers. "I hear you want to see your siblings," he said. "Well, you can't just yet." He stared at her, unsmiling behind his spectacles.

This refusal increased her resolve. "Why not? What have you done to them? They're children."

"We're still making enquiries."

"That's ridiculous. They don't know anything." She clenched a fist.

"That's for us to decide."

She resolved on a little theatre. Tears prickled her eyes. "You've hurt them, haven't you? What harm will it do if I see them? You think we're going to exchange secret messages?"

Impar scowled and shook his head. "Stop that, will you?" He appeared to reconsider. "Can you do anything with the Prince?"

"Why, what's wrong?"

"Come with me."

Maihara sprang forward with a sigh of relief.

Impar and soldiers led her up a narrow flight of stairs to the former servants' rooms at the top of the mansion.

"And what has happened to my ladies-in-waiting, and the other servants at the Palace?" she asked Impar's back, as they climbed.

He turned. "Who knows?" His face was a mask of indifference. "Have you names?"

"Yes—"

"Get me a list of names." He walked on.

Sihrima and Persis were in a bright but plain room painted all in white. It was furnished with wall cupboards, a table and a few hard chairs. Sihrima, wearing a red brocade dress that she favoured, sat with a book on her lap, looking bored while Persis rocked from side to side, staring at the wall.

Sihrima stood up quickly, letting the book fall, and the sisters embraced. Sihrima smelt of soap.

"Are you all right?" Maihara asked. "Have they done anything to you?" She touched a dark mark on Sihrima's cheek.

"No," her sister said. "It's been scary, and they're so rude." Sihrima's dark curly hair was tied back with a ribbon. She turned to stare pertly at Colonel Impar.

Impar leaned on the wall by the door, arms folded.

Both sisters turned to look at Persis. Maihara bit her lip. The prince had not been quite right since taking a heavy fall from his horse at a parade the previous month.

Maihara went over to her brother. "Have they hurt you?"

"I couldn't do anything when the rebels came," Persis said, in a small voice. "There were too many of them." He hung his head.

Maihara touched his shoulder. Persis looked younger than his fourteen years. His skin was pale and smooth, almost like a girl's, and fine straight hair hung down well below his ears. His face could pass for a girl's too, as they had found during childish charades and dressing-up in the past. She stroked his neck. "Nobody will ask you to fight any more, if I have anything to do with it. Nothing's your fault."

Sihrima tugged at Maihara's dress. "Did they ask you about ransom?"

Maihara turned her head. "No, but I would not be surprised if it's in their minds."

"I can't wait to get out of here. It's so boring. I hope they ransom me soon. What about you? Is it true that they arrested you?"

Maihara shrugged. "Yes."

"They locked you in a cell?"

"Yes."

"In a cell? They weren't lying? What was that about?" Sihrima's expression was eager.

"I was watching a strange-looking flying creature on the roof, when the secret service men grabbed me and accused me of all sorts of weird things."

Her sister gaped at her. "Why?"

"The war. They see conspiracies and spies everywhere."

"But why lock you up?" her sister persisted.

Maihara felt a growing irritation. "I told you." Sihrima was so slow that she wanted to slap her on the head, but the rat-faced Colonel was watching. She didn't know whether she would welcome being ransomed, given the contrast between the treatment she had received from the Empire and the rebels.

Her brother sat aside, withdrawn. She put her hands on his shoulders and shook him gently. "Don't think about what's past. Try to be positive. Talk to people." She felt sorry that she was unable to penetrate his distress, at the same time exasperated that he couldn't pull himself together.

While Maihara spoke to her brother in an effort to raise his mood, Sihrima paced about the room.

Maihara pointed to a black beam that spanned the ceiling. "If you've got that much energy, you could do some exercises in here."

Sihrima just scowled at her. "That's what common people do!"

Impar rapped on the inside of the door and beckoned to Maihara. "Come away. That'll do." As they descended the stairs he barked, "What's wrong with him?"

"He gets a black mood from time to time. Your locking him up has made it worse."

Impar shrugged.

Back in her room, Maihara moved with a lightness after confirming her siblings were safe and unharmed. She waited in trepidation for the servants to return from her rooms. If this worked, and she was able to trust them, she would see about sending them for the box.

A servant wearing a red armband returned with a couple of dresses and a few trinkets and told her the rooms had been pillaged.

Maihara thanked her and kept her feelings to herself. It would be foolish to shed any tears over her lost things. Some books from her bookshelf, works on history, warfare, adventure and the constitution, also arrived in a box.

The guards had told her this building was called the Anwar mansion after its previous occupants. She stood by her window and parted the net curtains. Unlike her rooms in the Palace, this place did not command views of the city, only the back of another mansion and beyond it the roofs of the Palace. The servants did not tell her much of what was happening outside, even when pressed. She supposed they had been instructed not to. It was worse than being confined to her chambers in the Palace.

There might be people in the adjoining buildings who were loyal to the Empire and wanted it back. They couldn't all be rebel sympathisers. With patience, the spy spell would enable her to seek them out. Then she would have to find a way to contact them and organise an escape. She'd head east to territory still held by the Empire. But first, to try spying, and to look for routes to escape on foot.

Demophon had evidently been a rebel. What would happen if she asked her captors to trace him and bring him here?

She half expected the General to summon her, but he left her to read and fret for several days. She supposed he had more important things on his mind, such as consolidating his ill-gotten gains and rounding up enemies. He had been extremely ill-mannered, but he'd not spoken to her as if she was a child, or let her be ill-treated.

Tutored lessons had not always been to her liking, but they had filled up the day. Now she occupied herself with spell-spying in the adjacent buildings and making a mental map of locations and who spoke well of the Empire and against the rebels. It was tiring work, and she dare not write anything down.

Her room faced another mansion, where there were people who, from what she overheard, were sympathetic to the Empire. Among them was a boy who sometimes played below her window, in a yard separated from the Anwar's back yard by an eight-foot-high wall. He looked the same age as Persis. She could start by contacting him. He was clearly present during their loyalist conversations.

She wrote a note on a scrap of paper, and weighted it with the only item she found to hand, a piece of costume jewellery. '*A lady needs your help*,' it said. She waited. After some hours, the boy appeared in the yard below. She opened the sliding window, her heart beating faster, and threw the note high, in the direction of the other mansion. It arced over and landed at his feet. He picked it up.

Using her spy spell, she watched in an agony of impatience as he unfolded the paper and slowly read, his lips moving.

Don't tell me he can't read.

He looked up. She waved. The freckly face split in a grin, and then the boy dashed out of sight.

She waited, racked with uncertainty, unable to see him with her spy spell. The boy might simply betray her, or he might fetch an adult with whom she'd have to work out a plan of escape. Resourceful men could trick the guards, or get her out by the window and into the other building. Then she, and she hoped her siblings, would have to escape the rebel-held city and make their way east. Once in Imperial territory it would be best to lie low till her father's mood mellowed.

A distant noise attracted her attention. A window facing her room lifted up with a scrape and the shutters, previously closed, were open. The boy leaned out, grinning and waving. "Hey!"

"Quiet!" she hissed, and put a finger over her lips.

The boy nodded.

Now she had to devise a way of communicating with him, silently. Written notes would be better than shouting. With a wave, she stepped back and hastily penned another note, just "Have you found someone?". She weighted it and attached a line of grey thread to the bundle. If she missed the window, she would haul it back.

By the time she was ready to lob it, the boy had disappeared. *Unreliable.*

He reappeared a few minutes later with another boy, darker-skinned, with curly black hair. They grinned and waved.

She threw the weighted note upward as hard as she could in the direction of the other building. It hit the building's brick wall and fell on the roof of a low extension, and to her relief the boy climbed out and retrieved it. He read the note and nodded, before pointing to the other boy.

Idiot. She shook her head and held a hand above her hair, to signal that she wanted a grown-up. The boy crouched down, doing something out of sight, and a minute later tossed out the weight, which dangled in mid-air. As she hauled in the thread, a double string came with it, clearly intended for hauling messages to and fro. Maybe he wasn't so stupid after all.

He'd written on the note in an almost illegible spiky scrawl. "This will be our secret."

Annoyed, she wrote. "This is not a game. I need a grown-up to help me." She cut away and disentangled the excess thread, and worked the twin strings to send the note back.

The brown-haired boy read the note. Maybe the other one couldn't read. His manner became less bouncy. The paper passed back and forth a few times, conveying personal questions, and answers. With misgivings, she gave them her real name. She doubted that the average person, however sympathetic to the Empire, would risk their necks for a mere noble. Abruptly, the boys dropped the string, closed the window and disappeared.

She sat, breathing quickly and collecting her thoughts. She so hoped this was going to work, but her accomplices did not seem reliable. Those boys just wanted to fool about and play secret agents, but this was a deadly affair.

-9-

A distant shouting infiltrated through the window from outside, disturbing Maihara's thoughts. The maid who brought Maihara's lunch to her room appeared distracted, and platters rattled as she shouldered the closing door. Maihara seized the tilting tray.

"What's happening?" she asked.

"The Dhikr have arrived in the city. Now we'll all be raped, robbed and murdered in our beds."

A chill of alarm shivered down Maihara's spine. This news confused her. "I thought the Dhikr were your people's allies?"

"They fought against our enemies. But they're brutes. And now they're being let into the city."

Maihara set the tray down. "But the rebels seized Calah. They won't want to let go of what they've stolen." Her stomach churned. Had there been some change in the balance of power between the invading factions? That would not be good.

The maid was silent, clasping her hands together.

Maihara tried again. "Have the rebels given the city over to the Dhikr?" The maid could have picked up some rumour.

"I only heard that they're coming in, Mistress."

So far as Maihara knew, the rebels alone held Calah, and their allies, or ex-allies, would not get in without a stiff fight. Yet, she had heard the Dhikr were seasoned and terrifying warriors who had crushed an Imperial army, while the rebels were no more than an armed militia. It was not reassuring.

She made herself eat the meal, remembering how food had stopped coming during the first invasion. Nobody came to escort her to visit with her siblings, and a tension pervaded the mansion. Sounds of distant shouting intruded through her window. Maihara sat with a history book on her lap till her legs became numb, the pages unturned. She read the same paragraphs over and over without taking in the words.

More shouting and thumping filtered through the floor from below. Two soldiers came and ushered Maihara politely down the stairs.

"What's going on?" she asked.

"You'll see, lady," was all they said.

Heart thumping, she wondered if they meant to hand her over to the Dhikr.

The soldiers pushed her into the mansion's main hall, an ornate space with a high coffered plaster ceiling. At the far side stood a dozen primitive warriors, clad in scale armour, with horned helmets. Maihara gasped. They looked alien against the wood-panelled walls, marble pilasters and chequered marble floor. On the near side of the great room stood Tarchon with his officers and around twenty mail-clad and armoured troops.

The barbarians glowered with narrowed eyes at the men opposite. Their skins were browned by weather and scarred by cuts. Their thick limbs, exotic armour, weapons at their belts and scowling faces all spoke violence. She shuddered. Easy to see why the Imperial armies had broken. Their leader, a tall, wide man with a black beard and scarred face, had a spiked mace hung from his belt.

Tarchon beckoned, and the guards ushered Maihara over to him. She caught her breath and her hands shook. It was a relief to be placed next to the General on the rebel side of the room. She really didn't want to stand near the barbarians. Tarchon wore his full uniform with decorations. He and all his officers were armed. A sour stench tainted the air in the room, a smell that Maihara presumed came from the barbarians, the reek of unwashed bodies and clothes.

"Is this fugging wench her, then?" the large barbarian

asked, in a guttural accent.

"This is Her Grace Maihara Zircona Cordana, the Crown Princess," Tarchon said. This was the first time he had used her full title in her hearing. "Your Grace, this is the warlord Barin, of the Dhikr."

So this was Tarchon's equivalent among the barbarians. Barin did not respond directly, but turned aside and said a few words to his men that Maihara did not understand. Several of the Dhikr chuckled.

"And is this one a woman yet?" Barin asked. Even though they were speaking in the Empire's Sar language, his accent made it hard for her to follow what the warlord said.

"Her Grace is seventeen, so another year."

"Another year of childhood?" Barin sneered. "In our land we make women of 'em at fourteen. I bet you've been rogering her already, haven't you?" He made a poking gesture with his finger that made it plain to Maihara what he meant.

Shocked at his directness, she kept her reddening face immobile.

"I'll ignore that offensive remark," Tarchon said, in a loud voice. A brief silence oppressed the room.

Barin glowered. "Empress, eh? She seems to have more spine than the fairy boy." He scratched his crotch, causing his scale armour to grate. "What you say, one of us marries the tart."

Marry a pie? It took her but a moment to catch his meaning, and tense with alarm.

While they were speaking, one of the barbarian warriors walked to a corner of the room and hitched up his armour skirt. A stream of wetness trickled past the man's boots.

"General, I don't mean to be rude or offensive, but in the interests of harmony, could you ask your men to piss outside our buildings, or in the garderobes provided?" Tarchon said.

"We'll piss where we fugging well please," Barin snarled. He put his hand on the handle of his mace.

A clink and clatter filled the hall as armoured men put hands to their weapon hilts, and her stomach clenched. If they started killing each other, she'd be caught in the middle of it.

Tarchon, chin held high, stared Barin down and raised his arm as if about to give a signal. "Then if you please, piss outside."

Seconds passed. Barin grunted and lowered his gaze with a shrug.

"We have no plans to have the Princess married, General," Tarchon said.

Barin looked blank. "Uh, marriage?" he said after a pause. He grinned. "Would she ride my stallion, then?" He fixed Maihara with a piggy stare.

"He wants to know if you'll marry him," Tarchon explained.

Maihara found her voice. "I'd rather die." She glanced at Tarchon, and with a mild shock saw his appraising look.

"What did she say?" Barin demanded, in a menacing tone.

Tarchon took a half-step forward and put a hand on the hilt of his dress sword. "What kind of answer did you expect, Dhikr?"

Barin scowled. "Am I bothered? She's ugly anyway. You can keep the sodding witch, Tarchon." He stepped two paces forward.

Maihara took a step back, colliding with an officer. Why was he calling her a witch? Merely an insult?

Barin peered at her. "Nice big titties, though." He pointed at Tarchon. "That's what he likes." Barin laughed, allowing Maihara to smell his bad breath. "I'm done here. We'll go where there's no fuggers looking down their noses at us."

A sense of intense relief swept over Maihara as Barin gathered his men and tramped out.

She waited till the door closed behind the Dhikr. "You're allied with him?"

"I'm afraid so. Not ideal, but he's manageable if kept in

his place. I hope that wasn't too distressing, but he insisted on having a look at you." Tarchon looked down at her with a half-smile.

Maihara shrugged. "I didn't understand half of what he said."

"He was using words well-bred young ladies shouldn't know," Tarchon said. The officers chuckled.

Maihara eyed Tarchon. She had revised her opinion of him. He wasn't quite a gentleman, but a decent man compared to Barin, the vilest brute she had ever met.

Back in her room, she placed her hands under her breasts and cupped them, gently. Being called ugly, even by an ignorant barbarian lout, had hurt. But, big titties. Tarchon likes big titties. Ha.

Even if General Tarchon was less repulsive than the Dhikr, the suggestion that he found her of sexual interest was unsettling. She dismissed the thought at once. All the more reason to recover her box and use it to make her escape. She had to get to the palace, and once there, she could make an excuse to explore the remains of her room, but there was no obvious way of bringing this about.

Within hours, however, the rebels collected Maihara by coach and drove in the direction of the Palace. As the coach moved off, her anxiety rose. This movement might be connected to the Dhikr visit. Perhaps the rebels had already hatched some deal to hand her over. The guards in the carriage refused to answer her questions. Her body tensed with fear.

A few poorly dressed people were moving from alley to alley, and signs of fighting still disfigured the streets near the mansion. Ominous stains marked the pavements and buildings had windows and doors boarded up or broken in. Furniture and other objects discarded by looters lay by the roadside. A fire-damaged building lay blackened with charred timbers showing through holes in the roof.

Doorways and side passages beckoned as the coach rolled by, and she thought for a moment of opening the coach door and jumping out. Her fingers touched the door handle.

With a cough, a guard reached an arm forward. She sat back.

Only when she sighted the palace outer wall did she recollect that she had hoped to enter the Palace to look for her box.

Four guards brought her to an ornate room on the ground floor of the Palace, next to the staterooms on the southern side. As the heavy door thudded shut behind her, Maihara found herself facing a twin row of metal sculptures and modelled figures on plinths, all jointed as though parts could be moved. A tall window shed a yellow light. The walls were decorated with gold pilasters and red flock paper, and a full colour allegorical painting adorned the ceiling.

Voices murmured. Tarchon, a couple of aides and the rat-faced officer, Impar, stood inspecting the exhibits. The setting confused her.

Tarchon still wore the green jacket with the gold epaulettes. His brown hair, too short to benefit from a comb, was neatly trimmed and his strong chin had the beginnings of a beard. He appeared to be in a good mood and eyed her with a disrespectful smile. "You scrub up nicely, Princess."

Maihara straightened her back and did not reply. Warmth rose to her face. She would have to think on her feet. What if he threatened to give her to Barin?

Tarchon beckoned her forward. Heart beating, she moved to join him.

"What do you know about these, Princess?" Tarchon asked, gesturing to the plinths. "Automata, they say."

"Yes," she said, uncertain what he wanted. Why would they be interested in automata? "Well, they move." She had seen them demonstrated to visitors on state occasions.

Tarchon did not seem too surprised. "What, clockwork? Is there a key?"

"Maybe behind the plinths. You're not going to smash them up, are you?"

Tarchon frowned. "We're not vandals, Princess."

One of the officers, apparently, was an engineer. He found a large key and cautiously applied it to a dressed doll-figure, with a clicking sound. He removed the key and looked at Maihara. "Now what?"

She pointed to an inconspicuous knob. "There, I think." Demonstrating the automata was not going to make her situation any worse, rather it might motivate the rebels to preserve the devices.

The officer pressed it. With a jerky motion, the automaton, a female figure in court dress, leaned forward and played on a small xylophone with two metal hammers which swung from side to side. The tune was quite recognisable.

One of the men swore and stepped back. "Magic," he muttered.

Maihara smirked. She knew better, but asides from a few clocks and a few automata belonging to great nobles, no mechanisms as sophisticated as these existed outside the walls of the Palace.

"The Nut Tree," Tarchon murmured. So he too knew that tune.

They moved to the biggest automata, which resembled a metal bird sitting on a bed of twisted glass rods.

"What does this do?" Tarchon asked by way of conversation as the engineer wound it.

"It all moves," Maihara said. She folded her arms across her chest. If they got it working, it would save her the effort of explaining.

The automaton clicked into motion. The waterbird extended its neck and undulated it as if it was alive, while silver and jewelled wings extended. The glass rods transformed into twinkling water in which painted fish bobbed up. This was her favourite of the automata. With exclamations, two of the men took a step back.

"What's inside it?" Tarchon asked, after the others had

recovered their composure.

"Clockwork." Maihara was enjoying this, watching the rebels awed by the automata.

The engineer found a panel in the plinth and opened it. He peered inside, with an oath. "This is mad. I've seen clockwork, but not like this."

The others bent to look. Over their shoulders, Maihara saw a mass of yellow metal shafts and toothy wheels that filled the entire interior. Most were in motion, in a simulacrum of metallic life.

"What is all this for?" Tarchon asked her, gesturing to the line of automata. "No, don't answer that. Come and explain these to me."

He led her to a table at the side of the room, on which several shiny objects lay. Impar followed.

"We found these things in a room next to the Emperor's bedroom and private audience room," Tarchon said. "What can you tell us about them?"

All the objects were of metal, but there the similarity ended. A metal model of a winged cat, with whiskers of gold wire and sapphire eyes, lay next to part of a human arm, with wires and rods trailing from the open end. It looked like the claw that had given her a shock, when she glimpsed it inside her father's workshop. But it was just an arm. Other bits looked like the innards of a mechanical clock, all spiky wheels. Tools lay in a pile. A large magnifying glass was set in an ornate metal frame.

She took a breath. Her impulse was to deny any knowledge of these mechanisms, but the rebels already associated these automata with her father, and suspected their significance.

"What room did you find these in? The one to the left of his private chambers?"

Tarchon nodded.

"We children were forbidden to go in there, on pain of severe punishment. It was always kept locked, but we knew it was a workshop. Can we go in there now?"

Tarchon glanced at Impar, who nodded, spectacles

glinting. "In a moment. Don't touch anything in there." He gestured to the table. "Do these things work?"

"Maybe."

"The cat flies?" Tarchon gave a snort. Unlike the larger models, the cat had no base.

"I expect its wings flap if you wind it. There are other models like that around the Palace if your men haven't smashed them all."

Tarchon narrowed his eyes. "I told you, we're not vandals."

"I've seen the damage," Maihara said.

Tarchon shrugged. "There was fighting."

Colonel Impar pointed to the metal arm. "What the devil's that nasty thing?"

"It looks like a man's arm," Maihara said, deadpan.

"There's a rumour that the Emperor threatened us with mechanical men," Impar said. "This looks as though he had his artificers make parts for one."

Tarchon stared at her. "What else do you know about this?"

"Nothing. We weren't supposed to know anything."

"Did anyone else talk about it?"

"Not in my hearing." She was not going to tell them what Lord Farnak had told her, that Cordan claimed to be developing an army of golim soldiers. A mood of defiance bubbled up to the surface. "If you think you've defeated my father, you'd better watch out."

Tarchon scowled, which made him look intimidating. "We are. Do you know where he might be hiding?"

She stared back at him. "No." Even if she did, she saw no reason to help the rebels.

Tarchon sighed.

"We'll keep searching the storerooms and cellars, General," one of the officers said.

"Very well, but get it done quickly." Tarchon picked up the mechanical arm and bent it at the elbow.

The door of her father's workshop stood ajar, the lock broken, and a rebel trooper stood on guard. Tarchon ushered her inside. A clear light came from a south-facing window. To one side were plain wooden shelves loaded with battered books, and to the other rows of cabinets. In the centre were benches littered with tools and incomplete mechanisms and metal parts. At the back was a desk with a couple of models on it, and more stood on top of the cabinets and bookshelves.

"Well?" Tarchon asked her.

"I've never been in here before. He liked to make things."

"Did anyone else come in here?" Impar asked. His long nose pointed at her.

"Only his special workmen, I think."

Impar grunted. "You know any names?"

She shook her head, glancing around the room. There were no humanoid parts. Perhaps Farnak was right, and no golims would trouble the rebels anytime soon. Her father had talked of distant workshops. If the Sar Emperor wanted workshops, he would get them, but from mechanical toys to armies of mechanical men was a big step. And if they did show up outside Calah's walls, that was the rebels' problem, not hers.

They led her along a short, ornately furnished passage lined with cabinets containing exotic ceramics, still unsmashed, to a room which she recognised as her father's study, though disorganised as if a storm had hit it, with ornate inlaid furniture in disarray and a litter of books and papers on the floor. The room had been hastily but thoroughly searched.

Tarchon seated himself behind her father's broad desk, of dark carved southwood inlaid with a pattern in paler woods. His aides stood alongside him while the guards grouped behind her. Seeing him sitting in the Emperor's place disturbed and depressed her.

"We have a few questions we need to put to you."

She struggled to control her thumping heart. They had chosen this setting to impress her after putting her at her

ease with the automata. What could they want to find out
that they hadn't asked already?

"You say you're not a sorceress, and you were merely
watching a flying reptile when the Fifth Bureau arrested
you?"

She took a breath and nodded. The mention of the
reptile incident unsettled her. So, they were picking at that
again.

"And why did this unnatural creature appear when you
went to the roof? Just a coincidence?"

Maihara met his gaze. "How would I know? Maybe
some male magician used to feed it there."

Tarchon made as if to say something, then closed his
mouth. "This is your handwriting, isn't it?" he said,
pointing to a paper on the desk. "It matches your other
jottings."

Maihara's jaw dropped. She recognised the parchment
as the same that she had drafted but not sent with the
messenger-bird. A chill swept over her.

She remained silent. What were they driving at? At least
it gave her a reason for being on the roof.

Tarchon smirked, and the officers glanced at each other.
Impar sneered.

"We found this when we searched the Fifth Bureau
offices. Their record-keeping is good. So, you were trying
to send a message to the Shardans?"

"What if I was?" Maihara said with ill grace. If they
knew so much, it was useless to carry on denying it.

"We're merely curious," Tarchon said. "I thought that
the Shardans were out of favour at Court. Things must have
been desperate if the Court was begging for their aid. But
why do it under your seal? Perhaps it was your idea?"

Maihara remained silent, and shrugged. She could claim
it was Farnak's idea, but what was the point?

"Will the Imperial command be pleased when they find
you planned to send a diplomatic message?" Tarchon
asked, fixing her with his grey-eyed stare.

"I think they're already aware of this," she snapped. She

would not be safe in the Imperial lands now.

"How pro-Empire is the Shardan principality, would you say?"

She remained silent.

"Their paperwork shows that they think you summoned the flying monster and sent it away by shouting a magic curse after it had done its work of clearing part of the wall. Charges were pending, when our attack came."

She found her breath caught in her throat. What else had she jotted on that paper? The room went a misty grey. *They know*. The attack, the defeat. The Imperials would blame it all on her.

One of the officers started forward. "Are you all right, Princess?"

"Yes." Maihara recovered herself, determined that she wouldn't cry. What now? Would Tarchon go on to accuse her of sorcery and have her executed? Her knees were weak.

Tarchon was smiling. "Either way, that beast helped us." He spun his pen on the desk. "By the way, we found a warren of sub-cellars and passages under the Palace. Is that where your father is hiding?"

She straightened her back and glared at him, tight-lipped.

"Still not talking?" Tarchon grinned as if she had done something amusing.

It annoyed her.

"You've no ideas? No family hidey-holes?"

The man was insolent. "Certainly not! Who do you think I am?"

"Well, what are we to do with you?" Tarchon asked, dropping his insincere smile. "You've been a naughty girl," he said. "You've been plotting to escape."

She gasped, and a chill ran through her. Surely, they'd punish her for this.

"We had the boy whipped, and moved the family out. If he'd been an adult, we'd have executed him. We won't tolerate any attempt to free our high-ranking prisoners. Do you understand?"

"Yes." She nodded. Whipped. That was cruel. How did they intend to punish her?

"Some of our more extreme supporters want you executed. Many of the poor backed us in hopes that we would relieve their poverty. When they find we can't do as much as they hoped, they'll be angry, and we may need some public executions to pacify them."

"And reduce the number of parasites," Impar said in a low voice.

She stared at Tarchon, frozen. This couldn't be happening. He couldn't execute her. It wasn't her fault.

"We could ransom you, if the Imperial side are willing to pay. They've plenty money in Chancungra."

Maihara dropped her gaze. So the Imperial state was still functioning and held the eastern capital. Being ransomed no longer held any attraction, not if the Emperor held her personally responsible for the collapse of Calah's defences. What did the man want of her? Clearly he wanted something.

"So, what do you want, Princess? Do you want to be ransomed? Or do you prefer to stay here?"

Maihara found the question impossible. She didn't want to stay in the hands of the conquerors, but being returned to the Imperial Court could be worse. If only she had someone to advise her.

"Did you capture Lord Farnak?" she asked. "What happened to him?"

"Farnak?" the General said. "We've got him. He'll be executed for his crimes against the people."

Maihara gasped. "But he's not a bad man!"

Tarchon shook his head. "On the contrary, he's a very bad man. Thousands of peasants starved on his lands last year in a famine he made worse, because he hoarded grain while prices rose, and he has executed dozens of our people who campaigned for justice."

Maihara clenched her fists. "Please don't kill him." The thought of this happening to someone known to her was horrible.

Tarchon shrugged. "Why make an exception for one criminal?"

She stared at him. This man was as brutal as a gladiator. She doubted he lost much sleep over sending people to their deaths.

Tarchon shifted a paper on the Imperial desk, indifferent to her reaction. "The Imperialists have shown an interest in ransoming your sister, but they don't want you."

Maihara flushed, irked by his sneering tone. He'd just asked her if she wanted to be ransomed. He'd been playing with her. "What about my brother?"

"They want him." Tarchon lounged back in his chair. "But since he's the Crown Prince, I think we'll keep him. But what are we to do with you? No obvious use, and the people like to see rich parasites executed."

Maihara looked away, into a dark corner. Executed? Surely he was playing a game with her. This was the point where she should offer to do something useful, but the words stuck in her throat. Despair dragged her down. They wanted to kill her, and her own father let her be thrown in a dank cell. Nobody alive cherished her. A wave of anger swept her up and made her reckless. "The Palace never allowed me to do anything useful, General. So you want to execute me for breathing?"

Tarchon lolled in his chair and smirked. "Ah, spirit! I didn't say I wanted to execute you."

Despite the mind game, she seized on a glimmer of hope. "I'd like to send word to Shardan," she said. "They might give me refuge. So far as I am aware, nobody there desires my death."

Tarchon shook his head. Her faint ray of hope dwindled. The General turned and exchanged glances with one of the other men, Colonel Impar, the one who had moved her to the Anwar mansion but seemed to have some bigger role. Impar kept an unreadable face.

"There is pressure from some of our supporters to put a compliant figure on the Imperial throne. People here have no concept of government, other than Imperial rule. The Crown Prince doesn't seem to be up to the job. What if you were to sit on the throne as our Empress while we perform the real business of ruling?"

The suggestion shook her, and for a moment she thrilled with excitement. To be hailed as Empress, with all the pomp and glory that entailed? She had daydreamed of such a day, but if she was to be a mere figurehead for the rebels, what was the point? She sensed he was testing her.

"I don't want to be your figurehead. The whole Empire would see me as disloyal. Trying to contact the Shardan was troublesome enough. Co-operating with you would be worse."

Tarchon slapped the table. "Don't you approve of our aims? Improving the lot of the poor, who starve and pay half their earnings to rapacious landlords? Or stamping out the rampant corruption and extortion?"

"What corruption and extortion?" she shot back.

"Didn't you know? There are Court appointees who seek out people with any money, noble or merchant, and haul them to a secret court on trumped-up charges. They are released if they pay a large fine or agree to be bound over for a large debt against their future good behaviour. Nobles are allowed to charge fees in their domains for anything from inheriting land to sanctioning a marriage, or managing the estates of orphans to their profit. Humble folk cannot afford to pay for legal hearings. There is no fair taxation or good law in Imperial territory."

"This sounds like rebel propaganda. Those claims are grotesque."

Tarchon turned to one of his men. "Larchis? What do you say?"

Larchis, a tall officer, clenched a fist. "Princess, my father was a merchant. Tax collectors from Calah accused him of hiding secret wealth, and imposed a large fine, which he could not pay. By the time we got him out by selling our assets and borrowing from relatives, he was a broken man and his business was gone. Bastards."

Maihara closed her mouth. She could not be sure this man did not speak true. Ars Demophon had made similar allegations. "But one bad case does not condemn the whole system."

"What about the game Farnak and other nobles played, of pressuring their peasants to sell their grain, and then hoarding it while prices rose the next year? While people starved to death?"

"I didn't know about that. But bad harvests happen."

"If you don't care about that, do you know how many children died of starvation in the past year?"

A loaded question. "No. But I don't believe you're helping, with your war."

Tarchon ignored her riposte. "What about all the other abuses? The lack of good law? The starvation wages? The excessive privileges accorded to nobles? The extortions they are allowed to practice in their districts? The raping of brides?"

"I can't believe everything is as rotten as you say."

"What will convince you? We can let you go out into the streets and ask the common people what they think. We'll give you a strong escort so they don't lynch you."

She shook her head. "All right, it may be as you say."

"Should not all this be swept away and replaced with fair law for all, and fair gathering of taxes?"

"Any caring person would support such measures. That's not sufficient reason to ally myself openly with you." Sweat dampened her body. This was an intolerable choice - shameful collaboration, versus uncertainty and the threat of execution.

"You're no use then," Tarchon said. "Impar will turn you out of your nice room and let you fend for yourself in the street."

She had wanted to escape, but to be thrown out on the street with no sympathisers to guide her? She might be attacked, murdered or enslaved before she made it east on her own feet. Her legs shook, and she gasped for breath. Some of her feeling must have shown on her face.

"No need to decide today," Tarchon said. "If you won't do it, we can try with your sister or the Crown Prince." He gave a small smile. "Take her back and bring the next one."

The guards began to usher her out.

"Since I'm here, may I go and get some things from my room?" Maihara asked quickly.

Tarchon turned and looked at her, frowning. "Certainly not."

Impar inclined his long body. "It's nearly time for the meeting upstairs, General."

Tarchon turned to him. "They can wait. But don't take this girl back yet."

An officer led her out. As she left the study, she heard the low buzz of a discussion, and Tarchon saying, "Bring the younger princess."

They would make the same offer to Sihrima. No, that was absurd. To enthrone the younger and female Imperial child would make the farce obvious to all.

Unless the other two had died. A wave of fear swept over her.

-10-

Some time later, Tarchon joined five of his officers, clad in their green dress uniforms, in an airy banquet room upstairs above the council chamber on the south side of the palace. His staff had set the central table with the finest cloth and plates the Palace could still muster. Apparently in more peaceful times the Emperor had eaten here in public. The roof was of glass, and tiles painted with scenes of hunting and music-making covered the walls. To his eyes, the room looked almost undamaged, though most of the fine rugs and animal-skins lay heaped in a corner, and an odour of burning hung in the air. A line of twenty rebel soldiers stood guard around three sides of the chamber.

Tarchon took his place at the head of the table, amid a murmur of greetings.

A senior officer raised his hand. "General, what's this about appointing another Emperor?

"There are two provinces, Sintheer and Rewar, whose governors or lords have not moved to support Emperor Cordan, or declared for us," Tarchon said. He stabbed the tabletop with his finger twice as he spoke. "They are more likely to declare for us if we appoint an emperor of the West. Also, our agents have no word that the Emperor is alive, or that he has reached the eastern Empire, so if we appoint one of our own, it should provoke an instructive reaction from the Imperials."

The thin-faced Colonel Impar was shaking his head. "Before the Empire seized it, Avergne was a separate country. It should be independent again. And the other provinces."

"We've discussed this, Colonel. We need unity to defeat the rest of the Empire."

Impar scowled, and his spectacles glinted as he glanced around the room as if seeking support.

Tarchon wished that Impar would keep his republican ideas to himself. Impar had numerous like-minded allies among the rebels' non-military supporters and some of the militias, people who wanted to sweep away every vestige of the Empire and replace it with new radical institutions. It had been hard enough to wrest Avergne away from Imperial rule without totally changing how the country was organised.

"You underestimate the conservatism of the countryside," Tarchon said. "The petty local leaders of Shardan, Avergne and the other Western lands we aspire to control would accept an emperor or empress of the royal line as legitimate. They know nothing of Emirs, or dictators or ruling councils." He glared at Colonel Impar. "We need a unifying figurehead. If it helps consolidate our power, we will give them an emperor."

"I still think this is a bad idea," Impar said. "It's simplistic and reactionary."

"We have a freer hand at the moment," Tarchon said. "We have the cities, and we have not begun to re-organise the country districts. But consider the Avergnian Guard, the provincial troops from around Calah whom we dispersed and disarmed. In the south lie the Port Cities and the oceanic coast - the richest part of the Empire of Sar and the seat of its power. If we go to war with the Varlord-officered forces of the south-east, I would rather not have to keep our troops guarding the Avergnians. I would have sympathetic Avergnian soldiers fight for us."

Impar shook his head.

"Let's see what our allies think of these ideas," Tarchon said. "Fetch them in, along with the elder princess."

Guards ushered the Princess into the banquet room and led her to an empty chair at Tarchon's left hand.

Half a dozen Dhikr, including the tiresome Barin, entered in a close group, clutching delicate glasses in their grimy hands and staring around the room. Barin apparently was the leader of a sub-tribe of Dhikr and had obtained his position by his leadership qualities, and violence.

Ten of the Dhikr's scale-armoured fighters followed and stood in a mob against the fourth wall. Maihara stared at them, clearly wondering what were they doing here.

The senior Dhikr took seats opposite the rebels, with the warlord Barin at the near end and the rest snarling at each other as they squabbled for precedence. Three hard-faced men in plain dress, representing the civilian radicals, seated themselves near the lower end of the table. Three turncoat nobles, distinguished by their elaborate dress, took up the remaining seats.

Hastily trained soldiers served the meal and poured wine liberally into crystal goblets. Tarchon signalled that they could all start eating. His rebel officers seemed to know what to do with the cutlery, but the Dhikr ate with their fingers. While they ate and drank, the Dhikr warlord confronted Tarchon, his battered and hairy face twisted in a scowl. "What are you after, Tarchon? What's this about a new emperor?

Tarchon saw Maihara tense. He set down his wineglass and turned to the ill-mannered Dhikr.

"We are thinking that a puppet Emperor of the West should be appointed, as a figurehead for our combined forces, and to court support from wavering provinces. We have three of the Imperial children captive. They could be candidates."

He hoped Barin was following this. The Dhikr warlord was not stupid.

"Sounds good to have an emperor under our control," This was a wart-faced Dhikr warlord apparently named Minyan. "But we'd rather have an emperor of our blood, not one of the infernal line of Cordan." Barin nodded.

Or empress. Maihara appeared to shiver.

"But we conquered the country! We can do what we like!" This was an old Dhikr with a long white beard, whom Tarchon had heard addressed as the Emir.

"This region was conquered by our joint forces,"

Tarchon corrected him. The eastern Empire was still firmly held by the Imperial forces for Cordan.

The Dhikr leaders hissed and scowled.

Maihara was clearly taking in this dissension among the rebel factions.

"Why would they fight for us?" Barin said. "We've invaded their country, screwed their women and looted their crops and goods!" The other Dhikr laughed in agreement. The sound made Maihara shudder with revulsion.

"You forget how much the Varlords are hated," Tarchon said. He had not forgotten the circumstances of his wife's death. She had been injured in the street by a carriage driven by some noble. A doctor was sent for, but failed to come as an arrogant Varlord being treated for a minor ailment had refused to release the doctor. By the time the doctor arrived, his wife was beyond help. Tarchon had neither forgiven nor forgotten.

They returned to the subject of an emperor. Tarchon's officers proposed him as the new Emperor of Avergne and other rebel provinces. Mutterings arose round the table from the radicals, the turncoat nobles and the Dhikr, while Tarchon affected surprise.

"I don't want the throne. I'm no emperor. And if I sat on the throne, I doubt that I'd last long before some radical comrade cut me down, crying 'betrayal!'"

Some of his officers chuckled.

The Dhikr failed to see anything amusing, and proposed their Emir as Emperor.

"That won't do," Tarchon said. "The people won't accept a Dhikr emperor. Do you want the Western Empire to rise in revolt again?"

A muttering arose from the Dhikr. Those standing by the wall clapped their hands to their mailed chests in rhythm, making a menacing noise.

Maihara watched this noisy circus in apparent bewilderment.

"You didn't want the position, so let us fill it," Barin

shouted. The noise grew till the room rang with bawling voices and fists thumping the table.

Tarchon sat shaking his head till the noise subsided. Now Impar gave a slight nod.

"Neither proposal will bring unity," Tarchon said, "Let us return to an earlier proposal, that we crown the Cordan boy-Prince as our puppet emperor."

Barin spat on the floor while his subordinates growled and muttered.

Maihara started and looked upset. "You can't do that," she said. "My brother isn't fit to make even a pretence of ruling. He'll probably be sick if you try crowning him."

"Be quiet, you tart," Barin shouted. "We'll not have a woman speak here."

Colonel Impar caught the eye of his leader.

Tarchon raised his arm. "No, let her speak."

"He made a fool of himself during a war parade, falling off his horse. That'll happen again."

"I see," Tarchon said with a smirk. "You want to propose yourself for the role." She was reacting as he had anticipated.

"I don't," Maihara said quickly. "You could have a High Council of lords. Even Cordan had a council of advisers."

"That doesn't answer all the General's points," said the officer to Tarchon's right. "I propose the young Prince."

"Not that fairy," Barin said, thumping the table. "No way."

They argued while rays of coloured sunlight crept across the floor. The Dhikr became more unruly, shouting at each other and throwing pieces of food. These barbarians were fine warriors but uncivilised. The Princess stared as if appalled.

"The Princess would be a more articulate and confident crowned head than her brother," Tarchon said, with a smile.

She eyed him, evidently wondering what was he up to. It was not his intention that the meeting end up electing her.

"Never," Barin shouted, and his compatriots growled

agreement.

More courses of food and fine wine were brought in, and the discussion paused. Maihara was being careful with the wine, as if she had been schooled not to drink too much of the stuff. Some of his officers were looking tipsy, and using the silver tableware on the latter courses of the meal as though they'd never learnt the proper etiquette.

"So how are we to proceed?" Tarchon asked, with a glance at Maihara.

"You should arrange for a ruling council, with all your factions sitting on it," Maihara said.

The Dhikr growled and glanced at each other and the three turncoat nobles stared at her. Impar and other officers exchanged looks.

Tarchon raised his arm and called for silence.

"It allows different factions to have their say, and allows ideas and expert opinions to be aired. Better than relying on one person." And better than enthroning any of her siblings or herself. She raised her voice as men frowned and talked over her. The three nobles looked serious.

Tarchon banged on the table for silence. "Thank you, Princess. I propose we move to a vote on these questions."

Colonel Impar glanced at Tarchon and pointed to the door.

Tarchon shook his head. "First, who wants to elect the Emir of our Dhikr allies? If in favour, raise your hands."

All the Dhikr raised theirs, except one who was slumped across the table and another who was too drunk to respond.

"Who is opposed?"

All six rebels raised their hands, in a swift movement.

"That proposal is defeated. Now, who wishes to elect the Princess here as our Empress?"

Maihara looked apprehensive. She clearly did not want this.

"Never! Not that tart!" Barin shouted. Other Dhikr growled agreement.

Tarchon raised his hand. Two other rebel hands were

raised.

"And who is opposed?"

Most of the Dhikr fists shot up, and half of the rebel hands.

"That proposal is defeated," Tarchon said. Maihara breathed a sigh of relief.

"I propose that we not vote on the younger Imperial sister," Tarchon said. "That would smack of desperation, if carried. Any objections?"

Nobody objected.

"Now who prefers to elect young Prince Persis as our Emperor?" Tarchon asked, looking at Maihara. "He won't cause us any trouble."

Maihara tensed.

One of the Dhikr, the warlord Minyan, raised his hand. Three more followed. Half of the rebels and the three nobles raised theirs. Tarchon counted hands.

"And who is opposed?"

More of the Dhikr, including Barin, and a scatter of rebels, raised their hands. "Not the girl-boy," Barin shouted, and several of his fellows jeered.

"That proposal is carried," Tarchon said. Several rebels applauded, while the Dhikr banged on the table and shouted among themselves. Plates jumped and cracked.

Maihara clenched her fists. "You can't do this!" she shouted. "He's a child! It'll crush him."

"It's time you returned to the Anwar mansion, Princess," Tarchon said. He had correctly anticipated the effect of bringing Maihara in and letting her speak, and now he had his boy-Emperor in the bag Maihara wasn't happy. He regretted that, but needs must.

When he detailed two soldiers to escort her, Maihara stood up with ill grace and glared at the head of the table. He wondered what a great lady did in this situation. This one dropped a minimal nod and turned her back.

"Good day, gentlemen." Grim-faced, she walked off between the two soldiers.

***

125

Maihara curled up in her room's battered armchair and struggled to regain her composure. A chill ran up her spine as she reflected how badly the day could have turned out for her. Men in that room would have been happy to have the whole Cordan brood executed and someone else appointed as their figurehead leader. They had detected her escape plot so easily, and that poor boy had been whipped because of her. She imagined red welts criss-crossing his pale skin, and winced. A feeling of shame oppressed her. The rebels were ruthless; she believed what Tarchon had said about executing any adults who tried to help her escape the city. But was the Empire any more merciful? She presumed that her grim father would do no less in similar circumstances.

And the offer of being made Empress in place of her brother? Days ago, she had imagined herself as Empress, but she did not want to be the rebels' puppet. The mere trappings of being an Empress were not what she wanted at all, and being involved in such a sham would ruin her chances of succeeding to the throne of the Empire, or what was left of it. She would hold to her dream of being a real Empress with effective power, and to that end she'd gamble that Tarchon had no intention of sanctioning her execution, despite his bluster. If she was wrong, the extreme rebels would have her and her siblings on a scaffold.

The election of Persis, which she expected they'd confirm, saved her from an invidious situation. But if they made Persis Emperor, the pressure would be too much for him. Yet if she or Sihrima were made Empress, the rebels might see Persis' existence as a problem.

What now? She was determined not to bang on the door and shout 'I agree, don't execute me.' Most likely, that General would do what he wanted with any of them regardless of what she said. She prayed that her resistance would not doom others she cared about, her siblings or her ladies-in-waiting.

And the Fifth Bureau thought she was a witch and had searched her rooms for evidence, but there was no mention of the box. Rather than risk the lives of sympathisers, her next step should be to make further efforts to recover the box and its contents and to see what she could do with them to facilitate her escape. She had already seen what havoc the box could wreak.

-11-

There was to be a grand procession through the city, ending at the Throne Hall of the Imperial Palace, where the coronation would take place. The guard officers told Maihara that she was to attend, and she should choose a suitable dress. The prospect of a public procession followed by a ceremony filled her with apprehension, but it was pointless to complain or think of not co-operating. She needed to be there for her brother.

She looked over the half-dozen dresses rescued from her old room that hung in the wardrobe. These were elaborately made, in sombre colours with much brocading. A little solemn for what she supposed to be a festive occasion, and the weather was hot. There was one, white satin with pearl trimmings that would just about do. Other dresses with semi-precious trimmings had disappeared, but the looters seemed not to have recognised the real Tifly pearls for what they were. Should she make a fuss and demand a grander outfit? Well, she didn't care. Her brother would be the centre of attention.

A double knock rattled the door, and before she was able to respond it was flung open. Tarchon entered with two of his aides, all wearing green rebel uniforms, and the aides swiftly checked in corners and behind curtains. Tarchon's forceful presence dominated the room. Uneasy, she retreated to the far side of the table that stood in the middle of the carpet. The General carried an object wrapped in purple cloth.

"You can wear this tomorrow," he said, placing a glittering circle of metal on the table and pushing it toward her. It was a coronet studded with precious gems, a gold circlet three fingers high, without spikes or arches, the mark of a middle-ranking noble.

"No thank you," she said, pushing the unexpected gift back.

"Why? Is it not grand enough? You'll do as you are told."

"It's got 'Shoot Here' written across the front of it. Some of the citizenry might not approve of this procession." She scowled at him.

Tarchon frowned. "I can assure you there will be troops along the route, and they will search the buildings. We'll allow nothing to interfere with this." He slid the coronet toward her with a forceful gesture.

The aides said nothing, but stood with their eyes darting about the room, taking in the piles of books, and the satin dress draped on her bed.

Maihara was unmoved. "Maybe it's got 'Shoot Here' written in Dhikr." She pushed the coronet away.

"They wouldn't shoot you. Anyway, they'd recognise the carriage, regardless." Tarchon pushed the coronet back. "Be ready tomorrow morning."

Maihara resisted the urge to flick the coronet back at him. She left it where it was, on the inlaid surface of the gaming table. Tarchon smiled and went out. She eyed the coronet. What had happened to the previous owner? She wouldn't wear it in the procession, but it looked like a valuable item, a handy piece of portable wealth. If circumstances fell out in a certain way, she could sell it.

She glanced at the ceiling. How was her brother reacting to this new order?

After breakfast next morning, a servant helped her put on the white dress and get ready. It left her lower arms bare and, with underskirts, flared out from her waist and hung to mid-calf length. The young curly-haired escort officer, Lieutenant Harayam, glanced at her. "Where's the coronet?"

"I'm not wearing that." She put her hands on her hips.

"You have to bring it."

She had him labelled as a malleable type, but no doubt he had been given orders to make sure she complied with the General's wishes. She was in a resistant mood, but the lieutenant looked obdurate. With a sigh and exaggerated movements, she retrieved the coronet from a drawer and slipped it into a pocket in the lining of her dress.

Her brother waited with an escort in the great hall below. He was splendidly dressed with gilded shoes, yellow tights, a gold belt and a red jacket embroidered and slashed to show the rich lining. A silver circlet balanced on straight dark hair that framed his pale, delicate features. He stood with shoulders slumped and head down, mouth quivering.

She took his soft, warm hand. "It's just a show," she told him. "Nobody expects you to do any ruling. They were even talking of using me instead."

"It's all right," Persis said in a whisper. "I don't mind."

Well, you should. A sense of guilt oppressed her. She was letting him down.

In the stable courtyard of the Anwar mansion, the guard escort led Maihara and her brother toward a shabby closed carriage, black-painted with tattered leather trimmings and lowered blinds on its windows. Maihara eyed it with alarm, fearing the worst. "Where are you taking us?" They clearly were not going on a grand procession in this.

"Don't worry," said Lieutenant Harayam, eager to offer reassurance. "The procession starts from the Temple of Victory, on Zar. General Tarchon wants you to get there without attracting attention on the way."

Maihara nodded. It made sense. If the procession started from her new residence, the whole population would know where to come if they wanted to demonstrate their hate. She could almost see and hear the violent mob as it surrounded the building, baying for her blood.

The temple street name, Zar, teased a notion into her mind, like a dry leaf blown on the wind. *Zargutal*. That was one of the keywords. She savoured it, and made sure she would not forget it again. This would give her that opening to the magic realm, and the few spells she had already tried.

They settled in the carriage, facing each other. Maihara carried a floppy hat. Her brother's fancy clothes and smooth, delicate features didn't make him look any more manly. He looked at her in dumb appeal. "I don't want to," he muttered.

She repressed her irritation. "I thought you didn't mind. I told them what I thought. They ignored me."

"I can't," he said. He looked down.

"You just have to sit and wave," she said. "I think we'll be in an open carriage." A surge of guilty affection moved her, and she leaned over and kissed him on the cheek. It felt soft and smooth on her lips. "If you can't bear it, they'll have to get someone else, sooner or later."

Persis raised his head.

The carriage set off. Through a crack in the blinds, Maihara glimpsed the exit passage, several guards and the street front of the mansion. They rumbled through grand streets, still littered with debris of disorder. The buildings of the rich here were faced with smooth pale stone and had carved detailing around windows and doors. Broken objects, discarded stones, sticks and abandoned loot lay in front of mansions with broken or boarded windows. Some city workers with a cart were clearing up the mess. The carriage entered a narrow alley where rebel soldiers stood guard. Anxiety dried her mouth.

The carriage door opened, and Maihara was obliged to descend and be led through a small door into a dim, high space. It smelt of damp, and of burning. Voices echoed. Fear rooted her to the spot. This was no temple. They'd been tricked.

"What is this place?" She shook off a guiding hand and headed for the door. Harayam shouted in a high-pitched youthful voice at the rebel soldiers, who grabbed her arms and forced her onwards. "Let go of me!" She struggled in their grip.

"We're in the back of the Temple of Victory."

Harayam's voice betrayed his tension. His tongue worried at his front tooth gap.

Indeed, the place did smell of incense. She allowed herself and Persis to be led onward, into a larger chamber. Lamplight picked out the faces of waiting guards and officers, and a glimpse of stone walls and an ornate ceiling with plasterwork. Rays of daylight streaked from the front of the main sanctuary, whence came the murmur of a crowd.

A figure emerged from the shadows. "You can put on your coronet now, Your Grace." It was the same aide who had accompanied Tarchon the previous day.

"Didn't bring it. Not wearing it. It'll just make me a target." Maihara raised her lace-trimmed hat and put it on.

The aide sighed and waved them onwards.

They exited from the temple front doors onto sunlit steps, in front of a large crowd of curious onlookers. From the temple portico, a wide street ran up toward the Palace. Tarchon was beside the carriage, wearing a fancy uniform with rows of gold braid on the shoulders. A couple of Dhikr were there, the Emir and one of their generals, but not, mercifully, the odious Barin. The Dhikr wore gilded scale armour.

Tarchon glared at Maihara. "No coronet? Can't you do what you're told?"

"S-she's got it with her, sir," Lieutenant Harayam said, stammering.

"Let's see it," Tarchon said. They all glared at her. Behind them the open carriage waited, with three rows of seats and four horses harnessed in front.

Maihara produced the coronet. "I'm not wearing this in an open carriage." She flicked the hand holding the coronet, miming a throw.

"You'll wear it at the coronation," Tarchon said, with a scowl. With his two hands, he gripped her around the waist. She gasped in surprise and outrage as he lifted her with effortless strength and shoved her into the middle seat of the carriage. He turned away to direct the Dhikr into the vehicle.

How dare he manhandle her Imperial person, the low oaf? Maihara glowered at his back, before reflecting that she'd won the argument over the sparkly coronet.

Her brother, white-faced, was placed in the front seat alongside Tarchon. Beside her, Maihara had a foul-smelling Dhikr. He looked straight ahead, not at her. On her other side a rebel officer got in, and Maihara saw to her surprise this was a woman. Another Dhikr and guard took the narrower seat behind.

The female officer turned to smile at Maihara. "Don't worry, Your Grace. We'll do our best to keep you safe. I'm Major Cleia Chavin."

Maihara eyed her. Cleia was tall, slim, and quite broad-shouldered, with long legs clad in tight uniform trews. Light brown straight hair curved in at her neck in a smart bob. Maihara wished she had an athletic body like Chavin's, instead of an awkward one that curved out at the hips and breast.

"I'm pleased to meet you," Maihara said, meaning to be polite. This was the second female rebel soldier she'd seen. Evidently the rebels thought women capable of more than soft indoor tasks. "How did you get to be an officer?"

The carriage moved off.

"I've always liked the outdoors, and when the rebellion started in our province, my brother couldn't go, so I volunteered to help in his place." Chavin's lightly suntanned face was oval and of pleasant appearance.

"But why did they accept you? And can you kill people?"

"They needed anyone who could help the cause. Soldiers have lots of jobs to do besides killing," Chavin said.

"What kind of jobs?"

"Women can do anything that does not require brute strength, from staff work to scouting or putting up tents."

Maihara shook her head. She already believed women had a place in political administration, but as military officers? If women could be soldiers, was there any task they couldn't undertake? Her head spun with the novel visions this opened up.

***

Sett slouched through the West Gate of Calah with a deadly bundle strapped to his back. His feet trod hollow on the planks of the moat bridge. Suspicious green-mailed guards stared at him as he passed. He sweated, fearing a curt word of command, the search, the blows. Other travellers shuffled along beside him. The guards did not call him back as he entered the tunnel-like gate or when he stepped onto the roadway beyond.

Once inside the Low Town, he glanced around him in curiosity. The streets were shabbier than he remembered. Gaudy paintwork on shops and taverns had faded and peeled and lay grey under the baking sun. He'd heard that deluded elements of the townspeople had risen in futile revolt not long before the rebels took Calah. In gaps between buildings, charred timbers poked up through the mud-brick rubble like blackened fingers, mute testimony of conflagration. Repairs had not begun since the riots and the sack of the city.

Further up, Sett passed the shuttered and silent houses and workshops of jade workers and artisans. There was little work for them here. Few had the money to buy their products. Only the weapon-makers were kept busy, he had heard. The rebels were buying more arms.

On his back, the dismantled weapon chinked and bulged in its grimy sack. He spat, cursing the rebels and turncoats who had taken over the city. Their alliance with the barbarous Dhikr showed their true colours and lack of scruples.

Higher up in the city, rags hung drying from the windows of a merchant's abandoned mansion. The rebels had stripped the great merchants and any surviving nobles of their wealth. The merchant class had fled, and there was little commerce now. Calah and the agricultural West were cut off from the ports and manufactories of the Empire of

Sar's Chancungra Shore in the east. Sett's south-eastern Imperial masters, resting in their opulent sea-girt palaces, had said the rebels had won their battles but lost the war.

The tinkle of glass rang in the hot dusty air as he turned his footsteps to an open square, a space perhaps fifty paces by fifty. Light dazzled him. Mobiles fashioned from obsidian and glass hung in the open area. The harsh white sun splashed from brilliant reflectors that moved in a slight breeze, sending out rays of many colours. They represented nothing but dreams, fancies, whimsical creations.

Four sleepy-faced spearmen, rebels or turncoats who had ruined the city of his birth, guarded the sculpture court. He hurried away lest the spearmen remark on the idle, loitering stranger and question him. Should they then peer into his sack they would drag him away for questioning, with a quick death the best he could hope for.

As Sett toiled higher up the city's breast-shaped mound, he met more people in the streets. Women hurried by, glancing around and carrying half-empty bags. Some were heading toward the procession route that led to the Palace. The streets were still littered with rubbish from the city's sack, and a row of buildings lay roofless with soot marks above the gaping window openings. A dead dog lay half under rubble, while a couple of men with grimy bandages on head and arm peered at the wreckage. "Damn their parade," said one as Sett went by.

Sett smiled to himself, reassured. The Imperial secret service had been correct. There was to be a parade before the coronation.

A thin crowd, herded in by troopers and sweating in the sun, lined the broad street leading up to the Palace. Here he found an unoccupied building that suited his purpose. He pushed open a broken door, climbed narrow stone stairs and entered a dusty, bare room. None would disturb him here, he hoped. If any did they would meet his sharp-bladed dagger.

He laid out the crossbow parts on the floor and checked that nothing was missing. First, he assembled the stripped-down stock, broken in two for ease of concealment, then attached the bow, a double-curved composite of wood, bone and sinew glued together. Next, he took up the heavy string, made of linen threads and with looped ends. He held the string in his teeth and jammed the bow into an angle of the walls, sweating to bend the curved bow enough for the linen cord to be hitched on. It would not reach. He cursed. Normally, stringing a crossbow was a one-man job. He tried again with all his weight and after a struggle looped the string onto the powerful bow.

He picked up the two cunningly shaped trigger parts of metal and slotted them into place, securing them with their pivots. With one hand, he tried the action of the 'goats-foot' arming lever, and fingered the half-dozen bolts selected in practice shoots for trueness. Lastly, he tested the trigger mechanism to ensure it worked smoothly.

The window here was jammed shut, and he dared not knock it out. He threw his sack over the weapon to conceal it as best he could. No-one would see him with it as he climbed the stairs.

The stair ended at an insecure door, opening onto a flat roof with a stone parapet on the street side. He crouched at a corner of the roof where a chimney hid him from any other aerial spectators. Sett leaned over the parapet, looking down onto the heads of the crowd lining both sides of the hot, noisy street. Unseen trumpets blared below, to the left, and a tramp of massed feet became louder and louder, till it shook the frail ledge of stone where he hid. A rank of trumpeters, bearing shiny metal horns, marched into view in near unison, clad in dress uniforms of bunched satin.

Sett uncovered his crossbow and armed it. He knew all eyes would be on the scene below. Behind the trumpeters marched a green-scaled glittering mass of armoured troops that flowed along the street on myriad legs, slanting aloft rank upon rank of tall metal-tipped spears. The building vibrated to its uneven dull-footed tread.

He pondered the first choice of missile before selecting a quarrel tipped with a square head of precious steel. It would pierce armour, or make a horrible lacerated wound in unprotected flesh. He set out the other five steel bolts on the tiles.

Sett squinted along the sights of his readied weapon. He caressed the trigger with his callused forefinger. On they came in serried ranks, rows of archers, troops of riders bearing lances, officers on fierce-pacing, snorting horses that clopped on the cobbles.

Sett, sweating, shifted the heavy crossbow from target to target. He began to panic. Which of these gaudy officers was Tarchon? An open carriage appeared down the street, and troops lining the pavements saluted it with a great roar. Ranks of green-capped rebel soldiers crashed past, carrying pikes and maces.

"Emperor!" they roared.

The to-be-Emperor was in his sights. Triumph flooded through him as he studied the brightly clad figures in the open carriage. That gaudily clad youth must be the Crown Prince. The man in shiny uniform beside must be Tarchon. He'd try for both. The men seated behind, in scale armour, had to be the leading Dhikr. That woman with her face and hair hidden by a wide hat might be a mistress, or the Crown Princess. His heart pounded as he slid his crossbow around and took careful aim. At this short range he could not miss.

-12-

Maihara's carriage moved along a street route lined on both sides with rebel soldiers, who kept back the crowd. Brick-built tenements towered above her, and ahead a long straight street ascended toward the Palace. Most of the throng were well-behaved or cowed, waving green rebel flags. A few shouted abuse.

"Liars!"

"Traitors!"

"Rebel scum!"

Maihara, exposed in the low-sided open vehicle, shuddered with alarm. What was going on? The rebels tolerated this dissent? Her father would have sent in the soldiers. Those people in the crowd bold enough to oppose the rebels might not have a high opinion of her being here.

She was seated next to the female officer, Chavin. Female officers? What else did she not know about the insurgents?

Her brother sat next to Tarchon with his shoulders hunched, hands fidgeting. Behind them Maihara had Chavin on her left, with a Dhikr beside her and another behind in the third row of seats.

Tarchon poked her brother on the arm, and Persis jumped. "Prince Persis, wave to the crowd."

Persis waved his right arm in a stiff gesture, then lowered it as shouting from the crowd increased.

Soldiers struggled to hold back a vocal group of protesters, seemingly pro-revolt, who waved hand-lettered signs that read 'Sellout' and 'Betrayal'. They sounded even angrier than the pro-Empire shouters.

Alarmed, Maihara leaned forward and tapped Tarchon on the shoulder.

He turned. "What?"

"If you tell the driver to vary the speed of the carriage - should anyone shoot at us, it'll put his aim off."

Tarchon turned and raised an eyebrow. "Whatever gave you that idea? You worry too much."

"I read it in a book of tactics."

To her vexation, he turned away with a snort and a shake of his head. A moment later though, she saw him lean forward and talk to the driver.

The hostile noises from the crowd continued. They'd be throwing things next. She concentrated, and entered the magical space she carried within her, calling up one of the few spells she could still reach. With a flick of her finger, she launched the spell for tracing things that flew swiftly through the air.

A small bird swooped and soared overhead. A very unreal-looking trail marked its path through the air, a series of bright orange curving lines, like a rope of red-hot wires. *Fantastic.*

The carriage bumped on in the procession till they were about a third of the way to the palace. The enclosing wall filled the end of the street. A gap had opened between the horses and the marching regiment in front. The driver flicked his whip, and the carriage lurched forward, throwing Maihara back. She grabbed at the seat in front of her. There was a bang, and the wood under her hand vibrated. A crossbow bolt had passed over her and struck and embedded itself in the door close to a Dhikr's hand, tail up. She shrieked.

Tarchon swung around, cursed, and turned back. "Incoming!" he shouted. His head jerked in swift motions as he looked for the shooter.

Maihara shuddered with shock, yet she raised her head and looked around. A straight tracer, a rope of glowing wires in the air, ran up from the carriage to the top of a tenement on her left, which had a recessed or flat roof. The other carriage occupants were reacting by crouching and looking left as they realised what had happened.

She raised her arm and pointed. "Up there!" she yelled as loudly as she could. "The roof! The flat roof!"

"Go!" Tarchon ordered Chavin.

The female officer glanced at Maihara then vaulted out of her seat into the roadway. She ran to the left, grabbed a couple of rebel soldiers and disappeared into the crowd. Maihara envied that leap. It was time to do likewise, rather than sit waiting to be shot at. She scrambled over the half-door and flung herself into the road, stumbled and landed on all fours.

The carriage was moving away from her. That was not what she'd had in mind; she wanted to take cover alongside it. She sprang to her feet and hurried after it. The crowd were laughing at her. Two soldiers grabbed her by the arms and dragged her along, almost carrying her. Tarchon turned around, mouth open.

"Let go of me!" she cried.

The soldiers ignored her command. "You're not going anywhere," one said in a nasty tone. The carriage was slowing. One of the soldiers opened the carriage's half-door, and the two of them tossed her inside. She landed on the floor, across the Dhikr general's mailed feet, and gasped with shock and outrage. Near her nose her brother, a shivering bundle of gaudy red clothing, lay partly under the front seats. It seemed that Tarchon had done the sensible thing and thrust her brother down out of harm's way.

The two Dhikr gabbled in their own language. She raised her head and looked up. Another glowing trace led roofwards, even though she had not heard it. So, they were still being shot at. The marching regiment ahead blocked the street and left them a sitting target. She lowered her head and clenched her fists. If only she'd had more time with her box.

"Way left! Clear the road!" Tarchon shouted, demanding that the regiment move out of their way. "Watch the rooftops!" A good idea, Maihara thought.

Most of the crowd were still cheering or shouting, oblivious to the attack. With a whack, another missile struck the carriage. Maihara saw the glowing trace flash above her face. She twisted her head to look. The bolt had just missed Tarchon and punched through the carriage side beside his legs. The Dhikr shouted louder. The carriage rumbled over the cobbles at increased pitch.

"Clear the way!" the driver shouted. His whip cracked. The carriage bounced, tossing her against the feet of the Dhikr seated above and behind her. The floor jolted and vibrated as the carriage gathered speed. A scream came from underneath. They'd run someone over. She opened her mouth to protest.

"Stop! We've—"

"Damn fool!" Tarchon said.

Did he mean her, or the victim? An orange trace flicked over her head, and a man cried out. She could not see who had been hit - either Tarchon or the driver. She glimpsed the upper floors of passing buildings of grander quality. The hammering of hooves and jolting of the carriage continued as it raced up the remainder of the processional route.

"Who's hit?" she shouted.

***

As the carriage passed through an arched opening in the Palace wall, Tarchon felt that the coronation had not begun well. The vehicle shifted on its springs as several passengers jumped down. He barked orders, and soldiers laid hands on Maihara and lifted her up and out of the carriage. She did not protest. Two soldiers helped Prince Persis down and assisted the driver, bleeding from a shoulder wound. Persis stood white-faced and trembling. The two Dhikr warlords dismounted and shouted at Tarchon, gesticulating back toward the procession route.

Tarchon was not in the mood for any complaints from the Dhikr. "It was Imperial resisters," he told them.

They were already inside the palace complex, in the outer yard bounded by a brick wall and lean-tos on one side and the architect-designed stone face of the palace buildings on the other, now like the carriage passengers looking rather the worse for wear with several broken windows. Tarchon looked round for his staff. They should be here waiting for him. He turned to look at Maihara for a moment. She stared at him with clenched fists and contorted face, and looked primed to cry or vent her anger, after being shot at, manhandled by soldiers, and laughed at by half of Calah, but she could keep these feelings to herself, for now. Her brother the appointed Emperor was safe.

Tarchon gathered his staff and made a gesture, indicating that they proceed through a grand doorway into the ceremonial part of the palace. They were early, so there was time for Maihara and the prince to have their outfits straightened and cleaned. Maihara's dress needed attention. It had two dirty marks low in the front of the skirt, as well as lighter patches of grime and a rip. They stood in a grand gilded hallway, surrounded by soldiers, while a maid tried to clean the dress with a brush and damp cloth. Another maid worked on the rip with needle and thread. He was reminded of how he had first seen the princess - flushed, dishevelled and grimy. The dress should be changed, but there wasn't time for that. She raised her right hand, reaching for something, then lowered it with a faint expression of disappointment. The hat she had worn at the start of the procession had gone missing.

A handsome young fair-haired officer was staring at her, open-mouthed. What was so interesting about that girl? She turned, at a maid's urging and Tarchon saw that she had lost a button in front and the dress had parted, revealing curves of uplifted flesh and a hint of lace. *Nice cleavage.* His male mind sprang to attention.

The ever-efficient Colonel Impar hurried up to Tarchon with a worried expression and saluted.

"Somebody attacked the procession?" the Colonel asked.

"From above, must have been crossbows." Tarchon made pointing gestures over his head, miming the crossbow shooting, while Impar nodded.

"I told you it wouldn't be popular, General."

"Why didn't we have men on the roofs?"

"That wasn't in my brief."

"Whose brief was it, then? Have our men on the ground caught anyone?"

"I've been securing the palace, sir." Impar threw up his hands in a gesture of resignation, before saluting and turning away.

What of the prince, the object of all this? Prince Persis stared, white-faced. "Please," he mouthed. He had a damp patch on his trousers.

The princess was trying to get his attention. He came over, irritated and loomed above her, with a frown. "What?"

"My brother. Can't you at least delay this farce till he's calmed down?"

Tarchon scowled. "No, we'll proceed. He'd better get used to it. I see that *you've* recovered." The maids had tidied her up and secured the revealing neckline. He looked round, toward the double doors to the Great Hall at the far side of the anteroom. "What the crot were you doing, trying to escape?"

"I wasn't. I was trying to take cover behind the carriage."

Instead of responding, he cast his gaze again toward the inner doors, which had partly opened. In the gap, a rebel flag was being waved. "They're ready. Where's your coronet?"

"Here." With sulky reluctance, she fished out the coronet from a concealed pocket in the dress and put it on. At least she was finally wearing the glittery circlet.

"Your place is with my officers. Behave yourself."

Tarchon took the head of a line formed of his staff officers, the Dhikr's Emir and other high officials and progressed from the anteroom into the Great Hall. Inside, the high-roofed space was a riot of gilded carving that glittered in light diffusing from above. Despite loathing its former owner, he had to admire the effect. Green-uniformed rebels lined the walls. A sparse collection of civilians stood around on the main floor - not a great show. The few Dhikr present elbowed in behind their leader, other guests giving them a wide berth. As Tarchon halted the procession near the throne at the east end, he prayed that nothing else was to go wrong.

***

Maihara reached inside herself to her personal magical space and turned off the tracer spell. There might be people among the rebels or the Dhikr who could detect it, and she needed to be careful.

She glanced around. Judging by their elaborate clothes, some of those present were from the nobility, minor nobles willing to support the rebels. Now minded by a pair of guards, Maihara was placed in a processional line next to a woman she thought she recognised, a lady-in-waiting from the old regime with a beauty spot on her left cheek. She looked rather tearful.

"What's the matter?" Maihara whispered.

The lady curtsied. "My husband. He's missing. I think he's dead, Your Grace."

"Oh." Maihara was confronted with the human reality of the invasion. The woman's grief and loss tore at her. Poor woman. What could she say? "Do you want me to see if I can find out anything?"

"Please, Your Grace."

"Then give me his name and residence, and a description."

The woman took out a pencil and a scrap of paper from a pocket in her full skirt and scribbled a couple of lines. "I'm Serina Aurian. Thank you so much, Your Grace."

A white hand proffered Maihara the paper, and she slipped the scrap inside her sleeve.

At the entrance to the hall, a bearded Monist priest in white robes embroidered with looping patterns waved a glass disc over the heads of the dignitaries as they passed him. The wind of it cooled Maihara's face as she processed by.

"Why is he doing that?" Maihara asked her bereaved companion.

"It's supposed to sniff out magic users, Your Grace. They'll not want anyone hexing the ceremony."

Sweat prickled under Maihara's arms. *Close.*

There were signs around the walls that the hall had been looted. Small niches that had held statues stood empty, darker patches on the panelling marked where cabinets had stood, and holes showed where gilded lampholders had been wrenched off. A litter of debris had been pushed into corners, but the decorations above head height were untouched and the scale of the place was such that the looters had made little impression.

The line of eminent supporters trod a path along a russet carpet, to where a gaggle of Monist priests in long white robes waited at the far end of the room. Apparently, the chief rebels did not like the Nine Gods priesthood. The carpet ended in front of the crystal throne, an ancient artefact fashioned out of a huge mass of translucent quartz, and used in the coronation of emperors. At night, lamps placed underneath gave it a flickering eerie glow.

Tarchon and his officers bunched below the raised dais, looking solemn. A chief priest of the One God led Persis forward and placed him on the throne. He sat gripping the arms with white fingers. An ermine cloak was draped over his colourful red jacket, yellow trousers and gold belt, causing him to look small inside it. His silver circlet glittered in the lights. His features twitched, and he looked ready to snivel.

Maihara's heart filled with love and concern at the sight of him. A small part of her wondered how it felt to sit on the crystal throne and look down on the crowd. But she wouldn't sit there at Tarchon's behest.

Tarchon moved to the steps below the throne and made a speech full of words like justice, reconciliation, freedom and brotherhood. He asserted that they had not come to rob and plunder, but to give back what the high nobles and Varlords had taken from them under the rule of the former

Emperor. "That's how those people gain their vast wealth, to build their palaces. By grinding the faces of the poor, weak and honourable. For them, you are merely prey. I say to you, to know is to be armed." It sounded just, but she was not convinced. The nobles were not all rogues, any more than the poor were all honest and hardworking.

The Dhikr scowled and muttered. Maihara wondered if it was the comment 'not ... rob and plunder' that displeased them.

"We will give you a new Emperor innocent of any crimes," Tarchon concluded. The rebels lining the sides of the hall cheered, while some minor nobles remained tight-lipped.

I wonder who writes his speeches, she thought, fanning herself with one hand. The air was uncomfortably hot.

One of the priests stepped up and intoned a long prayer. Maihara watched her brother closely. He'd gone pale as a sheet and was breathing quickly and deeply. *He's going to have one of his fits.*

***

Tarchon eyed Persis with unease. The Prince was very pale and Tarchon hoped the little brat was not going to embarrass him by fainting or throwing up.

A gaudily dressed priest, wearing embroidered yellow robes and a tall crown-like hat with a rounded top, picked up the Imperial crown from a cushion and advanced with it toward the throne. Persis cringed aside. Tarchon moved closer and hissed in the boy's ear. "Sit up straight, you brat."

Persis obeyed, and the archpriest placed the shiny, bejewelled crown on the Prince's head.

"Speech!" someone shouted, in a coarse accent.

Tarchon made an irritated gesture, and the outcry stopped. Persis lurched to one side, away from the General's waving arm, and the crown fell off. A young attendant, quick as a cat, grabbed it before it could hit the dais. Persis slumped sideways across the arm of the chair, his body shaking. Tarchon paused, nonplussed. "Fugging useless," he said, mainly to himself. He patted Persis's cheek then straightened.

Maihara, in the line-up, started forward, but strong hands gripped her arms.

"Is there a doctor here?" Tarchon shouted.

Maihara struggled, desperate to reach her brother. "Let me go to him!"

A roar of startled reaction filled the hall, and officers ran to Tarchon's side.

Guards moved to hold back the struggling princess. He could see she cared for her brother.

A man in grey doctor's robes appeared and held a jar under Persis's nose. He stirred, and sat up, looking around as if he didn't know what had happened.

"Keep still," Tarchon snapped. Everything was going wrong this morning, first the attack, then the princess jumping out, and then this brat fainting. Damned Zircons, they were more trouble than they were worth. "I give you Persis Zircon, Emperor of Avergne," he announced, in a parade-ground voice. The crowd murmured, drowning out what Tarchon was saying as he set the crown back on Persis's head. "Salute the Emperor."

Down in the ceremonial line he saw Maihara, still restrained by a couple of guards, clenching a fist. It was not hard to read her - she objected to Persis being subjected to this. Yet the boy was next in line to the *Imperial* throne. What did the spirited Crown Princess secretly think about *that*?

Tarchon raised his hands and clapped, signalling for applause. Persis sat, glassy eyed. The loyal crowd, led by Tarchon's officers, cheered and huzzahed, failing to make much impact in the great room. Embroidered wall hangings on the upper walls and strips of carpet prevented any echo.

Maihara lowered her head, and the guards relaxed their restraining stance. At a word from Tarchon, the arch priest beckoned, and compliant nobles came forward two by two to bow before the throne. Tarchon's officers followed. Maihara came up in turn with some lady she'd been paired with, and curtsied to her brother, who stared past her, gripping the arms of the throne with white knuckles.

This was the last part of the ceremony. The priests led the new Emperor off his throne, and the procession uncoiled back to the gilded anteroom. The high priest lifted the crown off Persis's head, and the priests bore it away. Tarchon kept his face bland, giving no clue to his chagrin at the prince's pathetic performance. Rebel guards hustled Persis away to an assigned side-room. Maihara tried to follow, but an officer barred her way.

Major Chavin had come in and was glancing around. Maihara went over to her, no doubt glad of a friendly face. In a sour mood, Tarchon beckoned the bob-haired female officer over. The Princess followed.

"How did it go, Major?"

Chavin bowed her head. "The princess did spot the attacker, and I went after him to find and stop him quickly. I got up on the roof with two fighters."

"And?"

"We flushed him. He tried to get away across the roofs, but he fell, and the militia caught him in the back street."

"Any sign of a second shooter?"

"No, General."

"All the same, good work." At least one of his subordinates had managed to do something right. "Where is he now?"

"Being taken to your headquarters, General. What happened with the carriage, sir?"

Tarchon scowled, pointing to Maihara. "She jumped out of it. She's a handful."

Chavin bowed again. "How did the ceremony go, sir?"

"A farce. That boy's useless. He's sick," Tarchon said.

Maihara's face twisted in anger. "I told you that," she snapped. "May I go to my brother, General?"

Around them, a stream of departing dignitaries shuffled past the painted walls of the anteroom, which featured a series of murals of rustic scenes.

He could not see any reason why she should. "No, you

may not."

Chavin said nothing, but pointedly raised an eyebrow.

"She tried to escape during the shooting," Tarchon explained.

Maihara's jaw dropped as she paused for breath. "I did not!" she protested. "I was trying to take cover. I don't like being shot at."

"Nor does anyone," Tarchon said. A fresh thought occurred to him, and he glared at her. "Did you know there was going to be an assassination attempt? Or was it to let you escape?"

Maihara stared at him in surprise. "Of course not! But any fool should have known it was likely. Surely you don't suspect me?"

He did. He had already foiled her attempt to use that common boy to organise an escape.

"But I warned you."

"General, the princess spotted the assassin and called his position," Chavin said. "She would not have done that if she was part of the conspiracy."

"Maybe she already knew his position," Tarchon said, unsmiling.

Maihara looked alarmed. "You're being ridiculous. You saw how the bolts fell. Do you think I'd risk my brother? Or myself?"

Tarchon made a face, as though considering. "So how did you spot the shooter?"

Maihara was quick to answer. "I happened to be looking that way, and I saw a flicker of movement. So I called it. It wasn't a time for hesitation or questions."

"I see," said Chavin. "And then you tried to take cover? I'm impressed. We should have you in the army."

Tarchon had to chuckle, and Maihara smiled, relieved the tension had been broken. But he had not finished. "I'm surprised you didn't try to shield your brother, with your quick reactions, since you love him so much."

Maihara stared at him. Her face reddened. "I didn't think. I couldn't imagine how."

"Evidently not," Tarchon said, meanly. "Please attend me at the headquarters, Major, with your detailed report." He turned away and called for his staff officers and an escort.

***

"I don't like that man," Maihara said to Chavin.

"He's under a lot of pressure," Chavin said with a frown.

Maihara dismissed that comment. 'Pressure' was no excuse for uncouthness. She sensed an opportunity. "I want to see my brother. Can you get me in there?"

"We'll try," said Chavin, moving off and gesturing for Maihara to follow. The two guards detailed to keep an eye on Maihara trailed after, along a long echoing passage that ran between palace and fortress.

Maihara wondered why she had acted as she did. Did some part of her mind calculate that trying to climb over the seats in an elaborate dress and shield her brother from a plunging crossbow bolt would be ineffective, or had she solely thought of saving her own skin?

The grey-robed doctor, a brown-skinned man of middle age, was with Persis in a little room off the passage. The plain white plasterwork and green-painted wood marked it as a service room. A clutter of domestic objects lay on shelves and tables. Guards stepped aside to let Chavin, Maihara and her escort pass. The curly-haired Harayam arrived, red-faced and panting for breath.

"How is he?" Maihara asked, addressing the doctor.

Persis, his fine coat removed, sat on a plain chair while the doctor examined him.

The doctor looked up. "I've given the Prince a sedative, and his breathing and pulse are returning to normal. He had a fainting fit."

"He's your Emperor," Maihara corrected the doctor. "So will he be all right?"

The doctor bowed his head to acknowledge Maihara's words. "The gods willing, he should be fine, provided he avoids any stressful situations."

Chavin excused herself. "I have to go report to the headquarters now, Princess."

"I hope I'll see you again," Maihara said.

Chavin nodded and walked away with brisk steps.

Persis was staring at Maihara. She wanted to take two steps and hold him, but it wasn't possible. One didn't go grabbing Emperors. What was stressful about dressing up and sitting on a throne? Persis could try a bit harder. No, that was unfair. He'd been shot at.

"I trust you'll relay that advice to General Tarchon, Doctor," Maihara said.

Harayam cleared his throat.

"Yes, your, er ..." The doctor stumbled, evidently unable to identify this personage to whom he was deferring.

"You promised I wouldn't have to do this," Persis said in a whining tone.

Maihara sighed, containing her irritation. "I've spoken to General Tarchon, but that's all I can do. I'm a prisoner, the same as you."

"Princess." Officer Harayam, who had recovered his breath, touched her arm. "Come away now, you shouldn't be here."

"I should stay with him." She didn't want to leave her brother like this.

Harayam overruled her, and led her out of the side-room, but there was something else she needed to do. She turned to face him. "You have orders to take me back to the Anwar?"

He gave a curt nod. "Yes." She glimpsed his tooth gap.

"I want to collect a few things from my old room. It's right here, just upstairs." She pointed ahead to the north-east corner of the palace.

"My orders—"

She set off toward the stairs and heard Harayam following behind.

"You're not afraid of me, are you? Bring the guards. What could go wrong?"

Harayam looked uneasy. "Very well, Princess. But we

haven't got all day."

In the north corridor, people were spilling out of the Great Hall. A staircase of fine polished wood, with moulded plasterwork decorating the walls, led upward.

"I thought you said your room was just upstairs," Harayam said with youthful petulance, as they climbed past the first floor.

"It is. Up here."

At third floor level Maihara set off along the upper north corridor. It overlooked the glazed roof of the Great Hall.

"You can't go wandering around the Palace," Harayam said behind her.

"Don't worry, I just want my stuff." At last, she reached the door of her room. She placed her hand on the handle.

-13-

Maihara flung open the door of her childhood room. Broken trinkets lay strewn across the carpet, and the writing-table was overturned. The looters had thrown bed coverings on the floor, taken drawers out of the dressing table and pulled books from shelves. The wardrobe doors hung open.

She stared, as a lump gathered in her throat. Strangers had poked their hands into private places, fingered intimate things from the drawers, and stolen her clothes. She could not live in the room again after seeing it like this. Her fingers curled over her heart. Her childhood had ended.

She had no time for regrets. Mindful of the watching escort, she scooped up trinkets and dumped them on the dressing table.

Harayam stirred the small ornaments with a finger. "Are these valuable?"

"Why?" She nearly asked him if he meant to want to steal some as well.

Harayam drew back his hand as though stung.

She rummaged in the bottom of the closet under fallen clothes. The better dresses not already retrieved to her Anwar room were missing. The box was still there inside the trunk, underneath some battered stuffed toys and childish fancy dress outfits. She caressed its smooth polished black wood and picked it up with reverent fingers. Best not draw attention to it. She put it on the dressing table, then looked in the wardrobes and dressing table drawers for other items that were worth taking. There wasn't much. The dresses not stolen were those she didn't care for so much, and the ornaments not taken by the looters were childish things. Alongside the shiny baubles, the box, the size and shape of a large thick book, looked old and ugly. Perhaps that was how others always saw it.

The curly-haired Harayam had picked up the box and was shaking it. "What's in this?"

Her body tensed. "It's nothing, some things from my mother."

Harayam turned the seamless box over in his hands, looking for a catch. "There's something loose inside it."

"It'll be mementos, or dried up scent."

He put the box down. "Open it please, or leave it behind."

She glared at him, fists clenched. "It won't open. I'm taking it."

Harayam shrugged. His mouth had an obstinate set. "We'll decide that."

Ill at ease, she continued to search the room for anything else worth bringing away.

Minutes later, the guards stepped aside to admit Colonel Impar. Maihara's heart sank.

He scowled at Harayam, spectacles glinting. "What's she up to now?"

"Collecting her things, she says, sir. But she wants this box." He pointed to it. "She won't open it."

Impar picked up the box with gloved hands. "How do I open this?"

Dismayed, Maihara struggled for words. To have this unpleasant man interfering with her precious box was a disaster.

"What's in it? A weapon? Poison?"

"Just mementos from my mother. The lock doesn't work," she said.

"It's got no lid or lock or anything, sir," said the soldier who had found it.

Impar shook the box. The contents rattled. He ran his fingers around the underside and turned the box upside down. "Tell me how to open this, or I'll break it open."

He was harming the box's contents, and she fought the urge to snatch it from his rough hands. "I can't. It doesn't open." There was no way she would let them see her magic book and scrolls. She knew she should be calm, but as his rough fingers pressed the box, a dizziness swept over her and it was as if she was becoming someone else. Her vision faded and objects in the room lost colour. She couldn't lose the magic book and mirror a second time. She drew herself up, straight-backed. "It's mine. Don't you dare break it, or you'll be really sorry."

Immediately she regretted her provocative outburst.

Impar's thin face became redder. "You what? Open the fugging box! The commonwealth rules here, not you."

Shaken into silence by his anger, she flinched back.

Impar gripped the box and threw it hard onto the table. It bounced off and spun across the room, coming to rest on the far side, on the floor.

She ran after it but stumbled on a pile of bedding and sprawled against the wall.

"Open the box!" Impar shouted again.

She couldn't remember how to get the box to open. "I c-can't," she stammered. "I don't k-know how." She crawled over to the box and reached for it, but a soldier footed it away and collided with her, brushing her side and kicking her hand. He picked up the box and handed it to Impar.

Impar turned the box over. He was quiet, then made an audible exhalation. "If you won't co-operate, I'll have to take it away for examination." He turned and took a step toward the door.

"No! You can't," Maihara shouted. She stepped forward, but the soldiers, all big men, moved with arms outstretched to block her path. Impar stared at her, a challenging look.

Impar had the advantage. He'd take the box away and open it by force, and she'd never get that object of power or its contents back.

"Wait!" She stretched out a hand. "Let me try." She fought for breath and the room resumed its normal colours.

Impar gave a nod, and put the box on the table. She picked it up and ran her fingers over it till she found the

155

secret place to press and slide. It didn't open. Her heart beat faster as she sensed Impar's impatience building. She tried again, with shaking fingers, and the mechanism yielded with a click. She opened the lid and held it so Impar could see inside.

"Take the stuff out." His voice was imperious, and he wasn't using any honorifics to address her.

With shaking hands, she pried out the magical book, and then the scrolls and mirror, laying them on the table.

Impar stirred them with a forefinger. "What is all this?" he asked in a cold tone.

"It's a present from my mother. She used to be amused by these relics."

He opened the leather-bound book and flipped a couple of pages. "What's this?"

"It's old."

"I can't make out a word of it. Why give you this?"

She hesitated. Should she say it was an heirloom, or what?

Impar's eyes narrowed. "I don't like mysteries. I'll have these looked at." He piled the items back in the box.

"They're just heirlooms. I told you—"

Impar took up the unlatched box and frowned at her. "So you say."

"Will I get it back?"

Impar shrugged, and went out, followed by a couple of the guards.

She stood with clenched fists, glaring at Harayam who avoided her eyes, and at the guards. As her breathing calmed, tears wet her cheeks. She had not eaten all day. If only she'd had something to eat, she might have acted more rationally. She was sure Impar did not like her, and this confrontation had not helped.

"Which things are you taking with you, Princess?" Harayam prompted, looking embarrassed.

She bowed her head and with a heavy heart showed them the things she wanted carried.

Down in the outer yard, there was a delay while

Harayam ordered a closed carriage. The yard had stables and outbuildings along the exterior wall side. Straw and bits of broken loot lay on the square cobbles. The soldiers, bored, made jokes to each other, one holding up a dress and mimicking a female voice. Silently, Maihara wished them bad luck.

"Sorry about your box, but we had strict orders to check for banned items," Harayam said, avoiding her eyes.

Maihara sighed. Remembering the lady at the ceremony, she offered the scrap of paper to the officer. "Could you find what happened to this lady's husband?"

"What's this?" He took the paper and examined it. "When did you get it?" he asked, bushy eyebrows crinkling in a frown.

"She asked me when we were waiting in the grand hall."

"Lady Aurian?" Harayam read. "We'll look into it." He pocketed the note.

"Thank you. And have you any word of my former tutor? Demophon."

"Demophon, was it? I'll ask some people, Princess. He might have perished during the attack or the street fighting."

Maihara nodded gravely. Though he had betrayed her confidence, it was sad to think of Demophon lying in a heap of corpses.

Some while later, back at the mansion, a maid arrived to help Maihara undress and retire to bed. She lay still, thoughts churning, with the loss lying like a lead weight in her stomach. Darkness crept in. A bright star showed in the sky beyond the window. She'd been a fool. If only she had kept her head and been smarter, she could have played down the importance of the box and avoided revealing so much. Now the rebels had it and were examining its contents. The unknown person who had sent her the box on her fourteenth birthday would be disappointed.

Why couldn't she have been calm and quick-tongued?

Because it was *hers*. She *wanted* it. She *needed* it. What a disaster.

But she had a ray of hope. They might give the box back if they couldn't make anything of it, and if she persuaded them its contents represented harmless occultism that she didn't understand either. And if she made no further trouble. She vowed to use all her charm to influence Tarchon and his followers.

A floorboard creaked outside her room. She heard the murmur of male voices, and slipped out of bed, padding over the carpet toward the door.

"What's she doing in there?" A well-modulated male voice, one of the officers responsible for guarding her.

"It's all quiet; probably asleep by now." A more raspy voice.

" ... Good call by young Harayam. When Impar seized the box, she behaved like a dream-chaser deprived of her drug pipe ... extraordinary."

If they mean I behaved like a mad thing, they're right. The words hurt.

The raspy voiced man chuckled. "What will Tarchon do? Get rid of her? A Zircon princess and—"

A shiver of unease went up her spine.

"No, too valuable as a hostage."

"Could be." Boards creaked as a man shifted his weight.

"Did you hear what she did during the attack today?" the better-spoken voice said. "Nobody else had any idea where the bastard was shooting from, and she was shouting, 'Up there! Get him!'" A jingle and rustle sounded as if the man had been miming her actions.

"You can tell like, she's the real thing - the look, and the voice of command," the raspy voice said.

"That's what centuries of privilege do for you. Are you an admirer?"

"No way. But she's got big ones. And those dresses..." A low chuckle.

Maihara's ears burned. Men were like dogs. Still, it was a relief that they did not believe Tarchon meant to kill her, and gratifying that they thought she had presence.

"I'm turning in now. Behave yourself."

"Aye."

***

Two days passed without any word of her box. It was a bright morning. Footsteps clumped in the passage outside Maihara's room and knuckles rapped on the door panels. A key rattled in the lock. She gasped and sat upright in her chair. *What now?*

An unseen hand thrust the door open, and two officers of the rebellion shouldered their way in. They wore smart green jackets, and were clean-shaven, with short-trimmed hair.

"The General wants you," said one.

Fear stabbed through her. Had they examined the box contents and decided she was too dangerous to be allowed to live?

"What for? What does he want?"

The other shrugged.

"Am I coming back here?"

"As far as we know," the darker-skinned one said. "They want some information from you."

She could only surmise whether it was a follow-up of the box affair or something else, and her heart fluttered. She smiled at him and tugged at the plain dress she was wearing. "I can't come like this. I need to change into more suitable attire." She needed to look her best for this encounter.

The first officer's eyes glanced over her blue house-dress. "Very well, Princess. But can you be quick about it?"

She gave a nod. "Can you call my maid?"

One of the rebel-appointed maids helped her into a more imposing dress in pale satin, with a wide skirt and semi-precious trimmings. The officers, with soldiers in attendance, took her in a closed carriage to the Palace. Her escort was not talkative, and she shivered with unease in anticipation of the meeting to come.

159

They led her into an upstairs ante-room at the Palace's fort. She judged it led to the fort stateroom, where she had come face to face with General Tarchon for the first time. She took a seat on a gilded and red-upholstered chair and took note of her surroundings. Double hardwood doors with inlays led into the next room. From beyond came a murmur of male voices. Her escort stood, watching her. She steeled herself to act calmly and to use her charm to dim the memory of the earlier debacle.

After the shock of the box seizure, she still had access to the three basic spells she had practised. She brought her passwords to mind, activated the spy spell, and sent it into the stateroom. If they meant her no good, at least she would be forewarned.

The room with its wood-panelled walls and richly coffered plaster ceiling, gilded and painted in blue and orange, was unchanged.

Tarchon, occupying the head of the central table, was talking politics about the various provinces to a Dhikr seated to his left. She closed in the spy view and flinched at the sight of the ugly and corpulent Barin. Their elderly Emir, with a gilded chain around his neck, sat next to Barin, listening. She inched the view around. Two more Dhikr warriors were on that side, one of them cleaning dirty fingernails with his knife. Sitting opposite them were rebel officers with gold rope sewn on their green-uniformed shoulders. A robed Monist priest sat at the far end.

Tarchon turned to his right and raised an arm. "Send the Princess in!"

The doors of the ante-room swung open. Hastily, Maihara shut off the spy spell.

Officers showed her to a seat at the table in the meeting room. The hoops of her skirt caught on the table edge and flicked upward as she sat. She worked them down and struggled to gain her composure, conscious of Tarchon's eyes on her. A servant placed a filled wine-glass in front of her, while the Dhikr warriors glared. She was the only woman present, and her siblings were not here. Neither fact boded well. She reached for the wine-glass and drained it.

One of Tarchon's officers reached over Maihara's shoulder and set two letters before her.

"Have a look at those," Tarchon said, from his end of the table. He sat with hands placed widely apart, dominating the group of rebel officers.

Maihara read over the handwritten letters, written with blue ink on fine paper. One was addressed to Sihrima, and the other to Persis, exhorting the recipient to be brave and expressing the hope that they would be released soon. They were signed 'Zircon' and it looked like her father's handwriting. Her hand shook. This was evidence her father had gotten away. There were tales of tunnels under the city that extended beyond the walls. Some said that snakes and toads lived down there. Ugh.

There was no letter for her. The disappointment was keen, though the rebels could have kept it back.

"What do you say?" Tarchon asked. "Are they from him?"

"Yes," Maihara said. Her throat was tight, and she could barely get the word out.

"Not a forgery?"

"No, it looks like his hand, his ink and it's the kind of things he would say."

Tarchon did not seem pleased. He made a hooking gesture, and the officer behind Maihara retrieved the letters.

"How did you get these?" Maihara asked, her voice shaking.

"The Imperials have contacted us. They want your siblings back."

"Where's my letter?"

Tarchon's expression softened. "They didn't give us one," he said in a quieter voice. "They seem more interested in your two siblings. I'm sorry." He turned to address the meeting. "We're making contact with the Imperials on a ransom for the Princess Sihrima. We are negotiating a price, and a place and procedure for making the exchange."

Maihara lowered her head. They didn't want her. She didn't get on too well with her frivolous sister, but the prospect of parting from her, perhaps forever, saddened her. It would be useless to protest, for these men wouldn't listen. At least Sihrima would be out of rebel hands.

The Dhikr's Emir got up from his chair and tottered around to Maihara's side of the table. She could hear his whistling breath behind her, and she hated it when people did things directly behind her. She scraped the chair back, stood, and turned.

"She's got child-bearing hips, and big breasts to make plenty of milk," the old man said. "I need a new young wife; I'd enjoy riding this one."

Maihara stared at the wrinkled barbarian with mounting fear and rage. He was balding, with white whiskers and a small beard, and wore rank-smelling leather trousers and jacket, heavily adorned with plates of metal and bits of jewellery, and with a gold chain about his scrawny neck. She couldn't imagine anything worse than being violated by this senile goat. She glanced at Tarchon, but could read no assistance in his expression. Along with her fear of rape, a mist of rage was building, and she was unable to resist its mad embrace. She pointed her forefinger at the old man. "You can just die."

There was an outbreak of shouting. The Emir took a step back. "Bitch," he mouthed.

"An insult to our chief," Barin bellowed. "Flog the fugging tart."

Tarchon banged his gavel on the table for silence, and shouted the Dhikr down. "She's *our* prisoner; *we'll* decide what we do with her."

The Dhikr muttered and snarled. Tarchon made a beckoning gesture to his right, and all the rebel soldiers guarding the meeting took one step forward. The floor quivered as they stamped in unison. The Dhikr subsided.

"Charming," said one of the rebel officers.

Colonel Impar turned his thin face to Tarchon and

grimaced.

"Princess." Tarchon caught Maihara's eye and gestured to her. "Sit down."

The rejected Emir was tottering back to his place.

"Witch," a Dhikr said, into the comparative silence.

A cold wash of fear swept over her. Surely no one would think she had cursed the Emir? She cleared her throat. "My apologies, Emir. I did not mean that literally. But, no thank you."

There was an amused murmur from the rebel side.

"That's not enough." Barin thumped the table.

"Enough of this," Tarchon said. "You're not in your horse camps now, my friends. You don't address an Imperial Princess in that common manner, so don't complain if you get a horse-camp reply."

The four Dhikr at the table merely scowled.

Tarchon rapped his gavel on the heartwood table. "We will have a short recess for drinks and snacks. Then we'll continue our discussions."

"Without the she-devil," Barin said, with a growl.

"As you wish."

As uniformed soldiers brought in pots of hot koosh and biscuits, Tarchon led Maihara out. "You've made our negotiations twice as difficult with that little outburst. You'll have to miss the rest of the meeting."

"Sorry," she avoided looking at him, "but the thought of being defiled by one of those barbarians was disgusting. What do they think women are, some kind of goat?"

Tarchon bent over and spoke in a low voice. "Actually, that's more or less what they do think. But they're our allies." If he was furious with her, his amused tone did not show it.

"I don't know why you dragged me here in the first place." She turned to look him in the face.

"To publicly verify the letters." They reached the double doors. "I hear you have been asking after your tutor, Ars Demophon. Do you know why he left the Palace's employ?"

"He disappeared and left a resignation letter. I assume he fled because he feared he'd be arrested for spouting his radical ideas."

"Were the Fifth Bureau onto him, do you know?"

"I have no idea, but I was shouted at by my father the previous evening for asking about the rebel agenda. I assumed Demophon must have got word."

"I see." Tarchon rested a hand on the carved door surround.

"You don't know what happened to him?"

"Quite a few people died or disappeared during the uprising and occupation."

Maihara sighed.

Tarchon beckoned to the soldiers and officer waiting in the ante-room beyond. If he was concerned about Fifth Bureau agents still being active and planning assassinations, he was not likely to confide it to her. The Empire's secret service was well placed to remain active and out of sight after the fall of the city.

Maihara spoke quickly. "May I go see my brother?"

Tarchon hesitated. "No, and don't go stirring up any more trouble."

Maihara had been reading in her room for an hour when tramping feet and voices made noise in the passage. A key clattered in the lock before the door was flung open. Colonel Impar entered, with a pair of soldiers at his back. She sprang to her feet, alarmed. His rat-like features bore a grim expression, and with a quickening heartbeat she tried to guess what bad news he was bringing.

Impar looked at her through his round spectacles without moving. "Still here," he muttered.

Why would he imagine otherwise? "What do you want?" Mindful of his previous aggression, she fought an impulse to back away and stood her ground.

Impar did not answer at once. He looked over his spectacles to read from the war history book she had open on the table. "We have a problem. We calmed the Dhikr down and had a discussion about a ruling council, but at the end of it the Emir got off his chair, fell over, and died."

"He's dead? Already? How?" He'd been lively enough that morning. "Oh." She trembled. The Dhikr would want her head for this.

"Oh, indeed. They blame you, and they want you executed for murder and witchcraft."

Maihara felt faint and cold, and colour faded from the room.

"There's no need to look so terrified," Impar said, without much sympathy. "I doubt that the General will give them the satisfaction. Don't go doing anything else."

He retreated and shut the door. The key turned in the lock.

She sat down and took a deep breath. If people thought she had killed the Emir by witchcraft, she was in big trouble. Images of ghastly methods of execution that she'd read in books including burning at the stake flashed through her mind. What would the rebels do? Impar's demeanour suggested that he didn't much care about the death. So why had he made that brief visit?

What had he meant by 'Still here'?

Maihara started. Of course, he meant she had not magically vanished.

-14-

Tarchon laid aside the papers he had been signing. Dusk was falling in this small room high in the Calah palace fort, and a yellow light from two oil lamps bathed the whitewashed brick walls. It lit the faces of the several officers who had just entered and who stood silently, awaiting his word. They had gathered to discuss the latest tension in relations with their troublesome allies, the Dhikr. Finally, Colonel Impar entered, head lowered to clear the doorway, and saluted.

"Take a seat, gentlemen, if you can find one," Tarchon said.

Some of the officers sat on a wood bench. Impar moved closer to Tarchon's desk. Tarchon awaited his intelligence officer's report with unease.

"Your report, Colonel?"

"Sir, I took two men and went to visit the elder princess. I found her in her room—" Impar paused. "I informed her of the Emir's demise. She showed signs of surprise and alarm."

"How did you interpret that reaction, Colonel?"

"Either she's a very good actress, or she knew nothing about it. The death, I mean."

"Thank you, Colonel." Tarchon strove to conceal his relief at Impar's verdict. He liked Maihara, and since the Emir's sudden demise he had feared the worst, that he had made a misjudgement that put them in all in danger from a powerful Imperial sorceress. A danger that would force him to give orders he did not want to give. Many of the radical faction wanted all the Imperial family executed, but Impar thus far had accepted the Army view that executing the children would not be wise and they were more valuable alive than dead. "Wasn't there some business with a box? And the rumour that she is descended from Vimrashan witch-queens?"

A two-stripe officer raised a hand. "We found nothing conclusive, so far."

"She looks like a witch," the youngest officer said.

Tarchon, displeased, fixed him with a chilly stare. The young man flushed.

"As the lieutenant says, there's no clear evidence," Impar said, pressing the bridge of his glasses. "She could still be a risk. I suspected those papers in the box were cyphers or cypher keys, but it appears they concern magic."

The major looked wide-eyed. "Real magic?"

"Do we believe in magic?" Tarchon asked. It was mostly old wives' tales and superstition.

Impar glanced around the room, at the officers. "A lot of people do. I prefer evidence."

"So we're not accusing her of anything," Tarchon said. He did not credit Impar's suggestion that the Imperials had planted the princess on them. "Do we know any more about the death?"

A fresh-faced officer spoke up. "Sir, the Dhikr would not let us examine the body. But the staff doctor's opinion is that he suffered an apoplectic seizure. Natural causes, in other words."

"It's unfortunate that it happened during our meeting," Tarchon said.

"I expect it was the shock of having a female defy him, sir," Impar said dryly.

Tarchon chuckled, his mood buoyed by the suggestion of Maihara's innocence in the matter. "That's very good. In fact, that's the line I'll use if they continue to rant and bluster." He composed his features. "What are the Dhikr doing?"

"They've made threats, sir," another officer said. "About what they'll do if we don't hang the girl."

"General Pendash's men are watching their camp," said a fourth man. A couple of men stirred to look out of the slit windows. The lamps cast dark human shadows shifting along the walls.

"Have the gates barred," Tarchon ordered. "Tell Pendash he's not to let a single one of them inside the city till further orders."

"Yes, sir."

"Are we overlooking anything, gentlemen? This could be important."

"Perhaps one of their own side poisoned the old brute, sir," the fresh-faced officer said.

Impar scratched his chin. "Who knows with savages? Maybe that's how they decide their leadership succession."

"Did you notice any suspicious actions during the meeting?" Tarchon asked the youth.

The youth lowered his head. "No, sir."

"Pity," Colonel Impar said.

"We could tell them we think one of theirs did it," said the second officer.

"No we won't," Impar said. "Don't give them ideas. They might accuse us of poisoning their Emir."

Tarchon tapped the table. "Colonel Impar is right. Natural causes will be our official line. Let's hope they calm themselves in a day or two."

"If they don't, shall we hand over the girl?" the fourth officer said.

"Even if she is a witch, and an over-privileged brat, that's a bad idea," Impar said. "We mustn't show those brutes any sign of weakness."

"No concessions," Tarchon said. He did not have the slightest intention of handing the princess over to the Dhikr, regardless of what they threatened or did. They were effective allies and brave warriors, but their customs were primitive. In the real world one had to have relationships with people one did not like, without behaving like them. Impar's opinion came as a relief. "We say it was natural causes, so no concessions. Anything else would imply our involvement."

"Very well, sir," Colonel Impar said. He found a stool

and sat down.

"We also need to plan for exchanging prisoners and ransoming the Imperial children," Tarchon said. "This will be difficult if the Dhikr remain troublesome." The younger princess Sihrima was likely to be ransomed, but even though crowning Prince Persis as a rival Emperor had failed to achieve any of the hoped-for results, they would keep the young prince for the time being.

He led the meeting to discuss the exchange logistics. It seemed to him that if Maihara wasn't a menace, she might prove useful at the exchange meet-up.

***

Next day, Maihara had a visit from Cleia Chavin. The tall female officer was in trousered male-style uniform and her nape-length brown hair was neatly brushed. Her cheerful manner and smile dispelled Maihara's apprehension. Bright light streamed in at the window of Maihara's room, illuminating Chavin's oval and lightly tanned face.

"What's happening about the dead Emir?" Maihara asked at once.

"Nothing much, yet. We're hoping it will blow over. So far as I know, the senior leadership believe his death was from natural causes. But the Dhikr are still blustering and complaining, and neither side wants to back down."

Maihara let out the breath she had been holding and relaxed in relief. She remained seated at her table and invited Chavin to sit in an armchair. After an exchange of social pleasantries, Chavin asked, "How well can you ride?"

Maihara looked up at her, mystified. "I've never ridden."

"Never ridden a horse?" Chavin leaned forward with a look of surprise.

"No." Maihara glanced out of the window, which showed a patch of blue sky.

"Now, that's a problem. Tarchon wants you to be present at the prisoner exchange; he thinks it will be helpful. And it'll be your last chance to say farewell to your sister."

"Can't I go in a carriage?"

"When they planned this, they assumed you could ride. Part of the route is across country, too rough for a carriage. Can your sister not ride either?" Chavin tilted her head.

"I don't know; she's tried it a couple of times. Is this far outside the city?"

"It's at the Kunn Hills; they wouldn't agree to meet any closer. We can manage the prisoners, but you have to get there by horse."

"I can't!" Maihara interlaced her fingers. She had never been closer to a horse than riding in a carriage required.

"You'll have to. Put on some plain outside clothes, and I'll take you down to the yard."

After Maihara had changed into a plain skirt and jacket, Chavin walked her down to the Anwar mansion's carriage yard.

"Why were those minor nobles at the coronation?" Maihara asked, as they descended the stairs. "Are they all traitors?"

"Don't call them that, Princess. A lot of the minor nobility support us. Tax promoters used to snoop around their estates looking for signs of wealth, and then filing a secret report. Then the landowner would get a demand for payment of an extortionate sum, with no appeal, so that some had to mortgage their estates to avoid debtor's prison. Or the promoter would take a bribe to look elsewhere. Till the next promoter came along." Chavin spoke with feeling.

"I see." Maihara had heard complaints about the Imperial tax system. She was silent till they reached an iron-studded door. Clearly the rebels had found real grievances to exploit, but those didn't seem to justify war and mass killing.

"When did you learn to ride?" Maihara asked.

"When I was five. My father put me on a mule and led it around the farmyard."

"That young?" Maihara was surprised. She tried to

assess the social class of Chavin's family. Prosperous farmers or small landowners, perhaps. They might rebel against unjust tax.

As they entered the square cobble-paved yard, Maihara's nose was assailed by the smell of straw and horse dung. There were six wooden half-doors, and horses stirred behind two of them. Four rebel soldiers idled in a corner, and looked over making comments as Chavin and Maihara walked across. At the far end of the yard, a dark horse was tied up near a stone water-trough. A stable-lad offered it a handful of hay.

"Do you have a side-saddle?" Chavin asked the stable-lad.

"Yes, Ma'am." He disappeared into a dark doorway.

"What do the men think of you being an officer?" Maihara asked. "Don't the male officers object?"

"Only the more stupid ones," Chavin said. "The intelligent ones realise that I'm not going to take their front-line jobs, and that I do jobs they might not want anyway."

"Such as teaching unfit princesses to ride?" Maihara asked.

Chavin smiled and shook her head. She pointed to the dark horse.

The horse looked very high, and when Maihara walked up to it, it snorted and moved its feet. It thrust its head at her.

She retreated. "Will it bite?"

"It's probably expecting a treat," Chavin said.

The stable-hand carried out a saddle and commenced fitting it on the horse. There was something odd about the look of the saddle.

"High-class ladies ride side-saddle in the Empire, so we'll start you with one," Chavin explained.

Chavin, with the aid of two soldiers, helped Maihara into the saddle and put her left foot in the footrest. It didn't feel secure, and the hard cobbles of the stable-yard were a long way down. To her left, the horse tossed its head.

Chavin led the horse by the reins while Maihara gripped the saddle's pommel. She feared the animal was about to tip her onto the cobbles but did not protest.

She was determined to master riding, at least well enough to stay on the horse. To go to Kunn meant to be with her sister till her release, and to be in a position to seize any chance of escaping, though the latter thought filled her with doubts.

All went well while Chavin led the horse around the yard, but soon Maihara had to control the horse herself. It circled the yard, head down, till Maihara gave the reins a shake and the horse, clearly bored with walking, broke into a trot. Maihara squealed and grabbed the front of the saddle. The animal turned a corner and changed its gait to a faster, jolting movement. "Help!"

Officers and soldiers ran to grab the harness of the errant animal. With order restored, a shaken Maihara sat on a mounting block while the horse was led away.

"Wasn't that brute trained?" Maihara complained. "What is this, a Dhikr plot?"

"No, Princess," Chavin said. "It's a fine horse but perhaps a bit lively for you. We'll get a more docile one."

Another horse, smaller, slower and less fine-looking, was led out, and the side-saddle transferred onto the replacement's back. Maihara was given a glass of wine to steady her nerves. She looked at it.

"I'm not supposed to drink."

"Never did me any harm, your Ladyship," said the stable-lad. "Drink it up, now."

Maihara did so. It gave her a glow and a relaxed feeling.

"Are you ready to try again?" Chavin asked.

Maihara would rather not, but if it meant being able to say goodbye to her sister at the exchange, she'd do her best. Hoisted onto the horse, she had to try making it go and stop. This horse, fortunately, was far more adept at the latter.

At last, the exhausting lesson ended. Chavin leaned

close to Maihara. "A word of advice, Princess. Some people still wonder if you murdered the Emir, but if I were you, I'd keep quiet and not protest my innocence too vigorously."

Maihara looked at Chavin, puzzled. "Why?"

"Some people don't take sorcery seriously. Others are afraid of any female power. It's 'kill the witch' with them."

"Like the Fifth Bureau?"

"If you say so."

Maihara had to be content with that.

***

A maid woke Maihara at dawn and helped her dress. She chose the same outfit she had worn the previous day for the horse-riding lesson. The curly-haired Harayam, now attached to her guard detail, led her down to the stable yard. In the courtyard a four-wheel coach waited. The officer motioned toward it.

"I thought I had to ride?" Maihara asked him.

The rebels still had not explained why she was being taken to this meeting. Perhaps they hoped her presence would trouble the Imperials, provoking fears that she had changed sides. Or they hoped the Imperials would change their minds and offer a ransom for her. For her part, the prospect of being so close to a group of free Imperials filled her with anxious anticipation and fear. The Court might have softened its attitude toward her, opening up prospects of ransom, rescue or escape. If the contrary, they could attack, and seize her for execution.

"Orders were to put you in this carriage, Princess," Harayam said in a monotone. He seemed ill at ease in her presence. She wasn't complaining if it meant she could take this last ride with her sister. Sihrima had already taken a seat in the carriage, which smelled of stale leather.

Maihara slid beside her sister and hugged her. This might be their last time together. "I'll miss you."

"I'll miss you too," Sihrima said, but looked away. Maihara sensed her sister's excitement at the prospect of release.

"Have you seen Persis?" Maihara asked.

"No, I think he's at the Palace. I suppose he's all right there."

Maihara sighed. She had hoped to learn how her brother was coping.

Lieutenant Harayam and two rebel fighters climbed in. Maihara released Sihrima, not liking to show too much emotion in front of the rebels.

"Did they ask you if you could ride?" Maihara asked her sister.

"Yes," Sihrima shrugged. "I had a go at the Aranish estate a year ago."

"Yesterday, they were talking about riding cross-country," Maihara said. "That female officer gave me a riding lesson in the yard here. It went on for ages, and it was hellish. They seem to have changed their minds."

"Probably because you were useless, Sis." Sihrima smirked.

Mindful of Sihrima's allegedly greater experience, Maihara bit back any reply.

The carriage tilted as men climbed on the outside, then it moved off. They descended the city's mound with brakes squealing, passing along a wide elegant street of the upper city, then narrow streets below, and she caught glimpses of grand houses and shops before they passed through an arched gate in the city wall. Out here on the plain, a detachment of mounted rebels waited to escort them. The landscape was flat with a collection of windowless huts nearby and fields of crops. Maihara kept looking out of the windows. Even before the uprising, as an over-protected princess she rarely had a chance to see what the world looked like outside the Palace, and being out here made her conscious of what she had missed. To the right was a distant village.

To the left, in the middle distance, a large camp of tents with pointed tops and banners spread across trampled crop fields. Horsemen milled around outside it. The Dhikr camp. Maihara gave a shudder.

The escort formed up around the coach, and without further delay, they moved off along the eastern road. The pace was much faster than in the streets, and alongside them the escort horses were cantering. Often the carriage would lurch and shudder as its wheels crashed through potholes, though the road was raised and well-made with a topping of bound gravel. Every few hundred yards, an irrigation ditch ran under the road. Maihara clung to a leather grab-handle without protest. The sooner they were away from the Dhikr, the better.

They passed farmsteads that were burnt or had animal carcases lying in the fields. The landscape remained flat with isolated clumps of trees and scattered silent buildings. A few birds of prey circled, looking for small animals hiding below.

"Something bad has happened here," she said to Harayam. "Who did it - you or the Dhikr?"

"The Dhikr," Harayam admitted, shifting in his seat.

"Your allies."

Harayam scowled but said nothing.

It was easy to discomfit him. Maihara felt that she had scored a hit, but sad for the empire's subjects. They were the ones who suffered most from invasion and warfare.

"Can't you tell them to slow down?" her sister asked, after another jolt that threw her against Maihara.

"They'll rest the horses when we're out of sight of the Dhikr," Harayam said.

Maihara did not respond. She was happy to be as far away from the Dhikr as possible, and Sihrima's mind might already be on something else.

"Is it far to the hand-over?" her sister asked.

Maihara glanced at the young officer. "They said it would be in the Kunn Hills," she said. "That's around four hour's travel."

Sihrima groaned and shifted in her seat. As usual, she disliked being made to sit still with no like-minded companions to entertain her.

"Where is Tarchon?" Maihara asked.

"The General's with the other group," Harayam said.

"What other group?"

The soldiers did not answer her, but the exchange had to involve more forces than she saw around the coach.

"What province does Tarchon come from?" Maihara asked. She knew little about the rebel leader.

"From Ankar, in the north-west," the officer said, showing his tooth gap.

That was where the revolt had started, so far as Maihara knew. "What was his family like?"

"They owned a corn business. Had a house and mill in Pamarken town," said a soldier with a moustache.

"Is he married?" Sihrima asked.

"Not any more," Harayam said. "His wife died."

"What happened to her?" Maihara asked.

Harayam shrugged. "I don't know." He folded his arms.

"Did he have any children?" Sihrima asked.

The soldier shook his head. "I understand he had a brother. The brother was to inherit the business, while Tarchon joined the Army."

"The rebel army?" Maihara asked.

"No more questions," Harayam said, frowning.

Maihara was left to speculate that Tarchon had trained with the Imperial Army before changing sides. Did that make him a treacherous person?

The carriage slowed to a walk. The sisters were silent. Maihara had things she felt she could say, about their childhood, and what might happen in the future, but it seemed awkward to speak. The presence of three rebel men was discouraging as well. Instead, the sisters held hands.

Maihara reached inside herself for her connection to the magical world. It was what she did from time to time to reassure herself. She felt nothing. Was it because she was out in the countryside? She tried again, closing her eyes with the mental effort, but it was the same. Not good.

The carriage sped up again. After a while, the sun streaming in the window left Maihara hot and sticky. The air in the coach reeked of old leather and male sweat.

The carriage and escort halted to water the horses at a stream crossed by a stone bridge.

"It's too hot in here," Maihara said. "I need to get out, or I'll faint." Reluctantly, the officer agreed.

The plains' breeze cooled her skin, but brought on a different need. Maihara went behind a bush, wincing at the indignity. She hoped the men would have the decency not to watch.

Horses crunched hooves in the river gravel and dipped their necks to drink. The countryside, flat in all directions, was divided into fields with crops of yellow corn and other green and ripening plants. A few clusters of distant huts broke the monotony. The road, wide enough for two carriages to pass, crossed the single-arch bridge and ran onward to the East. Sihrima patted one of the carriage team. The air carried a reek of warm horse and equine manure, making Maihara wrinkle her nose at the smell.

With the horses watered, the carriage set off again with its escort. Another carriage, long and black with barred windows, had caught up and followed behind. Some while later, her carriage turned off onto a smaller, rougher track where it went at no more than a trotting pace. The countryside here was only partly cultivated, with large expanses of scrub and weedy pasture turning back to scrubland, and only a few fields with rows of crops. They passed the remains of a hamlet, the cottages roofless, with gable ends sticking up into the blue sky and grass growing around the walls. Beyond it, weeds grew around rows of grey standing stones. They were the height of a small child and set in crude rows about two paces apart.

"Why does nobody live here?" she asked.

"This is where the Kunn harrying took place a generation ago," Harayam said.

"Harrying? I don't understand what you mean."

"There was unrest here, because of hunger." The young officer spoke with animation. "The peasants took up arms, there were various protests and disturbances. Instead of trying to fix the causes, the Lords sent in men to harry the whole area. They burnt crops, burnt or pulled down huts and houses and barns, and killed anyone who did not run fast enough. The country has never recovered. Few people live here now."

"Were many killed?" Maihara asked after a pause. She found it hard to accept that the nobility could do this. But the abandoned countryside told its own story.

"Thousands," Harayam said. He gave her a cold look. "See those tall thin stones. Those are grave markers."

She looked again at a group of the stones that had puzzled her, and sucked in her breath. The rebels had made allegations in her hearing before, but she had dismissed it as their twisted version of the facts. Now her conviction was shaken.

The carriage passed unidentifiable low stone ruins among which small trees grew and a couple of cultivated fields and then stopped. Maihara stared. They had arrived at a primitive hamlet of low stone-walled and thatched huts, beside a hill with outcrops of tawny rocks. She had never seen any place so dismal and poverty-stricken.

"What's going on here?" Sihrima asked.

"This is where you change to horses," Harayam said.

Maihara was not looking forward to this, but the carriage interior was hot. "May we get out?" she asked.

"Not yet."

The outriders milled around, and some, armed with lances, galloped out of sight. Maihara guessed they were scouting for any signs of trouble. The thought gave her a quiver of unease. Things might go wrong, and the Imperials make a pre-emptive attack, putting all their lives in danger.

After a wait, the riders returned, and a hand knocked on the carriage door. "Please get out now," the officer said.

Maihara stepped down, onto sandy ground with a few weeds growing in it. The area around the stone and wood huts was trodden and a few goats were tied up but the inhabitants were keeping out of sight.

Cleia Chavin appeared, leading the same placid horse with side-saddle that Maihara had ridden in the stable yard.

"Here's your horse." With the help of two troopers, she lifted Maihara into the saddle. Again, it seemed high up, but to her pleasure she could see over the top of the huts to the fields and ground beyond, which undulated in a series of sandy hills with scrubby vegetation. "Keep in the middle of the column and don't wander off," Chavin said.

Maihara saw that Chavin was wearing a sheathed sword. "Can you use that?" she asked.

"The sword? My father taught me fencing, with my brother."

"And in the army?" Maihara prompted.

"I had to do the same sword-fighting and lance drills as the men, but nobody's expecting me to fight unless we find ourselves under sudden attack by the enemy."

Nearby, Sihrima was also mounting up, on a grey horse, and Harayam, her personal escort, mounted and put his horse on Maihara's right. He clipped a line to the bridle of Maihara's horse and held the other end. Whether it was to lead her horse or stop her cantering off he didn't say. Either way it was humiliating. Everybody else seemed able to ride, but her father had decreed that there was no need for her to risk a riding accident. With much shouting and whinnying, the column moved off along a rough, dusty track at a brisk walk. Outriders rode ahead and on the flanks.

"This used to be forest," Harayam said with feeling, gesturing at random. A few grey flat-topped stumps stood out among the scrub. "Felling the trees has damaged the land, and let it erode out and become waste."

Maihara concentrated on not falling off and on keeping her horse on track with the other riders. After a while, she realised that if she didn't do anything, her animal would follow the escort. She could concentrate on looking at the dry, depopulated scenery and the other riders. The horse seemed to share her dislike of the trek, hanging back on the lead rope and huffing as it plodded up sandy inclines.

Tarchon was nowhere to be seen. Despite her brag about being able to ride, Sihrima was sitting side-saddle and allowing her horse to follow the others. Thirty or forty riders were strung out along a track that wound across sandy country part grown with scrubby bushes and thin grass. Hooves thudded, harness jingled and the warm air bore an odour of horseflesh.

Cleia Chavin was some way off to the right, wheeling her horse at a canter around a hillock. Maihara sighed. Even if she didn't dislike horses, there was no way she could look like that, seated astride and riding a horse as skilfully as the men. Cleia's horse looked like the same one that had given Maihara such a fright in the stable yard. She felt a twinge of shame.

-15-

Maihara and Cleia's column joined up with the larger rebel force that was meant to protect them from any Imperial mischief. Green flags fluttered above a mass of mounted troopers, and hundreds of hooves stirred up dust. Maihara hung back with Cleia while the commander of her column reported to Tarchon. Gestures animated their conversation. Tarchon wore light mail, and a pointed helmet hung by a strap from his saddle peak. He slashed the air with his riding-crop as the other man spoke. She found that seeing him here in martial gear at the head of an armed column was more reassuring than she anticipated.

The two mounted lines, theirs and Tarchon's, had halted side by side, in the midst of a scrubby waste. Yellow flowers crowned the spiky bushes, and a few long-tailed lizards panted in the scant shade. Flies rose to investigate the horses. A dozen men in clothing of good quality, mounted on nags and with hands tied, brought up the rear of Tarchon's riders. Maihara ached from the unaccustomed effort of riding and was sure she smelled of horse.

Tarchon beckoned them over. He pointed the crop toward Maihara.

"Is she managing that horse?"

"Yes, sir," Cleia replied.

Maihara glared. She harboured a list of resentments, about having to ride for leagues, being snacked on by flies, being dragged to an uncomfortable encounter with the Imperials and losing her sister.

He turned to his aides and the section commander. "We have to be doubly careful of any trickery. We'll advance, and after the scouts make initial contact, we'll pause while we verify each other's dispositions. Then we move closer as agreed and make the exchange. Do you all understand the procedures?"

The officers raised a chorus of 'Ayes'.

"Princess Maihara, I want you to remain close to me at the meeting, in case I have to ask you anything about the enemy. Stay two paces behind me."

"Aren't you afraid I'll mislead you?" Maihara asked, in combative mood. She was fatigued, sore, and about to meet in some diplomatic dance the same faction who threw her into a dank cell.

Tarchon narrowed his eyes. "You'd better not."

Irritation flashed through Maihara. "I'm a prisoner, not your Empire adviser."

Tarchon frowned at her. "You'll do what you're told. I don't have time to argue."

She kept silent. Tarchon was no doubt stressed by the dangerous situation they were entering. If the Imperials proved treacherous, they could kill or capture his delegation. An alarming thought entered her mind. Despite his words, did he intend to hand back his bothersome prisoner without a ransom? She should stop testing his boundaries.

"I don't want to be handed back," she said.

He looked at her in mild surprise. "You won't be."

The prospect of meeting the Imperial delegation was becoming less and less appealing. "What if they try to snatch me?"

"I'm calculating they don't want you badly enough to violate the parley terms. They didn't offer a ransom."

"You didn't tell them I'd be present?" Wind ruffled her hair. Fresh unease gripped her. The day felt less warm than a moment ago.

"We mentioned the possibility. I wanted you here, to see how they might react to your presence. They threw you in a cell rather than smacking your wrist for being naughty. I want to understand their thinking." He raised his head.

She stared at him. He might be testing her, judging her importance to the Imperial side. She feared this encounter and longed to be away from this desolate region.

Tarchon turned his horse away. The scouts ahead were signalling. Maihara tensed. She walked her horse after Tarchon over rising ground where clumps of thinly leaved scrub clung to the dusty earth. The side-saddle bumped and rocked with the motion of the horse.

They crested a small ridge. Below was a bare open space, and at the far side, soldiers in glittering armour, perhaps fifty in number, stood guarding a tented pavilion.

Maihara drew in a breath.

"I expect they have more troops than we can see," Tarchon said to her. "Our scouts will signal if all looks well."

Maihara looked away from him to the dry, undulating landscape, and glanced rearwards. The soldiers from their combined columns did not look many, out here. What if the Imperials broke their word? "There could be more of their troops beyond that ridge. Or even behind us." She wished she was back in Calah.

"You don't need to give us military advice," he said, in a brusque tone. "We have troops behind us in depth, to guard against any trickery from them."

Alongside the pavilion, Imperial household flags and Empire pennants of orange and yellow fluttered in the light wind. Rebel officers waved green flags, then a trumpet sounded from the Imperial formation.

Her heart beat faster. It was finally happening.

"Sound the reply," Tarchon shouted. A trooper fumbled a bugle out of his saddle-bag and blew on it. A blare filled her ears and echoed faintly from the hills.

A white flag waved from the Imperial formation.

"Wave the white flag," Tarchon shouted. An officer pulled a white flag on a stick from his saddle pouch and waved it. Tarchon ordered two of his officers to ride forward. Two riders in gaudy armour moved forward from the Imperial position. Their mail was in bright colours with shiny metal at knee and elbow.

With a jingle of mail, rebel troopers formed up forward

of Maihara, partly blocking her view and forming a defensive line.

"What's going on now?" Maihara asked.

"We're starting the agreed procedures," Cleia said.

Two riders from each side rode forward, passing far beyond the respective Imperial and rebel positions.

Maihara turned her head to watch the two armoured Imperial riders.

"Whatever are they doing?" she asked Cleia.

"They are checking behind us, to make sure we don't have more troops hiding behind the ridge. We're doing the same."

Maihara looked forward. The two rebel officers had separated beyond the ends of the Imperial line. "If those men had been bribed, we could be, ah..." she said.

"Stuffed," one of the listening officers supplied.

Maihara puzzled over the word. Wasn't that what happened to toy animals? The mordant relish with which the officer pronounced it made the meaning clear enough. She shivered.

They waited. Immobile in a persistent breeze, Maihara pulled her riding cloak closer about her.

The Varlord scouting riders and the rebel riders reappeared at almost the same time. As they re-entered the space between the forces, they made arm-signals to their respective leaders.

The two rebel officers rode toward Tarchon. She could not hear every word of their reports, only their calm voices.

"It looks like all's well," Cleia said.

Tarchon nodded and raised a hand. Flags waved on the rebel and Imperial sides, making coded signals. Two soldiers brought a man in trousers and silk shirt with his hands tied in front of him forward from the rebel ranks, on foot. Imperial troopers likewise brought a captive forward from the Imperial side. In the centre of the field, the two pairs of officers, now dismounted, conferred briefly, holding sheets of paper, before the minders allowed the freed prisoners to proceed. A man with ragged grimy clothes and drawn, unshaven face limped barefoot into the rebel lines.

The delegations repeated the same procedure another ten times. "Who are these men?" Maihara asked.

"They're senior rebels, captured or arrested by the Imperials," Cleia said.

"And the ones your side is releasing?" Maihara asked.

"They're Varlords who were trapped in Calah."

Maihara blinked. She had not known the rebels held any of the Imperial elites, but there had been no reason to tell her.

Behind her, freed prisoners were having their hands untied, asked questions and offered food and water. An officer scribbled notes. Mutterings of anger rose as the ragged and grimy men spoke. Maihara was not close enough to hear what they said, but she imagined they had not been treated kindly. She thought to have a few last words with Sihrima, but Harayam held the reins of her horse, and her sister was on the far side of the mounted group.

More flag-signalling played between the insurgent and Imperial groups. Now two troopers led her sister forward, on foot. Her hands were not tied, as befitted her high rank. She glanced around her, saw Maihara and waved. Maihara's eyes filled with tears. She waved back, and called, "Gods be with you, Sihrima."

From the Imperial line, two men were pointing at her.

"Goodbye, keep well," Sihrima replied. She turned away, looking toward the Imperials, and set out across the field, with the two rebels close behind. The Imperial officers approached again, but they had no prisoner with them. It puzzled Maihara, till she saw that one of the Imperials was carrying a large bag. Of course, the plan was to ransom Sihrima, not exchange her.

Sihrima increased her pace. One of the rebel troopers ran in front of her and forced her to stop.

"Wait here!" the trooper shouted.

Tarchon gave an order, and two archers discreetly readied their bows, half-hidden by the mounted men in front.

Fearful that violence was about to erupt, Maihara put her fingertips in her mouth. Her heart thudded in her chest.

The two pairs of officers had a conference in the middle of the field while two Imperial troopers brought out a folding table. The two troopers withdrew.

Maihara let out her breath and stole a glance at Tarchon. He waved a hand behind him in a negative gesture. The archers lowered their bows.

The procedure of counting over the money took time, an agonising wait for Maihara as well as the rebels, gripped by nervous tension. Rage burned through her. The Imperials had offered that great pile of yellow metal in exchange for Sihrima, and for herself, nothing other than the threat of prison.

At last, the accounting officer signalled he was satisfied, and Sihrima was allowed to go forward. She did not look back, but picked up her heels, and the Imperial officers went into a trot to keep up with her. Sihrima disappeared into the Imperial ranks. The two rebel officers, left alone, shovelled handfuls of coin back into the large bag with urgent haste.

The two officers returned to the rebel ranks. Men stirred and looked at each other with smiles. A murmur of talk arose.

"Is that it?" Maihara asked. She wiped away tears.

"No, there's a truce agreement to be signed," Cleia told her. "It will extend this truce for another thirty days."

Another wait, and a bustle in the Imperial position. More signalling. Maihara shifted in the side-saddle, realising she had been tensing up. In a body, the rebel contingent rode across the flat space, closer to the Imperials, before dismounting. A trooper helped Maihara from her horse. Stiff and sore from two hours in the saddle, she stumbled as her boots touched the ground. Her horse shook itself and made a small whinny of relief. She glared at it.

Maihara was led forward on foot, a pace behind Tarchon, the two of them guarded by a total of eight officers. She walked stiffly, relieved to be out of the saddle. The rest of their force, still mounted, was drawn up ten paces behind.

They were close enough now to see the faces of the Imperial officers. Her sense of dread rose. How would they react, if any recognised her? She saw no welcome here. Imperial household flags, yellow and orange with a black crown, fluttered from the corner poles of the pavilion. It was made from green and purple canvas, and the tie ropes and pointy tips of the poles were gilded with gold paint. Two troopers ran forward and planted two more of these flags at the sides of the table. A throne-like chair glistened behind the inlaid and varnished table. Varlord officers in mail painted in patches of green, orange and blue, glittering like the wings of butterflies, lined up at each side of the closed drapes in the pavilion front. Another ran forward and laid out a set of scrolls.

A horn blared, making them all jump. The pavilion curtains twitched back.

A figure in gaudy multi-coloured armour and wearing a velvet face mask emerged from the cloth pavilion, attended by two pages in elaborate court jackets with gold braid trimmings. The flanking officers fell on one knee. Maihara trembled and inched backward.

Tarchon turned to her in surprise.

"The Emperor," she said.

Tarchon made a sharp intake of breath.

The Emperor, her father, glanced along the line of rebels and his lips twisted in a sneer, visible through the small mouth opening in the mask.

A spark of anger mixed with the fear, as she looked at the man who had ignored her and put her in prison. What was behind his stupid purple mask?

Tarchon nodded to her. "All right." His face was sweaty and his demeanour tense as he stepped up to the table and raised his right fist in a rebel greeting.

The Emperor seated himself on the central chair. "We wanted to see what the chief rebel looked like," the masked figure said in a loud voice. It was her father's voice. "You do not look like much."

She saw Tarchon's back straighten, and his fingers clench.

"We will place our mark to this agreement," the Emperor said. "It will give you time to reconsider your position, rebel. Soon enough, you'll fall out with the Dhikr. They are better fighters than you, and they'll crush you. Then we will see."

The Emperor waved a mailed hand, and an officer hurried forward to unroll the scrolls flat on the table. "Think about surrendering to our lawful authority, rebel, before the Dhikr eat you."

Tarchon tilted his head back. "I'll place my mark on the document. But I do not feel intimidated by a man who dares not show his face."

"You dare insult us?" The Emperor made a twirling gesture, and his guard put their hands to their sword hilts.

Tarchon was silent, but kept his head raised.

With an angry gesture, the Emperor snatched the velvet mask from his face. Tarchon started visibly, then reached for the wax seals.

Maihara stared, shocked. It was her father's face, but made of metal. It shone dully, it had seams, and there were small screw-heads placed as if to hold the face together. It was another mask, but close-fitting. As the Emperor grimaced at Tarchon, his face flexed in a natural way. It was no mask. It did not make sense. What had happened to him?

Tarchon seemed distracted. An officer was helping him warm the seals and affix his mark to one of the treaty copies.

"I see you have the witch with you," the Emperor said, looking at her.

Her legs trembled. The metal lips had moved as though

they were real. There was something glassy and unnatural about the eyes. She'd been wrong. The golim work was far more advanced that she had believed, and it appeared that by some means her father had applied it to himself.

The Emperor's finger pointed at her. He wore white finely made gloves. "Get her away from me!"

Maihara took a step back. Tarchon turned in surprise. The Emperor's minions took a stride toward her.

"Take the princess back," Tarchon ordered his aides. He faced the Emperor. "What the hell is this?"

"Take care the traitress does not betray you, just as she betrayed us."

Tarchon's head jerked up.

The unjust accusation direct from her father's lips infuriated her. "I did not betray you," Maihara shouted. "I wanted to summon help."

"Lying witch, be silent!" the Emperor shouted. "You summoned a monster to attack the city wall."

"What!" She was shocked. "I didn't!" She had summoned the pterostrophe, but how could he know that? And she had not meant it to attack anything. Anyway, it had merely swooped low over the city wall.

"Get her away from me!" the Emperor repeated.

Tarchon turned and red-faced, made a down-sweeping gesture with his right arm. "By the Gods, be quiet!" He grabbed her by the arms and pushed her back into the line of officers.

An officer gripped her arm and stood in front of her, tense-faced, blocking her view.

A chill of fear swept over her. Her hopes of her return to the Imperial side lay shattered. She looked around the officer's braided shoulder and stared at Tarchon's back. Tarchon had finished placing his seal on the treaty document, and pushed it across the table, at the same time accepting the copy with the Imperial seal affixed to it. He took a step back. The officers at the table, facing their opposite numbers, all saluted.

Tarchon turned and frowned at her, before stepping

past. "Reverse and mount up!" he shouted.

In a swirl of purposeful movement, the rebel troopers back-stepped and looked for their mounts. Two officers hustled Maihara to her horse and pushed her up into the side-saddle. Leaders of platoons reported status.

"All ready," called an officer on the left.

"All ready," from the right.

Tarchon raised his right arm and swept it forward, signalling an advance. With a jingling and a clumping of hooves, the group moved off at a walk, a trot, a canter, sorting itself into a line. Riding side-saddle, Maihara was able to look back. The Imperial signal flags were waving a farewell.

Beyond the ridge, they were out of sight of the Imperials and out of danger of imminent attack. Tarchon halted the column and rode up to Maihara. "What did you mean by arguing with the Emperor? You could have ruined everything."

Maihara shook her head. She kept silent, sensing he wanted to ask her something else.

"What was wrong with his face? That face mask?" he asked.

"I don't think that was a mask. It looked like part of his face. He's had an interest in mechanical men; now he seems to have become one."

Tarchon gave a bark of disbelief. "That can't be. It's a fraud."

"I don't think so. I know what he looks and sounds like; you don't."

"You're both insane. Don't you have any reaction then, to your father becoming a machine?"

Annoyed, she stabbed a finger at him. "Why should I share my feelings with you? I've learnt to expect two things from my father; indifference and lunacy."

Tarchon stared at her, then with a curse wheeled his horse and signalled for the column to move on. He hadn't asked her about the pterostrophe accusation, not yet.

Somebody must have poisoned her father's mind

against her. A weight lay on her heart. He'd become more distant since her fourteenth birthday, but he couldn't really hate her. If only he'd listened, let her explain. And yet it was her fault for summoning the pterostrophe. But was it really her father? It could be a duplicate. It did seem unlike her father to come to a desert meeting with only a treaty force to protect him. He'd have sent a body double.

Once out of sight of the Imperial position, the rebels spurred their horses to a canter. Maihara clung to her mount, fearing it would throw her off the awkward saddle. Hooves threw up a cloud of dust, that got into her eyes and nose. She glanced behind. Through the billowing dust cloud, she glimpsed another mounted column, following in their wake. Her group increased its pace, and the chase carried on for several miles, till they had to slow the blown horses to a walk.

The column chasing them closed the gap. "What's going on?" she shouted to the officer, not Harayam this time, who held her lead rope. He yelled back words incomprehensible above the clop of hooves. Their pursuers wore greenish uniforms, but the Imperials and the rebel formations both had those.

The pursuing column reached their rear. Neither group was readying its weapons, so far as she could tell. Men shouted and waved spears. Her heart raced.

The pursuers slowed to a walk. Not Imperials, then. Perhaps she had been the only person to think they were. She took deep breaths as her heartbeat eased. They skirted a hill of tawny rocks and arrived back at the primitive hamlet where they had left the coach. Cleia Chavin helped Maihara from her horse. They scuffled across sandy ground with a few weeds growing in it. Her butt, legs and hands were stiff and sore and she was glad to get off the horse. The villagers were still keeping out of sight. She wrinkled her nose at a reek of equine manure.

Four troopers brought rations of weak beer and bread round as she stood by the carriage waiting for the horses to be harnessed. It pleased Maihara that Cleia Chavin, the only other woman present, was keeping her company.

The freed prisoners stood by the second vehicle, attacking the food and drink as though they had not eaten or drunk for days.

"Tarchon's in a mood," Cleia said, "but don't worry. He'll get over it."

Maihara finished a mouthful of fresh bread. "What did he tell you?"

"That you shouted at the Emperor. I heard you."

Maihara shook her head. "There's more than that. Could you hear what the Emperor said?"

"No, we couldn't. I hear the Emperor said things about the Dhikr. How would that monster know what our allies intend?" Her tone was indignant.

Four troopers led the coach horses past, their tails flicking at flies. Another man followed with a leather bucket of well water.

Maihara found a fly floating in her watered beer. With disgust, she poured the top part away. "He said the rebels would soon fall out with the Dhikr and be eaten."

"We're not concerned by the Imperials' bluster. That's what they want, to sow dissent between us and the Dhikr. Don't worry; it's just talk."

Perhaps the rebels had likewise tried to trouble the Imperials by taking her to the meeting. Maihara shook her head, mindful of the discord caused by the Emir's sudden death. "We need to get rid of the Dhikr. The Emperor's right."

"We?" Cleia's eyes widened.

Maihara corrected herself. "You need to get rid of the Dhikr."

"They're our allies."

"They're animals." She sipped her beer.

Maihara seated herself in the coach, along with three silent officers. Around the coach, a substantial mounted escort gathered. She leaned into the window and propped her chin on one hand. Why had she said that about the Dhikr? She would be no safer should the rebels split with their so-called allies.

There was an empty, silent seat where Sihrima had sat on the outward journey. A gloom settled over her, even though Sihrima was probably in a place of greater safety. Around now, Sihrima would be having a cheerful journey eastwards with her father, in a gilded carriage. A lump gathered in Maihara's chest at the thought of that happiness and security.

If the rebels and Dhikr fell out, she would be in danger, but her father and the Imperials had shown no desire to take her back and declare her innocence. The strength of her father's animosity shocked her. At least the rebels were treating her decently.

To distract herself from these thoughts, she tried to start a conversation as the coach moved off. The olive-skinned Harayam sat opposite her, along with two other officers older than him, one dark-skinned with a thin face, the other sunburnt and with a wart. "What does Cleia Chavin do in your army?"

"Staff," one of the officers replied. "Non-combat duties."

"What're they?"

"Paperwork."

Maihara tried again. "What happened to General Tarchon's wife?"

"That's a sad story," the sunburnt officer said. "She was pregnant with their first child, when she was run down by a carriage in a street accident. Passers-by summoned a doctor, but he was called away to treat a Varlord officer at the garrison for some trivial and non-urgent ailment. He wouldn't come back, even when Tarchon pleaded with the officer. By the time the doctor returned, she was dead. The carriage driver didn't even apologise, and the Varlord had abused his position. It filled Tarchon with grief and rage. He vowed to bring the bastards down, the Varlords and the nobility. As soon as he found others who dreamed of change, he became their leader."

Maihara nodded. If Tarchon hated the Varlords and nobles so much, he would have little care for herself or her brother.

The refreshments had restored her energy, but she ached, and the afternoon was well advanced. As fatigue washed over her, her eyes closed and her head drooped forward.

She awoke with a start. The carriage had stopped. Outside, men were shouting, "Clear the road."

A mass of throats was roaring a barbaric war-cry. They did not sound like rebels.

Before the officers could prevent her, she raised the curtain and looked out. They hadn't arrived anywhere; outside was a section of the Avergnian plain. The carriage had slewed off the road. Ahead and blocking the way, a large body of mounted Dhikr was forming up into a battle line, hundreds of them armed and menacing in their scale armour. The Emir's death, the brutality of the Dhikr and the Emperor's warning all flashed together in a wave of fear that left her weak-kneed and shaking.

To either side of the coach, rebel horsemen milled in the dust, more and more of them cantering and hauling in their mounts, forming an extending battle line to oppose that of the Dhikr. It looked as though they were going to fight, and her coach was right in the middle of the battle line.

-16-

Heart racing, Maihara shrank back from the carriage window. Being halted by the brutish Dhikr out here filled her with primal fear. Last she had heard, the Dhikr were still angry and hurling accusations over the sudden death of their Emir. Lieutenant Harayam and the two other guards seated opposite her peered out of the windows, faces taut with concern.

More rebels came into view, gathering around her carriage and cutting off sight of the pony riders who had intercepted them. A parley flag fluttered beyond; it seemed that a small group of Dhikr was approaching under it. Indistinct shouting arose.

The obnoxious growl of the Dhikr warlord, Barin, rose above the din. "So, where have you been sneaking off to, Tarchon?"

Maihara flinched, and her heartbeat quickened. She didn't want another encounter with Barin and prayed this was not an attempt to seize her. Tarchon had taken a risk in bringing her out to Kunn.

Tarchon's voice was calm and firm. "You know very well we've been exchanging prisoners, Barin. It was a matter that did not directly concern you."

"There was more to it than that, I hear," Barin said.

Dhikr voices growled in assent.

"The truce agreement?" Tarchon said. "As you say, I was also attending to that matter. We told you the Imperials wanted to extend the handover truce. Now we have a thirty-day extension, so there should be no fighting during the harvests, and we have a respite."

"Bah. Can we trust them?"

"For as long as it's to their advantage, and if there are

no provocations," Tarchon said.

"What kind of fool trusts the word of enemies?" Barin sniffed and made a spitting noise. "Maybe you were conspiring with them to betray us?"

A rebel horse and rider filled her view, a mere foot away.

"I have the treaty here." Tarchon's voice sounded strained, hurried. This wasn't good. "Look. There's the great Imperial seal. And here's a copy for you."

There was a pause. A horse snorted and harness jingled.

"No, the other way up," came Tarchon's voice.

Maihara suppressed a snort of amusement while opposite her Harayam and the other two officers were smirking.

"How do I know this isn't a fake?" Barin growled, sounding annoyed.

"It's an exact copy. And you can send one of your wise men to look at my sealed copy, at any reasonable time. Or, if you want to ratify the truce, we'll both approach the Imperials and ask them."

She still couldn't see Tarchon. Several rebel horses and riders blocked her view, close enough for her to smell them. Flies buzzed around them. The voices faded as if the leaders had moved farther off.

"We can use the time to regroup and plan our campaign," Tarchon was saying.

Maihara sat back and bit her lip. It might have been less troublesome to have taken Dhikr representatives to the meeting. On the other hand, Tarchon would not have wanted to alert the Dhikr to her presence. Nor could she imagine the Dhikr complying with the neatly choreographed arrangements the Imperials and the Empire-born rebels had set up.

"Impossible!" Barin's voice was louder. The rest of his remarks and any reply was lost in a clattering of hooves, clinking of harness and shouting of orders. A stab of panic struck her. Were they about to start fighting?

Harayam looked out of the window. "Sounds like the

barbarians are leaving."

She sagged into her seat with a sigh of relief.

The scale-armoured Dhikr moved away. The coach jerked into movement, screened by rebel troopers, and picked up speed, passing a mass of mounted Dhikr to one side. The escort alongside broke into a canter. Maihara gave a shaky laugh. Just as well that the Dhikr had not taken it into their heads to look inside the carriage.

Time passed. She looked out, trying to make out how far they had come on the return journey. They were passing flat fields with growing crops and isolated thatched huts.

"Where are we?" she asked.

"We're near Brinnog," Harayam examined his clean, neatly trimmed fingernails. "It's less than two hours to Calah now."

The carriage slowed, and no Dhikr were in sight. Drowsiness crept over her.

Noise roused her, the sound of the carriage wheels grinding over hard paving. Outside the window a row of dilapidated stone buildings filled her view. The carriage stopped and started. They had arrived at a small town Maihara had not seen on the outward journey.

They halted in a town square, surrounded by two-storey buildings of rough stone, filled with a bustle of men and horses. Maihara, preceded by the three guard officers, stepped down from the carriage. Mounts were tethered in lines, and groups of rebel soldiers stood around or strode across the square. Townsfolk going about their business carrying bags or bundles made their way past the soldiers. A few scruffy children chased each other with shrieks or stood staring at the soldiers. The place smelt of horse-dung.

"Is this Brinnog?" she asked.

Harayam flexed his shoulders. "Yes, it's one of our towns." The purpose of the stop soon became evident. The exhausted horses, foam-flecked, were uncoupled from the carriage and fresh animals put in.

Tarchon ambled over on foot, tapping his thigh, while a soldier offered Maihara a cake and a cup of hot, steaming *koosh*. She held the cup, waiting for the scalding Army brew to cool, and watched him approach.

The rebel leader acknowledged the salutes of the awed Harayam and the other two officers with a nod, and smiled at her pleasantly. He had taken off his helmet, but his mailed figure bulked large. "I hope the Dhikr road-block did not alarm you. Fortunately we had enough force to make them pause."

"It's all right. No worse than the Imperials."

"They really don't like you. The Imperials, I mean. What are they afraid of? Is it because you're a real sorceress?"

Her *koosh* cup rattled in its saucer. "They're crazy."

"What was that about you summoning a monster to attack the city wall?"

"I already explained all that. That's why you found me in a prison cell. Somebody must have fed my father with lies." She stared at the ground, tearful with disappointment.

"Or there's more to you than I thought." Tarchon paused. "Have you got enough to eat and drink there?"

Maihara shook her head. He seemed not to believe her.

"Ask them for more. Let them know if you need to go anywhere before we re-start," he hinted.

Maihara blushed at this thoughtful but embarrassing suggestion. She nodded, sensing he was trying to make up for his brusque behaviour at the meeting. *They caused his wife's death*, she remembered.

"All right." She took a bite of the cake. She could have eaten two. The men seemed much more relaxed here, relieved to be in one of their bases.

"So Barin was not happy?" she asked.

Tarchon's eyes narrowed. "He was suspicious of the meeting, but I think I managed to mollify him."

"I'm not surprised he was suspicious. Couldn't you have invited a Dhikr observer to the meeting? That would have saved all that shouting."

Tarchon shook his head and looked aside. "They weren't involved, so they didn't need to be there."

Maihara was not impressed. "So they are not party to this truce? How will that work?"

"They're not a signatory, but they are only in contact with the Imperial territory on a small Northern front. I've made it clear I can't control what they do there."

She shook her head. At least, making polite enquiry after her comfort was an advance on suggesting he could execute her to gratify his supporters. Why was he was bothering to tell her all these details? Was he beginning to think of her as one of them, or was it calculated? They had come face to face at least ten times now. It could be because he wanted something from her. His polite attentiveness made her want to reciprocate, but she fought the impulse. It was weak and disloyal to think of Tarchon as her friend.

If he had made any connection between the Emperor's appearance and the chatter about mechanical soldiers, he wasn't disclosing it to her. But she was making another connection. Why would an Emperor capable of building mechanical regiments react so violently to a daughter suspected of being a witch? Maybe *magic* was involved in this. That made it more likely that the mechanical soldiers would become real. That still wasn't her problem. If those things arrived and drove out the insolent rebels, that should be good. Wouldn't it?

"By the way," she asked, "why did the Imperial authorities arrest Lord Farnak? You found him already imprisoned?"

Tarchon gave a nod. "So far as we know, he was accused of criticizing the Emperor and plotting to influence the Imperial succession."

Maihara's heart gave a jump.

The sun was lower by the time Harayam ushered Maihara back to the coach. The journey resumed, and she fell asleep again. By the hour they neared the walls of Calah, the sky was darkening and cloud glowed red in the West. They passed within sight of the menacing Dhikr camp, and a dozen riders streamed from among the tents and galloped toward them.

Her escort fanned out, weapons at the ready. Maihara held her breath, and released it as the coach clattered under the great east gateway. The gates under the deep-vaulted brick arch slammed shut behind them, and the carriage rumbled at reduced pace through the city streets. By the time they arrived at the Anwar mansion, the stable yard was in deep shadow save for the glow of a few oil lamps.

In the evening, the guards allowed Maihara to eat with her brother, who had been brought over from the Palace. It was a consolation to have one of her siblings still with her. They dined in one of the Anwar's downstairs rooms. It boasted blue walls, plasterwork, and a long dining table with padded chairs, too grand for just two diners and their silent minder.

"Did Sihrima get released?" her brother asked, as soon as they sat down.

Tears wet her cheeks. "Yes." It came out croakily. "It all went smoothly. The officers took their time counting a great pile of money, though. Nine hundred thousand, they say."

"You don't look very happy about it, Mai."

"She didn't look back. Our sister - we may never see her again." She thought of her mother, whom she had last seen on her sickbed surrounded by doctors and ladies in waiting.

Her brother stared at her with unease. He never seemed to know what to do with crying girls. "Father will beat the rebels. Then we'll be together again."

"The rebels think otherwise."

"When are they going to ransom me?" he asked in a sulky tone. He picked up his fork.

She sighed. "They would have exchanged you today if that was going to happen. They've not said any more about you being Emperor, and I suspect they want you as a hostage."

"You seem to spend a lot of time with these rebels," her brother complained. "They're traitors. You shouldn't talk to them." He scraped a dish with his fork, an action that would have got his head smacked before the capture of the Palace.

"The Imperials think I'm a traitor too." Maihara wiped her eyes. "I saw Father today. He called me a witch. He doesn't want me back at all." The recollection hurt her.

Persis stared at her, open-mouthed.

The food was a little dried as if it had been kept waiting under a warmer. They were served wine, which was some compensation.

"Let's change the subject. What did you do today?" she asked.

"I spent the day playing cards."

"Who with?"

She learned that Persis had a new companion, a nobleman's son, whom the rebels had found for him. The family must have changed sides.

Maihara sagged with weariness. She ached from the long horse-ride, and she'd parted from her sister, and been called a witch and traitor by her father. It had not been a good day.

***

Tarchon leaned his elbows on the long table in the fort's upper hall, waiting for his staff officers to enter and take their places. There was one troubling matter he had to clear up, then the rest of this meeting should be routine. Yesterday had been a testing day, but he had emerged successful with prisoners exchanged, and a large ransom secured. He had faced Emperor Cordan and a troop of the troublesome and suspicious Dhikr, his so-called allies, and survived. This was the same room, wood-panelled and with costly coffered and gilded ceiling, that he'd used for the meeting where Maihara had shouted at the now deceased Emir. He preferred using this old fort building, as it was easier to make secure than the vast, rambling palace.

The Crown Princess was being ushered into the ornate

room now. She wore an elaborate flared wine-red dress, and her hair curled loose about her shoulders. She was a bit chubby, with a prominent nose, but he found her face and the untidy hair endearing. Nothing in her appearance suggested a threat to the Imperial regime or himself.

She hesitated and turned her head to look around the room before moving on, no doubt relieved that none of the Dhikr were present. Eyes followed her as she was led forward and seated at one end of the long table. Being rejected by the Emperor like that must have hurt. That was an issue he needed to explore, without alarming his people. One would expect the Emperor to leap at the chance to ransom the Imperial Princess, instead of acting as if he was disgusted with or even afraid of her.

He had a sudden warm impulse to hug her close and comfort her. No, this was an inappropriate line of thought, even dangerous. She was a prisoner, one of the Imperials, and half his age.

Various of his officers nodded to Maihara in greeting, Major Chavin among them. Chavin doodled with a pen and paper, while the civilian radical representatives stared at the princess with obvious dislike.

Tarchon rose and addressed the meeting. "As most of you will have heard, yesterday we concluded a hostage exchange and obtained a large ransom for the younger princess, Sihrima Zircona." The sackful of gold would be a significant contribution to the rebellion's expenses.

Eyes turned toward Maihara, who had lowered her head. It probably hurt her to hear her sister referred to as a traded item. He'd had her brought here because he needed answers to some questions about the Emperor.

"We have not made any such agreement for the other two Imperial children." He did not suppose that Maihara would like this either.

The leader of the 2nd Cavalry Corps raised his hand. "Why can't we ransom the other two, General?"

Lack of money was a frequent topic at rebel councils, and no doubt the cavalry officer had this in mind. Tarchon glanced at Maihara, who continued to look down at the table, and nodded. He did not want continual interruptions, but the question merited an answer. "In answer to that, we did crown the Prince as Emperor, and even if we have him abdicate, it will look inconsistent to ransom him so soon. As for Princess Maihara, there are difficulties mainly with the Imperial side."

It also made no sense to release potential successors to the Imperial throne, but did that apply, after what he had seen? The unnatural image came into his mind again, while the three-stripe cavalry officer raised his hand. "I understand that the Imperials think she's a witch. If we were to put her on trial, they might ransom her back if she's found innocent."

Several officers murmured "Aye," or nodded.

Maihara, mouth open and wide-eyed, looked appalled.

Tarchon felt a twinge of guilt. He did not wish to have her terrorised, but he could not rush to her defence too quickly in squelching this unwelcome diversion. He pointed a finger at the questioner. "What makes you think that the Imperials would believe the judgement of a rebel court? And the more open we make it, the greater the risk that she'd be found guilty, which would be most unhelpful."

"But, General -"

Tarchon gripped his lapels. "These supposed powers can't amount to much, otherwise she'd have disappeared by now, instead of being obliged to sit and listen to this."

"There should be an investigation, General."

"Enough. We have weightier matters to discuss than a Zircon family squabble." He had no intention of putting Maihara on trial, or of approaching the Imperials about ransoming the remaining two siblings anytime soon. He glanced at Maihara. She seemed upset but trying to put on a brave face.

He scooped up a sheaf of papers and held them up. "We also signed an important truce agreement with the Imperials, to cover the harvest period. Each side agrees to hold its present territories and not attack the other." He summarised the truce terms, and their implications. "We need to discuss how to exploit this breathing space."

"And what do the Dhikr think of this?" asked an infantry colonel from the 2nd Army.

"They'll be here soon," Tarchon said. "So we'll hear their views then."

There was a mutter of comment that swiftly faded. Maihara flinched and put a knuckle to her mouth. He'd have to ensure that she and the Dhikr did not meet.

"There is another matter I wish to raise," Tarchon went on. This was why he'd had Maihara brought in. "When I met the Emperor, his appearance was rather disturbing. In fact, his face appeared to be made of metal. It seemed too lifelike to be a mask, and the Princess, who should know him best, insists his face was of metal in place of flesh."

There was a murmur of astonishment around the room.

"When did you last see the Emperor, other than yesterday, Princess?" he asked her.

"About two moons ago," she admitted.

"And he looked normal then?"

"Yes."

"No metal face?"

"No."

"I had heard the Emperor was becoming frail and aged, and that was why he made fewer appearances," Tarchon said. "Could the Princess comment?"

"That's not true," Maihara said. "He was well enough for a man of his age."

"One moment," Tarchon said. "The man we saw yesterday was wearing armour. I didn't see him move much, but he seemed a fit and robust man. Could it have been an impostor?"

"The man had my father's mannerisms and voice. I'd recognise him anywhere," Maihara said.

Men shook their heads.

"Could be an actor," said a thick-set man of middle age. General Pendash was one of Tarchon's most trusted comrades. He had resigned from the Imperial Army after the northern massacres, and Tarchon had made him commander of the rebel 3rd Army.

Tarchon let the comment go. Pendash hadn't been there. "What makes you think it was anything other than a face-mask?" he asked Maihara.

"The Emperor has always had an interest in mechanisms," she said. "Lord Farnak told me that the Emperor planned to make golim soldiers to be used against the rebellion."

"Go on?"

Around the table his officers were making muttered exclamations and turning to look at himself or the Princess. This was a shade more than the Princess had revealed at previous questionings.

Maihara's expression remained calm. "That's all he told me," she said. "If you hadn't murdered Lord Farnak, you could ask him yourselves."

"He wasn't murdered. We executed him for serious crimes against the people," he said.

She shook her head and pursed her lips as if restraining herself from replying.

The Emperor had become a golim? It made no sense, but he did not care to raise alarm about it here. It was obvious that the princess and her father had not been close, so he doubted that she had much to reveal about what they had seen. "We need to investigate this further," he said. "Major Chavin, take the Princess out, and then we'll have the Dhikr in. Don't let them see her."

The door closed behind Maihara.

Tarchon eased his shoulders, then turned to opening a discussion of the truce. When Major Chavin returned, he kept her aside, against the oak-panelled wall, on the pretext of confirming Maihara's safe departure. He was still concerned by what he had seen at Kunn yesterday, and that he had under-estimated the sorcerous abilities of the Zircon family. The father - he couldn't even be sure what the father was. "You have spent time with the Princess, Major.

Have you seen any sign that she has occult powers?"

"No, sir." Chavin gave him an enquiring look.

"I need to decide how far to trust what she's saying about the Emperor's face. He called her a witch. That could be why he doesn't want her back. She could have the same powers - an Empress in waiting."

"I see, sir."

"And I need to determine what to do with her - send her back to the Empire side or keep her here. If I get it wrong, I could be wasting a useful hostage, or harbouring a dangerous person."

"I don't know, sir. She seems a nice girl."

"A nice girl who might have murdered the Dhikrs' previous Emir by magic. Do you know what Colonel Impar thinks?"

"No, sir." Chavin stood at ease, her face giving little away, her manner professional.

"He suspects that her imprisonment was a charade designed to plant her on us. For some fell reason." Privately, Tarchon thought this overly paranoid.

Chavin nodded. "I suppose that's possible, sir."

"So, the safest thing to do would be to send her back. But I didn't bring us this far by playing safe." Tarchon ran his fingers through his hair. "What's your recommendation, Major?"

He did not like the idea of handing Maihara over to people who might mean her harm. The cause should be more important than one over-privileged girl, but it would be at a cost to his humanity.

"If I might make a suggestion, sir. Win her over to our side."

"Oh?" Tarchon looked at her in surprise. Was she serious?

"She appears to have liberal sympathies and a knack of winning people over. If we win her trust, we avoid wasting a useful asset, and we might gain a powerful ally."

Tarchon breathed out in relief. Chavin's suggestion made sense. "Yes, we should." He wondered if Maihara knew more than she was saying about the metal men, the golims.

"She seems very well-informed," he said.

"She's well-educated and reads widely, sir." Chavin gave him a look, as though she was tempted to ask her superior an indiscreet question.

Tarchon glanced at the waiting officers, then back to the Major. "What do you think of her?"

"I like her. She's smart, level-headed and seems a decent person, unlike the other two. The younger sister was a brat, and the brother wants to be a girl, it seems to me." Chavin paused, and awaited his reaction.

Privately amused, he gave a nod. "Go on."

"She doesn't like the Dhikr though. She said the Emperor was right, and we should get rid of them."

Tarchon gave a short laugh. "They feel the same about her."

"The curious thing is, she used the word 'we'."

He leaned forward. "Did she now? What do you make of that?"

"That she identifies with us."

"Maybe she thinks we'll help her exterminate the Dhikr. That's not happening," Tarchon said.

He returned to his seat at the table, gathering his thoughts. The continued allegations of Maihara's supposed inherited sorcerous powers were troubling, but he had mitigated the problem by separating her from her magical box. Chavin's last remark confirmed his feeling that he should keep Maihara close. Despite their opposed roles he found it hard not to like this brave, quick-witted girl.

The Dhikr entered. Their warlord, Barin, was accompanied by a man of middle age in an embroidered cloak and polished boots. Possibly their new leader - Tarchon had not seen him before. He had a piercing gaze as he scowled at the rebel officers. Two Dhikr warriors in scale armour made up the rest of the party.

"This is our new Emir, Emir Vozzeg," Barin said, indicating the man in the colourful cloak. Tarchon murmured a diplomatic greeting.

The newcomers took places at the table.

"Our scribe read this treaty of yours," Barin said. "He told us what's in it, but it's just paper. We're not trusting these Imperial running dogs." Piggy red-veined eyes glared at Tarchon.

"This may be true," Tarchon said. "But the purpose of the truce is that the autumn harvests can be gathered in, which will benefit both us and them. They sought the extension, so it's likely they will honour it till their harvests are in. And we need a good harvest. Last year's was thin, so we don't want the common people's first taste of radical rule to be one of famine."

"This truce won't last," Barin growled.

"You're right," Tarchon said. "History tells us truces rarely last long, unless there is a balance of need and fear. The question is, assuming the truce holds awhile, what are our plans after?"

"War," Barin said.

"War. We'll conquer it all." the new Emir repeated. The Dhikr fighters rattled their weapons.

Tarchon raised a hand. "We pray it will be so. But a direct attack will be difficult. Many castles, rivers and strong-points bar our eastward advance, and there are large drylands difficult to cross with an army."

"Have you men who know these places?" Barin asked.

"We do. But let's consider other options. We can take the remaining provinces between us and the Southern ocean, and then raid the Empire by sea. Or the Dhikr could attack the Eastern Empire from the north." His ultimate aim, like that of many rebels, was to free the whole Empire from autocratic rule, but for that they needed the Dhikr.

"It'll be winter soon. Maybe you want the Dhikr to freeze to death?" Barin scowled with suspicion.

They had not mentioned Maihara yet. Perhaps the new Emir didn't want to pursue the death of his predecessor. Tarchon wondered why not. Standing, he looked into the faces of the men around the table, while an aide unrolled a cloth-backed map onto an easel. Satisfied he had their attention, he turned and gestured to the map.

"Here is the western part of the Empire. We are here. These provinces to the south are wavering. Sintheer province will declare for us. Shardan has not cast off its allegiance to the Empire. We need to advance south and take control of all these provinces. The Sintheer is navigable as far up as Debrish, here. We can send a force by river barge to reach Retis, here on the estuary. After that, we strike along the coast to Loomis and Licinus. God willing, we can capture ships and make a fleet.

"Our second army under General Pendash will march south-east to occupy Linyan province, here."

"And what do we get? We want to seize warmer lands," Barin said.

"The Dhikr can strike directly toward the Eastern Empire." Tarchon swept two fingers across the top of the map. "You could cross the Central Desert, which guards them to the north, or take a more southerly route, through the line of forts here. There's water." His fingers rested half way up the map.

Barin scratched his chin. "A pincer. I like that."

"The Imperial forces will have to divide their attention three ways, between the Dhikr attack, Pendash's attack in the central southern provinces, and their southern coast and islands. With the east defeated or contained, our western independence will be secure. Is the plan good?" Tarchon sensed that the Dhikr were interested.

The new Emir nodded. The morally compromised alliance would hold.

-17-

The evening after the meeting, Maihara sat in her room reading a book by the popular writer Ulrich, of dark tales of monsters, sorcery and betrayal when a rap on the door made her jump. She remained silent, pulse racing, and placed a hand over the book. The previous night, her sleep had been disturbed by a confused dream of mechanical soldiers with clawed hands, striding across a landscape of deserted and broken villages, with bloated dead animals lying in the fields and mossy gravestones by the roadside.

If the mechanical soldiers were as real as the Emperor's metal face implied, and not a figment of her dreamscape, the harvest truce would give the Empire a breathing space in which to manufacture them in quantity, and transport them forward to the next battlefield. Not a pleasant thought.

The door opened. It was the short-haired Cleia Chavin in green uniform.

"What is it?" Maihara asked, in a higher than natural tone.

"You needn't look so worried. I just wanted to reassure you about the outcome of the meeting. It seems that nobody has troubled to inform you."

For a moment, Maihara could not speak. It was nice of Cleia to come. Images of herself being put on trial had been running through her mind. Nasty deeds were done when people were afraid.

"There's no danger of you being tried as a witch." Cleia smiled. "Tarchon's against giving people troublesome ideas of that sort."

"Why would he care?" she asked. Tarchon had mocked the idea that she had any powers.

Chavin pulled out a chair and sat. She leaned forward.

"You're not seeing what I see. The General is very interested in you. In fact, he sees you as a significant person in the struggle between the radicals and the Empire."

"Me?" How could she be significant?

"I think he sees you as a disruptive force, one he'd prefer to keep in his arsenal."

Maihara shook her head. "That's ridiculous. I thought he merely found me annoying, and one of the class of people he most hates."

Cleia's lips quirked upward at the corners. "He doesn't hate you. But you keep surprising him. Things happen around you. He was most concerned that the prisoner exchange would go smoothly, and follow the proper protocols, not giving the Imperials any excuse to make difficulties. And then you started crossing words with their Emperor."

"You think I should have kept quiet." She lowered her head.

Cleia smiled. "That would have been wise. Few people argue with Emperors."

***

Summer had ended, and Maihara saw the great hall of the Anwar mansion being decked out for the harvest festival held annually on the 25th day of the ninth moon. Low sun streamed in and picked out the gilding on the east wall. Servants set flowers on tables around the walls, and at one end, they had laid a long table with ripe fruit, loaves of new bread and bowls of cooked food. An odour of spices and fresh bread hung in the air.

She wondered if she would be allowed to attend, and indeed soon she was included in a celebration under way, with many more people than usual in the house. The harvest truce negotiated at Kunn was apparently holding.

A drummer and string player sketched out a tune, and several couples weaved in a vigorous rustic dance. It all looked and sounded a world away from the dances Maihara knew from court. The soldiers present were meant to be watching Maihara and her brother, but appeared more interested in helping themselves to the food and filling glasses with foaming brown liquid from a wooden barrel, or in pestering servant girls for a dance.

Maihara helped herself to a glass of wine from a side table.

The double doors opened, and General Tarchon entered, flanked by officers and soldiers. The fiddler paused mid-bar, causing an abrupt hush, and the dancers looked around, slowing. With an impatient gesture, Tarchon commanded the musicians to continue.

As the dancing resumed in the hall, he made his way over to where Maihara stood.

"Good afternoon, Princess." He smiled. "I hope you find the festival pleasing."

Maihara nodded. "Yes, thank you."

"You don't find it too common for your tastes?"

She studied this remark for insult, veiled or otherwise. "No, it's just... different. Less formal. Do you read Zubertin?" Zubertin was a popular author of novels set among the country nobility, and Maihara had several of his volumes.

He nodded. "It reminds me of the ball scene in 'The Harvesters', where they have a dance in the barn for their peasantry. One of the few scenes where the common people are mentioned."

Apparently the General was literate. Something in his favour. "That's right, but one doesn't read him for the lower-class characters." Maihara was tempted to ask Tarchon what his rebels had done with the likes of Zubertin's characters, but before she decided if she dared, he asked, "What do you think of Karpaz? I find him more to my taste." His eyes were gleaming at her.

"'The Country Doctor'? I like those tales too."

The corners of his lips twitched. Well, if it was a test, she had passed.

Her eye was caught by a young couple who stood in a corner, kissing. She stared. By the way they were kissing gently and repeatedly, they must be in love.

Tarchon followed her gaze. "They're entering into the spirit of the festival," he said, in an amused tone.

Maihara could not think of anything sensible to say. "They say you're a widower."

"That's so." He looked sombre.

"Have you thought of remarrying?" The question came from nowhere, prompted by his unattached and bereaved status. Instantly she wished she could take it back.

"Such thoughts have crossed my mind, but I have more pressing concerns. The war. Why do you ask?" He raised an eyebrow.

His face had slight lines around the eyes and on his forehead. His chin and the skin above his upper lip bore a trace of stubble. Her mind was void of any words to say. She felt hot, and she was sure her face was going red. Her question had been indiscreet.

"Do you wish to dance, Princess?" he said, rescuing her. His lips curved in a smile.

She nodded. At least dancing would bring an end to this awkward conversation.

"May I offer myself as a partner?" He made a slight bow.

"Yes, General." She raised her arms to a starting position and awaited his response, surprised by his invitation. She enjoyed dancing, and there was no partner of suitable rank here. The General was the nearest available.

"They're playing a sarabel." He led her onto the floor, took her right hand, and put his other hand about her waist. In a moment they were performing the sedate steps of the sarabel. It was the best known of the court dances.

What was she doing? She had not meant to dance with him; he was just her jailer.

Her brother Persis had been allowed to come with his new companion. She caught a glimpse of Persis staring open-mouthed, and imagined what Sihrima would have thought. The other pairs of dancers, soldiers and servants, paid them little heed save to make space.

"In a general sense, Princess, have *you* had thoughts of marriage?" he asked.

"What? No, not really. Anyway, I don't have the good looks and slim figure that men seek in a bride." This was not entirely true. She had expected that her fate was to be married off to the son of some provincial satrap, to cement the Empire's power, and had hoped that her arranged husband would prove good-looking and kind. Her chilly father had said little of any negotiations, but she did not expect him to consult her.

"Self-deprecation is not an attractive trait," he said, interrupting her thoughts. "Your appearance is not so displeasing. In any case, millions of plainer women have felt the fond embrace of lovers."

His hand burned on her waist, and her face felt as though it was going red again. There must be something about dancing that led on to these embarrassing topics. She lowered her head, unable to meet his eyes. The twirling movements of the dance were pleasant, but it ended too soon, and she disengaged her hand.

"Would you like some refreshment?" he asked.

She did not reply, but took a step toward the table of food. The General didn't dislike her looks, and she enjoyed dancing with him. She needed to eat, and distract herself from these troubling feelings. Soon she had a plate piled with bread and cheese, and a bowl of vegetable stew.

The General picked up a glass. "Do you want some ale?"

"Beer? Yes, please," she said.

He put the glass under the spigot and turned the wooden tap.

What did he mean by those remarks about her appearance? 'Not displeasing' was quite flattering, but 'plain' was rather rude. Or had he meant she could get a lover even if she was 'plain' rather than 'not displeasing'?

A lover? Her eyes strayed to the young couple, still entwined. She wanted a handsome prince to hold her like *that* and kiss her like *that*. Her body tingled at the thought. No chance of that now, with her world shattered by civil war. Only rebels who eyed her up and down as though contemplating some barnyard activity.

She put her plates on a side table and applied herself to the food. It avoided the necessity of speaking.

Tarchon wasn't that bad-looking, and he had some manners. Enough for a dance partner. Maybe they would dance again when she recovered her composure.

He placed the glass of beer beside her plate.

"If you swore not to attempt escape, we could allow you to move freely inside the mansion, but not to step outside. Would you like that?" He raised a finger.

Mouth full of bread and cheese, she nodded. The offer felt patronising, but there seemed little point in refusing. Where could she run to, anyway?

"Do you swear, then?" With a crooked finger, Tarchon beckoned a couple of his uniformed aides to approach. The young men stared at her, but said nothing.

Tarchon's grey eyes bored into her, as if he suspected her thoughts. *Annoying*.

She finished the mouthful and swallowed. "I swear on my honour as a Zircon, not to try to escape."

"Very well," he said. He turned to the officers. "You've witnessed this. The Princess is to be permitted free movement inside the Anwar mansion."

Both young men saluted.

"What's your favourite food?" Tarchon asked, watching her eat.

She hesitated. She was partial to an exotic and no doubt expensive fruit cake, topped with cream, but Tarchon might be judgemental about that. "Grilled eels in sauce."

Presently Tarchon excused himself. "I'm neglecting the other guests." As the celebrations continued, she saw Tarchon and his aides approach Persis.

Back in her room later, she threw herself on her bed. What had happened? The General was interested in her,

Cleia Chavin had said. Perhaps she had misunderstood what Cleia meant. She had thought he was interested in her as a source of information. Did he admire her as a woman? An image rose unbidden to her mind, of the General holding her close and kissing her, just like the pair of young lovers. 'Not displeasing', he had said. A disturbing reflection. She thought he was about thirty, not impossibly old. So what, then? Was it just the power he held over her that gave her these unwholesome thoughts? He could do whatever he wanted.

The serving women had boyfriends, or so she gathered from their talk, but an Imperial Princess could not behave in that way. If she kept her dignity, her future was likely to be a lonely one.

***

Not long after the harvest festival, Maihara heard rumours that war had broken out again, rumours which she corroborated by discreet snooping using her spy spell. Imperial troops in the south had made an attack on a rebel position, and the rebels had retaliated. As she roamed the mansion, she overheard talk that both sides were mobilising their forces. The rumours troubled her. She had not objected to the truce; it meant that young men of both factions, like the earnest young officers she saw daily, were not marching out to battlefields to get themselves killed or maimed.

She climbed a rough stair to the roof. The roar of the city reached here, a murmur and clattering, mixed with distant shouts. It seemed louder than the day before. Over the rooftops, outside the city wall, she glimpsed a distant patchwork of fields and the country beyond now yellow with stubble or tan with parched earth. The wind bore a faint scent of straw and had carried a fine dust of chaff to the boarding at her feet. She should have been able to see the menacing Dhikr camp from here, but there was only a brown mark on the fields to show where it had been.

A noise near at hand distracted her. A soldier had gained the roof, and made his way toward her along the narrow boarded footway. She tensed, but the man merely called to her.

"Madam, you're wanted below."

She descended steps and carpeted stairs to the main floor and entered an ante-room with gilt and green plasterwork, furnished with upholstered armchairs and a deep carpet. The summoner was, as she had guessed, General Tarchon yet again. Handsome in his well-fitted uniform, he sat with two of his aides while a servant poured tea.

Tarchon rose and greeted her. His manner was courteous but not overly familiar. He gestured for her to sit, and she seated herself in a yielding chair.

Tarchon got to the point. "The truce has been breached, and our forces are mobilising for war."

She drew a breath before releasing it in a sigh. "People hoped it would last longer. Didn't your people want peace?"

"We did, but few expected it to last much beyond the harvest time. There are many who want war, especially on the Imperial side. Anyway, it was them who broke it, not us."

They would say that. "So this truce was about harvesting?"

"Armies have to eat, Princess. So do the people."

She took a filled cup offered by the servant. "I heard talk of mobilising. Yet you took the trouble to tell me in person. Is there some reason for this?"

She wondered, she hoped, did it mean he held her in some special regard?

Tarchon gave a nod. "There is. I am to leave the capital and lead troops in," - he paused - "a certain direction."

She narrowed her eyes at him. Of course, as a mere prisoner, she was not going to be told any detail of their military plans. "So, you want to spread your area of conquest further. Just what do you think this is achieving?"

"We will free the people from a corrupt and brutal regime, and bring justice and relief from want."

"So you say. Spreading death and destruction, more likely."

"No worthwhile gain is achieved without some pain. People were already dying under your regime."

"We're not going to agree."

He smiled and leaned back. "I wish you to accompany me."

"What?" The cup in her hand shook, spilling a few drops of brown liquid on the carpet. "Why?" If the golims existed, Tarchon would be taking her outside the protective walls of Calah, and directly into their path. Into the dead villages of the dreamscape.

"Splitting the hostages."

"I'll be separated from my brother?" Her voice rose.

"Regrettably so." Tarchon gestured with the back of his hand, and the servant and aides retreated to the far side of the room.

"But why me?" She bent forward.

Tarchon sipped his tea, looking at her over the patterned cup.

"Major Chavin says that you are interested in me," she said in a low voice. "What sort of interest? Is that why you want me with you?"

Tarchon frowned. "She said that? You're coming with me because I wish it. There'll be no discussion."

She let out her breath in a small gasp of exasperation. "Eeh!" She raised her voice. "I'm a Zircon princess. You can't drag me around the country like a parcel!"

He looked at her, scratching his jaw. "Your conversation pleases me. Your bold ideas. Your self-confidence. You'll make a lively companion." He drained his cup. "Till later, Princess." He stood and gave her a final glance. "We'll arrange transportation. Best put your things in order."

She watched him go, and buried her frustration by banging down the teacup.

What had just happened? He had bluntly informed her of his plans, but the explanation was suspect, and he had not exactly denied that he had feelings for her. Otherwise why not take her brother? What was going on here? He was the enemy, and an Imperial princess could not be friends with such a low-status person. And she hoped she had not got Cleia Chavin into trouble.

Belatedly, she realised she might have revealed to Tarchon too much of her own feelings.

"Will that be all, madam?" the servant asked in a monotone, after a pause.

"Yes, thank you." She waved the man away.

As she finished her tea, the servant sidled up to her, after glancing around the room. Nobody else was present, and his manner roused a sensation of unease in her. She had not seen him in this mansion before, yet he seemed vaguely familiar, with his dark hair and slightly battered features.

The man bent down and spoke in a low voice. "Your Grace, one hears that you will be forced to travel with Tarchon. You'll be well placed to rid us of the vile rebel. Just say the word, and we'll give you the means."

She stared at him in shock. "You mean, kill him? I couldn't! I've never hurt anyone."

"It's for the Empire."

"No!" She shook her head.

The man gripped her arm. "Don't start a row. I have a knife."

She smelt his foul breath. Trembling, she shook her head.

"Do you like him, you witch? You disappoint me, Princess, you really do," he said in a low, hard voice. "You'd better say nothing of this; we don't like traitors."

"What? Who are y—?" But the man was already striding away.

She trembled, and tried to get up, but her shaking legs would not support her. The noise of the street door slamming shut reached her ears. She got to her feet and dragged herself up the stairs. A maid passed her and stopped.

"You look pale, Princess," the maid said.

Maihara stared at the maid. Was this another of them? "It's nothing. I just need to rest."

Once in her room, she leaned against the panelled wall. An Imperial agent had got into the mansion and demanded that she kill Tarchon. That was her duty, to kill the enemy, but she had reacted without thinking. One could not kill a man after drinking tea with him. What should she do now? If she told Tarchon's people, she'd be placing herself firmly in the rebel camp, and in danger from the Imperial fanatics. Better say nothing for the moment. General Tarchon would be aware of the risk of assassination anyway if he had any sense.

If agents were able to infiltrate the mansion, they could get into this room. Those wooden panels might conceal a void in the building. Her eyes ran across her bed and the wardrobe. A bribed servant could plant a poisoned needle in her bed. Or in clothes. She touched her bodice.

The agent's threats had shaken her. It wasn't just that she couldn't murder Tarchon. Those were the same men who had menaced her after her arrest. She wanted no part of such vile people or their methods. Did she want to be an Imperial princess if it meant being soiled by their bloody hands?

She opposed Tarchon's rebellion against the Imperial state, and was sickened by the number of people who had died in the fighting, but what now? Should she warn Tarchon again about the golim menace? He had not made further mention of rumours of mechanical soldiers, and might laugh off her concerns. A girl with bad dreams? Warning him was not her duty; in fact, given her position as Imperial Princess, her duty lay in *not* warning him.

She crossed to the window and looked out at the building beyond. Enemies could overlook her room from there. Regardless of the golim threat, she might be safer on the campaign trail whether it led south or east.

-18-

With a grinding of brakes, the carriage lurched to a halt in a drizzle-dampened provincial town, forced to a stop by a press of rebel fighters jamming the wide street. The odour of unwashed bodies seeped inside the vehicle. Weathered buildings of brick and stone, two or three floors in height, huddled together on each side under roofs of scalloped red tile. Armed men peered into the grilles of closed shops.

"Where's this?" Maihara asked, hot and tired from the long journey from Calah.

Her chaperone, Lady Aurian, glanced out of the window. "I'm not sure, Your Grace." Aurian was small, round-faced, with a beauty spot on her left cheek and black hair tied back with a hair clasp. She wore a grey cloak over a brocaded yellow dress. So far as Maihara knew, Aurian had no children, possessed a pleasant singing voice and enjoyed doing embroidery. The unfortunate woman had never found her husband, but the rebels had given her a new role. Tarchon had been solicitous in ensuring that Maihara was properly chaperoned on her enforced journey. Opposite her sat two officers of her escort, Lieutenant Harayam, young and with short, curly hair, and Colonel Selvar, older and balding. Maihara's personal maid, one of the red-faced females from the Anwar Mansion, sat beside Aurian.

"This is Debrish, Princess," Selvar said. "It's on the river Sintheer."

Aurian had been appointed the day after Tarchon's surprise announcement that Maihara was to accompany him, not long after the harvest dance. Maihara had been surprised that Tarchon should appoint a noblewoman and initially suspected that the chaperone was there to report on her every move, but she had soon warmed to her new companion.

"You need to be escorted by someone of suitable rank, Your Grace. I attended that ridiculous coronation ceremony, and that will have been noted, so I am not anxious to return to Imperial territory. My husband is still missing, and my estate overrun, so I need a position."

Maihara agreed. She had not liked being enrolled as Tarchon's companion.

"General Tarchon briefed me on Emperor Cordan's attitude toward you. I think Cordan fears you have magical powers that could unseat him. You have consorted with rebels for months, and your radical views have been noted."

Maihara had protested. "That's absurd! I don't have that kind of power, and I..."

"He thinks you do, even if he's wrong, and he commands an Empire and a secret service. Take care, Your Grace, or you may find yourself in an unmarked grave."

Maihara had been silent, stunned. The hint that the Fifth Bureau was watching both of them had not passed her by. But her father couldn't, wouldn't harm his child. If only she could speak to him and explain. It must be that Tarchon and Aurian wanted to deter her from escaping.

"I don't have any magical powers." She had the distinct impression that her protective chaperone believed otherwise.

"If you say so, Your Grace."

Maihara thanked Selvar for his geographical information while Aurian stared out of the window. Debrish lay in the southern province of Rewar. Past the carriage streamed mailed rebel warriors on their brown ponies, and an assortment of more exotic fighters. A troop of bowmen and women in green-and-brown garb caught Maihara's attention. Both men and women had black hair gathered in top-knots, and they carried long bundles slung on their shoulders.

She pointed at the bowmen. "Who are they?"

"Archers from Zis," Selvar said.

"Where's that?" Support for the rebels must be more widespread than she had imagined.

"The West. They're another minority persecuted by the Empire." Selvar's voice betrayed an edge of emotion, anger.

She glanced at Selvar, then back to the bowmen. They looked weary.

Two days earlier, they had crossed from the province of Avergne to Rewar, travelling through a region that had been hotly contested by local militias. The countryside here was greener than around Calah, with lush fields of corn and vegetables, stands of broad-leaved trees and occasional meandering streams. With the aid of the Box and its contents, she might have found spells that could reach from Calah as far as here. Their carriage passed the detritus of war in the form of a burnt town, wrecked farmhouses, charred fields, a wounded child, occasional corpses and rows of freshly dug graves. Refugees with hopeless eyes camped near the roadside. Maihara had slept badly.

The carriage moved on at a walking pace. Maihara leaned out of the open window despite the drizzle. Alongside tramped men in long brown robes, with what looked like lengths of rope slung over their shoulders.

Lieutenant Harayam noted her interest. "They're trackers. They hunt using whirling stones linked with rope."

Maihara examined his boyish features. Was he testing her credulity? Harayam appeared serious. She nodded.

The carriage turned a corner, and its wheels rang on a hard stone road. The taller buildings were left behind, and she glimpsed masts and the gleaming water of a river.

They stopped in front of a large brick building, slit-windowed with towers and crenellation. Soldiers milled to and fro, shouting. Lieutenant Harayam got out and held the carriage door. A warm wind caressed her though it was late in the year. The drizzle had stopped. Maihara imagined herself making a run for it, to disappear into the confusion on the streets of Debrish. She sighed. Even if she had anywhere to go and her awkward legs outran the portly Colonel Selvar, Harayam looked fit, not to mention the soldiers of the guard.

Aurian grabbed Maihara's hand in hers. They descended and stood together as Harayam turned to give orders for their luggage to be unloaded. Aurian was a head shorter than her charge. She turned to Maihara and whispered in her ear, "Remember what I said earlier."

Maihara nodded. The older woman had been evasive on her exact role, but at earlier halts in their journey had been exhorting Maihara to listen out for any information that might be of interest to the Imperial forces. Maihara was not sure she ought to do that, even though Aurian denied any connection with the obnoxious Fifth Bureau. Aurian had left a nephew in Calah, so she might be under pressure.

The tanned faces of the locals passing by or looking on were guarded, unwelcoming. Even here in Debrish, she hoped her guards would be careful to keep both extreme rebels and angry Imperial sympathisers away from her. It would be hard to tell who posed the greater threat.

If she had her box, she could have hoped to use its secret lore to protect herself. Had Tarchon left it in some deep, secure vault in Calah, or taken it with him? A spark of resentment glimmered.

The officers pushed the crowd aside and led her into the fort, along with Lady Aurian and the maid. They passed under a brick arch, defended by great metal-studded doors and a suspended wood and metal portcullis, and came to rest in a courtyard cluttered with waiting troops and piles of equipment.

"Orders are to wait here," Selvar said.

"Can't we get on the battlements and look at the river?" Maihara asked.

"My orders are to wait *here*," the overweight Selvar repeated, frowning.

Lieutenant Harayam, hands at his sides, looked up at the tower tops. Sunlight glinted on his blond moustache.

"Do your orders specify which part of the fort we are to wait in?" she asked.

"No," Selvar admitted with a scowl.

"Then there's no reason we can't ascend." Maihara fixed him with a stare.

"It's at my discretion," Selvar said, drawing himself straight.

Maihara got her way with a smile and some girlish persuasion, and climbed to the top platform of the small fort. Lady Aurian trailed behind, grumbling about the ascent.

Maihara looked down. On this side the Debrish fort commanded the river Sintheer, around thirty yards wide at this point. A medley of voices and clatter drifted up to the battlements. Below, a long dockside swarmed with men and carts. Bright-mailed officers led horses that baulked at the sight of the water transport. Big boats with masts lay against the dock in a long line and as she watched, men, stores and animals were going aboard them.

This was no boat trip, but a fist aimed at the parts of her Empire so far unoccupied by rebels. From the snippets of misery she had glimpsed through the carriage windows, she conjured more bleak-eyed prisoners, more dead soldiers and civilians, more burnt villages, more maimed and homeless children. Maihara clenched her fists on the worn stone. Did she want the Empire to win? She wanted it to remain, but any sense of pride was pushed aside by the memory of her father's glaring metal face and of the cell he'd had her locked in. Her instincts rebelled against fighting, and from the thought of more ruin. There was nothing she could do to stop it, not without her magic and its province-wide potential. If she had been born a boy, they would have taught her about war, and how to manage armies. Her brother had no interest in such things.

In theory it was her duty to escape, but even if she got away, there was no prospect of a warm welcome in the

Empire. Their Fifth Bureau had locked her up as a witch and traitor, and her own father had rejected her. She still had not told anyone about the Fifth Bureau's approach to her - to do so felt like changing sides. Dragged south, she had to endure the separation from her brother and sister, and the nagging fear of ambush by Cordan's annihilating golim warriors. She fidgeted with her sleeves as she pushed the thoughts away. She had to be strong. At least she had Lady Aurian to fuss over her. Though Aurian was a lot older than Maihara, she was an educated person and they got on well.

Booted feet sounded on the stone stair. Her escort saluted smartly. It was Tarchon, hatless but looking smart in his green uniform with gold shoulder stripes. Two of his staff officers followed, Impar wearing dark glasses, and another man she did not know. Tarchon smiled and came to stand beside her. A warmth infused her, despite her misgivings. How should she respond?

"Princess, we are travelling southward by barge tomorrow. Forces in this province have declared for us, but we need to be on our guard for signs of resistance." He spoke in a firm tone. "Please obey the instructions of the officers guarding you."

Maihara eyed his profile. "I don't know why you want to drag me into a war zone at all."

He frowned. "We've been over this." His voice softened. "You don't want to be left in Calah near the Dhikr, do you?"

"No."

"Or left in some wayside fort?"

"No."

"Or handed over to the Imperials?" He touched her cheek with two fingers.

"No." Maihara felt herself flushing.

"General..." Lady Aurian began, in a warning tone.

"Very well, then."

"The food on this trip's awful," Maihara complained. "A lot of coarse bread, and overcooked stew with nameless things in it. Is this what you all eat, or is it some special torture for captive nobles?"

Tarchon frowned. "It's what we all get. If you got special fare, word would get around and the men wouldn't like it."

"The food was perfectly palatable, under the circumstances," Aurian said.

"Ha." Maihara folded her arms.

"You seem lively enough on it," Tarchon said, cracking a smile.

Maihara leant against the brick parapet. "Can't someone show me how to use one of those crossbow things? I could help defend the barges. My brother got to learn, and he didn't even like it." Crossbows were supposed to be easy, and she was sure they would allow Major Chavin use one.

Tarchon appeared amused. "Certainly not. We don't let prisoners near any weapons."

"Wooden sword practice?" Maihara suggested.

"No. Anyway, I don't think you have the right physique for sword-play. It requires agility."

Maihara narrowed her eyes at him. "Are you saying I'm fat?"

Tarchon recoiled. "No, not at all. You're perfectly slim."

Lady Aurian put a hand over her mouth and was clearly trying not to laugh.

Maihara giggled. She had no illusions. If she wasn't well-rounded, the General wasn't a rebel.

"Well, excuse me, I have a war to fight." Tarchon turned to Lady Aurian. "Try to make her behave."

He turned and descended the steps, boots crunching.

Maihara put a hand to her chest. What was that over-familiar cheek touching about? Was it meant as a sign of affection, or merely to show her who was in charge? Teasing him was such fun. And, distracted by his touch, she had again put off the opportunity to tell him of the Imperial agent and his threats. So far, there had been no word of any golims or mechanical soldiers.

She turned at a footstep as Colonel Impar approached her. His round darkened glasses hid his eyes, giving him a sinister appearance. His narrow face was twisted in dislike, and he stopped where Tarchon had stood. He lowered his head and spoke close to her ear. "I've noticed you getting your Imperial claws into our General, witch. If you harm our cause, I'll kill you myself."

Fear swept over her. For moments she did not know what to say, how to respond. He wouldn't get away with murdering her, but she had to deflect his anger and malice. "I'm not! I won't! I admire him, that's all. I gave my word."

Impar tapped a hand on the wall. "I'll be watching you, witch."

Selvar led a shaken Maihara away and down to the riverside, where a barge awaited them, gleaming with varnished wood and polished metal, in contrast to the battered working vessels moored near it. This, apparently, was to be their transport for the next few days.

She would have to be wary of Impar on this journey. His prejudice against her, and his willingness to harm her, ran deeper than she had realised.

Selvar hailed the barge, but the crew shouted back that they weren't ready.

Maihara found a crate to sit on while they waited. The fort loomed close at their backs, its shadow touching the quayside. Impar's threat had shaken her. Not all rebels were her friends. Her thoughts drifted to spying, and whether Debrish was one of the magically-active places. It was days since she had looked inside herself for her magical powers. This was as good a time as any to try it again. The surroundings were not promising, but at least if she tried, she would learn what kind of places harboured magic.

To her surprise, she sensed the prickle of magic almost at once, and invoking her passwords found her way to a magical space with rows of symbols, slightly different from the design she had experienced in Calah. The numbers of rows and columns of symbols seemed different, but here was a slightly modified sigil for that spying spell that had so alarmed her when she first tried it.

The semi-transparent picture generated by the spying spell persisted even when she closed her eyes, so it was for her alone. Likewise, as she had found at Calah, nobody else could hear the relayed sound, even if she set it at a high level for herself. No hand gestures were required, and so long as she did not forget herself and mutter spell-words aloud, or use a spell that generated any strange sounds, she could work in front of others while pretending to read or rest.

"I'd like a cup of tea," she said to Aurian. "If they have any in this place."

Aurian sent their maid off to procure some.

Maihara pretended to watch the activity on the dock while in actuality launching and directing the spying spell she had used in Calah. She did this by thinking of touching parts of the bottom of the image that were marked up in the obsolete language as direction controls. She could also slide her finger in the image itself but that would make her look weird to any onlookers. Soon, she was watching and listening to a group of soldiers talking to Lieutenant Harayam alongside a barge. She was not really spying, she told herself; she was seeking news from the Empire that could inform an escape plan.

"So we're going on these down the river? Better than fugging marching."

Their conversation, full of strange oaths, was not what she hoped to hear.

"Princess?" A hand touched Maihara's shoulder, startling her. The serving-woman stood beside her with a mug of tea. Maihara took the mug, and glanced up, but the other two women seemed oblivious to what she was doing.

She spied around the boats at random, learning little. She spotted Colonel Selvar striding toward the fort, and followed him with difficulty. She found it hard to move the spy to track a moving person. He passed among sheds, heading for the fortification, and her spy followed, blanking as it passed through the thick brick wall while Selvar entered at a postern.

Selvar greeted the men inside, with a sloppy salute. She did not know any of them, save one or two, who she had seen around the fort in Calah, but they had the shoulder flashes of senior officers.

She was getting a headache. It was a strain to operate and listen to the spell while behaving like normal on the quayside. She took a mouthful of tea.

"How are the ladies?" said one after some military talk.

"Well-behaved so far," said Selvar. "What's the military situation, sir? I don't know much myself."

"We know that at least one Imperial regiment is manoeuvring to the east of us. And landowners hostile to us are raising militias. But where are they, and what do they mean to do?" A man with the shoulder flashes of a major-general was speaking.

"The scout reports?" another officer queried.

"By the time we get reports, those bastards are already somewhere else. We can't be sure if they mean to block the roads, or take us in the flank."

This was concerning. If Imperial forces were in a position to attack the barge fleet, she could be exposed to danger.

"Tarchon's swift move downriver should take them unprepared," the second staff officer said.

"I hope the scouts and messengers are up to the job," said the major-general. "We need to secure the ground behind us while we advance on Retis."

"Is there a plan for taking Retis?" Selvar asked.

"Yes, there is. We will land a squadron of cavalry upstream to cut the town off. Then the main landing will be just above the town, while the barges attempt to enter the harbour and river docks. We'll also have our agents inside to stir up disorder. With luck the place will fall with little resistance."

Rebel agents? So the Imperials were not alone in using agents and spies.

"Is Retis walled?" Selvar asked.

"It is, but word is that they are in poor condition."

The discussion switched to how long it would take to clear Imperial resistance in the countryside around them and to the south. They seemed to be anticipating a swift campaign.

Maihara continued to listen to her spy, until the officers exhausted the subject of their campaign and commenced putting papers into leather satchels. She had a headache and sagged with tiredness as if she had been working at her books all afternoon. She shut off the spell, not wanting to know any more of their low thoughts about drink and women. The sun had shifted around. Aurian sent the maid off in search of a sunshade.

Presently she and Lady Aurian were allowed on board their barge and were led to a cramped cabin in the bowels of the vessel. It looked pleasant enough in the daylight, with a round glass port that faced the shore, walls and fittings of luxurious smooth, reddish-brown wood, and a washbasin glazed with bright paintings of fish. There were two berths, one above the other, with fresh linens and soft blankets, but there was barely enough floor space to stand and turn around in. To her vexation, she had to struggle out of her travelling dress by herself, as she had earlier given the serving-woman some free time.

So the rebels intended to capture Retis. She didn't want that, with its attendant misery, but what should she do? If she told Lady Aurian, it might restore her own credibility with the Empire, but she might need to explain in detail how she acquired the information. And she would be betraying the rebels' trust. A defence of Retis would at least slow the rebel campaign, but there was no assurance it would reduce the amount of death and suffering. On the other hand, one might think the defenders of Retis should be offered the choice.

***

The barges cast loose at dawn. After a breakfast of grilled fish and bread served in a cramped and crowded saloon that reeked of cooking odours, Maihara found her place on a comfortable deck seat, where a couple of rebel officers kept watch over her. Mud-banks topped with reeds slipped by. A few native boats were drawn up on the bank and reed-thatched huts stood among trees. Between the stands of trees she had glimpses of reed beds and of slightly higher ground where green crops grew in rows. On the water, a fleet of barges ahead, behind and alongside them, laden with men, animals and stores made way downriver. As well as tall triangular sails, most had flat boards that could be dropped over the side, apparently to arrest sideways drift under sail. So far, this felt more like a pleasure cruise than a military expedition.

Tarchon paid her little attention, for he was constantly on deck watching the river banks and shouting orders. Their eyes met twice, but his expression remained unchanged. It seemed that she was less important than his duties. He had paid her more attention when they waited out the truce in Calah. What had she expected?

What was happening with her brother, back in Calah? She doubted that Persis shared her mixed feelings about the rebels. Tarchon had a brother, but according to Cleia Chavin the brother had before the uprising betrayed Tarchon's meetings with rebels to the Imperial authorities. That might have left a scar on the General's character.

A *pok* noise distracted her attention. She couldn't identify it. Was that a fat drop of rain? The sky looked bright. The noise came again, and the two officers near her straightened and looked around.

Another *pok*, and a small rip appeared in a sail.

"Get down!" Tarchon was shouting. She turned. He was waving in her direction, red-faced. "Get her down! Now!"

Stung into action, the two officers grabbed her roughly and hustled her to the varnished wood stairway leading below. She struggled, outraged. Below deck, they released her with mumbled apologies. One ran back on deck, while Colonel Selvar remained with his bulk blocking her way upward.

"What's happening?" It was a silly question. Somebody was shooting things at them. Overhead, feet pattered on the deck and the *thwack* of other impacts rattled through the hull. From nearby, broken glass tinkled.

"Enemy incoming," Selvar muttered.

She shivered. She had never before been this close to the war. It must be an Imperial attack, and they were shooting at *her*.

-19-

Maihara was obliged to remain below decks till nightfall, lest the attack be repeated. Lady Aurian, despite not having been on deck, was more disturbed by the assault than Maihara herself, and crouched low beside her bunk.

"We could be trapped down here," Aurian complained, not for the first time. She wrung her hands till her knuckles showed white.

Maihara suppressed a prickle of irritation. The prospect of being trapped below did not worry her too much. She could have been hit by an arrow or crossbow bolt, or executed as a witch, or thrown from a horse, or killed by drunken rebel soldiers, or beheaded for treason by her father's men, but the death god Tabor apparently did not want her in the underworld yet.

Eventually Aurian, soothed by a nightcap of thick red wine, fell asleep. Maihara lay in the lower berth, in the dark, listening. Water chuckled, feet tramped above, men talked, and water-birds cried. In the opposite berth, Lady Aurian breathed heavily.

A knock came on the cabin door.

"Who's that?" Maihara said, her voice wavering.

"It's Tarchon."

"General?" What on earth could the rude man be wanting now? This intrusion was rather improper.

"May I come in?"

"You're the master here." It came out more sharply than she intended. Lady Aurian was present, should there be any question about his presence. And she did want to see him. "Give me a moment." She grappled with her dressing-gown, unlatched the door and retreated to her bunk.

Tarchon eased his way in. He wore his green uniform,

now stained and rumpled. The jacket fitted close on him, emphasising his lean and well-muscled body. He wore black boots, splashed with mud and with a strand of dried river-weed stuck to one.

Maihara eyed him silently from her blanket refuge.

"I'd like to apologise for my rudeness of earlier," Tarchon said. "I should have spoken sooner, but there has been so much to do, and I did not want to be seen chatting to you in front of the men."

Lady Aurian slept on, breathing steadily.

Maihara felt an impulse to tease him, and leant on one elbow in the berth, making a frown. "You should apologise. You have shouted at me or ignored me these past few days."

He looked at her, with a faint smile, His face looked tired in the lamplight. "Then I apologise. I didn't mean to expose you to fighting. I hope you weren't frightened."

"It was alarming. I don't like being shot at."

"I'm sorry. Our scouting was deficient."

"And you were exposing yourself. If you'd got yourself killed, I'd have nobody amusing to talk to." She smiled.

He made a mock salute. "I'm touched that you care."

She laughed. "Not that much. But your officers are no fun." The air in the cabin was hot. "You can sit down."

Tarchon's eyes widened. He had gone quiet.

What was with him? Perhaps he also found this situation a little awkward. "How did you let that attack happen?"

He cleared his throat. "An isolated group of shooters had taken a position among trees two hundred paces from the river. It was a nuisance attack, and we had a mounted force pacing us on shore who soon dealt with them."

"And will this happen again?"

Tarchon shrugged. "The scouts are supposed to prevent it."

Lady Aurian stirred and opened her eyes. "Gods above!" She scrambled from her bunk and wrapped a blanket around Maihara's shoulders.

"I don't find this proper, General," she said, scowling up at Tarchon. "You can speak to her tomorrow."

Tarchon mumbled an apology. "It's late." He backed out of the door, making a swift bow.

The door closed.

"Huh. He couldn't get out quick enough." Maihara shook off the blanket. "It's warm enough in here."

"Your Grace!" Lady Aurian scolded. "You shouldn't let him see you like this."

"Like what?"

Lady Aurian pointed at Maihara's chest. Maihara looked down. The nightgown had a rounded, low-cut neckline. And she was still wearing her breast-support. Tarchon, standing three feet away, must have got a good eyeful of her cleavage.

"Oh!" That explained Tarchon's reaction. How utterly embarrassing. She felt herself reddening. At least he had not lingered or made remarks.

"Your Grace! What were you thinking? You should be more careful."

She was not entirely ignorant of male natures. "I doubt if he sees me in that sort of way."

Lady Aurian's lips tightened. "He's a man. And one of the lower class."

He's a man. That gave Maihara much to think about. The idea of Tarchon admiring her cleavage was distinctly unsettling. She'd been distracted by his presence, and mishandled the situation.

***

Around midday an outburst of urgent shouting interrupted the downriver progress. The barges slowed as sails descended to the decks with a rattle. Crude anchors splashed into the water and held the barges still as the river moved past, or they tied up to trees on the riverbank. Men went ashore over planks or using small boats, wearing armour and carrying weapons.

"What's happening?" Maihara asked, as sailors brushed past her on the deck.

"They say there's a fort round the next bend with catapults that can shoot over the river," Colonel Selvar said. "It looks like it's resisting our passage. Tarchon's given orders that it be taken, so that we can pass safely."

"So where is Tarchon?"

"He's gone ashore to direct the attack, they say."

The thought of Tarchon putting himself in danger made her insides tighten with anxiety. If he was killed, she would be in a difficult position, with few friends among the rebels. That was true, but if he was dead, she'd miss his words, and his mild eyes, and the promise of amusing flirtation. What were these thoughts?

She stood up. "I want to go ashore." She could see nothing from here.

Selvar blocked her way with an outstretched hand. "The General has given orders that you stay on the barge, Princess."

With a sigh of irritation, she sat down again. A group of soldiers with mules and horses stood on the bank fifty feet away where the troops had disembarked. The river curved here, and the water was deeper close into this bank. On the far side it was shallow. Inland lay fields of stubble with stooks of straw collected at intervals, separated by narrow strips of woodland, and a cluster of wooden farm buildings. Long-legged birds pecked in the stubble. If anything was happening, it was behind the trees and beyond the river bend.

Tired of waiting, and mindful of the flying arrows of the previous day, she descended to her cabin and found a book.

"What's happening?" Lady Aurian asked from her bunk.

"Nothing I can see."

Maihara tried to read, but images of Tarchon in the middle of fighting kept coming to mind.

At a shouting on shore, she dropped the book and raised her gaze to the cabin window. Men on horseback and on foot were milling about on the bank. An unseen object hit the barge's woodwork with a thunk that reverberated inside the hull.

"It's happening again," she said. Her heart beat faster. Aurian gasped.

Selvar stood guard in the cross-passage outside her cabin. "They can't get to us here unless they swim," he said.

She exited the cabin. Selvar was looking through a small round glass set in the boat's side. Unable to see past him, she hurried to look through the glass at the other side of the boat. Three men jumped into the water from the far bank, with a series of splashes. She stood on tip-toe to see where they went. One lay face down with an arrow through his neck, and floated away, while the other two dove beneath the grey water.

Maihara's heart thumped. "Something's happening on this side. Is anyone in command out there?" The raiders could easily cause chaos among a mass of moored and grounded barges. If only she had her Box, she would not feel so helpless.

"Of course," said Selvar. His footsteps scuffled behind her and he put a hand on her arm to move her aside.

She let him look.

"Damn. Keep your head down."

More shouting broke out, much closer at hand. Fear stirred in her. Unable to see, she went to the other side, then moved forward. From the front cabin window, just above deck level, she saw a man standing in the bows of the barge, now pointing upstream, and aiming a bow at the water. He released his arrow, which shot into the river, but the shouting continued.

The barge gave a faint lunge, then the banks and other barges moved. No, their barge was moving downstream.

"Some bastard cut us adrift," said a coarse voice, outside the cabin.

For a moment, Maihara was pleased that the rebels were not having everything their own way. "Why don't they do something?" she called to Selvar. "Don't they have a spare hook?" She left the forward cabin.

With a crash, the barge slowed. The impact threw Maihara off her feet in the passage, and she fell against the wooden cabin wall. "What was that?"

Selvar pushed himself upright. "We hit another barge." Maihara got up, wincing, and peered out of the side port. A cabin top and mast slid by a few feet away. Sailors fended off her barge with a long pole.

The collision was unnerving. "Is this thing going to sink?" she asked. Her heart was pounding. The hot lower deck felt very confining. "I want to get outside."

Colonel Selvar moved quickly to block the stairway to the deck. "I don't think that's a good idea. Keep down." He grabbed her arm and pulled her downward. Above, men's voices made an incoherent din.

"Are we sinking?" Lady Aurian cried from inside her cabin.

"Not yet, Ma'am," Selvar replied.

Sounds from outside diminished. They were drifting in mid-river, heading around the bend to where the Empire-held fort blocked their advance. This wasn't good. The expression on Selvar's face showed that he thought the same.

The commotion on deck became louder. Disturbed, Maihara moved to the port side at a crouch and looked out. The barge had turned partly around, and to her dismay an open rowboat full of armed men, not in uniform, was heading straight toward them. Several pairs of oars churned the water.

"We're being boarded." This wasn't supposed to be happening. A chill of alarm swept over her.

Selvar drew his sword, his face pale.

The commotion intensified. A thud shook the barge, and feet trampled on deck. Shouts, screams and the clash of arms penetrated into the cross-passage from above. Fear gripped her now, a terror of being struck down or dragged off by unthinking attackers. The action was all out of sight. With a bang and clatter, an arrow pierced the other window, showering them with fragments of glass. Maihara cried out. In her cabin, Aurian was whimpering and praying.

After some minutes the shouting increased with the Imperial war-cry of 'Hail Cordan' audible over the din. The noise of fighting lessened. The attackers were winning.

A sharp banging attacked the hatch above the stairwell to the deck, and it was flung open, admitting a flood of light. A man with a sword descended, with a mob of desperadoes behind him, dressed in motley agricultural garb and armed variously with knives, clubs and vicious looking agricultural implements. With heart racing, Maihara retreated behind Selvar and grabbed his coat.

Selvar stood his ground, sword in hand.

"Don't resist, Selvar!" Maihara shouted, fearful. "They'll kill you."

"Surrender!" the leader of the mob shouted. "Drop your weapons!" He was clean-shaven and wore an Imperial junior officer's uniform jacket.

"Please drop the sword, Selvar, it's over," she said.

With reluctance, Selvar laid his sword on the floor. A desperado pushed him into a corner and menaced him with a knife.

"We're prisoners," Maihara told the Imperial officer.

The brown-haired young man looked slightly surprised. "Yes, Ma'am, you are our prisoners."

Maihara was a touch relieved. At least he understood that much. "No, we are rebel prisoners. We're Imperial ladies."

The officer looked confused.

A violent looking ragged man kicked open the door of Maihara's cabin. Inside, Aurian screamed.

Maihara raised her voice. "Don't panic, Serina, they're on our side."

Lady Aurian was pushed out into the passage, looking terrified.

"So who are you?" the officer asked.

"That's Lady Aurian, and I'm Lady Maihara Zircona."

The officer's face twitched. "And who's that bastard?"

He pointed his sword at Selvar.

"Him? He was guarding us." Her voice came out high-pitched.

"I'll have to ask you to come with us," the officer said. "Don't worry, you'll be treated with respect. What should we do with him?" He pointed at Selvar.

Selvar looked at Maihara, face white and hands raised.

"He's a prisoner of war, an officer. Haven't you got protocols for that sort of thing?" She looked the young officer in the eye.

"Yes, your ladyship."

Out on deck, several bloodstained bodies lay around in attitudes of sudden death, and sullen sailors and rebels sat with their hands tied. Maihara looked away and grasped at a rope for support. The thought that people whose faces she knew had died as she was freed hit her like a blow.

The barge was drifting downstream in mid-river, and a large rowboat was tied up to it. The banks were higher here, and the river moved more swiftly. A stone fort built on a rocky outcrop loomed over the right bank. Men stood below the fort, pointing. She felt exposed, and not just to the river breeze. Somebody might decide this barge was the enemy, and start shooting. And where was Tarchon? How could he have allowed this to happen?

"We'll take you ashore in our boat, your ladyship, once we're out of sight of the fort," said the Imperial officer.

***

As dusk fell, the group of riders entered the grounds of a country mansion with a long pale frontage, pillared portico and a darker wing extending rearwards. Rows of tents disfigured the lawns around the house, and groups of men, some in green uniform, idled.

"This is Radukamaris," the young officer, whose name was Lieutenant Ferris, told her. Unlike his men, he spoke with a well-bred, educated accent.

In the stable-yard, Maihara slid from the back of the horse on which she had sat for hours, balanced uncomfortably on a standard saddle. Every part of her was sore. They had ridden through cultivated countryside, still untouched by war, alongside fields yellow with cut stubble, or green with winter vegetable crops. She'd had time to reflect on Aurian's earlier warning of being captured by the Empire. Aurian, on another horse, looked anxious and had been silent. Her rescuers, if that was what they were, had passed no comment on Maihara's status, but soon she would find out what the local command knew.

But what should she do now? After being imprisoned, and after her father's shocking rejection of her at Kunn, and the sinister approach from the Fifth Bureau, allowing them to return her to the eastern capital at Chancungra seemed a bad idea. If only she could speak with her father freely and find out what the problem was. Somebody must have whispered accusations in his ear. He'd called her a witch. She was one, but she had never tried to use her magic against him.

Perhaps it was her fault for being too outspoken and dabbling in magic. Her father might have got wind of it somehow. After what she had seen on the journey, her pride in her Imperial heritage had waned, but it would be wise to allay suspicions that she had been 'turned' by the rebels. And if word had reached here that the Emperor had turned against her, she could say that the rumours were greatly exaggerated. She would have to wait to see if the officers here knew anything.

She followed the young officer through a low doorway and along a passage, before entering a series of increasingly grand rooms. Lady Aurian limped behind. They entered a grand saloon, carpeted, with gilt patterned wallpaper, furnished with opulently padded and upholstered chairs and lit by two chandeliers.

Ferris hurried forward, saluted, and spoke to a distinguished-looking man in an Imperial uniform with shoulder stripes and medal ribbons on his breast. He had a small beard, receding, greying hair and a florid, squarish face. This senior officer looked in Maihara's direction and made a beckoning gesture.

The soldier escort urged Maihara forward. The officer waited, and made a bow.

"Milady, am I addressing *the* Maihara Zircona?"

Maihara straightened her back.

Aurian stepped forward. "Yes, the Imperial Princess Maihara Zircona Cordana, Duchess of Avergne."

The officer went down on one knee. "Welcome to our humble mansion. I am deeply sorry that you have been troubled. The experience must have been terrifying. I'll have our best suite made ready. I'll arrange at once a suitable meal, washing facilities, a change of clothes, and female servants to wait on you."

Maihara signalled for him to rise. "Thank you, maybe later. May I know whom I am addressing?"

The officer bowed again. "General Katan, commander of the provincial armed forces, at your service."

"Thanks for your kindness, General. But first, we need to talk."

"About what, Your Grace?"

"About the war."

"With great respect, Your Grace, a young lady need not trouble herself over that. You can leave it to—"

"This young lady is troubled over it. I have important military information."

The officer's expression changed, losing the fawning smile and becoming more businesslike. "I see, Your Grace. Please take a seat. I'll have refreshments sent in." He beckoned to Ferris and spoke in a low tone. Ferris departed.

Maihara looked round for an armchair and beckoned Lady Aurian forward. "This is my companion and chaperone, Lady Aurian."

Aurian curtseyed, and General Katan bowed. "Charmed, Milady."

Katan glanced at Maihara, who directed her gaze at Aurian. Maybe Aurian would reveal to this Imperial officer that she was more than a chaperone, that she had some connection with Imperial agencies. Aurian however remained demurely silent.

On the wall, Maihara spotted a set of official portraits. There was her father, a younger Sihrima, a small Persis in uniform - and a good likeness of herself. No wonder the General had accepted her identity at once. There wasn't one of her mother. A pang of longing for earlier times touched her.

Maihara settled herself in a comfortable armchair that supported her upright. "First, may I ask what your responsibilities are here, General?"

Katan leaned forward in his chair. "I command the 9th Brigade and various militia and irregulars, defending this district against the rebels."

"Thank you. Are you in communication with the Imperial Central Command?"

"Communications are difficult, but we should be able to get a message through. You wish me to inform them that we have freed you?"

Maihara raised a hand. "Don't trouble about that. It can wait. I'm sure army couriers have more urgent duties." In the absence of word that she was forgiven, the last thing she wanted was for him to tell the Imperial court that she was in Imperial hands here. If rumours of her arrest by the Fifth Bureau and suggestions of witchcraft had reached Katan, he was not letting it show.

General Katan rested his veined hands on the arms of his chair. "You have information?"

When she set eyes on the grey-haired Katan, Maihara had decided what her conscience and divided loyalties would allow her to do. "I have become aware of the rebels' general war plan," she said. "They intend to strike southward, down the river and quickly take the port of Retis, so that they have a base for sea operations. Then they will strike along the coast eastwards, it seems, by land and sea."

She had done it now. A sense of guilt bothered her about revealing the rebel plans, after they had mostly been kind to her. But the Imperials would find out all this sooner or later, the hard way, and an early warning ought to crimp the rebel advance, reduce the area overrun by war, and reduce suffering. She had to hope her intervention would not simply prolong the conflict. And she needed to counter whispers that she was a rebel sympathiser.

She glanced at Aurian. Her chaperone looked a little surprised, but pleased.

Katan scratched his nose. "We suspected that they were aiming for the coast. But it should be easy to strike at the river, and cut them off from their base."

"I should think they are aware of that prospect. You should take care, General."

Katan puffed out his cheeks. "They're just a bunch of amateurs, agitators. We should be able to deal with them."

Maihara shook her head. "No, General. I have observed them at first hand. Many of their officers formerly served in the Imperial forces, and from what I have seen they have made themselves into an efficient army. As for the Imperial forces, I hope you don't take this badly, but have you heard about the disaster with the Northern army?"

The general nodded, looking glum.

"And the rather rapid fall of Calah, without any support arriving?"

The general nodded again.

"And what have you done since?"

"We have had to regroup. And as for the North, there are rumours that the rebels were aided by some savages, the Dhikr."

Maihara tapped the arm of her chair. "General, I've met the Dhikr, and whatever you have heard about them, the reality is worse. If they showed up here, I expect most of your irregulars would run away."

The general fiddled with his fingers. "I see."

"I don't know how the rebels plan to protect their advance south, but I'm sure they've thought about it. Retis is some way from here."

"You say they intend to take Retis. But Retis has a garrison and walled defences. It should resist them."

As the general talked, Maihara sensed that he was not

getting the message. If the town was not to be taken unawares and put to the sword, she had to advance another game piece. The lives of the inhabitants were more important than her scruples.

"General, I do know they have a three-point plan for taking Retis."

The general steepled his fingers. "Go on, Your Grace."

"They intend to arrive before the defence is alerted, and strike by land, as well as by sea through the harbour, and be aided by their agents inside the city."

"Agents? I see. If you don't mind me asking, Your Grace, how did you obtain this information?"

Maihara looked him in the eye. "I was lucky enough to overhear some of their officers talking about it."

Lady Aurian raised her head sharply, but said nothing.

A uniformed servant approached with a tray bearing a teapot, cups and cakes, and placed it on a low table in front of them.

The general dismissed the servant and waited till he had left the room before speaking. "If that's the case, Retis should be warned as soon as possible. We should send a messenger."

"You don't have a messenger-bird for Retis, General?" Maihara picked up a cake and bit into it.

"Regrettably, no." He lowered his head.

Outside the tall windows, the night was black save for the glow of a campfire. Maihara allowed herself a yawn. She would accept the general's munificent hospitality for one night at least.

"General, has any more military equipment arrived to end the truce?"

Katan raised an eyebrow. "What have you heard, Your Grace?"

"There was talk at Court that the Emperor hoped to introduce some advanced weapons that would turn back the rebels."

Katan didn't react. "The Central Command orders us to hold our positions and await strategic developments."

"What kind of strategic developments?"

Katan did not answer. No doubt he suspected her of being a chatter mouth girl, incapable of keeping a sensitive secret.

"I have one more question, General. What will you do with the rebel officer you captured when I was freed? Your Lieutenant brought him to your headquarters."

"The prisoner?" Katan gave her an enquiring look. "He's a traitor. We'll toss him in a cell."

"The rebels treat their prisoners decently. I'd like to think that you'll do the same, General. You'll all have to live together after the war."

"They're rebellious scum, Your Grace."

"They're people, with different political views to yours, General."

Katan nodded, with reluctance. "As you wish, Your Grace. I'll give orders that the fellow be treated correctly."

The suite was lavishly furnished, with a four-poster bed topped by an azure dome, and yellow wallpapered walls with a frieze of brightly coloured birds. There was a marble bath which a relay of servants filled with buckets of hot water. Maihara sank into the hot bath with relief. She was not happy with what she had done, but she might still find herself in an Imperial prison, and any unwelcome revelations of her imprisonment and allegations that she was a witch or pro-rebel needed to be countered in advance.

Aurian sang to herself as she looked over some garments that the General's servants had found for them. Maihara's baggage had not followed her from the barge, but the servants found her a fine dress in cream and red that was not too tight for her. During these preparations, Aurian followed Maihara with her eyes. When they were alone, and ready to descend for the formal dinner, Aurian pounced.

"I'm pleased, of course, that you informed the general of the rebel plans. But how did you come by this information, when I heard nothing?" Her tone betrayed resentment.

Maihara offered the best excuse she had devised. "My ears are quite sharp. I overheard a few things at Debrish and elsewhere, and pieced it together."

"How, exactly?" Aurian was vexingly persistent.

"I don't want to talk about it now."

"And why did you not tell me at the time?"

Maihara looked away. "The rebels were kind, and we had sworn not to make any trouble, in exchange for comparative liberty. I was not happy about betraying their trust." This was all too true.

"It was your duty as a member of the Imperial court," Aurian said in an accusatory tone.

Maihara said nothing.

General Katan hosted the dinner in a room that looked far too opulent for a military headquarters. A long, highly polished table of dark wood occupied the centre of the room. The walls had friezes running around below the moulded ceiling, which bore a centre painting of the Nine Gods arrayed for battle. Dark flock wallpaper lined the walls, which were hung with oil paintings of battle scenes and uniformed figures.

Maihara was seated to the right of General Katan in the guest of honour position. Lady Aurian sat further down to the left, looking weary. Along with the general's senior officers and their ladies, they sat at the long table that groaned with the weight of silver centre-pieces which glittered in the light of many candles. The cutlery was silver and the painted plates piled with exotic foods. She wondered if they ate like this every day, and how much they spent on feeding the soldiery.

Maihara had one more set of questions for the general.

"General, what can you tell us about the situation in the principality of Shardan?"

The general wiped his mouth with a napkin. "Shardan, eh? What prompts your interest, Your Grace?"

"My father thought they were politically unreliable.

Even when Calah was threatened with siege, he was unwilling to ask that they send troops to our aid. The rebels hoped to persuade Shardan to declare for them, but that came to nothing. So what is happening there? Have you any news?"

"Only that there are many rascals there who subscribe to rebel ideals, but the Prince holds for the Empire."

"But do they have troops there? And what are they doing with them?" She tapped the table with her fork.

The general seemed unsure. He spoke in a low voice to an officer on his left, and signalled for a waiter to refill their wineglasses. "We had a report a while ago that they had several regiments under arms, for defence of the principality and keeping civil order."

Maihara sucked air through her teeth. She was not getting a sense that the Imperial forces were well co-ordinated. She had heard plenty from the rebels about the corruption and inefficiency of the Imperial civil society, and the failures in the North and at Calah indicated that the problem extended to the army.

But an idea was forming in her mind. She liked the idea of Cordan's regiment of golim soldiers less, the more she heard what excesses even human fighters could commit, and she was minded to pit her influence and her magic against them. As she understood it, Shardan was independent, and if she got herself to the principality, she could hole up there, away from both the Empire and the rebels. She still harboured the long-term ambition of succeeding as Empress, and doing some good for her people. She could hardly do worse; she had the impression that Farnak and others had blamed Cordan for the Empire's poor state of defense, and she would need backers and advisers. It might be a long game.

Next morning, Maihara sought an early meeting with General Katan. She had slept badly again. It had been the same dream as before, except that this time one of the metal monsters had sunk its claws into a child. Along with

Aurian, she had herself escorted to Katan's office, in another of the tall ground-floor rooms with a view of the park. Sunlight lit up rows of shelves lined with books, and a collection of animal heads and other hunting trophies. It did not look much like how she imagined a military command room - plain and with maps and papers, like Tarchon's office at the Calah Fort.

The general bowed low and invited her to take a chair.

"Is there anything I can do to make your stay more pleasant, Your Grace?" he enquired.

"It's been very pleasant, thank you. No, I wanted to talk more about Retis. We agreed that they ought to be warned."

The general nodded.

"I've been thinking. I ought to go to Retis myself. If I speak to the commanders there myself about what I overheard, it might give them more vital detail than they'd get from a message alone."

"Possibly," the general conceded. "But surely you wish to return to the eastern Empire as soon as you can?"

That was a question she wished to evade. After Aurian's warning, she had no intention of going to the eastern Empire anytime soon. A map of the Empire hung on the wall behind the General. "The rebels still hold my brother. And isn't there a desert in the centre of the continent?"

Katan scratched his chin. "There is, Your Grace."

"And the most direct route is across the desert, is it not?"

"Along the southern fringes, to be exact, Your Grace." He steepled his fingers, waiting for her to come to the point.

"It appears that the rebels are expecting the Dhikr to rampage across the central desert in their winter campaign. If you think I'm going that way, you can think again."

"But surely, with an adequate military escort—"

"I've met the Dhikr and I have no wish to renew the acquaintance. Not even with an escort."

"Your Grace, please reconsider—"

"No." She glanced at Aurian, who had a peculiar

expression on her face. She hoped Aurian would keep quiet. Aurian ought to know why she did not want to go east. It was true that Maihara had heard something of the Dhikr being encouraged to campaign in the central desert, and that was a good enough pretext for her objection. If the general thought her a nervous, obstinate and unreasonable female, so be it. The overland route was too close to places where officials might have heard about her arrest. Why General Katan did not know already she wasn't sure. Maybe the Emperor preferred to conceal the scandal.

Katan sighed. "What are Your Grace's wishes?"

Maihara stood and walked over to the map. She traced a line, down and to the right. "I'd like to go to Retis, and then to the eastern Empire by sea. So far as I know, the rebels have not reached the sea, and don't have armed ships, so it ought to be safe enough, if I don't delay."

Katan sighed again. "What Your Grace proposes is not unreasonable. But are you sure you don't wish to remain here?"

"I'd feel safer on one of our eastbound ships, General. The rebels threaten this area."

"I am merely concerned with Your Grace's safety, and with your speedy return to the Imperial court."

Maihara waited, anticipating a 'but'. If anything happened to her on Katan's watch, his career would be over.

Katan steepled his fingers. "If you will permit me, Your Grace, what exactly did you hear the rebel officers say? About Retis?"

"I don't remember all the exact words now. They talked of the three elements of their attack, and one said 'if we arrive sooner than they expect, and attack at multiple points, it'll leave them in disarray.' They mentioned a canal, a Fowler's headland and the Eastern Beach, which must mean something to the locals. I'll get it written down."

"Yes, we should draft a communiqué and alert the Retis garrison to your observations, Your Grace. Then they can act as they see fit." He made no move to do so.

Maihara was not at all sure that she would be taking ship for the East at Retis. Once at the coastal port, she would have to find a pretext to instead travel overland to the neutral principality of Shardan, where she might get a warmer welcome than in the Empire.

"And what's the quickest way of getting to Retis?"

"The roads between here and the estuary are not good, Your Grace. Most people use the river."

"The river?" That did not sound good. "So I'll have to get on the river ahead of the rebels? And they've already had a day's advantage."

"I suppose that's true, Your Grace." He eyed her with renewed interest.

"So, a communiqué?"

"I'll get one of my aides to help you." He beckoned.

Maihara agreed. It would be helpful to have the message written on military paper, with Katan's name on it. Retis needed to be saved from fire and plunder.

-20-

The same morning, Maihara and Aurian were alone for a few minutes at their breakfast.

Aurian set down her fork. "Your Grace, I don't believe in this willingness of yours to return east. You're planning to go somewhere else, out of the Emperor's reach, and meddle, aren't you?"

Maihara stared at Aurian in surprise. Her chaperone's suspicions were close to the mark, and she needed to be sure that Aurian was on side and would say nothing to Katan that would wreck her plan. "It's a long way to the East. And what do you mean, meddle?"

"Your Grace is far more interested in politics and warfare than is proper for a young lady."

Maihara pushed aside a plate of cold meats with a sharp movement. "By what right are you advising me on politics? I only intend to meddle with the rebel advance. You're just my chaperone, and a chaperone appointed by the rebels, at that."

Aurian's cheeks turned red. "The rebels have nothing to do with the matter. Perhaps because I'm a little older and wiser than you?"

Maihara shook her head. "Wiser? Since when have you ever taken an interest in politics? You were just the mistress of some small country house."

Aurian's eyes widened, and, she clenched her small hands. "You should be careful, Your Grace."

Maihara pressed her lips together with an effort. There was more she wanted to say, but it might not be wise to say it. Aurian was the only friend she had around here, and things said in heat might not easily be unsaid. Aurian's remark about meddling annoyed her, not least because she hoped to be free to act.

Aurian took up her fork and poked at her cold meat, looking upset. They ate in silence. Sounds of domestic activity filtered into the small breakfast room.

Aurian reached for a glass of fruit juice. "I have not seen you like this before, Your Grace. You're trying to assume command."

Maihara contemplated this for a moment, examining the remark for possible insult. Aurian's expression showed an irritating concern.

"That's because I am finally free. I have never been free before." The revelation had not come to her before this moment. Till now, she had been under the control of the rebels, of the Imperial Bureau, of her father, of a succession of tutors and nannies.

Aurian opened her mouth to say something and then closed it. She set down her glass untasted.

After further polite but firm requests to the general's staff, Maihara got her Retis message written and sealed. Now she just needed an escort and transportation to Retis. From the languid pace of events at the general's headquarters, she feared this might take time to arrange, and with every hour that passed, the Fifth Bureau was more likely to get word of her presence, and the rebel barge fleet sailed a couple of miles further down river.

Questions revealed that General Katan and his staff were considering by what route they might send her, and what size of escort was appropriate for an Imperial princess. And how many uniformed troops they could spare.

Meanwhile the rebel force was an unseen threat. Would they stop to search for her, once they realised what had happened? Different scenarios ran through her mind, the rebels shrugging off the attack and pressing on, or a furious Tarchon urging his men to scour the countryside for her. Surely he would be concerned about her. There was no way of letting him know she was unharmed. If she suggested sending a message, the Imperials would immediately suspect her loyalty.

Horns blared outside. Maihara pulled aside the drapes of a tall hall window, but saw nothing new among the tents and park trees. Minutes later, a sweaty and dishevelled man in military uniform and riding boots entered the hall of the mansion, asking for the general staff. Maihara followed him into the staff office, with Aurian at her heels.

General Katan was there, in his dark green uniform, bent over the desk of a subordinate. He looked up, frowning, as Maihara entered. "What is it, Your Grace?"

For answer, she pointed to the messenger.

The horseman saluted. "Message from Colonel commanding 14th troop, sir." He held out a crumpled paper sealed with red wax.

The general glanced at Maihara, then meaningfully at the door. "If you'll excuse us, Your Grace, we need to examine this message."

"With respect, General, I'd like to hear it. It might concern me."

Katan tightened his lips, but nodded. He took the message and handed it to the seated staff officer. "Read."

As she listened, she learnt that a land-based rebel force was advancing on their position. For a moment, she imagined being re-united with Tarchon, but a tightness in her chest replaced this pleasant fancy. She would be ashamed to face Tarchon after her impulsive decision to betray his campaign plan. And being in the midst of a military clash would be dangerous for her. No, she had to get away, and before a message arrived ordering her detention.

"How long before they get here?" Maihara asked.

Katan pursed his lips. "We hope we will stop them from getting here at all. But from their reported position and likely rate of advance, they could reach this area in a day, unless opposed."

Told you so, Maihara thought. "If this is going to be a war zone, I'd like to leave without delay." The thought that this column might be searching for her tugged at her heart.

Katan frowned. "We are still discussing this. You need a suitable escort."

"Of course," she said. "But you have drafted the message to warn Retis. Perhaps you have an officer in mind to deliver it? I'll take responsibility for leaving with a small escort. I don't wish to deprive your command of valuable soldiers."

"We should not put your person at risk, Your Grace."

She sensed an opening. "It will be a severe embarrassment to the Empire if I'm captured here a second time," she said. "Even if I was by some chance uninjured."

Katan flinched. "Are you determined on this scheme, Your Grace?"

Maihara glanced at Aurian, who had remained silent. "I am. Unless you have a sensible alternative."

Some while later, Maihara and Aurian, now with fresh baggage, were put on two side-saddle horses and escorted by the ubiquitous Lieutenant Ferris in the direction of the river. She asked again about the welfare of the rebels captured during the raid, and Ferris reassured her that they were being well treated.

"Are you sure this is wise?" Aurian asked Maihara as they left.

"I hope so. Do you think Tarchon will hold back his attack if he suspects I am here?"

Aurian shook her head.

Ferris wore a dark green uniform, rather fancier than that of the rebels, with blue piping on the trousers and bits of braid and redundant shiny buttons on the jacket, topped by a flat cap. Of medium height, he had a build that suggested muscular strength and moved with the confidence of a man able to handle himself. He had short brown hair, a small moustache and a nervous smile that suggested he was both proud and apprehensive about being selected to escort the Princess. The soldiers had a similar outfit with less braid.

Ferris, she had discovered, was a younger son from an

aristocratic family, and had entered the army after a term at a military college. All his friends and family supported the Imperial regime.

Maihara questioned Ferris on their destination.

"We're heading for a village some way south of where we found you," Ferris said. "The river flows in a loop so the distance is not so far by road."

"And what was that fort by the river?" she asked. "Will that hold them up much?"

"Montfer? It depends on how long it can hold out. They might bypass it." Ferris looked away and kneed his horse into motion. Their route took them past fields in which thick-stalked plants with long curling leaves lay in yellowing heaps, and fields in which skinny cattle grazed, flicking away flies. They rode by mean-looking wattle and thatch farmhouses where carts and ploughs made of unpainted wood and crude agricultural implements lay outside.

By dusk, they reached a small village on the riverbank. A street of timber-boarded houses straggled down to the shore, most of them single storey huts, unpainted and in a poor state of repair. The column of over a dozen smartly uniformed soldiers descended a street that was no more than a strip of stones and mud. Country folk dressed in dull, patched clothes gaped at them and stepped back between buildings or into doorways. None of them looked over-fed. Maihara was conscious that the cost of her outfit or the soldiers' elaborate uniforms would probably have outfitted the whole village. If this was what country life was like under the Empire, maybe the rebels had a point.

At the shore, a wooden platform on poles stuck in the mud and water jutted out into the river, which looked around forty yards wide here. Several small boats were tied up to it or pulled up onto the riverbank. A muddy street and a single line of huts and mean houses ran along the shore. A few nets dangled from poles.

A thin-faced trooper called Calcas helped Maihara from her horse, and she stood on the landward end of the dock, one of the few patches of ground that wasn't muddy. Ferris went to ask about hiring or commandeering a boat and disappeared from view. A stout man outside a hut with an ill-painted sign was trying to attract the attention of the soldiers. She looked again. This seemed to be an inn serving the village and the riverside pier. Several of the soldiers disappeared inside, but Maihara, mindful of the accommodation she had quit earlier that day, had no inclination to follow.

Aurian stood beside Maihara, looking around with disdain. "This is a miserable place. I hope we're not lingering here long." Aurian looked upriver. "Which way are we going?"

Maihara pointed downriver.

"And where is the rebel barge fleet?"

Maihara pointed upriver. In the gloom, the reedy banks curved to the right. "If we can believe Ferris, they may be up there." She showed Aurian the first and second fingers of her right hand, crossed for luck, a gesture she had picked up from hcr maids.

A group of grubby and ragged village children had gathered to stare at them hopefully. They whispered among themselves, jostling and squelching their bare feet in the mud.

"Have you any money to give them?" Maihara asked in a low voice.

"Not a good idea," Aurian said. "They'll just swarm us, asking for more. Ferris can deal with them."

Maihara nodded, with reluctance. "What's keeping him, anyway?" She caught the attention of one of the soldiers still guarding them and the horses. "What's keeping Lieutenant Ferris?"

"He be looking for a man with a boat, Ma'am."

Ferris presently appeared, accompanied by one of the village men, and strode out onto the pier. They were looking down on one of the larger boats, which had a long, low cabin on it and two masts. Ferris jumped onto the boat, disappeared for a moment then returned. The two men were arguing.

Maihara waited with impatience, then strode along the pier. Planks rang hollowly under her riding boots. Words of the argument became clearer.

"What's the problem?"

The boat owner, a black-haired, stocky, brown-faced man wearing shapeless trews and an open leather coat over a grimy pale shirt, looked up.

"He's objecting to having his boat commandeered," Ferris said. "Says he'll be beggared. I've explained twice that he can make a claim." He tapped his sword. "I don't want to use force."

Maihara spared the boat a glance. This shouldn't be the issue. "Look, Ferris, you'll need him and one or two of the local men to work the boat. Hire them. They can bring the boat back here. Give them some money. Now can we get on with this?"

Ferris's mouth fell open. She could tell by the glint of his teeth. "Yes, Your Grace."

Ferris engaged in further discussion with the boat owner. Pale water-birds swam by. Maihara tapped a boot on the planking. It occurred to her that Ferris might have limited funds for his mission. Katan had not given her any money, but her outfit had pearls and a brooch.

"He'll take us," Ferris announced. He ran a palm over his forehead. "We can stay here overnight and leave at first light."

"Here? Where?"

"At the inn." Ferris pointed ashore.

"Is that a joke?" Maihara's lips tightened. "I don't think so."

"It looks dirty," Aurian chimed in.

"Then we can sleep on the boat, and sail at dawn," Ferris said in a weary tone. "I'll get your baggage aboard."

Maihara glanced upriver, into the gloom of the river bend. A prickling of unease crept up her spine. "The rebels can't be far away. We should sail tonight."

"You said they don't move at night," Ferris objected.

"But they might still scout. After what you did, they'll want to make their positions safe."

"We should move," Aurian said, voice edged with anxiety. "I agree with the Princess."

"It's getting too dark to see where we're going," Ferris objected.

"I can still see which way is downriver," Maihara said. "What does the boatman say? He should know his river."

The boatman grumbled when the question was put to him, but conceded that it could be managed. "But if we run on the mud, we could be stuck there till first light," he concluded.

Maihara's sense of unease increased as the baggage was put on board, another villager found, and eight soldiers selected to come with them. The remainder would take the horses back to the Army headquarters in the morning. Ferris had managed to buy some local produce and a few fish to supplement the Army rations from the saddlebags.

"If they haven't drunk that inn dry," Aurian said, with a wry smile.

All appeared to be ready. Maihara looked down on the shadowy boat.

"We could order grilled fish to take with us," Ferris suggested.

Maihara's patience snapped. "No, we'll go now!" The Imperials were too complacent over the position of the rebel barges, and the rebels might be much closer than Ferris assumed.

Ferris looked hurt. "Very well, Your Grace. I thought you might be hungry."

"It's fine. Let's go." She had not thought about food since they arrived at the village.

"I don't want anything," Aurian said from below. "Let's go."

A soldier with an unusually flat nose helped Maihara down a slimy ladder into the boat. She sat on a hard bench as the boat cast off and slipped away from the dock. The boatmen hoisted a sail.

Almost silently, the boat slid downriver. The outlines of trees on the bank showed dark against the sky. The night was mostly clouded, but a few stars and a sliver of moon peeked out.

After they had been moving for some minutes, her acute feeling of unease had not diminished. She looked astern, straining to make out anything in the gloom.

The boatman was looking in the same direction. "There be another boat," he announced, in a low voice.

"What?" Maihara's fears were re-ignited. "A barge?"

"No, a smaller boat. I think it be making for the jetty at my village."

It could be rebels, still searching for her. "Ferris, there's another boat," Maihara said.

"Where?"

The boatman and Maihara pointed.

"I see it. Keep quiet, all of you. No noise, no splashing."

The boat slipped downriver, with a faint chuckle of water under the bow. Maihara thought she could see a second boat behind. It too headed for the jetty. Was there a third? The distance was increasing, and ahead the river made a shallow bend.

***

Maihara stirred and came fully awake. Her bed rocked slowly. She was aboard the boat on which she had got away from the grimy riverside village. Morning light shone through small round windows, illuminating the forward cabin she shared with Lady Aurian. A bunk bed was fitted on either side, and most of their luggage remained in leather cases on the cabin floor. Her leg and side itched where something had bitten her during the night. The bunk was hard, and the air in the cabin smelt sour and stuffy.

It was the fifth day of their river journey. As they'd left the first riverside village, other boats had emerged from the gloom and landed. So far, they had seen nothing more, but each evening her unease at being overtaken and recaptured grew. What was she trying to do? Initially, she had dismissed Tarchon's denunciation of the Empire as rebel bias and slander, but she had seen the state of an Imperial regiment for herself, and witnessed abject rural poverty. It looked as though the rebels were right, and she did not want the Empire to continue like this. But she could not bring herself to wish for the defeat and overthrow of all that she knew, nor, after seeing the carnage on the barge, the crushing of the rebels, who were mostly decent and had good intentions. There ought to be a middle way.

Was Tarchon thinking of her? They had seemed on the brink of a significant relationship. She had worried about being disloyal to the Empire when courting a friendship with him. Now she felt she was being disloyal to him. Would he believe she had not tried to escape? Fate, in the form of the Imperial raiding party, had intervened. She was, with luck, on her way to Shardan, where she could make her own fate.

She pulled on her dress and went up onto the deck. The river was wider here with a slick of mud below either bank, and the air bore a taint of salt, of rotting weed as they neared the sea. The sky arced white with thin cloud, and a fresh breeze tousled her hair. Two soldiers tugged at a sail rope. Ferris sat on the cabin top, head bare, chewing on a piece of dried fish. They had taken food with them, but were sustained by fish caught from the river and flat bread bought from riverside halts each day. The boatman stared ahead, shading his eyes with one hand. Soon they would be reaching Retis.

A soldier pointed. "What's that?"

Maihara looked. A white line stretched across the river from bank to bank, some way ahead. It was moving closer.

"A wave!" the crewman from the village shouted.

The wave, for that it was, foamed closer. It was high, higher than the boat's side, rushing toward them as fast as a horse could run. Maihara stared, fingers in her mouth. This couldn't be natural. A magical attack? Some magician had tracked her. Her guts clamped with fear.

"'Ware water!" the boatman shouted. "Close hatches!"

The wave was upon them. The front of the boat reared

up. Maihara lost her balance, fell, rolled sideways, slid off the cabin top with a wail, down onto the narrow side deck and just as the boat was about to pitch her into the water, she caught hold of a taut rope tied to the deck side.

She clung there, heart hammering, as the boat pitched and shuddered in the rough water behind the wave. Trooper Ostein reached down and grabbed her arm, hauled her from her awkward position.

"A water-horse. We've been attacked by a water-horse!" a soldier cried. "I knew this was a bad voyage."

"Nonsense, man," the boatman said. "It was the tidal bore."

"What?" Maihara said. "You mean it wasn't... weird?"

"No," Ferris said. "That was a tidal bore. Never seen one, but I've read about them. The incoming tide gets funnelled into the river."

"How can that be?" Maihara, eager to hide her momentary panic, wanted details.

"It's what happens when a fast tide floods up a narrowing estuary, Your Grace."

She hoped he was right.

By afternoon the same day they reached the estuary and sailed past flat reedy marshlands swarming with pink and gold oyster birds. They had nearly been swamped by the tidal bore, and some of the baggage had got wet, but they had been able to sail on. Now, ahead, there was no riverbank, just a low grey line where sea met sky.

The riverboat, rolling uneasily in waves that came from the sea, hugged the left-hand bank. Plantations of small trees, planted in regimented rows, sloped down to the waterside. Birds with white and grey feathers soared above, making a curious keening cry, or stood with webbed feet on mud banks.

"The water's disappearing," Maihara said. "There's more mud."

"The tide's going out."

"Oh, tides, right." She felt a little foolish, and slapped

her forehead. Ferris smiled back. The water ahead sparkled silver in the afternoon light. Barges navigated up and down the wide river, and several larger vessels lay at anchor downriver. Smoke rose inland and drifted east. She hoped it was from industry, not war.

As dusk fell, a large town lay ahead of them on the left bank. Yellow light already glimmered from a mass of buildings rising above the river. Soon, Maihara's boat slid into the harbour at Retis, alongside fishing boats and coasters. She had completed the first part of her journey. The harbour smelt of fish and sea-salt, and bits of garbage floated on the water alongside the seagoing vessels and an assortment of small boats. She looked around, taking in the forest of masts, the stone harbour wall and lighthouse tower with its brazier, and the wood sheds that ran along the inner side of the harbour. Men bustled along the quays, loading and unloading carts, hauling bundles of goods off and on boats, and shouting.

Beyond the crumbling harbour defences, the town rose up a slope. A handful of stone-built buildings of better quality stood out from the lines of mean-looking tiled roofs.

Being in harbour raised the prospect of getting off the cramped and uncomfortable riverboat and into someplace better appointed.

"What a disagreeable place," Lady Aurian said. "I hope they can provide us with some proper accommodation."

"If there is any," Maihara said. Her chest tightened. Instructions concerning her might have reached the authorities here, but she had little choice but to make a bold face of it.

An Imperial flag fluttered above one of the buildings. Maihara gave thought to her mission here. Many people would die or be left destitute or bereaved if the rebels continued their advance across the Empire, capturing cities by force. If they failed to capture Retis, their violent advance might fizzle out. After that, they might reach some truce or compromise. A middle way?

She felt badly about betraying the rebel plans. Her

loyalty should lie with the Empire that had created and formed her, she told herself.

Ferris bore the official message, and they would have to contact the military authorities and warn them of the rebel attack plan.

The boat tied up at an outer pier, and the crew lowered the sails. The boat's galley smoked, preparing another basic meal for her escort and the crew. Ferris sent a soldier to buy some fresh shellfish to supplement their so-far unvarying fare.

"Can we get off and talk the military authorities?" Maihara asked Ferris.

"Of course, Your Grace. At once."

By the time they reached the landward part of the harbour with their baggage, the sky had darkened and oil lamps flared around the few boats that were loading or discharging cargo. Ferris hailed a two-horse carriage, and they set off with a reduced escort in search of the military headquarters. They crossed two wooden bridges arching over water, possibly the spiral moat about which she had read, constructed by stages as the town grew.

"Why a spiral?" Maihara wanted to know.

"I suppose they found it easier than filling in the original moat and starting again," Ferris said.

After several false turns the driver took them to a stone-built building where glowing lamps showed a couple of soldiers guarding an arched entrance in a windowed frontage.

Ferris shouted an enquiry. The reply confirmed that this was the right building. The place did not look to Maihara like a hive of military activity.

She and Aurian followed Ferris as he went to the guard office under the arch, which led to a shadowy courtyard.

A young officer with a single rank stripe on his shoulders put down a book and looked at them from behind a desk. In the lamplight, his face registered a mild surprise.

Ferris entered the office with a confident step. "I have urgent military intelligence for the senior officer commanding the Retis district."

The young officer hesitated. "I don't think he's here. Most of the senior officers will have returned to their residences by now. I'll see if I can find anyone." He rose and disappeared through a doorway in the back of the room, calling, "Trooper!"

Maihara heard muffled orders being given, then the officer returned. "I've sent to see who's available."

She sighed. It seemed that the brave defenders of Retis did not do much soldiering after dark.

The officer picked up his book, then lowered it again. "What's your message about?"

"A rebel advance," Ferris told him.

"What? Where?" the officer said, wide-eyed.

"Down river. Toward Retis," Ferris said.

"Are they close?"

"Close enough."

After several minutes, the soldier returned. "Colonel Vexis will see you now."

-21-

The lieutenant jerked his head toward the green inner door, and Ferris, Maihara and Aurian followed the soldier along the dimly lit silent passages of the Retis military headquarters. The turns confused Maihara and chills pricked her spine. She did not know what reception she would get here at the end of these cream-walled corridors.

They entered a plain, lamplit room where three men in green Imperial uniforms sat at desks scattered with papers. One rose as they arrived; a man with thinning fair hair.

"You're the fellow with the message?"

"Yes, sir," Ferris said, taking a step forward.

"And who are these ladies?"

"Witnesses," Ferris said shortly.

Maihara's breathing quickened.

"And what's the gist of this?"

"The rebels are advancing downriver. They intend to take Retis by a surprise attack, sir." Ferris held out a folded paper. "Perhaps you'd like to read this, sir. General Katan's message."

Colonel Vexis took a minute to read the paper, while Maihara tried not to hold her breath, then he looked up. "So, you're Ferris?"

"Yes, sir."

Grey eyes under sandy eyebrows eyed Maihara and Aurian with renewed interest. "And these ladies are?"

Maihara, dry-mouthed, nudged Aurian who spoke up. "This is Her Grace the Imperial Princess Maihara Zircona. I am Lady Aurian."

The colonel started with surprise, and stared at Maihara, before going down on one knee. "My sincere apologies,

Your Grace. I didn't realise. The fellow didn't say."

Maihara, relieved, put on her most courtly voice. "It is of no consequence, Colonel. Please rise."

The colonel stood and made a quick bow. "Do you require any refreshment, Your Grace?"

Maihara waved a hand dismissively. "That can wait. Will you act on this?"

"Certainly. But I can't act on my own authority. This will have to go before General Xaris, commanding, and he isn't here till mid-morning." He paused and glanced at the paper again.

Maihara tapped her foot on the floor in irritation. She wanted the man to take the message and act on it, protect Retis, not stand there raising pointless objections. She needed to eat and rest.

"You overheard the rebel plans yourself, Your Grace?"

Maihara contained her annoyance. "That's right."

"How did you overhear this, Your Grace, from whom, and what exactly did they say?"

"It's summarised in the report, Colonel," Maihara told him. "I'm not entirely ignorant of military talk. I've heard enough of it these past months. Their intentions were perfectly clear." She clenched her fists.

The colonel turned to Ferris. "You saw the rebel barges, Lieutenant?"

"Yes, we scouted it before making our raid. It looked like a substantial force, in brigade strength."

The colonel put down the paper and tapped it with a forefinger. "I'll bring it to the General's attention as soon as he arrives."

"Colonel, can't we find this general tonight and show him the message? We sailed day and night to get here ahead of the rebel fleet, but they may be only hours behind us."

The colonel hesitated. "Well, you are at liberty to do that, Your Grace. I understand that the General is hosting a dinner party at his residence. I'll give you directions, but I don't know how readily he'll respond to this message."

Maihara snorted. She suspected that the general might be drunk.

Ferris stretched out a hand for the message. "With your permission, sir, I can escort the Princess there."

"As you wish." The colonel kept his hand on the paper. "Before you go, I'll get this copied so that I can present it as necessary."

"Yes, sir."

"Very well," Maihara said. It would be a small price to pay for keeping the colonel onside. "And can't you at least raise an alert or send scouts on your own authority?"

"I'll alert the sentries and put men on standby, Your Grace," Colonel Vexis said, with a vague gesture.

The copying took longer than Maihara had anticipated, and despite a cup of Army tea she was chafing with impatience by the time the colonel returned the original message. Lady Aurian was nodding over her cup.

"Let's be off," Maihara said.

Ferris saluted. "With your permission, sir?"

Ferris pocketed the message, and they set off back to the gatehouse.

Half an hour later, after crossing another long wooden bridge over the old spiral moat whose waters glittered blackly in lamplight, their carriage arrived at a mansion on the outskirts of the town. A fuming Maihara took in the scene with a glance. The yellow glow of lamps lit up a long facade of dressed stone. Wheel tracks marked the gravel of the carriage turning space in front of the pillared portico. Half a dozen carriages were parked to one side of the space, their carriage men squatting beside them in a group.

This was Retis's state of readiness for attack, and they expected her to sort it out herself.

A footman in an ornate civilian servant's uniform approached, boots crunching on the gravel. "Are you expected?" he intoned.

"No, but I have an urgent military message," Ferris told him. "And I'm sure he will admit this lady." He indicated

Maihara.

"May I have a name, sir?" the servant asked.

"Her Grace the Imperial Princess Maihara Zircona."

The servant made an audible gasp. He hurried off and disappeared through the main entrance.

Maihara waited under the portico with thumping heart, hoping that details of her differences with the Imperial regime had not reached the general. Faint sounds of music and merriment came from within.

Minutes later, a grey-haired, red-faced man in dress uniform, decked with medals and shoulder stripes, emerged from the hall. He stopped on sighting Maihara and bowed low.

"Your Grace, I presume?"

"Indeed, and you are General Xaris, I assume?"

"The same. This is a great surprise, and a pleasure. Welcome to Retis. May I serve you in any way? I am sorry you were kept waiting at the door."

"General, we have an urgent message for you. Lieutenant?" She beckoned to Ferris.

"Oh," the general said, indicating this was of less interest than an Imperial visitor.

Ferris produced the paper and offered it to the general.

The general held it under a lamp and read it, lips moving.

"The rebels are advancing downriver," the general said, looking up from the document.

"Yes, sir," Ferris said. "They threaten Retis."

"Yes, yes, but when?"

"Imminently, sir."

"When were they last sighted?" the general asked in a querulous tone.

Ferris stood his ground, looking confident but respectful. "Six days ago, sir."

"Where?"

"At the Montfer fort, sir."

"And any evidence that they've advanced?"

"It's in the message, sir. The Princess overheard their

plans."

The general blinked. "How could that be?"

"I was their prisoner," Maihara said, "till an Imperial raiding party freed me. I had plenty of opportunity to overhear their plans."

"Which are?"

"A rapid advance downriver, and seize the coastal town on the estuary with a multi-element attack."

"But she's a girl, with respect." He glanced at Maihara. "She could have misunderstood what she heard."

"We already had this conversation at the barracks," Maihara said, further annoyed that the general was addressing Ferris rather than herself. "I am familiar with military talk, and I am in no doubt about what I heard."

The general frowned. "Who else saw or heard anything?"

"I witnessed a large number of barges filled with rebels, sir," Ferris said.

"Anyone else?"

"One of our scouts reported a rebel force advancing by land, sir."

"I have guests. I'll discuss this with my staff tomorrow morning."

"Tomorrow morning?" Maihara said, her temper rising. "The rebels intend to strike before your defences are ready. They could be at Retis by tomorrow morning."

"With great respect, Your Grace, you should leave military matters to those who have experience of them." The general's words were slightly slurred.

Maihara pressed her lips together, repressing an urge to say something very rude. She could smell wine on the general's breath. Shouting at this drunken fool was not going to help.

"We'll call again tomorrow morning," she said.

The general swayed in the lamplight. "Why not join our party here, Your Grace?"

Maihara glanced at Ferris and Aurian, then nodded. "That would be most gracious."

"Where are you staying, Your Grace?"

"We don't know yet," Maihara said.

"Then you must stay here," he said. "My wife and I would be most honoured."

Maihara was developing a dislike of this general, but it would make sense to stay here instead of trailing around in the dark finding suitable accommodation. Actually, she had no idea what accommodation was available or how they were going to secure it.

"You are most kind, General, I'll accept your gracious invitation."

With an expansive gesture, the general bid them enter. They passed through a pair of glazed inner doors, into a double-height hall with a grand staircase. Light and noise spilled out of rooms to their right.

"Come meet my wife, and our guests," the general urged, making a sweeping gesture in the direction of the noisy rooms.

"I would really like to freshen up first," Maihara said, favouring the general with her best smile. "It has been a long and disagreeable journey."

"The Princess needs to change out of her travelling clothes," Aurian said.

Ferris had turned and was beckoning his soldiers forward with the baggage.

"Oh, yes, of course, Your Grace." General Xaris summoned a servant and ordered him to show Maihara to the best guest suite.

Upstairs, the servant showed Maihara into a grand bedroom with a four-poster bed, dark wood furniture of fine quality, and soft furnishings in matching fawn and green colours.

"I didn't know our generals lived like this," Maihara said to Ferris. The rebel officers certainly did not. Ferris said nothing.

Aurian explored the adjoining rooms. "There's a bathroom in there, and a small room through that door."

"We can put the bodyguards in there," Maihara said.

"You'll need to change quickly, Your Grace," Aurian said to her.

"I'll take all the bloody time I want," Maihara said. "I want a wash, and then I'll go down. I'd rather go straight to bed."

Aurian clicked her tongue. "Your Grace, if you want to get these people to listen to you, it would be better not to start by snubbing them."

Maihara sighed, and shrugged. She had to go downstairs and influence hearts and minds. She turned to the general's servant. "Can we get hot water up here?"

Some time later, Maihara and Aurian, now changed into more showy dresses, descended the main staircase escorted by Ferris and one of his soldiers.

"Where's the General?" Maihara asked a passing servant. He bowed and pointed to one of the function rooms, from which light and a chatter of conversation spilled.

Maihara stepped into the room with Aurian at her side. She paused, noting its opulence as a score of eyes turned to stare in her direction. The long saloon had a coffered ceiling with chandeliers, paintings hung on papered russet walls and there was a lot of gilt. Other senior officers might be present, and if so, delivering her message a third time might provoke quicker action, if aided by her Imperial authority.

A servant, bald and wearing an elaborate servant's uniform, sidled up to her. "Whom shall I announce?" he intoned.

"Her Grace the Imperial Princess Maihara Zircona," Aurian said.

"Her Grace Imperial Princess Maihara Zircon," the man declaimed in a loud voice.

"And the lady Aurian," Maihara added.

"And the lady Aurian."

A murmur of anticipation went around the grand room. Maihara stepped forward. There ought to be something to eat or drink in here, and she felt famished. Through the crowd, she glimpsed a side-table with an array of glasses and bottles on it, and made purposeful steps in that direction. Several richly dressed gentlemen and their ladies got in her way.

"So glad to meet you, Your Grace," said one, making a deep bow. "Can I possibly be of service?"

She turned with a slight smile. "You could fetch me something to drink."

"Of course, Your Grace. Wine?"

"Yes, sweet white."

"At once." The fellow turned on his heels and pushed his way through the crowd.

"And is there anything to eat?" she asked a remaining gentleman.

"The dinner's finished, Your Grace, but I'm sure we could find something—"

"There's fruit tarts and cake in here," the man's lady companion cut in.

"That will be most welcome."

"At once, Your Grace." The gentleman turned and pushed others out of his way.

Maihara had a glass in her hand and was fending off a dozen questions when the general wove into view.

"Your Grace, I am so glad you could come down. May I introduce you to my lady wife?" He looked around for a moment, puzzled, till a grey-haired woman in an expensive green silk dress, adorned with pearls, made her way forward.

The general's wife curtsied low, displaying a wrinkled cleavage.

Maihara was answering the inevitable question of how she came to be here when the plate of fruit tarts arrived. She turned to look for Ferris, who stood directly behind her, seemingly at ease with the distinguished gathering. "If you could hold these for me, Lieutenant?"

"The rebels held me prisoner by for some time," she said, "but while they were moving me south, their expedition was raided by the gallant Lieutenant here, and I was rescued. It seemed wise for me to head for Retis, as the Lieutenant had some military intelligence to deliver."

"Nothing to worry about," the general interrupted.

As various guests expressed their horror and fascination about her capture and escape, Maihara took a fruit pie and crammed part of it into her mouth. Her stomach felt as though it and food were strangers. Ferris tried to deliver a warning look.

Maihara did not agree that there was nothing to worry about. She saw nothing wrong in spreading a bit of panic, to underline the seriousness of the message. Her chance came almost at once.

"Where are those rebels now, Your Grace? Did the Lieutenant bring you far?"

"We don't know where they are," she said. "We last saw a large force of them several days ago near Radukamaris, travelling downriver toward Retis."

Her audience made startled exclamations of unease.

"It's nothing to worry over, I assure you," the general said, scowling at Maihara.

She resisted the temptation to reply. The guests did not seem reassured.

Maihara found that her wineglass was empty. She accepted another.

"Go easy on the wine," Aurian said in her ear.

"You were a prisoner of the rebels? Were you dreadfully mistreated? It must have been awful," a bejewelled lady in a heavily embroidered cream and gold gown said.

"It was dire," Maihara said. "The accommodation was sub-standard, and they never got my titles right."

Lieutenant Ferris chuckled. Some of her audience did not seem to get the joke.

"We should execute all those rebellious brutes," one of the noblemen said.

"I find that kind of talk unhelpful," Maihara said, in a sharp tone, remembering Tarchon, Chavin and others. "Most of them are decent people. They just have different ideas on how the Empire ought to be run. We need a settlement, not a massacre."

There was an awkward silence.

"I'm not sure the Princess meant exactly that," Aurian said.

"In the contrary, I meant exactly what I said," Maihara said. Tiredness and anger made her less cautious than she might have been. "It was answering legitimate complaints with a massacre that caused the revolt in the first place. We need more talking and listening, and less killing."

The general swayed toward her, scowling and red-faced, looking drunker and more aggressive than before. "I wonder how you got free, Princess. Maybe the rebels sent you here to spread their ideas and spread panic."

Maihara stood her ground and looked him in the eye. "I don't find remarks of that sort at all helpful, General."

"How do we know you're not an impostor?"

"I know how my father would react to that sort of remark," Maihara said.

"We know Her Grace is not an impostor," Ferris said. Maihara glanced around. He had his feet planted well apart and his right hand covering his sword hilt.

"Bah!" The general turned around and stumbled off.

A buzz of scandalised chatter rose.

"That went well, Your Grace," Aurian said. "Shall we retire before you start another civil war?"

"I'm hungry," Maihara said, reaching for another fruit tart.

"We can get room service," Aurian said.

Upstairs, Maihara kicked off her strappy shoes and threw one across the room. "That man's a drunken idiot. If our generals are all like him, I can see why the Imperial side is losing the war."

"And your remarks didn't help," Lady Aurian said.

"I'm tired. It feels as though these people want to stir up rebellion and be overrun. Am I the only one who cares? Where's Ferris? Tell him to wake us if there is any sign of the rebel attack."

-22-

Next morning, Lieutenant Ferris called in again at the Retis army barracks. His charge, the Imperial Princess, was being escorted to the mansion of a nobleman who had been at General Xaris's dinner party, the previous night. His understanding was that Her Grace planned to remain there for the rest of the day, at least. The noble had extended his invitation at the party, and Her Grace had accepted, leaving the General and his wife a polite note of thanks on her departure. After Ferris finally put Her Grace on a ship, he supposed he should stay to help defend the town. An Imperial officer should not think solely of saving his own skin.

Ferris straightened his cap and checked that his uniform and personal grooming were in order, then asked for the colonel they had spoken to on the previous night. As he entered the Colonel's office an orderly wandered by with a sheaf of paper files. Colonel Vexis regarded him with bleary eyes, while Ferris saluted.

"What can I do for you - Ferris, isn't it?

"Has the General given any new orders, sir?" Ferris asked.

The colonel put a mug down on a pile of papers. "I had a message this morning. He has given orders to raise the alert level, which I had done already, and he requested that a military surveyor be sent out to look at the town's defences and report back. We could defend the town from behind a bastion of paperwork."

Vexis seemed a kindred spirit. Ferris grinned in sympathy. "And that's it?"

"So far. We can't get any naval support. Leave is being cancelled till further notice. Were you expecting more?"

"The Princess is," Ferris said. "She expects that a three-part attack will take place very soon. If she is correct, what do you think the chances are of the town repelling a well-planned attack in brigade strength?"

The colonel shook his head. "Let's hope she's wrong. Where is she? Still at the General's?"

"No, sir. Some local noble, Lord Arcenio has invited her to his mansion."

"Oh? Did something happen at the General's mansion?"

Ferris wondered how quickly gossip travelled in this town. Unwilling to make any criticism of the Imperial Princess, he straightened and in a more formal tone said, "We delivered the message. Words were exchanged after the Princess expressed certain political views criticising the repression. Some people were not pleased."

"That's not good. What if she tries to overrule the General? Who are we supposed to obey?"

"I looked up her date of birth back at headquarters in Radukamaris," Ferris said. "She's still under age."

The Colonel audibly released a breath. "Well, that's a relief. She'll not be exercising Imperial prerogative then."

"I suppose not. But she seems to have a keen interest in political and military matters, that one would not expect in a Court lady." Ferris had found most young ladies to be empty-headed creatures. The Princess was disconcertingly different, but it was not his place to judge a member of the Imperial Family.

"Just try to keep her out of trouble, Lieutenant."

Ferris took a carriage back through the town. Buildings in the outer parts of Retis were low and whitewashed, with gardens containing a lot of scorched greenery as well as small trees. People in the streets seemed untroubled by imminent war, and despite the late season, flowers of red, yellow or blue brightened some of the suburban plots.

At Lord Arcenio's mansion, a compact white building rather smaller than the General's, Ferris found the two ladies in a comfortable sitting room. The Imperial Princess received Ferris's report on the military situation with a frown. "There's a provincial governor. Could we not speak with him?"

Ferris was unsure. "I think he's based in some other part of the province. Also, I doubt if he can overrule military decisions."

"And there's a city mayor," the Princess said. "My hosts want to invite him this evening."

"He won't be able to do more than request military assistance, I should think."

She tapped on the inlaid side-table with her fingernails. "That's no good. It'll be nearly a day since we landed, and they're not doing anything. The rebels could arrive any time now."

"That depends of how much we outdistanced them. If they are not sailing by night, we should have half a day yet, or more."

"So they could arrive at first light tomorrow."

Ferris nodded.

"And there's no ship leaving today?" Lady Aurian asked.

"Nothing suitable," Ferris said. He couldn't put the Princess on some tub manned by cut-throats.

"You'll have another chance to influence people this evening," Lady Aurian said, examining her fingernails. "Try not to talk like a rebel."

The princess gave her a sharp look.

Ferris was mindful of the Colonel's exhortation to keep the princess out of trouble. He was already a little alarmed by her willingness to interfere in matters of grave importance. "If I may make a suggestion, Your Grace," he said. "We could go look at the beach to the south and see what the state of preparedness is there. I have never really seen the ocean."

In a flash her displeased expression was replaced by one of pleased anticipation. "Nor have I," she said. "Let's go."

Ferris summoned a hire carriage and his soldiers, and

they proceeded toward the shore, skirting the side of an impressive stone-faced defensive moat that curved through and around the town. Previous rulers of Retis had extended the spiral moat in stages as the town expanded, rather than fill in the existing defences and start again. Afternoon activity in the cobbled streets seemed normal. They passed along streets of low white-painted buildings, shops and humble residences busy with people.

At the seafront, a line of sea wall set with stout stakes defended the land, and a broad expanse of yellow sand stretched out to the waves over a hundred paces distant. The outward-facing, pointed stakes did not look to him like an impregnable defence. To the east, cyclopean blocks of fused stone tilted at angles stuck out of the waves, the sea-wrecked remains of some giant structure of the ancients. The crinkly water extended without other interruption to a low, flat horizon. As Maihara and the others got out of the carriage, a party of soldiers in Imperial uniform approached and asked if he brought any orders.

"I'm showing these ladies the sea," Ferris explained. "This is Her Grace the Imperial Princess Maihara Zircona."

Round-eyed, the soldiers saluted and stepped back. One of the soldiers had a crutch. On Ferris's enquiry, it emerged that they were all recovering from wounds. Not confidence inspiring.

The princess and Lady Aurian stood on top of the sea wall, staring at the water. A brisk wind from the sea flapped at the princess's heavy, russet velvet gown and bent and rippled the grass on the long dunes behind the shore. It stirred grains of sand on the wide, clean yellow beaches, and tore white caps off the grey waves in the estuary. Seagulls soared overhead making a mournful keening noise.

"It's so big," he heard the princess say. "Water as far as I can see. And where are those waves coming from?"

"From out there," Aurian said.

The princess pointed to the wide expanse of sand left by the receding tide. "That sand looks as though it's never been walked on since the beginning of the world. How can that be?"

Ferris could not hear Lady Aurian's reply over the wind and sea noise. She looked at him and said something in the princess's ear. The princess giggled.

Aurian gave her a sharp look.

Her Grace turned. "I don't see much here to stop the rebels coming ashore, do you?" she said.

"No," Aurian said. "We hardly need to ask Ferris his opinion."

The princess glanced across the beach at the group of Retis soldiers who had resumed their position at the top of the sea barrier. "They're not an impressive bunch, are they? This looks as defensible as a mud-castle."

Ferris had to agree. It was as if Retis was a convalescent camp. Were the rebels to arrive in force, these defenders might not be much use.

"Can you get that Colonel to send more men here, Ferris?"

"Yes, Your Grace." If there were any.

The princess pointed to the beach. "Can we walk down there? Is it safe?" Her face was flushed.

"We can if you wish, Your Grace," Ferris said. He was reminded of how young she was. He enjoyed being in the princess' presence - she was spirited and charming, but anything more, considering the difference in their social ranks - he crushed the dangerous thought.

They got down to the beach over a ramp of rubble and dry sand. The water was a hundred paces further out.

The princess hung back to speak to Ferris. "Let's walk further out. Is this sand good for landing armed men and their heavy gear, do you think?"

"Good point." He glanced at the armed and armoured escort following on their heels. The princess and Lady Aurian walked ahead over the damp sand. So far as he could hear, they chatted about unwarlike things.

Partway to the water, the princess stopped and turned abruptly. She pointed to the six soldiers of her escort, now closed up behind her and all uniformed and armed with short swords and pikes. She spluttered with laughter.

"They should be enough to guard me from the fish," she said to Aurian.

"Are you all right, Your Grace?" Ferris asked. He felt awkward, disconcerted by her high spirits. She was much less arrogant and snobbish than he would have expected of an Imperial Princess.

"Yes, it's nothing."

Closer to the water, the receding tide left the sand moist and smooth. Scattered over it lay brown wrack thrown up by the sea. The waves had disgorged a long, dark object onto the sand, left behind by the ebbing tide. "Down there!" the princess cried, pointing.

She tramped resolutely toward it, across a bank of clattering pebbles. Their boots splashed across a wet, water-rippled flat of drying sand. The dark object glistened. It was some kind of creature, most likely dead. Shells crunched under the boots of the soldiers.

Soon, the princess stood over the dead thing, staring at it with revulsion and bewilderment. Wind whipped at her hair and clothes, and there was a prevailing smell of seaweed.

As the guards tramped to her side she looked to Ferris, as if he ought to know what this meant. "What is it? Is there sorcery in this water?" she asked.

Ferris had no idea what the thing was. The dark-skinned corpse resembled a naked man, save that slits, with the tips of pale, feathery gills protruding, gaped from either side of its chest. He shivered. It was real, but it shouldn't be. The creature's skin had assumed a bleached, salty hue in the sun, while lidless, drying eyes stared dully upwards.

He stood back as the soldiers, less imaginative, crowded around the body, probing and examining it. One of them ventured to speak.

"It's an Aquan, Your Grace!"

"They're real?" the princess asked, looking surprised.

In his landlocked childhood he had read of such beings.

Trooper Calcas hesitated. "Sailors say they live deep in the sea, in great cities of rock and seaweed, and they got fabulous piles of gold down there."

Ferris glanced at the dead Aquan again. The tale seemed incredible, but the corpse was real enough. It stank of dead fish. Other such strange half-humans were said to walk the Earth: leopard-people, men who were half lizard and other creatures spawned by sorcery.

"Why did it die?" the princess asked.

"Perhaps it drowned in the air, Your Grace."

With a backward glance at the corpse, the princess walked further toward the water and a lump of pale jelly, only to retreat with a shriek as a wave broke and foamed up the sand. "It's frothy!"

On the way back from the beach a sensation of being watched made him turn. A man in a fisherman's plain clothes carrying a rod was behind them. Further up the street he glanced back again. The man was still there, following them. Not good. He could have the soldiers drive him off, but that might attract further attention.

***

"So much for the southern defences," Maihara said to Ferris, as they climbed back into the carriage. Her first sight of the ocean and one of its stranger denizens had exhilarated her.

"Maybe they intend to rush reinforcements in from a central point, if the rebels land there," Ferris said, in a reassuring tone. He fingered his small moustache.

Maihara shook her head. "Will that spiral moat help with that? What if they attack at a couple of other points a little earlier? That's the cleverness of the rebel plan. The reserves will be drawn to the first attacks, and the rebels will storm ashore here unopposed. Especially with that old drunk in charge."

Ferris didn't laugh, which caused her to think she was right.

"What about the other defences?" she asked. The state of the defences indicated she might have little time to make her escape should the rebels arrive without further warning, and she hoped her escort could be induced to take her by land, rather than putting her on a ship.

"You saw the harbour side yesterday. We could go look at the northern walls."

It sounded good to her. Ferris gave an instruction to the carriage driver.

Some while later, after detouring around the moats through the quiet eastern streets, past folk tending little gardens with flowers and late fruit, they arrived at the northern edge of the town. A weed-grown stone wall three times the height of a man blocked it off, and dozens of soldiers were working here, clearing the area behind the rampart and moving a heavy catapult and a pile of rounded stone missiles into position.

"Looks like they are taking action here," Ferris said. He led them to the top of a quieter section of the wall.

She stood on tip-toe. "What's on the other side of this?"

"Marshland, and a suburb." He pointed. "Mostly built on stilts."

"You're not serious?"

"It's cheap land. It floods when the river is high."

Maihara was mindful that the walls of Calah were a lot higher, and the rebels had still got in, apparently with assistance from within. There was less reason to worry about the golim menace here. Her conversations at General Xaris' party had turned up no further information, and the terrain around Retis, with its marshes and canals, did not seem suitable for the automatons that had disturbed her dreams.

"This might hold, if the rebels split their forces," Ferris said, brushing some wall grit from his uniform. The soldiers with them said nothing.

"All we can do is pray," Lady Aurian said.

Praying seemed a good idea. It might help her clear her mind for the soiree this evening, where she intended to alert the leading townspeople to the danger that faced them. And not mess up by pointing out the rebel grievances.

"Yes, let's. Is there a sanctuary of the One God in the town?" The last time she had prayed, it had been to the One God.

The others stared at her in surprise.

"You don't follow the Nine Gods?" Ferris asked. He seemed taken aback. The soldiers stared and a couple of them muttered.

"That's my private affair." She had never felt close to the Nine Gods' worship, and after her experiences in Calah the new religion had some meaning for her. She was uncomfortably aware that Monism was associated more with the poor and the rebellion than with the Imperial Family.

Aurian pursed her lips. "Visiting that place does not seem proper, Your Grace."

"Why not?" Maihara felt obliged to justify herself. "We should find out what the mood of the Monists is. Somebody might be preaching revolt in there."

"If you say so, Your Grace," Ferris said with a frown. "I just assumed you followed the official religion." The official religion was that of the Nine Gods, worshipped by the powerful and the conservative elements, while the poor, radicals and rebels followed more the newer creed of the One God. The reaction of Ferris and the soldiers made her uncomfortable but not willing to back down.

"I'll ask the driver," Ferris said, in a reluctant tone.

The route took them past battered shop fronts and wary citizens to a poorer part of the town, where a plain hall with a double front stood in a back street. There were a lot of shabby whitewashed tenements and small shops with faded paint here. Was this what most of her Empire looked like, outside its opulent palaces?

Ferris made a brief enquiry at the entrance, while the rest of the troop hung back, eyeing her with surmise. Left to her own devices, she might have walked away, but did not want to look fickle in front of the others.

"There's a service in progress," he announced. "We can go in."

In the doorway, a knot of men in scruffy working clothes obstructed her progress. "Make way for Her Grace the Imperial Princess Maihara Zircona," Ferris said in a loud voice.

The men stepped aside on seeing the Imperial uniforms, but scowled and stared at her. One detached himself and ran inside.

"What the Tab do they want?" a male voice muttered behind her.

Maihara's heart sank. Didn't they understand that she just wanted to make a quiet prayer?

Inside was a plain rectangular space with whitewashed block walls, spanned by triangular wooden roof trusses of dark wood. A mass of citizens stood or crouched, facing the far end where a white-clad servant of the God stood on a dais, intoning a prayer. Maihara and her escort stopped at the back. Worshippers turned to stare at her escort, and edged away from them.

Unhappily, she waited. Surely they would stop staring and whispering if the soldiers did nothing. It had not been like this when she attended the small One God hall in Calah, some time after her capture. One of her escort brought her a hard chair. Gradually, the disturbance died.

Maihara closed her eyes, blocking out the soldiers and others standing around her. The priest was speaking of the need for brothers to help each other, to attend to the words of the Prophet and his wife the Prophetess, and to fear the judgement of the One God which would be visited on the unjust. At intervals the worshippers responded with a mass mumble of "Let it be thus."

Soon she also filtered out the priest's words. She needed guidance. Was it right to use her magic to spy on the rebels and betray their secrets, when she had promised not to escape? If people died as a result, would their blood and angry souls accuse her? What would the One God say to her? She admired the Empire's ambition, order and opulence. But she was losing faith in an Empire that was decadent, incompetent and left most of its people in want.

The rebels promised something better, but their methods led to destruction, death and anarchy. Should she be loyal to the Empire which had created her, whose leader and servants had not treated her kindly, or to rebels who had? If only there was a middle way.

The fresh air and the walking, together with the droning priest, made her sleepy. Her eyelids drooped.

She imagined herself on a metal throne with sculpted arms. A man in Varlord uniform brought her a report denouncing a corrupt noble, and bowed low. "Have that criminal arrested," she ordered. Another brought her reports of famine. She gave orders for granaries...

She opened her eyes, and tuned in again to the priest's words. "A man may strike a blow in a just cause. So says the Prophet. A man may not strike to satisfy his anger, so says the Prophetess."

Was that it? She had to follow her true feelings, and act in a just cause? That was an answer of sorts. But the priest also said that men should treat each other as brothers and be just. And the daydream was just a daydream. She could find no answer here that satisfied her, save to seek a way of ending the fighting.

They exited when the service ended. The common people emerging behind them were all staring and pointing at her, and talking among themselves in a murmur of voices. A few called out, not in a hostile way.

Ferris had made the carriage wait. Now he eyed the crowd with a wary look. "We are not far from your lodgings, Your Grace. Shall we return?"

She nodded. "Did you hear anything seditious?"

Ferris shook his head. They set off and soon reached a more opulent part of the town. The carriage approached a temple of the Nine Gods, though the frieze outside only represented the sea-god Laogonus. The building, of cut, smoothed and carved stone, was bigger and more richly endowed than the One God sanctuary, as befitted the Empire's approved religion. Maihara had the carriage stop, and got down, unsure whether to go in. If it got about that a member of the Imperial Family did not support the Nine Gods, it would cause a scandal she did not need right now.

The sea-god statues outside the carved doors had been damaged, perhaps by looters removing gems or gilding. One of the three-pronged fish spears was bent. Perhaps the rebels were causing dissension and violence here even before the arrival of their attacking army. A priest with a dark robe embroidered with symbols and the mark of the Nine wielded a broom outside, sweeping up.

Carved designs adorned the upper front of the temple, including a cross and cup she had noted in her magic book back in Calah. Magical designs? She sent out her magical sense to probe the location, preparatory to trying a spell. There was magical connection here, most likely not just in the temple but in all this part of Retis. Her spirits lifted. The presence of a magical connection was reassuring. She wondered though why magic was only available in certain places, generally urban areas.

As Maihara stood in front of the temple, the priest lifted his head and made the sign of warding against evil in their direction.

She tensed. "Why is that old fraud making the sign of the evil eye at us?"

Ferris had spotted the gesture and immediately had the escort block off the priest's retreat, and confronted the man. "What are you making that sign for? Do you mean to insult the Imperial forces?"

The priest flinched, but pointed a wrinkled finger in their direction. "It's her. She carries the mark of a Vimrashan. It's unnatural for a woman to practise magic. They're dangerous and uncontrolled."

A tingling of alarm swept over Maihara, as a prickle of sweat damped her body. How could this fellow pick her out? No, he appeared to be shouting at her chaperone and his gaze fixed in that direction. Maihara whipped her head around to see a look of fear and confusion on Aurian's pale face. So far as Maihara knew, Vimrashans did not have a distinctive appearance that would stand out in a crowd. The assertion that she was descended from Vimrashan witch-queens was not generally known to the population, and she wanted to keep it unknown.

Maihara pointed at the priest. "A lie," she shouted. "You just don't like women."

"Clear off, you windbag." Ferris gestured to the soldiers, who thrust the priest backwards into the temple doorway.

Maihara glanced again at Aurian. Her chaperone seemed to have recovered her composure. She couldn't be one, could she? She had to find out. If Aurian wasn't, the priest had sensed her own effort to link to the magical field, and that wasn't good.

"I'll not go in there to be insulted," Maihara declared, turning back to the carriage.

Silence reigned in the carriage as they set off to drive the short distance to Maihara's hosts for the night. Lady Aurian looked uneasy, Ferris seemed thoughtful and Maihara was not asking any questions.

The white mansion fronted onto the street with a pair of lamps marking the doorway. "We're here," Ferris said.

In the double-height entrance hall, Lord Arcenio greeted her warmly, after bowing. Their noble host was a vigorous man of middle age, brown-haired, olive-skinned and with a friendly expression.

"How was your excursion, Your Grace?" he asked her.

"The ocean was amazing, so big. The beach was great, and we saw a weird dead thing from the sea washed up on the sand."

Arcenio nodded, smiling. "What kind of sea-creature?"

"Like a man, but with fish-gills."

Arcenio gave a patronising smile. "The common folk have stories of such things. I have never seen one myself. And what of the rest of the town?"

"We saw various parts of the town, and some of the defences and the moats. The military appear to be preparing."

"That's good," Arcenio said without enthusiasm.

Oil lamps and a chandelier lit the stairwell. Maihara and Aurian went to their room to change for dinner. Arcenio had given her the best guest suite, finely furnished and decorated, in accordance with her status.

Maihara waited till the soldiers had brought up their baggage and departed, before confronting Lady Aurian.

"Serina, when that priest outside the temple was shouting about Vimrashans, he was pointing at you. Is there anything you want to tell me? Why would he shout at me? He definitely meant you, unless he had squint eyes and a wonky finger." She touched Aurian's arm, forcing her companion to look up and meet her eyes. "I don't like the idea that these priests can detect us."

Aurian was silent for long seconds, then nodded. "It's true. I do have the Vimrashan blood. It's dangerous for me if anyone knows. You don't think that priest will talk?"

"I can understand that. He'd better not." A great hope blossomed in Maihara's breast. "But can you sense anything? Do anything?"

"No, Your Grace," Aurian said quickly. "Don't say anything about this. The Emperor—"

Maihara's grip tightened, till Aurian's expression changed into a wince. "Cards on the table, Serina. Can you access the portals, do stuff?"

Aurian stared at her. "So you know about that? You can work magic?"

"Maybe." Maihara lowered her head, heart pounding. Revealing secrets was scary.

"All right. In some places, like back in Calah, I had the sensation that a presence was there. And I can influence animals - cats. Oh, and your mother once gave me a password. I saw something more."

"My mother?" Maihara released Aurian's arm and sat heavily on the bed. "You knew my mother?"

"Yes, I was there at that time, but I was not one of her inner circle."

"What was she like?"

"She was a very gracious lady, and beautiful. She looked a bit like you."

Maihara was silent. It had been a long time, and her childish memories of her mother were fading. She still missed having a mother. "And what— No, tell me about the password. What did it unlock? What did you see?" Perhaps together, she and Serina could—

"A kind of frame. Not like anything I'd seen before." Aurian massaged her arm where Maihara's fingers had gripped.

"You still have the password?"

"No." Aurian shook her head sadly. "I forgot it ages ago. My husband—"

Maihara clasped her hands and was silent. Aurian had lost her husband and her home. Maybe she really had forgotten the password, and was unable to work any magic, but Maihara was not convinced. Couldn't Aurian have told her sooner? Didn't she trust her? Obviously not, and why expose herself needlessly? If Aurian understood magic, Maihara should be careful.

Maihara raised her head. "So you can't do any magic?" she asked gently.

"No, Your Grace."

"I'm sorry. But I have one more question. Since you knew of my mother's circle, did you know anything about the box?"

Aurian looked puzzled. "What box?"

"The box that I got on my fourteenth birthday."

"Oh, that box? So you had it?" Aurian's gaze defocused. "I remember. Your mother wanted to be sure you received the knowledge at the right time, and I overheard her discussing with her closest companion about making a legacy for you. In case something happened."

She shifted, and gazed at Maihara with a speculative look.

A chill went down Maihara's spine. That, as far as she knew, was indeed the purpose of the box. There had perhaps been a whole coven of these Vimrashan women, and she had no clue that any remained at Court, or even still alive. There was much more she wanted to ask, and should she give Aurian a password and find out what she could do?

"In case what happened? What exactly did she say? Do you remember?"

"We have to talk about this later," Aurian said. "But first, let's put on our best dresses and go make an impression."

With extreme reluctance, Maihara agreed. She was determined to find out more from Aurian, but she needed to tread carefully.

When they descended, other guests in nobles' clothing were in the hall, and their host was ushering them into the dining room. The light from a chandelier and wall oil lamps reflected from the table settings. The walls glowed yellow with white mouldings, and a long table glittered with silver and glass centre-pieces, and patterned plates and sets of shining cutlery laid for a dozen people.

To her embarrassment, a servant ushered Maihara to a seat at the head of the table. Their host sat at her right, and the usher seated Lady Aurian next to him. The remaining places were taken by people whom Maihara did not know, and whose names mostly passed in a blur. They stared at her as though she was an object of immense fascination. She looked round for Ferris, who had not been seated at the table. He stood at ease at one side of the room, along with one of his soldiers.

Maihara was obliged to give an account of her adventures, which the company accepted with suitable expressions of horror and astonishment. She concluded by mentioning the dead Aquan she had seen on the beach. To her surprise, the company was sceptical. "Are you sure it wasn't an ordinary corpse, tangled with seaweed, Your Grace?" her host asked, smiling. "The port is full of tales of strange things seen at sea. Sailors tell these stories in exchange for drinks."

Maihara made a non-committal reply.

Their host brought the subject around to the subject of the rebel advance. He had already heard the sharp exchanges at the General's mansion.

Maihara gave an outline of the rebel overall plan and their intention to take Retis. A murmur of disquiet ran around the room and guests argued over whether to flee, surrender the town or resist.

While they argued, Maihara reviewed her astonishing conversation with Lady Aurian. Would it be wise to give Aurian the passwords? She wanted to know what Aurian was able to do, but then Aurian would know what abilities *Maihara* possessed. And she'd be able to perform the same spells that Maihara did. A vision came into her mind, connected with her future romantic hopes. With the spy spell, Aurian would be able to watch Maihara's most intimate moments. The idea was appalling, yet shockingly erotic.

"How many rebels are coming?" a bewigged nobleman asked.

"You should ask Lieutenant Ferris that," Maihara said, returning her attention to the present. She turned to look for Ferris. He had moved, and stood beside one of the wine serving tables by the wall.

Ferris bowed toward Maihara. "Your Grace. My lords, ladies, I estimated the rebels as being in brigade strength, perhaps a little less. We had a count of the number of barges."

"And what about the number of rebels in the city?" another man asked in an alarmed tone.

"You should know that better than us," Maihara said. She reached for another plate of the first course. She shrank away from the idea of giving Aurian all her passwords. That woman had too many secrets. Maihara wanted to keep hers. In particular, there was no way she was going to admit to the existence of the spying spell, much less give Aurian the keywords for it.

"I'm sure that the vast majority of Retis people are loyal

to the Empire," a third man said.

"That's reassuring," Maihara said. "Elsewhere many, perhaps most, of the common people appear to sympathise with the rebels." She set down her loaded plate with a thunk.

A silence descended on the table, and the guests stared at her with various expressions of disbelief and dismay. Too late, she realised that she had created the very effect she had been trying to avoid.

"It may be different here," she said quickly. "And whatever they think, they're not armed and the local garrison is."

"And we have our spiral moat, even if they breach the outer defences," their host said.

Maihara was not impressed. "The rebels are aware of the Retis moat. And they are coming by *boat*," She had overheard a rebel discussion about the prospects for attacking along the moat to cause confusion.

"They will be picked off from the banks if they venture into the moat," a noble with cropped hair said.

An approving murmur spread around the room.

"But placing troops to stop them will spread our forces too thin," the noble said.

Ferris nodded.

"How soon do you think the rebels will reach Retis, Lieutenant?" their host asked.

"Hard to say, Milord. If they continued their advance at the observed rate, they might arrive any time in the next couple of days. Your general is making preparations for a defence."

"And how many troops has he got?"

Ferris stood straight. "About a battalion, I understand."

A murmur of dismay ran around the table.

"I assume the defenders have an advantage?" Maihara asked, looking to Ferris. That had been the case at Calah.

"That is so, Your Grace. How much, depends on the quality of the fixed defences."

"A battalion should be enough to see off a rabble of

disorganised rebels," said a white-haired man, in a dismissive tone.

"That would be true if the rebels were disorganised," she said. "But I heard that they have some of the best and most innovative minds from the military academies in their ranks, men angered at being passed over for promotion because they were not of the noble class."

Again, a deadly silence fell on the room, and several noblemen scowled. She had said too much again.

"The town can be defended," Maihara said. "But not if you think it will be easy. Or if you expect an ill-organised attack."

At the end of the dinner as cups of hot koosh were served, and the ladies began moving to the adjoining music room, their host said, "It seems we should press for more energetic action to defend the town against any attack, and ask for volunteers."

There was a murmur of agreement.

Their host turned to Ferris. "Lieutenant, be honest now, how soon do you expect the rebels could attack?"

Maihara and Ferris exchanged glances. Ferris fingered his moustache. "Early tomorrow morning. We did our utmost to out-pace them, but we have already been here a whole day."

A murmur of shock ran across the room. Soon, guests were leaving.

Somebody found a lute, and Lady Aurian performed some courtly songs for the family and guests who remained. It reminded Maihara of happier days in Calah. Maihara was wondering if Aurian was able to perform any magic that Maihara could not, and how she might find out.

Back in their room, Maihara sat and propped her chin on one hand. "Do you think I'm meddling? It will be awful if the town was attacked without warning."

Aurian gave her a look. "No, Your Grace. I'm sure it's the right thing to do."

"We should leave the town by the east gate tonight,

before the rebels can get here," Maihara said. A sixth sense was arousing her unease.

Aurian stared at her in surprise. "Our new friends will think we're deserting them."

"You think we should stay? If there is a panic, and they cut the bridges over that spiral moat, it will be impossible to get out."

"We should stay, Your Grace. Everyone is tired, and one cannot travel by carriage in darkness."

Maihara frowned, but allowed herself to be persuaded. She was tired, and the night was dark. And she had another matter on her mind.

"Serina, if you don't mind me asking, how many Vimrashans were at court in my mother's time, and what could they do?"

Aurian tilted her head to one side, as she looked into Maihara's eyes. "And what can *you* do, Your Grace, if you don't mind *me* asking?"

A jolt of fear and anger spiked through Maihara's body. "Do?" She struggled to speak, shaking her head. She dared not reveal those secrets. Her stomach cramped. "The Emperor accused me of witchcraft. I can't say."

Aurian sighed. "As you say, Your Grace."

She took several deep breaths. "At least answer my question, Serina, please."

Aurian's nose wrinkled. "About six, that I knew of." She began removing her dress.

The sensation of unreality receded. "And were they close to my mother, or what?"

"You mean in her inner circle?"

"Yes."

Aurian was making this rather hard work.

"They were all in her inner circle of companions," Aurian said, folding the dress she had taken off.

Maihara leant forward. "And what could they do? That ordinary people couldn't, I mean."

Aurian slowly unfastened her undershift. "I don't recall that they did much, not that affected the real world. A couple of them had the ability to send each other messages, I recall."

"They *what*?" Maihara wondered if she had misunderstood. Aurian had not hinted at this earlier. Nobody had. Did Aurian just mean secret messages?

"Serina, what do you mean by 'send messages'?"

Aurian looked up from her task. "They sent messages from mind to mind, or so I was led to believe."

"But how?"

Aurian shook her head. "I don't know."

Maihara waited while Aurian undid the back of Maihara's dress. Maihara struggled out of the dress and folded it. As she changed into her night-dress, she thought about what to ask next. "Do you remember any of your passwords?"

Aurian shook her head again.

Maihara was not sure she believed this. "Did you each have your own sets of passwords?"

"I don't know. I think your mother had her own access, and maybe others did. But I shared a set of passwords, as I recall."

A more informative response this time. Perhaps Aurian was opening up. "And what sort of things did you do?"

Aurian looked away. "I don't recall now."

A likely story. Aurian was holding back. A different approach was needed to pry her open and learn what she was able to do and what threat she posed. Maihara laced her fingers and faced Aurian. "Can you call up the magic now?"

Aurian looked away. A brief silence extended before she spoke. "There's something there. Retis is one of those places, but I can't—"

Maihara resolved to take a small risk. "Try *Arisa*."

"What?"

"*Arisa*. It should open it."

Aurian mumbled to herself for a while, then her expression changed. Her gaze de-focused and her eyes moved as if she was looking at something Maihara was unable to see. "Oh... thank you."

"Can you do anything with it?"

"No, I need another password." Aurian's face fell. "It's gone. I couldn't hold it."

Maihara folded her arms. "Sorry. I don't want to rush into this." Aurian might be working for the Imperial Army Intelligence, an organisation for which Maihara had no liking, and she had no intention of enabling Aurian's spy powers. Or on allowing Aurian to report to Cordan on the extent of the Imperial Princess's magical powers.

They stared at one another. "Not yet," Maihara said.

-23-

Early next morning Maihara woke with her heart racing. What was wrong? Opening her eyes, she struggled to remember where she lay. This four-poster was in the second mansion in Retis. Serina Aurian was a witch. A noise of clanging and horn-blowing filtered in from the window. That did not bode well. She put on a dressing gown and shook Aurian, who slumbered in a narrow bed at the side of the room.

Aurian stirred. "What?"

"Go find Ferris and ask him what's happening."

"Yes, Your Grace."

Her breathing quickened. She did not want to fall into the hands of rebels again, or risk being in a town that was being fought over. She might not fare so well being captured a third time. Tarchon had detailed the variety of people, including merchants and minor nobles, who had reason to resent Imperial rule. Matters might not be as simple as she had imagined while secluded in the Palace.

After a couple of minutes, Aurian returned with a dishevelled Ferris, who wore trousers and undershirt and looked unshaven. He sketched a salute. "Your Grace."

"What's going on outside, Lieutenant?"

"That noise is a general alarm. I surmise that the rebels have been sighted, Your Grace."

It was what Maihara had expected. Imminent danger sharpened her senses, and she had to make a decision. "Can you get us out of the town, in an easterly direction?"

"Yes, Your Grace." Ferris snapped to attention, back ruler straight, with his thumbs in perfect line with his trouser seams.

Aurian stared at her in surprise. "Our hosts will think

we're deserting them."

"Perhaps, but what if the rebels find me in their household?" She spared her hosts a moment's regret. "I've done what I can here, and I don't intend to be caught like a rat in a trap." Already an impulse to be moving pressed her. "I doubt if the Lieutenant wants to see me recaptured after all the trouble he's gone to."

"No, Your Grace, I do not."

Aurian wrung her hands together. "What about the port? You said—"

"The rebels will be attacking there," Maihara said.

"Your Grace is right," Ferris said.

Maihara turned to him. "Give us a few minutes to dress, then be ready to carry our bags down. We'll need a carriage."

Ferris saluted. "Yes, Your Grace."

A few minutes later they were all gathered at the top of the grand staircase. Her stomach rumbled. "I don't suppose we have time for breakfast?" Maihara asked Ferris.

Ferris hesitated.

"I expect not," Maihara said.

Their host was in the hall, along with servants, looking distracted. He hurried to intercept her. "You're leaving my house already, Your Grace? Please stay."

"My escort advise me that the rebels are attacking. I have to leave while I can."

"Please don't abandon us, Your Grace." He pulled at his wig.

She looked aside, face flushing. "I've done what I can. It's up to the garrison now. I can't be captured by the rebels again."

"Please save us, Your Grace."

"Sir." Ferris moved the lord firmly aside. "Let Her Grace pass." Maihara bid their host a hasty farewell over her shoulder, and hurried away, head bent, carrying her shame with her.

As their carriage rattled through the damp early morning streets, shopkeepers were shutting their stores and a few citizens stood on the pavements asking each other for news. Ferris and his eight soldiers occupied outside seats on the roof, alongside and behind the driver. There was just one arm of the moat between them and the East gate. Maihara prayed that the bridge spanning it was still intact. Her bid for freedom could not end here.

The carriage gathered speed, swerving around a delivery cart and making pedestrians jump aside. Ahead was the rising arch of the wooden bridge, still intact, but occupied by a platoon of soldiers, with axes. On the far side of the moat, creepers with yellow flowers hung down over the stonework. The carriage had to halt while another platoon of soldiers crossed at the double, heading for the southern end of the town.

Ferris argued with the soldiers holding the bridge, till they allowed the carriage to cross. Green water rippled some twenty feet below. The moat was a substantial obstacle, with steeply sloping sides faced in stone, but it only protected the inner part of the city and the rebels could get into the spiral at the outer end. The sound of the carriage wheels changed as they regained the solid ground on the eastern side, and entered another street lined with houses and shops.

"Why are we heading for the east gate?" Aurian asked. "Will it be safe?"

"I'm not aware of any plan to attack on that side," Maihara said.

Aurian ran a hand through her hair. "Should we not stop to ask what is happening?"

"We know what is happening," Maihara said sharply. She did not want any delay, not after abandoning her new acquaintances. "The rebels have arrived, and they are going to carry out their plan."

They skirted a town square where an Imperial flag had been hoisted and a mob filled the open space. Indistinct shouting filtered into the carriage. Maihara lowered the window and shouted up to Ferris. "What's happening here?"

"Looks like they are trying to form a militia."

Perhaps her words of the previous evening were bearing fruit.

Within minutes they neared the Eastern gate. Buildings two or three floors in height lined each side of a narrow street packed with vehicles. Ahead was a jam of carriages waiting to leave the town through the arched gatehouse.

"What's the delay?" Maihara called to Ferris.

"I can't see. They're all held up behind the gate."

"Is it open?"

"Looks open."

Minutes passed. Their carriage edged forward a few feet. Maihara tapped her fingers in an agony of impatience. At this rate the rebels could be cutting the road to the east before they were able to escape. She leaned out to shout at Ferris again. They didn't have time for this nonsense.

Ferris looked down. "I think they are checking each carriage, Your Grace."

"So go and tell them to stop it. We need to go." Her heart was thumping.

The carriage tilted on its springs as Ferris dismounted. Within minutes, the carriages ahead lumbered into motion and moved forward at a steady pace. Maihara saw the inner side of the stone and brick wall getting closer and closer. With a jerk, the carriage halted, amidst shouting. A mob of roughly dressed men swarmed alongside the carriage, wielding sticks and knives.

"What's going on? Maihara shouted. A chill of alarm swept over her. Where was Ferris? This looked like part of the rebel multi-point plan - to use sympathisers inside the town to seize control of the gates. She looked forward, trying to see if Ferris was about to re-board. Ferris, sword drawn, was confronting two of the men. If she told him to have the gates shut now, she'd be sacrificing her own escape.

"We're looking for noble rats," one of the mob shouted. The gap-toothed face was staring in her direction. "You're not getting away."

She glimpsed a few garrison soldiers guarding the gateway, being menaced by the mob. The mob seemed to be impeding the fleeing carriages more than the soldiers.

"They're rebels! Cut them down! Drive on!" Maihara shouted. Lady Aurian's fingers dug into Maihara's arm.

Ferris turned at her shout. "What?"

Maihara pointed forward. "That's an order!"

"To me! Clear the road!" Ferris shouted.

Maihara sat back and pushed up the window. The carriage jerked forwards by a few feet, lurching over an obstacle. Outside, men shouted and screamed. Men in Imperial uniforms hacked at those in plain clothes, driving back men from the sides of the carriage and attacking a group trying to block the road in front. Maihara glanced to her other side. Aurian sat in the centre seat, wide-eyed with fear. The carriage moved forward again and stopped under the shadow of the gate arch.

"No," Maihara whispered. This was bad. The carriage had to clear the gates. Ferris was shouting. Weapons clashed outside the window. The left-hand door swung open. Fear lanced like a spear in her guts as a scruffy man lunged at her. The intruder grunted and fell back out of the door with a cry. A soldier loomed behind.

The carriage lurched forward into the bright light beyond. and hit something with a crash. Aurian cried out and Maihara gasped. The carriage veered to Maihara's side and edged out onto the open road, where it kept moving at a walking pace. A muffled voice filtered through the roof - somebody cursing the driver. It sounded like one of her soldiers, the one with the moustache.

Thumps and scuffling came from the back and from the roof. Maihara, heart in mouth, hoped it wasn't rebels. A soldier glanced inside and slammed the left-hand door. A last soldier scrambled up the outside. The shouting and screaming diminished behind. They had fought clear.

"Drive on!" Ferris shouted above. "Fast as you can." The carriage picked up speed, and rocked and bounced accompanied by the grinding of the wheels and the patter of galloping hooves on the road surface. A little way beyond the town, the carriage slowed as it climbed a hill, past lines of vines supported by wooden trellising. At a shouted command from Ferris, most of the soldiers jumped off the two-horse carriage and ran alongside. At the top the carriage gained further speed and the soldiers re-boarded. Looking back, she had a glimpse of the sea below, and the roofs of the town. No rebel troops were in sight.

Maihara turned to Aurian. "What happened back there, outside the gate?"

"We hit another carriage," Aurian said. "I looked back and saw the soldiers turning it and its horses into the ditch. Those poor people."

"What the devil was it stopping for?"

"I don't know. It must have broken down. Ours shot out of the gate and hit it."

Maihara felt somehow responsible. She was getting away, abandoning the less fortunate.

Ferris leaned over, looking down from his outside seat. "Are you all right, Your Grace?"

"I'm fine," Maihara shouted back. And she did feel fine. They had evaded capture by the treacherous rebels at the gate, and she'd made the right decisions. But why the bumping and screaming before the gate? The unpleasant certainty grew that they had run over one of the mob.

And what of her guard? She leaned out. "How are your soldiers?"

"Two wounded," Ferris replied.

They had been hurt defending her. Her buoyant mood deflated further.

"Have they shut that gate?" Maihara shouted.

"I can't see, Your Grace. We cut through the rebels, but I didn't see a lot of gate guards. It's General Xaris's problem now."

She glanced at Aurian. Aurian looked upset. Maihara took her hand.

The carriage raced onward, past vineyards and

evergreen orchards, while Maihara contemplated the cost of her departure. Two wounded soldiers, an unknown number of dead and wounded rebels, and an open gate. Her eight soldiers might have helped to guard the gate and close it. At intervals they passed a slower carriage on the paved coastal road.

They entered a road-cutting, of proportions such it could only have been made by the ancients, a reminder to her that the Empire was a transient thing and the Builders had accomplished greater works in the distant past. A modern track veered off and straggled up the hill. Abruptly her view closed in to dimly lit walls. Ferris had elected to take the Builders' road tunnel that pierced the hill. They were in darkness, and the close sound of the wheels cutting through dirt and puddles poured through the windows along with cooler air. A small circle of daylight shone far ahead, calming her fears.

"Where are we heading?" Lady Aurian asked. "We were going to take ship for the east."

"We can't. The rebels will have seized the Retis port."

Aurian gripped the door catch. "We should have left earlier. Where is this tunnel taking us? To another port?"

"Not anywhere close. We'll go to Shardan." Maihara awaited her chaperone's reaction.

"Shardan? Not the east? Was this what you planned all along?"

Maihara ignored the question. "I doubt that I'd get a warmer welcome in Chancungra than I received at Kunn. I'm not going there to be shut up in the Palace. We'll go to Shardan and seek refuge there."

"I forbid this," Aurian said, red-faced. "You're planning to meddle."

Maihara was unmoved. Ferris and the guards would obey her, not Aurian. "Forbid all you like. We're going to the principality."

They emerged from the ancient tunnel into daylight. The carriage clattered through villages with white walls and tiled roofs that lay silent, somnolent in the heat. Hamlets sloped steeply up hillsides, with houses terraced high above the red roofs below. In the fields, golden corn waved, and vines grew in neat green rows. They were never far from the sea. At last they slowed to an ambling pace. A strained silence reigned inside the carriage.

They halted in a small town, un-walled, with dusty buildings of yellow stone, their doors and windows painted red or blue. Maihara stepped down while Ferris enquired after a change of horses. The four animals, dusty and foam-flecked, were exhausted and needed water.

The driver wanted to return to Retis with his vehicle.

"You're a fool," Ferris told him. "The rebels will be attacking it by now. They'll confiscate your carriage and make you a pauper."

The driver hung his head. "I can't abandon my family."

They stood in a group in front of what appeared to be a coaching inn. A soldier wiped down the horses. Maihara spoke to the two wounded soldiers. Calcas had a slashed arm, and Tilis had a stab wound to the chest and a knock to his head. They had already been patched up, and Ferris wanted to carry them further rather than leave them behind to be captured.

Aurian stared, wide-eyed, at the bloodstained and bandaged men.

"They can ride inside," Maihara said.

The men looked grateful. Aurian was silent.

"Can we get breakfast?" Maihara asked.

"There's time to order food while they sort out the horses," Ferris said. "But you should get something we can take with us, Your Grace, not a two-hour sit-down meal."

"All right." She did not want to delay too long either. The rebels might send cavalry to chase her. That business at the gate suggested that the rebel agents knew she was in Retis.

They stepped inside the inn, and ordered rounds of bread with a selection of cheese, vegetables and meat pieces baked onto the top.

"I hope you were not too frightened by that affair at the

gate, Your Grace," Ferris asked.

"There wasn't time to be frightened," she told him. "It happened so quickly. You did well, Lieutenant."

Ferris made a small bow and smiled. "It's my duty to defend Your Grace. I'd do anything."

Maihara sensed his ardour. Yes, he probably would.

Soldiers downed glasses of beer. The hot food started to arrive from the kitchen. She folded her freshly baked hot round and bit into it. The mixture of flavours and textures included a tang of blood. She put the snack down.

Aurian watched her. "You're not hungry?"

"That fighting at the gate. So many people hurt so we could escape."

"They wanted to capture us. There was no way we could let that happen." Aurian chewed. "They were a violent rabble. What do you think would have happened if they'd dragged us out of the carriage?"

Maihara nodded. A movement outside the window caught her eye. The driver was turning his carriage around. Around? A rcalisation shot through her mind.

Ferris was quicker. "Soldiers! The carriage! Stop that man!"

The soldiers looked outward, then with an oath, three of them ran outside. Two restrained the horses while the third climbed up and grappled with the driver.

When Maihara stepped out of the inn into the road, it was all over. Two of the soldiers had dragged the driver from his seat and were holding him by the arms, while a third held the horses.

Ferris stepped close to the driver in a confrontational stance, feet spread. "What have you got to say for yourself, fellow? We hired you, and we need your carriage."

"My family. If Retis is being attacked by rebels, I need to be with them." The driver's voice choked with emotion.

The thought of being stranded in this hamlet with rebel cavalry on her trail was unappealing, but Maihara felt for the driver. This was why she hated the idea of rebellions and war, for what it did to the lives of people like this man.

"We already warned you not to go back there," Ferris said. "They'll seize your carriage."

"My family are more important." The driver spoke in a sullen tone. He hung his head.

"Bastard was stealing our kit," another soldier pointed out. The baggage was still in the carriage boot.

"That's a serious offence," said the third, looking at the sweating driver.

Ferris glanced at Maihara. He seemed reluctant to act in her presence, and the soldiers under his command looked eager to see the driver severely dealt with.

"Can we get another carriage here?" Maihara asked.

Ferris shook his head. "It doesn't look like it."

"We can't stay here," Lady Aurian said.

Maihara glanced around. The street, with its humble buildings, and a handful of gawping locals, did little to recommend the town as a refuge for a fugitive princess.

"So where can we find another carriage?" she asked the group. "When we do, we can let this fellow go."

The driver glanced at her, turned his head eastward, and mumbled a place-name.

"Where's that?" Ferris asked.

"A few leagues further on, Master."

"Is this your wish, Your Grace?" Ferris asked.

Maihara nodded.

Ferris turned to the soldiers. "Hold him."

"Where do you want to head for, Your Grace? This is the Loomis road," Ferris said, out of the driver's hearing.

"Loomis? I want to head for the capital of the Shardan principality."

"Not Loomis port, Your Grace?"

"No, Shardan."

"Very well."

Aurian pursed her lips.

***

The driver was obliged to take them to the next town, where they paid him and hired another carriage and driver. On the road again next morning, they passed an ancient stone pillar erected beside the way, its carved base marked with illegible inscriptions. The road was busy, with more people heading east than west. Later they turned onto the north-east road which bore, in the form of embankments and cuttings, further marks of the cyclopean hands of the ancients, a reminder that the past hid more than present-day savants knew.

"We're crossing the border into Shardan," Lieutenant Ferris said, pointing to the pillar. It marked the boundary between the Retis province and the principality of Shardan, which did not support the rebels and claimed to be independent of the Empire.

The Shardan countryside was hilly, growing corn and citrus fruits, and marked here and there by cyclopean ruins. Another two days and four more changes of horses later, they reached the city of Halamar. The capital city of the principality of Shardan was smaller than Calah but spilled out beyond a protective circuit of stone walls. There was no sign of war here, and no soldiers on the sunlit streets. To Maihara, the place looked prosperous and the buildings that were not faced in stone or brick were rendered and painted in bright colours. Having reached her refuge, she was in a buoyant mood. She felt for her magic, and discovered that Halamar was a magically active place. She supposed the Builders had settled it in ancient times.

Ferris found a comfortable-looking inn that offered rooms to wealthy travellers and pressed an Imperial Army credit note on the reluctant innkeeper. "Are you saying that the Imperial Army is not credit-worthy? In the Empire they'd call that treasonable talk, and a hanging offence."

The innkeeper gave in.

After a meal in their carpeted suite, they discussed their next move. Aurian was still annoyed over Maihara's change of plan.

"What exactly do you intend to do here, Your Grace?" she asked.

"First, establish myself here so I don't get sent back to

Chancungra or captured by the rebels again. Second, if I meet anyone of influence, I'll urge them to keep Shardan out of the war."

Ferris raised his eyebrows.

"You're meddling again, Princess," Aurian said. "It didn't work so well before."

Her annoyance flared. "That wasn't my fault. That general was an old drunk."

"You're only seventeen years old. People won't take you seriously."

"They would if I was a prince. What am I supposed to do? Stand around wearing pretty dresses? Wait till I'm married off to some ruler in waiting?" She sighed. "Not much chance of that happening." With a war, her brother in the hands of rebels, and her father hating her, the prospect of a dynastic wedding seemed remote. And the threat loomed of her father's animosity and his regiment of mechanical soldiers.

"But do you know what's happening here, Your Grace?" Aurian said.

"I know well enough," she said, irritated. She had done her best to find out. "The Shardan are trying to stay out of the struggle between the rebels and the Empire, or so they said in Retis."

"Do we know that's really true?" Ferris asked.

"It looks that way," Maihara said. "In Calah neither side could get any message of support out of them."

"Your Grace," Ferris said, "How do you intend to contact the authorities here? Will they listen to you?"

It seemed to Maihara that anybody should listen to the Imperial Princess.

"If I might make a suggestion?" Aurian said. "Tomorrow we can walk around like ordinary visitors, ask questions and try to find out what the situation is here. And maybe you should not tell everyone who you are."

"I shouldn't?" Maihara rolled her eyes at Aurian. "I suppose not." Spies from the Fifth Bureau could be operating here. The rebels would want to recapture her, and who knew what the attitude of officials of the principality might be?

Ferris clapped a hand to his chest. "My soldiers and I will defend Her Grace with our lives."

"Thank you for your loyalty, Lieutenant," Maihara said. Thought of the two wounded soldiers darkened her mood.

"If she keeps quiet, you may not have to," Aurian said tartly.

"All right, we will explore the centre of the town tomorrow," Maihara said.

Once they were alone in their bedroom, Maihara turned to Lady Aurian. "You're being a bit bossy this evening, Serina."

"I don't want you getting into serious trouble. And I think I'm the only adult here." She placed a hand on her chest and imitated the Lieutenant's words. "'My soldiers and I will defend Her Grace with our lives.' That young man has it bad."

Despite herself, Maihara giggled. "He's very loyal."

She moved to the window and drew back a silk-edged curtain. The street was dimly lit, and buildings three floors in height of smoothed stone lined the far side. Half a dozen smartly dressed men ambled below, talking loudly in what sounded like north-eastern accents. Rebels? Refugees? She peered down. A couple of them wore what might be rebel officer uniforms, but it was too dark to be sure. Rebel representatives here? A shiver of unease went through her.

-24-

With an embarrassed look, Ferris displayed the contents of his Army purse. It was nearly empty. Ferris, Maihara and Lady Aurian were breakfasting in the inn's dining room, where servants brought food and refilled their cups with steaming *koosh*.

"Where's it all gone?" Aurian asked.

Maihara stifled a yawn and cut open a regional item, a greasy bun with bits of fruit in it.

"On getting us to Retis, hiring carriages and so on," Ferris said.

Maihara wrinkled her nose and held her counsel. Budgeting was not something she had ever had to do.

Aurian put down her cutlery. "So what are we going to do about it?"

"Lord Farnak knew a noble in the provincial government here," Maihara said. "Lord Nardone. I'll try to approach him and see if he's helpful." Nardone's name had come up in Maihara's discussions with the deceased Chancellor. Nardone was the man she had tried to message by carrier bird, but the letter had not got through.

"Oh? What was his connection with Farnak?" Lady Aurian asked.

"Farnak said they'd met on State business," Maihara said, not liking Aurian's keen interest. Farnak had been arrested before the fall of Calah, and she did not want insinuations of court plotting to unsettle the loyal Ferris. So far, nobody in the provinces seemed to have the least inkling of any problem between Emperor Cordan and his Chancellor, Lord Farnak. If the Fifth Bureau had accused Farnak, this news might have been buried by the fall of Calah and Farnak's execution by the rebels as a criminal.

"What's Nardone's position?" Aurian persisted.

"I have no idea," Maihara admitted. If Nardone was not helpful, he might at least be discreet about her affairs.

"Do you know where Lord Nardone's office lies, Your Grace?" Ferris asked, rubbing his moustache.

"No, we'll just have to go out there and find out, discreetly." She rested her chin on her palm. "So who should I be, out there?"

Aurian swivelled in her seat. "If you don't mind, Your Grace, you could be my niece, Mai Aurian."

Maihara nodded. Serina had mentioned some while ago that she had a niece. "That'll do." It would fit with their respective ages. Maihara was both taller and heavier, so might pass more credibly as Aurian's niece than as a daughter. "You had both better stop calling me 'Your Grace.' Out there, that will really get people's attention."

"Yes, your G—" Ferris halted, embarrassed.

"You can address her as 'Milady', Aurian told him.

Ferris had another bombshell to deliver. "Milady. If there is an Imperial Army office or garrison in the city, I ought to report to them."

Maihara did not like the sound of this. She had not expected any Imperial Army presence here. "Oh? Why, Lieutenant?"

"My orders from General Metis were to escort you to Retis. Facilitating your escape to Halamar is a permissible extension. Now that I have carried out those orders, if I don't report to the nearest superior officer of the Army, they could accuse me of idling, or even desertion."

She stared at Ferris, not liking this at all. It was as if he was deserting her. If the Army confined Ferris and his men to barracks, that would leave her without protection in a strange city till she was able to get the support of Lord Nardone, or whoever. Also, in reporting his presence, Ferris could be obliged to disclose her name, which might not matter, but on the other hand might tip off a Fifth Bureau determined to make her life unpleasant.

She'd better not alarm Ferris by hinting that he shirk or

abandon his duty to the Army. He had already sent the two soldiers wounded at Retis to be treated by local doctors. "Lieutenant, can you not delay at least till we have contacted Lord Nardone? I don't want my name mentioned before that. Your standing orders from Metis should cover this. Or am I supposed to go there alone?"

"I really should report without delay, Milady."

"We don't know how dangerous this city is, do we?" She fixed Ferris with an appealing look.

Ferris chewed his lip. "Very well, your G—, Milady, I'll escort you till we contact him."

She breathed a sigh of relief.

Soon they were ready to venture out on foot. Maihara wore her travelling clothes.

"Mamer!" Ferris shouted. A small, mustachioed soldier with a scarred cheek stepped forward. "With us!" The trooper checked his sword, dagger and pouches were at his belt and followed them.

Out on the street, Maihara confirmed her impression that life here continued as usual. Well-dressed people strolled along the thoroughfares, looking into the multi-paned windows of emporiums, and carriages and delivery carts clattered by. In one direction, their street led into an area of old buildings and streets too narrow for a carriage. Up it she glimpsed an antique castle with timber upper parts, and a weathered temple to the Nine Gods.

The government buildings lay in the opposite direction. Away from the old centre, the road led into a long, wide avenue with a line of flowerbeds and small trees planted along its centre. Set back from the roadways were buildings whose scale and architecture indicated they were designed to impress.

Further on was a grand emporium with expensive dresses in the window.

"We need to sort out the money first," Aurian said, dragging Maihara away.

The avenue terminated at a massive and ornate building decorated with flutings and pediments. To the left and right formal entrances lay behind railings. Maihara led the way as they approached for a closer look. At a gap in the front railings a pair of guards barred their way.

"What's this place?" Ferris asked, stepping forward.

"It's the Halamar Palace, sir," one guard said.

"And who lives here?" Ferris asked.

"It's for the provincial government."

Maihara looked past the guards to the ornate doorway. As Imperial Princess, she could state her business and walk in, but she took a step back.

"You're not going in?" Lady Aurian asked.

Maihara looked aside. "Not through there. We'll look for a more discreet entrance."

At the side of the building numbers of people, some poorly dressed, were walking in and out of a smaller arched entrance. The tall double doors stood open to reveal a busy hall beyond.

"This must be the entrance for public business," Ferris said.

Maihara took a step forward. "Good."

Aurian frowned. "We're going in the public entrance? With the commoners?"

"Where else? I don't want to attract too much attention. Let's do this."

Inside, the hall had walls of smooth cut grey stone, with wooden panelling up to head level. She craned her neck to look up. Long, rectangular roof-lights gave light to the room. Desks of dark wood took up space around the walls and in the centre, and at the back a carved wooden railing divided off a smaller area. People of all skin shades, mostly beige, and some in exotic or brightly coloured ethnic dress moved in all directions across the flagged stone floor, lining up at desks, standing in groups, or just standing and looking around them.

They joined a queue for a booth marked 'Enquiries'. There did not seem to be a separate queue for nobles. Some of the people in line were shabbily dressed, and smelled. Lady Aurian rolled her eyes. After an irritating wait, a clerk beckoned them forward.

"Rich scum," someone muttered as they passed a handful of the lower orders still waiting. Maihara reached the polished desk.

The waist-coated clerk eyed her and her escort. "Yes?" he asked in a brusque tone, as if he couldn't see that they were a better class of visitor.

Maihara sensed Aurian and Ferris bristling at the clerk's brusqueness. Fuming, she let the rudeness pass, not wanting to draw attention to herself by demanding the courtesy due to a princess.

"Does a Councillor Nardone have an office here?" she asked.

"He does," the clerk admitted. "Are you a constituent?"

"No."

The clerk eyed her with suspicion. "You'd need to contact his staff and make an appointment."

She waited, but no further enlightenment was forthcoming. "How? Can you take a message?"

"Write a letter requesting an interview. If the Councillor wants to see you, he'll get back to you."

"And where do I hand it in?"

"The mailroom's over there."

"Thank you, I'll do that." She turned away from the desk, her escort following.

"What rude people," Aurian said, with a backward glance.

It was a relief that Nardone did exist and was contactable. "Forget them. Can we get a letter written?"

***

Evening found them back at their inn, still moneyless. During dinner, a letter for Lady Mai Aurian arrived at the inn's reception. In their suite upstairs, Maihara tore open the sealed letter and scanned its contents, written in a clear hand.

With a broad smile she waved the letter and related the

317

gist to Aurian and Ferris. "It's from Nardone. I am invited to attend a general audience at the tenth hour tomorrow. Now we're getting somewhere. If I meet Lord Nardone, that should be a step forward."

"Will you tell him who you are?" Aurian asked.

"If I have to." In her letter she had simply described herself as a noble lady from Calah.

"What exactly are you hoping to do, Milady?" Ferris asked.

"I'm hoping they'll give me residency here," she said in a lower voice. "So that I can't be extradited or deported to anywhere."

Ferris frowned. "They won't if I can prevent it, Milady."

"And I'll encourage them to resist a rebel invasion."

"Since there's an Imperial Army presence here," Ferris said, "shouldn't you let them handle the problem of resisting the rebels? They have the staff and will be familiar with the local forces."

"The Lieutenant may be right," Lady Aurian said.

"The Imperial Army?" Maihara shook her head. The Imperial Army had not impressed her. She sensed her jubilation slipping away. Why couldn't these two support her? She set her lips in an obstinate line. She'd have to marshal arguments to persuade them, but Nardone was the first priority. "Well, I still want to meet these people and ask about residency. I need an allowance and somewhere to live, if I'm to stay here."

"That much is true," Lady Aurian said. Ferris nodded.

As she lay in bed, Maihara reached for her magic. She launched her spy spell and sent it out, tracing the streets she had walked earlier that day. There was the bank, with its imposing frontage, raised entrance and guards, the halls and grounds of the Arknane University with its students and greybeards, the Monist sanctuary, the elegant shops, and the double-fronted Halamar Palace.

She fell asleep, and dreamed that she was trapped inside rooms walled with the magical interface panels. Alone, she passed from room to icon-walled room, but could not find a way out.

In the middle of the night, she woke in darkness, perspiring. Across the room, Aurian breathed steadily. Faint sounds came from a street outside, and an adjoining room. The magic had shut down as she passed into slumber.

***

Next morning, a short carriage ride from the inn brought the two women and Ferris to the side of the government buildings. Maihara wore the best dress she had with her, a russet one with white lace trimmings and a bone-supported flared skirt.

At the back of the entrance hall of the previous day, a clerk admitted them through a wooden barrier and double doors into another top-lit hall. Here many people in formal dress were standing around waiting. Maihara stared around her, confused. So many people to see Lord Nardone?

By degrees she established that the various doors around the hall led to the chambers of different lords. She found Lord Nardone's clerk and presented her letter.

He made a mark on a paper. "You'll have to wait, Milady." he informed her in a less than obsequious tone.

Maihara bridled. "For how long?"

"There are others before you. You'll have to wait to be called, Milady."

Maihara turned away with a nod and a mumbled "I see," resisting the temptation to tell the fellow what she thought of this treatment, and came face to face with an officer of the Varlord Order. She recognised the shoulder flash on his Imperial officer uniform and strove to conceal her shock of unease. Her assumptions about her safety in Shardan were unravelling.

"Good morning," he said, looking her in the face. "And who might you be? I surmise that you are new to Halamar society?" The officer was tall and slim with fair, short-cropped hair, a long face and firm chin.

Ferris made a salute. The Varlord officer gave him a

curt nod.

Maihara recovered her composure. "Yes, we've come from Retis. I'm Mai Aurian. And you are?" She strove to decipher the officer's shoulder flashes. Some mid-rank.

"Colonel Attarlay Vardish, of the Imperial Army special forces." He made a small bow.

Maihara introduced Aurian and Ferris.

"We've had bad news from Retis this morning. I hope I am not about to ruin a charming lady's day?"

"No, we heard earlier at our guest house," Maihara said. "Awful news." Word was spreading that Retis had fallen to the rebels.

"Quite so. One did not expect the rebel rabble to be so efficient."

"A lot of people didn't, I think," she said.

"So, you left Retis before the rebels attacked. The Aurians are not from Retis, though? I'd hazard from Calah?"

The man seemed disagreeably well-informed.

Lady Aurian interposed. "North of Calah."

The officer eyed Maihara, with a faint smile. "Lady Mai Aurian? You've come a long way."

"Indeed," Maihara said. Let the nosy fellow deduce their flight himself.

"Mai's become a modestly popular name of late. My sister named her eldest daughter Maihara, after the Imperial Princess."

"How charming," Maihara muttered, wishing her magic could make her vanish from the spot.

"You do look like the latest official portraits. A pure coincidence then?"

"It must be."

"So, Lady Mai, you're not the princess who was rescued from the loutish rebels on the river Sintheer?" The officer raised enquiring eyebrows.

"No, I'm not," Maihara said, wishing she had chosen a better alias.

The officer bent forward and lowered his voice. "If the

Imperial Princess did arrive here, I doubt that she would want to advertise her presence too widely. Some people close to the Imperial court are most displeased with her."

"Is that so?" Maihara said, heart sinking. This man was playing with her.

"We Varlords are not concerned with this squabble. If the Imperial Family start publicly disagreeing and locking each other up during a war, that kind of thing is bad for public morale, wouldn't you say?" the man said with a straight face.

"Quite," Maihara said. Her anxiety diminished a notch. Maybe she had not so much to fear from the Varlords, who were a closed military society also involved in Imperial administration, but she did not intend to declare herself to this officer. "If you don't mind me asking, what are the Varlord Order doing here?"

"Oh not at all, Lady Mai. We are attached to the Imperial Army office, and keeping a watching brief on Imperial interests here in the principality."

She saw an opening. "And are you pushing them to enter the war on the Imperial side?"

"You are interested in politics?" He did not register much surprise.

"I wondered why they did nothing when Calah was overrun by the rebels."

Colonel Vardish kept his voice low and assumed a serious expression. "We advised against it. Calah is over fourteen days' march away, and we would most likely have lost another army and left this region unprotected. We heard what the Dhikr did to the first one."

"So they wanted to help?" A feeling of outrage about the consequent fall of Calah filled her breast.

"Mostly they didn't. I've rarely seen a bunch of brave and upright citizens so pleased by our advice."

"Is that so?"

"And then the rebels made a bumbling attempt to win them to their side," the Varlord officer said with a sneer. "Not a chance."

"Are the rebel representatives still here?"

"I believe so. They want to maintain relations with the principality. They'll no doubt be requesting the return of the Imperial Princess, should she turn up here."

"Is anyone else looking for her?" she asked.

"We're not aware of anyone, but that doesn't mean nobody is."

Maihara's heartbeat quickened. To cover her anxiety, she changed the subject. "Isn't there unrest among the lower classes here?"

The Varlord gave her a sharp look, then shrugged. "They're not armed."

Ferris stirred.

Maihara allowed concern to show in her voice. "But what if the rebels come here, after Retis?"

"Then we'll encourage the principality to put up resistance, using the local levies. It'll be easier to keep the rebels out than to dislodge them once they're in."

She nodded. This, at least, conformed to her wishes.

"Why not use the Imperial Army?" Maihara asked, with heat. "Why can't they defend Shardan?"

The Colonel frowned. "We have only a token presence here. Shardan is an independent principality. Until this spring, the Empire didn't foresee any need for a large standing army anywhere, and then we lost one of the corps fighting the Dhikr."

"I see," she said. "There are rumours that the Emperor hopes to produce an army of mechanical soldiers. Have you heard anything?"

"If any such project existed, it would be a state secret." The Colonel looked severe. "Where did you hear this?"

"At Calah."

"And we wonder how the rebels are gaining territory." He sighed.

"What do you know about Councillor Nardone?" she asked.

"Him? Recently ennobled, humble origins, a plutocrat with his finger in various pies. Probably wants to enrich himself further."

"I see." Not an ideal contact.

"Well, it's been interesting talking to you, Lady Mai." The Varlord made a salute, as if she outranked him, and backed away.

Maihara felt as if she was something small that had been trodden on. What was she doing here? Besides seeing through her alias, the Varlord officer had given her a lesson in grown-up politics.

"You don't look well," Lady Aurian said.

"I'm sure he guessed who I am. Why would he talk like that about defence policy?"

"He didn't call you out. That's good, isn't it?" Lady Aurian said in a bright tone.

"I suppose so." The officer could still report meeting her.

Maihara turned as the clerk called another name. She rallied herself. Since she was here, she might as well keep to her plan, and ask for residency. That Varlord had not denied that golims existed, or expressed surprise. The Varlords were said to have secret rituals and interests not identical with those of the Court or the nobles. If they were favourably disposed toward her, there was hope for her yet.

After an age, the clerk called her name, and she entered a small room which appeared to be lit from an internal courtyard. Maps and book-cases lined the walls and a couple of clerks worked at desks. A youngish man in minor noble dress, a shirt, waistcoat and tight breeches, asked her name and business.

Maihara showed him the letter. He glanced at it, crossed to an inner door, and knocked. A muffled voice came from within.

"The Councillor will see you now," he announced, and opened the door.

Maihara, Aurian and Ferris entered. Councillor Nardone, a florid man in an elaborately tailored suit, embellished with lace on the cuffs and hems, rose from his seat behind a large darkwood desk.

He was tall, well built and exuded an aura of power which instantly put Maihara on her guard. Her father exuded such an aura, and so had to a lesser extent Lord Farnak. She had to remind herself of who she was, and that she did not have to act like a foolish female in front of this man. "Mai Aurian? What can I do for you?"

"Councillor Nardone? We are refugees from Retis. We hoped that you would be able to give us some assistance, if we contacted you. No doubt other noble refugees have come here—"

Judging by his unsmiling expression, Nardone was unimpressed. "But why ask for me by name? I don't know you."

Maihara tried again. "We're originally from Calah. This is my aunt, Lady Aurian, and our bodyguard. I understand that you knew Chancellor Lord Farnak."

The Councillor's expression darkened. "Farnak? I did know him. But that was some while ago."

"You heard what happened to him?" Maihara prompted.

The Councillor frowned. "It's reported that he fell into rebel hands and was murdered."

Maihara gave a nod. "Executed, according to them." She was still reluctant to accept all the accusations the rebels had made against Farnak.

"I see," Lord Nardone said. He gestured Maihara and Aurian toward a pair of upholstered chairs. "So how did you know Farnak?"

"We met him at the court in Calah," Maihara said. "We moved south to evade the rebels, and fled Retis just before the rebel attack there, and we hope that we can seek refuge in Halamar, and gain resident status here."

"It should be safe enough here," Nardone said in an indifferent tone. "You don't need any permission to reside here, but I hope you have brought your own funds. Unless you have anything useful to offer. Anyway, you could travel further east, to Imperial territory."

"I see." She sighed. How to angle this conversation to

her advantage? Lord Nardone had not seemed pleased by the mention of Farnak's name. "I knew Farnak well. I liked him." She paused. "Unfortunately, others did not. The Emperor accused him of disloyalty and conspiracy, and the rebels executed him as an enemy of the people."

Nardone winced.

"The rebels seized Farnak's estates, but they are still looking for much of his money. The Empire, meanwhile, are still keen to investigate and question Farnak's contacts to trace the extent of his conspiracy. There's a Fifth Bureau—"

"I know of the Fifth Bureau." Nardone's face assumed a pasty hue.

She gave Nardone her best smile. "It seems that friends of Farnak should stick together."

"Indeed they should," Nardone said quickly. "Is there some way that I can assist you ladies?"

Maihara attacked swiftly. "We don't have unlimited funds, and we need somewhere to live. We also need guidance on achieving residency status."

"Please help us," Lady Aurian said.

Nardone's eyes turned to her. "We don't have bags of money to hand out. But I could advance a small sum for your immediate expenses and recommend you for a loan."

"That would be most kind," Aurian said.

"And the residency?" Maihara prompted.

"I'll explain how to apply, and I'll sponsor you."

"Thank you," Maihara said, and paused, giving Nardone an expectant look.

Nardone took the hint and tinkled a handbell on his desk. The young man from the anteroom appeared. Nardone went to the door and spoke to him in a low voice. The clerk nodded and exited. Nardone re-seated his bulk at the desk.

"And there's a rumour that the Imperial Princess Maihara Cordana was rescued from the rebels and brought to Retis," Maihara said. "One wonders whether she will reappear in Halamar."

"Why would we care?" Nardone said with a scowl.

"If the Imperial Princess Maihara Cordana is in the city, she will no doubt want to have discussions with leading officials."

Nardone's eyes bored into her. "Oh? What about?"

"About the terms of Shardan's neutrality."

"I see. What terms?"

"That would best be discussed at a meeting between the princess and the Shardan leaders," Maihara told him. "If she shows up here, she will be interested in ensuring that the rebels don't gain power here. I hear that there are Imperial soldiers stationed in the city," Maihara added.

Nardone looked impassive. "They're just a liaison, protecting Imperial interests."

A knock came at the door. The clerk entered with a small bag closed by a drawstring, and several papers, all of which he handed to Councillor Nardone.

Nardone passed Maihara the bag. "Here's an advance of immediate funds." It had weight, and it clinked. He handed her a sheet of papcr with printcd tcxt. "Hcrc's a loan application. Fill it in and take it to the bank named at the top. And here's the residency application. Fill these in and take them to the desk in the main hall."

Maihara nodded. "Thank you." Her hopes rose. Being offered free money was good. Perhaps Lord Nardone was going to be a useful contact after all. She handed the purse to Aurian, and gave Nardone a smile. "Thank you for your help. And you may have my address, in case the Imperial Princess shows up and you need help to facilitate a meeting."

"By all means," Nardone said. He reached a claw-like hand for a sheet of stationery and noted the name and street of the Luxor inn.

"Is there anything else I can help you with?" Nardone asked.

"No, thank you," Maihara said.

Nardone nodded. "I'll speak to my people. We may be in touch with you ... Lady Aurian."

Outside, Maihara breathed a sigh of relief. "How did you think that went?"

"Well, he didn't have you arrested," Lady Aurian said.

"How much money did he give us?"

Aurian undid the purse and looked inside. Ferris looked over her shoulder. "I don't know these coins," she said. "It's better than nothing."

"Do you think he'll arrange a meeting?"

Aurian looked toward the grand avenue. "You'll have to wait and see."

-25-

"How does it look with the shawl?" Maihara asked, twirling for Aurian's inspection. She caught a glimpse of herself in the shop mirror.

She needed an outfit in which she would feel confident and powerful, and this red dress, suitably expensive and ornate, with patterns of black beading, frills, a wide floor-length hem, short sleeves and a modest cleavage made her look grown-up but not too old-fashioned. Red had been her mother's favourite colour. Some money from their loan would pay for the new dress. And it came at a discount, the dressmaker having made it for a lady of similar figure who had failed to pay for it.

"It suits you," said Aurian. The dressmaker echoed her approval.

The previous evening, Maihara had received a note inviting her to a meeting today, at Lord Nardone's home on the outskirts of the city. Ferris meanwhile had stated that he had to present himself at the Imperial Army office in Halamar. She could order him not to go, but the situation would have to be faced sooner or later. The problem caused her to sleep badly.

At noon she arrived at the Nardone address, which proved to be a mansion in a tree-lined avenue. The full complement of soldiers had come with her, together with a smartly turned out Ferris who meant to visit the Army headquarters later, and Lady Aurian. A wooden fence ran along the roadside, and behind it were lush green gardens that spoke of heavy watering. A few men in livery, perhaps guards, patrolled the grounds. The house itself had a central block of mellow stone. The wings were of newer construction and did not match the original, their bigger windows and curling traceries standing higher than the older part. Maihara's first impression was of Nardone's wealth, and the second that the man who commissioned the extensions had no taste.

She glanced at Ferris and Lady Aurian for their reaction. "It's big," was all her chaperone said, with a slight grimace of distaste.

A stone-flagged path led to the main entrance. At the door, a liveried servant confirmed that this was Lord Nardone's mansion and yes, Maihara was expected. The hallway with its honey-coloured ashlar walls and round-log ceiling beams was pleasant in an architectural way, but was cluttered with showy furniture that was too ornate for her taste. Or perhaps she was used to plainness, having spent much of her life in a palace where private spaces were relatively austere and well-worn. In a prominent position was a bronze statue of a human figure, heavily corroded and with the upper extremities somewhat melted. It was ancient, a relic of the time of the Builders, another reminder that not everything from that time had perished. Her soldier escorts stared around, open-mouthed, till a sharp word from Ferris called them to order.

A servant ushered them into a plushly furnished room with a marble fireplace at one end, and a carved overmantel of white limestone that looked tall even for this chamber. As they entered, several people in noble dress rose from around a polished table that occupied the centre of the room.

"Her Grace the Imperial Princess Maihara Cordana, Duchess of Avergne," the servant intoned. She had misgivings about dropping the alias, but soon too many people would know of her presence in Halamar for the pretence to be maintained.

Lord Nardone came forward to greet her. If he was surprised that his visitor of the previous day was the Princess, he hid it well. He smiled in a knowing way and bowed.

The waiting nobles also bowed, save the sole woman, who curtsied. They all stared at her. Maihara acknowledged their greetings with a nod, uncomfortable from all this attention. She had not become used to it in Retis either. The woman, who was middle-aged and rather hard-faced, looked back at her with curiosity and a confident air.

Ferris and his men positioned themselves at the entrance to the room.

Nardone indicated a balding man on his right. "Lord Wixos of Largue, the leader of our little group."

Maihara met Wixos' gaze and nodded to acknowledge the introduction. "I am pleased to make your acquaintance."

Wixos was older than Nardone, and balding. Dark blotches spotted skin that was lined by age. His round, fleshy features made her think of indulgence and dissipation. Small eyes roamed over her, lingering on her bosom and neckline. She was suddenly conscious of the pale skin and necklace exposed by the V-neck of the red dress.

Nardone introduced the remaining three guests, who had business interests in property, country estates, manufacture and mining and were not purely politicians in the Council. That gave her the impression that they were forward looking rather than traditional land-holders. The hawk-nosed woman owned a mine. Lord Nardone, whom she had already met, owned many blocks of property in the city.

For a moment, she felt naïve and ill at ease. They were powerful and worldly people. Why would they pay attention to anything she said?

"Please, be seated with us. We are deeply honoured by your visit today, Your Grace," Nardone intoned. "May I offer you some refreshments?"

Maihara accepted, and a servant hurried forward.

The meeting started with small-talk, and Wixos asked why she had come, and filled in some details about the

Principality of Shardan. Maihara fielded questions on the proposed length of her stay, and the Emperor's attitude to her visit.

"There is something you could help us with," Lord Wixos said. "Just an idea, but soon we hope to call a vote in the Council for an election of councillors. We hope to increase the representation of our group." He glanced at the richly clad figures seated around the table.

"Who gets to vote?" Maihara asked. She did not see any pitfalls here.

"The eligible Lords of the principality vote on who gets appointed to the Council, to advise the Prince."

"I see." That sounded much like the High Council at Calah. "And what will you do with your increased number of councillors?"

"We will push for policies which I am sure you will approve," Nardone said smoothly. "Repress rebel agitation here, so that we can free up troops to help the Empire elsewhere, carry out public works that will provide employment for workers, that sort of thing."

Maihara nodded. This sounded hopeful, but she'd want to discourage any active intervention in the war.

Nardone went on to outline a number of problems and proposed solutions. They would deal with wide-spread support in the countryside for rebels by expelling the rebel sympathisers over the border. Troublesome workers who withdrew their labour and made demands would be dealt with by passing laws making it illegal to organise and incite withdrawal of labour. A red-faced man applauded.

She was surprised to learn how little the workers were paid - less a day than Ferris spent when they took tea.

Nardone also had grand plans for increasing amenities and providing employment, by redeveloping large parts of the city.

Many of these plans sounded good to Maihara. They clearly intended her to endorse their schemes, but she needed to ask what they would do for her. "But what if the owners don't want to sell?"

"They get offered compensation," Wixos said, eyes lingering on her chest.

"And where are they supposed to go, after you demolish their buildings?"

"They can buy further away from the city." Wixos seemed to have an answer to everything. She found it hard to like him.

Nardone leaned forward. "It would be helpful if you publicly endorsed our group. Speak at a gathering of electors."

Here it was, their demand. "Well, I suppose I could," she said. "But I need to know more about the situation here. If people sense that I'm ill-informed, my endorsement will not carry much weight."

"Of course, Your Grace," Nardone murmured. "We can brief you."

As Imperial Princess, she ought to meet with Shardan's Prince, but that might be too far, too soon. Word of a high-level Prince-Princess meeting was certain to filter back to the Emperor, and her father was sure to see it as crossing a red line. "A briefing would be welcome." So would some alternative points of view.

"Excellent." Wixos looked pleased. He glanced across to Nardone. "We could arrange a meeting with more of our people for tomorrow."

Nardone nodded. "But tell us, Your Grace, what are you hoping to secure in return?"

She took a breath. "First, I want to have protection from any attempt by the rebel diplomats here to extradite me to Calah, and likewise I do not wish to be forced to return to the Empire before the line of succession is confirmed."

Wixos raised his eyebrows at this last.

"Secondly, financial support for my residency in Shardan, and in time, some sort of position."

Nardone smiled, in a way that appeared studied. "Be reassured on all three points. We can frustrate any diplomatic moves to extradite you. We may be able to offer you a palace—"

Lady Aurian's jaw dropped. Maihara strove to conceal a childish astonishment. A palace? She was a princess. Of course she deserved a palace. "Go on."

"—and a regular subsidy for your expenses, if you continue to lend your name to us. And if you have achieved the age of majority, who knows? We could create a suitable position for you."

"Is there a problem with the Imperial succession?" Wixos asked.

Maihara paused, weighing her words. "My brother, the notional heir, is in rebel hands, and I do not have the warmest relations with my father. My presence could be troublesome."

"Ultimately, the position of Prince is electable, in special circumstances," Nardone murmured.

Aurian stifled a giggle. Maihara glanced at her in surprise.

Wixos reddened and slapped the table. It took Maihara a moment to realise that he was angry with Nardone, not Lady Aurian.

"Nardone, don't say such things, even as a joke."

Nardone glared, then forced a smile. "My apologies, I meant it purely as a constitutional point. Not implying any disloyalty to the Prince."

Maihara strove not to show her surprise. Nardone seemed to hint that they could elect her Princess of Shardan if something happened to the current Prince. Perhaps the Prince did not have much power, or was Nardone just playing her along? "I see," she said, not daring to say more. The cards in this game were all face-down.

Wixos was shaking his head. "But how will the Emperor regard all this? Has he approved your visit and activities here?"

"Not as such," Maihara said with reluctance. "The Emperor ought to be kept informed, but if it's helping hold the Empire together, he should not object."

Wixos looked grave. "We should not do anything that troubles the Emperor."

"Of course not," Nardone said. "The Emperor should be told that his eldest child has arrived safely here, and that we are treating her with the respect her status deserves."

After Aurian's warnings, the thought of telling her parent her whereabouts made Maihara uneasy. Maybe revealing herself as Imperial Princess here had been a mistake.

"And it could be mentioned that we are taking measures to keep Shardan safe as an ally of the Empire, and hint that Her Grace approves," Nardone said. "We are a long way from Chancungra. By the time any reaction comes back, the electors will have met, Her Grace will have spoken, an election will have taken place, and our group will be putting into place measures of which the Emperor ought to approve." He turned to Wixos. "What do you say?"

Wixos nodded his bald head. "That's well argued, Councillor."

Maihara found the argument only slightly reassuring.

"We will set up a meeting with our group for tomorrow, then?" Nardone said.

"At my mansion?" Wixos said. He struggled out of his chair. Nardone gestured for one of his servants to help him.

"Indeed," Nardone said. He turned to Maihara. "By the way, Your Grace, you don't need to seek a loan. The Imperial Treasury maintains accounts with banks in the city, and as a Crown Princess you can simply present a written money order."

Maihara greeted this news with relief. "How do I do that?"

"I'll show you." He called for ink and paper. A few minutes later, she had an official-looking money order.

"As Her Grace leaves, I would like to show her the palace we have in mind," Nardone said. "It's nearby."

Maihara rose. "Yes, thank you. That would be most interesting, your Lordship." It was more than interesting. Nobody had offered her a palace before, and she was consumed with a desire to see what it was like, and whether it measured up to the picture in her mind.

A little way down the avenue, a long white building lay partly concealed by trees. Behind the foliage, Maihara glimpsed a central portico and two wings, rambling roofs and turrets. Weeds grew on high parapets, paint was peeling and the gardens were overgrown. But she saw that it could be beautiful. She liked it at once.

"It needs a little attention," Lord Nardone said. "But it's sound inside, and fully furnished."

"Does anyone live in it?"

"An old lady occupies a few rooms. Do you want to see what it's like inside?"

"Yes, of course." She was avid to see if the interior looked as elegant.

"We can't disturb her, but if we move quietly, we can look through a window in the left wing. That will give you some idea."

"Yes, let's."

Maihara, with Aurian, Ferris and a trooper, followed Nardone along a weedy path. As they approached a more open space, Nardone turned and beckoned with his hand. "This way, Your Grace."

Slightly out of breath, Maihara arrived at a tall, uncurtained window. Inside, the room was well lit by daylight. The walls were finished with pastel-hued wallpaper, tall mirrors, and vertical plasterwork panels, and the coffered ceiling had a central painting. Two elegant green-upholstered Empire chairs peeked out from under dust sheets.

"It's lovely," she breathed.

"I'm glad you like it, Your Grace. But let's not linger here and upset the servants."

On the way to the Imperial Army barracks, Maihara asked Aurian and Ferris for their reactions.

Ferris fingered his moustache and looked uncomfortable. "I can't comment on political matters, Your Grace. But it could be to these men's advantage to have you endorse their political party."

Maihara had come to the same conclusion. "Thank you, Ferris." She looked to Lady Aurian.

"That palace was impressive," she said. "If they are offering you that, they must be serious people, and they must want something from you. But you should inform your father before you do anything that might cause trouble."

"And what about their policies?"

"It sounded good, but I hope you know what you are doing," Aurian said.

Maihara nodded. She'd stopped listening to Aurian, her mind filled with the swish and ruffle of ladies' dresses across the polished floors of her refurbished palace. Maybe even being made Princess of Shardan when she reached the age of majority. The backing of the Nardone-Wixos faction would be very useful, and the prospect filled her with an enthusiasm she had not felt for some time.

Ferris pointed ahead. "That's the Imperial Army office."

Maihara's good mood evaporated at the sight of the Imperial flag flying above a plain building. She had to deal with the issue of her Imperial Army escort, and perhaps defend the loyal Ferris. Her father knew nothing of her presence here, but the more contact she had with the army, the sooner he would find out, and direct his army to return her to Chancungra. It made her think of her siblings. And then about Tarchon, who might be still looking for her. None of this raised her spirits.

Rows of rectangular windows on two levels faced forward, and at the centre was an entry for wheeled vehicles. Above the entry, the Imperial flag dangled on an angled pole.

Like a good officer, Ferris also intended to enquire after the men wounded at Retis. As he presented himself at the front door, he looked nervous.

An orderly led them to an office with whitewashed brick walls in the rear of the building, looking out onto a small grassy square. A tall man, with a stubble of greying hair, rose as they entered. A clerk sat at a desk behind him.

Ferris saluted, with a quick movement. "Lieutenant Ferris reporting, sir."

"At ease." The senior officer turned to eye Maihara and her chaperone. He bowed to Maihara, a quick, precise movement. "Her Grace Maihara Cordana, I presume."

"Yes." Maihara nodded.

"And Lady Aurian. The lieutenant's descriptions were accurate."

Maihara thought she was becoming disagreeably well known in Halamar.

"I am Colonel Sarkis, commanding the Imperial barracks and detachment here." He pointed to a pair of chairs. "Please be seated, Your Grace. May I offer you some refreshment?"

Maihara took a chair. "Nothing, thank you." As soon as she sat, she sensed that it put her at a disadvantage. The colonel was quite tall. Aurian stood, with her hand on the back of Maihara's chair.

"Your Grace, we are honoured by your presence, and we hope you are enjoying your visit to Halamar. Please forgive me for raising the question of your escort, but the Army provided it on the understanding that you were returning to Imperial territory. Is this still the case?"

Maihara shifted uncomfortably in the chair, her throat tightening.

"I was hoping to remain in Halamar for a while, Colonel."

The colonel nodded his head in acknowledgement. "Then we have to examine the continuation of your escort. Forgive me, but I understand that Your Grace has not yet attained the age of majority?"

Maihara's discomfort increased. "No, I haven't."

The colonel seemed to relax a fraction. "Under the constitution therefore, you cannot command us to provide an escort."

Maihara's heart jumped.

The colonel raised a hand in a pacifying gesture. "But do not be concerned. We cannot allow an Imperial Princess to go unguarded. We will continue to provide a suitable escort, but with great respect, I have to suggest certain conditions."

Maihara doubted that the colonel would be so forthright if she was a prince. She was not going to like this. "So what are you saying?"

"If you reside quietly in Halamar for a short time, that should not be a problem. But we hope you will not engage in any activities that would cause difficulties, like engaging in local politics or harming the reputation of the Imperial court."

She tried to mask her reaction as her throat tightened. This directive directly clashed with her discussions with Nardone and Wixos. Rather than say anything, she nodded.

"Your Grace's position here seems somewhat irregular. We would be happier if you agreed to return to Imperial territory in the near future. Escorting you there would best fulfil our duty to the Emperor. Otherwise we will be obliged to make a report."

"But I don't want to go back there." Maihara tapped her foot hard on the floor. The colonel raised an eyebrow.

"My father and I don't get on." As soon as she said it, she was aware that it made her sound like a schoolgirl.

"I'm sorry to hear that," the colonel said, not smiling. "Fathers and strong-willed daughters often don't."

How had he deduced on such a brief acquaintance that she was 'strong-willed'? The answer was obvious. Ferris. She glanced at the lieutenant, who stood by the colonel's desk, looking ill at ease.

"Can I enquire if you have any particular plans for your stay, Your Grace?"

She had anticipated that question. "I hope to meet some of the leading citizens and find out their views. Perhaps encourage them not to let the principality be drawn into conflict."

The colonel stiffened. "That's hardly a task for a young

Princess. I think we already have the Varlords here on a similar mission."

"If they were making a good job of it, Shardan would have come to Calah's aid and I'd still be in the palace there." She spoke with some force.

"With respect, Your Grace, that's a matter of judgement. Even if they'd arrived in time, it's questionable whether they had sufficient forces."

Maihara nodded, not wanting to argue with a professional officer about this. "I see. By the way, there are rumours that the Emperor hoped to produce regiments of mechanical soldiers. Have you heard anything?"

"I've not heard any more than you appear to have, Your Grace. They'd have to be magical."

That wasn't a bad guess. "Yes, Colonel."

"And I would prefer to see that you had the Emperor's explicit backing for speaking with the local civic leaders."

Maihara's lips tightened. She guessed that he would not dare go so far as to explicitly forbid her. "I note your concerns, Colonel. I'll try not to cause any scandal."

The colonel continued to look at her. She shifted under his gaze.

"Colonel, perhaps you can tell me what you make of the setup here? There's a Prince, but also councillors, and some talk of elections."

The Colonel nodded. "After some popular unrest fifty years ago, they tried to introduce a more modern system of government. Their business, of course. The Prince is head of state, but does not have much executive power. He has to rule with consent of the Council, which means he needs their agreement to create laws or declare war. As for the councillors, there seem to be various factions, one made up of the old nobility, and another the new money. People like Wixos. Some of these people are hardliners, and others are bleeding hearts who think the common people should be helped. The latter views are spread across the other factions to some degree. There are also people in the various groups who favour closer links with the Empire, and encourage our token presence here."

"Wixos is a Lord," Maihara commented.

"You can buy titles here, Your Grace."

"And there's an election soon? Who are you hoping will win?"

"I'm hoping I won't have to sort out their squabble for them." The colonel turned to face the door. "So you consent to be provided with an escort, Your Grace?"

She assumed this was an official protocol. "Yes," she said in a low voice. "The same escort, if possible."

The colonel bowed his head. "As you wish, Your Grace. You may retain Ferris and his six soldiers until further notice."

They waited for Ferris beside the carriage, with the corporal and the five soldiers. "What a tiresome man," Maihara complained. "If he was going to let me keep the escort, why all that fuss? He doesn't want me to do anything here except shop."

"He was covering his back," Aurian said. "If he gives you an escort to go around conspiring, he could find himself in serious trouble. But he can't refuse you a bodyguard. And now the Imperial Army knows that you're here."

Maihara gave her a look. "Conspiring? That colonel doesn't want me to talk to the locals, but I need to make a deal with Nardone and his friends. If I don't, I'll find myself being escorted back to Chancungra, back to a man who wears a metal mask and called me a witch." The thought of it, and the Fort dungeons, gave her a chill.

***

Maihara stopped at the door of her room. The place felt different. She and Aurian had left it untidy, with garments draped over the bed and a chair back, and wrapping paper in a corner. But this untidy? It looked wrong. It had not been like this when she left it. A sinking feeling gripped her stomach.

"Somebody's been in here," she said to Aurian, behind

her. "Thieves?"

"The inn servants will have come in to clean the room," Aurian said.

Maihara shook her head. "No, it's less tidy than it was before." She ran across to the chest of drawers below the window and yanked open the top drawer. It was still filled with undergarments, but items she had folded were rumpled and turned over.

"Somebody's been through this!"

Aurian ran to the smaller chest where she had put her things and pulled open a drawer. She turned, with a distressed look on her face. "Somebody's been in mine, too."

"Guards!" Maihara shouted.

Trooper Ostein entered at once. He stopped and glanced around the room before turning to Maihara with an animated and uncertain expression. "Ma'am?"

"A thief has been in here. Please check the other rooms, and fetch the Lieutenant." Disturbed and angry, she spun around to see that the wardrobe near the door was ajar.

Another trooper and Corporal Streit entered at Ostein's heels. They sprang into action, one wrenching open the connecting doors to the dressing room and the other disappearing into the passage. Within a minute they had checked the other rooms for intruders and called for Ferris.

Ferris appeared from below, at a run. "What is it, Your Grace?"

"A robber has been in here while we were out," Maihara said. "Could you have the inn staff questioned, in case they saw anything?"

"Or did it," one of the soldiers muttered.

"Has anything valuable been stolen?" Ferris asked.

"I don't know yet. But they have moved things, turned them over."

"If you could check, Your Grace?" Ferris said. "I'll question the staff." He detailed two soldiers to accompany him, and exited.

Shock, anger and fear rippled over Maihara as she

looked through her other possessions, mostly clothing. The intruder had disturbed everything, but nothing appeared to be damaged. Her few items of costume jewellery were still in the small upper drawer where she had left them. Only a pair of gilt bangles was missing, but that did not diminish the sense of violation.

She turned to Aurian, who was seated at her side of the room looking tearful. Maihara went over to her. "Has anything been taken?"

Aurian shook her head. "Somebody has fingered all my things. It's horrible. I don't want them."

Maihara took Aurian's hands. "We can get your things washed. I wonder how the thief got in?"

Aurian did not reply. Maihara squeezed her shoulder.

The curtained window looked undisturbed, and it was high above a yard. She crossed to the door, and bent to inspect the lock.

Corporal Streit cleared his throat. "May I examine that, Your Grace?"

She stood aside while he crouched to examine the door lock.

"There are scratches on the outside. Probably not significant. It's a good lock, Your Grace, but a professional thief could open this."

She clicked her tongue. This wasn't proving anything.

"And the inn staff have a key?"

"Almost certainly, Your Grace."

"How else could they have got in?" She glanced at the door to the small wash-room.

Corporal Streit took the hint. "I'll look around, Your Grace."

Maihara heard muffled voices downstairs. She beckoned to Trooper Sangha. "Follow me."

Downstairs, in the lobby, Ferris was haranguing the innkeeper. "Your security is inadequate. I'm holding you responsible for this."

"Ferris," Maihara said.

"Your Grace?"

"We've checked for anything stolen. There's only a pair of bangles that I can't find." Taking deep breaths, she fought down the anger that flushed through her body at this vile intrusion.

Ferris nodded.

"My humblest apologies, your Ladyship," the innkeeper said, bowing. "I am sorry for your distress and loss. If there's anything I can do to make amends?" He sounded anxious.

"Well," Maihara said. She turned at a sound behind her. Two troopers had several of the inn workers penned in a room off the lobby and were arguing with them.

"Have you questioned the staff yet?" she asked Ferris.

"They're trying," he said, pointing across the lobby. "So far, nobody knows anything."

It was as Maihara expected.

"I can offer a free extra night, or free meals," the innkeeper offered, in a desperate tone.

"We'll take the free meals," Maihara said quickly. She felt that the inn was liable for this outrage, but she did not want to be vindictive. She crossed the lobby to speak to the soldiers questioning the staff.

"Only two bangles are missing, as far as we know," she told them.

Hibbett pointed an accusing finger at a frightened-looking woman in a maid's outfit. "That one was cleaning your room, they say."

Maihara did not respond. She was not convinced that the intruder was one of the staff. She turned back and took Ferris aside.

"Ferris, do you think the intruder came from outside? Your corporal says a criminal could have undone the lock."

"Why do you suspect that, Your Grace?"

"I'm sure Aurian locked it. Someone searched the room thoroughly, disturbed lots of things, but took almost nothing. As if they were looking for something they didn't find. Maybe they thought I arrived laden with cash and left it in the room? The inn staff would not have left a mess if they wanted to take something."

"Why take the bangles, then?"

Maihara shrugged. "Impulse? Or to make it look like robbery. I don't like it. It's as if they knew who we were."

"The innkeeper may do," Ferris pointed out. "And some of his staff."

"Were any other guests robbed?" she asked.

"We don't know yet," Ferris said. "Not till they return and complain."

By nightfall the investigation had petered out inconclusively. No other guests reported a theft or intrusion.

Prompted by Aurian's distress, Maihara had asked Ferris to have herself and Aurian moved to another room. She herself had no desire to sleep in the burgled room again.

"You should apologise to the inn staff," Maihara told Ferris at dinner. The waiters were serving the meal in a rather sullen manner, banging down plates and cutlery.

Ferris ran fingers through his hair. "Why? We don't know they're innocent."

"We don't know if any of them is guilty. It's better not to leave all of them with a bad feeling."

Ferris nodded. "Yes, Your Grace. I'll offer a discreet reward for information, if I get the chance."

"Who do you think did this?" Aurian asked, in a low voice.

"Either professional thieves, looking for high value, or somebody's secret service," Ferris said.

Maihara glanced at Aurian. It could have been anyone, including her father's Fifth Bureau, and it left her with a sinking sense of insecurity. Colonel Sarkis' attitude about the bodyguard had left her anxious and tense with annoyance. And now this. Disclosing her identity and presence here had been a mistake. The sooner she got herself safely established with people of influence in Halamar, the better.

-26-

Next day, by appointment, Maihara arrived by carriage outside Wixos's mansion. It was as big as the dilapidated palace she had been offered in the next street, and newer looking than Nardone's mansion, with large expanses of smooth, blank stone and a portico with a single angled roof plane. It shouted wealth, confident but restrained taste, and modernity. A tremor of excitement and apprehension ran through her. She needed to make a good impression here.

"It looks like a Chancungran building," Maihara said, as their hire carriage turned onto a gravelled driveway. She recalled the modern Imperial Palace at Chancungra from a visit years earlier in her childhood. Her mother would have known the palace well.

"If you say so," Lady Aurian murmured.

They were received by half a dozen liveried servants, who brought a carpeted stool to help Maihara down from the carriage, and ushered her party through the towering main doors with many obsequious bows. Lord Wixos, clad in a glittering robe of coloured silk, waited inside the doors, along with a much younger blonde woman in a long sweeping dress, also of coloured silk that reflected the light.

Lord Wixos bowed and welcomed her to his home. His eyes flickered over the escort of Ferris and six soldiers, but he did not comment.

Turning, she saw that behind her hung a huge portrait of Wixos, in formal dress, with his trophy wife. In the portrait his skin blotches barely showed.

"Thank you," Maihara said, a little distracted. Her eyes glanced around the entrance hall, huge, high, brightly daylit from above and its walls decorated with pastel colours and several gigantic portraits. Pale statues of human figures, mostly nude, posed at the sides of the floor space.

Lord Wixos and consort led the way, along a wide, high corridor lined with paintings, occasional furniture with rich decoration, and sculptures. Several of the portraits resembled Lord Wixos. Scared-looking servants scuttled away. Maihara glimpsed richly furnished rooms, and an indoor pool, all blue surfaces and still water, with steps leading down into it. It looked as though the designer had seen the Imperial Palace at Chancungra and tried to outdo it.

They arrived at a room panelled in dark wood. Wixos' consort slipped away. Half a dozen men and one woman were seated here in dining chairs around a long white-draped table set for a meal, and they rose as Wixos entered. He waved an arm for silence.

"May I introduce Her Grace the Imperial Princess Maihara Cordana, Duchess of Avergne."

Maihara recognised one or two people in the room from the previous day. Anxious to create a good impression, she struggled to remember names as Wixos introduced them.

Introductions completed, they sat around the table. Lord Wixos called for servants, who served tea and small round cakes. Maihara glanced again at a lord seated near her, who had now placed his arms on the table-top. His right hand appeared to be made of shiny yellow metal, with joints for the fingers, and many finely-cut screw heads. An ornamental prosthesis? It reminded her of her father's face at Kunn. She shivered.

The man saw her looking, and flexed his metal fingers. It was a working hand. A giddy feeling of shock swept over her, and she steeled herself not to faint. This was the kind of work of which her father had boasted, and which she suspected she had seen at Kunn. But here, in Halamar? It meant that the machine-men she feared were becoming real.

"Milord, what happened to your hand, if you'll pardon me asking," she managed.

The man smiled, a little smugly. "This?" He raised and turned it. "I had this done in the East. It was a special favour, but I still had to pay a fat purse for the work. It's amazing what they are doing with the magical arts there."

A magical hand? She had a strong impulse to touch it, to feel if it was real. "But, why?"

"I lost the original in an accident. I did not want to live as a one-handed man, Your Grace."

The thought of such a limb loss made her wince. "I'm sorry. That must have been very unpleasant. Are there others like you? Was that made in the Imperial workshops?"

"I was privileged. I understand only a small number of people have had work done."

"And what is it? How—?" She shivered

"A blend of man and machine. There are rumours of artificial men, or complete machine bodies, but nobody is allowed to see inside the Imperial workshops."

Her spine tingled. "But, if you don't mind me asking, how is it done? How is this possible?" She reached out, wanting to touch the shiny hand.

The man smiled. "I was not in a state to note what they did, but I understand they have rediscovered some magical knowledge of the ancients. They've been working on it for years."

Maihara was unable to compose a polite response. Only men were allowed to work with magic. Women who tried were abused as witches, dangerous creatures.

"You knew nothing of this, Your Grace?"

She shook her head, dizzied, as if the scene were behind glass. "Did you see or hear anything of golim soldiers there?"

The man looked at her as if finding her question sharper than he expected. "They don't say. But it is no secret that the Imperial army is small in numbers. They need a mechanical reinforcement."

Maihara nodded. "Quite." Lord Farnak had spoken of her father boasting that a golim army would soon throw back the rebels. The revelation that it was not just talk did not please her at all; it was an Imperial version of the Dhikr.

Wixos encouraged his guests to get up and sample sweetmeats and drinks placed on tables around the sides of the room. Beside the tables stood easels with sketch plans of new buildings.

"Please refresh yourselves and look at the plans," he said.

Maihara rose to her feet with Aurian at her elbow. Here was her chance to press Wixos' group for details of their plans, but she was far more interested in learning more about magical blends of man and machine parts produced in the East. She saw no one else with obvious modifications, but Wixos' blonde trophy wife glided so smoothly that she might have had wheels instead of legs under her long, bell-shaped floor-sweeping dress. What a horrible thought.

A man in a plain grey robe greeted her politely, enquiring about her escape from the rebels. He was middle-aged, balding and otherwise unremarkable, with a broad face. She related a by now well-rehearsed story, and dared ask him what he knew of magical body modifications in the principality. "Like that esteemed Lord's arm," she added.

"I am surprised such things are not known in Calah." His face gave nothing away.

"I only knew of automatons, which were not magical at all," she said. "There were amazing automatons on display at the Palace."

The man raised a hand. "I have heard of such things, Your Grace. I was thinking of magical works. You are sure there was nothing?"

"Quite sure." She was not sure what he was getting at, and she had no intention of disclosing her own exploits.

Her anonymous questioner looped his thumb and mid-finger. "I apologise for mentioning it, Your Grace, but there is a rumour you were gifted a magical box on your fourteenth birthday."

She strove to conceal her shock. Who was this man and how did he know this? On the other hand, Sihrima had blurted before the whole court that her sister was a witch and had received a weird box. And others must have known, including the person who delivered it.

"Oh, that. It wasn't really magical. And it disappeared after a while." She avoided his gaze. "I don't know what happened to it."

"You don't remember what was inside?"

She shook her head. "I couldn't even open it. There was no visible catch."

The man made a surprised face and did not press her further on the subject.

Wixos had left the room. Instead, Lord Nardone was there, glaring for some reason at Ferris. Lord Nardone greeted her respectfully. "Lord Wixos has introduced the others, I believe?" he said.

"Yes, thank you. These are your plans for rebuilding the city?"

Nardone pointed out features of the plans for a couple of minutes. As soon as Nardone's attention switched to another guest, Ferris sidled to Maihara's side.

"There's another meeting going on, down the passage," he said in her ear.

"Ah," she said. That explained where Wixos had gone, and why Nardone had looked annoyed. He had seen Ferris exploring. So why had they not mentioned this other meeting to her? She reached inside herself to contact the magic in this part of the city. Pretending to look at the architectural drawings, she launched her spy and sent it out into the passage. The spy view superimposed itself on the drawings before her. A few false moves into empty rooms, and it showed her another table of refreshments, and Wixos's torso.

In the other room, Wixos was talking. "I have asked the servants not to attend. I hope you don't mind serving yourselves."

"It's fine. We can talk freely with no nosy bastard

servants listening". The other man was the red-faced noble with waved hair who had the previous day approved removal of rebels.

"How are you really going to make the rebel sympathisers in those rural districts leave the principality?" Wixos asked, with a laugh.

"Set fire to their huts and crops," the man said without hesitation. "Let the militia kill a few of those who fight back. We can blame the rebels."

Maihara strove to hide her shock. She had imagined some kind of enforced travel.

"Do the militia know which ones are loyal to the Empire?" Wixos asked.

The man merely shrugged.

Maihara moved the spy behind two men who were examining a city map which apparently showed a planned development. One jabbed a finger at a central area, well away from the sector outlined in red. "Here's the next scheme. The Vincis warren's ripe for development. You can't drive a cart through those alleys, and it's full of Vees. I never liked them anyway."

"Foreign tricksters."

"There's something alien about them."

"It needs a good riot. Denounce them as baby poisoners."

"Good plan. No compensation needed if we can winkle them out."

The men laughed.

Maihara muted the spy and turned her attention to her surroundings. In the room with her, she recognised the hard-faced noblewoman from yesterday's meeting. She edged toward her, trailed by Aurian and Ferris, and caught the woman's eye. A more pleasant expression crossed the noble's face, and she turned.

"It's pleasing to see a woman engaged in politics," Maihara said by way of an opener.

The woman, Lady Rygard, made a small curtsy. "Thank

you, Your Grace. I am merely continuing the work of my late husband, who was on the Council."

"I hear you own a mine. What does it produce?"

Lady Rygard tipped her head to one side, examining Maihara with interest. "Your Grace, it produces red oxide that can be refined into metal, for tools, weapons and things."

"And do you manage it yourself?"

"Yes, it's the best way of ensuring I'm not being robbed or cheated. People think a woman can't manage a big estate, but I soon show them they're wrong."

With a shock, she spotted Lord Nardone in the spy view. She looked around, heart thumping. Nardone was no longer in this room.

Instead, he was speaking to somebody in the other meeting.

"Lord Nardone, what's the story of that palace you offered to the Cordana girl?"

"The story, sir?"

"Why is it neglected, with one old lady living in it?"

Lord Nardone smiled, rather like a sea-monster baring its teeth, she thought. "It was built by a wealthy and illustrious family, who lost their money through poor investments. The old lady is the last of the line. My son has been diligent in visiting her, and the poor old lady relies on my dear boy to such an extent she has insisted on leaving it to him....."

"That's lucky. But has she no heirs at all?"

Nardone shrugged. "There are nephews, once removed. I'm afraid they are ne'er-do-wells. Drunkenness and gambling. Never visit. The dear Countess has wiped her hands of them."

"Would they have inherited if she hadn't left it to your son?"

Nardone shrugged again. "What would they do with a palace? They don't have money to maintain it. We're doing them a favour. Anyway, the Countess is quite happy for my son to have it."

Maihara's pleasure at being offered a palace evaporated. It would almost be like receiving stolen property. She ground her teeth. Tarchon was a nicer man than any of these people.

She moved the spy on to another conversation.

"...plain and overweight," a richly dressed man was saying. "She's falling for it. And whatever happens, we'll be good. If she goes home to complain, she'll probably end up in a cell."

The young man he was talking to laughed. "Naïve. She totally went for Nardone's palace, I hear."

Maihara clenched her fists. Eavesdroppers never heard anything good about themselves, but this was beyond intolerable. They had all been lying, and they were laughing at her.

"Are you feeling well, Princess?" The lady mine-owner was eyeing her with concern.

Maihara snapped her attention back to the room and the conversation she was supposed to be having.

"I, er—"

"You look a little flushed, Your Grace."

"It's the heat." Maihara grasped at some straw with which to continue the conversation. "There's been talk of trouble with workers. Have you had any? The kind of thing Nardone mentioned yesterday?"

Lady Rygard shrugged. "They tried withdrawing their labour. My overseer said we should just hire more, so that's what we did."

"What were they demanding?"

"They complained about accidents, ground-slips. But they were after more money, an extra obol a day."

"And the mine couldn't afford it?"

"There are swarms of them. If I paid an extra obol per day, I'd be tens of thousands of obols a year out of pocket."

Attuned by the conversations coming through the spy link, Maihara did not like the tone of this.

"I see." She was not here to argue, but she was sure the workers needed those obols more than the Countess Rygard.

Lord Wixos was in her room again and calling the meeting to order. More people, whom she had glimpsed in the other meeting, were filing in and taking seats around the dining table. Maihara shut off the spy, now showing an empty room. The effort of using the magic had drained her.

Servants came in with plates and tureens of food, which they placed on the table, and more bottles of drink. Maihara took a seat between the lady mine-owner and the man in grey. Maihara did not register a mouthful of what she ate or drank during the meal. She would be expected to give some response to the Wixos faction's overtures and, mindful of the possibility of extradition, she dreaded making remarks that would offend her hosts.

At the end of the meal, Wixos rose to his feet. "We have all met Her Grace," Wixos said smoothly. "She has met us and been briefed on our plans. Perhaps she has some remarks to make."

Maihara got to her feet. Her mouth was dry as she looked around the expectant faces.

"I am concerned by a few things I have heard in the past days," she said. "The original revolt in the North started because there were complaints about low wages, anger about repression and anger about a famine which some claimed was caused by grain speculators. The response of the authorities was to send in troops to deal violently with those responsible, and many people died. And what was the result?" Despite herself, she found her voice rising, and becoming more impassioned. What she had just overheard had offended her too much. "Part of the army mutinied, and the revolt grew till it engulfed the Western capital and forced the Emperor to flee."

She paused, while the lords listened grim-faced, all eyes on her. "And what is happening here? It seems that the same conditions that encouraged revolt in the North persist here in the principality – low wages and so forth. And what

353

is your answer? It seems you intend to violently crush dissent. The same tactic that totally failed in the North."

An outbreak of muttering interrupted her speech. She let it continue, and then rode over it in a louder voice. "So what is your answer?"

The mutterings grew angrier. Lord Wixos called for silence. "As I understand it, Your Grace, the Dhikr invaded the North and seized whole provinces."

"That was after the revolt started," she said.

"The revolt might have been put down if the Dhikr had not invaded," Lord Nardone said. "It's different here."

"You think the Dhikr won't come here?" Maihara said. "True, they are a long way off, but there is not much between their conquests and Shardan, just the central desert. I have seen the Dhikr. They are savage brutes and seasoned fighters. If they come, you are doomed. The crows will feast in your palaces."

Her words chilled the room.

"Repressing unrest has worked in the past," Lord Wixos said. "What do you suggest, Your Grace?" His tone sounded faintly patronising.

"Address the complaints of the poor in a more constructive way. Then the principality will stand together if attacked."

"They'll do that in any case," said one of the nobles.

"They didn't in the North," Maihara pointed out. But they did not seem to be listening.

"We hope to have means," Lord Wixos said.

"That's the same old answer," she said. "More violence." She clenched her fists in frustration. During the dinner, the man in grey had hinted that the Empire's researchers were developing new war-machines. Mechanical men. After seeing the hand, Maihara no longer thought the Emperor's plan of golim armies a joke.

Lord Wixos rapped on the table, not looking at her. "Shall we adjourn and consider our positions?"

***

"Those people were awful," Maihara said, as soon as the carriage moved off.

"I wouldn't argue with that," Lady Aurian said. "So your answer was 'No'."

Maihara turned in surprise. "I told them I would have to consider it further, that I had doubts."

"I thought you made it clear that you didn't like their policies and weren't interested."

"Are you sure?" She had assumed that despite the frank exchange of views it would still be possible to repair relations.

"They did not look pleased."

Maihara bit her lip. "I didn't want to leave them with that impression. I just didn't like what I heard of their plans."

Lady Aurian raised an eyebrow. "I didn't hear anything unacceptable."

"I know what they really intend. They want to wipe out villages with rebel sympathisers in them by burning them down and having the militia kill them. They want to make money by grabbing people's houses on the cheap, or for nothing, and redeveloping. They think the poor are there for them to exploit. And that palace they are offering me, it doesn't belong to them. They're planning to steal it from an old lady's nephews."

"You overheard something you weren't meant to, didn't you?"

Maihara was silent.

"Look, Maihara, we are both Imperial noblewomen. We enjoy a nice lifestyle, with comfort and money and good food. You have a proud name to maintain. If you want this to continue, you know what you have to do. Just hold your nose and do what others do."

The carriage turned a corner and headed into a more mundane and built-up street of the city. The two soldiers beside Ferris swayed into the bend, maintaining impassive expressions.

Maihara shook her head. "I can't give my name to

burning the poor out and exploiting them." She had met many rebel supporters, and to her they were just people. "I want reform, not more of the same vicious stupidity and greed. I'd rather starve."

"Then unless you find some other support, you'll be going back to Chancungra under escort, unless the rebels persuade the Prince to hand you over to them. Your father will be more convinced than ever that you're a threat, after you spent months being friendly with the rebels. You had better keep talking to Wixos' people."

Maihara slumped in her seat. She didn't want that. The trap was closing. Either the horrible Shardan nobles or a return to Chancungra and her father's crazed animosity.

Aurian's eyes narrowed. "I hope you're not thinking of going over to the rebels. To that Tarchon."

"No! I can't, whatever my opinions. Not as Imperial Princess. That would be treason."

"I'm glad to hear it, Your Grace. Better make your mind up quickly. Accept their offer."

"You sound like that Countess," Maihara said resentfully. "She only cared about her income."

Aurian went red. "Look, Your Grace. I'd be more like that Countess if it wasn't for your rebels. I'd have an estate. And a husband."

It was true. "I'm sorry. I should not have said that." A surge of frustration and anger swept through her. She clutched her hair and pulled it till it hurt. "I don't know! I don't know what to do!"

Aurian folded her arms and sat back, waiting till Maihara had subsided. She turned to Ferris. "Have you anything to say, Lieutenant?"

Ferris shook his head. "No, milady. I'm only here to guard the Princess against danger. As the Colonel ordered. Nothing else."

"I could find out what the other politicians are like," Maihara said. "There must be at least one other group on the Council."

"There are," Aurian said. "While you were talking to

those people, I heard talk about the others. There is a group of more liberal councillors, who want to introduce policies that would please the rebels. That's what this whole election thing is about."

Maihara raised her head. "That's it. I should talk to this other group."

"I don't think so," Aurian said sharply. "You encouraged Wixos and Nardone, you let them believe you would support them, and now you go talk to the liberals. How do you think the first lot will react?"

"I'd look untrustworthy," Maihara said in a small voice.

"More than that. If the liberals block their schemes, members of the first group could lose a lot of potential profits. They won't like that. And they will be annoyed if they fail to get more candidates elected without your endorsement."

"So what might they do?" Maihara asked, with a sense of unease.

Their carriage was now approaching the new city centre.

"They would not dare to attack you physically, the Emperor's daughter. But they could make things difficult. They might turn people against you and make it hard for you to remain in Shardan. Maybe encourage your extradition instead of blocking it."

Aurian turned to look at Ferris, so Maihara did the same. He was tight-lipped as he met Lady Aurian's gaze.

"Shall I turn the carriage around?" Aurian asked. "So you can tell Wixos it's a yes? I know you're ambitious."

"No," Maihara said in a faint voice. What would Tarchon expect her to do?

"Your mind is made up?"

"Yes. I don't care if I have an awful life. If they contact me, I'll tell them I meant no."

"And you won't be contacting the liberals instead?"

"I don't know. I know nothing about them. Did you get any names?"

"Yes," Lady Aurian said.

"I should be more careful next time. The liberals may turn out to be as bad as the others, or useless."

"Fine," Lady Aurian said. "So what are you going to do?"

"I don't know. Avoid the Wixos group while we find out about the others." None of the prospects that passed through her mind seemed appealing.

Earlier, guided by Lord Nardone, Maihara had drafted a handwritten money order to draw cash from an Imperial bank account. Nardone had persuaded her this was better than taking out a loan.

She handed the signed document to Ferris now. "So where can we cash this?"

"It's drawn on the Marisa bank," Ferris said. "I think that's the same one we passed a couple of times."

Maihara nodded. It was the imposing bank she had mistaken for a government building.

As their carriage entered the grand avenue, she recollected that the bank was almost opposite the Monist place of worship. She needed to sit quietly and collect her thoughts, without Aurian urging a course of action on her.

She spoke to Ferris. "Drive over there. I want to go into the Sanctuary and pray for a while."

Ferris looked at her in surprise but ordered the carriage to turn across the avenue. They all stepped out onto the broad pavement, under a pair of flowering trees.

"Are you sure you want to go in here?" Aurian asked. A flower petal had settled in her hair.

Maihara waved the objection aside. She had enough conflicting thoughts in her head already. A few men in the coarse clothes of lower-class city workers loitered outside the temple, in the shadow of its white lime-washed frontage, but she and her escort ignored them. They pushed past a pair of solid, arched doors of close-grained wood. The interior was high, echoing, silent, the walls a plain white and the roof beams black.

She knelt by a painting showing the Prophetess in a

typical pose, hand upraised in blessing, and gathered her thoughts, mostly of Tarchon. She missed Tarchon, his grey eyes, his stiff smile. He liked her a lot, cared about her. Nobody here did. What would he want her to do in Shardan? He would not want her to support Wixos's plutocrats. The Wixos group could not be all-powerful if they were seeking the support of a visiting princess. Perhaps the liberal group was equally influential. Satisfied that she was safe inside the temple, she sent Ferris across to the bank.

After half an hour, Maihara rose stiffly, dissatisfied but not inclined to reverse the decision she had made in the carriage. Ferris had still not returned.

"Well?" Lady Aurian said. "Have you changed your mind?"

Maihara shook her head.

Outside, she turned to the corporal. "The bank."

Flowering trees and passing carriages partly blocked her view of buildings on the far side. "Shall I bring up the carriage, Milady?" the corporal asked.

"No, we can walk across," Maihara said. She looked forward with pleasurable anticipation to being free from financial worries for a while.

Having crossed the dual roadway they halted at the foot of the bank steps, below the pillared entrance. The two uniformed bank guards looked down, while Maihara and Aurian loitered outside. Well-dressed citizens passed by. A few leaves fluttered from the avenue trees.

Ferris emerged, scowling. He half-ran down the steps, looking harassed. A bank clerk stood at the doors calling after him. The two bank guards took a step to follow but halted on seeing the three soldiers standing near Maihara and Aurian. Ferris joined them but barely broke his pace. "Come! Hurry."

Maihara and Aurian almost ran to keep up with him. "Ferris? What's the matter? Did you get the money?"

Ferris looked over his shoulder, cap awry. Maihara followed his gaze. The clerk had not followed them, but was watching from the steps.

"No, I didn't get any."

Maihara held out her hand. "And the bank order? Have you got it?"

Ferris looked down. "No." He continued walking up the avenue.

Maihara muttered an unladylike word, then hurried after him. "Lieutenant, why didn't you take it back? What were you thinking?"

Ferris glanced at her. "I handed it over at the counter and everything seemed normal. I expected them to give me notes or coin without any fuss. But the note had gone to another room, and then they asked me questions. Who was I, what was I doing in Retis, why was I cashing this order?"

She felt a clutch of alarm. "Is this about me?"

"No, but I had to explain that I had come from Retis escorting Your Grace. They had the insolence to ask if I had reported to the Army command here. They clearly suspected I was a forger."

The group crossed the avenue in front of a passing cart to regain their parked carriage. Ferris turned to Maihara. He brushed his uniform as if removing dust or dirt. "I tried to convince them I wasn't a forger. I had to show them my tag and identity papers. Then the manager said the draft was a clear forgery."

"That's nonsense! We saw it signed," Lady Aurian said.

"They said it lacked an official stamp, and the signatures were forged. It's absurd. Then the rogues threatened to call the militia and have me arrested." His voice rose. "I told them I was an officer of the Imperial Army, a gentleman, and showed them my sword. I told them that if they wanted blood in their bank, they should have some."

Maihara's heart sank. "I should have gone with you, Lieutenant. Unless it was all a trick."

Ferris opened the carriage door for her to climb in.

"They've had enough time to send a messenger stopping payment," Aurian said. "If we hadn't gone to that rebel temple—"

Maihara ignored her. Squabbling was useless. Somebody in power had blocked the payment. "Who owns that bank?" she asked. "Who controls it?"

Aurian and Ferris did not know.

She slumped in her seat, gripping her hands together as chills of dread crept over her. She was in a foreign country and had alienated a powerful group of people. They might not stop at cancelling her bank order. There was nobody to defend her if she did not throw herself on the mercy of an Empire that regarded her with ill will and suspicion at best. The Imperial Army could snatch back her small bodyguard at any time.

"Let's hurry, Your Grace. The sooner the rest of my soldiers rejoin us at the inn, the better."

Their carriage brought them back to the inn within minutes. As the carriage halted, Ferris detailed Hibbett and Mamer to check their rooms. He and Ostein escorted Maihara and Aurian inside.

As they entered the lobby, four men in dark plain clothes moved forward from behind the innkeeper's bar and from shadowy corners of the room. Sheathed knives hung at their belts and two carried clubs.

One placed himself in front of Maihara and held a sheet of paper in her face. "Mai Aurian, you are being detained for fraud and treason."

-27-

Maihara drew back with a gasp, and tried to read the summons held out by the dark-clad intruder. She had half expected something like this, but not so soon.

Ferris snatched the paper, glanced at it and thrust it into a pocket. "You're not arresting anyone," he snapped, fists clenched. "Who are you?"

Maihara stared at the menacing quartet of armed men confronting them. Scruffy clothing and partly masked faces. Her heart thudded in her chest. She glimpsed the moon-faced innkeeper behind his desk. Nobody else was in the lobby.

"No questions," growled the hard-faced man who had waved the paper. "Better come quietly."

Maihara pushed Lady Aurian toward the stairs. "Run! Get the soldiers!" The rest of the escort ought to be upstairs. With a startled look, Aurian turned and ran.

The intruders stirred into movement. "Stop her!" One man drew a dagger and started after Aurian.

"Look out!" Maihara shouted.

Ferris snatched out his sword, with a shout of "At them!" and lunged at Aurian's pursuer. All at once the remaining trooper and the four men reached for weapons, shouting. Ferris's sword struck home, piercing the back of Aurian's pursuer. The man gave a grunt and fell to the floor, bleeding.

Maihara gasped and jumped aside.

Trooper Ostein staggered, hand on his just-drawn sword. A club had struck him on the head as he drew. Ostein's knees buckled and his sword drooped.

The three thugs still on their feet turned on Ferris, one younger-looking man swinging a club, the others with daggers drawn.

"Ferris!" Maihara cried. He swung his sword in an arc to keep them back, his face twisted in anger.

Maihara picked up a four-legged stool and swung it, hitting the hard-faced leader on the head from behind. The man staggered and swore. He half-turned, shaking his head.

Ferris slashed at the arm of the other dagger-wielding man, drawing blood. The man yelled and fell back, clutching his arm.

The man she had hit, still shaking his head, turned to face Maihara. His face twisted in rage. "Bitch!"

Maihara readied the stool again. Her heart thumped. Movement seemed slowed, the fear making her hyper-aware.

Her assailant lunged at her, dagger raised. She swung the stool, hitting him in the face. With a groan, he lowered his dagger and fell back.

She stepped back. She had not thought that she had hit him that hard. Ferris lunged at her attacker with his sword, leaving himself exposed. He reeled as the club wielder hit him on the neck and shoulder. The other man she had not hit swapped his dagger to his left hand and stabbed Ferris in the side.

Ferris lowered his sword and slumped to the floor. "Sorry," he mumbled.

"Ferris!" Maihara cried, stricken with shock and dismay.

Two assailants turned to face Maihara, one with a bloodied knife, clasping his side with blood trickling between his fingers, the other younger man with the club. Vicious expressions twisted their features.

"Drop that, you bitch," said the one with the knife, waving the blade.

Maihara took a step back. She was out of options. Fear iced through her. Perhaps the death god Tabor wanted her after all. They would overpower her easily, but a Zircon did not surrender.

The club wielder grabbed the stool by its top and ripped

it from her grasp. It fell to the floor with a clatter.

She took another step back. Fear left her dizzy. Her eyes were on the bloody dagger blade.

"Hey, what's going on here?"

All turned to see who had called out. A tall soldier stood in the street doorway. His expression changed as he took in the scene, the bodies lying on the floor, the raised weapons.

"Lieutenant!" The trooper dropped his packages to the floor in a scatter, and in a swift movement drew his sword and sprang forward. The club wielder staggered back with a howl, his arm half severed, and the backstroke cut a bloody gash across the dagger assailant's face.

The man Maihara had hit dropped his dagger and ran for the door and out into the street. The club wielder tried to follow, clutching his arm, but the soldier was too quick for him. He spun around and slashed, and then continued to stab and slash in a frenzy till it was obvious that the dark-clothed man was dead.

Maihara took a deep breath. The immediate danger was past, with three assailants on the floor, two wounded and one very dead. Her rescuer, Trooper Warga, knelt and bent over his lieutenant, opening his eyes and feeling his neck for a pulse.

Ferris moved feebly and turned his head as she knelt beside him. His blue eyes flickered open. "Sorry," he murmured. "I couldn't—". His eyes rolled up and he spoke no more.

Maihara raised her hands to her face. "No!" Footsteps thundered and more Imperial soldiers surrounded them from the stairs and the street. A small cry made Maihara look up. Lady Aurian stood on the top step with a hand over her mouth. "What happened?" she asked in a faint, high-pitched voice.

"The Lieutenant's dead. Stabbed in the heart," the kneeling soldier said.

A collective growl came from the surrounding soldiers. "Bastards," one said.

Maihara met Aurian's eyes. "It got violent. Ferris tried

to defend me." Saying this made the disaster real. She'd lost her loyal aide and defender. That cheerful young man would never speak again. Her eyes filled with a rush of tears.

The soldiers were talking in raised voices, demanding and offering answers.

"Who are these bastards?" asked Hibbett, kicking a fallen black-clad figure.

Maihara raised her voice. "Find out who these men are. Search them. If they can still speak, make them talk." Men so quick to resort to violence could not be genuine public servants.

The soldiers knelt and got to work, searching the men on the floor. A scream filled the room as the questioning started. It seemed that the soldiers were not gentle in their interrogation techniques, but Maihara did not have it in her to care.

She sank onto a stool.

Lady Aurian clutched Maihara's arm. "What will we do now?"

Maihara's eye fell on the innkeeper, who all this time had been sitting frozen behind the unlit reception desk. She caught the eye of Mamer, and pointed.

The soldier forced his way behind the desk and grabbed the balding innkeeper by the shoulders. "What do you know about this, you bastard?"

The innkeeper remained silent, face twisted in fear.

Mamer shook him. "Talk!" With a dull clunk, Mamer head-butted the innkeeper.

The innkeeper gasped in pain. "I don't know anything," he gabbled in a high-pitched voice. "They told me to be quiet and not move."

Streit handed Maihara a few scraps of blood-smeared paper he had taken from a fallen thug. Too shaken to make any sense of them, she passed them to Aurian. "Ferris got the warrant they shoved in my face," she told the corporal. She stifled a sob.

Aurian turned over the pieces of paper. "I can't make

much of these. These are nothing. They could be receipts for meals."

"So who do you think these men are?"

Aurian put the papers down. "I'd say it's rebels, attempting to seize you and pretending to be court officials to catch us off guard?"

"Not Wixos's Lords playing rough?" Maihara asked.

Aurian shook her head. "They've no motive go this far."

"Or the Fifth Bureau?"

"It could be. I just imagined they'd be more professional." Her voice quivered.

The corporal came across the foyer to her, avoiding the dead attacker's blood-soaked corpse. "We couldn't get anything useful out of them. It seems the leader got away and the rest are low-grade thugs."

"We have to report this. Don't they have forces of law here?"

Streit shrugged. "Haven't seen any. We're taking the Lieutenant's body to the Imperial Army post. We have to report his death there. You're our princess and all, but we can't guard you from another attack like this. Beggin' your pardon, but you should go home."

"You're not abandoning me here?" she said sharply. "Some of you can stay?"

"We all need to report," Streit said in a dogged tone. "You can come with us, yer Grace, and get them to send you home."

Maihara looked at Lady Aurian. After this, being left without an armed guard was not an option. Her plans here were in tatters, but going east was not an appealing alternative. An uncertain fate awaited her in the eastern Empire, but it was better than being dead.

"We're running out of options," Aurian said. "We'd be safer at the Army base, and you can try persuading them to believe you rather than the Fifth."

Maihara would have preferred to approach the Varlord

Order office, since the officer she met had hinted at support. But the Varlords might prove equally treacherous.

With reluctance and sad at heart, she turned to the corporal. "I'll come with you. Can a couple of you guard us upstairs while we pack?"

With a faint air of relief, the corporal nodded. "Very well, yer Grace." He called two soldiers out of the side room.

Grief and disbelief weighed Maihara as she climbed the stairs. Ferris had died protecting her. Her options were closing. She did not want to go to the Imperial Army base, but could not think of an alternative. She would think while she packed, and maybe delay the soldiers a while longer. They were clearly shocked and disheartened by the death of their lieutenant, but she would appeal to their loyalty to her.

She halted at the door to their suite, Aurian behind her, and directed Mamer to go in and check it.

"You think there might be someone in there?" Aurian asked.

Maihara did not reply. Anything seemed possible.

Mamer entered first and checked that the room was clear. Maihara threw items into her travel chest.

"You're splashed with blood," Aurian said, pale-faced.

Maihara looked down. Her red dress was wet with scarlet blotches. "It's not mine." She stared at it in sick dismay. "Help me change." Aurian sent the soldier out while Maihara changed out of her best dress into a plainer one.

Back downstairs, she stood on the bottom step of the stairs and addressed the five soldiers. The one who had taken a knock to the head was sitting up, and the sixth was apparently outside hailing a carriage.

"I am grateful to you for escorting me so far. I am sorry that it has turned out like this." Her eyes fell on the body of Lieutenant Ferris, now rolled anonymously in a length of cloth. She looked away. "But I remain your princess, and it is your duty to guard me till you are relieved from that duty. You need to return Ferris's body to the Army. Very well. Let us do that first."

The soldiers nodded, murmured agreement, and the corporal sketched a salute.

She turned to the inn-keeper, who still cowered behind his desk.

"There is nothing else to pay, is there?"

A couple of soldiers glared at the inn-keeper and bunched their fists.

"Nothing to pay," the inn-keeper assured them in a shaking voice.

They had to wait till a second hire carriage was found. The body of Ferris and four soldiers and their kit went into the first, and Maihara, Aurian, their travel chests and two soldiers into the second.

The corporal waved his arm from the first open carriage, and the two vehicles set off. She did not know the way, but the carriage drivers ought to.

A closed black carriage fell in behind them. It was and long and squarish, resembling a delivery wagon. For no particular reason, its appearance made her uneasy.

"Keep up," Hibbett ordered the driver of Maihara's carriage. A gap of several yards to the leading carriage had opened as they approached an intersection. The first carriage crossed, but a light carriage and an empty cart cut across in front, on the intersecting street. Maihara's carriage squeaked to a halt.

"Move it!" Warga shouted. The driver plied his whip, cutting into the traffic and earning curses. The first carriage was now several vehicle lengths ahead. An empty delivery cart followed it, separating the carriages. The reactions of the soldiers fed Maihara's anxiety. They were tense, looking around them. She gripped the edge of her seat. The closed black cart was just behind.

The street was narrow, with old buildings on one side and shops and tall houses fronting the pavement on the other. Daylight was fading. The cart ahead stopped, and their carriage was forced to halt behind it. Another delivery cart was parked on the other side of the street making it impossible to pass. Maihara stood up, a hand on Aurian's shoulder, to look over the cart and its solitary occupant, the driver. In front of her, Warga had also stood up, shouting after the lead carriage.

A movement in the corner of her eye made her turn. Three men had exited the black carriage behind and were running forward, weapons in hand. One had a sword, another a club.

"Look out behind!" Maihara shouted. A crippling fear gripped her. It was happening again.

"Stop in the name of the people," the leading man shouted. "You're all under arrest."

"You bastards," Warga shouted, displaying his sword. "You're dead meat."

One of the attackers leapt into the front of the carriage and gave the driver a blow that sent him toppling into the road. Hibbett swung his sword and hit the attacker in the back of the neck. Another assailant wrenched open the rear half-door of the carriage on the offside and reached for Aurian. With a scream, she huddled against Maihara. Warga swung around and engaged the man. Maihara gasped and ducked as a sword hissed over her hair.

Another assailant appeared and jumped onto the carriage to engage the two soldiers, lunging at Hibbett with a knife. Hibbett cried out, and blood stained the breast of his uniform.

If only she had a weapon. Instead of surrendering, she should run. They had just passed an alley among the old buildings. Maihara opened the nearside carriage half-door and scrambled to the ground, dragging Aurian with her. One of their assailants saw the movement. Shouting "Stop!" he lunged at Aurian with his blade as Maihara dragged her forward in the direction of the lead carriage. Aurian cried out.

Alongside the obstructing cart, Maihara could not see the lead carriage in the street ahead, but a narrow alley opened beside her, its further reaches filled with a menacing blackness. She dragged Aurian into it, till the

369

gloom enveloped them, and paused to look back. The alley's mouth showed dimly as a rectangle of light grey. A dark-clad figure appeared silhouetted in the greyness, looking around in confusion and apparently unable to see her. while a shout came from the street.

A ginger cat trotted past her feet and headed further up the alley. Her gaze followed the cat as it glanced back at her with a flash of green eyes and then disappeared through a solid brick wall.

There was magic here. Not waiting to consider it any further, Maihara gripped Aurian's arm and ran for the spot where the cat had vanished. The alley-side wall looked like solid brickwork. Heart sinking, she stopped and looked back. The dark obscured the end of the alley, and sounds of fighting filtered through.

"Fugging bitches got away," a barely distinguishable figure shouted. "Vanished into thin air."

Maihara gasped, shaking off the acute terror that had gripped her.

The other thugs joined him as dim shadows. Maihara froze, holding her breath. The men looked, but did not see her. "Witches," said one, and they turned away.

The sounds of struggle outside had died away, leaving street sounds mixed with angry and indistinct voices.

She took a breath to calm her racing heart. Beyond the buildings that fronted the main street, brick boundary walls hemmed in the alley, then further on stood a series of mean looking houses, all dark and closed tight. The cat appeared again at her feet, glanced up at her and vanished.

She reached out her right hand. It sank into the brick, met a yielding surface like wood, then nothing. Surprised and relieved, she pushed forward, dragging Aurian with her.

She stood, breathing heavily and listening with trembling limbs for sounds of pursuit, but nobody came after. Around her extended an urban garden, with small trees, shrubs and flower beds. Walls ran along two long sides. From the garden, the gate looked like a tall wooden gate, half open. Quickly she moved to shut it, trying not to make a noise. They were alone.

She had escaped these assailants for the moment, but she had lost the soldiers, and her baggage. Aurian moaned. Maihara released her tight grip on Aurian's arm and turned to her.

"I'm sorry—" Even in the shadowy light, she saw that on Aurian's other arm blood darkened the material of her embroidered jacket, and the material was slashed. "Serina, you're hurt."

Aurian gave a slight nod and moaned again. She did not try to pretend that the wound was slight. Blood was dripping from her arm.

Maihara clamped a hand over the wound and gripped tightly. What was she supposed to do now?

A scuffling further up the garden caught her ears. A dark-haired, bearded man wearing a dark cloak with light trim was staring at them and frowning.

She eyed him with apprehension. Another enemy?

"What are you doing here?" he asked in a well-modulated tone.

His words not seem very friendly. "We've been attacked. My friend is hurt."

The man made no move to assist. "How did you get in here?" His voice carried a hint of accusation.

"I followed a cat. Through your fake wall."

"That's unfortunate." Rather than move to help, the man took a step back.

"I saw one of our attackers looking in. He didn't see me watching him."

The man's expression changed, relaxed. "You can see through it?"

Maihara nodded.

He beckoned with one hand. "You'd better come."

Maihara followed him through the garden, supporting Aurian. She glimpsed a single-storey extension to a gloomy building before the man opened a door decorated with peeling blue paint. They followed him into a kitchen, warm and smelling of boiled cabbage and hot grease. Heat radiated from a black range with a couple of pots simmering on top of it.

A plump woman, grey-haired and dressed in a dark skirt and blouse, rose and stared at the newcomers.

"Strangers?" the woman said, in a wavering voice.

"It's all right, Cook. At least one of them seems to be of the blood. The other is injured."

Maihara started. Blood? Did they detect her as a Vimrashan?

"Oh?" The woman's eyes fixed on Aurian's arm. "Should I help her?"

"Yes, Cook."

With the woman's help, Maihara got the jacket off Aurian's wounded arm, revealing a nasty slash wound. The cook prepared a wash, with water from the steaming kettle, and a brown powder, and dabbed it over the wound. Aurian whimpered.

Soon the wound was bandaged. Lady Aurian sat sipping a medicinal tea. "It will ward against shock," the old woman explained. Colour was returning to Aurian's face.

"What people are you?" Maihara asked. "What's with the magic wall?"

"We prefer to keep ourselves to ourselves." Their host gave her a cold look. Of early middle age, he had a small forked beard and an olive complexion. He was handsome, clad in a neatly tailored jacket, dark trousers, buttoned waistcoat and cream shirt, and exuded a confidence and sense of presence. "And who are you? You are dressed like wealthy people, nobles even."

"That's right," Maihara said.

"May I have a name?"

"Names can get one into trouble," Maihara said.

"But how should I address you?" the man asked.

"You can call me Kafnis." It was the first name that came into her head.

"And your friend?"

Maihara nudged Aurian.

"You can call me Lady Onetree." It was a name from Aurian's estate, or former estate, Maihara knew.

"My name is Mardax. Excuse me," the man said, standing. "I need to fetch someone."

By the time Mardax returned with a well-dressed woman, evidently his wife, Aurian was spooning down a spicy broth.

"Lady Kafnis?"

Maihara turned. "Yes?" Grey eyes met hers. She resisted the urge to look away.

"This is my wife, Miriam," he said in an elegant drawl. "Perhaps you can explain how you came to be here?"

Miriam Mardax wore a brocaded gown, had several rings on her slim fingers and had her brown hair fastened back in a bun.

Maihara faced them. "Armed men attacked our carriage. They were getting the better of our escort, so we fled into your alley."

The man's eyes widened a fraction. "I expect they have gone by now. Have you any idea who they were?"

"We don't really know." It seemed best not to tell the whole story.

"Perhaps you can find your way back now to your home or friends?"

Maihara shook her head. "We are not residents in this principality, and we appear to have run out of friends. And money. And anything." She slumped in her hard chair, keeping one eye on her questioner.

Mardax frowned, as if disappointed that he could not get rid of them so easily. He glanced at his wife.

"What are you people afraid of?" Maihara asked, and before the man could answer, "Are you Vimrashans?"

The man hesitated. "We are. As you are, it seems." The man's eyes widened. "And your friend."

Whoa, she thought. That had been an inspired guess. She had thought she was the only one, then Aurian revealed herself, and now these people. But would they be willing to help her?

Evidently Vimrashans were able to sense each other. And that priest in Retis had sensed herself and Aurian. But she had totally failed to sense Aurian. This needed investigation, before she let slip that she could not sense their hosts, and made them suspect her anew.

Aurian meanwhile had finished her broth and was listening, her face relaxed.

"People are suspicious," the man said. "They distrust anyone with unusual abilities. We choose to keep to ourselves and discourage the others from entering our quarter of the city."

"So do you have any special abilities, then?"

"Surely you know?" he countered. "Some of us can sense the soul of this city, here."

She could, too. "And you can get into it? Do things?"

"Some have claimed such things." He was not giving much away. "And yourself?"

It was time to perform for her supper, without giving too much away. "A moment." She entered her magic space, found a harmless spell and snapped her fingers. The light level in the room suddenly increased, bathing the room in a bright white glow.

The other people in the room, including Aurian, gasped, and the old cook pressed her palms together, fingers upward.

"Clearly you are a magician of some ability," Mardax said, unmoved. "Anything else?"

"That's it, really," Maihara said. "There's nothing else to show." Just to show off, she changed the hue to a warm yellow before extinguishing the light.

"Do either of you have any affinity with animals?" Mardax asked.

Aurian shrugged. "I quite like small dogs."

The man gave Maihara an enquiring look.

"What sort of affinity?" she asked.

"Being able to sense their mood. Even summon them."

I wonder how they'd react if I told them about the pterostrophe. "I'm not sure." *Where's that cat? Kitty Kitty.*

"How's your arm?" she asked Aurian. Aurian's colour had returned.

"It hurts a bit, but I feel better now."

Maihara squeezed Aurian's hand. "Sorry. This is all my fault."

The dark-bearded man raised an eyebrow.

A scratching came at the kitchen door. The cook went to open it. The ginger cat stalked in and checked them with greenish eyes.

"Kitty," Maihara said, stretching out a hand. The cat trotted forward and leapt onto her lap. She stroked it. It purred.

"That cat rarely accepts strangers," said Mardax, with a faint smile. Maihara indulged in a modicum of triumphalism. She might be as powerful a magician as anyone else here. Could they make lights, spy or summon nasty flying reptiles? Maybe not.

They stared at Maihara as she petted the cat. She half expected the creature to speak.

Miriam Mardax tugged at her husband's sleeve and whispered to him.

Mardax inclined his head. "You can stay in my house overnight."

Maihara greeted this offer with a sense of relief. She and Aurian followed him along a short white-painted passage and into a sitting-room.

"Wait here," Mardax said, gesturing to upholstered armchairs. The cat had trotted after them, and hopped onto Maihara's lap.

The room, panelled and yellow-lit with oil lamps and tastefully furnished with good furniture, spoke of discreet wealth.

Maihara had a more urgent concern than their host's intentions. She leant forward. "Serina, what's this about being able to sense other Vimrashans? Can you do that?"

"Yes. But one needs to know how. You have to seek and then be able to recognise what the sensation signifies."

"Did you know I was one? Before Retis?"

Aurian gave her a look. "I assumed you were a Vimrashan, like your mother."

Maihara flushed. "So how do I—"

Somebody was coming. The door opened and Miriam Mardax entered, followed by a maid with a laden tray.

"We always try to help those of the Blood, when we can," their hostess told them. "I'll have a room made up for you. In the meantime, I thought you would like some refreshment."

"That's most kind," Maihara said. "Thank you."

Miriam Mardax turned to Aurian. "Is your wound paining you?"

"Not so much," Aurian said.

Hostess and maid withdrew. The tray bore cold cuts of meat, bread and a bottle of wine and glasses. Maihara realised that she was hungry.

While she ate, she savoured her feelings of magical empowerment, before more serious questions brought her back to ground. What was going on outside this protected enclave? What was she to do? She pictured her own father ordering the brutal attacks, and dismissed it. How could he shed her blood? But in view of Aurian's warnings she feared being taken back to the Empire.

Before the attack, she had decided to abandon Wixos and try to contact the more liberal elements of the ruling classes and get their support lest the rebels, or anyone else, seek to extradite her. Her present situation would make that difficult, but she could hide among these Vimrashans and seek their aid.

As for contacting the Imperial Army or the Varlords, even if one or the other was warmly disposed toward her, they might crumble under direct orders from the Emperor, or a hostile briefing from the Fifth Bureau.

Or there were Tarchon's rebels. A small voice whispered, 'Return to the rebels. Some of them like you, they are decent people and they mean to help the poor and clear out corruption.' But as Imperial Princess she could not support a rebellion against the Imperial State. And their advance brought death and chaos in its wake. And which rebels? It seemed possible that an extreme local rebel faction who wanted her alive or dead had attacked her.

Outside, darkness fell. Their black-bearded host, Mardax, reappeared. "Please come through to the dining room. We are having dinner."

In a dark-panelled room lit by oil lamps, an oval table, glinting with silverware, was laid for a formal meal. Miriam Mardax was there, directing the maid to set out laden plates and tureens.

"Please sit." Mardax gestured to the unoccupied chairs.

During the three-course dinner, Mardax and his wife gently probed them for details of where they had come from and who they were. Maihara disclosed that she had fled from Retis just before the rebel attack. She sought to entertain her hosts with an account of the dead Aquan she had seen at Retis. To her surprise, they were as sceptical as the Retis nobles.

"Our folk here have tales of little people who suck milk from cows, or steal children and replace them with ugly halflings. Just like sailors are notorious for telling fanciful sea stories. Perhaps you were expecting something strange, and mis-interpreted a corpse that had been in the sea a while. Rotting and half-eaten corpses of dead whales have been taken for dead sea-monsters."

Maihara nodded, not wanting to argue, but she knew what she had seen.

"Have your people always been here?" Maihara asked.

"We come here from villages and small towns," Mardax said. "We rely on not attracting attention, and on magical barriers that discourage outsiders from coming in."

"What if they follow a cat, or chase a ball?"

"So they may do. The darkness you saw is just to discourage people from entering our sector at night."

"And the fake brick wall? Will that keep them out?"

"A conceit. How many people touch a wall to see if it's real? If outsiders put a hand to mine, their minds will tell them that it's solid."

What a wonder. She would have felt at home, if only she dared tell them who she was. During the dinner, Maihara became increasingly uncomfortable about deceiving her hosts. How might they react if they discovered that they had harboured not a distressed noblewoman, but the Imperial Princess, sought by some very determined thugs? The longer she delayed telling them, the more deceived and angry they would feel. And then what would happen?

***

As she lay in the unfamiliar bed that night, unable to sleep, she sought out the city's magic with her mind, engaged her passwords and sent out her spy spell. She had already been to the Imperial Army's Halamar offices, so with an effort she was able to trace her way there, and slip the spy inside the building. Had they buried Ferris yet? In one room, officers were talking about her disappearance.

"It's an outrage," said one. "Why aren't we acting?"

"The Commandant has made a formal complaint to the Shardan government, and demanded that she be found," said a second.

"We should bring in men and search ourselves," said another. "Damn their sovereignty."

"I heard that they've sent for more men. We should take over the whole fugging country," said a fourth.

"We don't have enough forces to take over here," said the second man. "Otherwise we'd have done it years ago."

She was both shaken and touched by their vehemence. If only they were sworn to serve her and not the Emperor. The conversation was yielding little new, so she looked into other rooms, mostly dark and silent at this hour. One contained racks of weapons, another stores. In a corner of a weapons room a shiny object caught her eye, and she turned up the sensitivity of the spy view. It was a man-like figure all in shiny metal, stood upright in an up-ended wooden crate in which it had clearly been brought here. Straw packing lay heaped on the floor. At the top of the crate a label hung - painted in black brush-strokes it read

'Golim 002'.

At the sight of it, a chill of fear ran up her spine while a series of recollections passed through her mind - her father's purported boast of an army of mechanical soldiers, his metallic face at the Kunn meeting, the man with the metal arm, Lord Wixos' cryptic remark about soon having 'means'.

Clearly the scheme was nearing realisation. There seemed to be just one of these golims here, and she supposed it had been sent here to be discreetly shown to the Shardan allies. Perhaps just to stiffen the resolve of a wavering ally. Or perhaps Cordan had ordered it sent here so that numbers of them could be sold to the Shardan principality, raising funds for the cash-poor Imperial state. Should the golims threaten the empire, Cordan was wily enough to retain means of shutting them down.

The thought of ruthless and corrupt men like Nardone and Wixos gaining control of golims sent for the defense of Shardan and turning them loose to slaughter those who stood in the way of their profits filled her with horror. She had to stop them.

-28-

Maihara sat in the downstairs room with Lady Aurian, trying to read in the dim light that filtered through translucent window drapes. She had eventually slept, falling into a nightmare in which metal handed figures rampaged through narrow streets, killing and burning. Faint sounds came from other parts of the house, a thump of feet upstairs, a clatter from the kitchen. Lady Aurian sat with eyes closed. A knocking at the front door, out in the hall, made Maihara lower her book. Voices murmured.

Maihara started her spy spell and positioned it in the hall, to hear more clearly. "...news of a missing princess."

"What's this?" Mardax's voice.

The spy's eye revealed a man's back and the silhouette of an unknown visitor.

"Is there any description?"

"Yes, here." The visitor handed over a crumpled sheet of paper.

The front door closed and Mardax moved back out of view. Moments later, the door of the sitting room opened. Hastily, Maihara shut off the spy.

Mardax came in and stood in front of her, holding the paper. His face was creased in a frown. "There's news from outside. The Imperial Princess and her companion have gone missing, and the Army is looking for them."

"What does it say?" she asked.

For answer, her host handed her the paper. The crudely printed notice announced that the Imperial Army were concerned over the whereabouts of Imperial Princess Maihara Cordana, believed to be in the city under the assumed name of Mai Aurian, and her companion Lady Serina Aurian. It gave a description of the princess as 'well-built, with dark curling hair', and her companion as 'shorter and slighter.'

Maihara looked up. There seemed no point in saying anything. Even without the descriptions, her failure to register any surprise would have been admission enough.

Her host's lips tightened.

"I'm sorry," she said.

"*Sorry*! The highest-ranked woman in the entire Empire comes here, with troops looking for her, leading the Imperial Army in here, and you're *sorry*? We thought you were in distress, we took you in and fed you, and you've tricked us. Do you realise what the Army could do, if they think we've kidnapped you? Do you?"

Maihara stood and raised a hand to stem the flow of angry words. "You don't have the whole picture. I may be the highest-ranked woman in the Empire, but I'm not popular at the Palace. They know that I am Vimrashan, that I am a witch. They threw me in prison, and I only escaped because the rebels took the city, and then they too stared murmuring against me. I was looking for a way to remain in Shardan."

Lady Aurian stirred and sat up.

Mardax remained silent, face flushed, but his lips set in an angry line.

Maihara hastened to explain. "Because I was desperate not to fall into the hands of either the Empire or the rebels, I made contact with a group of State Councillors whom I hoped would help me, but when I attended a meeting with them I did not like their views."

"Why not?" Mardax asked, in a cautious tone.

"They seemed intent on enriching themselves by grinding down the people. They bragged of dishonest property deals, including one that might concern you. They mean to clear and develop some of the poor, crowded districts—"

"Which ones?" Mardax asked sharply.

"The Vincis, for one."

"They plan to grab the Vincis?" her host interrupted.

His face looked older, his voice heavier. "Which of them is planning this?"

"Wixos and others. That's what they said. That's here, isn't it?"

"It is. I'd be even more disappointed in you, if you had lent your name to those criminals. Why did you not approach our Prince? That would have been appropriate for a person of your rank."

Maihara was digesting the confirmation that the people who had taken her in were a target for the Wixos group's rapacious plan. "The Prince?" she echoed. "I didn't want a State visit. I didn't have an introduction to your Prince and did not want to expose myself to the risk of being extradited; I needed to find support in your country first." She glanced at Aurian, who said nothing. "Do you see why I was not anxious to reveal my identity?"

"You were not frank with us, Princess. A foreign Royal taking refuge here exposes us to reprisals from your enemies. I fear their power and malice."

Aurian had opened her eyes. "There is Vimrashan blood in the Imperial Family. On both sides. Her Grace means you no harm."

"Maybe she doesn't, but this could harm us. I beg you to leave. Go back to your Army." He made a sweeping gesture. "Let them look after you."

Maihara met his hostile gaze. "I'm sorry we misled you. But the Army might return me to the eastern Empire, to the Palace." *And to the cells.* "I want to know what is really going on, what my danger is, before I move. There are others who might be able to help, if I could contact them." During the night, ensconced in a soft bed, she had not been able to locate the Varlords' office and listen in on them.

Miriam Mardax came in, attracted by the sound of raised voices. "What's happened?"

"We've just found out who our mystery guests are. Meet the Imperial Princess Maihara Cordana and her chaperone," he said in a sarcastic tone.

His wife gasped, and made a swift curtsy, remaining

with head bowed. "Your Eminence, please forgive my husband. He speaks without thinking. Have mercy on us!"

Maihara waved for Miriam to desist. "Please rise. The fault is mine. I'm sorry for deceiving you."

The woman stood, but curtsied again. "You could have told us, Your Grace," she said in a soft voice. "We would not have betrayed your confidence."

Maihara nodded, feeling regret for not trusting them. Things would have gone better if she had taken them into her confidence. She had disappointed them and put them in danger.

Within half an hour, a small but excited crowd of two or three dozen men and women, mostly dressed in humble working class clothes, had gathered outside. It appeared that Mardax was not the only one to see a copy of the printed notice, and rumours of her presence had already leaked into the community. The atmosphere in the house had not improved.

"Is somebody going to speak to them? Should I go?" Maihara asked.

"No, I should address them, Your Grace," Mardax said. "But not in the street. We have a meeting hall."

"Just tell them it's a false rumour," Aurian said.

Mardax frowned. "I won't lie to them." He went out, and through the doorway came muffled sounds of him addressing the crowd, and sounds of them dispersing. Her tension eased. Apparently Mardax had influence in this community.

He came back into the room where Maihara and Aurian waited uneasily. "They're going to the hall. I'll speak to them there."

"You want me to come with you?"

"If you insist, but I'd prefer you did not. I don't see how that would help your situation."

Maihara felt a tremor of unease. "What are you asking me to do?"

"I'll explain your presence to our people, and then you

can address them, if you insist. I doubt that they will welcome you here, however."

Her body tensed with apprehension. "I'll come speak to them." This was her last chance to retrieve the situation.

They followed their host along a narrow street. "Here we are," Mardax said, pointing. Maihara could not see any hall.

They had stopped in front of a row of houses with the usual doors and windows. Inside however, a narrow lobby gave onto a long, high room, its floor crowded with people. Maihara and Aurian followed Mardax up a short, narrow flight of stairs that gave onto a stage at one end of the hall. A sea of expectant faces looked up at her. She flinched under their scrutiny and avoided their eyes. From here, she saw that the ground-floor windows were false or magicked, because the lower walls were panelled. Only the street doors were real. The upper floor windows lit the hall. Effigies of the Nine Gods were fixed high up under the plaster ceiling. A murmur of expectant voices filled the room.

Mardax raised his arms and called for silence. The murmuring diminished.

"You will have heard rumours of an unexpected event today, a crisis. My friends, let me share the facts with you. A visitor whom we took in yesterday claiming to be a fugitive, one of our blood, turns out to be something more. In the city, soldiers are hunting for the Imperial Princess Maihara Cordana, said to be missing. This woman is she." He indicated Maihara with a dramatic gesture, and the crowed ooed and murmured.

She flinched but remained silent, straight-backed, trying to judge the mood of the crowd, sensing that Mardax had not finished having his say.

"She deceived us, and her presence here puts our community at risk. Soldiers could storm in here searching your houses and accusing us of complicity in her business, or of disrespecting her Imperial person. My question is, do you want to give this interloper sanctuary, or do you want her to leave?"

"Leave," audible voices responded.

To protect his people, Mardax was turning them against her. He paused to glance at Maihara, and she took it as her cue to speak, to fight back. She stepped forward with hand raised, and forced herself to look into the faces below. These were ordinary humble folk, anxious, ready to listen. She tried to remember how her father had spoken in Court, and what tricks of voice and word he used to hold attention and to persuade. "I regret that I did not reveal my true name when I came into your quarter. I should have trusted you more. But I had my reasons. I came to Halamar privately and was seeking sanctuary from trouble at Court. Why? Apparently, the Emperor sees me as a magical threat."

As she spoke she engaged in opening her virtual portals to start some magic. "Like you, I am of the Vimrashan blood." As she pointed upward, a white light brightened the room. Gasps and murmurs ran around the crowd. "That may be one reason I am not liked at Court. I was accused of witchcraft, thrown in a cell, and only released when the rebels took the city. Some of them wanted me executed. Then I was nearly assassinated by some anti-rebel agent." The light reddened. "After fleeing to Halamar, I attended a meeting of your State Councillors, one of your political parties. I learned that they have plans to redevelop the Vincis district, turn the people of Halamar against you and drive you from your homes."

The hall erupted into noise. Several people shouted questions at Mardax.

"Is it true?" one man near the front called out.

Maihara raised her arms, and the room gradually quieted. She had to find the right words before they turned on her. Borrow some ringing phrases she had heard in another place, from Tarchon. "Of course it's true," she said. "That's how those people gain their vast wealth, to build their palaces. By grinding the faces of the poor and weak. For them, you are just prey. I say to you, forewarned is forearmed."

Noise erupted, but this time of concerned outrage. Again she waited for it to die down before raising her arms for silence.

"But you want to know why I have fled into Vincis. Somebody in your city wishes me ill. Immediately after I visited the State Councillors, armed thugs attacked my party. So I fled into your alleys, and I claim sanctuary with you. I do not wish to trouble you for any longer than I have to, but I need a little time to identify my enemies and plan what I have to do next. I hope that in the future I will have power to help and protect all those of the Blood. I don't want to be one of the exploiters. I want to extend a hand of hope."

"We don't want you here," a heckler shouted.

"Is that what you say to your friends?" she shot back.

A small ripple of applause welled up. She looked to the back of the hall. Faces there were turned to her. She was sure they could all hear. "I do not want to be sent back to Chancungra, or the Eastern territories. And that will not help you. I cannot help you there."

The ginger cat had appeared from somewhere, and rubbed itself against her calves. She extinguished the reddish light.

Mardax stepped forward. "So let us know your opinion. Who wants to speak?"

Hands waved and voices shouted out. Mardax called up a man and a woman in dull-coloured and frayed clothes, their hands and faces worn by work, who became ill at ease when they stood on the same boards as the Imperial Princess and faced the crowd.

"I say, let her stay," said the man.

The woman shook her head. "What about our children? She's putting us in danger."

Mardax called a halt to these conflicting contributions after some confused debate. "My friends, let us take a vote. Raise your hands if you want to offer the Princess sanctuary."

Maihara stood with her hands at her sides, palms turned

toward the crowd.

More than half those in the hall raised their hands.

"And if you want her to leave at once, raise your hands."

A small number raised theirs.

"I think that's a clear result," Maihara said, to the crowd. She placed a hand over her breast. "Thank you from my heart for your kindness."

A few of the crowd applauded.

Mardax looked grim, but he lifted his arms and spoke. "We will shelter the Princess for a time, until she is able to leave. You must not speak of what you have seen or heard here to outsiders. Swear this by the One God."

Maihara breathed a sigh of relief. She had retrieved the situation, but now scores of these people knew who she was and where she was. She sought out Aurian, who was staring at her open-mouthed.

The meeting ended, and a number of people pressed forward and found their way to the lobby, hoping to speak to her. Mardax addressed her in a low voice. "I need no more proof that you're a princess. You're a dangerous woman, Your Grace. Just what did you mean by helping us?"

She looked him in the eyes. "I intend to have power. If my enemies win, that will be a loss for defenceless people everywhere."

People pressed around with worn, anxious faces, asking questions, many of which she deflected.

"How long will you stay?"

"I don't know yet."

"How can you help us?"

"I hope to use my power."

Soon Mardax leaned close. "Please return to my house, Your Grace."

Maihara followed him. She took Aurian's arm. A trail of people eager for her attention followed.

Back at the house they settled in the sitting room. Mardax finally sent away the more persistent princess-worshippers and closed the inner door.

"What do you want from us that will help you decide what to do next?" A faint resentment tinged his tone.

"I need to know what's going in the city," she told him. "And the progress of the rebels' war. Have you any way of finding out what's being said at the Army barracks? And the Varlords? Where is their office?"

"The Varlords?" Mardax shook his head, a shadow of fear passing across his features. "We desire no attention from them." He sighed. "I will pass on to you any news from the city."

"Thank you."

Maihara wanted some undisturbed time to spy on the Imperial Army office, the provincial Government office and, if she could find it, the Varlord Knights' office. But undisturbed time was what she did not get. Even after her host ushered out the first round of visitors, there was a trickle of significant people in the community who wanted to be presented to her, and a stream of questions about how she had arrived here and what she hoped to do next.

More worryingly, her host brought her a series of reports that soldiers were searching buildings along the road where the thugs had attacked, and were looking down alleys. In daylight, the occult blackness offered no deterrent.

"It's only a matter of time before they venture further in."

He did not say it, but she knew what he wanted. He wanted her to be gone.

As darkness fell, she contrived to be alone with Lady Aurian upstairs, on the pretext that her chaperone was tired. Aurian winced as she lay down on her bed.

"How is your arm?" Maihara asked.

"It hurts a bit when I move it, but it's no worse than before."

"I'm sorry I got you into this. What do you think we should do now?" Maihara reached out and touched

Aurian's shoulder.

"We're in serious danger, and I don't know what to do any more."

Her chaperone's admission chilled Maihara more than anything else that could have been said. "I just have a bad feeling. What if you're right about my father's attitude? What the Emperor said to me at Kunn wasn't very nice."

"Yes, I wonder if he ordered those thugs, or if it was local men, trying to do what the Fifth Bureau wanted and get a reward."

"Or local rebels, thinking Tarchon would welcome my corpse. All the more reason to be wary," Maihara said quietly. "Surely my father would not authorise such a vicious attack? I need to know what's going on."

"I hope you're not thinking about that man Tarchon," Aurian said. "You're not thinking of rejoining the rebels, even after this attack?"

"I was thinking of him," Maihara admitted, red-faced. "But I can't rejoin the rebels. That would be a final break with the Empire. Their uprising is a challenge to Imperial order, and I'm not ready to support that."

Aurian turned her head to look at Maihara. "If we could reach the Army, we should be safer with them, and you could try to delay your return east."

Maihara was not convinced. The Army were unlikely to harm her, but might receive orders to escort her east to her doom.

The ginger cat lay on the bedspread. Maihara reached out a hand and petted it. She did not mind cats, but the way this one followed her around and stared at her with its green eyes was unsettling. Maybe it was spying on her.

She shook her head. "We should get our story straight in case they burst in here. We are really pleased to see them, because we did not know what to do except hide with these kind people."

"All right, but better still if you—"

"There's also the Varlords," Maihara said. "I don't know so much about them—"

"Nor do I," Aurian interrupted. "What of them?"

"The one I spoke to hinted that they did not care for the rift between me and the Palace. They might be helpful. I was just alarmed that he recognised me, but—"

"That's just speculation. Anyway, they are subject to the Emperor's authority, like the Army. You may as well go to the Army. At least we know more about them."

This conversation was not leading to anything constructive. "But I need to know what's going on." Maihara clenched her fists. "Do you think the Vims are listening to us?"

"Why? I don't hear anyone outside the door."

"I meant magically."

Aurian shifted on the bed to look directly at Maihara. "What makes you ask that? Can you do anything like that?"

"No," Maihara said quickly.

"Well, you could ask them what they can do, if you're so anxious to find out what's happening."

"That's an idea." Maihara regretted her impulsive question and hoped the conversation was moving on.

"I really am tired," Aurian said, and turned her face upward. "You were good earlier, at the meeting. I knew you had spoken in public at the Calah palace, but that was surprising. You were charismatic. Before you spoke, they wanted to throw us out, but now they can't get enough of you."

"Thanks." She was pleasantly surprised by Aurian's praise, but not unaware of her ability to charm. She had used it on the rebels, on people she had met while free, and now on the distrustful people of the Vincis. "I've had to sit through plenty of speeches."

A servant called them to dinner. Aurian descended the stairs slowly. Maihara had been hoping that only their host Mardax and his wife would be present in the dining room, but to her annoyance two more local worthies were guests, an old man with a white beard, dressed in a light cloak with patterns embroidered into it, and a plump balding man whom their host introduced as a merchant. Mardax introduced the old man as Vannis Veneris, a magician, and pulled out a chair for him, treating him with a degree of respect that he did not extend to the merchant. Veneris was of slight stature and had the kind of facial features including lightly bronzed skin and a sharp nose that Maihara had come to associate with the Vims.

Despite the presence of guests, she resolved to ask what the Vims could do about spying.

Mardax seemed unusually energised and showed Maihara to her seat without his usual frown. "I have news for you, Your Grace. A couple of women answering your description have been sighted in a sector of the city a mile from here, and the troops are concentrating their searches there."

"What?" Maihara dropped her fork with a clatter. "You mean you fixed this?"

Mardax nodded, looking pleased with himself. "It will be safe for you to remain a little longer."

"Thank you," Maihara said with feeling. "That was very clever."

The cook served the main course. Maihara leaned over to cut up Aurian's food so that she could eat it one-handed.

"These impersonators," Maihara went on, "Were they a close resemblance?"

Their host nodded smugly.

Maihara suspected that illusion was involved. "That's excellent." It would be even better if a false trail led out of Halamar. She was tempted to ask how it was done, wanting to create illusions for herself. She glanced at the two guests.

The old man was smiling.

Their host offered wine, from a dusty bottle.

Maihara accepted a half glass. "I need to ask you, what else is happening out there? Is there any news of the rebel advances?"

Mardax nodded again. "There are rumours that they have advanced along the south coast almost as far as Loomis. And that they have encouraged insurrection inland. Messengers have been seen entering and leaving the Varlord Knights' building with unusual frequency."

"Where is the Varlord building?" Maihara asked.

"It's on Valgard Street," Mardax said.

"And where's that? What's it near?"

"It's north of here, just inside the old city wall," the bald merchant said sourly.

"Near the Army barracks?"

"It's a few minutes' walk."

"Do you have somebody watching those places, or do you do it magically?" Maihara asked.

The old man gave Maihara a sharp look and lowered his fork. "Such things can be done magically, you understand. But one has to be very careful. Spying is one of the accusations often levelled against us by our persecutors, and if certain people got even circumstantial evidence that we had spied on them with magic, the results would be disastrous."

Maihara shivered.

"What we have just told you of the rebel advance is widely known in the city," their host said. He and the old man exchanged glances.

"I see," Maihara said. "What persecutions have you experienced?"

"Did you mean here? There is a larger proportion of Vimrashans in one of the eastern provinces," Mardax said. "But there are communities of them in many of the major cities. We tend to stay together because we can use small magics without fear, as you did earlier today, Princess. But being a closed group leaves us open to envy and hate, especially if we are successful in business. When there are riots, our homes and businesses are usually the target."

With discomfort, Maihara wondered who had suffered the most in Calah.

"You mentioned that you hoped to help the Vimrashan communities in the future," the merchant said. "What had you in mind?"

"I can't predict what influence I might have in the

future, but I hope to encourage tolerance and stability."

"And how might you do that? What could a woman do?"

"There is nothing in the constitution to prevent a woman becoming Emperor," Maihara said.

All stopped eating and looked at her.

"Empress," Aurian said.

"Is that likely?" asked Mardax with a laugh. Miriam Mardax gave him a warning look.

"Our Emperor may live a long time," Maihara said. *One never knew what ears incautious words might reach.* "We all hope so. But after him there's my younger brother, who has a weak constitution and remains in rebel hands. Or another dynasty might establish itself. Or there's me."

Silently, they regarded her as if she was one of the nine gods. She looked down at her food.

"Some might not want this. Is that anything to do with your present difficulties?" the old man, Veneris, asked. "Is anything said at the Imperial Court?"

"If anyone wanted to seize the Throne, they might want to discredit the Imperial Princess first," Mardax said in a quiet voice.

Maihara's fork halted in mid-air as she contemplated this. After the latest attack, Aurian's simpler but more horrible theory seemed equally likely. Too many disagreeable incidents had befallen her at Imperial hands. First her father's obvious dislike of witches and, by inference, herself, then imprisonment for the pterostrophe incident, then the bizarre reaction and insults at Kunn. It annoyed her that magic was only considered safe in male hands. It was more pleasant to believe that some unknown hand was working through the Fifth Bureau, than to accept that her own father had ordered the Bureau to eliminate her as a threat, but such wishful thinking could be bad for her health.

-29-

Maihara helped Aurian climb the narrow stair. Inside the bedroom, Aurian fixed Maihara with a determined look. "This talk of magical spying. That's something you can do, isn't it?"

Maihara, cornered, looked away. Her stomach tightened.

"I wondered how you managed to overhear so much of the rebel plans. You used your magic, didn't you?"

She had hoped Aurian would not think of this. "If I did, I certainly would not want to tell anyone about it."

"So you can? You might at least have told me, a fellow Vimrashan and your friend. I'm disappointed in you." Aurian was frowning.

The judgement was hurtful, but Maihara felt driven to defend herself. "You heard how evasive the Vims are over using spy magic. They don't want anyone to know about their spy powers either."

"But I'm not going to tell anyone else." Aurian extended a hand. "Just give me the passwords."

Maihara sat and folded her arms across her chest. "I can't give you my own passwords. You'll have to find another set." She did not wish Aurian to know details about how the spy magic worked. The magic space was personal. With visceral feeling, she did not want Aurian poking around in it, even less the idea that Aurian could watch her.

"Why not?" For a moment, Aurian seemed bewildered. She put up a hand to wipe her eyes. "You're afraid I'll find out your secrets?"

Maihara looked on in baffled silence. She did not want to hurt Serina like this, but she could not give way.

Aurian's expression hardened. "This is about you and

Tarchon, isn't it? You don't want me watching you with him. I'm your chaperone. That's what I do."

Maihara felt a flash of annoyance, and frowned. All she had done with Tarchon was talk, even if her imagination had ventured further.

Aurian pointed a finger. "But I wouldn't use it to watch you and Tarchon doing intimate things, however I disapprove. That would be very low of me. And it's low of you to imagine I would. Do you even have any friends?" Her eyes glittered with anger.

Maihara recoiled at the hurtful jibe, conscious that she had servants and admirers, but hardly anyone she could call friend. "I'm sorry, Serina. That's not what I was thinking. But I want to protect myself. Anyway, I don't expect it will work. From what you've said, you can barely sense the magic in the middle of the city, or hold onto it. I think few Vimrashans can." Unless they have a magic mirror, she thought.

Aurian lowered her head. "So you won't help me?"

"Why do you want it so much?"

"Because it's our birthright. Our power. And I can do nothing with it. Nothing."

Maihara sighed. She tried to think of a way out that would not cause a breach or be insufferable, rejecting alternatives till she had an inspiration, an idea marginally less objectionable. "You could ask the Vims. If they give you a password, for your own space, I won't object."

Aurian's expression brightened. "Why would they? Do you think they will?"

"They're fellow Vims. You can ask."

Aurian nodded, and the corners of her mouth turned upward. "I will ask them. But if they refuse, then—"

"Sorry I'm being difficult. Still friends?" Maihara stretched out a hand. Aurian did the same, and they interlaced fingers.

Aurian's grip tightened. "Have you been spying from here already? Did you find out anything?"

"Yes. Last night, I found the Army office and listened.

They were making a big stink about our disappearance."

Aurian sucked in her breath. "But the Army office must be a mile away. That's insane! I see now why you kept this quiet. And since then?"

"No, I haven't; the Vims can't leave us in peace. It takes time."

***

Next morning, Maihara requested a private meeting with the old man, Vannis Veneris, who had come to dinner. She understood from Mardax that Veneris was a guardian of the Vimrashan's magic lore, and hoped that he was not one of those who thought that women were too emotional or weak-minded to be allowed to deal with magic. To her relief, he accepted the invitation with alacrity.

When the white-bearded old man arrived, wearing the same occultly patterned cloak as before, Maihara offered him herbal tea in her upstairs room. Lady Aurian infused the tea and poured the sweet-scented liquid into glazed cups. Veneris accepted the tea with thanks.

After the courtesies, Maihara wasted little time in asking him for a set of magic-space passwords.

"Your Grace, I regret that we cannot give these out, for our spaces, as you call them, are all in use from time to time. But I can tell you that if we need more spaces, we mine for the passwords."

Maihara stared at him, cup poised in her hand. "Whatever do you mean?"

"We believe there were vast numbers of these magical spaces, and that in the distant past they were in common use. And some had rather simple passwords. So we guess what form a password might take, and keep trying different combinations."

Maihara leant forward. "How does that work?"

"We had some success in trying ancient names, with a number or numbers attached. That sort of thing."

This made sense to Maihara. "Right. Thank you." Mindful of her missing box, she asked, "I don't suppose you have any instructions for using spells? They can be tricky."

"All the magical spaces offer instructions," the old man said. "If you find the right command, you will instantly know how to work everything at that level."

"Huh? How?"

"The knowledge becomes lodged in your mind."

Maihara digested this strange assertion. "Weird," she murmured. It had not occurred to her that finding help could be that simple. Aurian had assumed an expression of keen interest. Maihara did not press the point further.

"While I was at a meeting with the Wixos nobles," she said, "A man asked me about a magical box gifted to me on my fourteenth birthday. He wanted to know what was in it. I wondered how he was aware it existed, so I pretended to have forgotten about it. So have you any idea who he was, and why he was interested in my box?"

"What did he look like?" Veneris asked.

"A middle-aged man, with an anonymous face, short brown hair, wearing a plain dark blue robe."

"Him?" Aurian said. "Fifth Bureau, I'd say."

Maihara looked at her in surprise. That answer made the most sense.

"Other sorcerers might well be interested in your box," Veneris said. "You have no idea what was in it?"

"There were handwritten notes, a strange mirror, and a ring."

"Wasn't there anything else?" Aurian asked. "A book?"

Maihara shook her head. "No, that was later. Just a funny round stone. I'd forgotten that. I left it lying about my room and someone stole it. I didn't know what it was for."

"You don't have the box now?" Veneris asked.

"No, the rebels took it." She turned to Aurian. "You were in Court at the time, and you knew about the box. Have you any idea what the stone was?"

"Not really." Aurian screwed up her face in an effort at recollection. "I think – there was something about the box containing your mother's memories. I'm not sure."

"That makes no sense. I don't remember any diary or anything like that. Just the stone."

"Maybe it did contain your mother's memories," Veneris said. "What I explained earlier. It can be used in the opposite sense, to store what's in your mind into a magical vessel, for instance."

"You mean the diary was in that stone? No, you mean my mother's actual memories?" Excitement rose in her.

Veneris nodded. "Yes."

"Oh!" The implications struck Maihara a blow. If she had been quicker or less careless, she could have shared her mother's experiences, her thoughts, felt her love... She covered her face with her hands and stifled a sob. How to use magic, how to handle men, embarrassing secrets about her father. All this, her mother had meant to gift her.

She lowered her hands to see Veneris and Aurian staring at her in concern. "Are you all right, Your Grace?" Aurian asked.

"Yes. No. If I hadn't been such a stupid, frivolous girl, I could have had all that."

"Your Grace has never struck me as being either stupid or frivolous," Aurian said. "It was fate, or somebody did not want you to have it."

"But why all this interest in my box?"

"It may have contained some other object of power," Veneris said.

Maihara said nothing. She suspected he meant the magic mirror, which amplified or concentrated magic, not the box itself, which she knew to be a channel of power. But she saw no reason to tell these two.

Aurian toyed with her tea cup. "If that's the case, it makes it more likely it's the Emperor himself who fears you and wants you eliminated. He believes you have magical power, he sees you as a threat."

Maihara shook her head. *Not her own father.* "Eliminate! That can't be. He couldn't. He wouldn't."

"You don't know how far a man will go to hang onto power," Aurian said.

Maihara thought back over various incidents. That Varlord officer she had met a few days ago dropped hints of something like this. But why pursue her box? What do they know? In the far-away palace, at her fourteenth birthday, her little sister blurted out that she was a witch, and her father had reacted with anger and suspicion. It was hard to accept that her own father meant her serious harm. What did he fear she could do?

"I understand your mother was a witch," Veneris said. "And so are you. If you had remained in possession of the box, your unknown adversary would have a great deal to fear."

Maihara leaned toward Veneris. "What is this stone? How does it work? You have to show me."

Veneris shook his head. "It requires preparation. Please calm yourself. In any case, I don't have one at hand now."

"Yes, you do. I can see it in your face. I don't have time for preparation. I might have to flee this quarter at a minute's notice, and I need to know this in case I ever get my hands on my mother's stone again. And I want to learn this *now*." She reached forward and gripped Veneris' wrist in a firm grasp. His face twisted in discomfort.

She relaxed her grip. "Please."

"Very well, Princess. If you insist, come to my house. But if it goes badly—"

***

Veneris' house was small and old-fashioned, a narrow tall house squeezed between two others. Inside, he led them up a dark creaking staircase and bade them wait while he fetched something from a locked room he would not let them enter. Maihara, tense, activated her spy to watch what he was doing. He was opening a small cupboard built into the wall. She shut the spy off, wary of being discovered.

Veneris led them up to an attic where a skylight let in a shaft of sunlight, brightening the shabby space. The floor was of bare dusty boards and over her head ran rough-surfaced apex beams with plaster between. "We're in luck. The sun favours us with its rays." He brushed dust from a

399

piece of junk furniture and set down a stone with a shiny upper surface in the area bathed in sunlight. Its size and shape struck a chord of memory.

"Let us wait a minute or two for the sunlight to activate it," Veneris said. "Then you can try to reach to it. Follow my directions. The opening word is *vikigris*."

They waited minutes, before she became aware of an entity close by. A magical entity. Not the set of icons she had experienced before, but a half-seen ball bigger than a red pumpkin, flickering with sparks of light. With excitement, she sought to force her way into it, but it barred her way. She offered it the word *vikigris*, and a magic space similar to that of the spells snapped into her consciousness, half overlaying the sunlit room. She raised two fingers as a signal to Veneris.

"You see the names of the memories?"

Words in the ancient language appeared inscribed on a series of shields. She nodded and kept her fingers raised.

"Good. You can come out now."

But she was already translating the ancient words on the shields that represented the stored memories. *Machines.* That could be valuable knowledge of what Cordan and his savants were doing in the east. In a flash she had activated it. She staggered as a buzzing inside her head distracted her.

"What have you done?" Veneris cried. "Stop! It's dangerous!" He tried to push past her, reaching out for the shiny crystal, but she resisted him, and she was the stronger. She held him off while the process continued inside her head. Beside the shields, a tall glass filled with coloured liquid. A progress marker, perhaps.

Aurian looked on with an expression of confusion and alarm. "Your Grace! What are you doing?"

Maihara looked over the remaining memory names. One translated as power magic. That was too enticing to let pass. Her head cleared, the progress marker gone, and at once she activated the second memory. The buzzing in her head re-commenced.

"Stop!" Veneris cried again, pushing against her. "If you write over your—, you could go insane, or even die."

She ignored him, holding him away from the crystal, as she translated more names, despite the interference in her head. The sense of his warning percolated by degrees. Better not take too many, anyway she saw nothing else essential in the list.

Her head cleared. To continue was too risky. She released Veneris, who stumbled forward, snatched up the crystal and tucked it inside a pocket.

"What did you do?" he cried. "Are you—?"

"I'm perfectly well," she told him. "There's nothing wrong."

He said nothing, his face working angrily. Aurian stared at them, bewildered.

"You could have destroyed yourself," he muttered.

"You should have said that earlier. Did you really think I would get that close and let the opportunity pass?"

"You tricked me."

"I did not. I did not know what I would see or do once I experienced this."

"What have you done, Mai?" Aurian asked.

"I'm not sure yet. I'll explain later."

"Enough here," Veneris said in an angry tone. He collected his stick and limped toward the attic door. Maihara, with the agility of a young person, got ahead of him and opened the door wide. She descended a few steps and waiting for Veneris to catch up, offered her arm to help Veneris descend. He ignored her, struggling to descend and leading with the same foot at each step. Further down, he took her arm.

On the lower floor, he shut the door on them while returning the crystal to its secure place.

"What did you do up there?" Aurian asked in a low voice.

"I managed to collect two stored memories into my head." She tapped her forehead.

Aurian's eyes widened. "Why was he panicking, trying

to stop you?"

"Seems he thought that if I collected too much, I might displace the memories that make me Maihara Cordana. Or he didn't want me to do it at all."

An odd expression flitted across Aurian's face. "You were reckless, then." Aurian touched Maihara's arm.

"Years of waiting. No box. My book seized. I was not going to let this chance pass."

At the foot of the stairs, inside the front door, Maihara tried to restart a conversation.

"Are there many besides you interested in these occult matters, Master?" Maihara wanted to know.

Veneris turned on her with a scowl. "I'm not making small talk with you, you stupid, reckless girl. Now, I'll escort you back to your lodging."

Aurian raised her eyebrows at his rudeness. Maihara kept quiet.

As they neared Mardax's house, Maihara attempted an apology. "I'm sorry, Master. I know it was reckless, but the temptation was too much."

Veneris left, pleading another engagement. As his walking stick clunked down the street, Aurian leaned close to Maihara. "Please tell me what was that about mining for key-words he spoke of earlier. It did not sound helpful at all."

"No, it was very helpful."

Once upstairs, Maihara seized a piece of paper and a graphite pencil, and wrote out a series of words and characters. "These are common names in the ancient texts, and these are numerals. If I put them together," she scribbled, "you have a typical secret name and password. He said that large numbers of people had these spaces. He implied that the owners had to create the passwords. Dumb people would have dumb passwords." She tapped the paper. "Now, do the opening word for the magic, *Arisa,* and try this name and password."

Aurian's nose wrinkled and her eyes seemed to defocus. "It doesn't work," she said after half a minute.

Maihara pushed the paper at her. "So keep going. Try another one."

"How do you know these weird words?"

"I told you, I studied ancient languages with my tutor at the Palace."

Some time later, in the same room, Aurian beckoned to Maihara. Aurian was silent, lips moving slightly, for a quarter of a minute. "I can't do this. It keeps fading." Then she gasped and broke into a delighted smile. She reached out to grab Maihara. "It works!"

Maihara tolerated the hug. "What can you see?"

"It's like you said earlier. A wall with pictures. There's that funny writing."

"Alright. So try things. You can't do any harm there, I hope."

Aurian's face fell. "It's gone again."

It was becoming clear that Aurian did not possess a fraction of her own strength and facility with the magic, but Maihara would rather not have done this at all. She had skimmed through her new stolen knowledge overnight and learned that there was more to the magic than passwords and levels. A skilled magician of intellectual ability could bypass passwords and block other users. And some individuals had a greater sensitivity to the magical auras than others. She felt awkward about not telling Lady Aurian what she knew sooner. But to her mind, allowing Aurian any access to the magic workings was only going to cause trouble.

-30-

After Tarchon reached the southern coast and captured Retis, mutinous sailors of the Imperial Western fleet stationed further west surrendered their ships to him. Badly fed, their pay in arrears and with the deadly flux decimating the crews, they offered little resistance to the seizure of their ships. To his satisfaction, included in the seizures were several untried 'great ships', tall sailing vessels armed with cannon fired by alchemical powder, as ordered by the Emperor.

Freshly crewed and provisioned, the first task of the rebel fleet was to escort transports full of elite rebel fighters, newly tagged as Marines, along the coast as part of Tarchon's land-sea campaign. So far, their progress at sea was unopposed. In the days after leaving Retis, they had intercepted a few merchant ships in their path. After capturing and looting them, the rebels attached these ships to the convoy.

One night, the sound of alarm horns roused Tarchon from his cabin on the *Cerow Fleetstar*, one of the untested three-masted warships. The decks trembled as men ran to their battle positions. Concerned, he dragged on outer clothing before hurrying on deck into the chill damp air. Many lights moved over the dark sea ahead. Marines on the flagship shouted and cursed as they fumbled with their armour.

The lights were bright, as if nearby, but the vessels carrying them appeared short and low in the water. Beside him the shapes of several officers looked out, one holding a spyglass.

"Those boats look small," Tarchon said.

"They're fishing boats," said the ship's captain.

"Good, then we can buy fresh fish for our crews," the sailing-master said.

"No," said Tarchon. "They'll betray our position. We should signal for the fleet to seize them."

"We should wait for the Admiral," the captain suggested.

Tarchon received the suggestion with displeasure. Catonne had not appeared, and so far as Tarchon knew was sleeping off a bottle of wine in his cabin. It was obvious what needed to be done here, and he saw no need to follow the agreed command structure to the letter and rouse the Admiral. Admiral Catonne was a well-connected officer from a ship-owning and naval dynasty, and while Tarchon was in overall command of the rebel forces, Catonne had insisted on being in tactical command at sea.

"We are seizing ships in our path to prevent them warning the Imperials," Tarchon said, irritated. "We can proceed without him. Pass the order."

"Aye, General, if you say so," the captain said.

The sailing-master peered out into the gloom. "That'll be the fishing fleet out from Skene," he said.

Loomis was the port Tarchon hoped to capture, while Skene was a small harbour partway along the southern coast. "We can't let them go back there," he said. The boats were all drifting stern to wind, trailing nets. The fishermen had lit flickering lanterns that hung from the masts, setting a galaxy of yellow lights swinging over the darkened sea.

The forward galleys had reached the boats and marines were boarding them, with peremptory commands and warning shouts.

Admiral Catonne climbed up to the rear deck now, and with a cursory nod to Tarchon, set about questioning the captain and lookout, while staring ahead.

"What's going on here?" Catonne had a head of greying hair, a neat grey beard and wore a fine uniform jacket with shoulder stripes, braid and two columns of shiny buttons.

Tarchon pressed his lips together. He wished that

Catonne had stayed in his berth.

"We've run into the Skene fishing fleet, Admiral," the captain said.

Catonne looked out into the dark. "That's the lanterns? What about it? Why all the alarms?"

"The General is minded to seize and detain them," the captain said.

Catonne looked around the darkened deck and fixed his eye on Tarchon. "What are you playing at, General? This is pointless! Those boats can't harm us! Surely they can't fly to Loomis before we reach it?"

Tarchon faced down the angry Admiral. "We are seizing ships that could give us away, Admiral," Tarchon said. "We can't endanger our plan by being soft-hearted."

"With respect, General, this action is entirely unhelpful. These boats and men will be an encumbrance, and if those fishermen weren't Varlord supporters before, I'm sure they will be soon. I spent years watching fisher boats at Loomis, so don't tell me how fast they move."

Catonne stared at Tarchon while the General matched his gaze.

"You agreed I would make all decisions relating to fleet engagement, while we were at sea," Catonne said.

To his annoyance, Tarchon knew he had given this undertaking. "Are you sure those boats can't betray our course?"

"They can't. And they have a living to earn."

He could overrule Catonne, but the problem of what to do with the boats and crews remained. With reluctance, Tarchon nodded. "You're the sailor. I'll defer to your judgement." He turned away from the Admiral and captain, to hide his ill temper.

Catonne leaned toward the captain. "Signal the ships to abort boarding and stand by."

The captain shouted down to the main deck. Sailors ran back and forth, horns blared, and a pair of coloured lanterns began a jerky ascent of the mast, swinging to the motion of the ship.

Tarchon returned to his cabin, smarting from the encounter. He was tired, too tired. If swift riders set off the moment one of those boats raced to shore, that would be Catonne's fault.

Unable to sleep with the argument jangling in his head, he wondered what Maihara was doing. He hoped that she was not in danger. Several people in captured Retis claimed to have seen her there at various locations before the town fell. A report of an altercation at the east gate suggested she had escaped eastward. From there, the direct route led to Loomis, which he intended to capture. In such troubled times, even with a military escort, she could be in personal danger. Various worst-case scenarios of harm preyed on his uneasy mind.

Or she might have headed north-east, into the principality of Shardan. She had mentioned the principality when he questioned her in Calah. Anxious to get her back, he had sent several agents in pursuit, with instructions to follow her trail until it entered Imperial territory.

He liked her very much, enjoying her youthful energy, and she seemed to like him. They even had interests and sympathies in common. A suspicion nagged at him that she had simply been playing him, gathering information before escaping to her own side, unlikely as his reason told him it was. If it proved correct, other generals eyeing his position would be swift to sneer and whisper against him.

If Maihara was brought before him, he would soon know if her rescue had been opportunistic, or if the Empire and their Princess had been playing him for a fool. Could they possibly have known of the emptiness inside him and laid an elaborate and cruel trap?

Yet it seemed doubtful that they would use their Imperial Princess as a pawn in that way, even if the rift between her and the Court was genuine. Unless she was an unknowing pawn. If only he knew what was really in her heart and mind. Apart from his wife and first love, he'd had little experience of women of his own class or above.

He sighed. He should concentrate on managing his land-sea campaign and the control of the freed provinces, and not moon over a girl.

He lay awake, listening to the tramp of feet on deck, and the creaking of the ship's gear. Now his fleet had started the swift and covert progress eastward, he dared not make contact with the land lest the Imperials learn of his course and position. He would have to wait longer for any news of Maihara.

***

Maihara, Aurian and their hosts sat around the oval table in Mardax's dark-panelled dining room, softly lit even at midday, the windows hidden by russet curtains. "We hear rumours of an attack in the south by rebels, and disorder elsewhere," Mardax announced over their lunch. "And several people have been arrested in the city for conspiring with the rebels, against the principality."

"Not good," Maihara said.

Lady Aurian lowered her fork. "Is the principality in any danger?"

"There seems no danger as yet," Mardax said. "Though news of this sort is never good."

The candlelight flickered, glinting on the silverware.

"I do hope nothing worse happens," Miriam Mardax said.

After dinner, Maihara and Lady Aurian retired to the lamp-lit sitting-room to read one of Mardax's books on the history of the Vimrashans. As soon as they were alone, Maihara turned to her companion. "It appears Shardan is likely to fall to the rebels, sooner or later. We have to decide how this affects us, and what we should do."

Aurian frowned. "That's not what Mardax said. You know something more, don't you?"

Maihara nodded.

"And I don't need to ask how?"

Maihara shook her head. She felt awkward about not taking Lady Aurian into her confidence sooner.

Aurian's eyes narrowed. "So, what do you know?"

"From what I overheard, the Imperial officers here think that Shardan is in danger, and they don't think the Empire is able to send troops to defend the principality. That fits with what Mardax told us."

Aurian held her arms wrapped around her body.

"So I have to decide, go or stay. If I stay in hiding, I could be trapped by the rebels. Even if I mend bridges with the Wixos party, I may have allied myself with the rebels' enemies at the wrong time. If I surrender to the Army, I may find they have new orders from the Imperial Court to send me back to the Empire."

"You wanted to contact the more liberal politicians in Halamar," Aurian pointed out.

"I don't know how to contact them. And even if I do, they could be persecuted by the Wixos group, or the rebels may overrun the whole principality. It's really too late. I've totally failed here, haven't I?" She had hoped to establish herself in Halamar, make contact with those in power, keep Shardan out of the war and find out more about the golim menace. So far, she had little idea how to counter the golims, which might spearhead an Imperial fightback with an army of metal monsters dealing indiscriminate death, far from the peace she hoped to promote. She put her hands over her face. Despair and disappointment welled up within her and tears flooded her eyes.

Aurian reached out and touched Maihara's arm. "No, I think you've done well in dealing with people much older and more experienced than you. And in handling some frightening situations. I haven't always agreed with you, but you have a wise and brave head on your shoulders. So why do you think we should leave?"

Maihara raised her face. "How can I contact the liberals now? I'd need an armed escort if going out as the Princess, and the Vims are not likely to form one. I'd have to avoid contact with the Army. And I am more inclined now to believe that the Emperor means me ill. If we don't go soon, we could be cut off, or arrested, and not be able to get out of Shardan at all. I'll be in danger of being handed back to the rebels, to appease them, or to the Imperials, for the same reason."

Aurian gave Maihara's arm a brief squeeze. "I do have the names of some Liberal councillors."

A sharp knock came at the front door, and Maihara started. Hinges creaked, and the unseen visitor spoke to their host in a low voice. In the pause, Maihara realised that she did have an idea of how to deal with golims. If the Empire meant to use them, that implied some effective means of control. That could be magic - the same kind of magic she used to start and control her spells. The insight must have come from the memories she had stolen from Veneris.

The front door closed, and Mardax opened the door of the sitting room.

"What is it?" Maihara asked.

"A contact has brought the names of several of the people arrested," Mardax said, running fingers through his hair. "They are councillors of the liberal faction."

Maihara muttered a rude word she had learnt from the Imperial soldiers.

Aurian's face registered shock. "What?"

"It's a plot," Maihara said. "The Wixos faction have seized a chance to attack the others. I doubt that the liberals have been conspiring with the rebels. More likely they merely support some radical demands. I've read about this sort of tactic in the histories."

"Does this matter?"

"It does. It makes it far more difficult to engage with the liberals now. By the time I make contact and get them to trust me, they may all be arrested."

"I see what you mean," Aurian said, after a pause. "But as I said before, you could approach the Wixos group."

"I won't. And after this the Wixos group may be less interested in my support. They won't need me to help win places at the election. If the election happens at all."

Aurian's face fell, showing that she got the point.

Mardax left the room.

Maihara's confusion fell away. There was only one way forward. It would be difficult, but it had to be done. Get out of Halamar and into Imperial territory, and avoid detection long enough to work out the detail of how to resist the golims, and travel to the locality where she could put her knowledge into effect. Maybe that kind of defiance was what her father feared. "It's too late to make this work. Shardan's not my country; the Empire is. We need to get out as soon as possible, to the east."

Aurian stared. "Leave now? Eastwards? You mean to Imperial territory?"

"Yes, but if we go as two noble refugees, no-one need know who we are. In time, things may change." Her swift survey of her stolen magic knowledge had given her confidence. Magic might aid their concealment, and her way forward. Identifying herself as Imperial Princess in Halamar had not turned out well. She had learnt a hard lesson here; if she meant to be Empress it was not enough to be the Imperial princess and have magical powers, she had to have supporters who shared her ideals. But the game was not over.

Aurian nodded, but said. "And what will we live on?"

Maihara hesitated. She had not thought about this, never having been in such a situation, but surely something would turn up. "Let's speak to the Vims about leaving. I think Mardax is keen for us to go. I don't altogether blame him."

***

When they put this to him, Mardax accepted her declaration without comment, but his manner hinted at a certain relief. Within two hours, he had a plan for them to get out of the city and the principality.

"We know a fellow Vim with a trading business. His yard is on the eastern outskirts of Halamar, so we will have to lead you there. Tomorrow he can conceal you in a cart and take you out of the city, and eastwards."

Maihara nodded. "That sounds good. Can we trust this man?"

"Implicitly."

411

"Very well."

As Mardax left the room, an idea nagged at Maihara's mind, something suggested by her audacious theft of Vannis' information. The spy spell magically showed her vivid views of places around the city, with sound, but what lay below? Magic worked in some locations but not others, but she had discovered no feature above ground to explain it. Was the answer underground? She sent the spy point downward, commanding it to pause at whatever it found.

The house had a cellar, but that did not interest her. Below the cellar floor the spy descended blackly through yards of ground. Beyond this were glowing lines, and further down the screen broke up into a scribble of ancient script. Something down there was blocking it.

"Maihara?" Aurian said.

"Mm? I'm resting."

With Aurian reassured, she concentrated on the spy again. The layer it refused to penetrate was of uneven depth. Curved? A vault? A huge artefact? her mind filled with wonder. This touched on other mysteries, the nature of what the ancients had left behind, what was being rediscovered in the east, and how the magic worked. Since it functioned in some places and not others, the magic had to be associated with devices underground left by the ancient Builders.

Mardax burst into the sitting room. He stood for a moment in the doorway, panting for breath. "Your Grace, soldiers have made their way into our quarter and are searching houses. You need to decide now - do you wish to surrender, or leave at once?"

Maihara stared up at their host in surprise, realising that time had passed, and the shadows of dusk lay all around. She shut down the spy spell. Her heart beat faster. "We'll leave," she said, with a glance at Lady Aurian, who had jerked forward in her chair. "Do you have a bag, for our things?"

"A bag? Yes, we put aside packs for each of you. Let me fetch them." He hurried away, to reappear along with his wife, who carried two bags with shoulder loops.

Maihara stuffed the few clothes she had into one of the bags, while Aurian did likewise. The clothing they now wore was plain enough for them to pass as ordinary women of the town, and she wore no brooch, rings or hair ornament. Miriam Mardax added warm cloaks and a pack of dry food, and Maihara, embarrassed, thanked her for her kindness.

She pulled on her boots while their host looked up and down the narrow street. He led the way as distant shouts and yells filtered around the buildings, seeming to come from different directions. Maihara stumbled over uneven cobbles. They reached a shabby building and waited in a neglected unlit hallway, while Mardax found their guide, a thin and shabbily dressed youth.

Mardax bade them farewell while the youth lit a lantern. They descended a flight of brick stairs, then passed along a vaulted passage. At intervals dark cellar openings gaped.

Aurian bumped into Maihara several times before taking Maihara's arm. Aurian's unease was infectious; anything might be lurking in those unlit cellars. The lantern gave barely enough light to avoid tripping, and their guide did not look reliable. It occurred to her that for the first time in her sheltered life she was venturing out without a protective entourage of courtiers, servants or guards. She missed Ferris.

Maihara activated her spy spell. It amplified light, and now she could follow their guide as if the passage was well lit. The lantern glow lit up dark cellar rooms filled with barrels, racked bottles or dusty junk.

They descended further, below the level of the cellars, into a tunnel vaulted with brick and stone.

The youth halted and retraced his steps.

Maihara grabbed at him. "What are you doing?" she whispered.

"I took a wrong turn," the youth mumbled. "We have to go back."

They retraced their steps for a couple of minutes. She

thought she heard other footsteps and voices, but did not want to stop and listen.

The youth turned into another passage. "This is it."

They had only gone a few yards when a voice echoed from behind. "Is someone there? Hey, who's there?"

She flinched, and her heart raced as she fought an urge to panic and run.

The sound of clumping boots echoed as though the shouter had increased his pace. In response their guide extended his stride, and Maihara trotted to keep up. Aurian panted and scuffled behind.

Maihara reached for the controls of her spy spell again and sent it back, with flurried thoughts. It frightened her more not to know who was behind them, shouting. About fifty yards behind, around a couple of deviations of the way, she had a vivid glimpse of an Imperial soldier. Were there more?

Her vision part obstructed by the bright spy screen, she stumbled on the uneven floor and fell to her hands and knees. She shut off the spell before rising and hurrying on. She'd seen enough.

With a sprint, she caught up to their guide and grabbed him by the shirt, forcing him to stop. "This is no good," she said in a low voice. "We'll hide."

The lantern light showed darkness to one side. She shoved the youth into it, collected Aurian as she came up and dragged her chaperone into the cobwebby dark. They listened, as she held her breath. Perhaps they could ambush the soldier, but they had no weapons, and he looked as strong as the three of them. And, from the clumping of boots, there were more than one of them.

Another plan - she knew now that she could send the witch light she had shown the Vims away from her at will and vastly increase the brightness. She started the light, and sent it back along the passage till she judged it must be beside the soldiers.

"Shut your eyes," she told her companions. She pushed the brightness of the witch light as high as it would go, seeing swirling numbers in the control. A bright red glow pulsed through her closed eyelids and died.

Cries of fear and distress echoed along the brick-lined passage.

"Now." She hauled Aurian and the youth out of the alcove and thrust them along the passage. "Hurry."

The guide stopped with a cry as the tunnel ahead went dark. On her square of spy vision she saw him crouched and scrabbling on the grimy floor.

"It's all right, I can see him," she said to Aurian. "What's the matter?" She poked him in the back.

With a yelp of fear, the youth flinched away. "I dropped the lantern."

"Calm yourself," she told him. "Wait a moment."

A hand brushed her backpack and took hold. "Mai," came Aurian's voice, with a tremor.

Maihara turned on her witch-light, and filled the space with a white glow.

"Aah!" The youth started, then reached for the fallen lantern and picked it up, along with the smouldering candle.

"Let's go," She turned to Aurian and moved the witch-light forward. "The light, first level, second row," she said in a low voice.

"What?" Aurian whispered.

Maihara moved on. After a minute, a second pale, steady glow lit the tunnel walls, then went out. Aurian made a disappointed noise. Shouting echoed through the passages from behind, coming closer. Maihara didn't dare try the blinding light trick again, lest they associate it with their quarry. Where had she got that from? It must have been part of the knowledge she stole from Veneris.

At last, she found herself ascending on aching legs, and their guide unbolted a door. Beyond it was a shadowy street, paved with dirt. Maihara doused her light.

Their guide pointed. "It's down that street. Look for a tavern, and the sign with a wagon wheel. Ask for Auraxis."

"You're not taking us there?" Maihara was incredulous.

The youth looked away, unable to meet her eyes. "I can't. They know me here."

"But - you want money?"

The youth shook his head.

"What, then?" She glanced at Aurian.

"They'd get me," the youth said.

"The soldiers?"

"I can hide from them, ma'am."

This was not getting her anywhere.

"So what will happen to us out there?"

"Probably nothing, ma'am."

Maihara was not going to waste time trying to learn what this youth feared. Outsiders, other youths, or persons he had stolen from, probably. Her body tensed. With any luck, nothing would happen and their clothing should help them pass unnoticed.

She glanced at Aurian again. "We should walk separately, in case soldiers or agents are looking for two women answering our general description."

Aurian nodded, looking apprehensive. "I suppose so."

"Very well. Wait till a count of twenty, then follow me. Keep me in sight. Let's go."

Aurian mumbled, "Yes, your — ma'am."

With a glance in Aurian's direction, Maihara pulled the door further open.

Mardax had given her a password: 'Alexa is twenty-six today.' The man she was to meet should reply with "No, twenty-seven."

A chill settled over her. What if the password got the wrong response?

They had plenty time to reach the transport yard before the appointed hour. Too much time, for they had left much earlier than previously arranged. She slipped out into the street unnoticed.

Heading right, she found that the street forked. None of the streets were named. Afraid of losing her way, she asked for directions and the man she asked was overly keen to show her the way. She had to speak firmly to get rid of him. Aurian should be following, but she dared not look back.

This was a poor district. The shops and houses were shabby and the people dressed in dull or ragged clothing. She spotted the tavern she had been told to look for as a mark. A sign with faded and peeling paint hung over the street. The image on it looked like a wheel. As she hesitated, a well-dressed man sidled up and made an indecent proposition. She turned on him.

"Get lost!"

The man took a step back.

Rattled, and with ears burning, she hurried on, confidence shaken. Men here wanted to abuse her in disgusting ways. And if they knew who she was, they would most likely want to do worse. She turned down a narrow alley running alongside the inn, and glanced through an open door grimed by a thousand hands. In the dim interior, men sat at plain wooden tables with glasses of drink before them, or stood at the bar. Several seemed to be staring at her. She hurried on. Belatedly, she remembered to check for Aurian. Her chaperone's small figure was entering the alley, head down.

She made her way into an open space, rutted, with two parked carts, and a shed beyond with a wagon wheel sign. To her left, two thin-faced men in loose, grimy workmen's clothes responded to her presence with ill-mannered remarks. Red-faced, she turned to them. "Is Mr Auraxis here?"

In response, one came over to her. "Will I do?" he said in a coarse voice. A hand insinuated itself onto her bottom. She spun and confronted the short, stubble-faced man, who breathed beer fumes.

"Stop that!"

He recoiled.

Another man had emerged from the shed. "Somebody wants me?"

Not wanting to waste any more time on the groper, she walked up to the presumed Auraxis. "Mr Auraxis? Alexa is twenty-six today."

The man looked surprised. After a pause that seemed to last an age he finally responded, "No, twenty-seven."

She sighed with relief.

"Not here!" the man hissed. He opened a door behind him and beckoned for her to follow. She waved Aurian forward. The idlers stared.

-31-

Red-faced, Maihara stood inside the long wood-boarded wagon shed as Auraxis turned back to dismiss the two labourers, who wandered off through a rutted wagon exit leading to another street. After an eternity, the men moved out of view. She beckoned to Aurian who was lurking in the inn alley.

Auraxis, a middle-aged man in a grey workman's smock, peered at them with disquiet. His face was tanned by weather, and stubbly.

"Mardax sent us," Maihara said. "He said you'd help us."

Auraxis frowned. "You're early. I'm not ready till tomorrow."

"There was a problem," Maihara told him. "May we wait here?"

The man sighed and edged further into the building.

"Soldiers started searching the quarter, so we had to go," Maihara said.

"The wagon won't be loaded and ready till tomorrow morning," the man said. "You should come back then."

"We can't go wandering about these streets," Aurian told him. "Can't you hide us till morning?"

The man shook his head. "I don't have rooms for fine ladies."

"Anything will do," Maihara said. "We don't want to attract attention."

With reluctance, the man showed them up a narrow stair to a small shabby room where paint was flaking from the timber walls. The only piece of furniture was a double bed, made up, and covered by a dark bedspread. The room smelt stale and unaired.

Lady Aurian made a face.

"It'll do," Maihara said. "And in the morning?"

"My wagon is inside my shed, out of sight. It's a box wagon, and there's a smaller box under the frame. You can stay hidden in that till we clear the city, and then as you like. I am taking goods over the eastern border. I can take you there."

"What do you want in return?"

The man shrugged. "You're one of us. I can tell. Have you eaten?"

"This place is awful," Aurian whispered later, as they ate sliced cold meat and bread from a plank balanced on their knees. "Can't we go to the Army?"

"We already tried that," Maihara said. "It didn't go well." She meant to be firm, but despite her resolve, tears wet her cheeks and a sob shook her as she remembered Ferris's dead face. Aurian stroked her back.

"Have we any money?" Maihara asked.

"Some. I asked Mardax for some travel money as we left. He couldn't refuse after being so anxious to be rid of us."

"Good." Aurian had common sense.

During the night, Maihara woke. Her lower leg itched. The bedclothes smelt musty. Something had bitten her. She twisted, trying to reach it and scratch the itch without waking Aurian. Persis and Sihrima would both be sleeping more comfortably this night.

A horrible life. That was what she had said a few days ago. *I'd rather have a horrible life.*

***

With a fair breeze filling its sails, Tarchon's fleet neared the coast, menacing the town of Loomis. From the stern deck of the flagship, he surveyed the scene with tense anticipation. Officers shouted orders, and men ran to adjust ropes or clear hatch covers. Sunlight sparkled off the water, and rigging creaked as his ship rolled in a light swell. Twenty supply ships and oared galleys followed the flagship. All this was happening at his command. The galleys he had brought with him were driven by two rows of twenty-five oars at each side and carried a hundred rowers and over thirty marines each. As was the custom of the time, the rowers were slaves, criminals or captives. A narrow central gang-deck ran fore and aft above the rower's benches, and two slave-wardens paced up and down it, each with a long lash of bullock-hide under his arm. On either side, the slave-rowers laboured in their chains. The unfortunates were of many races, stray barbarians, olive-skinned men from the south and east, or dark-haired men from the western plains, but a good many were Empire loyalists who had refused to change sides. One could smell these galleys when they were to windward, the stink of sweat on the rowers and excrement in the bilges.

To seaward rolled a line of supply ships which mostly relied on square or lateen sails. Tarchon had to rely on the naval officers to operate all these ships, but failure of the expedition would be laid at his door.

Through his spyglass, he scanned the shore for signs of an armed force. According to the plan he had laid earlier, the advance part of his land force should have reached the town by now. Cut off from contact on board ship, he had to rely on his officers doing their part. He trusted them, but not having reports of their progress raised his anxiety. As the ships moved nearer, he adjusted the spyglass, straining for a sharper view of a dark patterned mass covering the land beside the town. Occasional flashes of light came from it.

He lowered the spyglass with a sigh. "A land force seems to be in position beside the town," he remarked to his Admiral. Catonne wore his uniform jacket with the two rows of buttons, and his three-cornered hat.

As they approached, the dark mass resolved into a besieging force surrounding the town on the landward side. A few men with pikes stood on the harbour wall, and the defenders had fastened a great boom of logs and chains across the entrance to the harbour, preventing any ships from entering. Tarchon's mood darkened, for his attack plan called for the warships to enter the harbour, though the Admiral had warned him there might be a boom in place.

"There's a boom across the harbour."

"They're expecting a seaborne attack," Admiral Catonne said.

Tarchon gave Catonne a meaningful look, but the Admiral did not respond. Tarchon had been concerned, despite the Admiral's assurances, that word of their advance would spread along the coast. His plan had included a swift advance and a two-pronged assault on the land walls and through the harbour. He curled his fists in frustration. There was no point in upbraiding his Admiral, and it was possible that the barrier had been closed in response to the arrival of his land force. As the general in sole command of this attack, he had to adapt his plan and press forward. Concealing his disappointment, he turned to his staff officers. "We need to signal to the forces on shore. Get them to identify their units." He needed confirmation that the designated units had all arrived. And, of course, that they weren't the enemy. More than one commander had made that fatal mistake.

The ship's deck crew hoisted a string of signal flags. In response, a signaller on shore started signalling with a pair of white flags, and unit banners were held up so they were visible from the ship. A fresh-faced aide turned a spyglass on them. "It's the 2nd cavalry and the 4th foot," he reported.

"So far, it's good. We need to send someone ashore and make contact with them," Tarchon said. "Ask the captain if he'd be kind enough to provide us with a boat. And have the marines stand to for a landing." The *Cerow Fleetstar* was not venturing any closer inshore. The naval staff did not care to risk the sailing ship in confined waters with a partly trained crew.

Two staff officers stepped away to carry out these orders.

"Ficke, take the boat and contact the command on shore, tell them our plan, then report back to me," Tarchon said.

The young officer saluted and hurried off.

While the marines on the various smaller ships armed themselves and got ready the ship-mounted catapults, another small boat approached the flagship from the beach, carrying rebel officers to confer with Tarchon.

"We've been in position since this morning, General," a bearded young rebel said. "We don't think the garrison is large, but they're being defiant."

"And they have walls," Tarchon said. "You've already demanded that the garrison surrender, I assume?"

"Yes, General."

"What can you tell me about that chain across the harbour? Is it well defended?"

"We can't see it from our positions on land, General."

Tarchon sighed. "If we don't receive any further signal from you, we'll launch a seaborne attack into the harbour in an hour. When you see us going in, the major-general is to start a land assault at once."

The officer saluted. "Aye, sir."

Tarchon watched as the boat returned to the beach. A few arrows arced out from the town walls, but fell well short. On the flagship, marines in armour wound up the catapult in the bows and stacked a pile of missiles.

An hour dragged on, without any sign that the town was ready to surrender.

"This is exciting," said Catonne with apparent irony.

"I don't seek excitement, Admiral."

Catonne looked at him for a moment. "As you wish, General."

A flag signal from the shore indicated that the shore force was ready to attack.

"Admiral, please have the attack galleys move against the port," Tarchon said.

Catonne saluted, and spoke to the captain. Men ran, signal flags snaked up the mast, drums and horns sounded, and with a splash and creak of oars, and the thump of the pacing drum, the lead galley moved shoreward. A score of other galleys followed. Catapults at their bows fired pots of inflammable liquid plugged with burning rag into the town.

Tarchon eyed the floating barrier across the harbour mouth as they closed on it. "What think you of this boom?" he asked Catonne. "Should we land troops at each end and try to cut or release it?"

"Probably," Catonne said. "But I'll have the captain of the *Herga Star* ram it. We'll soon see how strong it is."

Flag signals and shouted commands instructed two galleys to be ready to land troops at the ends of the boom. Ahead and to their right, the galley *Herga Star* got under way, oars foaming the water at a high stroke rate. Tarchon held his breath as she headed for the middle of the chain at speed. When she was a ship's length from the floating timbers, the oarsmen stopped rowing. With a clack, the ship's bow bit into the barrier. It whipped back as the two halves straightened, and baulks of wood jerked clear of the water, till the boom was angled like a taut bowstring. But it held, stopping the galley and forcing it back, to drift a few yards clear of the boom. Spray settled across the water.

"Strong enough," Catonne said. "You'll have to capture the ends."

"I agree." He saw no other option. Getting into the harbour was becoming more troublesome than he had hoped. If he couldn't breach the chain barrier, it would severely compromise his attack. He'd have to rely on the land force, plus whatever marines he was able to put on the beach. He tried not to show his anxiety to his men.

Two galleys moved forward to land marines at the ends of the floating barrier. Arrows landed among them, then defenders ran out from hidden positions to attack the marines. A man on board one of the assault galleys lost his balance, fell into the water, and disappeared with a scream, weighed down by his armour and equipment. Tarchon watched intently across a few anchor cable lengths of water. If they could not force the chain, the capture of the city would be delayed.

His strategy relied on fast movement, to take towns before the Imperials could concentrate to protect them. If he did not take Loomis quickly, a relieving Imperial force would arrive and his strategy would unravel. The cannon-armed 'great ships' he had captured were not ready for battle, their new crews still in training.

With Catonne, he had two more galleys close in and use their boarding-planks to get men ashore on the outer harbour jetties. Tarchon directed his spyglass to the battle around the chain anchors as the struggle intensified and moved a few yards inland. Shouts and screams carried across the water, and men fell. Combat engineers protected by shields from a rain of arrows worked to release the chain. They pried at the stone where it was anchored to the base of a wall, before concentrating on a large rusted shackle. The shackle pin yielded to a crowbar and hammer, and the engineers redoubled their efforts. One engineer fell, hit by an arrow. The rest carried on working.

Tarchon directed his attention to the harbour basin. There were ships there, but he saw no warships prepared for battle. A cheering arose to his left. The boom was slipping sideways as the left end chain dropped into the water and sank.

"They've cut it," Tarchon said.

Catonne raised his arm. "Forward!"

Oars struck the water, and sixteen galleys made their way into the harbour. The defenders, a couple of hundred in number, fell back, and soon Tarchon's men gained the harbour and the few ships in it. A high crenellated wall with small towers and two closed gates sealed off the harbour from the town. Defenders with bows, swords and crossbows waited along its top. The foot of the wall did not look a good place to be.

Tarchon called his officers to him and they made a swift assessment. There was plenty of wood in the harbour, in the form of huts, boxes, masts and the like, that could be used to make scaling ladders or rams and shelters for attacking the gates.

Smoke was rising from beyond the town wall. Men atop it ducked as Tarchon's marines loosed arrows at them from the dockside. Marines dismantled a pair of sheds and used the flat sections as large shields. Under their cover, a long mast hammered on the gate. Men swarmed up the harbour seawall and from there used short ladders to climb on top of the town wall. All around the harbour, bodies of the dead and wounded littered the quays.

The flagship backed off so that Tarchon was in a line of sight to receive flag signals from the land army about the progress of their attacks. Several attacks on the walls were under way.

Two hours later, the defenders were holding out, the marines having been unable to force an entrance at the harbour and, to his concern, assaults by the land force on the circuit of walls had likewise failed. Without cannon and heavy siege equipment, the advantage lay with the defenders. More of Tarchon's marines had fallen to a persistent rain of arrows from defenders shooting from behind crenellations of the city wall, and he became increasingly frustrated. Before his eyes, his marines were taking steady casualties; a man spinning from his attack group transfixed by two arrows, a marine dragging himself back under cover leaving a long slick of blood behind, crumpled bodies of men who would never rise again. Tarchon swore to himself. "Get them back under cover," he shouted to his aide. "Pass the order."

Tarchon summoned officers from shore to the flagship to consult on their next move. A lengthy siege of Loomis would give time for the Imperial side to bring up a relieving force. They needed a new plan. Perhaps they could bombard the harbour with the *Cerow Fleetstar's* cannon. It would be the first time the guns had fired in anger.

***

Maihara stumbled up the pass, trying to keep pace with the other walkers, while Lady Aurian tramped beside her.

The sky was a deep blue, flecked with cloud. Around them lay loose rock, with thin, tough-looking plants growing in the cracks. A few purple flowers bloomed. Above the valley sides, jagged peaks mottled with white scratched at the sky.

She paid little attention to the view, concentrating on putting one foot in front of another on the uneven track. Her feet hurt, her legs ached, she was hungry, and she needed to pee. If she stopped, the rest of the marchers would just leave her behind along with Aurian. The escape had not gone smoothly. Fighting between Imperial and rebel forces at the south-east border of Shardan had blocked the wagon road, forcing Maihara to take a more northerly route through the mountains that lay between the principality of Shardan and the Imperial province of Triano, and on foot. There were rumours that a column of rebel horse had penetrated Shardan from the south and was attempting to raise the countryside in revolt. There was talk of a military disaster in the south of Triano, closer to Loomis, where an Imperial force apparently dispersed rebel militias only to pursue them into an ambush by rebel mounted forces. Perhaps she had been wise to leave.

This was the third day of the trek, led by a mountain guide. They had spent the previous night huddled together under a sheet of canvas in a shallow cave, with rocks for a bed. There were about twenty people in the party, all bundled in coats or cloaks. Some were refugees trying to get to Imperial territory; others did not care to state their business.

Imperceptibly, the track levelled out, and the valley widened, giving a view of the peaks to each side. Slivers of silver water threaded down expanses of soaring dark rock. The strain on her leg muscles eased. Water... heather for bedding... She stumbled against Aurian. She was falling asleep on her feet. The aching in her legs lessened on the level track, but the sky was swiftly clouding over, from white to grey. It began to rain.

"Why can't they stop?" she asked Aurian.

"There isn't anywhere to stop. We'll just get wetter. I wish they'd walk at our pace, not theirs." She missed her escort, and thought with sadness of Ferris.

After a couple of hours, the path sloped downward, which brought Maihara a new misery. Each downward step jolted her knee as it took her weight. It hurt more than going uphill.

She was falling behind. Before her, the score of marchers straggled down the mountainside. A series of huts loomed out of the rain ahead. A dark figure stood at the side of the track, waving them on - their guide. Maihara maintained her pace till she reached him.

"Is this it?"

Her narrow-eyed mountain guide nodded and showed his teeth in a smile. "We can rest here."

Now she was eager to get out of the wet. She followed Lady Aurian and the other refugees as they squelched down a muddy track between stone-built huts. From some of them, an orange light glimmered behind window coverings.

Their guide knocked on the door of a hut and they entered a space dimly lit by a lamp and a glowing open fire. It was at least warm and dry. Two individuals in layers of peasant clothing smiled and gestured her toward a chair. Exhausted, she sank into it with gratitude and soaked up the warmth from the fire. Her cloak dripped water. It was a relief to stop the painful jolting of her knees, the ache in her legs from hours of walking, the pain in her feet. Her feet still smarted, the blisters and sore places having become more raw in the past hours.

Lady Aurian hunched in the other chair near the fire, looking tired and miserable.

Their guide made his farewells.

"Thank you so much for taking us this far," Maihara told him.

Aurian fumbled in her bag and handed over the balance of the agreed fee.

Their new hosts offered them food. Maihara accepted with eagerness. She did not care what it was, she'd eat it to fill the gnawing emptiness in her stomach.

The family placed a pot over the fire and tossed various ingredients into it. By degrees, the smell became more enticing. While they waited, the peasants offered them warm beer served in misshapen pots.

After over an hour, the meal was ready. The stew, poured into clay bowls was placed before her on a low table. The peasants produced two shiny spoons, clearly treasured possessions. The stew was far too hot, so while she waited for it to cool, Maihara unlaced and eased off her boots. Her feet were sore and the bandages covering the previous blisters were stained, but removing the boots offered a slight relief.

The stew was cool enough to eat if she blew on each spoonful. It didn't taste bad. She had downed most of the stew when she heard the muffled sound of hooves and male voices barking questions outside.

She looked at Aurian. "What's that?"

Aurian looked up from her stew, round-eyed. "Are we expecting to be met?"

The door burst open, and five men in dark leather clothing forced their way in, knives in hand. Swiftly they crossed the room, threatening the peasants and frisking them for hidden weapons. More men blocked the doorway. One man, clad in leather and with a metal breastplate, menaced Maihara with his knife.

"Who are you?" he demanded.

Her heart thumped as fear clamped down on her. "Who are you people?" Militia or robbers?

"No fugging games. Your name, woman?"

"Lassa Onetree."

The man sniffed. He glanced over to where another man was questioning Lady Aurian.

"Lady Serina Onetree," the other man repeated in a coarse voice.

The man in front of Maihara shook his head. "It's them." He bent over Maihara, pointing his knife. "Are you the Princess?"

"What princess?" Maihara said, meeting his eyes.

"Bullshit." He grasped Maihara's hands and examined them, with a grunt. She was too frightened to protest at the *lèse-majesté*. He straightened. "We're arresting these two," he announced to the room at large. The peasants looked away. He gestured to the door with his knife. "Out!"

Her captor tugged Maihara's arm. She stood. Her feet met the cold floor.

"I'm not going anywhere." She couldn't go outside without her boots. "Who are you people?"

For answer, the man jerked her forward over an extended foot. She fell on the dirty floor. A kick landed on her side, tumbling her over, and another in her stomach, winding her. The man seemed to consider, before kicking her in the face.

Winded and shocked, she lay there, before touching her throbbing cheek. Not a princess, just a captive woman. She tasted blood, but nothing felt broken. She got to her knees and crawled toward the fire.

"Where the fug are you going?"

"My boots!"

"What about them?"

"I need my boots."

"For fugsake. Put them on, then."

Maihara sat and struggled with her boots. She got them on, then sat with the laces in her hands, mind a shattered blank. How to tie them?

Her captor barked an order at the man holding Lady Aurian. "Tie the Princess's boots for her." The other man knelt and quickly tied Maihara's bootlaces. She stared over his back at the fire, thoughts whirring. Arrest? What charge?

Her captor pulled Maihara to her feet and dragged her out into the darkness of the muddy alley. Aurian was already outside. Dim shapes of horses and men moved in front of her.

"Who are you people?" she asked, again.

"We are a militia of the Radical forces."

Her heart sank. She was back in rebel hands again, and this lot might turn out far less friendly than Tarchon's staff.

"I thought the Empire controlled this area." It made no sense.

"Not any more, they don't."

Maihara's shoulders sagged. All that walking, all that effort had been in vain. The province to which she had hoped to escape was falling into rebel hands. Her plan to stay free and oppose the golim menace for the benefit of all the people threatened by war had come to nothing. Protesting or explaining anything to these louts would be futile. She needed magic, and there was none here. She needed to be free to act, and this was not in prospect.

Her captor put her on a horse in front of him, and they moved off at a walk into the dark. A strong arm around her waist kept her in place. She could see little, but smelt damp pine woods, horse, an ill-cured leather jacket and unwashed male. At intervals, men called to each other, alerting their comrades to turns in the dark, descending trail. Her captor was not talkative.

"Where are you taking us?" she asked him, as drips of light rain hit her face. It cooled the throbbing in her cheek.

"We're handing you over to the regular forces. They can decide what to do with you."

"What happened here? I thought this province was Imperial territory."

"The Imperials gathered an army here to strike at the radicals besieging Loomis," he said. "But they met with an accident on the way. So now nobody's in charge of this part of the province." The man chuckled to underline his meaning.

"Who told you where to find me?"

"Your mountain guide, of course."

Maihara's spirits sank further. They must have let slip some clue to their identity, or at least that they were well-connected nobles worth betraying. Or the carrier could have been indiscreet. She could trust nobody.

Later that night, they arrived at another, larger village,

where her captors lifted Maihara off the horse and led her into a low stone-walled hut. The leader argued with the occupants, before a woman showed Maihara to a box-bed built into an internal wall. Here she lay damply for a while, nursing her bruises, before falling asleep. When she awoke, the space was still almost dark, but a clattering, the lowing of animals and human voices signalled that it was morning. She concentrated, and searched for a magical aura, but found nothing. Would it be any different if she had her Box?

She emerged, to find her captors alert. Lady Aurian sat at a scarred wooden table, eating a grey broth with a spoon.

"How did they know where to find us?" Aurian asked in a low voice.

Maihara glanced at their captors. "The mountain guides betrayed us for money, the brutes. Do you know where they are taking us?"

"To Loomis, I overheard."

-32-

Some days later Maihara was in a carriage approaching Loomis, a city which her captors clearly believed to have fallen to the rebels. Upland forests had given way to fields of stubble where the crops and straw had been gathered in, to groves of evergreen olive trees and citrus and low farmhouses of yellow brick. Her apprehension grew. She had not been further mistreated, but the demeanour of her captors was unfriendly. The latest escort, from the regular rebel army rather than their resistance militia, was aware of her escape from the barge convoy and dropped unsubtle hints that she would be called to account.

Lady Aurian sat opposite her, blank-faced, beside a guard. Maihara had not heard her sing since the troubles in Halamar, and the reflection of what she had dragged Aurian through made her mood darker.

Tarchon would probably be in Loomis. The thought of being brought before him caused a worm of ice to clamp around her heart. They had been getting on so well, before Ferris and his men had rescued her from the barge. Ferris, that fine young man, dead in Halamar. Now Tarchon would be angry with her. There was no telling how he might react to her recapture, and she hoped there would be no retaliation against her captive brother. Things might have changed, and she recalled Tarchon's chilling remarks in Calah about having her executed as a parasite. Perhaps, urged on by the likes of Colonel Impar, who hated her, he would succumb to pressure to carry out those threats.

As the carriage climbed a hill, the towers and walls of Loomis became visible by degrees. Slim towers at the city centre soared high above the walls. The carriage stopped on a rise, blocked by troops filling the road ahead. Vineyards lay on each side of the road, the ground between the rows of trellised vines littered with falling leaves. A row of burnt-out peasant houses smoked near the road. Her fists clenched. Further along the coast, past pines and sand dunes, lay the city. To her right a fleet lay at anchor in the bay, close to the harbour.

As she watched, a dozen galleys slowly moved behind the stone piers of the harbour and out of view. The troops blocking the road ahead lessened in number. With the carriage window open for air, a faint murmur of clashing and shouting reached her ears. They were taking her to a centre of the enemy's power, from where there would be no escape, leaving her helpless to influence the war. No followers, no magical box.

Under the sun, the interior of the black carriage became stiflingly hot. The escort sent a messenger ahead for further instructions. By the roadside nearby, an enterprising trader had an open canvas shelter put up to shade customers from the sun, and had lit a brazier to grill meat and vegetables on skewers. The succulent odour drifted past her nostrils.

"It's suffocating in here," she complained. "And I'm hungry."

The guards glared or ignored her. After some argument they allowed her to step out and go to the food stall with some money begged from the guards. She sat in the shade where, eating from a skewer and trying not to get grease on her face, she listened to the officers' speculation about the hold-up and the disturbance ahead as Lady Aurian huddled beside her, silent, with a drawn face, apparently more frightened than herself.

"There are some things we should not mention, if they question us," Maihara said in a low voice. "Any warnings I gave. You agree?"

Lady Aurian nodded.

The officers of the regiment blocking the road stared at them for a while, before returning to their grilled snacks and beer. Maihara stood and looked out over the bay toward the distant city.

Tarchon's master plan, as she had overheard, was to advance swiftly and in force, shocking towns like Loomis into surrender. Here the relief Imperial army had evidently failed to arrive, leaving her people in the city to face the horrors of siege, with starvation and fighting. After that would come the storming, raping and pillaging she had read about in books. But those were real people behind those walls, who had done nothing to deserve this suffering. She dug her fingernails into her palms. In no way would the rebels' promised reforms be sufficient compensation.

The road cleared, and the escort made her and Aurian get back in the carriage, which rolled past bivouacs and drowsy, resting men toward the town.

When the carriage neared the walls, she saw with sinking heart that a section of wall had been thrown down as though struck by a giant fist. A line of shanties stood half-wrecked, the surrounding vegetable gardens trampled. Two bodies lay unburied. The carriage headed for an open gate. A few soldiers wandered around, and it was obvious the rebels had already taken the town.

As they entered the town, she glimpsed piles of weapons abandoned outside the walls, presumably given up there by the surrendering defenders. A sense of foreboding swept over her as the carriage rattled through the echoing gate passage and into the subjugated streets. Rebel troopers escorted the carriage, and soldiers lined the streets, but there was no sign of the townsfolk. Doors were closed and windows shuttered.

She searched for a magical aura and found one at once, but it was not a form she recognised. Disconcerting, but given a day here she should be able to solve the problem and connect with it. The city's history extended back for millenia, its slim pre-Fall towers famous. The towers at the city centre, closer now and hundreds of feet in height, resembled colossal pastel-coloured temple columns.

Close to the port, she stared in shock at the damage on the streets. Loose tiles littered the pavements, buildings were burnt. Shops and houses lay open with their contents scattered in the street, and dead bodies lay at the side where they had been dragged. Pools of dark blood marked the roadway. A few scared-looking civilians were recovering their goods or nailing up their properties.

Lady Aurian leaned forward to look out of the carriage window. "How awful. Who did this?"

"I think they were bombarding this part of the town from the ships," the chief guard said.

"Where are we going?" Aurian asked.

"They have requisitioned a mansion near the port. We're to take you there," the officer in charge said.

"Is it safe?" Maihara asked. "What's going to happen to us?"

"Just following orders," the fellow said.

Maihara was not reassured.

When they stepped down from the carriage in a guarded courtyard, it was like being in Retis or General Katan's house at Radukamaris again; a strange and opulent mansion, confusion, a late meal and finally rest in an unfamiliar luxurious room with guards outside the door.

Not long after dawn, two men in uniform came to question her. Guards led her to a room in the service wing, unadorned by anything other than cobwebs, and made her sit at a small scarred table while the officers seated themselves facing her. More guards lounged in the doorway.

The interrogators were both clean-shaven, looking in their thirties, with officer shoulder flashes. One had fair hair and light skin, the other black, with a swarthy skin. They stared at her as though they disliked her already. She shivered, despite the warmth of the weather. Of what crimes against their cause would they accuse her?

"Your name?"

The question seemed absurd, but it emerged that they wanted formally to confirm her identity. She resisted the temptation to give pert replies.

"Maihara Cordana Zircona, Duchess of Avergne and

Crown Princess."

The fair-haired one wrote out her full name and titles.

"Why did you escape from the Sintheer barge fleet?"

"I didn't. Imperial forces attacked and captured the barge, and freed me."

"Why did they only attack the one barge, the one with you on board?" the black-haired, swarthy officer asked.

"I have no idea."

"Obviously they knew which barge to attack. Were you aware of a plan to rescue you?"

"No." She had wondered this at the time, but Ferris and his men had clearly not expected to find her, and the other person under suspicion, Lady Aurian, had appeared equally surprised and never admitted that she knew of a plan to free the Imperial Princess.

They carried on with this line of questioning for a while, before changing tack.

"We have a complaint that your party murdered several citizens who tried to prevent you leaving Retis on the morning of the attack."

Murdered who? The thugs at the East gate? "I don't know what you're talking about."

"Then let me remind you," the dark-skinned officer said. "As your carriage reached the East gate, it was stopped by a group of citizens who wished to prevent your escape. You ordered your guard to cut them down and drive over their bodies."

This was not far from the truth. With a chill, she saw the danger. The rebels could put her on trial for murdering fine and public-spirited citizens, if they were so inclined. The penalty might be her death.

"We were held up by some thugs at the gate. They were just a mob, and had no right to prevent Imperial citizens leaving an Imperial city."

"You ordered your soldiers to cut them down."

"The Imperial Army's soldiers, not mine. I don't recall giving any such orders."

"We have a witness report that says you did."

She tried not to show her dismay. "There was a lot of shouting and screaming. He must have misheard. Or he's just lying."

The dark-skinned officer frowned. "And why would he lie?"

"A lot of rebels hate the Imperial family."

"With good reason, Princess."

"But it's not my fault."

The fair-haired officer tapped his pen on the table. "We're getting off the point here."

Maihara hoped they had not questioned Lady Aurian and got a different story. Poor Ferris was forever beyond their questioning. "Those thugs attacked my escort. If they attack armed Imperial soldiers in uniform, they've only themselves to blame if they get killed."

The fair-haired officer rapped the table again. "Can we move on?"

The other officer shuffled his papers.

"So what were you doing in the principality of Shardan?"

They questioned her on her stay in Halamar until, after two hours, they ended the session. Maihara was exhausted. She hoped that she had not told them anything of importance. She did not see her chaperone again and assumed that Lady Aurian was being questioned separately and put in another bedroom. Alone in a strange room, she missed her companion and worried over what Aurian might have told the interrogators.

The next day, two more officers questioned her, going over much the same ground. She was tempted to warn them about the golim threat to their people, but hesitated. After being hauled across two provinces, sold, and treated as a war criminal, she felt resentful. Lady Aurian had seen the metal hand, but let the interrogators ask about it if Aurian mentioned it.

She wondered if the reports were being passed to Tarchon, if he still had the authority to protect her, and if she would ever see him again. He had seemed fond of her.

Did he still feel the same, or was he now angry and wishing he had never tried to befriend her?

***

Tarchon had cleared himself an office in the captured Loomis fort. He had kept the furniture left by the previous occupants, ordered the place cleaned and pinned a map of the south coast to the wall.

An aide entered with a handful of papers.

"Do you have a report of the Princess' interrogation yet?" Tarchon asked before the man could speak.

"Yes, sir." The aide handed over the papers.

Tarchon glanced through them. "She's not giving much away."

"No, sir. The other woman, Lady Aurian, was more forthcoming. She says they spoke to various people in Retis about our advance downriver, while their military escort was delivering his report. And the Princess met local politicians in Halamar, trying to make a deal with them. Then they visited the Vimrashan district in Halamar. It's all in the other report, sir."

Tarchon thumbed through the second, thicker, pile of papers.

"Colonel Impar suspects that both of them are witches, sir."

Tarchon shook his head. He was not convinced by this allegation. Impar disliked Maihara, and hated nobles in general. Even if she was a witch, that was not why she was a problem. The problem was what to do with an Imperial Princess whom he personally liked, and who might or might not be sympathetic to his cause.

"I'll study these," he said. He wanted to see her, but he had to be certain of what she had been doing, or plotting, while she was on the loose. His people would suspect him of being overly partial to her if he tried to resume the same friendly relations as before. And she had reverted to supporting her own side the moment she escaped.

An hour later he was in consultation with the lanky

Colonel Impar. They sat at a battered table in Tarchon's bare, damp-smelling office.

"That escape was pre-arranged," Impar said, stabbing a finger at the papers. "Look at what she's been doing while free, even if it came to naught. That girl's a meddler, shoving her long nose into political matters beyond her limited understanding, but she does have a great degree of confidence, or arrogance, and she can influence people. That makes her potentially dangerous."

"There's no evidence of pre-arrangement here," Tarchon said. "But she gave her word not to escape, and then she does, and does her utmost to thwart our campaign. That's what rankles with me."

Impar pressed the bridge of his glasses. "The justice committee want an example made."

Tarchon looked away and shook his head. The extremists would call for Maihara to be beheaded, but the thought filled him with horror and nausea.

***

Next day, Lady Aurian was let into Maihara's room. She had not seen Aurian since before the questioning. They embraced.

"What about you? Did they question you?" Maihara asked in a low voice.

"Yes, for hours."

"Did you tell them anything?"

Aurian shook her head. "You?"

Maihara indicated a negative.

Her chaperone looked relieved.

Maihara put a finger to her lips. "They might be listening now."

Aurian nodded. "Let them. It's been unpleasant, being locked up alone and not knowing what they intend to do with us."

They talked in low voices for some time about what the future might hold.

A clattering and clumping of boots sounded outside in the passage, and a knock came at the door.

"Who—?"

The door opened, and Tarchon entered, with two bodyguards. He was in his green uniform, with the same shoulder stripes, and a collection of medals pinned on his chest. She stared at him without speaking. He looked much the same, perhaps more stubbly and tired. He wasn't smiling, and she could not read his expression. An apprehension grew in her breast.

"Good morning, General," Maihara said. "This is ... awkward."

"Good morning, Princess." He paused. "I'm disappointed that you fled our custody during the barge journey. In Calah, you swore you would not seek to escape," he said in a tone of suppressed emotion.

"I didn't try to escape. I found myself in the middle of an Imperial attack." Her anger flared up.

"That's what your interrogators said," he responded in a calmer voice. "And did you know anything about it in advance?"

"No, I didn't."

He turned to Lady Aurian. "And what about you, Madam?"

"I knew nothing," she said. "It was a complete shock."

He nodded. "And what were you trying to do, in those places you visited?" he asked Maihara.

"The short answer? I was trying to stop my people being killed."

"I've read what you told the interrogators." He paced across the room, between the curtained bed and the padded armchairs. "Do you swear that you won't try to escape or make mischief?" he asked, staring into her face.

She hesitated. She'd sworn not to escape, back in Calah, and she did not feel she had broken her word. And it appeared that she had run out of places to escape to. She raised her head. "Only if I'm treated decently, properly protected and given immunity from malicious prosecutions."

He sighed. "I can guarantee the first two."

"Are your people going to put me on trial on some made-up charge?"

"I'm discussing this with Impar. Some people are very angry."

"They are?" She raised a hand to her face. Impar was her enemy; if he was involved in any trial, she was in danger.

"I'm not in favour of a trial, but they have sent for witnesses from Retis."

She tensed and was silent, too unsure of him to make a pert reply.

"Excuse me," Tarchon said, and swept out before she could ask about Persis, or Sihrima.

-33-

Tarchon was pondering how to deflect the moves for a trial of Maihara when an officer burst into the fort office and stopped before the General's desk, panting for breath. "Somebody's attacked the Princess!" the intruder exclaimed, before anyone could speak.

"What!" Tarchon was on his feet, a splinter of fear in his heart. "Is she hurt?"

"I don't know, sir. She's still alive."

"Who's there? At the mansion?"

"Colonel Impar, sir."

Tarchon pulled on his jacket. "I'm going over there."

Minutes later, he dismounted outside the stone-built Lumin mansion and handed the reins to a soldier. He ran inside, finding the ornate rooms busy with soldiers milling around.

"Where's Colonel Impar?" he shouted.

"Upstairs, sir." A soldier pointed up the gilded main staircase. Tarchon took the steps two at a time. He found the intelligence officer in a red-flocked corridor outside one of the bedrooms.

Tarchon confronted him. "What's going on?"

Impar saluted. "An intruder got past the guard into the Princess's bedroom and attacked her. She yelled, and the second guard disturbed the intruder."

"Is she badly hurt?"

"No, General." Impar gave a faint shrug. "Just bruised."

"How by the hells did this happen? Wasn't she guarded?"

"I'm sorry, sir. I assessed the risk as low. It's a solid building, and she was locked in. I had one guard outside and another in the ante-room."

A medical orderly was tending to a soldier lying on the red-patterned carpet. Tarchon pointed. "What happened to him?"

"He was unconscious when we found him. The intruder must have done something to him, sir. Either a drug or using a pressure point. There's a bruise on his neck."

"Have you caught the intruder?"

"We have him."

Something in Impar's tone hinted at another problem.

"You're questioning him?"

Impar shook his head, his eyeglasses glinting momentarily. "The Princess stabbed him during the mêlée."

"But surely—?"

"She's clearly got a strong right arm. She stuck several inches of steel into his guts. He's in severe pain, and I don't think we're going to get much out of him."

"But who was this man? Why attack her?"

"That's what we're trying to establish, sir."

"I want to see her."

In response, Impar extended his arm toward the ante-room and bedroom in a gesture of invitation.

Tarchon strode forward, head filled with inexpressible concerns, and stopped in the doorway. Maihara, looking shaken, was massaging her throat with one hand and holding in the other a half full wineglass which a maid had just handed to her. An ornamental screen was pulled across the middle of the room and beyond it, out of the Princess' view, a doctor was working on a man in dark plain clothing who lay on his side. The doctor had cut away clothing, revealing pale skin and a mess of blood. A dagger still protruded from the man's stomach.

He took a step toward Maihara. She looked slimmer than before her escape, but with the same untidy hair and smooth-complexioned face, prominent nose and the attractive blue-violet eyes.

"Are you all right?"

She looked up at him, and her eyes widened. She took a large swig from the wineglass. "No."

Clearly she was not seriously hurt, save for a bruise forming on her neck.

"They say you stabbed him? Why?"

"The bastard tried to kill me." Her vehemence and the soldierly language startled him.

"But didn't the guard—?" he began.

"The guard followed him in and started grappling with him, but he might have been another of them."

"Another of who?" He could get a complete account of this later.

"I don't know. Rebel fanatics?"

"Looks like the work of a professional assassin, the way he got past the first guard. You didn't hear anything?" he said.

"When he worked the lock." Her expression suggested that she had suspects in mind.

He had an impulse to go over to her, but conscious of Impar's eyes on his back, he did not. "I'm pleased that you're all right. Our apologies." He turned and went out.

After fearing far worse, his relief at finding her on her feet and coherent was immense. He still felt the same desire to protect her, but the cool and wary look she had given him had hurt. He might have betrayed his feelings by rushing in here, and dared not hope that relations between them could ever be the same as before.

***

An hour or so later, Tarchon was in conference with Colonel Impar back at the fort. Sheaves of hand-written reports in black ink lay across Tarchon's desk. Thinking of Maihara, he shifted in his chair and fidgeted as Impar made his verbal report.

"I've re-read the women's interrogation transcripts," Impar said. "No clues there. I don't think he's one of our supporters who got over-enthusiastic. His clothing and shoes, and the coins, suggest he came from the East."

"The Empire?"

Impar nodded. "The way he rendered the door guard unconscious suggests professional training. It's lucky the

Princess made a row. For her, that is."

"And she stabbed the attacker with his own knife while the guard was grappling with him. But why would the Empire want to kill her? It makes no sense."

"Maybe they're afraid she'll tell us something she found out while she was with them," Impar said.

"Or it's as Lady Aurian claims. The Emperor wants her eliminated. But why go this far now?" He twisted in his seat as a tremor of anxiety ran through his body. The assailant had been determined and there might be others.

"Perhaps they didn't feel threatened before," Impar said. "Look at what she seems to have been doing while she was free, even if it came to naught. Perhaps they too think she's a troublesome meddler."

Tarchon turned to face Impar. "If the Emperor's against her, we should keep her safe. You know the old saying, that my enemy's enemy is my friend."

"Not too close," Impar said, looking serious. "She knows how to use a knife."

Tarchon compressed his lips. He disagreed with Impar's hostile opinion of Maihara.

***

A rapping sounded at the door of Maihara's room before it opened, and the guard ushered in Lady Aurian. Maihara hurried to her, and they embraced.

"Did something happen?" Aurian asked. "There was a commotion yesterday, and a soldier came in to check my room."

"Somebody got past the guards and tried to assassinate me."

Aurian's mouth was a perfect O. "Were you hurt?" She held Maihara at arm's length.

"My neck's sore, otherwise I'm all right."

Aurian fussed, examining the marks on Maihara's neck and uttering condolences.

"And the assassin?" she asked after a while.

"He was stabbed." Maihara did not want to discuss what she had done. Nor did she want to think about what had guided her hand to unsheathe the dagger and stab. There were things in her head now of which she knew nothing till they sprang into her consciousness or directed her hands.

Maihara and Aurian talked in low voices for some time, circling around the incident.

A clattering and clumping of boots sounded outside in the passage, and a knock came at the door.

"Who—?"

The door opened, and Tarchon entered looking more stubbly and fatigued than the day before, and accompanied by two bodyguards. She stood, her heartbeat quickening. This had to be about the assassination attempt.

"I apologise again for the attack on your person, Princess," he said stiffly. "Our security was inadequate. That should not have happened."

A bubble of anger surfaced in her. "You call that security? I survive all sorts of danger and now this."

"Have you found out who sent the assassin?" Aurian asked.

"Not for certain, but there is evidence that he came from the Empire."

Maihara was silent, and a lump grew in her throat at the thought that her father was trying to kill her. It was not unexpected, but still hard to accept. She prayed that her sister was safe from similar attention.

Next morning, grey cloud blanketed the sky and rain whipped against the windows of Maihara's new room in the Lumin mansion. The bedroom had silk wall hangings, movable screens painted with eastern-style pictures, and furniture inlaid with small pieces of pattern-figured woods. She had learnt from the guards that Tarchon had departed on a sea mission. They told her nothing of Tarchon's voyage, but she assumed he had sailed eastward into Imperial waters. A gloom settled over her that matched the weather. With Tarchon gone, there would be nobody to oppose the Justice Committee's moves to impeach her for treason against their new state. The only consolation was that she and Aurian were to be let out of the mansion, but under guard.

***

Tarchon was roused from his cabin by the violent motions of the flagship *Cerow Fleetstar* and the howling of wind. He struggled up a tilting and rolling stairway to see what was happening. He was hoping to isolate the defences of the coastal towns east of Loomis, by making a landing at the city of Licinus, a hundred sea-miles to the east. Unless the Imperials were particularly stupid, they would have figured out his fast-moving land/sea strategy by now. On a personal front, the sooner he defeated the Empire, the better his chances of repairing relations with the Imperial Princess Maihara. This bad weather though was not helping. As he reached the raised stern deck, wind and rain whipped his face. Grey lumps of land showed across the turbulent sea.

Admiral Catonne in full uniform was on deck giving orders to the captain. Sailors ran about, struggling with the sails and hoisting signal flags.

Fleetstar was one of four 'great ships' seized from the Imperial Navy, with a dozen sails set on three masts, high wooden castles at the bow and stern and a score and a half of heavy cannon on her lower gun deck.

Tarchon made his way over the tilting deck to the ship's first officer, who stood at the rail with head bowed, watching the Admiral. "What's happening, Sailing-master?"

The grizzled sailor, distinguished from the rest of the crew only by the tattered sea-jacket he wore over his grey shirt, sketched a salute. His sunburnt skin looked weathered as the wood of his ship. "Enemy ships sighted, General."

Ahead, a ship in the leading formation was flying a red flag.

"The enemy?" Tarchon said, his heartbeat quickening. "I can't see anything."

At the weather side of the stern deck, Admiral Catonne had cupped a hand above his eyes to observe the other

448

ships of his fleet. He nodded to Tarchon and came over. His admiral's blue sea uniform managed to look well pressed despite the rain which ran down his clean-shaven, ruddy face.

"I don't see any enemy," Tarchon repeated. He did not feel in control here. The sailors were operating the ships and the sea and poor visibility defied him.

"We're at deck level, and that ship's half a league farther out," Admiral Catonne pointed out. "Sailing-master, is this rain likely to clear?"

"Aye, sir," The sailing-master, Baundes, pointed to windward. "It's brightening."

"Six ships!" the lookout in the crow's nest high up the foremast shouted, pointing.

The fleet was not yet formed up for battle. The *Cerow Fleetstar* was in the middle of a straggling group of eighteen ships, four of them tall ships powered by sail and armed with the new cannons, fourteen war galleys with their square sails up, and three unarmed transports under sail. A few of the galleys, being lighter, had got ahead of the great ships, but one of the tall ships, the *Nightstar*, apparently a better sailer than the others, was in the lead. Astern and to the left was another, indistinct group of ships under Vice-Admiral Jusmer. All had their bows pointed eastwards. The rugged shore of Nussa Island lay to the south, a mere league distant.

"Have the red flag hoisted!" Catonne said to the captain. "General, no doubt you'll want to order your marine soldiers to arm."

"Of course." Tarchon leant over the drop of the stern deck and shouted below.

"Twenty ships!" the lookout shouted, while the marines were still arming.

"Where did they come from?" Catonne asked. "I've had no reports of such a large squadron in the area."

"It could be the Empire's Eastern Fleet," Tarchon said. "We have not had recent word of their position."

"I am minded to attack," Catonne said. "We could try to evade them, but there's not much sea-room. Even turning to run could have consequences."

It was a tactical question. Catonne merely sought his agreement, for the ships already sighted did not match his force. Tarchon glanced around at the indistinct shore, and the scattered ships, and found no answer there. "Admiral, can you defeat the ships you have sighted so far, and any others behind?"

Catonne gave a swift nod. "I believe so, if I can get ours in line of battle soon enough."

"Very well then. We have to fight, and take out their fleet. We can't carry out our landings with a large Imperial fleet in being in our rear."

Catonne turned to the sailing-master. "Hoist the signal to close up in line of battle!" He turned to Tarchon. "I hope we have enough time to form up. We're strung out all over."

"Would it not be quicker to form them into two lines?" Tarchon said.

The Admiral stared hard at him.

"I'm thinking in land terms," Tarchon admitted. Catonne had been delegated to handle marine matters.

Catonne paused. "We're not on land. Let me handle this. I want the great ships in an open line across the channel, and the galleys in a line abreast behind. We'll see how much driftwood the great ships can make of them."

The Emperor Cordan had given orders for the development of the cannon and the bigger ships to carry them. After seizing them in the shipyards, Tarchon ordered their commission.

"Won't the great ships be overwhelmed by the enemy?" Tarchon objected.

"Let them try." Catonne's eyes were flinty. "I hope they'll draw in the galleys and decimate them with their cannon fire."

With reluctance, Tarchon raised a hand in acknowledgement. The great ships carried many more heavy guns than the galleys, but they had yet to see this advantage tested in battle. He had to trust that the Admiral's tactical judgement was correct. "Of course." He still feared that the Admiral was wrong, and some of the more manoeuvrable galleys should protect the great ships.

Flag signals relayed the Admiral's commands to the other ships of the fleet, which acknowledged by hoisting cones of basketwork up their rigging. The decks trembled as armed men ran to their stations, their war-hardened bodies protected by armour of metal links or toughened leather.

The ships pitched and rolled as they surged over the long, heaving waves.

Tarchon hastened below to his wide sea cabin in the ship's stern and had a marine help buckle on his armour of black lacquered steel. Running feet slapped on the timber deck overhead. The armourer offered him the Sea-General's black cylindrical helmet.

Tarchon felt a kind of relief, now the battle was to begin, a clean battle against a visible enemy whom Catonne could ram with his ships, burn with his flame hurlers, and deliver to slaughter with waves of Tarchon's war-hardened marines. Every blow and every death strengthened his own cause, the safety of the Western rebel lands. What would Maihara think if she saw him in armour?

And when it was done, the sea would swallow the dead.

Back on deck, he looked on with unease as the fleet arranged itself according to his admiral's orders. The gusting wind was behind them. The *Blackstar* ahead had hove to, waiting for the other three great ships to move abreast. All the galleys were dropping their sails, and several had reversed course and were rowing westward to get into position. The visibility had improved and the enemy fleet was visible, spreading out to span the channel ahead, which had a width of over ten miles. Advancing against the wind, they had no sail hoisted. Those he could see outnumbered his fleet.

The *Cerow Fleetstar* bore him toward *Blackstar's* line, ahead of the galleys. His position felt increasingly exposed in one of just four ships confronting the enemy as the flagship surged forward. The movements of the rebel fleet neared completion. As the admiral had proposed, they split into two lines, the great ships in a wide-spaced line of four ahead, and behind, the galleys in a line that spanned the channel. Each great ship was over a mile from the next, so there was no danger of being hit with each other's shot.

Ships had moved close to the mainland and the island of Nussa to prevent their line being turned by the enemy. He assumed that Catonne had knowledge of the depth of water inshore.

The rebel fleet moved slowly eastward with the wind behind them, toward the enemy. The forms of the enemy ships grew more distinct, as they advanced into the wind under oars. The enemy would try to surround and board the great ships, and break through the line of rebel galleys behind. Shading his eyes, he tried to pick out the armament of the enemy vessels, but could not see any special features. The sun broke through cloud and caught the flash of bright metal on their decks.

Catonne had a word with the ship's captain, who turned and ordered the ship's guns to be made ready. Sweating inside his armour, Tarchon awaited the testing of his admiral's battle plan with unease. What had seemed sensible with enemy vessels just sighted was less reassuring when they were one ship in a line of four facing a swarm of galleys. If it did not work, he and the Admiral faced death or capture.

"Are the marines ready?" Tarchon shouted from the stern deck.

"Aye!" The mail-clad Master of Marines on the main deck waved his fist.

Tarchon did not ask if the ship's guns were ready. Below him, gunners were loading the swivel guns on the fore and stern castles, and shouts and rumblings from the lower deck indicated that the heavy muzzle-loading cannon were being loaded and run out.

"The Devil's weapons," the sailing-master said to Tarchon. Tarchon said nothing.

The line of Imperial galleys moved closer. There were over forty of them in sight. Their oars foamed the water, and he made out the shapes of sailors and armed marines on their decks.

Smoke puffed from the bows of the distant *Nightstar*, and a second later the boom of her bow guns reached his ears. Soon, the bow guns of a galley approaching the *Cerow Fleetstar* gouted smoke, and then he heard the crack of the shot. A line of foam skipped along the water and the *Fleetstar's* bow shuddered under Tarchon's feet. He flinched.

"Bastards have hit us," Baundes, the sailing-master said.

The bow guns of the *Cerow Fleetstar* replied with a roar and a puff of smoke. The balls hit the bow of the galley, punching two holes. Its mast tottered and the beat of its oars ceased.

Beside Tarchon, the Master of Marines raised a mailed fist. "Gutted the bastards!"

Tarchon nodded, imagining the hideous carnage among the rowers as the balls passed from stem to stern.

The flanking galleys came on, passing the stricken Imperial warship and heading for the *Cerow Fleetstar*, whose guns were temporarily unable to bear at that angle. He could make out the helmets of Imperial marines on the galleys. Tarchon gripped his sword hilt. This was what he had feared, that the enemy would brave the cannon fire and close in to board *Fleetstar*.

This was the moment of the Imperial catapulteers. Tarchon saw them clearly as they wound back the sling arms against the tension of twisted ropes. Sailors dropped flaming balls of pitch-soaked rope into the cups at the end of the sling arms, and bombardiers crouched, peering along crude sights. Missiles arced upward toward *Fleetstar* as the sling arms were released, and he flinched as balls struck her high wooden sides and dropped into the sea, others arcing over, or landing on the decks or rigging.

"Ward fires!" the captain shouted. Sailors dashed to douse the missiles with sand or hook them over the side before they could start fires.

A flaming ball landed at Tarchon's feet. "Fire!" He lashed out with an armoured foot, sending it rolling and dribbling a line of flame. The sailing-master, cursing, kicked it through a square hole in the bulwark, and stamped on the line of burning pitch.

An oncoming galley fired its pair of bow guns, hitting *Fleetstar* in the side. Wood splintered, and men below shrieked. Several galleys closed in on each side of *Fleetstar*, aiming to close and board. Tarchon's heartbeat quickened.

"Draw arms!" the Master of Marines shouted. Gunners worked the swivel guns on *Fleetstar*'s upper deck, firing on the packed decks of the galleys. Armoured men clutching swords and pikes looked up at the great ship's high sides. For the moment, *Fleetstar* held the advantage. As Tarchon looked down, enemy attackers stumbled, hit by arrows. Lines of men fell in a spray of blood as swivel guns blasted their ranks.

The galleys, now on each beam, closed in on *Fleetstar*'s sides. With a ragged boom, the main guns on the right side fired, followed a moment later by those on the left, under Tarchon's feet. Before his eyes, wood shuddered and flew up as the heavy balls tore through the galleys approaching on that side. Screams filled the air, oars ceased their stroke and poised at odd angles, and a bare mast swayed.

Grappling hooks flew out from the nearest galley below, and the maimed ships attached themselves to *Fleetstar* like wounded dogs seizing a boar. They pulled closer, while *Fleetstar*'s sailors and marines worked to unhook the grapples or cut the lines. On the splintered galley decks fallen men, severed limbs and splashes of bright blood marked the passage of the cannon shot.

Crossbowmen and swivel gunners shot down at the men

still crowding the decks of the galleys.

The Imperial marines made frantic efforts to escape the sinking hell under their feet and board *Fleetstar*, setting ladders against her high sides and throwing up climbing lines. Some tried to climb through the gun ports and attack the gunners. A dozen reached her main deck and fought the rebel marines till they were cut down.

Tarchon, fists clenched, cursed his impotence. He had set these fleets in motion, and now it was the Master of Marine's job to repel boarders and Catonne's job to direct the fleet battle. The cannon took too long to reload, and he had allowed the galleys to come too close. Where was Catonne? It seemed that the Admiral had prudently retreated under cover. No rebel galleys were close enough to come to their aid, but this was part of Catonne's plan, as they would have got in the way of the great ship's gunfire.

After two minutes of reloading the *Fleetstar*'s main guns boomed again, cutting swathes of destruction across the upper decks of the six or seven galleys lying on each side of her. More boarders climbed up at the stern. Sword in hand, Tarchon helped marines force them off the stern deck as unarmoured sailors at the ship's steering wheel cowered back. One Imperial boarder fell, and with a cry landed across the side-rail of the galley below, before toppling into the water. Leaning over and panting for breath, Tarchon glimpsed the evil work the fresh broadside had done, smashing away the galley's rails and leaving blood, torn limbs and maimed bodies in its wake. Men screamed as they lay with lost limbs or impaled by splinters.

Two more galleys arced in, heading for the *Fleetstar*'s stern quarters and hoping to avoid the broadsides that had mangled their compatriots. Tarchon held his breath. The great ship had no large rear-facing guns, and if the galleys approached from the stern they would be able to bring their large bow cannon to bear. As they closed with oars churning, the main guns in the rear of the ship fired a ragged volley, smashing through the hulls of the approaching galleys. One limped closer and threw grappling lines as the swivel gunners and crossbowmen shot down onto the open decks. The other settled in the water, oars stilled. Its marines stripped off their armour to avoid drowning, and cries for help drifted across the water.

Elsewhere, several galleys swarmed around *Nightstar* and the other great ships, shrouded in clouds of smoke. One galley seemed to be on fire. The other Imperial galleys had passed, and, rather depleted in numbers, were closing on the advancing line of rebel galleys.

A score of attackers swarmed at Fleetstar's stern, trying to board. Her high sides and the anti-boarding nets impeded them, but some made it to the stern deck and gained a foothold there. Tarchon took blows to his armour as he fought shoulder to shoulder with his marines to force the attackers back. He feared the plan was miscarrying, and the galleys had been allowed to come too close before the great ship could disable them with gunfire.

"Won't they ever stop coming?" the Master of Marines exclaimed, letting his blooded sword droop.

Tarchon shook his head. The naval officers had taken refuge below. "How far can we depress the main guns?"

"I don't know, sir." The Master of Marines ran to a hatchway and shouted into it. Swivel guns fired down on the attackers as fast as the tired gunners could reload between waves of boarders. A minute later a main gun fired, followed by another, and another.

At last, the furious attacks waned as the two attached galleys settled low in the water and the others cut themselves loose and drifted away. Several were sinking, just as Catonne had intended, and the others had their upperworks shot to pieces or on fire. As they drifted away, the *Fleetstar* continued to fire on them.

Behind, the two lines of galleys had come together, and pairs or knots of galleys were locked in battle.

"What now?" Tarchon asked the Admiral who had reappeared, hatless. "Do we aid our galleys?" He pointed westward.

"That's upwind," the Admiral said shortly. "We'll try to aid *Nightstar* and the ship beyond."

Fleetstar turned under sail, leaving behind a mass of disabled and sinking galleys, still full of men hoping to board *Fleetstar* and fight her, or just save themselves from the sea. She made way crosswind toward the *Nightstar*, still engaged in battle. Around Tarchon, marines checked the bodies lying on the decks and threw the dead overboard. They spread sand on the pools of slippery blood.

After some time, they neared the *Nightstar*, still under attack from six large galleys.

"Pass her to windward," the captain ordered the sailing-master. This would take *Fleetstar* past the other ship's stern, in a position to attack any galleys attacking that vulnerable area of the other great ship. Tarchon supposed the captain meant to rake the galleys with cannon fire, while avoiding hitting the *Cerow Nightstar*.

Tarchon watched, biting his lip. At last the guns were able to bear, and they fired a half-broadside that rocked the ship. Several balls enfiladed the galleys from end to end, splinters flew, and the crash of shot and cries and screams of wounded men came across the water.

"The Devil's weapons," Tarchon said.

"Thank the One God that we seized them," Catonne said, overhearing.

On the other flank of the *Nightstar* the enemy was forewarned. As they passed the stern, the two galleys closed in on that side were cutting themselves free and turning away under oars. A half-broadside tore into one and missed the other.

The battered Imperial galleys still afloat limped off eastward away from the battle, hoisting their square sails, and Tarchon turned to look elsewhere. The other Imperial galleys that had attacked the great ships at the ends of the forward line were also breaking away, some escaping to the east, others heading for the main line of battle, a line that had come closer, especially at the ends.

"We're turning their flanks," Catonne said.

"Can't we get closer?" Tarchon demanded.

"No, they're upwind."

Cerow Fleetstar held her position downwind of the battle while Tarchon tried to make sense of the melee of fighting along the double line of galleys. They gathered in pairs and knots, with smoke part obscuring the scene. The wind bore a murmur of sound, a mixture of crashing and screaming, mixed with the intermittent rumble of bow cannon.

"Are we winning?" Tarchon demanded. He was mindful how Maihara hated the carnage of war.

"It's early to tell," Catonne said. "They outnumbered us by at least twenty galleys, but our great ships shot up or sank at least that many, and we're holding our line." He aimed a spyglass at the centre of the battle. "There's a small group of enemy that seems to have broken through, but a couple of galleys are hoisting our flag."

"We've taken them?"

"Looks that way. Let's hope Vice-Admiral Jusmer and the Commodore keep their heads. It'll be a fight to the finish. If the enemy try to retreat eastward, they will have to pass our guns again, and they can't break westward and upwind with exhausted rowers."

***

In the battle line, Lieutenant Harayam, late of the enemy princess's river escort, thrust in desperation at a snarling Imperial marine, one of a mass of boarders. Three times the enemy had swarmed aboard the *Gulen 1* from one galley or another, and three times the rebel marines had forced them back. Now most of the rebel marines had been killed or wounded, and the survivors forced to retreat to the stern deck. The Imperials had command of the rest of the galley and were butchering the wounded rebels and sailors, with cries of "Traitor!" The defection of the Western fleet had infuriated loyalist Imperials.

As his opponent fell down the poop steps, Harayam snatched a glance at the wider battle, hoping to see some friendly galley approaching. If none came, his chances of survival were slim. The air was thick with pitch smoke. Fierce fighting continued between the rebel line of galleys and the Imperial galleys which had advanced past the four great ships to intercept them. Harayam's ears were filled with the clash of weapons, the cries of warriors about to be dragged underwater and drowned by their armour, the crunch of splintering timbers, the clack and whine of catapults.

Several galleys nearby clung together in a deadly embrace, held by grappling-irons and boarding planks. Archers and crossbowmen clustered on bow and stern platforms, sniping as marines fought bloody battles across the decks.

Another rebel galley was closing to board their attackers. Its speed signalled that it meant to ram, or shear off the other galley's oars.

"A ship's coming," Harayam gasped to a comrade. The man grunted and sank to the deck without replying. An arrow was buried in his breast. Harayam's left gauntlet was dripping blood, and it seemed to be his. He ducked as arrows flew over from the Imperial galley's bow platform.

With a crash, the rebel galley buried its beak in the side of one of the besieging galleys, smashing oars. Armed men swarmed onto the Imperial warship, overcoming the sailors and marines who remained on board. A pair of swivel guns barked, slicing bloody swathes through the boarders massed on the *Gulen 1's* deck.

In minutes, the tide of battle had turned, with the Imperial galley taken and its rowers freed, and the surviving boarders on the *Gulen 1* surrendering.

"We're winning," Harayam said to one of his few remaining comrades.

"Not yet," his companion said, pointing. A pair of Imperial galleys had passed through the line and were circling for the attack.

"Where's the captain?" a rebel officer from the relieving ship shouted.

"Hit," Harayam shouted back.

"Why don't those great ships come? We need their guns here," Harayam's companion said.

Harayam nodded but said nothing. In front of him the lower deck was bloody and littered with maimed corpses and the dying. Entrails hung over a grating. Below, he glimpsed the pale eyes of terrified rowers.

Smoke billowed low over the sea abeam, where six ships were locked together in pairs, the crews fighting hand to hand. On one, a rebel flag jerked upward to the masthead. Harayam muttered a prayer to the One God.

-34-

The weather cleared, but Maihara's mood did not. She was held in Loomis, and though she was allowed outside under guard, the prospect of another assassination attempt occurring meant she rarely felt at ease. With Tarchon gone, there would be no possibility for several days of easing their strained relationship.

So far, doing magic in Loomis was hard work. There was magic here, but the design of the magic grid she found was entirely unfamiliar, differing from that found in all the previous locations, and she could not find a spy spell or anything else useful among the pink and blue windows, annotated with ancient text, that appeared in her mind. Aurian would be expecting her to provide further intelligence on the rebel plans, but Maihara had none to deliver, and no means of overhearing any.

Her confidence in being able to direct the results of her interfering had taken a blow since Halamar, and she did not want to pass on any more information, not if it meant more prospective deaths, and Imperial efforts still failing to stop the rebels.

"I've not heard anything interesting," Maihara insisted.

"Are you sure? Do you even need to overhear our minders talking? You can use spy magic."

"It doesn't work here. You should know that."

Aurian's face bore an obstinate expression. "I only know that mine won't."

"I don't see that I'd be doing any good. The rebels took the towns despite our efforts, and many of our subjects died in pointless fighting. You saw that blood in the streets."

"Of course there will be losses. It's a price worth paying

461

to hold back the rebels for even a day. Hamper them, and we'll win."

"Losses are people," Maihara pointed out, thinking of Ferris.

"My husband was 'people'. They killed him." Aurian's lips tightened.

Maihara became alarmed lest Aurian, who seemed not to accept her reasons for not performing any spying, would feel provoked into disclosing to the rebels the full extent of Maihara's spying abilities. And then Maihara would be in big trouble with rebels terrified by the notion that she could watch or listen to any conversation, anywhere. Spies were tortured, or beheaded. Losing Tarchon's protection would be just one of her worries. If she tried to keep Aurian happy, a fresh leak of rebel plans might point back to Maihara.

She had no idea how to solve the Aurian problem without making the situation worse. Telling Aurian to try solving the Loomis magic herself had just made her companion angrier. She suspected that Aurian was actively spying, and if the rebels arrested Aurian, she would denounce the workings of Maihara's spy magic, willingly or otherwise.

Tarchon had still not returned to Loomis port after his abrupt departure. During Maihara's closely guarded excursions to the markets or the seafront she tried to find out what he was doing. There was a rumour that the Imperial Eastern Fleet had sailed west and that Tarchon was seeking to bring it to battle. Her mood darkened and anxiety arose. Her protector might be drowned, and then she would be left at the mercy of Impar and the Justice Committee, the same people who had executed the former Chancellor, Lord Farnak.

While Lady Aurian helped Maihara undress for the night, they held a whispered conversation.

"Have you heard any more about the rebel plans?"

Aurian asked.

"No. There's word the Imperial Eastern Fleet has come west. That would explain why Tarchon has disappeared. There seem to be fewer warships in the harbour."

"You think Tarchon is seeking to battle the Eastern Fleet? Can't you find out?"

"How? How can I, if they won't tell me, or talk about it in my hearing?"

"We both know how you can do it, my dear." Aurian passed a comb through Maihara's thick hair.

Maihara tensed with frustration. "I'm not hearing anything. It isn't working here. I told you."

"I know you have the power to do this. Perhaps more so, after what you did in Halamar. Why don't you do it now?"

"It's like I said. It doesn't work in this city. The magic is different. I don't understand why."

"I'm not sure I believe you. Are you sure you're not leaning to the other side? You seem very fond of General Tarchon." The comb snagged. Aurian tugged.

"Ow! Mind what you're doing."

"You are, aren't you? I saw the way you and he looked at each other."

"You misunderstand. I don't dislike Tarchon. He's an amusing man. But that's not the point here. I'd like to learn their plans for my own interest, but I can't. Besides, I'm not happy passing on information I glean here to the Imperial side. It's a breach of trust. Why do you think we're in these nice rooms, and not in a damp cell? It's because we promised to behave."

Anyway, how was Aurian going to pass on any information? When they went to the markets, or Aurian went to a Nine Gods temple, they were closely supervised by guards. For some reason, Aurian had recently developed an interest in religion, despite not having expressed any interest in the Nine Gods in any of their previous long conversations.

"Behave?" Aurian hissed. "Our side won't be pleased if

they think you're siding with the enemy. And what will the rebels do if they hear what you passed on already?"

Maihara felt a chill, then a flush of rage. She had a strong impulse to hit Aurian, a fight she would most likely win as she was stronger and heavier. With an effort, she restrained herself. "I can't believe you said that, Serina. I thought we were friends."

Aurian lowered the comb, and hung her head. "I'm sorry, Your Grace. I should not have threatened you. I've had a letter passed to me from Imperial Army intelligence. They are angry that I have been able to feed them almost nothing since we left Calah, and they're putting pressure on me for results. They've got my nephew."

Maihara stared at her. "They do? The swines. They threatened you here? Have you thought of asking the rebel regime for help?"

Aurian scowled.

"How did they reach you?"

Still Aurian did not answer.

"I could talk to our minders. Tarchon's officers aren't going to discuss anything of importance in my hearing. The IAI should find someone else." She squeezed Aurian's hand.

After retiring to bed, Maihara lay in the dark, thinking. It was sad that the question of espionage which she had started with good intentions was driving a wedge between her and Aurian. She ought to aid the Imperial side, but she had sworn not to cause trouble, and had little heart for aiding the Imperials after what she had seen and heard on her journey. Still less after being advised that an organ of the Imperial state, or even her own father, was conspiring to kill her. Passing information could cause a military disaster for the rebel side. She did not want piles of dead on her conscience, not when her prime aim was to bring an end to violence. Her warnings to Retis had not saved that city.

If Aurian carried out her threat to expose Maihara as a

witch and spy, that would mean the end of her relationship with Tarchon, the only rock in a shifting sea of danger. If all the rebels found out the full story of the warnings delivered to Retis, she did not imagine that she would survive long. Between a desire to punish her, and conviction that she would betray more of their plans, she supposed that she would be dealt with summarily. A mob eager to kill the witchy Imperial Princess would make an end of her quickly. Dark fear made her thoughts race, driving out sleep.

Even if she wanted to provide more information on the rebel plans, that would be dangerous, and she still had to find and translate the instructions for working the local system of magic. The ancients of this Southern city must have liked to do things differently.

The situation was intolerable. If she was to be sure of avoiding the rebels' Justice Committee, she had to do something about Lady Aurian and her compromising spy network. She had become used to Aurian's company but if it was a choice between her death or Aurian's removal, Aurian had to go. A future Empress would not hesitate. But what to do? She could not let Aurian be arrested and tortured. That would be horrible. If she told the rebels that Aurian was an agent, Aurian could retaliate by denouncing her as a spy and witch. And she did not want to think of being brought face to face with Aurian after denouncing her.

Maybe she could distance herself from Aurian by urging her to find another employer and recruit another inside agent, but Aurian might not react well to such rejection. Would Aurian flee if given a fake warning? Maybe, but it would rely on her being easily startled into flight. No, it needed to be something cleverer, that would give Aurian a chance to get away while allowing herself to feign shocked innocence. And how did Aurian communicate with her handlers? It was too late to ask now without arousing suspicion. Aurian was unlikely to tell her, anyway.

Next morning, Aurian wasn't around. The servant woman provided by the rebels helped Maihara dress.

"Where's Lady Aurian?" Maihara asked.

"Gone out, Your Grace," the woman said, tugging Maihara's dress straight.

"Where?"

"Heard her say she was going to the temple."

This was not the first time Lady Aurian had gone out without her. She was a paroled prisoner, and allowed to come and go, if escorted. Now she was attending the temple so she could join in the singing of the services. Odd.

Looking out of the window, Maihara slipped her fingers into a pocket below the waist of the dress. Her fingers encountered a slip of paper. It was a letter, addressed to her in crude script, and sealed with a rough blob of wax.

Princess - we suspect that the traitor Tarchon is about to sail from Loomis. We warn you that this is your last chance to prove your loyalty by ridding the world of him. You did not respond to our previous note. To proceed, arrange a walk to the cloth market today and we will contact you with instructions.

Her hand shook as she held the note. More threats. Was the serving-woman another agent? But the message did not make sense, for Tarchon had already sailed. Perhaps the note had been put in this dress some time earlier.

How many in the grand mansion were working with the Fifth Bureau, or Imperial Army intelligence? Her sense of being under threat intensified. First Aurian, and now this. But if she was smart, she could use this note. She would have to time things with care, and hope that Aurian responded in a rational manner.

Lady Aurian returned from her walk. As soon as she entered the hallway, Maihara ignored an idling guard and went over to Aurian. She spoke into her chaperone's ear. "You're in danger. I received a note from the Fifth, threatening me and demanding that I assassinate Tarchon."

She showed Aurian the note. Aurian's eyes widened. "It wasn't me. There must be Fifth agents here."

"It's a trick, or just meant to frighten me into co-operating with them. What they are demanding is too crude. I think they meant this note to be found by the rebels, to cause me harm. They may have planted other notes. I can destroy this one, but if the rebels find another - do I have to spell this out? They'll looking for a source."

"You mean?" Aurian pointed to her own throat.

"You'd better clear off now, before they suspect you."

"But what about you?" Aurian said in a low, strained voice.

"I'll tell them it's a Fifth plot, nothing to do with me. They believe the Fifth want to kill me, but if there's more of this, you could fall under suspicion. And Tarchon likes me. He'll take my side. Now go, before they see you."

She embraced Aurian, kissed her on the forehead, and gave her a gentle push. "I'll make up something." She raised her voice. "That ornament we looked at—"

Aurian, looking shaken, headed for the doors, then turned and forced a smile. "I'll get it at once, Princess," she said more loudly. In a moment she was gone.

Maihara headed for the stairs, heart pounding. How long would Aurian need to contact her handlers and go to ground? Half an hour might be enough. In her room, she sat in the armchair and took up a book, but was unable to read. A ray of sun came in at the window and painted a line on the floor. When it had moved a little across the pattern of the carpet, she took out the note and looked at it. Should she destroy it, or show it to her guards? Saying nothing would give Lady Aurian more time to flee. Disclosing this note would deflect suspicion from her should the rebels find other planted notes. The dilemma had no easy answer.

Tears filled her eyes. Her confinement would be lonelier without Aurian's company.

After half an hour she left her room and looked down the stairwell. A guard idled below.

"You! Get one of the officers. Now!" she shouted.

The man turned his face upward with a startled look, and hurried off, calling to one of his comrades, who came into view and with double steps climbed partway up the staircase.

"Whaz'up, Princess?"

"I found something."

Minutes later an officer of the guard detachment appeared, a man who had escorted her into Loomis. She showed him the note. He read it, with lips moving.

"This is bad. We need to inform the General's staff and the security bureau, in case anything else happens."

"Can these people get in here?"

"Don't worry, Ma'am, we'll be watching. If anything serious happens, it'll be my neck that gets stretched." The man tapped his teeth with the note. "Show me exactly where you found it."

Maihara pointed. "It was lying just inside the door, as if it had been pushed under and then swept aside as the door opened."

"I see. And you found it just now?"

Maihara nodded.

"You'd better stay in your room. I'll post a guard."

Maihara had half expected that they would insist on leading her to the cloth market to lure out the Fifth Bureau agents. Instead, left alone, she paced the room.

At the bedroom window, the port spread out below, partly obscured by a red-brick fort. A dozen ships were moving, two in the harbour, and others in a line heading out into the estuary. Several waited in a cluster, out on the grey water. A galley, oars stroking, towed an oar-less and tall-masted supply ship out of the harbour entrance.

The door rattled and opened. "You're required downstairs." She did not recognise the man, who wore an officer's uniform.

"What's this about?" she asked as they exited the small room.

"Colonel Impar wants to question you about that note," the officer said.

Her heart skipped a beat. What had it to do with Impar? That extremist officer was the last person she wanted questioning her.

The rat-faced Impar was in the main hall, in uniform, with a group of five officers. He greeted her with a nod, but continued talking for another minute.

Impar beckoned her and her escort forward. The corners of his mouth were upturned.

"Good morning, Princess. I hear you found a note urging the murder of General Tarchon," he said in a serious tone. "This is so?"

She managed to nod.

"First, the note. It says 'today', but is undated." He held a scrap of paper, but did not let her look at it. "Do you know what date this refers to?"

She met his eyes. "No, but as I found it today, I assume it means this day."

"And how often does this cloth market take place?"

"It's daily, I think."

"Correct. And it's a morning market." Impar thumped his fist on the hall table.

"We could take her there," one of the officers said.

Impar scowled. "Incompetents. It's too late to stake out the market now." He turned to Maihara. "Is this the first note?"

"Yes. But they threatened me at Calah. They demanded that I try to assassinate Tarchon."

"And you did not report this at the time?"

"I could not see any point. No, I meant to tell the General, but the Imperial raiders rescued me before I found a suitable moment." She gestured to the stony-faced officers. "I don't see my guards anywhere."

Impar adjusted his glasses. "We've exchanged your entire escort, as a precaution. We don't know yet who delivered the note."

Her unease grew. She had not foreseen this drastic response.

"Where's Lady Aurian? I hope you're not being beastly to her."

"Like I said," Impar said. "Do you have any reason to

suspect her?"

A chill of unease curled up Maihara's spine. If they had rounded up the whole escort detail, why omit to ask her where Lady Aurian was? "No, certainly not. I don't see how she could have received it. And don't throw her in a cell and shout at her. The poor woman's suffered enough."

Impar scowled. "She's an Imperial noble. A weak link. She should not have been appointed in the first place."

Impar's men locked Maihara in a tower room at the Lumin mansion while they continued their investigation. After what felt like hours of nervous boredom, the door lock rattled and the heavy, rivet-studded door opened.

It was Colonel Impar again, with three officers and a woman, none of whom Maihara recognised.

Impar sat down opposite her and fixed her with a hostile stare. "First, did you spy on radical discussions and communicate information to the enemy, the Imperial forces?"

"How could I? I was a prisoner, and under guard." She had, but it would be idiotic to admit anything before the investigators laid out their irrefutable evidence.

"Are you sure?"

"I am sure."

"Did anyone discuss confidential matters in your hearing?" His glasses glinted.

"I don't know what you'd consider 'confidential'."

"Any discussion of military matters."

Maihara assumed an innocent air. "Well, people did tell me about some military things, but only after they'd happened. If I asked what was happen*ing* or about to happen, they'd clam up."

"And did you observe any military activity?"

"One or two things, but not close up."

"What things?"

"Men boarding barges, troops on the river bank, ships outside the harbour."

Impar's face had assumed an expression of suspicion.

"Where?"

"Well, I was being dragged around with the Army."

"Oh, I see." Impar regained his composure.

"Did you mean Imperial military activity?"

"Yes, but we already questioned you on that. Or have you more to add?"

"No."

Impar made a note. "Several witnesses say that you pressed them for information on General Tarchon's whereabouts recently. Is this true?"

Maihara shifted in her seat. "I might have done."

"Did you? Why?"

"I was interested."

"I know you and General Tarchon got on well, but this behaviour seems rather odd."

"We were quite good friends. I missed him."

Impar narrowed his eyes. "Is there anything else concerning you and General Tarchon I ought to know? Has he ever discussed military matters with you?"

"No, certainly not." She managed to sound shocked.

"Have you ever been alone with him?"

Maihara did not like the direction this questioning was going. "Not like that. Why are you asking me this, and not about the note?"

"I am more interested in your friendship with General Tarchon. I suspect that you have encouraged it in order to collect information and find an opportunity to assassinate him."

"That's totally not true. Why would I hand over the note, in that case?"

Impar scowled. "Where's that bitch Lady Aurian? You were the last to see her. The guards say she left the mansion, returned, spoke to you and went out again. What was that all about?"

So they had not caught Aurian yet. Maihara thought quickly. Impar was smart, and thorough. He had probably questioned the serving-woman already, and she might have told him that Aurian went out to visit the temple, and even that she had told Maihara this.

"Apparently she visited the temple early in the morning."

"Which one?"

Should she be vague or misleading, or use some genuine-sounding information to allay Impar's suspicions? "I never went with her, but I assume she used the Temple of the Nine Gods, the one dedicated to the sea-god Laogonus." Aurian went there to sing, or so she claimed.

"Where's that?"

It seemed Impar did not know everything about Loomis. "Near the markets?"

"And why did she go out again after you spoke with her?"

Maihara took a breath. "I had asked her to buy an ornament that I saw in the market the day before yesterday, but she forgot, and I asked her to go back for it."

"What sort of ornament?"

Maihara thought quickly. "How should I describe it? It—"

"Please do." Impar scowled and folded his arms.

"It was of glass, made with several colours and with a fancy top part. It was lovely."

"And what stall was it on?" Impar said, in a tone that implied he was not convinced.

"In the middle of a row of glass stalls. Near the — I'm not sure." She saw the trap that Impar was preparing for her. "Actually, I've no sense of direction."

"And how was Aurian supposed to find this?"

"She was with me. Now I remember, we looked at several. I hope she knows which one I wanted."

Impar was silent. He elbowed the officer next to him.

"Sir." The man turned and left the room.

"We now know that Aurian slipped away without an escort," Impar said. "Now, let's go over this again."

Impar went over various aspects of her story several times, making her repeat it and disputing various points.

So this was how interrogators got their results. The

pressure made her acutely uncomfortable. It was just as well that most of what she told him was true, and they really had looked at ornaments in the market. She could be involving an innocent market trader in this mess. If Impar had her dragged down to the market, she might have to convince them she'd forgotten exactly where the stall was.

***

Impar's men locked Maihara in the bare tower room again, with too much time to worry over what she might have overlooked. After several hours the door lock rattled as a key was turned.

She was surprised to see the tall figure of Cleia Chavin, in her green uniform. The short-haired blonde female officer sidled into the room and shut the door.

"Cleia-?" She was unsure what to make of this. During the month or more of peace, she had come to regard the officer as a friend.

"Good afternoon, Maihara," Cleia said, looking serious. "I've heard about your adventures."

"Oh, you have?" Her heart beat faster.

Cleia took Maihara's hands while Maihara remained seated. "It's good to see you."

"Likewise." She was pleased to meet again her friend from Calah but disconcerted to encounter her here.

Cleia pulled up a chair. "I haven't seen you for a while. Are you well? You're slimmer."

"Yes."

"They've not mistreated you?"

"No."

"When the Imperials freed you on the river, were you expecting a rescue?"

That suspicion again. "No, I don't even think it was a rescue attempt, just a raid."

"And while you were free, were you working against us?"

Maihara shifted uncomfortably in her chair. "I just wanted the fighting to stop."

"But what were you doing in the principality of

Shardan?"

"Trying to get away from the war." She looked into Cleia's face, trying to guess where this was leading.

"Impar and his team are suspicious of you, but they are puzzled by these latest developments. Why would somebody try to assassinate you, and what is that note about?"

"Do they know who the man was?"

"The assassin? They believe he came from the Empire, which increases the mystery. Do you think that anyone in the Empire is plotting against you?"

"I do."

"That man, your attacker, has just died by the way."

"I'm sorry." Maihara had a twinge of nausea, remembering the man's groans. "I didn't mean to kill him, exactly." Her hands were shaking, and she was unable to go on. She gasped for breath, and tears came into her eyes. She had killed another human being. To her humiliation, sobs of grief and shame shook her.

Cleia embraced her in strong arms, and rocked her. "It's all right. *I know.* It must have been a horrible experience." She lifted a hand to touch Maihara's neck. "He's left marks."

After a few minutes, Maihara recovered her composure. Cleia held Maihara's hands in a warm grip. "Don't feel guilty. He'd almost certainly have been executed after questioning, anyway."

Maihara nodded. It did not make her feel any better about destroying a man's life.

"And what of the latest note?" Cleia asked gently. "What's with that?"

"The same people," Maihara said. "Trying to make me look bad."

Cleia questioned her further over the notes, and Maihara gave the same answers she had given Impar.

She leaned closer. "Impar suspects you were trying to form a relationship with Tarchon so you could get information, or even harm him."

"So he said, more than once."

"Has Tarchon ever told you anything he shouldn't?"

"No." Indeed Tarchon had not been indiscreet.

"Is that on your word of honour as a Princess?"

"Yes."

Cleia relaxed. "I still have to convince Colonel Impar. Various witnesses have seen you talking to Tarchon on over a score of occasions."

"I enjoy talking with him, He's a nice man. When he's not around, I miss him." Maihara slapped the arm of her chair. "Why is Impar interested in me and Tarchon?" She made a face.

Cleia looked away. "Colonel Impar has directed the line of investigation."

"What has all this to do with him, anyway?"

"Don't you know? Colonel Impar is responsible for all our agents and military intelligence in this region."

A chill ran up Maihara's spine. "I didn't know." She was not the only person in danger here. Impar had contacts and support outside the military, and she belatedly realised he could have more power in the revolution than his relatively lowly rank suggested. Perhaps he aimed to discredit Tarchon and advance his own power.

Cleia relaxed her stance. "If you didn't know that, you're not much of a spy. Now tell me the truth about you and Tarchon. I don't want to cover for you and then be made to look a fool when the real truth emerges."

Maihara hesitated. As her friend, Cleia deserved the truth and would be angry if she was misled. But the real truth, that she saw in Tarchon's eyes, was dangerous and she dared not utter it. After the failed attempt to kill her, Tarchon had appeared remarkably quickly, looking more than a little concerned. Tarchon was romantically interested in her, and Impar must not find out. If he did, he would do everything in his power to prevent any further contact between Tarchon and herself. One of his minions could have his ear to the door now. She turned and glanced at the metal-studded door.

"Would you find it easier to talk somewhere else?" Cleia asked.

Maihara nodded. "Yes." It would give her a pause to reconsider.

A few minutes later, they were on the flat roof of the Lumin mansion, with a view of rooftops, the harbour and the sea beyond. It was windy up here, and noise coming up from the streets blocked any small sound. Two soldiers lurked out of earshot, blocking the way back to the stairwell. A stone parapet was all that stood between Maihara and a large drop to the courtyard. She doubted that Impar would grieve if she threw herself over it.

Cleia repeated her question concerning Tarchon.

"I do like him a lot," Maihara said. "I didn't at first, but he's a decent man, and quite good-looking, and fun to talk to. When he's not around, I really want to see him."

"And what do you talk about?"

Maihara looked out over the town. "Silly things, mostly. I like to see him smile."

"Have you ever had strong feelings for a man before?"

Maihara turned. "I don't know. What do you mean?"

"Love."

"That's ridiculous." The suggestion that she was in love with an enemy general was somehow insulting. Even if she did have feelings for him.

"I think you have a schoolgirl crush on Tarchon." Cleia smiled.

Maihara held her tongue, resisting the impulse to assert hotly that it was not a crush, or more than a crush. Being suspected of a crush did not seem dangerous. She looked away, her face heating. "I don't. You're being silly."

Cleia's smile deepened. "And what about Tarchon? What does he feel toward you?"

Here was the big lie. "How would I know? Obviously he finds my company amusing, otherwise he would not keep showing up. I'm a well-educated young woman and a good conversationalist." She lifted her chin.

"And do these conversations include military matters?"

"Do I cross-examine him on his next campaign? No."

Cleia worried at this topic for a while, Maihara maintaining denial.

"No. Why are you going on about this? Why suspect me?"

"You said the Fifth Bureau tried to recruit you in Calah to assassinate Tarchon. Impar suspects you may have agreed to assist them, and you are conspiring with others."

Such suspicions might be credible to somebody like Impar. "I haven't."

"One of Impar's men wonders if you killed that man to silence him."

A shock ran through Maihara. "I did not! That's absurd!"

"Fantastical, is what Impar said." Cleia gazed toward the distant sea. "We'll go down now. I'll make my report to Colonel Impar."

They approached the stairwell. "What was Tarchon's first wife like?" Maihara asked. "The one that died."

"I never met her. But I understand she was well liked. A sturdy girl, and a little younger than Tarchon. I think she was seventeen when they met."

"What?" Maihara concealed her shock. So she was the same age now as his first wife had been. That partly explained his interest.

"You should avoid being alone with him. How many women attendants do you have?" Cleia asked.

"I only had my chaperone, Lady Aurian and a woman who brought the bathwater and sometimes helps me dress."

Cleia frowned and made a *tsk* sound with her tongue. "When this enquiry is over, I'll see if they'll give you some female servants. You should have several, for a proper establishment. That should discourage any misbehaviour from male visitors."

"I suppose so, but won't your women here hate me?"

"I expect most will be too glad of the money to worry over your politics. But don't raise your hopes too high. I'll have to persuade Tarchon or his people to employ them, and I don't know how much time I have here."

Maihara nodded. Having maids would be good, so long as they weren't there just to spy on her.

-35-

By Cleia Chavin's insistence, Maihara was allowed the run of the mansion and permitted to explore its passages and opulent rooms, though trailed by a couple of guards. The plasterwork was ornate, and in some reception rooms painted in colours with an absence warmer hues like red, and the upholstery of the twisty gilded furniture was similar. It made her think of being underwater.

She missed Lady Aurian. By now a reaction had set in, and heavy-hearted, she felt she had done a terrible and not needful thing in driving her companion away and allowing suspicion to fall on her.

But it was done, and a further reason to seek some accommodation with the rebels, and Tarchon in particular. There was no shelter for her in the Empire.

And she would finish her work on the local Loomis magic.

By late afternoon, word of Tarchon's return changed the mood of both Maihara and her minders, from tension to anticipation. There was to be a victory banquet, with selected representatives from the town invited. The banquet was being held in one of the finest rooms in the city, the Lumin mansion's salon overlooking the harbour. Her unease did not diminish. The professional attackers might try again. Or Tarchon might treat her as coldly as before.

She had put on a fine new dress of blue silk, and a coronet of silver inset with pale gems balanced on her hair. The serving-woman held up a gilded hand mirror.

The brooch and rings set with rubies that Tarchon had sent up for her to wear lay on the dressing room table, the gems glowing red. Had they been a gift, her heart would have trembled, but they were a loan, and she wondered where Tarchon had got them. From the city, or loot from his expedition? Yet it must mean something, that he wanted her to dress well.

In her mind, possibilities shifted. She could accept the protection of Tarchon and the rebels while waiting for new circumstances. Perhaps she and Tarchon could work together on common goals, on countering the golims. Clashing with this was her dream of becoming Empress. She did not see yet how to have both him and that other dream.

"Why are they putting me on display, after that attack?" Maihara said to her new servant, Kallie. Resentment that her safety appeared of secondary importance soured her mood.

"You'd have to ask them. You look every inch a princess, Milady." Kallie told her. "They must have their reasons." The blonde-haired Kallie was one of the servants Maihara had acquired at Cleia Chavin's instigation. She was a local woman in her twenties who had formerly worked in another noble house in Loomis.

"It's foolish." Maihara shivered. "Some of the guests could be Imperial secret service agents, with knives in their boots." Perhaps it was her talk of compromise and reconciliation that aroused the hatred of shadowy extremists. She thought now that the attacker had muttered 'Traitor' as the guard ran in.

"I'm sure the General will have selected the guests, and bad people will be kept out. Don't worry, Princess."

Guests milled in the main hall at the foot of the curving gilded staircase. As she descended, Maihara had a view of heads. Tarchon stood at the foot of the staircase, smartly uniformed, with several of his officers behind him. He looked up, and as their eyes met, he raised a hand in salute.

"Good evening, Your Grace. I hope you are well."

"Very well, thank you." Despite the formal exchange, her heart warmed at his smile and her resentment at having to wear the items he sent up melted away.

His eyes ran over her. "Those ornaments pleased you?"

As she reached the bottom step, he took her hand. A tingling went through her. "They did, thank you." She lowered her eyes.

"Now you look like a princess," Tarchon said, echoing Kallie's words.

She warmed under his praise. He had wanted her dressed for his own eyes, not just to impress the defeated townsfolk. "Thank you. I hope you're guarding me like one."

"I'm guarding you like the most precious thing."

"But why do you want to show me off here, General?"

"It's to underline our message to the worthies and minor nobility of the place. We want change, but we won't hang all the nobles, or send all the citizens out into labour camps to till the fields." He gave a cheerful smile.

"I'm sure they'll be relieved." Things must be bad, if a city could be so easily wooed, she thought.

The banquet awaited in a long, ornately decorated room with gilded plaster work, darkly gleaming furniture and a fine ceiling with painted mythological figures of the Nine Gods mythos looking down on the laden table. Officers in green uniforms and a handful of crestfallen dignitaries from the town stared as Maihara entered with Tarchon. Four soldiers with short weapons discreetly trailed her. She glanced up. Two soldiers with armed crossbows crouched behind the fretwork balustrade of the small minstrel's gallery. She took her seat near Tarchon, with some lady of the local nobility at her side. Loud voices filled the room as the victorious officers celebrated still being alive. A few stared morosely at their cups as if remembering fallen comrades or absent kin.

She turned to the officer next to her as the first course was brought in. It was Colonel Impar, or, as she privately thought of him, Rat-face. He was her enemy, but it would be prudent to engage him in polite conversation, rather than blanking him or talking across him to Tarchon and causing tongues to wag.

"Were many people killed in the fighting here, Colonel?"

Colonel Impar eyed her with caution before replying. "Casualties were light, Princess. Resistance collapsed as soon as our alchemist blew a hole in the city wall."

"How did you get so much fire-powder?"

"Ah." Impar shrugged and did not explain further.

"What of the city people, the civilians?"

Impar pressed the bridge of his round-lensed spectacles. "Not much trouble, as far as I know."

"And your army is not looting and sacking the city?" She was being impolite, but Impar deserved a little payback.

"Certainly not." The officer managed to appear indignant. "General Tarchon made it clear that we would punish any lack of discipline. We have deployed elite troops to curb any looting and violence against the population. Our mission is to free the province from the Imperials."

"Indeed? While my carriage was passing through the streets near the mansions, I saw plenty of damaged buildings, scattered goods and dead bodies."

"As I said, it's our policy to curb such excesses. Perhaps what you saw was the result of the bombardment from the harbour."

"Why was that necessary?"

"We invited them to surrender. They wouldn't." Impar forked up another mouthful of the rich food.

She changed the subject. "I heard that the Imperial forces intended to defeat you, by launching a surprise counter-attack during the siege." The interrogators had questioned her about this. "But instead, you attacked them. Did you have spies?"

Impar belched and gave a smirk. "No, it's because we're smarter than the Imperial army."

"You are? But someone said—"

"The defenders had a defiant attitude. Our General

wondered why, and sent the cavalry, which we didn't need for a siege, northward post-haste to see if they could contact any enemy. The cavalry commander gathered local auxiliaries, as General Tarchon suggested."

"And?" Maihara dipped a chunk of fish in the rich sauce.

"He prepared an ambush in a wood several leagues north of Loomis. It was a success. They ambushed the Imperial column, and the enemy became most discouraged."

"But - scouts?" Maihara began.

"Didn't use them, or didn't listen," Impar said with a sneer. "That's why your side's losing."

The account brought her little joy. The rebels would remain in firm control of this part of the coast. Yet she saw better now why the rebels followed Tarchon. Men were drawn to a leader who displayed such a combination of luck and skill. If she did not feel a duty toward her people, rich and poor, she would have little reason to retain any loyalty to the Imperial side.

So where else had Tarchon been clever? "And you won't tell me why I was taken to those secret meetings with the Dhikr leaders?"

Impar glanced around, and leaned close. "Because you annoyed them. We needed an Imperial target for them to hate." One corner of his mouth twisted up.

Was he serious? She had annoyed the Dhikr?

Tarchon spoke to her from the head of the table, asking if she liked the food.

Her heart lightened at this excuse to talk with him. "Yes, I do." She had been helping herself from plates of seafoods both cooked and raw, exotic vegetables, and small rolls of rice wrapped in seaweed. This was Imperial seafood cuisine, as unfamiliar to her as the spicy Shardan fare.

"Is it true what your Colonel says about the ambush in the woods? Your idea?"

"It was an obvious move," he said, before modestly

confirming his role in halting the Imperial relief column.

They turned to small talk about the region. "What's inside those old Loomis towers?" she asked, like any tourist. They were constrained by the company, and she was conscious of Impar at her elbow listening for any impropriety. But she and Tarchon were able to look into each other's faces without inhibition, exchanging glances.

Servers brought round a blue drink served in tall glasses. Maihara downed two of them before realising, from its giddying effect, that it was wine.

The room grew noisier as officers drank and shouted out toasts to Tarchon and to the dignitaries. She did not enjoy being among noisy strangers. A trio of musicians started to play, and a couple of the civilians danced with their women. Maihara wished that someone would ask her to dance, but nobody did, and it would be improper for her to ask.

As the town guests were funnelled out, Maihara waited in the front hall with her maid and the ever-present guards, when a scuffle broke out between two groups of drunken guests. The guards piled in to separate and eject them from the hall. One of Maihara's guard detail hurried out her maid Kallie, while Tarchon caught Maihara's eye and made a nod of his head to one side. She followed, feeling a little unsteady from the effects of the blue wine she had drunk. They slipped out of sight behind a painted screen and into an anteroom.

He stepped closer and stretched out a hand. She moved to take it in hers, but he touched her hair, and gently stroked her cheek. A shock ran through her at his touch. Confused by the change in his mood, she edged back.

"You troublesome girl," he said in a soft voice, withdrawing his hand. "What will I do with you?"

A wave of warm emotion swept over her. He still liked her.

Maihara leant closer, unable to control her smile.

Tarchon put his arms lightly about her and then stroked

her hair. "You're beautiful."

Startled, she pulled back. This was sudden. But she felt safe in Tarchon's arms. His touch excited her.

He loosened his grip. "I'm sorry if—" he began.

"I'm not a child," she said, and raised her head.

Their lips almost met, but both of them drew back, she unsure she should kiss an older man, a rebel, he perhaps feeling he shouldn't take advantage of a young female prisoner. Even if the guards were looking aside. His breath was warm and smelt faintly of wine. A tingling shot through her, through her brain, her breasts, her lower region. She gripped him, pulling him closer. More gently, his arms came around her back and held her. She enjoyed the embrace, the sensation of his hard body against hers.

Long seconds later, they broke apart. "I should dislike you, but sometimes I have strange thoughts." She ran a hand over his tunic.

"Maihara, my victory at sea has given me a stronger hand to protect you. There'll be no trial." He eased back, slipping out of reach. "I wish I could be your friend and companion, but I'm the leader of a rebel army."

"And I'm the Imperial Princess," she finished for him. "Why do you care about me? I'm not so pretty."

"I'd be happy to look at your face all day. You're a clever and charming young woman."

Sounds of the ongoing altercation in the hall filtered through the closed door.

"Indeed?" This pleased her, even if it were flattery.

He nodded. "I thought of you, often, after you went missing. At first, I feared that you might be killed or taken and horribly abused by the irregular attackers. I had mounted troops scour the country along the river, but we found nothing. Later, after we took Retis, I heard you had been there a day earlier as the Imperial Princess, and I was much relieved."

He pushed her away. "Quickly now, before someone sees us." He touched her face in a brief caress. "Sleep well."

In a daze, Maihara stumbled out of the room and past the screen. She clenched her fists in excitement. At last, it was out in the open. He did care for her, and he knew now that she cared for him, even if it was mad and wrong.

Rather unsteadily she followed her maid to her silk-hung bedroom.

'You look every inch a princess', Tarchon had said. 'Beautiful'. He must be in love with her.

Lying in bed in a room that felt less steady than she liked, she replayed the memory of that fond embrace, the heady joy. If only they were married, there would be more than kisses and embraces. Adult embraces, without clothing, the kind of thing she'd read about in those books. Thinking of it made her body warm with unfamiliar sensations.

***

In the commandeered Loomis mansion, Maihara saw nothing of Tarchon next day, which served well, given her anxiety that she had done something rash under the influence of the blue wine. She had pushed forward her relationship with the handsome General, and that excited her. But it could be a ruinous mistake. Who was to blame? She had no experience, no compass to guide her, and she dared not ask Cleia Chavin, who was certain to be shocked, or the maids who had been hired expressly to protect her from any intimate contact. Outside, the rebels consolidated their hold on the city, on her people.

As she prepared to retire to bed, a rapping came from a section of wall near the bed. "Who's there?" she exclaimed, with sudden fear.

"It is I, Tarchon," came a muffled voice. The wall there had a rectangular set of marks in the silk wall-hanging as if it hid a secret door for servants or assignations.

"General?"

"May I come in?"

Should she? She had already embraced him. Where were the servants? The guards? What if someone saw?

Curiosity and caution warred in her. "I suppose so."

The door opened on oiled hinges. He stood in the opening, dimly lit by the single lamp, dressed in a rumpled shirt and uniform trousers. "I apologise for the intrusion, but I cannot speak of a personal matter with others present."

"What is it?" she asked, with increasing unease. The last time they had been alone, they had almost kissed. What if he wanted more now? This was not the safe arm-in-arm walk in a garden that she had imagined as a next step.

"Don't be alarmed." He remained by the door. "I merely wish to speak. These words are for you alone."

She let out the breath she had been holding. His expression was mild and his demeanour unthreatening.

"My maids should be present."

"I'm sorry, Princess. I dare not risk loose talk." The shirt hung close to him, emphasising his well-made body. On his feet were light shoes. "I had enough trouble slipping by the guards. Many people will not welcome us having a close relationship."

Maihara lowered her head. It all made sense. She was the one becoming wound up, while he had such concerns and also his duties to attend to.

"I see. Your Colonel Impar already suspects there is something between us. He doesn't like me."

"I'll speak to him," he said. "He needs to be reassured that you won't stab me."

Maihara flinched. The memory of the stabbing was like a nightmare.

Tarchon's tone implied that Impar suspected other things.

"May I sit down? It's been a long day."

"Please sit." Then she realised that despite the otherwise elaborate furnishing there was no chair.

He crossed the room and sat on the chest at the foot of the large bed. "I've been thinking how we could be together openly. Have you any thoughts about marriage?"

"Not really." Her capture had dashed any prospect of a

regal arranged marriage. Her heartbeat quickcncd.

"You know, I'm not sure how to ask this. I have thought of marrying again, but I have not met a woman whom I cared for, who was clever and sensible, and interested in things that interest me. Until I got to know you. I know my feelings about you, and I dare hope that you return them."

He turned to face her. "Princess, the real campaign will begin soon. We will have less time to spend together as matters stand. There may be danger. There is a way that I can best protect you from extreme radicals in our movement. I want you to be - I mean I want to ask you, will you be my wife?"

"Your wife?" She gasped, and raised a hand to her face. His words were sinking in. He cared enough to want to marry her. "But, I'm..." Her heart beat louder.

This is going too fast. "But there's been no formal negotiation. And we've spent no time as each other's special person. I'm just your prisoner."

"Does the idea not please you?" His face betrayed a sincere anxiety.

Noble ladies were rarely allowed to marry for love. Their families would consider suitable suitors, and if she was lucky, the lady would be allowed to veto the least appealing. And at her level, an Imperial marriage was also a political treaty. Words like *boyfriend* and *girlfriend*, used by the lower orders, were not in the vocabulary. Should they be on first name terms now? Melis Tarchon's sudden proposal smacked of business rather than love, but that was forgivable. She would have preferred him to be motivated solely by love, but she had a tumult of warm feelings for him, and in her situation there could be worse suitors.

"It does please me." Her heartbeat quickened. "But surely there are many difficulties in the way. I'm the daughter of the man you're fighting. And I'm much younger than you."

Tarchon's expression lightened. "So you might? If these difficulties were set aside?"

"I might." As she said this, she believed that she could

marry him, and hoped this showed in her face.

Tarchon smiled. "I don't think of you as very young. You seem to have a grown-up head on your shoulders."

"What would your parents say?" She had learnt that his parents lived, but that the Varlords had burnt their house and mill as a reprisal.

"I'd hope for their blessing, but I need not seek it. The only such impediment is that some will say to marry you I'd need the consent of your parents —"

She smiled, and shook her head.

"Quite. But we can work around such things, if we get legal advice. Or if we wait a few months, once you are eighteen your marriage can no longer be opposed on those grounds."

She nodded. That seemed better, and she would not have to do this alarming thing right away.

Tarchon looked pleased. "There's just one thing. I can't marry an Imperial princess. You must give up your titles."

She took a sharp breath, shocked. *No.* "I don't know." Her instincts baulked at the suggestion. "If I'm not a princess, what am I? A prisoner? A minor noble? Some kind of entertainment girl?"

Tarchon's face fell, betraying disappointment. "No, you'll be an ordinary citizen, my wife."

Ordinary? The word burned her. She wasn't ordinary. She had the latent power to perform potent magics. And, ever since she had spoken to various people about the succession, she had clung to the idea that *she* could be Cordan's successor. It wasn't likely, she would almost certainly be prevented, but when confronted with it, she could not let go of that duty, that dream.

"So, will you abandon the title?" he persisted.

"I can't."

Tarchon's face registered surprise and disappointment. "You don't understand. I'm the leader of a rebel army. There's no way I could marry a titled Imperial Princess. People would see it as against the spirit of our revolution. It would outrage our fighters. Other factions would seize the chance to conspire against me."

She pressed her lips together and looked at him in frustration. "*You're* the one putting your army before *us*. I'm not *ordinary*. I can't just give up my titles."

"You're not seriously thinking of being Empress? That's very unlikely to happen."

"Unlikely or not, so long as I have the titles, I have the potential to influence events, or to pass the title of Emperor to a worthy successor."

"It won't happen. You want the Imperials to win this war, so you can become Empress in time, don't you?" His face twisted in frustration and disappointment.

"I don't wish that. I want peaceful reform. What will be, will be. But I can't give up the titles and abandon the Empire to idiocy."

Tarchon turned around and stared at the wall, head bowed.

Distressed, she waited for his next words.

He stood and faced her. "If you don't wish to marry me, you can just say so. You don't need an excuse." His voice was sad.

"No, that's not it at all, Melis. Suppose the Emperor died tomorrow." She clicked her fingers. "Would you still want me to give up my titles?"

Tarchon's mouth dropped open a fraction, and his jaw worked as he considered the implications. He shook his head. "They're already rejecting you. It'll be the same."

"That's just one faction. What if another faction supported me?"

He shook his head again. "Name them. I know what you hope, but it's a dream."

"I don't believe so." The Varlord officer and his hints. "Can't we wait?"

"You'd be safer as my wife. But if you have to choose between being Empress and us, you'd choose the Empire?" He stretched out his hands.

"I want to have both." Her heart beat faster. She found it hard to meet his eyes. "Can't we try? There must be a way."

"My colleagues want to abolish the Empire, and call it something else. A Commonwealth - awkward word. Would you want to be a mere figurehead, or just sit on a ruling Council?"

She threw up her hands, and with a short laugh, let frankness overcome discretion. "No."

"You're impossible."

"If I was Empress, those changes we both want, I could just — order them."

"It wouldn't be that simple. You could introduce reforms, but in a system of absolute rule, the next Emperor could just as easily set about undoing them. It's no solution. But what if there's no Empire? Will you marry me then?"

She nodded, unable to trust herself to speak.

Tarchon straightened and raised his head. His eyes smiled. "I'll wait for you. But please reconsider." He stretched out his arms again, and this time she let him hold her. She leaned into him, breathing in his male scent, as his arms pressed against her and his hands caressed her back.

"Make me Empress. Let's try."

"You can hope," he said with a small laugh.

His lips pressed on the top of her head, then he released her. "We mustn't speak of this outside this room. It would be very dangerous for both of us. Officially, you're our prisoner, and a hostage."

Hostage or not, he wanted to marry her, and that gave her some power over him. "Can you return my box? It was my mother's."

"Your box?" He paused. "I don't understand."

"It was a precious gift I received on my fourteenth birthday, willed to me from my mother. When I tried to retrieve it, your man Impar thought it was suspicious and seized it."

He nodded. "I will. Once I'm satisfied you can't harm us with it."

"And help find a round polished stone that was lost from it."

He stared at her, confused. "What is this stone? I know nothing about a stone."

"It came with the box, but it disappeared. It was my mother's, my connection with her. Find it and—"

Tarchon shook his head. "When we are back on Calah. I can't do anything now. I must go now, before I'm missed." He swung round and with a few steps reached the secret door. He turned once more, smiled and went out.

She flung herself into an armchair, elated. He'd proposed. He wanted to marry her.

But she couldn't, not yet. Tears came to her eyes as doubt seeped in. What had she agreed to? The thought of surrendering to Tarchon filled her with both excitement and misgivings, but declaring herself rebel, commoner and wife was a step too far, too soon.

But if Tarchon thought they had an understanding, her ambitions were still in play. She still wanted her magical box, and the power it represented. And she really needed to tell him about the golims.

-36-

A firm knock sounded at the door of Maihara's room.

"Come in."

Two officers in green rebel uniform entered. Maihara recognised neither of them.

"Princess, you have an invitation," said one. "You wanted to see the famous Loomis towers?"

She had mentioned it, at the banquet. "Yes," she said, wondering.

"I'm Lieutenant Ficke, of General Tarchon's staff," said the speaker. He was a pleasant-looking young man, with cropped brown hair. He bowed. "Please come with me."

Behind them she glimpsed two soldiers. She stood and went with them. As they descended the stairs, she tried to look at their uniform badges to identify their unit. The narrow stone-flagged street was busy with townsfolk going about their daily business.

"Where are we going?"

"The Sloan Tower," said one of the soldiers. It meant little to her, but presently they reached the base of one of the Loomis towers. This one was duck-egg blue, rough and weathered when seen close up, and had a modern timber door fitted at its base. The lead officer indicated that they were to enter.

Maihara's heart beat faster. Perhaps they intended to frighten her into confessing, by holding her over the drop to the streets below.

The men led Maihara down stone stairs into a semi-basement of the tower. A lamp supplemented the dim light from a half-blocked window. A few papers and a sword lay on a table.

Tarchon was here, along with a couple of aides.

Anxious thoughts spun through her mind. She had almost mastered the local magic scheme, translating the help messages and the labels of many of the sigils from an obsolete dialect. Had he brought her here to confront her about spy magic, or deliver a final judgement of guilt about the Retis incident? He looked up as she descended the last stone step.

"Excuse the drama, Princess. Please be seated." He gestured to a wooden chair.

"What's going on?" Her mouth was dry. Tarchon's formal tone in contrast to their bedroom encounter increased her unease, and she hoped it was merely because of the presence of the aides and guards.

Tarchon moved aside a handful of papers. "We have had more reports from the Empire, on what we spoke of earlier. It's as we thought, they have declared you an enemy of the regime. I suspected that Impar might not tell you, so I'm telling you now. His witnesses from Retis are still awaited, much good may they do him."

Heat burned through Maihara's body. "I've known for some time that my father, far from honouring me as Imperial Princess, would rather keep me locked in a prison cell. And now this." The sense of being betrayed and spurned cut like a knife. "There are many customs and practices in the Empire that I don't like."

Tarchon frowned and scratched his jaw. "That's the only reason? He doesn't like your opinions?"

She shook her head. "No, there's more. You're aware of the rumours of mechanical soldiers?" She had to make him believe.

Tarchon nodded.

"You remember when you took me to the hall of automata in the Palace at Calah?"

He nodded.

"I may have misled you about what they meant. They are wonderful, but they have little to do with Cordan's promises of mechanical men. You remember the Emperor's appearance at Kunn?"

"Yes. It's hard to forget."

"At Halamar I saw a man with a complete working metal arm, that he says the Empire sold him."

Tarchon's eyes widened.

"There's more. The Shardan nobles talked of buying mechanical soldiers for their army, so these golims clearly exist. Cordan's work is behind it all. He promised a golim army that would lift your siege of Calah. I think he is using some kind of ancient magic to create these things, and that his ultimate plan is to make enough of them to reverse all your advances and destroy your rebellion."

"I see." Tarchon glanced at his aide.

"So why is Cordan pursuing me? He fears I could undo his magical plans. He knows I would oppose him. I am his daughter, and some at Court supposed my mother to be a witch."

Now she had his complete attention. Her heart beat faster.

"You are admitting that you have magical power?" he said.

"He probably fears that I could set that pterostrophe on him."

Tarchon barked a laugh.

"He fears that I have power. So which do you fear the most, Cordan's magic or mine? I promise you, I have no powers that can harm a person. Nor does my father, but he commands armies, and a swarm of golims waiting to attack."

She thought he had gone paler in the lamplight. "I heed your warning. I'll want to know more of these things. But why are you telling me this?"

"You don't want my help?" She held her breath. He could still fear her powers.

"Oh, I do." He flashed a fleeting smile. "But what are your terms?"

I want to be loved. "I want security. No questioning about what I can do. No trials. No denial of my status as Imperial Princess. And the return of my personal

495

possessions."

Tarchon made a small nod. Apparently, he remembered the personal possession to which she referred. "Very well. There'll be no trial; my victory at sea has given me extra leverage against the radical faction who want to remove all Imperial institutions and execute the nobles, so I can promise you that. But our accord must be kept quiet. Those people would be quick to accuse me of having Imperialist sympathies." He looked at his aides, who nodded in response. "I'll make a public statement about your status, though the radicals won't like this. And returning your personal possessions will be difficult. If they're in a vault in Calah, they're safer there than if I send word for them to be brought here."

She released the breath she had been holding. "Thank you."

"Enjoy your sightseeing tour. Ficke will escort you."

***

Safely back in her room, Maihara threw herself into a soft-padded armchair to rest her aching legs. Escorted by Lieutenant Ficke, she had climbed the worn spiral staircase of the tower. The steps were worn by centuries of feet and in semi-darkness, save where a hole in the wall admitted light and glimpses of roofs. After many loops of the stair, she had become aware of light glaring on the walls above. She paused for breath. In another turn of the stairs she reached an open platform surrounded by a circular waist-high wall.

She had stared in wonder at the city, a maze of roofs and streets, sprawled map-like below. Beyond the harbour, the sea rippled in a crinkled expanse of grey and blue. Wind tugged at her clothing and whistled around the tower top, much stronger than at street level. The men with her gazed open-mouthed at the view. None ventured close to the cracked stone parapet. The thought of the drop below made her giddy.

To the south lay the harbour, with the arms of quays and jetties enclosing the ships looking small from this height.

On a large warship a sailor was climbing up latticed side-ropes to the masthead, looking for all the world like an ant climbing a spider's web attached to a short twig. Outside the harbour was glittering grey water, dotted with a few rocks and an island. The coast stretched away to the right. Ahead, the water rippled out to the horizon, sparkling like beaten silver, with a few small specks that were ships.

It had been worth the climb to see this, even though it had left her breathless and with aching legs. The descent added the pain of jolted knees, but she had carried on, not wanting to show any feminine weakness.

While her maids fussed, she wondered what Tarchon was doing. The tower was nearby. By now, she had penetrated the city's unfamiliar magic and decoded enough of the labelling to reach the spells she wanted. She found the spy spell, and in a minute or two she had started it and found the tower. Several soldiers stood around the base on guard, but the basement room was empty. With the magic, she followed the spiral stair upward.

Rebel officers stood on the platform, conferring and pointing seaward. She recognised several by sight, including Impar wearing his dark glasses - and Tarchon. Several men stared aside at the view, standing back from the vertiginous edge.

Even at second hand, the view and the drop to the streets below made her dizzy.

Tarchon raised his arm, and at once the others fell silent and turned to face him.

"Gentlemen, I have received a report from Colonel Impar about a security problem. We have suspected leaks of our plans in the past. There is evidence that the Imperial Army operated at least one spy circuit in Loomis, and that the Princess's chaperone, who has fled, was involved. One of the Nine Gods' temples has been identified as a meeting place for Army spies."

This isn't new, Maihara thought.

"Colonel Impar has found no evidence that the Princess

was involved, and I therefore decree that the Princess's status as a trusted prisoner shall be unchanged. I have judged that the Princess is a strategic asset in our struggle against newly disclosed threats from the Empire, discovered by our forces in Shardan, and there will be no question of any distracting trials or impeachment."

Maihara's heart leapt. They were not going to hold her over the railing after all. She turned her view to Impar. He was scowling.

Tarchon continued to speak. "However, I concur with Colonel Impar's prudent action in rotating the Princess's guard in its entirety, and I compliment the Colonel on his excellent and painstaking work in protecting us from spies." He glanced at Impar, who assumed a neutral expression and gave a slight nod.

For the moment, she had maintained Tarchon's trust and survived Impar's unwelcome scrutiny.

Tarchon was still talking. "Our naval victory three days ago cleared away half of the Imperial Eastern Fleet." He paused, and several of the officers applauded. "When, the One God willing, we find the other half of that fleet and bring it to battle, the sea road from this port to the coasts of the Empire will be ours." Tarchon pointed to the sea with an expansive gesture.

She turned her magical view to look out over the shining waters of the broad river estuary. Fishing boats floated out there as though stuck on a mirror.

"Our war galleys shall pour out of the estuary of Sintheer and from Loomis, to scour the southern seas. We shall harry the Imperial ships, and attack towns on the islands of the Chancungran Sea that hold allegiance to Cordan. By attacking the arteries of Southern trade, we shall hasten the downfall of the luxurious East and its arrogant Varlords," Tarchon said.

The staff officers applauded in agreement.

She was not going to voice any support of this vainglorious scheme, though by including her in his briefing Tarchon was demonstrating to his people his continued belief in her harmlessness.

Tarchon pointed to the stair head. At once, the assembled officers moved to the arched stair entry. Tracking them partway down, she heard one of the officers ask, "What do you think of the General's words, Ficke?"

"It's a big ocean. Who knows what's lurking out there?"

"Nothing our marines can't handle, Lieutenant," said the other.

ABOUT THE AUTHOR

Kim Cowie has worked as a technician and as a technical author, and has sold articles to non-fiction magazines, as well as two short stories. Kim has always enjoyed reading and writing SF and fantasy stories. Currently he is working on a series of fantasy novels.

Kim was included in the June 2017 list of "14 Exciting New Authors to Try Over the Summer" on the SFF Chronicles forum.

Author website: kimjcowie.com

Other books by Kim J Cowie:

The Plain Girl's Earrings
Deadly Journey

Printed in Poland
by Amazon Fulfillment
Poland Sp. z o.o., Wrocław

53418368R00298

Fiona lives in the small town of Airdrie near Glasgow with her husband, Liam, and their two daughters, Erin and Sian.

She works as a deafblind guide/communicator and a British Sign Language facilitator, learning British Sign Language after the birth of her second daughter.

This is Fiona's first novel, and she hopes to go on and write many more.

Free

Fiona Morgan

Free

Vanguard Press

VANGUARD PAPERBACK

© Copyright 2017
Fiona Morgan

The right of Fiona Morgan to be identified as author of
this work has been asserted by her in accordance with the
Copyright, Designs and Patents Act 1988.

A CIP catalogue record for this title is
available from the British Library.

ISBN 978 1 843863 20 7 4

Vanguard Press is an imprint of
Pegasus Elliot MacKenzie Publishers Ltd.
www.pegasuspublishers.com

First Published in 2017

Vanguard Press
Sheraton House Castle Park
Cambridge England

Printed & Bound in Great Britain

For Liam, Erin and Sian.
Thank you for giving me everything.

Mum and Dad,
thank you for helping me make this possible.

Acknowledgements

I started writing this book simply to prove to myself that I could, and here it is done and dusted. I couldn't have written it without the help of family and friends.

Firstly, my mum and dad, they instilled in me the work ethic to complete what I start and the belief that if you work hard enough at what you want you will achieve it. My mum (and the girls of the Witness Service in Airdrie Sheriff Court) for helping me with the details of the court system (any mistakes are mine), and for giving me my love of books, and my dad for giving me my love of cars, hence the reason for so many gorgeous cars in the book.

My sister for constantly believing in me and boosting me, or booting my bum whenever I've needed it. Also for my gorgeous photo for the book and every other photo you have taken of me and the family, I am so proud of everything you have achieved with Lemonjelly Photography.

Eveline, thank you for letting me adopt your name and for answering all my questions on hospitals and ward security.

Gary, a massive thank you for answering all my weird questions about policing and domestic violence. Again, any mistakes are mine, or details may be smudged to fit.

Katie, I have so much to thank you for not only for proofreading and agreeing that I could do this, but for accepting me, being my 'bf', and personal cheerleader.

My two girls, Erin and Sian, for being the most amazing

daughters I could ever want, for constantly telling me how great my book is after reading that one line, and pushing me to get it published.

I've saved the best to last, as is tradition, I would like to thank my husband, Liam. Thank you for believing in me throughout everything, for giving me your opinion, even though you had no idea what I was talking about, and for our amazing conversations of a night, I know what every shoulder shrug and grunt means. I love you with my whole heart and more.

Oh and Mum, I am sorry for all the swearing!

CHAPTER ONE

"Are you ready yet, Ava?" Nathan shouts gruffly from the bottom of the grand gold and red staircase that dominates the very large very ostentatious hallway in Nathan's large seven-bedroom mansion. It has every mod con in it known to man and no expense has been spared on decorating it, but it is a cold heartless house. Upstairs, in the pristine and very clinical looking white bathroom, Ava stands in front of the mirror. She is small in height, just getting to five feet, blue eyes, with shoulder length brown hair, and the pain dancing in her eyes is noticeable even to her. The bruises on her arms are already starting to emerge. She is going to need to keep her stole on to cover up the finger marks he has left on her porcelain skin, she doesn't want anybody asking questions of the amazing Mr Low, the six foot, toned, black haired, green eyed bully that is her boyfriend.

Taking a last look in the mirror to check that her make up isn't too heavy and her lipstick isn't too bold, Ava thinks to herself, why?, Why do I always manage to get him so upset, what is it that I have to change to make him happy? Can I make him happy? Is it actually me?

Another shout from downstairs breaks into Ava's musings; she jumps at his tone and swallows her fear down, taking a deep breath she answers,

"Coming honey." So with a strained smile painted on her face she walks out of the bathroom, picking up her stole from the bannister and glides down the sweeping, red-carpeted staircase.

"You look stunning," Nathan compliments her, and he sounds genuine, though he always is after he has gotten rid of his temper. He is always loving, sorry and remorseful after he has beaten her, then her heart starts to lift again. The change in Nathan's temper is complete, well at least enough for Ava to think that this time he means it, he really is sorry and he does love her. That is until he sees her walking down the last of the stairs and sneers at her,

"Maybe, if you didn't flaunt yourself with your whore-red lipstick and come to bed eyes, I wouldn't need to remind you that you're mine so much!"

Ava's heart freefalls to her stomach, 'and there it is' she thinks, his temper is still there, just under the surface as always. The small voice in her head reminds her that he is probably going to be like this forever, that he isn't changing and he never will! Putting her head down Ava walks from the mansion and climbs into the back of the waiting silver 1965, 2.5 V8 Daimler.

The driver closes her door and she is alone for a minute, but not long enough. Nathan enters the other side of the back seat and places his hand on Ava's knee. She flinches slightly but enough that Nathan feels it. She closes her eyes and can feel the sly grin on his face and the feeling of power emanating from him; she knows that tonight is going to be a long night.

In the Daydream Club, all of the staff are ready for the big charity ball starting, there are already a few guests milling about, champagne in hand, gossiping about the entertainment for the night and who the big spenders may be.

Neil is satisfied that everything is as it should be and

everybody knows what they have to do. Even though Neil owns the club he leaves the management to Jack, his best friend. It's easier that way so certain people don't know about his business. Although he keeps a hand in and always does his shift. Tonight he is working the cloakroom (he would never expect anybody to work anything he wouldn't work, so he does everything from the meeting and greeting to cleaning the toilets).

"You ready for all the glitz and glamour of the rich and powerful?" Jack asks, bringing Neil out of his thoughts,

"Eh? Oh aye, well, all the big wigs will be here so there is bound to be some drama!" The men roll their eyes at each other.

"You all right boss? You seem a bit…urgh?"

"Aye, well, Julie's been back on the phone wanting to get back together!" Neil sighs and slumps over the cloakroom counter.

"You are kidding me! Please tell me you are not considering going down that road again, Neil for God's sake!" Exasperation oozing out of every pore in Jack's body.

"No, Yes, Maybe, I don't know!"

"Why the fuck do you want to go back to that batshit crazy girl?" Jack looks about making sure that no one on the elite guest list heard his cursing.

"She says she's pregnant!" Neil closes his eyes and shakes his head slowly, "You know I need to be there for her if she is!"

"Oh mate don't—" Out of the corner of his eye Jack notices a silver Daimler has pulled up, more guests arriving. He straightens up and clears his throat, motioning for Neil to do the same,

"Right you, get up off your elbows and get on with what I

pay you for!" Jack says with a tongue in cheek tone to his voice and a wink that only he and Neil understand.

"Yes Boss!" Neil chirps back with a salute to his manager.

Outside the Daimler has pulled up and the driver gets out to open the door for Nathan. He steps out and comes round to the other side opening Ava's door, he puts his hand in and takes Ava's. She puts her hand in his shakily and steps out into the chilly night. Autumn is starting early in Glasgow, it is the end of September but there is a definite chill in the air.

Walking up to the club doors, Ava feels the usual pressure of being the perfect girlfriend. Nathan always expects her to be so much more than she feels she is; he expects her to have poise and sophistication and she tries, she really does try – shoulders back, stomach in, and chin up…well that bit never happens as she isn't allowed to look at other men – but it never seems to work, Nathan is always asking her "Why? Why can't you be like the other women? Why do you always seem to disappoint?" Even in all the finery that Nathan buys her, "To make you at least look like you fit in." She knows she won't be enough. With a deep breath and a heavy heart, she walks through the open doors and into the grand hallway of the club.

"May I take your coat sir?" Neil asks, his voice full of polite service as he looks up at Nathan and Ava. His eyes rest on Ava and he loses all his breath, as he realises that he is looking at the most beautiful woman he has ever seen. He also realises that she is scared, hurt, and feeling very uncomfortable.

Nathan clears his throat impatiently to get Neil to tear his eyes from Ava.

"Yes, here." He dumps his coat on the counter. Neil hands

14

him his ticket and turns to speak to Ava.

"And you Miss, do you..."

"No she doesn't!" Nathan snaps at Neil cutting him off mid-sentence to Ava.

"Okay then." Neil is taken aback by Nathan's abruptness, but doesn't show it. He glances at Ava and catches her eye, he gives her a quick smile, and she looks away quickly, but not before he catches the briefest of smiles from her.

"Come!" Nathan growls and pulls on Ava's hand roughly.

Neil watches her leave and vows to find out more about her and who the arrogant prick she is with is.

"Ah, Mr Drake, how nice to see you." Nathan smarms over people he wants to get land from, so he can build his famous luxury apartments. Unfortunately, people smarm their way over Nathan because he has the money to make friends and influence people.

"Nathan Low, how are you? Still building those stunning apartments?"

"Yes, in fact a piece of land has just caught my eye in Glasgow, quite near your house actually."

"Oh, that sounds interesting; my house price might increase if you build there!"

"Yes, hmmm maybe." Nathan isn't normally in the business of boosting other people's fortune but if he has an end goal then he can let it slide.

"And who is this gorgeous creature you have on your arm tonight Nathan?" Mr Drake turns his eyes to Ava and leers, she can actually feel him undressing her with his eyes and he is old enough to be her father!

"This is my girlfriend, Ava." Nathan also notices the leer and is puffing out his chest at his accomplishment of having such a beautiful, curvaceous lady on his arm. He pulls Ava closer to him and gives Mr Drake a grin that screams, she's mine!

Taking their leave, Nathan walks Ava over to the table that has their names on it,

"Sit!" he growls, "You can have one drink, so I'm guessing it will be a red wine?"

"Yes please." Ava sighs.

Nathan lowers his stance until he is face to face with Ava who has sat, as per her instructions.

"Don't you dare go into one of your moods, you selfish little mare, I have brought you to this lovely place and spent thousands of pounds on your outfit for tonight, not to mention the money I'm going to need to spend whilst we're here and probably on you! So quit with the sulking, you would think I was cruel to you or something!"

He is so close to her she can feel his breath and spittle on her face. The sweat has started running down her spine and she feels like screaming, 'You are cruel to me you bastard!' but all she can do is look up all doe eyed at him and say sorry, that she would love a glass of wine and thank you for everything that he does for her.

"Good." Nathan smirks as he stands up, "That wasn't so hard now was it?" And he strides off to the bar, people acknowledging him all the way there.

While alone, Ava starts to think about her life and why she stays with Nathan. She is tired, tired of being afraid, tired of worrying, she is even tired of just breathing.

Neil watches Ava and Nathan walk away and find their table, he can see that something is going on but he is too far away to hear what is being said, whatever it is it doesn't look good. He is making it his mission tonight to find out who that couple are and what the deal is with that prick and his attitude.

Once everybody is in, Neil leaves the cloakroom to find Jack, if anyone knows who they are he will, Jack knows everyone.

"Jack, who's the woman sitting at table three? She came in with the prick at the bar!"

Jack is standing at the stage where the auction will be making sure everything is set up,

"Table three, ehh not sure, and what prick? Personally I think there's a lot of them in here tonight." Neil snorts his laugh

"Aye well that is very true, but this one in particular is standing at the bar in the black suit,"

"Really! A black suit? Every man in here is wearing a black suit you idiot it is a black tie dinner!"

"Shut up, I know that, let me finish, the one carrying the red wine back to table three."

"Smart arse!"

"Yip! Now do you know him?"

"Aye, that's Nathan Low. He's a house builder, well, a luxury apartment builder. He buys up ground, builds apartments and charges extortionate amounts of money for them, he is like a trillionaire"

"Uh, so someone I can compete with then?" Neil feels the air leave his lungs when he realises who Nathan is, there is no way that he can compete with him and his money. The club keeps Neil comfortable but it doesn't give him crazy money like Nathan has, but there is still a flicker of hope in Neil's heart that says she isn't happy with Nathan and so maybe money isn't the be all and end all to her world, unlike some women.

"Well," Jack starts to say, his tone full of the promise of

gossip, "your description of him being a prick might not be far off the mark, apparently, he has a temper like nothing else and is known for his fists. Wait, why would you want to compete with him, you don't build houses, you don't build anything!"

"No, I know, I just didn't like the way he was treating the beauty on his arm." Neil's eyes drift over to look at Ava, just as she looks up and catches him looking, and again he sees the briefest of smiles pass her lips towards him. His heart actually stutters and he inwardly laughs at himself.

"Mmmm, and you think you can treat her better?" Jack is teasing slightly, but can see that his pal is quite serious about this, that is when he starts to get the knot in his gut!

"Well, I wouldn't mind trying."

Jack pats him on the back and walks away with a smirk, Neil is left standing there knowing full well he wants more than to try.

Nathan hands the wine to Ava and sits down with his hand on her back, rubbing very gently. It should be a sensual, comforting touch but instead every stroke makes Ava feel sick and worried, lulling her into a false sense of security and all. The auction starts in a flurry of action and the bids are going crazy, people bidding millions of pounds like it was single notes. Neil makes his way round the club collecting glasses and making small talk to some of the clientele. He gets to table three, Nathan has left the table to get another drink for himself and Ava is sitting looking down, twirling her wine glass slightly between her fingers, even the look of her slender fingers twirling the glass is enough to make Neil hard.

"Having a good night?" He aims for a pleasant customer service tone but instead ends up sounding like an awkward teenager. What is she doing to him, she is just sitting there and he can hardly string a sentence together in a proper man voice.

"Yes, thanks." Ava looks up from her glass to see the guy from the cloakroom, she smiles, he has the same look of desire in his eye as he did when he looked at her when they arrived. Blushing, she looks back down, inside she is torn, one side pleading with the rather handsome man in front of her not to linger talking to her as she doesn't want Nathan to see her talking to another man. His jealously would mean another argument, but, on the other side this guy's easy way, cute looks and those eyes that make her feel something that isn't fear, means she doesn't want him to leave.

"Can I get you another drink?" Neil asks now that he has regained control of his voice so he at least sounds like the twenty-five-year-old that he is and not the sixteen-year old he is acting like.

"No, No, I'm not allowed, em, no sorry my boyfriend won't let me, I mean he is at the bar." Ava lowers her face so this gorgeous guy can't see her shame. "Thanks anyway," she says softly as she peeks up through her lashes and smiles shyly at Neil, her whole face relaxes momentarily then it's gone and the anxious, wary, worried look is back as she looks to the bar. Neil follows her gaze to the bar and realises that the prick is staring at them; if looks could kill, he is pretty sure that he would be six feet under at that moment.

"Okay, just let me know if you need anything, I'm Neil." He holds his hand out for her to shake, but instead she looks to the bar again then snaps her head back,

"Thanks but I'm okay." The panic is rising in her throat, she tries to keep it from coming out in her voice or showing on her face but she is sure she doesn't quite manage it. Neil can feel the panic, stress and worry coming from her in waves, he nods slightly smiles and walks away. In his gut he knows something isn't right with this girl and her relationship with the prick, and he knows he will find out about them, he just isn't sure how!

The night continues with millions of pounds being spent left, right and centre, at the end of the night Neil is collecting glasses again, the auction has finished and most people are making their way home. Nathan and Ava are still sitting at table three when Neil walks past, he can hear a slightly muted argument, the prick is doing most of the talking with the beauty mumbling sorry every now and then. Neil brushes past Nathan and slightly bumps him. Nathan snaps, he pushes out from the table and starts raising his voice to Neil, "Watch what you're doing you idiot," he pauses for a bit, "Oh it's you, and who exactly do you think you are, talking to *my* girlfriend?"

"Oh I'm sorry, Sir, I didn't realise that we were still living in the eighteen hundreds and that your girlfriend needed permission to talk! And for your information, I am a manager here and so it is my job and privilege to talk to whomever I wish! Now if you don't mind the night has ended and we are trying to close up, thank you."

He turns to say goodnight to Ava as Nathan grabs his arm, "Excuse me, but, do you know who you are talking to?"

Neil can see that the guy is starting to lose his cool, his eyes are wide with anger and he is practically foaming at the mouth trying to rein himself in.

"To whom!" Neil says, his face is poker straight.

"What. What are you talking about?" Nathan's face is getting redder by the second much to Neil's amusement.

"To whom. What you should have said was 'do you know

to whom you are talking?' And yes I do Mr Nathan Low, but I do not really care, you are in *MY* club and you are being disrespectful to the beautiful woman on your arm."

Neil looks at Ava and smiles then looks back at Nathan with a smug look on his face – impressed with his witty comment– just in time to see Nathan's fist flying towards him. He manages to move, but not quite quick enough and Nathan's fist makes contact with his cheek. Even though Neil is a few inches smaller than Nathan, he has enough self-defence training under his belt. He grabs Nathan's fist and has his arm up his back and is frog marching him out the front door within seconds of the punch landing. Once they get outside Neil let's go of him.

"Stay!" Neil is growling now. "I will escort your girlfriend to you momentarily." He turns to the bouncers standing at the front doors and growls, "Keep him here!" Walking back in Neil thinks to himself, bouncers, huh, couldn't bounce a fucking ball! When he is back inside the main hall, Ava is standing at the table, she looks so worried it breaks Neil's heart looking at her.

"Sorry about that..." Neil stops for her to tell him her name, "Ava," she says so gently, everything about her is sweet and gentle and innocent.

"Ava," Neil says loving the way her name feels in his mouth.

"I would like to offer my apologies for the scene with your, eh, boyfriend. I refuse to have violence in my club." Neil realises that he has said, my, but he doesn't think that Ava has registered it; she just looks as if she is going to be sick.

"Are you okay Ava? You look a bit..."

"I'm fine." Ava cuts him off, she is trying her hardest to

sound and look fine but she doesn't think she is pulling it off, considering she can see the way she is shaking in the mirror behind the bar and the way her breathing is getting more rapid.

"Okay," Neil says guardedly, then he lowers his voice so it is just Ava who can hear him, "But, I think maybe you're a bit worried about how the rest of the night is going to go when you get home, so, I'm going to give you my card with all my numbers on it, home, here and my mobile. If you need me at any time, day or night, phone and I will be there for you, I promise."

Ava inhales sharply at his offer, then clears her throat,

"Oh, ehmm, sorry but what exactly do you think will happen when I get home, Neil?" Ava can't make up her mind if she is pissed at him or relieved that someone has noticed Nathan's behaviour towards her and is willing to give her support, and maybe even a way out?" Shit, maybe he has read the situation wrong, Neil thinks but his gut is still telling him otherwise

"I'm not sure Ava." He tries to keep his voice steady and reassuring, "But if your boyfriend's temper is anything to go by then, I just want you to have someone you can turn to, who, God willing, can protect you if need be." Neil looks down, frightened that he has said too much, looking up again, he sees Ava relax into a smile,

"Thank you," she says, her voice thick with emotion.

"Yeah, well, em, let me walk you to the door." Neil puts his hand on the small of Ava's back, he can feel the electricity spark between them. The need to save and protect this gorgeous woman doubling by the second. Ava feels the electricity and she also feels safe with his hands on her, she is completely overawed by these feelings and not sure what to make of them, but, she does realise that seeing Neil and feeling his hands on her has awakened feelings in her that she had forgotten were possible. It is with a heavy heart that she walks through the comfort of the gold and red lavish foyer of the club and out into the chill of the late September night and back into Nathan's arms.

CHAPTER TWO

By the time the Daimler pulls up outside Nathan's mansion, Ava feels sick with the silent brooding coming from Nathan. Ava walks through the front doors and starts up the very grand stairway, she jumps and stands absolutely still at the slam of the door and the roar of Nathan.

"And where the fuck do you think you are going you little slut?"

Wincing at the hatred in his voice, Ava turns on the stairs to speak, "I'm...I'm going to change." Her voice is low and timid, she avoids eye contact and starts to turn again, trying to escape up the stairs, or so she thinks. It doesn't take Nathan long to stride from the door to the first few stairs where Ava is turning. With one swift move, he has a hold of her hair, pushing her up the stairs. The growl coming from deep in his throat is a threat of what is to come. Once upstairs in the master bedroom, Nathan strikes out hard and fast with the back of his hand to her cheek. Ava's head reels from the blow, she tries to duck, move, anything to get out the line of fire, but she is not quick enough,

Nathan grabs her roughly by the wrist and drags her back towards him, "You little whore, who the fuck was that? Who was the fucking guy eh?"

Tears streaming down her face she tries to explain, "I don't know, honestly, I don't know!" Ava doesn't know where the blows are coming from anymore; they are just raining down on her. She continues, trying to explain that she doesn't know who he is or why he was speaking to her. But, it is to no avail, Nathan isn't listening to her, instead he is screaming obscenities at her, emphasising each word with a slap or a punch or a kick, spit flying everywhere with each insult of slut and whore and any other disgusting name he can think of. All Ava can do now is get into a ball and wait until it stops, protect her head and wait. Time seems to stand still for Ava, the blows coming down on her body are slowing, Nathan's breathing is hard and guttural from the exertion of the fight. He stops. Ava stays curled up in the foetus position wondering if he is done, doing mental checks in her body. Arms, sore but moving, legs, same, as long as she can move she will be fine, she can carry on, hide the bruises and make sure nobody notices – we don't want Nathan's business being affected by her being useless, he has his reputation to keep. She can hear Nathan breathing hard, she makes herself stay still – made that mistake before, getting up before he either says so or leaves the room, it just means an extra kick

"Stand up!" The hatred is still in his growl, normally the exhaustion takes it all away, she shakily gets to her feet, but obviously not quick enough for his liking,

"I said, fucking stand!" He grabs her elbow, grabbing clothes and skin in the process, dragging her up. "You really don't know who that wanker is then?"

"No," Ava tries to make her voice sound believable and not scared, but it just comes out as a squeak. Nathan exhales loudly and dips his head; he reaches out for Ava so tenderly her heart breaks another bit,

"I'm sorry, I really am sorry, it looked like you knew him, and he was looking at you…you know how I feel about other guys looking at you, and then he put me out and you were taking your time getting out, I thought, well you know what I thought, I thought you were WITH him."

Ava is staring at the floor; Nathan puts his finger under her chin and raises her head up to look at him. His face looks sorry but his eyes still have the hardness to them that frightens her, the thought flashes through her head, this might not be over!

"He was just asking if I had a good night," she lies, hoping that Nathan doesn't sense the lie, "Then he walked me out to the car."

"Okay, I believe you, you know I don't want to do what I do but sometimes I just can't help it. You know how much you mean to me. I can't take the chance that someone will come in and take you from me."

Ava just mumbles as the pain coursing through her makes it too sore for her to say much more. Nathan gives her a chaste kiss on her lips and leaves her standing to go and pour himself a drink.

Ava moves slowly into the en-suite off the master bedroom that they share. Looking in the mirror, she is astounded at what she sees, Nathan has never hit her face before, but tonight he has and what a mess he has made of it. She walks into the shower and gingerly washes her face, body and hair. She gets out, dries and climbs into bed and closes her eyes, only then does she break down – silently – the question of why going round and round her head until she falls into a fitful sleep. Nathan climbs in beside her in the early hours of the morning; he cuddles in and starts to rub his hand up and down her leg. She just lies there, awake, but praying he doesn't push the matter any further as her body and soul are too battered and tired for sex, plus she has lost all interest in Nathan in that way.

"Come on Ava, let me make it up to you, I want to apologise in the best way possible." Nathan's voice is husky and full of want. Knowing that that can change if he doesn't get his own way, Ava tries to appease him

"I'm tired Nathan."

"I know but I need this, I need to know that you forgive me and that you still love me!" He sounds like he is almost begging, so with a heavy heart, she turns around slowly and Nathan climbs on top.

****

Walking back through the club after seeing Ava out and locking the doors, a heaviness settles on Neil, he can't get the perfect face of Ava from his mind, but he also can't shake the feeling that something bad is going to happen to her because of him.

"You coming to cash up?" Jake is asking from the office door, but Neil doesn't hear him, he has too much going on in his head,

"Oi, dreamer, Neil, do you hear me? NEIL!" Jack is shouting now and laughing at the same time. He has seen his friend go a bit sloppy over women but this feels different, he seems to be on a different planet with this one and not all of that planet is good by the pain and fear that is crashing over his features.

"Neil!" he shouts again and this time Neil looks up,

"Eh, what?"

"I said are you coming to cash up or are you going to stand there dreaming of your lady in black?"

"Aye, I'm coming." Neil blows out his cheek and enters

the office. Technically, it is Jack's office because he runs the club, so it is Jack's pictures on the desk and photos on the walls, any paperwork Neil needs to do for the club is done at the office in his house. Jack has decorated the office very minimalistic, with a black and white colour scheme; he is sitting behind his black desk counting the takings from tonight,

"Here you check they bundles, a thousand pounds each." There are four bundles and Neil checks them all.

"We've had a good night don't you think?" Jack says, more of a statement than a question.

"Mmm? I suppose, though I am totally pissed at the bouncers, that incident with Ava never should have happened!"

"Oh Ava is her name, is it? How'd you get that information out of her, that Nathan prick wouldn't let anyone talk to her?"

"I know, I put the prick out on his ear for starting his pish, then told him I would walk Ava out to meet him."

Jack is laughing and shaking his head, "That, my boy, is a sly trick! Well done."

Neil smirks at his shrewdness, "I wanted to talk to her by herself, make sure she was okay. I have a horrible feeling that even though Nathan was pissed at me, he is going to take it out on her, and probably with his fists!" Saying the words aloud makes Neil want to throw up.

"How'd you work that one out then?" Jack is frowning at his friend, not liking what he is hearing.

"I saw some bruises on her arm when her shawl thing slipped a bit. They looked like finger marks."

Jack could feel concern mixed with worry starting in the pit of his stomach, trying to find another reason for the bruises he surmises out loud, "Well, maybe she likes the Dom/Sub thing, you know tied up and that?" Jack winks, trying to lighten the mood and ease the worry in his stomach, and the fear on his friend's face.

"I don't think so, but, anyway let's get this lot counted and get home."

Neil drives home, his classic 1985 red BMW E30 M3 making him feel loved, it might not be the flashiest Beamer on the street, but it's his and he loves every inch of it. He bought it dirt cheap as it was for the scrap heap and he has been working on it ever since, one day she will be perfect and Neil is looking forward to seeing her perfect but he is also not wanting it to finish as then he will no longer have anything to work on.

Driving always settles his brain and lets him switch off from any problems he has, but tonight there is still a scrap of thought about the beautiful Ava in his mind. Her black, pencil dress that came to mid-shin, her porcelain skin – except for the bruises – on show, the blueness of her eyes, the way they glittered when she smiled at him and those lips, tinged red with her lipstick. He gets out of his car, fixes himself, the thoughts of Ava has made things uncomfortable for him to walk in his jeans, and walks in to his house. Normally he would have a beer and something to eat but not tonight, tonight he grabs a beer from the fridge and heads to the shower, really wishing that it wasn't a shower on his own. He drains his beer, has a quick shower, gets dried and climbs into his queen size bed, where he lies awake, tossing and turning, not able to get the thought of Ava and what Nathan might be doing to her out of his head, until dawn when the exhaustion takes over and he falls into a fitful sleep full of dreams. Dreams of Nathan looming over Ava and Neil helpless behind glass, he is screaming like a lunatic for the prick to stop, as he rains blows down on her beautiful skin, turning the beautiful porcelain angry colours of red and black. Then the glass breaks and he has Ava in his arms, just them in a dark room, he is kissing her, hard, his kisses full of passion and desire, want and need, he feels himself hard against her and she is rubbing him, the full length of him, quicker and quicker until... the scream that rips from his body wakes him and he realises that it was a dream, a dream that got very wet very quickly. He laughs at himself, and mutters to the empty room,

"God what age am I, fifteen? Having wet dreams and waking up covered in my own spunk, Jesus!" He looks at the clock and realises that he has only been asleep for two hours, it is six o'clock in the morning and he is fully awake. He gets up and pads downstairs into the kitchen for a drink; all he can think about is Ava, how gorgeous her curves are, the way she looked down when he spoke to her. He desperately wanted to lift her chin until her eyes, those sparkling blue eyes, met his. He would touch, feel, kiss and cherish her until she screamed with pleasure, but first he needs to find out why she has those bruises on her and if that prick is involved. If they are down to his hand then God help him, Neil is going to have his head, and his balls.

****

Nathan has left by the time Ava wakes, she sighs with relief that she is alone. She feels crap inside and out. Getting out of bed, she winces as pain shoots through her body. Aching all over, she goes into the en-suite and looks at her reflection in the mirror, what she sees makes a whimper escape from her swollen lips. She doesn't recognise the girl staring back at her, her eyes are black and swollen, her lips burst and have crusts of dried blood on them, and the bruises emerging on her arms and torso are black. She crumples to the floor and cries, deep, heart-wrenching screams coming from her belly, deep, deep down in her soul. All she can think is why? Why, why, why her?

Nathan goes about his business all day making deals, buying ground, seeing over the new apartments that his company is building. All day he has this nagging feeling at the back of his head. To a normal person they would recognise the feeling as guilt, but to an egotistical, power-hungry, abusive person like Nathan, he thinks it is just the feeling of pity for the stupid cow whose fault it is that he lost his temper a bit last night. He has done nothing wrong; she pushes his buttons making him angry at her and HIM, Neil, the asshole in that crappy club. Fucking cunt, thinking he can touch his property, thinking he is good enough to fucking talk to him let alone tell him what to do and then putting him out the club like a common drunkard, well he'll show him, he will be coming for that crappy club, he will shut it down and leave the asshole to rot in the gutter!

Ava busies herself with tidying up, they do have someone to do all of the cleaning, but it helps to keep her mind off Nathan and his fists. Every time she catches sight of her reflection in a mirror or a window, she breaks down another bit. Going through her handbag from the night before, she notices the business card that the guy, Neil, from last night gave her. She takes it to the bed and climbs in, she has her mobile in her hand, she stares at both of them, just sitting there for what feels like hours, but is actually only about five minutes, staring at the name on the card – Neil Alexander –

thoughts whirling about her head, *"Could he help me?"* Ava thinks to herself, *"No, nobody can help me, Nathan knows everybody, and anyway why would he want to help me, Nathan is right I'm not all that and what can I offer him other than being a nuisance?"* But the worry in his eyes last night when he gave her his card, the hint of concern in his voice when he said to contact him if she had any problems, the feeling running up and down her spine when he had his hand on the small of her back, and the smile he gave her when she walked in to the club at first, surely they all mean something? She inputs his number, but doesn't press dial. She is still having an internal battle about whether or not to phone Neil when her finger slips and she hears the ringing sound coming from her phone, she can't move, she didn't mean to press the dial button – did she? – Then she hears his voice, muffled because she is holding her phone in her lap,

"Hello? Hello? This is Neil here, can I help you?"

Ava put the call on speakerphone, "Hello," she squeaks,

"Hi, who is this?" His voice is soft and she can tell that Neil has clicked as to who has phoned him.

"Is that you Ava?" Silence for a heartbeat, "Don't worry you don't need to say anything if you don't want to, or can't, but please know that I'm glad you phoned, if you want to talk, we can, but if not, then at least you know I am here at the end of this phone whenever you need me."

She cuts him off from talking anymore; she needed to talk before she lost the small amount of nerve she has managed to build up. "I think I may need help." Her voice is quiet and quivers with emotion, but under it all Neil can hear a determination to fight – even if she can't.

Neil holds his breath, he can't believe that she has actually called or spoken,

"Okay, what do you need? Do you want me to come and get you?" Neil closes his eyes, worried he might have pushed her too quickly,

"I, I, I, don't know, exactly but he hit my face last night, he has never hit my face before, that's not good is it?" Ava needs to get all of this out in the one breath or she won't say it at all, she needs to hear someone not connected to her or Nathan tell her that she can do this, she can leave, it's not her fault, it's not her and she isn't worthless!

"Hitting you anywhere is wrong, and if this is the first time he has hit your face then yes he is escalating which means he is probably only going to get worse, he may have broken his own rule about hitting your face and if so it will get worse, believe me, I know!"

There is something in Neil's voice that makes Ava stop, he sounds like he actually knows what it's like to feel like this.

"How do I know it's not me? I mean, I make him so—" her voice breaks and she can't go on, at the other end of the phone, Neil's heart is breaking listening to this gorgeous woman blame herself for getting a beating, it makes his blood boil. Knowing it can take years to get the thoughts out of your head, he is desperate to get a start on removing them from Ava's and proving to her just how worthy she really is.

"I promise you, Sweet, there is nothing you do or don't do to make him go there and do that to you, it is all him, I promise."

Ava can hear the front door close downstairs, she flicks her eyes to the clock, three pm, is that him?, She listens, hardly breathing, then she hears Nathan call her name, panic sets in and she whispers down the phone that she needs to go and then hangs up. She puts Neil's card in her underwear drawer and gets off the bed, leaving the room and going to the top of the staircase,

"Oh there you are darling; I thought maybe you were out." Nice Nathan is back, he always is nice after he beats her. Ava's heart slams into her chest, praying that Neil understood her mumbled end to their conversation and not try to phone her back.

****

Jack walks into his office, he knows Neil is in there as he can hear him talking on the phone, he can only guess that it is to the woman from last night, and from what he can hear she is in trouble and his friend is going to move heaven and hell to help her. Jack feels the worry he felt last night only this time it is for the girl and his friend. Something has started with Neil, and he hopes that Neil can get through it relatively unscathed, as Nathan Low isn't the type of man to mess with, he has the money and the friends to get away with murder.

"Hello, hello, Ava, are you there? Shit!" Neil throws his phone on the desk and puts his head in his hands, exhaustion washing over him, mostly due to the lack of sleep, but also with the worry and the adrenalin leaving his body.

"You alright boss?" Jack asks as he walks into the office, he can feel the air is heavy with worry when he sits down.

"That was Ava." Neil points to his phone, then looks up, "She said he hit her face last night, that that was the first time he has done that, you know what that means don't you?"

Jack knows that was more of a statement than a question, he knows the history of Neil and his dad, he has spent countless nights drinking with Neil while he tried to get the ugly thoughts of uselessness from his head, the need to understand why his dad beat him and his mum and also beat the fear that he would turn out the same as his old man. Thank God for BMW, and the re-building of his car or their livers would be pickled!

"What you gonna do?" Jack asks warily, not sure he wants to know the answer.

"Help, somehow, I canny phone back, I think Nathan just came home and that's why she hung up"

Jack nods, "So are you just going to wait till she gets back to you?"

"Yeah, think so, unless I can find her."

CHAPTER THREE

A week has passed since Ava phoned Neil, she has picked up the phone to do it again many times, but she has never had the confidence to actually go through with it. Nathan has been on his best behaviour, he hasn't come near her, violently or sexually and for that, Ava is very happy. It is the first Friday night in October, so Nathan is going out with friends as they do every month. Normally, Ava's only friend comes to see her on these nights but her face is still bruised and swollen so she has cancelled, feigning illness

Ava is relaxing in the huge bath with her book when Nathan enters to say goodbye, "I think it's best that you stay in yourself tonight, don't you?" His tone is questioning but also accusatory. He doesn't want anybody to see Ava's face, so he has banned her from going out all week.

"Yes, I have cancelled on Claire again and I'm just staying in with my book."

"What do you mean, AGAIN? You say that like you have had to cancel on Claire all the time!"

Ava can see the anger rising in Nathan's eyes, "No I didn't mean that, it's just I cancelled last month because I wasn't well," the panic in her voice is as clear as a bell.

"And that was my fault was it?" More accusations from nowhere – maybe from his own guilt but Nathan doesn't give heed to guilt.

"No, I didn't say that," Her panic taking over now Ava starts to get up out of the bath, Nathan pushes her back down, water splashing over the sides of the bath,

"Listen Cow, I never made you sick last month so you can stop your fucking lying."

"When did I lie to you?" Confusion and panic make the words come from her lips before her head realises she is talking.

"When don't you fucking lie to me?" Nathan snarls at her, "You lied when you said you didn't know that idiot from last week, but you both looked very friendly when he walked you out of the club"

"I told you I don't know—" the rest of her sentence is lost when the back of Nathan's hand makes contact with her cheek. Pain explodes in Ava's head, water flying all over the bathroom. Nathan's hands are on her shoulders, pushing her down under the water, she is struggling for grip, trying to find something to hold onto, anywhere on the bath to stop herself from going under but there is nothing, nothing but pain, panic and water, water in her mouth, up her nose, everywhere. He drags her back up out of the water, she is coughing and choking water streaming from her nose and mouth as she tries to get the water out her lungs and the air in,

"Stop fucking pushing my buttons you stupid cow, one of these days you are going to make me do something a lot more serious than a slap and you will only have yourself to blame! Now, look what you have done, I need to go change, as you've got me all wet. So once I've done that I'm away."

Nathan stands, straightens his suit jacket turns and walks out of the bathroom; he is hardly even out of breath.

Ava sits there in the half-empty bath until she hears the front door close, then she explodes into a mass of screams and crying, until there is no sound left in her. She eventually gets out the bath dries, dresses, then gets her phone. Hands shaking she texts Neil. *Can I come to you?*

She presses send, then stops dead, "What have I done?" She is talking aloud to herself, panicking in case Neil gets back to her but worrying that he doesn't. Thoughts running through her head of why? Why text this guy? She only met him a week ago, why not Claire, her friend, then she remembers, how Neil made her feel safe, he seemed to understand, also he isn't connected to Nathan or anyone who knows Nathan. Maybe, she hopes, that Nathan can't or won't get to him. Her woman's intuition is screaming at her that her way out is Neil, so she is going to listen to it, and hope that this stranger is her answer.

Neil's phone buzzes just as he parks the car outside the club, he is about to start a shift to help out with the party that is in full swing inside He lifts his phone from the passenger seat where he threw it after he spoke to Julie. The crazy ex-girlfriend is still banging on about being pregnant, but won't prove it or tell Neil how far gone she is. Considering they haven't had sex in two months he is pretty sure that the odds are the baby won't be his, that is if there even is a pregnancy, and not just a ploy to get money! Looking at his phone his heart starts slamming into his chest as his stomach free falls to the floor of his BMW. The text from Ava staring back at him, his mind is in a spin, what has happened? has he hit her again?, has she decided to leave him, and if so then why? He starts to phone her then hangs up quickly, confused if he should text or phone, maybe he is there, and listening in, because of that thought he decides on a text,

Of course, do you want me to pick you up? Phone me if you can.

Seconds later his phone goes.

"Are you okay, what happened, has he hit you again?" Neil's voice is changing from panic to sheer anger.

Ava on the other hand sounds calm, serene almost, "Can you come and get me please?"

Neil is taken aback by just how calm Ava sounds, he suspects something has happened and she is working on shock and or autopilot.

"Yes of course I can where?"

"The Oaks, Royal Gardens, Bothwell. I will be at the end of the drive way outside the gates."

Wow Neil thought, that is an address and a half! "Ok, I can be there in about twenty minutes, stay safe, I *will* get you. I take it he isn't there?"

Neil is out of his car and pushing into the club, he needs to let Jack know that he won't be in tonight and why. His adrenalin is pulsing through his veins making everything seem unreal and too fast.

"No, he is away out for the night, he won't be back till late, please come, I don't want to change my mind!" Her plead pulls Neil to a standstill, he knows that feeling exactly, he knows that when you are trying to get away the slightest thing can knock your confidence about leaving and make it all too hard and scary.

"I'll be there," his voice is steady and sure, "I promise, I will get you away from there."

"Okay." Ava sighs this last word and then there is silence.

Neil rushes into the club searching for Jack, he spots him at the bar, but, just as he gets to him, he notices Nathan standing talking to him. Nathan turns slightly to see Neil and smiles, even his smile is vile looking, he thinks, he just looks sly and sleekit and like a prick! Neil plasters his service smile on his face and says good evening, and turns to Jack, "A word boss"

"Aye, whits up?" Jack knows there is something wrong with his best friend; he just wasn't expecting what came next.

"I canny work tonight, I need to go." Neil has Jack by the elbow and is dragging him towards the front door.

"What'd you mean you, canny work, is it because of that arse at the bar?" Jack is confused, Neil has never blown of his shift before, obviously, he doesn't need to work, it's his club, but, never has he just pulled out last minute like this!

"Yes, no, kinda, I need to go and collect Ava, she called me, I think something else has happened and she wants out."

The bad feeling in Jacks stomach has returned, "You do realise her boyfriend is standing in there, in your club, at this party?"

"I know, I saw him, but I need to get her. Can you please just keep him here? I'll get Ava and take her to my place, then I'll text you when we're home."

Jack rolls his eyes and takes a deep breath. "Okay...are you sure you know what you're doing, and why you're doing this?"

"What'd you mean?"

"Are you doing this to be the white knight in shining

40

armour, saving the damsel in distress, 'cause, pal, this ain't Disney and you will get hurt. She won't want a relationship with anyone after getting out an abusive one, and if she does will it be because you saved her?"

Jack doesn't mean to sound as bitchy as he is making it sound, but he is worried about his friend and the uneasiness in his stomach is growing!

"I can't leave her in danger!" Neil knows he is snapping but he can't help himself he needs to be on the road getting to Ava and think about all this crap later, but he does know his friend is just looking out for him, "and anyway I'm not taking her to my house just to get my leg over, I want her safe – end of!"

Jack holds his hands up in defence, "Okay, okay, I understand, I just don't want you getting hurt, physically or emotionally, and Nathan Low has the money and the status to know bad folk, and he doesn't like losing! But you know I always got your back, so, go, go save the girl" Jack is waving his hands in a shooing motion.

Neil slaps him on the back and smiles, "Cheers man, let me know if he leaves before I get back to you." And with that, Neil is running to his car and screeching out of the car park.

With a sigh and a shake of his head, Jack turns and walks back into the club. Looking up he see Nathan walking towards him, his hand outstretched for a hand shake.

"Jack." His tone friendly, but with an undertone of calculation mixed in.

"Yes, how can I help Mr Low?" Jack is full of smiles, but the uneasy feeling is still there and still growing with every second of this conversation.

"I was wondering if I could have a word with you, just a

bit of business."

"Of course, step into my office. Would you like a drink?" Jack motions to one of the waiting staff – ever the professional – and thinking to himself, 'what a great time to have a meeting with the enemy, since my crazy best friend is away saving his girlfriend'.

"Have a seat Mr Low, what can I do for you tonight?"

"I was wondering Jack, would it be yourself that I speak to about buying the club."

Shock flashes over Jack's face, did he hear right, Nathan Low is asking to buy the club. The chill of worry that has been gnawing away at Jack has doubled, he knows this has something to do with Neil and the other week; he is just not sure what Nathan knows or what his plan is.

"The club isn't for sale, Nathan." No more pampering to this prick calling him Mr Low, and trying to be respectful, he doesn't deserve the respect,

"I have a sleeping partner and so I wouldn't consider any offer on the club." Nathan's face hardens slightly, but then the smarmy smile takes over.

"I would make it worth both you and your partner's time. Money is no object Jack, name your price!" Confidence and smarm oozing out of every pore.

"Money doesn't interest me, Nathan, or my partner. I am sorry to disappoint, but, the club IS NOT for sale, end of story!"

"Okay, Jack, if you won't sell me the club then maybe you could help me with a member of your staff!"

****

Neil races to the address in Bothwell, Ava is standing outside the gates just like she said she would be, one small holdall sitting beside her on the pavement. Neil jumps out and runs to Ava bundling her into his arms and holding her close to his chest. Ava lets herself be held and breaks down, the stress leaching out of her body as a warm safe feeling seeps in. Once the sobs wracking her body slow, Neil pulls back slightly so he can look into her face, the need to kiss her is overwhelming, but Neil resists, he bends, picks up her holdall takes her hand and walks her to his car.

Ava climbs in, settling in to the soft leather of the BMW, knowing she should probably be feeling something, but she doesn't, she is just numb.

"What happened?" Neil asks when he gets in the driver's side.

Ava looks down, "He crossed another line, he, he—" She breaks down again; Neil just sits quietly but reaches out and gives her hand a squeeze.

"Take your time, it's okay."

"Do you mind if we drive please, I just want to be away from here?"

"Aye, no problem, buckle up."

The drive to Neil's house in Kings Park only takes eight minutes, as the roads are so quiet; even so, Ava is sleeping before they arrive. Neil strokes her arm gently and she comes to with a start, but relaxes slightly when she realises that she is in Neil's car and not at the house.

"You okay Sweet?" Neil's voice is soft and warm.

"Where are we?" Ava is still sleepy and her voice is thick with sleep.

"My house, in Kings Park, Nathan is at the club, so don't worry he doesn't know where you are."

She nods silently.

"Do you want to go in or is there somewhere else you would rather go?" Desperate that she says she happy to be with him, Neil is holding his breath. The desire to protect this gorgeous woman in his car is like nothing he has ever felt before.

"If you don't mind can I stay here?" Ava's voice is quiet and unsure, "I mean it will only be for tonight, I'll organise something else, I just didn't know where, or who else to turn to."

Neil turns in his seat so he is facing her and takes her hands reassuring her, "Ava it is okay, you can stay here as long as you need. You will be safe here, I promise, come on in to the house out of the cold." They get out of the car, Neil lifting her bag and they walk into Neil's house, "I'm sorry it's a bit of a mess, I wasn't expecting company, erm, I know it's not what you're used to, but, it's home to me." Neil looks down feeling embarrassed at his house. This is a first for him, he is normally happy with his lot in life, he works hard, his club does well, he has never wanted more than what he has or what he has worked for, but knowing what Ava is used to is making him doubt his worth.

"It's lovely, you don't need to worry, this is a house that is lived in and not just existed in! Do you live alone?" Looking around, Ava can't see any signs of anybody but Neil in the cosy living room.

"Yes just me, I do have a spare room, don't worry about the, eh, sleeping arrangements" Neil is actually feeling embarrassed and can feel his cheeks going red, he hadn't thought about the sleeping arrangements when he dashed to save Ava, he just wanted her safe.

The smile that shadows Ava's face relaxes her features and lights up her eyes, "It's okay, the couch would be fine, I wasn't expecting you to give up your bed for me, but if there is a spare bed then that's even better."

Neil picks up her bag and takes her to the room she will be using.

The room is set up as a bedroom with a double bed and decorated in browns and creams, all thanks to Julie, his crazy ex, but it was only ever used when she fell out with Neil and she made him sleep in the spare bed in his own house, and he did it to keep the peace. Neil stands at the door,

"I'll just go back downstairs, let you get settled. Em if you need me I'm just downstairs. Oh the bathroom is just down the hall." He turns to leave but stops and turns back, "Would you like a drink or food or something?" He was floundering like a fish out of water and he knew it, he just wanted to help, but wasn't sure what was best for Ava.

"Yeah a drink would be lovely, a brandy or a whisky would be perfect, I'm just going to get changed, if that's okay."

"Yeah that fine, I have Highland Park, twenty-one years, is that okay?"

"Oh you don't have to get out the good stuff just for me; I'm fine with a blended whisky, Grouse or Bells." She looks to the floor, "I'm not normally allowed to drink anything but one glass of red wine and definitely not a whisky, that's a man's drink, and women shouldn't drink men's drink!"

Neil's eyebrows draw together, the disbelief on his face visible,

"So if whisky is a man's drink than what the hell is a women's drink?"

"Gin and Tonic!"

They both burst out laughing at the stupidity of what has been a rule that Ava has had to live by, and for that very reason, she is looking forward to having a rather nice whisky to relax with for the first time in too many years.

"It's fine, I have a club, and anyway I don't drink blended whisky, so I'm afraid it is Highland Park or Irn Bru."

"Well I guess it will be a Highland Park then."

Amusement dances in Ava's eyes, she can see how hard Neil is trying to make her feel at home and can see how tense he is, but seeing her laugh seemed to make him relax ever so slightly, maybe it was her imagination, but she didn't think so.

"Ok then, I'll go and get it sorted, take your time though you don't need to rush, it's okay. Okay, right well...I'm sorry I'm just aye!" And with a shake of his head, he closes the door and starts to walk downstairs, berating himself for being so antsy.

In the room Ava sits on the bed and puts her head in her hands, she fully expects the tears to come but they don't, she must have used them all, or maybe it is because she is glad to have some time on her own, after all it was only two hours ago Nathan had pushed her under the water in the bath tub and now she is standing in Neil's spare room after only talking to him two or three times on the phone and only actually meeting him once. Crazy? Yes but she couldn't think of anyone else who would help and he made her feel safe, something she hadn't felt in years.

Neil is downstairs in the kitchen sorting the drinks; he brings them into the living and sit on one of the couches and phones Jack.

CHAPTER FOUR

"Neil, how's things?" Jack is still sitting in his office, after getting rid of the pompous, arrogant arsehole that is Nathan. Wanting to buy the club, who does he think he is? Thinking he has got nothing better to do than click his fingers and the club will be his, aye that will be right!

"I've got her home, she is upstairs getting…I don't know, whatever women do. She was upset and shaking when I picked her up but she seems to have calmed down a bit now. How's things there?"

"Party's going well, but, I had Nathan in here asking questions!" Jack was feeling anxious about telling Neil about his conversation with Nathan, but knew he had to tell him, it is his club after all, so his only hope is that Neil is too busy saving the girl to come down to the club to take Nathan's head from him. Jack knew Neil would never sell the club; it was proof to himself that he wasn't useless; he could do something with his life other than be a punch bag for his father.

"Oh aye, what kind of questions?"

Jack could tell that his best friend's hackles were up even through the phone. "Eh, well questions about the club, he was asking about buying it," Jack held the phone away from his ear in anticipation of the explosion that he knew would be coming from the other end of it, but all he heard was silence, eerie silence, no explosion. Jack put the phone back to his ear, "Neil? You there?"

"I'm here"

"Did you hear me? He wants—"

Neil snaps in, "I heard! Why does he want the Daydream? What the fuck is he playing at?" The anger in Neil is bubbling up, threating to explode and he is fighting hard to suppress it, as he knows he has to keep it together, Ava is upstairs and frightened as it is with violence, so the last thing she needs is the person who is saving her from the violence to explode in an angry rage.

Jack continues, "He says that money is no object, and he can make us an offer we can't refuse, we just need to name our price."

"US? What do you mean US? Did you tell him about me? Jack you know—" Neil can really feel the tension in his shoulders increasing with the anger that he is barely controlling,

Jack interrupts, Neil's rant, "Why would I do that ya wee dick!" He is nearly shouting at his best friend now, not through anger but frustration, Neil knows he would never mention his name in connection with the ownership of the Daydream club, "No, I said I had a sleeping partner and that neither of us are interested in selling the club or money."

Neil lets out a sigh, "Thanks pal, I know you wouldn't say anything, it's just him, he's a prick!" Neil's breathing and tension had eased slightly with Jack calling him out and calling him a dick. He is the only one who can call him that and even more, so that is what Jack says to rein Neil in when his anger is getting the better of him.

"What did he say to that?" Neil is calmer now, "I guess he's not used to hearing the word no, and likes it even less."

Neil hears the living room door open behind him; he turns

round to see Ava standing in the doorway. She has one of his jumpers on and a pair of his jammie bottoms, she looks so vulnerable standing there in his clothes, he never thought that seeing his jammies could be a sexy sight, but, seeing Ava's gorgeous curves filling them out in all the right places has him hot under the collar. His breath catches in his throat, and then the thought of anyone hurting her makes his heart break.

"Neil, you there?"

Neil has zoned out of his conversation with Jack as he looks at Ava standing there, he clears his throat. "Eh, aye, what're you saying?" He mouths to Ava that it's Jack on the phone, and stands to go into the kitchen, motioning for Ava to sit on the couch. Once in the kitchen he could carry on with the conversation, "He said that if I wouldn't sell the club then I have to get you fired or he will get the club shut down!"

Neil bursts out laughing, "No shit, he wants me fired from my own club, aye very good. Right leave it with me; tell him you will look into it. I better go Ava came downstairs, so I'm going to try to get her to eat something."

"Okay, you coming in to cash up?"

"No, not tonight, you come over here when you've locked up and we can do it here."

"Cool, see you later, and Neil," Jack's tone is full of warning, "be careful, this guy knows folk!"

Neil smiles, his friend always does have his back. "I know, I know, it'll be alright." The confidence in Neil's voice is a lot stronger that any of the men actually feel.

Neil puts his phone on the kitchen table, lifts the drinks and returns to the living room. Ava is still sitting on the edge of the brown leather couch, wringing her hands together. Neil sits beside her and puts the drinks on the coffee table in front of them, he takes her hands in his, "How you doing Sweet?"

His voice is soft and full of concern.

"Erm, okay, I think. I'm not exactly sure how I feel to be honest."

"I know, Sweet, I know, it will get easier, you will realise that you are better off away from him, and you will start to believe in yourself again, I promise."

Ava relaxes slightly; she picks up her drink, takes a sip and puts it down,

Neil continues, "You want to talk about it, about what happened?" His voice is gentle.

She turns slightly in her seat, reaching out for her drink, then places her other hand on Neil's, "Well," she starts slowly and quietly.

Neil stutters in, "You don't need to if you don't want to, or can't, it just might help to get it out. I'm sorry, I'm a man I'm rubbish at this sort of stuff."

She smiles, a real smile, the first for a while. "It's okay; I think you deserve an explanation about why I phoned you. As I said he crossed another line," Neil stays quiet, but does notice that she is still holding his hand. "I was in the bath, I was meant to be having a friend round but I had to cancel due to this mess." She points to the fading bruises on her face and arms, "He came into the bathroom to say goodbye as he was going out. He said about Claire coming over, or not coming over, I explained to him that I had already cancelled, but this was the second time I had done this to her, as I cancelled last month because I was unwell, and he went off on one, shouting that it wasn't his fault I was unwell and had had to cancel. I can't really remember the rest of what he said because he back handed me, then grabbed my shoulders and pushed me under."

Neil was mid sip of whisky when Ava said about Nathan pushing her under the water, the warm liquid felt like it had got stuck in his throat, he swallows hard and then the bellowing is out of his mouth before he realises that it is coming from him.

"The fucker did what?"

Ava jumps with the shock of Neil raising his voice; she pulls her hands away and shrinks into herself.

Neil mentally kicks himself for his outburst, but, the thought of the him pushing her under the water was more than he could handle, "Oh Ava I'm so sorry, I am so, so sorry, I didn't mean to frighten you, it's just – urgh – him!"

Ava tries to relax and manages slightly, "I know, it's okay, but yeah, he kept pushing until I was completely under, he held me there for a few seconds, but it felt like more. I was thrashing about and then he stopped and pulled me back up, growling something about being wet and left to change. I thought about what you said, about him and his violence escalating and I thought what is the next step for him? Would he not pull me up but just keep pushing me under? I've stayed too long and put up with too much, but, when he starts threating my life, well—" She leaves the sentence hanging in the air between them; she takes a sip of her whisky.

Neil is slightly stunned at hearing what happened to her and it brings back bad memories of his father, many he had thought he had buried, "Why phone me? I mean, I don't mind and I'm glad I could come and get you, I wouldn't just leave you in that situation, but, you don't know me, we've only met once and spoken twice, three times if you count tonight."

"I know, but, I don't have anybody else. Nathan made sure of that. My mum and dad died four years ago." There is sadness in her voice and tears welling in her eyes, she drains her glass and then continues, "Plus I had a feeling that you understand the feeling of being in an abusive relationship?" Ava looks up at Neil, he stiffens and shuffles in his seat, clearing his throat, but he refuses to look down or lower his head, he is not that wee boy anymore.

He looks Ava in the eyes, pure determination shining out, "Yes, unfortunately I do, so please don't worry about anything. You needed someone to be there for you the way Jack was there for me, so here I am." Neil opens his arms to show he is there for her.

"Thanks," Ava's voice is cracking and her eyes are welling again.

"Do you want to contact the police?" Neil knows how difficult this decision is, so he is making sure his voice is level and that he asks the question very carefully.

"I don't know, to be honest. Part of me says yes, as he has gotten away with beating me for too long, but another part of me says no, as I have only ever involved the police once and it was worse for me in the end, and in the end, it is his word against mine. It is Nathan Low we are talking about, he has the money and the friends and everything to get away with it and make life hell for all of us. The thought makes me feel sick!"

"I understand, I do, but, I do think you should get it documented, just in case, I mean I don't think we've heard the last of him."

Ava thinks about this for a bit, "Yeah, you're probably right, but tomorrow please?" It is almost a beg coming from her lips,

Neil gives her a hand another gentle squeeze, "No trouble, I'll drive you to the station tomorrow."

"You don't need to do that, surely you have work to go to, I can get a taxi or the bus."

Neil is shaking his head, "Eh naw, I promised you I would support you through all of this and I will, anyway I can come and go with the club whenever I want."

Ava gives him a strange look but doesn't question him about his work at the club. Which he is thankful for after all his slips of the tongue.

"Right I'll go get us another whisky, would you like something to eat?"

Ava straightens and stiffens as she tries to get off the couch. "Oh, I'm sorry, I probably should have had dinner started, I'll do it just now." Panic washes over her.

"Hey." Neil keeps his voice soft as he gently pushes her back onto the couch, "I didn't ask you to make dinner, I asked you what you wanted for dinner, I'm making dinner, or phoning it, depending on whatever you want, and…" He puts his fingers under her chin lifting it slightly so she would make eye contact with him, "You have nothing to apologise for, you have done nothing wrong, okay?" Anger starting again in his belly at the thought of Nathan making her this fearful, she tries to smile, her eye shinning with unshed tears,

"Yeah, just force of habit I suppose. Em I would like Chinese if that is okay?"

"Well Chinese it is then!"

****

Nathan slams through his front door, "Ava? Ava? Where are you?" He is furious at the conversation with that idiot in the club. Telling *him* he's not selling the club, well he'll see about that, that club will be shut down whether it's because he owns it or he has it arranged!

"Ava, where the fuck are you?" his anger is at boiling point and quickly turning towards Ava. He storms upstairs, taking two at a time, screaming at the top of his lungs, slamming doors open to all the rooms in the upper floor. "Where are you, you little slut?" He slams into the only room that he hasn't checked, the master bathroom, the one he left her after he pushed her under the water in the bath. "You in here cow?" Silence, Nathan stops in his tracks, his breathing hard from running up the stairs and shouting so much, looking about the bathroom shelves at the sink he notices something missing, her toothbrush. A cold shiver runs up his spine, "She wouldn't!" he growls under his breath, his anger getting the better of him he raises his voice, "She wouldn't fucking dare!" he shouts, his words echoing round the empty bathroom. He slams back out into the hall and into the master bedroom, kicking the door open as he goes, wrenching the huge wardrobe doors open he steps inside, checking for missing clothes, from there he grabs her drawers emptying their contents into the middle of the king size bed. He sees the card sitting in the middle of the little bundle of underwear that Ava had left. Picking it up he turns it round in his fingers, reading the name embossed on it – Neil Alexander. "You bastard!" he roars at the ceiling, Pulling his phone out of his pocket he speed dials his lawyer, "That club I was speaking to you about, the one I want, well you get me it or you find a way of getting it shut down, and you get it done for tomorrow!" Nathan is foaming at the mouth with anger and hatred as he shouts down the phone at his lawyer.

"Nathan I can't just—"

"Just get it fuckin done you have one week!" He cuts the call and then dials the number on the card.

Neil's phone rings, he lifts it from the coffee table and answers it, "Hello."

"You bastard, where is she?" Nathan is snarling the words down the phone at Neil

"I'm sorry, but who is this?" Neil knows who it is, and he is up out of his seat heading towards the kitchen and closing the door behind him. Ava is lounging on the couch continuing to watch the film that they have put on. The last thing she needs is to know who it is on the phone.

"You know who this is, so tell me, is she with you?"

"I don't know what or who you are talking about." The mantra in Neil's head is, keep calm and deny, keep calm and deny.

"Like fuck you don't know, Ava where is she? She better not be with you or so help me I will mess you up."

"I haven't heard from her, but I'm guessing she's left your sorry arse then? Well good, she deserves so much more than an abusive prick like you. So if you don't mind, I am going back to watch my film, and please NEVER, contact me again!" Neil manages to keep his voice calm and cuts off the call. He sits down at the breakfast bar, his legs turning to jelly. How the hell did Nathan get his phone number, does that mean he knows where he stays? "Ah shite!" he mumbles. He walks back into the living room trying his damndest to act natural so Ava doesn't suspect anything is wrong, but he doesn't have to worry about that as he is faced with her sound asleep on his couch. He stands and watches her breath in and out, this is the most peaceful he has seen her, no frown, no stress, just completely relaxed.

He lifts her up and she wakes slightly, "Shh, it's okay, I'm just taking you upstairs to bed, I don't mean that the way it came out."

She smiles a shy smile and closes her eyes again.

Neil takes her upstairs and lays her on the bed in the guest room, after placing a gentle kiss on her forehead he turns and walks out, closing the door behind him. He goes back downstairs and pours himself another drink. He settles down on the couch and starts to think.

At two o'clock, the front door opens and Jack walks in, he sees Neil sitting on the couch, his head in his hands.

"You okay boss?"

Neil looks up at his best friend. "Aye, well," he lets out a strange chuckle, "Got a phone call from Nathan asking where Ava is and if she is with me."

"What! Where did he get your number? What did he say? Does Ava know?" Jack's questions are coming at Neil like a machine gun.

"I don't know where he got the number, my best guess is the business card I gave Ava, I didn't really give him a chance to say anything, I told him I didn't know where she was and hung up. And no Ava doesn't know about the call, thank God!"

"Mmmm, okay, so what we going to do then?"

Neil looks up at Jack, "Us? You don't need to get involved in this, this is my problem, it's my choice to get involved, in getting her away from him and the abuse."

"Eh, I don't think so, I'm obviously going to help you, I've never abandoned you any time before when you have needed me, so I ain't going anywhere this time…ya wee dick!"

They both burst out laughing, a nervous, strained and stressed laugh but a laugh all the same. Laughing always gets them through their tough times.

They count the takings and Neil puts it in the house safe, then they sit down to plan what they should do about Nathan, Ava and the Daydream.

CHAPTER FIVE

Ava woke feeling rested, she opened her eyes and looked about, she didn't recognise the brown and cream double bedroom she was in, it took her a second to remember where she was, and why. She got out of bed, and padded down the stairs in the baggy jumper and PJ bottoms she'd found in the master bedroom next door to the one she was in. It was decorated in reds and greys, she's not sure if this colour scheme was picked by Neil, it didn't seem to suit him. As she was pacing the bedroom, she noticed that the bed hadn't been slept in, and panicked a bit, did he leave? Walking into the living room she is confronted by the two men spread out on a couch each, that explained why the bed wasn't slept in, both of them are sound asleep. Shaking her head at the sight of the pair of them, she walks into the kitchen and starts hunting for the kettle and the coffee. She sees that Neil has a machine, one of the fancy coffee making things that make all different types. Neil walks into the kitchen behind her, stretching his hands above his head, showing off his slightly toned stomach.

"Morning, Sweet how you feeling today?"

Ava turns around at the sound of Neil's voice; she notices his bare skin where his T-shirt has ridden up with his stretch. She quickly averts her eyes, "Sorry, I didn't mean to wake you." She can feel her cheeks flush at seeing his stomach. "Is it okay to make some coffee?"

"Aye of course it is, do you know how to use it?" Ava nods, there was a similar one at Nathan's house, though she only used it a few times.

"It's okay, you didn't wake me, I've always been a light sleeper," he lies, he normally sleeps soundly, but last night he hardly got any sleep thinking about Nathan, his threat and what to tell Ava. "You don't need to apologise, and you don't need to ask for anything here, please treat this place like your own home."

He is standing right beside her and places his hand gently on her arm, she flinches slightly, but catches herself, her nerves are still on edge from any human contact. A slight amused noise leaves her lips, "You forget where I called home, I had to apologise for everything and ask permission for anything I wanted, from food to cosmetics."

Neil blows out his breath and shakes his head slowly, "I'm sorry, I never thought, but please don't feel like that here, as you can see there aren't many rules to this house." Neil points to the closed swinging door behind him, indicating the sleeping man in the living room. "

"Okay." Ava relaxes a bit, "I will try. Would you like some coffee whilst I'm here?"

"Yes please, I can't function until caffeine is thrumming through my veins."

Neil gives Ava a smile, she smiles back and then busies herself making the coffee for both of them. Putting the coffee in front of Neil, who is sitting at the breakfast bar in the middle of the kitchen, Ava slides into the bar stool next to him. She can feel the stress coming from him in waves, she tries to think of something to say, just to fill in the silence, Neil has gone quiet and silence makes Ava nervous as she doesn't know what is coming next,

"So will Jack surface anytime soon?"

"Probably not, we were up pretty late talking business."

"Oh, okay, well, what are you doing today? When do you need to be at the club?"

"The club doesn't open until tonight so me and Jack will take you to the police station, if that is still what you want to do. Then I was thinking that we could go and have some lunch, there is some stuff we need to discuss with you."

Panic flashes over Ava's face, the feeling that something bad is going to happen is rushing through her system.

"Okay, but you don't need to take me to the station, I can get a taxi, and I, eh, I don't have any money, to go to lunch, or clothes, and while we're at it I don't have a job or anywhere to stay."

The realisation of how bad her life is now, that she has left Nathan slams in to her. The thought that maybe she has made a mistake crosses her mind, but she pushes it away as quickly as possible, she must be in a better place now that she doesn't need to worry about getting a beating every second of the day. With everything that is going through her mind, she starts to shake, violently. Neil takes her into his arms in a warm embrace, after a second he pulls back.

Ava looks up into his deep hazelnut eyes, and all she sees there is kindness and his voice is full of it too.

"Hey, don't worry, I would never let you get a taxi to the police station, you will need someone to be there with you, for support, and that is why I'm here, to support you all the way. Also, the reason Jack and me want to take you to lunch is to talk about a few of those things. So everything is going to work out, Sweet, I got you, don't worry!"

Ava nods slowly, fighting the tears that are threatening to

fall from her eyes, nobody has been this kind to her in years, it takes her breath away, she can't understand why Neil wants to do this, but kinda hopes he doesn't stop.

"The only thing I need from you, is the promise that won't go back to him, to Nathan, no matter what."

Ava's eyes widen, how did he know that she had thought about going back, maybe he didn't.

"You don't need to worry about anything," Neil continues, "nothing but getting back on your own feet and getting back to that strong independent woman that I suspect is still in there."

Ava is staring at him, amazed that what he has just said, it really does sound like the truth, like he really means it, she is starting to nod.

"Promise me, please." Neil knows he sounds like he is almost begging but he doesn't care, he just needs her to promise this one thing, he went back home once and it was the worst thing he could have done; he really doesn't want that for Ava.

"But what about money and stuff? I haven't worked since Nathan made me give up my part time job when I was nineteen and that was five years ago, who is going to employ me, I'm useless, I have no talent there is nothing that I am good at!"

Neil shakes his head, but smiles knowingly, "Those are some of the things that we are going to talk about at lunch, just please promise me, never back to him!"

"Ok, but—"

Neil puts his finger to her lips to stop her in her tracks. Ava smiles, it really does amaze her how relaxed she is starting to feel being with Neil, not just in his company but in his arms too, in a comforting way.

Just at that, Jack stumbles through the swinging doors from the living room to the kitchen, rubbing his eyes like a toddler, "Mmmm I smell coffee, someone hit me." He stops dead where he stands and slaps his hand to his mouth, mumbling behind his hand he sits, "I'm so sorry, I didn't mean, I just mean, eh, I didn't mean anything violent, oh God I am sorry."

Ava has started to giggle and Neil's shaking his head at his friend.

"It's okay," Ava says chuckling at the horror still on Jack's face, "I know what you meant, honestly Jack, it's okay."

Jack lets out the breath that he has been holding in, "Right, aye. I am sorry though."

Neil is still shaking his head and Ava is still smiling at Jack, "Anyway, what time are we going to the station?" Jack looks between the two people standing in front of him, Ava's face has turned to shock, she wasn't aware that Jack was coming with them,

"What do you mean, we, I thought it was just me and Neil that was going?"

"It can be if you want," Jack starts, "but I am here if you need me. Truthfully, I rarely let this numpty out on his own, he can get a bit confused!" He motions over to Neil whilst winking at Ava, who smiles again. She likes Jack's easy way and the way he manages to relax the atmosphere with his humour, which is normally aimed at Neil, he comes across as a really nice guy and a very good friend to Neil.

"Thanks for that pal!" Neil stands and clears his coffee cup, his tone is full of amusement at the ribbing he took from his best friend, "Right I'm going to get ready. You my friend can drive us to the station and then drive us to lunch!" Neil

61

isn't pissed at Jack, he knows what he's like and loves him even more for offering to help Ava.

Ava and Jack are left in the kitchen, Jack is making himself a coffee, "You want another?"

"Yes, please, if that's okay?" Ava is fiddling with her mug,

"Of course it's okay, the only problem is, I need your cup"

Ava looks up at Jack, he is smiling, and again his smile relaxes her,

"Oh, sorry, here." She hands over her cup, "You must think I'm a leaching cow" The statement comes from nowhere, and takes Jack and Ava by surprise, slowly he walks back over to the breakfast bar, taking the stool next to the one Neil was sitting in, so he is diagonal to Ava.

Putting her cup down in front of her, Jack asks, "What makes you say that?" Confusion clouding his eyes.

"Well, I met your friend once and now it looks like I have latched on to him, making him rescue me."

A low chuckle comes from Jack, "Listen honey, Neil never gets made to do anything, also he knows how bad it is to be in a domestic abusive relationship, he would never leave anybody in a hole like that. I don't think you're a leach at all, I do think that you need help, and both Neil and I are here to do that." His expression darkens slightly, "Although I do know that Neil has probably already said to you, but just in case he hasn't he will ask you to promise that you will never go back to that prick." Ava is nodding, Jack continues, "That will be a deal breaker for him!"

"Yeah you're right; he has said that to me. I don't want to go back to him; I just don't know that I have the strength to be on my own!"

Jack gets up from his seat and walks round to Ava's side,

putting his arm around her shoulders, "Hey listen, you ain't alone, you got me an the numpty upstairs, even though we don't really know each other, okay? You take your strength from us until you get enough of your own back."

Ava's blue eyes glisten with tears, the kindness of these men blows her away, knowing she can't talk over the lump in her throat, she nods, furiously, Jack puts his other arm around Ava and gives her a cuddle,

"Right, move your arse upstairs and get ready, your knight in black jeans hates waiting!"

Giggling despite the tears Ava asks, "How do you know he'll be wearing black jeans?"

"Because honey," Jack has put on a very camp voice, "that's all that man wears!"

Ava is laughing out loud, something she hasn't done for far too long, and she is enjoying the feeling of freedom, and happiness? Is that what that feeling is?

Neil walks into the kitchen, through the side door from the hall, "What's all the hilarity in here?" Neil ask.

Both Ava and Jack turn to look at him, Jack turns back to Ava, "See, told ya!" Then flounces from the kitchen.

Ava explodes with laughter again, Neil stands watching the scene before him, not sure why all the hilarity or why it's aimed at him, but enjoying the sound of Ava's laugh all the same.

CHAPTER SIX

Walking into the station, Ava's stomach is in knots, she is shaking and panic is starting to get a grip on her. She stops walking, standing stock-still. Neil notices she has stopped, but is a step in front, so he turns round, "Ava?"

Ava is shaking, sweat running down her spine, she desperately wants to say that no she isn't okay, but the thought of talking makes her feel sick, if she opened her mouth then she would throw up so she just stands there. She looks up at Neil, but the movement of her head makes the world spin. Her breathing is coming hard and fast now; her vision is closing in from the sides until there is nothing but a pinhole of light, then blackness takes over.

"Ava, are you okay, you don't look—"

Neil is cut off as Ava's legs give out on her and she falls to the ground. Neil lunges forward, managing to grab her before she hits the ground. He shouts for someone to help, and a policewoman rushes through the door that is behind the counter. Looking at the scene in front of her, the woman grabs a chair and takes it out to the couple.

"Do you need an ambulance?" the officer asks as Neil lifts Ava and sits her on the chair, gently putting her head between her knees.

"No, I think she has had a panic attack and fainted. This is a big step for her, coming here."

The policewoman's voice is gentle as are her actions, she kneels down in front of Ava, making sure she is okay, "Ah, I see, I'll get you some water." She gives Ava's knee a pat and gets up to get the water,

"Thanks," Neil says, then turns his attention back to Ava rubbing her back and saying her name until she feels able to talk,

"Alright Sweet?" Neil is on his hunkers holding her hand gently between his own.

"What happened?" She is still feeling dizzy, and her voice is weak.

"I think you had a panic attack then fainted."

The door behind the counter opened again and the policewoman comes out with a glass of water, Ava looks up and tenses at the sight of the officer,

"Erm, fainted, but I've, eh, never fainted, ever!"

"That's okay," the officer says, "It can happen at any time, especially if you are under stress, worried, or uptight.

"Ava's head snaps up, "What'd you mean uptight, what makes you think I'm uptight?" Ava is being very defensive,

"Well to start, if you don't let go of this guy's hand you might break some bones!"

Ava looks at where her and Neil's hands are connected, she sees that she is holding Neil's hand so tight that his fingers have turned white and they are squashed together, she lets go quickly, "I'm so sorry Neil are you okay, have I hurt you?"

"I'm fine, Sweet, I'm worried about you, are you okay?" Neil is still hunched at her side, his legs going numb, as numb as his hand was a few seconds ago, but if getting Ava to report Nathan and what he has done to her over the years and the attempt on her life then it will be worth it.

"Still feel a bit panicky, but other than that I think I'm okay." She looks at Neil again, "You can stand, you know, you look like you're in pain hunkered down like that. A smile grazes Ava's lips.

Neil chuckles slightly, loving the way that even through her own worry she thinks about other people, about him! "I'm not sure I can to be honest." He starts to get up, feeling the pins and needles of feeling shooting up and down his legs and feet. The officer is still standing in front of them,

"So, can I help with anything?" Neil, who is standing up now, shaking each leg in turn, looks at the officer and then they both look at Ava.

She takes a deep breath, closing her eyes, breathes out and starts, "I have just came out of an abusive relationship, and I was wondering...if...eh, if I could put in a complaint or report him, or just get the abuse documented." She stops talking and takes another deep breath, in and out.

"Okay," the officer starts, "I'm Officer Young, Sian Young. First off, well done for getting away. If you are wanting to put in a complaint, then we will need to do some investigating and ask some questions, we will need for you to give us a statement about the abuse."

Ava's face pales again, "I, eh, I'm not sure, I mean, I don't want him to know where I am."

Guilt hits Neil in the stomach, hard, knowing he hasn't told her about the phone call from Nathan, he just didn't want to add any more stress to her this morning. He closes his eyes listening to Ava.

"I just want to tell you, so...I don't know, maybe I shouldn't be here. I've got out, so maybe I shouldn't kick the hornets' nest." She stands quickly and the room spins again, grabbing out for Neil's hand to steady herself, he takes her arm in one hand and puts his arm around her waist, steadying her with the other. "I'm okay, I just, I've changed my mind." She looks up at Neil, pleading with her eyes, "I want to go, I don't want Nathan questioned, it will only make things worse, for me, for you and the club, no, I don't want to do this, I need to go." Panic starting to creep back into her voice, she can feel it creeping back up her spine.

"That's okay," Officer Young starts, her voice soft and full of concern, "but if you give me Nathan's surname, I can just have a wee look into him, nothing official."

Ava is shaking her head,

"No, I can't he knows too many people, he can influence people, I can't I'm sorry, no, Neil can we go please?"

Neil nods, still holding onto her as if their lives depended on it; he starts to turn towards the door.

Officer Young puts her hand on Ava's shoulder to stop them, "Please, if you change your mind, or if he threatens you in anyway, come back and see me, okay, just ask for WPC Sian Young, please?" Her eyes are pleading, Ava feels a connection with the officer, she has a feeling that Sian knows what she is going through, just like Neil. She nods, then turns and walks back out into the crisp autumn day.

Jack is sitting waiting in his car, a red 2015 Mazda 6 TS2, he has settled down for a quick nap, late nights and early mornings catching up with him, thinking they would be a while in the station. When the doors open. Jack's eyes fly open and he sits upright, "What the hell?" He sees Neil getting into the front seat and looks behind him to see Ava in the back, looking very pale and shaken, "Eh, that was quick, was it not?"

"Sorry," Ava says quietly.

"There is nothing to be sorry for, please Ava, it's okay."

Neil turns to Jack, "Ava took unwell when we walked in, a panic attack and fainted, she has decided that she doesn't want to put a complaint in."

"Okay, was the police alright with that?" Jack gives a quick glance behind him to Ava then back to Neil.

"Aye the WPC was lovely about it, and has said that if anything else happens, to get back in contact with her."

Jack is staring at Neil, trying to gauge his emotions, but he can't get a proper look as Neil has turned to stare out of the side window. He peers back, looking at Ava again, she is sitting with her head bowed slightly, her eyes closed and she is shivering, though it is not cold in the car, as Jack has had the car running with the heating on.

"Listen honey," Jack's voice is soothing, "If you don't want to go through with the complaint, that's okay, but I would say that if you do have any more contact with him, then it might be an idea to keep a diary of any incidents."

Ava lifts her head, looking at Jack, she is amazed that he isn't annoyed at her; in fact, his face is full of sympathy, and worry as he smiles at her. "Yeah, that sounds like a good idea." She give Jack a small smile, then the silence resumes in the car. The air is heavy with unsaid words, Jack turns back to face the steering wheel and puts his seatbelt on,

"Right, lunch, where we going?"

****

Nathan wakes up, his head screaming at him due the amount of alcohol he consumed last night after he spoke to that idiot Neil. The thought of alcohol sparks a wave of nausea starting from the bottom of his stomach and sweeps up and over him. He puts his head back down on his pillow and closes his eyes. Wondering where he went wrong, why did Ava leave? The only answer he can come up with is she was having an affair with that idiot and thought the grass was greener. Surmising in his own head, he ticks off a list of things he did for her, gave her, like – a splendid mansion to live in, tick, expensive designer clothes to wear, tick, more jewellery than a queen, tick, nights out, tick, weekends away, tick, exotic holidays, appropriate friends, never needing to work, and a great sex life, tick,tick,tick and tick! And what did the ungrateful cow do? She would question him, answer back, push his buttons, to the point where she made him snap and gave her a slap or two. A couple of bruises here and there, nothing too bad except her stupid skin was so pale that they always looked worse than they obviously were. It was never his fault, it was always her, she started it, she pushed, and pushed or she wouldn't do as she was told. That is how real men, like the men in his family, deal with their women, keep them under control, yes, it was always her fault, he has never done anything wrong! Settled in his own head that he was free of any guilt, he vows to himself that he will get Ava back, and he always gets what he wants! He starts to plan how to make this happen, starting with getting the club and shutting it down. Picking up his phone, Nathan phones a few friends that owe him some favours, time to start the ball rolling.

CHAPTER SEVEN

In the restaurant, Ava is sitting at the table as Neil and Jack are at the bar getting drinks.

"You okay…? Neil…? Haw, you alright?"

Neil has a faraway look in his eye and isn't listening to Jack. Jack gives him a playful punch on his shoulder to bring his attention back to the here and now and away from the dark place of his past.

"Eh, aye." He lets out a sigh, "Just memories and shit." He pauses a beat, "I just don't want him to get away with it, but I canny push her to do anything that is going to reduce her to an unconscious heap on the floor. I mean she totally freaked out walking into the station; we weren't even through the door when she collapsed. Hopefully he'll do the right thing and just let it all go, let her go."

Jack looks at Neil in disbelief, "Aye right!"

Neil looks back at his friend with the same look, but also with sadness in his eyes. "I know, but if I don't have hope, how am I meant to get her through it?" He motions with his head towards Ava. She is sitting with her head in her hands, Neil can't see her face but he doesn't need to, he knows what is going on inside her head, the berating she will be giving herself, it's the same thing that went on inside his head when he'd done something wrong and made his dad go off on one. "You okay here, I'm going to sit with her?"

Jack looks over at Ava then back to Neil, "Aye, I got it. You want a pint?"

"If you're driving then aye, but if not just get me an Irn Bru, and get Ava a single malt."

"Ok." Jack turns to order the drinks as Neil walks over to the table.

"Hey Sweet how you doing?" He sits in the seat next to her putting his hand on her back, rubbing gently. Ava looks up hearing the softness of Neil's voice. How can this guy be so nice to her, why is he not angry at her, at her behaviour in the police station. She embarrassed him and herself with her shocking behaviour, not that she could help it, when she fell she had lost all control of her legs, of her whole body, but, not once did he raise his voice, or his hand! He never made any comments about her being an embarrassment, or tell her to get a grip of herself. In fact, thinking back, he never said anything that made her feel worse, or made her think that her reaction was her fault or done on purpose, if anything he soothed her, made sure she was safe, and even now sitting in public rubbing her back, making sure she is okay. Is this how it should be? Is this how you should be treated? She looks straight into his deep hazelnut eyes, expecting to see anger, or disgust, but sees nothing like that, the only things she can see is the need to help, hope and strength. She really hopes that she can absorb some of that strength and use it for herself.

"Alright, kind of, I guess." She gives him a wobbly sad smile, "I am sorry though, you went to all that trouble of coming to collect me when I phoned, taking me in, letting me stay and taking me to the station and all I can do is freak out and faint!"

Neil gives her a wry smile, "Hey Sweet," he takes his

hand from her back, Ava feels a sense of loss from his touch, but it is short lived as he takes her hands in his, she has lowered her head again when she was apologising, habit again, "Hey, look at me." She reluctantly lifts her head until their eyes meet again, she can still see kindness there, but she can also see worry and some pain, did she put that there? "You have nothing to be sorry for, and I mean nothing. You didn't make him treat you the way he did, it was never your fault when he beat you, and your reaction going into the station was not something you could control. It was something your brain and emotions couldn't cope with, your brain didn't want to deal with the situation and what the consequences of reporting Nathan could be, so it shut down, fight or flight. You did nothing wrong, please believe me." Ava barely nods. "I will never make you do anything you aren't ready to do or don't want to do. I am a bit pissed that he might get away with beating you, but, I'm not angry or upset at you or anything you have done." He pauses trying to rein in his anger at Nathan and the want to take Ava into his arms and never let go, "Listen, I know how hard it is to take each step away from the person who has abused you for years and made you believe that it was all your fault, I understand I promise."

Looking at Neil, Ava starts to think that maybe she wasn't the one to put the pain and hurt in his eyes, someone else did, someone he loved, but she is sure that saving her is bringing back the memories.

"Thank you," she manages to squeak out as her emotions are threating to take over again, and gives Neil as grateful a smile as she can. Neil's heart breaks and melts all at the same time.

Jack arrives with the drinks, he can feel the emotion at the table so clears his throat as he sits down, making the other two break their eye contact. Neil grins at Jack and Ava looks down, red patches covering her cheeks.

"Right we ordering then?" Jack asks clearing the air and getting the conversation started on a safer path.

After everyone has finished their meal and the server has tidied up, Neil orders more drinks and then starts the conversation that him and Jack were planning last night.

"Ava, me and Jack were talking last night, and as you know we are both here for you, I – we, know that you don't exactly know us, and you're not sure why we are doing this, but we are and we are not looking for anything in return. The only thing we ask for is your promise that you won't go back to that pric… him."

Ava has lowered her head again and is playing with her rings, twirling them round and round her finger and then taking them off and putting them back on again.

Jack picks up where Neil left off, "We just need you safe. It was the one condition that I gave Neil when he was going through this."

She looks over to Neil and he gives her a lopsided smile, and a shrug of his shoulders.

Jack continues, "So if you can promise us that then we have a job for you at the club."

Ava's head shoots up, her eyes darting from one man to the other and back again, not believing what she is hearing.

"But why? I can't, I'm not worth—"

Neil puts his hand up to stop her talking, "No, stop right there, you can accept the job, you are worth it, it will give you some independence financially as you will be earning your own money, another step away from Nathan, but just to be on the safe side you will always be with one of us. More than likely me as you will be staying with me for the time being. We are in the position to do this to help you and so we are doing it, no argument." His tone turns emotional, "If Jack didn't help me, I would be either dead or in jail, so I am doing this for you!"

Holding Neil's gaze, Ava starts to nod her head, "Okay, I promise, I won't go back to Nathan, but how can I work in the club, I've not really worked, never mind in behind a bar, and I don't want to take anybody else's job."

Neil saw determination in her eyes when she started talking, but the more she spoke about the job the more it slipped away and was replaced by fear.

"I'll train you, and you are not taking anybody's job."

"Aye, don't worry," Jack has a glint in his eye and his voice is full of cheekiness, "We know the bosses!" Neil loves the way his best friend can break the seriousness of a situation when it is getting too much.

"You will learn all parts of the business, not just behind the bar, then you can decide what you like doing best. We will start slow, one step at a time." He smiles at Ava, and she smiles back,

"Yeah, one step at a time," she repeats after Neil, thinking to herself that that could be her mantra from now on.

Jack stands, "You want one more before we go?"

Ava looks at her empty glass, normally she wouldn't be allowed more than one, two at a push, but she's free to allow herself to live, "Why not, if that's okay?"

Jack nods and heads towards the bar, Ava turns to face Neil again, "Thank you, again, I really appreciate everything you are both doing for me, but I can't live with you for free, people will talk and Nathan will find out and it will be really bad for you, and Jack and his club. I don't want to put you in danger." Ava looks up at Neil and opens her mouth to ask him a question but closes it. Neil can tell she is about to ask something that she feels awkward asking,

"You can ask me anything Sweet, it's okay."

Ava opens her mouth again and this time she asks. "Is the club yours as well?"

Neil tries to look shocked and even thinks about denying it, but in the end he doesn't, "What makes you ask that?" He knows he should be panicking at this moment, panicking that someone has worked out his connection to the Daydream, but he doesn't, he feels in his gut that he can trust her. She has trusted him with her life and her safety so the least he can do is be honest and trust her.

"A couple of things, you've said, things about the club that only someone who owns it would say. Like 'my club' and 'I can sort things' and that you can work whenever you feel like it and so will I!" Ava looks back down at her feet, frightened that she has crossed a line.

"Ah." Neil had been so desperate to help this gorgeous girl in front of him that he has let his defences slip and his mouth run away with itself. "Well no it's not also my club, it is my club but it is not common knowledge. To the world it is Jack that owns it and I am a worker only."

"Why don't you want people to know it's your club? Why are you hiding? Is it a legal thing?" Panic is starting to claw at Ava, she has trusted this guy with her freedom and life, she is staying in his house, she knows nothing about him and has just found out that he is hiding a huge part of his life from the world, what else is he hiding? Should she trust him?

All of the questions and emotions that have gone through Ava's head played out on her face, Neil could see the panic, uncertainty and fear flash over her face and he hates the fact that he put it there, he has to explain why he has to have his connection to the club under wraps, but how?

Neil sighs and scrubs his hand over his face, "Ava," he starts, his voice unsure, "Sweet, listen, yes the club is mine, Jack does own a share in it, and he runs it for me. I don't want certain people from my past knowing the club is mine, not because I'm hiding anything or doing anything illegal, but I had to cut ties with my, him, the person I don't want to know the club is mine." Neil takes a deep breath and continues, "They have taken everything from me once, well twice in different ways, and I refuse to let it happen again."

Ava takes a breath, a deep soul searching cleansing breath, then she looks up and looks Neil in the eye, holding contact,

"Is it the same person that beat you?" Her voice is soft, but still slightly unsure.

Neil wants to break the eye contact they have, so she doesn't see the hurt that he still feels over his past, but he can't, she deserves the truth, if he is to gain her trust, he has to be open with her, tell her everything. He also refuses to shy away from the thought of his father, even though it still hurts, he WILL NOT be that cowering wee boy again!

"Yes, it was the same person. It was my father."

Ava gasps audibly and reaches out to touch Neil's hand, not sure why, but she just feels she needs to make contact with him. "He beat me and my mum."

"I'm sorry Neil,"

He shakes his head, "It's okay, you didn't do it! Yeah, my father beat me until the day I left the house when I was seventeen and Jack took me in. I started the club three years after that with money that my mum left me when she died. My father wasn't happy as he didn't know that my mum had money put aside for me and he expected me to hand it all over to him, said it was rightfully his. I refused and he thought he could beat and bully it from me like he did everything else in my life, but I had started training in karate by then and I got the better of him. That made him even angrier, so he involved some unscrupulous lawyer to try to get the money through threats of shutting me down, and trumped up accusations of money laundering, and he even sued me to get my inheritance. I started to pay a bit, but then thought about it and refused to be bullied and used by him again. I closed the club for a bit and got the police to investigate his allegations, they found nothing, because there was nothing to find. They wanted to arrest him for wasting police time, I'm not sure what happened after that because I cut all communication and contact, re-opened the club 'Under new management' gave Jack his share, changed all the paperwork, and now on the surface my father has no claim on the club because it not mine!"

Ava is astounded at what she has just heard, how could a father, someone who is supposed to love and cherish and protect their blood be so evil and selfish, it was disgusting.

Jack had arrived back at the table while Neil had been talking, he sat quietly knowing full well that if Neil was interrupted he wouldn't finish his story, and it is good that he is talking about it. Jack also knows that Neil still feels responsible for his father's actions, that it still hurts and that he is terrified that he would be the same as him, that is why he rarely dated. He might see someone a couple of times but nothing serious.

Neil looks at Jack. "And if it wasn't for this idiot I would probably be a down and out alcoholic, in the mad house or in the Big House. He introduced me to my BMW cars and taught me how to fix them up, and he agreed to help me out in the club, and put up with all my shite!" He smiles at Jack with so much appreciation and brotherly love it is palpable.

"You are very welcome, ya wee dick!" Jack tips his glass at Neil. Ava gasps at what Jack said and looks between the two friends, frightened at what Neil's reaction will be, but all she sees is brotherly humour between them.

Neil looks at Ava and chuckles at the confusion on her face, "It's okay it means he loves me!" The confusion Ava feels remains, but she relaxes as she can see how much they mean to each other, they are closer than some brothers, it is amazing to see.

Neil takes Ava's hand and the air around them changes, making the mood of their conversation turn serious again, "Right, Sweet, time for the difficult part."

Ava stiffens in her seat, "We're going to talk about Nathan, aren't we?"

Neil nods and gives her hand a squeeze, "Aye, but it's okay, we're going to get through it, we're here for you."

Ava looks pleadingly between the two men, mentally begging them not to mention him or what he has done to her.

"He contacted me last night, demanding to know where you are and if I have seen you."

Ava flinches, "How did—" the realisation that he knows where she is and how he worked it out hits Ava hard, so hard she doubles in two, as if she has been punched in the stomach.

"Your card, I left your card in my drawer." She tries to take her hand away, but Neil doesn't let her go.

"Hey Sweet, it doesn't matter how he found out, he would have found out sooner or later. It's not a problem, I promise."

Jack is nodding and puts his hand on her shoulder and

gives it a squeeze. "Listen girl, between the three of us, we will get you through this, you will move on and then he can get to!"

Looking at both the men sitting at the table with her, Ava can feel their strength emanating from them and seeping into her bones, giving her the strength she needs, the strength she will use to get through all of this crap and away from Nathan.

CHAPTER EIGHT

Sitting behind his desk in his home office, Nathan is waiting on some people getting back to him on the whereabouts of Ava, and who the sleeping partner is for that bloody club. He is trawling through the internet reading anything he can about the Daydream Club, Neil Alexander and Jack Bale, though there isn't much coming up. He is getting very frustrated at how little information there is on any of them. He picks up his crystal brandy glass, draining the last of the amber liquid, looking into the glass, staring intensely expecting the answers he desperately seeks to be at the bottom, they're not so he hurls the glass at the wall beside the open door to the office, letting a growl escape at the same time. The crystal shatters into a thousand pieces and the last drop of the brandy starts running slowly down the wall. His anger not yet satisfied, Nathan picks up the picture of him and Ava that sits on his desk, looking at Ava smiling up at him in the picture makes his anger double, and again he throws it across the room shouting and cursing her with every ounce of venom he has in him.

"You fuckin' stupid bitch. Where would you be if it wasn't for me, eh? In the fuckin' gutter where you fuckin' belong that's where!" He stops his rant when he hears a female clear her throat, his head snaps up expecting to see Ava standing in the doorway, tail between her legs begging for forgiveness, but instead he sees Joan, his housemaid. "Oh sorry Joan, I eh, had a bit of an accident."

Joan eyes him cynically, "Oh right, I'll get right on it and clear it up before I go home. Would you like me to get the photograph re-framed?"

Nathan pauses for a second, taken aback by the question. Does even the staff think she has left him for good? Never to return? The niggles he has felt all day make him think that maybe yes this is true but, he refuses to believe that someone as needy as Ava would have the balls to dump him! I mean he is Nathan Low; nobody gets the better of him!

"Yes please Joan, but place it in the living room, it distracts me in here!"

Joan mentally rolls her eyes at him, she may not be a fan of her boss, but she is certainly not stupid enough to upset him. He pays her wages and pays her well, so her mouth, eyes and ears will remain, as always, tightly closed!

"Yes, Sir." And with that she is scurrying away to fetch the brush to clear up the broken glass.

Nathan walks out of his office and heads to his home gym, phone in hand as it starts to ring. "Low!" he answers gruffly,

"Nate it's Mark, I've been looking into the Daydream for you." Nathan changes direction and heads for the living room, sitting on a wing backed chair looking out at the crisp October afternoon, he hates people calling him Nate, that is not his name, but he lets it slide this time he just needs information.

"Yes, and?" His tone is still gruff, but his stomach is in a spin, desperate for the information he is hoping his contact will have.

"Aye well on the surface the club belongs to Jack Bale

and he runs it, but a couple of years ago Neil Alexander owned it but he had problems with his old man trying to get money out of him, the club shut and then re-opened and, ta-da, Jack owns it and Neil is a lowly worker. I'm still digging though, 'cause that just don't smell right to me!"

Nathan smiles wryly to himself. "Good work Mark, keep digging and look into the dad as well. Oh and get a tail put on Neil, see if he does know where Ava is!"

"Okay, how long for?"

"Till I fucking say so!" he snaps, "What about Ava any news?"

"Not that I've heard, I do have someone looking, but nothing as yet. If she is with Neil we'll find out and I'll let you know."

"Great, keep in touch, I need to know everything."

"Okay, you're the boss!" Mark hangs up.

Nathan thinks how great it is when his staff just do as they are told, no questions asked. Mark has always been his go to guy when he needs dirt on someone. Mark works hard to get the information and he doesn't mind getting his hands dirty when investigating and he never asks Nathan for a reason! Smiling to himself at this new information Nathan goes to his gym in the basement, before the phone call he wanted to do some serious damage to one of the punch bags, but now he needs to think so he goes on the treadmill.

Two hours later Nathan has trained, showered, re-dressed and thought about everything that he has discovered. He makes some phone calls, some about Ava and some about business, he is still trying to get the land next to that old codger, Mr Drake, the problem isn't the buying of the land, it is the buying it for the right price and nobody asking any silly questions, like do you have proper planning permission? Or may we have more money for the planning permission? Why can't people stop being so greedy and just accept the bribes that he deems fit for them! His anger starting again, he phones his estate agent to see if they are any further forward on buying the land.

"Have you got this sorted yet?" Nathan is his usual gruff self, but his estate agent has worked with him long enough to know what he is like and how to deal with him.

"Yes Nathan, I have just heard that you have the land and the planning should be in the bag by tomorrow."

Nathan lets out a small sigh, "Thank the Lord for that, at least something is going right. Keep at it I want that planning permission as soon as possible!" He cuts off the call without a goodbye or a thanks. Feeling slightly better that at least one thing in his life has been restored to normality, well a closer version of normality than the past twenty-four hours have been anyway.

Another few hours later, and Nathan has been behind his desk doing some work, but is starting to feel restless, with no Ava in the house to help him out with his urge, he texts one of the 'girls' he keeps on his payroll for his own personal pleasure. Tonight he needs to be in charge, to be in control and not take any more crap from anybody, and this daft bint is the best girl in the business for just that.

Be here for 7pm, wear the green dress

Not even a minute passes when the reply comes through.

Yeah, no problem.

He smiles; this girl is starting to make him feel better already.

CHAPTER NINE

The next day, Ava wakes up feeling relaxed, that is until she remembers she is starting work in the Daydream today and her nerves kick in. She has never really worked a proper job and certainly not one in the five years she was with Nathan. The thought of working, finding out if she is good at anything or more likely, finding out that she is crap at everything, is making her feel sick to her stomach, pushing the thoughts to the side she dresses. Pulling on her black pencil skirt, black blouse, stockings, and a pair of black ballerina pumps, she looks in the mirror and sighs. These were the only smart clothes that she lifted when she left; she really hopes that they are suitable enough for work. Her heart heavy with worry she walks down the stairs to get some coffee. She starts working about in the kitchen making coffee and putting things anyway, it's then that it hits her that even though this is only her second morning here she is relaxed enough to move about the kitchen as if it is her home, and it is all thanks to Neil, he has made sure that she has felt at home. He has been a perfect gentleman, giving her space when she needs it, listening to her like she is the only person worth listening to, giving her silent support when she talks about Nathan and why she stayed and why she eventually left, and understanding why she called him. She is overwhelmed at his trust in her with the truth about the club and his dad. Jack explained that Neil just doesn't talk about any part of his life especially his past, but he has told her, at least parts of it. It really did make her feel special, something that she never felt with Nathan.

She goes into the living room through the swinging doors and sits on the couch; minutes later, she decides she might want some toast. Walking back into the kitchen she notices Neil has come down and is standing at the coffee machine. He has put on some music, the Foo Fighters, she thinks, then notices he is dancing, whilst he waits on his coffee getting made. She stands there watching him move in time with the music, his black jeans hugging his very tight backside perfectly. Ava is surprised to have even had that thought, even though it was only for a second. She makes a small coughing sound to get Neil's attention, he turns and smiles, a genuine happy to see you smile, until he realises that Ava has been watching him dance then his smile turns to embarrassment, not used to having anyone live with him, he forgot himself for a bit and let loose. Ava smiles back, she realises that it feels like forever since someone smiled at her, a real genuine smile, a smile just for her, just because she was there. It felt really nice, she had forgotten how nice it was to have someone who was happy to see her, and not be angry at her.

"Oh, hi, eh you been there long?" Neil's voice still has a slight hesitation to it.

Ava's not sure if that is because he is unsure around her, frightened or walking on eggshells around her or just the embarrassment of her seeing him dance. Ava suspects it might be a bit of everything. "Long enough to see you shake your shammie!" She is laughing, humour glinting in her eyes.

Neil looks down to study the wooden flooring in the

kitchen, his cheeks feel like they are burning, and he only hopes that they aren't as red as they feel. "Ah, too long then!" Neil brings his eyes back up and sees the smile on Ava's face, he grins back noticing how easy things are becoming between them, and in such a short space of time.

"You want one?" Neil asks pointing to the coffee machine.

"Yes I would love one, thanks, though I'm not sure it will stay down." Ava tries to keep the humour in her voice, but Neil notices the worried look in her eyes. Handing her, her coffee he stands next to her putting his hand on the small of her back for reassurance.

"You know it's going to be okay, today. You'll be with me."

Ava turns where she stands and looks at Neil, she wasn't sure what she expected when she looked at him, but it certainly wasn't the kindness, or the belief in her that was shining back at her. Every time she looks at Neil, she is astounded at what she sees, or doesn't see to be more precise. She never sees any hatred, disgust or annoyance; it is such a change from being with Nathan. Is it meant to be like this, being with someone? Though she's not 'with' Neil, in that way, so maybe she should just stop that thought right there.

"Well that's easy for you to say, you've worked there forever, it's your business, I've not really ever worked" Fear flashes across her blue eyes making them dull slightly with the shame of her confession. She really felt like a spoilt bitch, but the truth of her position was that she wasn't allowed to work. When she got together with Nathan, she had a Saturday job in a cafe, but Nathan convinced her to leave, saying that 'no woman of his needed to work, especially in a greasy spoon!' She tried to broach the subject once just to give her something to do during the day, but the argument and beating that followed wasn't worth having the conversation again.

"Well, I'm going to show you the ropes to all parts of the business, my business, and you don't need to learn it all by tomorrow so it's okay." He is rubbing her back in that ever so slight way he does, making her nerve endings tingle. She tries her best to ignore the feeling, she really doesn't need to go there, she can't go there, just now.

"Good, I was worried that there might be a test or something." The sparkle is starting to return to her eyes, making the blue shine again as the humour comes back into her voice.

"Oh there will be a test, just not tomorrow." Neil eyes are also glinting. He is enjoying the easy banter between them, that they can go from something that is worrying Ava to joking about it. Ava smiles, a full easy smile that relaxes her entire face. Neil muses at how beautiful she is.

"Well thanks for the heads up, I will remember to take notes." Ava lifts her mug of coffee and tips it in a 'cheers' motion towards Neil and then sits down at the breakfast bar.

"What will we be starting with? I wasn't sure what to wear, so went for business, although my wardrobe is limited at the moment anyway. Is this okay?"

The uncertainty is back in her voice and that reminds Neil to take her shopping for some new clothes. Her lack of confidence makes Neil angry that someone who supposedly loved her ripped it all away, but in the back of his mind he remembers being that way after he left his family home. He knows it will take time, time, patience, and finding something meaningful, something she can do that she can glean some success from. That is why he is going to teach her all aspects of his business, to see if there is something that she can make her own. Finding something that he could make his own saved him, hopefully it will be the same for her.

"Aye, you look stunning!" The words were out of his mouth before he knew what he was going to say, he really doesn't want her to think he is only doing this to get her into his bed, yes he would love to have her there, and on the couch, and in his office, damn it he would love to have her on top of the breakfast bar right now, but that is not what this is about. Hopefully, one day, but not just now.

Ava looks down shyly, pink spots appearing on her cheeks, she feels shy about the compliment, but that is not why she looked down. She is expecting a 'but', you look stunning, but, a little less lipstick/makeup/leg showing, it always happens, but, the more the seconds pass by and the 'but' doesn't come, she realises that it isn't coming, he isn't going to say it. She can feel that Neil honestly means it; she can also see that he is feeling shy about saying it. Not because he didn't mean it, but because he does mean it. That thought should be scaring the life out of Ava, that Neil thinks she is stunning but it doesn't, and it is that thought that scares her.

"Thank you." She gives him a shy smile, but hopes that it also communicates how grateful she is for the compliment.

Neil clears his throat and smiles back. "Aye, well it's the truth." Neil, reprimands himself internally for letting that last statement come out. It is the truth, but he doesn't want to scare her away or find out that she doesn't see him in the same way, then the embarrassment kicks in, his confidence seeping away "Eh, aye." Neil starts to move towards the swinging door that leads into the living room, "I'm just gonna go get....aye." Shaking his head and mentally slagging himself off for turning into a teenager who just bottled it after the girl he fancies spoke to him! He leaves the kitchen and goes into the living room and then into the hall where he sits on the stairs and laughs silently to himself, he really must have come across as an idiot. He pulls his Doc Martins boots from the shoe rack at the front door, pulls them on and starts to lace them up.

In the kitchen, Ava is also laughing to herself at the way Neil reacted to the compliment he gave her. She realises that he might like her. The thought that that is the only reason he is doing all this pops into her head, but she pushes that thought away as quickly as it came. Neil has never touched her, at least without there being a legitimate reason, like comforting her when she was crying. So, he can't be doing all of this just to get her in bed. She's not one hundred percent sure why he is doing it other than his past, but she won't look a gift horse in the mouth.

She drains the rest of her coffee when Neil walks back into the kitchen through the adjoining door from the hall,

"You ready?" Neil asks leaning against the doorframe. He seems to have found his grown man voice and actions again, thankfully.

"Oh yes, just my jacket to get." Ava slides of the bar stool and takes her cup to the sink. She turns to face the doorway that Neil is standing in; he is holding her jacket up all ready for her to slip on, she smiles and walks over, turning to push her arms into the sleeves. Neil helps by pushing the jacket up Ava's arms, she feels his hand skim her arms and she feels sparks running up and down her spine at the same time. She tries to ignore her body's reaction to his touch; she can't allow herself to feel anything emotional or sexual in the touch. She turns to face Neil; they are so close, close enough to kiss.

"Ready." She smiles, keeping eye contact with Neil,

"Good." He stands to the side to let her pass first then follows, watching the sway of her hips and her backside. Was that a moment there, when he put her jacket on or was it just his newly formed teenage mind playing tricks on him? Whatever it was he needs to ignore it, this is not what she needs right now and if things with Nathan go as bad as he feels they might, he needs to have a clear mind and that means he really shouldn't go there. Locking the front door behind them Neil climbs into his BMW and drives to the Daydream.

CHAPTER TEN

Nathan had his night of fun and games with the bint, and it was fun for a while, but he grew bored of her, his head – and other parts of his anatomy – weren't there, weren't up to the business at hand so he sent her away. She left with a sting in her tail for the audacity of her questions, questions about him and his ability. Slut, how dare she question him, it was her fault anyway, not being able to keep him interested enough, and she still took his money. Well not after last night, no fucking way in hell will she be coming back here! He makes a mental note to have her removed from his payroll.

He gets up from his king size bed leaving the sheets a rumpled mess from his fitful sleep, and walks into the en-suite for a shower. One hour later, showered, shaved and dressed, Nathan walks down the grand sweeping staircase, all reds and metals, and into his modern state-of-the-art stainless steel kitchen. His housemaid, Jean, has left his breakfast of croissants out for him and has started the coffee machine. He eats his breakfast and drinks his coffee at the kitchen table and then steps out into the cold, crisp, autumn day and into the waiting Daimler. On the drive to his office, he starts to make notes, about Neil, his connection to the club, his dad and his past. His mobile buzzes to life just as the Daimler pulls up outside his office in the Broomielaw area of the city centre that looks over the River Clyde. He looks at the screen, seeing that it is the hired thugs that are tailing Neil he answers the call. "Low!" he growls down the line.

"Aye." The gruff sound of the first hired thug comes from the phone, "Yir girl's there, way that guy, Neil. They left the hoose this moarnin 'bout hawf eight, an they drove ta that club he works at. He hid the keys oan him and opened up himsel'. It's jist them, in the place. Ah mean it isnay opened yit."

Nathan rolls his eyes at the uncouthness of the hired thug, but if you want something done with no questions asked then sometimes you need to lower your standards.

"Okay, keep in touch I want to know everything they do, and everywhere they go." Nathan barely hears the answer from the thug as he disconnects the call. The rage inside him is starting to grow again, all because of that stupid bitch Ava and her new found idiot Neil, but he doesn't have the time to do anything about it at the moment, he has a meeting with the builders for the new apartments he is starting, provided the planning permission is agreed, which it should be today, he has spent enough money to get it. Then the builders could get on with things next week.

Nathan gets out his car and enters the building, his receptionist gets up out of her chair already talking to him about people who have called and mail that has come in that he needs to go through, but Nathan isn't really listening, he is still trying to get his anger at Ava and her betrayal under control, but it's not really working. He stops walking, turns around and looks at the blonde who was following him, she is the complete opposite of Ava. Ava is small in height, she has curves in all the right places, dark shoulder length hair, blue eyes that sparkle and pale porcelain skin. The blonde woman – who Nathan has looked at every working day for years but has never really seen – is taller, though not as tall as Nathan's six foot one, she is slender, very slender, little to no curves. Short, bobbed, blonde hair and emerald green eyes, which are made up to perfection each and every day. Nathan wonders why he has never noticed this woman before, she is cosmetically beautiful, and more his taste than the bint last night. Making another mental note to himself to get this blonde into his bed, he looks her in the eye, and turning up all his charm, says thank you, smiles his full watt smile, turns again and walks into his office, closing the door behind him. The blonde who had stopped in her tracks realises that that is the first time her boss has smiled at her, or looked at her, or even said thank you in a meaningful way, smiling to herself, she walks back to her desk and sits down.

Once behind his desk, Nathan lifts the phone and dials his lawyer's number. He is only on for ten minutes, which is long enough to know that the planning permission has still not came through, cursing, he puts the phone back into its cradle. His intercom buzzes and the blonde announces the arrival of the builders, he tells her to see them in and get coffees organised. Seconds later the door to his oversized office opens and the two giant, burly men walk in. Nathan stands, walks round his desk and shakes hands with the builders, motioning for them to take a seat on one of the black leather couches. The three men sit and the blonde comes in with the coffee, asks if they would like anything else then takes her leave, closing the door for the meeting to start.

"Good morning gentlemen. I trust all is well this fine Thursday morning?" Nathan is in full business mode. Both builders nod, grunting that they are fine, they both look very uncomfortable sitting in their suits, they would much rather be on the building site getting their hands dirty doing 'proper' work.

The first builder starts, "So, is the planning permission in place? Can we get started on Monday?"

Nathan shifts slightly in his seat, he knows that they don't have the permission to start, yet, but, he knows he will have it by end of play today, even if it costs him even more money, so a wee white lie just now wouldn't hurt anyone.

"Yes, came in this morning we are all set for Monday. What about you, are you ready?" He uses an accusatory tone to shift the conversation away from himself.

The builder takes offence to his tone and his hackles rise, but he remains calm, "Aye, all our workers are in place and are eager to get to work…as long as the paperwork is in place and above board." The builder eyes Nathan. He has worked with Nathan many times before and never had any problems. He knows that the legalities aren't always top priority with Nathan at the start of the build but that they are in place by the end of the build, but this time Nathan seems really jumpy, something just isn't right this time.

"Of course it is!" Nathan snaps, "What do you take me for, a cowboy? Just make sure first thing on Monday you break ground, I have a schedule to keep!"

The builders' eyes widen at his outburst, cementing his suspicions that all is not right with Nathan.

"Right, on you go I've got other things to do!" Nathan shoos the builders away with his hand, already walking around behind his desk and looking at the paperwork sitting there. The builders look at each other, completely insulted at being dismissed in such a manner, they leave the room, glad to be out of the meeting.

Nathan phones his contact in the planning office, his

temper barely in check. "What the fuck is going on over there? Why don't I have the planning for my apartments yet? What the fuck do I pay you for if not to get me the planning I need when I need it?"

His contact is panicking slightly on the other end of the phone, stuttering and stammering at Nathan about someone getting fired for taking bribes and investigations and needing to lay low for a bit, but Nathan isn't listening and his anger is starting to bubble over. "Just get it fucking done, I'm starting the foundations on Monday and I need at least a promise of planning, do you understand me?" The man mumbles something incoherent and Nathan slams the phone down growling as he does it, "Fucking imbecile!" He stabs his finger into his intercom and growls for the blonde to come into his office. Seconds later the receptionist walks in looking picture perfect with a smile plastered to her face. A smile touches Nathans lips also, knowing what he has planned for them.

"Close the door and sit down please." As he did with the builders he motions to the black leather couches, they still have a slight heat in them from the burly men.

She sits, crossing one long leg over the other. "How can I help Mr Low?" she is almost purring.

Nathan smiles slowly thinking to himself of all the things she could do to him and him her!

"I would like you to contact this person." Nathan hands the blonde an address card with the name and number of the girl from last night, "and tell her, her services are no longer required, that she has never to contact me or anyone connected to me. Please remind her that the privacy clause of the contract remains in place and continues to be enforceable."

The blonde nods, her brow creased, not quite understanding the meaning behind her boss's words, but knowing not to question,

"Yes, of course Mr Low, anything else I can do for you?" She looks up at Nathan through her mascara-coated eyelashes. She feels the heat coming for her boss's eyes, he is staring right at her, running his stare over her body, openly admiring her, his eyes full of desire, his sly smile full of lust, he licks his lips whilst looking at her cherry red lips.

"Yes, what are you doing this evening? Could you be at my mansion about seven?"

The blonde feels that this was more of a demand than a question, but it was not one that she was going to ignore. One reason being he is her boss, and the second being if he is offering what she thinks he is offering then there is no way she will be saying no, to anything. The man is as sexy as hell and more money than God!"

"Erm, yes, Mr Low, Sir, I'm sure I can manage that. Is there anything I will need to bring with me?" She hesitates, not wanting to jump the gun at what he might want her for.

"No just you, but please wear something…sexy!" He grins his knowing sexy grin and his eyes glint as he undresses her with his eyes as she sits on his couch. The bulge in his trousers straining, and getting very obvious, he catches the blonde looking and he winks at her. He can see the blush rise in her cheeks and can tell that she is unsure, maybe even slightly embarrassed at Nathan's blatant eyeing of her and his arousal, and that she is completely turned on.

"Ah, yes Sir, of course, is that all, Sir?"

"Mmmm, for now." Nathan makes an amused sound in the back of his throat, and with a shake of his hand she is dismissed from his office, exactly like the builders.

CHAPTER ELEVEN

In the club, Neil is showing Ava the ropes of pouring drinks and using the till system. He hasn't seen any sign of pain, worry, anxiety, or panic on her face all day, all he has seen is concentration, determination, questions and maybe even some fun.

"Right, you know how to pour a pint, even a Guinness, I've shown you how to work the till, although using it is the best way to get to know it, it can be temperamental. Any questions so far?"

Ava looks at Neil, trying not to show how overwhelmed she is with all the information that he has given her, but the fun that she is having. "Don't think so, but who knows when there are actual customers involved." She smiles. Neil is starting to love seeing her smile, it lights up her blue eyes making them sparkle even more, it relaxes her features from the almost constant panic look, to make her even more beautiful.

"I know what you mean, and don't worry, the first few times you are working with real people I'll be right here beside you." He gentle touches her arm reassuring her. "Right, we'll start on the business side of things in the office. Bookings for functions and the accounts and stuff."

Ava nods in agreement and they start towards the office. Neil's phone starts playing the Metallica song *Enter*

Sandman, his ringtone, "You go on I'll just answer this and be right in." Ava continues into the office and Neil looks at who is calling him, Nathan. He added the contact after Nathan made contact the first time, he wanted to be able to keep tabs on all the calls Nathan made to him, just in case.

"What d'you want?" Neil is trying his very best to keep his tone level and his anger reined in.

"I want to speak to Ava."

"Who?"

"You know fine well who I am talking about, my girlfriend, the stupid mare who thinks she has left me. I know she is with you, so I want to talk to her NOW!"

Neil's anger level at the way Nathan talked about Ava, was getting dangerously high, he is finding it increasingly hard trying to keep it together and not shove his hand through the phone and choke the life out of the excuse of a man on the other end of the phone, so he takes a deep breath. "I'm sorry, but she's not here, I don't know where she is, but my guess is she wouldn't want to talk to you anyway. Now I have already asked you to never contact me again, so if you could refrain from phoning me again, it would be much appreciated." He cuts off the call before Nathan has the chance to reply. Putting his phone back in his pocket he walks into his office.

Ava is sitting in one of the cream leather chairs on the outside of the black wooden desk, she looks up as Neil walks in. "Everything okay?" she asks, not a hint of worry in her eyes,

Neil is desperate not to put the worry or fear back there, but doesn't want to lie to her, he knows he needs to gain her trust, and being truthful with her is the only way to do that.

"Well," Neil sighs, "That was Nathan on the phone."

Ava gasps, her hand flying to her mouth, "What, how does he know where I am?"

Neil closes his eyes, hating the fear that he has put back into her eyes. "I don't think he does know, for certain." Neil starts, trying to take some of the fear back from Ava, "He keeps asking to speak to you, but I continue to tell him I don't know where you are." He walks over to Ava sitting half on half off the desk he takes her hands in his, "Please don't worry, you're safe, okay, you're with me, I promise, I'll keep you safe."

Ava nods slowly but on the last nod, she lowers her head to the floor and the tears that have been threatening since she heard Nathan's name coming flowing, dripping on to her hands and thighs.

Neil moves off the desk and kneels in front of her, he puts his fingers under her chin and lifts her head up gently, taking both his hands, he places them on Ava's face, wiping away her tears with his thumbs. "Please don't cry, you don't need to cry over him anymore. I'm here to help, we'll get through this. I have you, Sweet." The need to kiss her tears away is thrumming through every part of his body, but he fights the urge, this isn't the time or the place to act on his feelings for Ava, no matter how hard it is.

Ava looks at Neil straight in the eye, her eyes are still glistening with tears, but they are not flowing anymore, only one word comes pleading from her lips, "Promise?"

That one word held so much need and pain and hope in it, it breaks Neil's heart and steels his resolve to get her through this, get her away from Nathan, once and for all, and to show her how she should be treated by a man who will love her entirely. Even if he isn't that man at the end.

"I promise!" He takes her in his arms and just holds her

close to him, her head on his chest where she breaks down again, sobbing, heart breaking, soul destroying sobs, soaking his black T-shirt right through so he could feel the warmth of her tears on his skin.

After a bit, she calms and pulls back, but not enough to remove herself from Neil's embrace entirely, her eyes are red raw with tears and pain, she lifts her hand and puts it on his chest, covering the wet patch. "I'm sorry, I've put you out and now you're on Nathan's radar and he doesn't stop until he gets what he wants, especially if he is pissed off."

"Hey, you don't need to apologise, I've told you, I'm not frightened of him, I'm not frightened of anyone anymore. I was only ever afraid of one person in my life and he is out my life and doesn't scare me anymore either! I refuse to afraid of anybody, I spent too many years being afraid and that shit aint happening again, okay!"

Ava nods, not trusting her voice. She knows that he is talking about his dad, she may not know the whole story, but she does know that he understands her situation.

"Okay." Her voice is still wobbly from crying, she clears her throat, "But I made a mess of your T-shirt."

Neil looks down at where Ava is rubbing the wet patch on his chest, he swallows hard, desperate that the teenage boy that has taken up residence in his head and trousers doesn't make an appearance. "Yeah, well that I canny forgive, it's a very expensive T-shirt." His eyes are glinting with humour, and there is a smirk on his face.

"Oh dear, well I better go then." Ava stands and Neil stands at the same time, still holding onto her arms from the embrace,

"Eh naw, I don't think so, you need to work off your debt of ruining my very expensive clothes."

Neil is laughing and Ava's eyes soften and her body relaxes, she grabs him by the shoulders and throws him into her arms, holding on to him as if her life depended on it. "Thank you! Thank you for coming to get me, for recognising my problem, that night in the club, for the support, for making me laugh again, for everything really, but mostly for treating me like a human and not a victim, never tip-toeing round me!"

Neil envelopes her in his arms again, loving how well she fits there and how good it feels to have her there. "Anytime Sweet, anytime."

Ava looks up at Neil; they are both standing neither wanting to break the spell. Neil drops his eyes to Ava's lips then back to her gorgeous blue eyes, their lips seem to draw closer together of their own accord, but just before their lips touch Neil senses that Ava may be swithering over the kiss, so before he can change his mind, Neil presses his lips in a quick chaste kiss on hers, and then pulls back. "Right, business plans next," he croaks out in the squeaky teenage boy voice that has decided to make a comeback into his life.

"Erm, yes, business plans." Ava isn't sure if she feels hard done by at the chasteness of Neil's kiss, or glad. Neil had read her feelings right, she did want to kiss him, but was frightened, and he seemed to understand that, and she was yet again surprised at how a man could be so kind. Butterflies were starting in her stomach over the near kiss, and Neil, but she wasn't going there, she was not going to analyse these feelings.

****

"The fucking arsehole hung up on me again!" Nathan is

screaming out loud to himself in his office, "Lying bastard!" He punches a button on the phone on his desk, and thug one answered after two rings. His voice booming out of the speaker into the spacious office.

"Aye, Boss?"

"Where are they?" Nathan demands, his tone ensuring the thug knew of his mood.

"They're still inside boss, how, whits up?" The thug ignores the mood Nathan is emanating down the phone.

"Right, as soon as they open that club you get in there. If she is there, you make sure you talk to her. You make sure she understands the situation she has started and that she will be better off back here with me. If she's not there find out where she is and when she will be back, but do it discreetly!"

Thug one understands exactly what Nathan is meaning, "Whit 'bout him?"

"Just make sure he sees you and make him feel uncomfortable but don't talk to him if you can help it."

"Okay, boss consider it done!"

Nathan cuts the call without so much as a goodbye, hoping beyond hope that the thug could pull this off.

Next, he phones his guy in the planning department, the phone just rings out then goes onto voicemail, Nathan growls down the phone for him to phone him back ASAP or trouble of a biblical sense would befall him. He disconnects the call and closes his eyes, feeling his anger taking over again he tries to regulate his breathing, in through the nose out through the mouth. Eventually he calms enough to make more phone calls, starting with Mr Drake. Time to ask the old goat some important questions.

****

Neil and Ava have been working on the ins and outs of the business all morning, only stopping for lunch. Neil looks at his watch and realises that it is nearly opening time and Jack would be there soon.

"You want to go for dinner, or grab a take-away and head home?"

Ava had managed to calm down after the phone call from Nathan and had been focused all afternoon on the paperwork. Being busy has managed to keep her mind from wandering and worrying, but getting asked her opinion or what she wants is still something she's not used to so resorts to her bog standard answer. "Anything, it's up to you." She was always giving the wrong answer to Nathan so stuck with this answer for every situation, and nine times out of ten, it worked.

Neil shakes his head and takes Ava's hands in his. "I'm asking you, what do you want to do? You do have opinions you know, and you are fully entitled to your opinions and preferences, and even express them!"

Ava smiles shyly, she loves how Neil can say things to her without it sounding like a lecture or a child getting into trouble like when the friends she did have at the start of her relationship with Nathan would tell her to leave him, that he was bad for her. She did know all of that but was too scared and downtrodden to leave him, because her friends used the same tone of voice Nathan used when he was telling her she wouldn't be able to live without him. Not Neil though, he gives her choices, asks her what she wants and supports her decisions when she does make them.

"Well, dinner out sounds like a nice ending to a busy but nice day…if that's okay?" She is staring deep into Neil's eyes and she sees what she thinks is a flicker of desire there, and she then feels it in her stomach too.

"Of course that's okay, I know a nice Thai place on Argyle Street." Neil smiles warmly at her then releases her hands so he could get their jackets, helping her slip hers on. Ava smiles to herself, she is starting to enjoy the feelings she is having about Neil, she hasn't felt this way for anybody in a long time, if ever. Thinking back to meeting Nathan she had thought she had had these butterflies and the warm fuzzy feeling she is having with Neil, but she now knows that it wasn't the same, it was always tinged with worry and fear, she knows that she should have realised that at the time, but Nathan could be so charming and never took no for an answer, so her life of hell began.

Neil notices the faraway look in Ava's eye and gives her a light tap on her forearm. "You okay? Ava?"

She blinks and turns to face him. "Sorry, yeah, just thinking back and wondering why, that's all, I'm okay. I got out and I'm here, so I must be fine!" She gives Neil a lopsided smile, as he pulls her into a cuddle, leaning his mouth towards her ear, her shoulder length dark hair tickling his nose as he whispers,

"I'm glad you're here and that you're fine." he holds her for a fraction of a second longer than was he thought was probably normal for friends before he can bring himself to release her.

Ava brings her head up to look back into his hazel eyes, "Me too." Then she stretches up and kisses him gently on his cheek. She can feel the heat from her blush rush from her toes to her face, but refuses to lower her head. She meant what she said and has thought about the very quick kiss they had already shared all day.

Neil's jaw is twitching with the effort he is needing to put into not grabbing Ava and locking his mouth to hers and kissing her until neither of them can breathe. He has to silently remind himself that it was just a peck on the cheek and not to read too much into it, but wow, she kissed him and now he can't get the smitten grin off his face – God he really is digressing into a horny teenager again!

"Come on, dinner awaits." He takes her hand and walks out of the club locking it up behind them.

The evening air is chilly for October, but Neil doesn't feel the cold, all he can feel is the warmth on his cheek from Ava's lips. Just as they arrive at the restaurant, Neil feels his phone buzz in his pocket, he takes a quick look at the contact name and sees it's Julie, so let's it go to voicemail, really not wanting the crazy ex-girlfriend to make his mood dip any. Once seated and drinks ordered, Neil excuses himself, saying he is going to the toilet, so he can text Julie. He notices that she has left a message and decides to listen to it,

"Why are you ignoring me? We need to talk, you are going to be a father and you don't care! Phone me, NOW!"

Neil puts his head against the cool tiles in the bathroom, groaning to himself – what is he going to do? Is it possible that he is going to be a father, they used protection every time...didn't they? He quickly types out a text,

Sorry for disbelieving you, but, I'm really not sure that I can trust your word for it, make an appointment for family planning and I'll go with you.

Putting his phone back into his pocket, Neil opens the bathroom door to return to Ava, his phone buzzes again, he reads Julie's reply.

You don't believe me? You're a dick head! Fine, I'll let you know when and where, but when I do prove it we WILL be back together, I am NOT bringing your kid up on my own!

Neil sighs out loud, what did he ever see in that girl, she always was a crackpot.

Aye right!

Putting his phone on silent without vibrate he walks back to the table, back to the girl he wants to spend his time with, the girl he is hoping he will spend the rest of his time with.

CHAPTER TWELVE

Nathan has finished up for the night, tiredness washing over him and starts walking out of his office when the phone goes, the blonde comes over to him, meeting him just as he is closing his door.

"Mr Low, there is a gentleman on the phone for you."

"Who is it?" he growls

"He, erm, he wouldn't say, Sir, he just told me to let you know they've left." Nathan's ears prick up at this piece of information and his tiredness wanes slightly,

"Okay, I'll take it in my office." He turns and breezes back into his office, lifting the receiver and making sure he hears the click of the blonde replacing hers before he speaks, "Low!"

"Ah Mr Low, how's it goan?"

Nathan rolls his eyes and bites the inside of his cheek. He desperately hates dealing this piece of scum or his partner in crime, but reminds himself that unfortunately he needs them at the moment and so reminds himself he has to keep it together. Taking a deep breath, he continues the conversation. "What's happened?" he keeps his tone level.

"Aye well, they've left the club, an that, an went in tae a swanky place an they're eatin the now."

Another deep breath, the nasally whine grating on Nathan's nerves. "Okay, is there any news on his father or the club?"

"Aye, I think we might 'ave found his faither, tryin to git his number the noo, an that, naw!"

"Let me know if they go back to the club or back to his house." He hangs up and sits for a bit thinking, planning.

Getting up from his desk, Nathan walks from his office to the reception area and over to the blonde. She doesn't hear her boss coming up behind her as she is busy fixing her desk for the morning. She jumps when he sidles up to her and wraps his arms around her waist and kisses the her neck, not expecting the sensual touch or feeling the bulge pressing into the bottom of her back, but enjoying them both anyway. Nathan's hands start to move, one roaming up towards her breasts and the other moving down, stoking the fire that has started raging between her thighs.

"I think I might want you to leave with me right now, if that is okay with you Miss?" Nathan has turned up his charm to nearly full watt, he will have her tonight, and preferably sooner rather than later, as he has plans later to scare Ava and her idiot boyfriend.

The blonde pants lightly under his touch, she has fantasised about her boss touching her like a lover, but never thought that it would actually happen, she had always thought that he had preferred brunettes and women whose dress sizes were in double digits – God forbid – she is a size four and does everything in her power to keep it that way, even if it means not being happy. Swallowing away her self-doubt she makes a pact with herself that she will show Nathan that she is much better than that doormat he called his girlfriend.

"Mmmmm," trying for a seductive tone she whispers, "Whatever you need Sir." Those five words were all he needed to hear for his manhood to start its own dance.

"Well you had better get yourself downstairs and into my Daimler then hadn't you?" As he says this, he gives her nipple a quick pinch and then rubs over the hard nub again making the blonde take a sharp intake of breath as he continues pinching and rubbing while he kisses her neck until his hand moves to her backside and gives it a playful skelp. "That's a good girl. My driver will be in the car out the front of the building, I'll be just behind you in a minute." Nathan taps her bottom again as she moves towards the lift. She turns back to Nathan and bats her eyelashes, looking lustfully at him, "Don't be long," she crows as she enters the lift.

Nathan is still standing at the reception desk shaking his head, the daft cow actually thinks she is going to be something important in his life other than another notch on his bedpost whenever he fancies it, women are so easy! He picks up the phone and calls thug one back. "I will be busy for the next two or three hours, so if they move, text me, do not phone me, do you understand?"

"Eh aye,"

"Good!" He hangs up before the thug can ask any questions, there never is any niceties with Nathan, and even less when it came to Nathan speaking to people he considered scum. Grumbling about being surrounded by idiots Nathan heads to the stairs and out the building to the blonde waiting in his car.

****

The meal was lovely and Ava is still sipping on her red wine, their conversation had flowed naturally between them and it felt like she had known Neil all her life and not just for a few weeks.

"Are you going back to the club?" Ava looks at her watch and is surprised to see that it is quarter to eight; they had been in the restaurant for nearly three hours. Neil is looking at her with complete admiration in his eyes every time they had locked eyes through the night. Ava flushes as their eyes lock onto each other again, and again she feels the butterflies in her stomach take flight. She tries to dampen the feelings she is having for Neil down by reminding herself that Neil didn't save her from Nathan for that reason and that he probably wouldn't want a romantic relationship with her as she is tainted now, broken goods, used, who would want her?

Neil can't help but stare into Ava's deep blue eyes, they have sparkled all through dinner because she has been relaxed and even happy. He really hopes that he has helped to make her relaxed and happy and not just the wine. Mentally he chides himself again as he remembers Jack's words, "This isn't a fairy-tale pal, you don't get the girl in the end just 'cause you saved her." And he's right, Neil needs to stop thinking about getting romantically involved with Ava, she probably won't want another man anytime soon anyway.

"Well I was going to drop by to see if it's busy, if you want we can try out your new bar skills for an hour and then maybe grab a drink with Jack and then home, if that sounds alright with you?"

"Sounds perfect." Ava is excited to try out what she learned today and get her new independent life started. Neil stands and helps Ava into her jacket, he pays the bill and they walk back out into the chilly night. It has started to get frosty and they can see their breaths in front of them in the cold air. They talk all the way back to the club, neither of them noticing that they had linked arms. It's only when they reach the front doors of the club and they have to disentangle themselves from each other that they notice. Ava blushes and opens her mouth to apologise, but closes it again as Neil smiles at her with the same look of adoration that he has looked at her all night, and if she's honest with herself she's not sorry that she took his arm, it obviously was a natural gesture for her.

Putting his hand on the small of her back Neil escorts Ava behind the bar to the bemused looks at some of the other staff members and lets Ava get to work. Neil stands beside her encouraging her and giving her gentle reminders if and when she needed them.

Jack comes out of the office, surprised to see the pair of them behind the bar, he stands and watches the couple working together, seeing how relaxed Ava is around Neil and seeing Neil smile like he has just won the lottery. It really is a lovely sight and Jack is happy for his best friend, but he's still a bit worried about Ava's ex. Smiling, Jack walks over to the bar. The club is quiet as there isn't a party booked for that night so it is just the regulars, and a few passers-by. Neil sees Jack walking over from the corner of his eye and looks up from the pint that Ava is pouring,

"What's up way you, you're grinning like the proverbial Cheshire cat!"

Jack makes his grin wider, just for Neil's benefit, "Just happy I guess."

Neil nods at his friends answer then glances back at Ava. "You got a minute?" Jack brings Neil's attention back to him, as he motions towards the office.

Neil gives him a bemused look but nods, "Aye," he turns to Ava, "You be okay for a bit on your own? Jack wants a word."

Ava looks up and smiles at both men,

"Of course, I'll be fine." When the men have walked away Ava takes a second to appreciate the normality of the situation and how relaxed she is feeling in her own self, even though she has only been away from Nathan for a short time.

****

Nathan is in his master bedroom, the one he used to share with Ava, getting changed for his night of hot sex with his receptionist. The blonde is downstairs sipping on a glass of the red wine that his housemaid, Jean, has opened for them and Nathan is just about to join her when his phone buzzes. Growling at the interruption he takes the phone from his pocket and looks at the screen, thug two, this time, Nathan stabs the answer button and growls "Low!"

"Eh, aye, eh, Mr Low." Thug two sounds younger and not quite as sure of himself as thug one, Nathan rolls his eyes at the stuttering on the other end of the phone and tries not to shout at what seems to be a young boy on the other phone, "Well, eh, the pair ae them went intae that club after thir dinner an that."

Desperate for the thug to stop talking in that awful whiney voice Nathan butts in, "Fine, one of you go in and see what they are doing. If you can, then get Ava on her own and let her know she belongs to me and only me." His anger bubbling in his stomach and coming up to his throat, "Keep me informed, but by text only, I have company tonight!"

"Aye, nae bother, you're the boss." The thug disconnects the call and repeats the instructions to his pal next to him.

Nathan walks down the stairs wearing nothing but gym shorts, showing off his tight abs and perfectly waxed torso, his anger dissipating with each step until he reaches the living room and his vision is filled with the sexy blonde siting crossed legged on his couch. Walking over to her he lifts his glass of wine that has been poured for him, before taking a sip he says,

"I'll just check on dinner then I'm all yours." The blonde lifts her head to look at her boss and gasps. Not able to find her voice as she eyes Nathan's naked chest, she nods her head. Not quite believing that she is sitting in Nathan Low's living room drinking his wine and is hopefully going to get to lick those stone hard abs just before he slips the full length of himself into her.

CHAPTER THIRTEEN

In the Daydream office, Jack is getting Neil up to date with what has been happening at the club, what's booked, what bands have been booked for the Friday nights and how the takings have been. Neil is sitting on the couch with one foot sitting on the other knee,

"So everything's going alright then?" As much as Neil trusts Jack implicitly with everything, including his life, and Jack deals with most of the management that the public sees, he still likes to know exactly what is going on in the club when he isn't there – it's still his club at the end of the day and he still has the last say in everything.

"Aye ticking along nicely. How's our girl doing?" Jack smiles, he knows Neil has a thing for Ava and he also knows that calling her 'our' girl will wind him up, in fact it might even kill him if he thought that Jack saw Ava in a romantic light never mind a sexual one. The look on Neil's face is priceless and was so worth the ear bashing that Jack knew he was about to get.

"OUR girl? I don't think so pal, you can get tae, wae that one right now! Not only did I see her first, but she isn't your type and you know how I feel, so you can just get—" Neil stops ranting when he looks at his friend.

Jack is laughing so hard he is holding on to his stomach like it might explode. "You're a dick, you know that!"

Neil shakes his head at Jack realising that he is getting wound up.

Jack tries to stop laughing and nods, clearing his throat he tries to talk, "Aye, I am that, but you love me anyway, but seriously how is she?"

Neil scowls at his friend then smiles, "She's doing good, really good actually. She's picked up serving at the bar really quickly and we went through the business side of things. She's been really relaxed all day, not jumped once. Here's hoping she can move on and that he leaves her to get on with her life like she deserves."

Jack nods in agreement of the last statement then frowns, "Do you really think he will though? I mean he has phoned you a few times."

"I know, and honestly no I don't think he will, he's too much of a control freak, especially where Ava is concerned, to let go and she has taken the control over her away from him by leaving, so no I expect him to start something, and if he does then we will deal with it," Neil sighs, "But a guy can live in hope." He smiles but it doesn't reach his eyes.

Ava is working away behind the bar, serving the few customers that have come through the door. She can't believe how relaxed she is feeling, how happy and safe she feels. She notices a guy walking towards the bar, he doesn't look like the normal clientele that she has been seeing tonight. He looks scruffy, even a touch dirty, like he slept in his clothes last night and hadn't had time to go home and get washed or changed. She feels a chill run up her spine. There are other members of staff on the floor and the bouncers are on the door and have allowed the guy in, so maybe she is just being paranoid but her eyes dart to the office door, praying for Neil to come out.

The guy sits at the bar and slumps down on one of the wooden bar stools. He smiles at Ava showing off his crooked teeth, and the gaps where there should be teeth at the side of his mouth. "Awright!"

Ava nods. "What can I get you?" she says trying to stay professional and keep the panic from her voice.

"Pint a lager please hen."

Ava smiles quickly and pours the pint. She hands him it and tells him the price, the guy pays and she turns to put the sale through the till. The guy takes a drink of the pint and about half of it is gone after the first swallow.

"So Ava, how do you like working here then?"

There is humour in his voice which chills her blood, slowly she turns round to answer the guy at the bar. She doesn't want to react, to give the guy the knowledge that she is rattled, but she doesn't quiet manage that, her eyes are wide and she is starting to tremble. "I'm sorry, what did you say?" her voice wavers but she tries to regain control of her emotions.

"I said," thug one is loving the effect he is having on this cow. "How do you enjoy working here Ava? Cause you see Nathan isn't too happy that you left him, you are his after all and he wants you to return home, to him." Thug one lifts his pint and takes another slug from it leaving a quarter left.

Ava is terrified, she knew from setting eyes on this vagrant that he was bad news, but the fact that he has given her a message from Nathan makes her sick to her stomach. Again, her eyes dart to the office door, then to the front door, imploring anyone to come and help her.

Thug one's eyes follow Ava's and he smiles at her, loving the feeling of power he has over her, making her quiver with fear, even though she thinks she's hiding it. "Oh aye and another thing, Nathan has put the wheels in motion to get this place shut down and a whole lot more nasty stuff will happen to that 'friend' of yours – Neil – if you don't go back to him pronto." He drains the rest of his pint, leans over the bar grabbing Ava's wrists, he tugs her towards him until she bumps into the beer pumps and bashes her pelvis into the sink underneath.

Not wanting to let the thug know he has got to her she swallows the scream that is in her throat, as the thug growls his next threat, "And if you still don't get your sexy little arse back to him, he will find you and it won't be a fuckin pretty reunion, understand?"

Ava nods, the pain in her pelvis, the shock of the threat and the tears in her throat making it impossible for her to speak. Thug one releases his grip but moves it up to tap Ava's cheek, he chuckles when she cowers from his touch, then he turns and walks away right out the front door without even a second look from the bouncers. Ava watches him walk away and then calmly walks round from behind the bar and over to the office door and gently raps her knuckles on it.

Neil is closest to the door as he is sitting on the couch and Jack is behind the desk, he stands and opens the door. Neil is confronted with Ava standing there looking like she has just been told some life changing news. Neil's stomach drops, her face is pale and she is shaking, fear emanating from her.

"Ava, what happened, are you okay?"

Tears start running down her cheeks as she tries to talk, "Neil." She stumbles over her words trying not to lose herself to the overwhelming emotion coursing through her, "There was…I think, Na—"

Neil takes her hand and walks her into the office, sitting her on the couch that he just vacated; he sits on the edge of the desk. "Ava what happened?"

Jack is still sitting behind the desk in the swivel chair that he personally picked for the office, the cold feeling in his stomach returning, he hadn't felt the sickening chill for a few days as there hadn't been any mention of Ava's ex but he knew that Nathan had to be behind what had upset Ava so much.

"Nathan knows where I am." She puts her head in her hand, shock seeping into her, making her body shake from her head to her toes. Why did she think it was okay to relax, to move on with her life, now she had got more than just herself in danger.

Neil and Jack look at each other, "How do you know this?" Jack is the one to ask this question the chill of worry coming through into his voice.

"A guy came into the club, he told me that I've to go back to Nathan, or, or—" This time Ava does break down.

Neil jumps up from the edge of desk he had been perched on, and starts pacing the small office, anger emanating from him, "Some guy just came into MY club to tell you, you had to go back to that piece of crap?" Neil has raised his voice, though not quite at the point of yelling, but Ava still shrinks back into herself at his outburst.

Jack watches the whole scene play out and knows that Neil's reaction is not good and not what Ava needs, even though he can understand why he is reacting this way. Walking around from the desk Jack stops Neil in his tracks by grasping onto his shoulders and making him look at Jack face to face, "Haw, ya wee dick, quit it! Look at Ava!" Jack growls and spins Neil round so he could see Ava sitting on the couch crying and shaking, her head and her eyes to the floor.

The view in front of him is enough to stop him. His heart sinks to his stomach he feels like such an arse for making her cry like that. Jack goes over to Ava and takes her hands in his and speaks gently, "Ava, what exactly did this guy say to you?"

Ava lifts her head and looks straight into Jack's emerald-green eyes, then she looks round to Neil, who has calmed down and is next to Jack, both hunkered in front of the couch. She can feel their strength and tries to use some of it; taking a deep breath, she tries to control the wracking sobs coming from her and the panic threating to overtake her senses. "He said that, eh, I, I belonged to him, Nathan, and that I had to go back to him—"

Neil lets out a growl, but Jack shoots him a look and he stops, turning his attention back to Ava as she continues talking. "He said that Nathan has already got things in motion to shut the Daydream down and if I still don't go back to him then he will do worse to all of us, and it won't be pretty!"

Neil looks down knowing what that threat could mean, then gets up and walks round to the back of the couch, putting his hands on her shoulders, "Listen Sweet, please don't worry about this, about him, we will sort this okay, you will NOT be going back to him."

Ava stands abruptly and spins round to look at Neil, her face set with scared determination. "No, he is going to close your club because of me, you and Jack and the rest of the staff will lose their livelihood because of me, that's not fair, especially when I can do something to stop it. It's not just me he will go after, he will go after you and Jack violently and I can't have that on my conscience." She places her hands on Neil's face, feeling a connection with him she has never felt before. "I don't want you hurt." She tries to let go, remove her hands but her body won't let her.

Jack is the first to talk, cutting into the intense moment with his voice. "Don't worry about us, or the club, we can get you away from him for good."

Ava turns to look at Jack who is standing behind her, forcing her hands to leave Neil's face, she sees pure determination there in his eyes and the way his jaw is set, there is no changing his mind. She turns back to Neil and sees the exact same look on his face. Ava wonders to herself fleetingly how two guys can be so supportive to an idiot of a girl they've not long met?

Neil speaks, bringing Ava out of her musings, "Jack is right, we will do this, get him out of your life, and we will do it together Sweet, I promise!"

Ava swallows, "Okay," she manages to choke out, "But how?"

All three of them look at each other for a moment until Neil answers, "Not really sure about that one yet Sweet, but we will."

"Okay," Ava sighs.

Neil takes her hand and heads towards the office door, looking back at Jack, Neil nods towards the bar, "You coming? I promised Ava a drink and we need to think of that solution."

Jack looks at Ava and then back to Neil and shrugs. "Moan then."

Jack closes and locks the office door behind him as they walk out into the main bar area of the club. Jack walks over to the bar and orders the drinks from the staff member there and then takes them over to Neil and Ava who has picked a table in one of the alcoves built into the wall, so they could have some privacy for their deliberations.

CHAPTER FOURTEEN

Thug one phones Nathan then remembers that he had to text instead, so quickly cancels the call then texts him.

Spoke to the burd, to tell her to get her arse back to you or else, will follow them

Nathan and the blonde have had dinner and moved back into the living room to relax. Nathan has changed drinks to brandy but the blonde is still on red wine and is starting to feel the effects of it, so she decides to excuses her herself to use the bathroom and freshen up, she wants everything right for her night of passion with her boss. "I'm just nipping to the toilet."

"Okay, don't be long."

She stands and squeezes in between Nathan and the coffee table, just before she gets out of reach, Nathan playfully slaps her backside, but hard enough to make her jump and let out a yelp. Nathan hears his phone as the blonde leaves and he pulls it out of his pocket to read the text. Laughing he murmurs to himself, "Bet that put the wind up the daft cow." He places his phone on the coffee table and stretches out, taking up the entire couch to wait on the blonde coming back from primping herself. Just thinking about what he was going to do to her got him going, and the blonde did not fail to see the definite bulge in his shorts when she returned, making eye contact she licks her lips.

"Close the door, then come over and stand here." Nathan points to the exact spot he wants her to stand and a smile dances over his lips when she does exactly what he says without hesitation or question. She reaches out to touch his chest and Nathan takes a small step back. "Oh no, not yet, first I want you to undress, slowly." His eyes are shining with pleasure and he is hard with excitement. The blonde starts unbuttoning her cream, silk blouse, slipping it over her shoulders and down her arms to puddle on the floor behind her. Standing there in her cream lace bra, black pencil skirt and black pointed stilettos. Nathan is still on the couch looking on with appreciation in his eyes,

"Now the skirt, but keep the shoes." The blonde obeys and shimmies out of her skirt leaving her standing in front of her boss with just her matching lace underwear and her stockings on. Nathan swings his legs round and stands, drawing his finger down her arm, leaving goosebumps in his wake until he finds her hips and then he stops and smiles. "Mmmm, yes, very nice." Leaning forward slightly, Nathan whispers how sexy she is in her ear then traces his tongue round it's edges then takes her lobe in his and nibbles, drawing a gasp from her. Moving his hands up her back then round to caress her breasts whilst kissing and nibbling his way down her neck to her collarbone, he then bares her breasts and starts an onslaught of sensations, rubbing and plucking until they are tight buds. Moving down with his mouth Nathan ups the sensations on her breasts, she lets out another gasps and then starts to move her hand round to his shorts.

Reaching in, the blonde realises that her boss isn't wearing anything else, "Oh, Mr Low, going commando."

Nathan lets out a growl and pushes his pelvis into her, "Always!" They both let go of the rest of their inhibitions along with Nathans shorts and the blonde's underwear. The blonde spends the next hour groaning and writhing under Nathan, until he spins them round so she is on top,

"Mr Low, please, take me."

Nathan lets a growl out, "Hearing you call me Mr Low is the sexiest thing I've ever heard." He enters her and they both thrust in time with each other until she screams his name again, making Nathan go over the edge as he thrusts in one last time.

She lays her forehead on his, both of them breathing hard, "Well thank you Mr Low," she purrs as she nibbles his neck,

Nathan gives her a quick squeeze, his way of a cuddle, "Well I aim to please." Kissing her chastely he lifts her off him and stands, reaching for the box of tissues he has sitting on his coffee table he pulls some out and hands them to her,

"Here, you will need to get yourself cleaned up and dressed." Then he dismisses her with a flick of his hand as he pulls his shorts back on. She walks over to her clothes and starts to get dressed, feeling the heat in her cheeks from the embarrassment of the dismissal, and the coldness in tone. She excuses herself and goes to the bathroom. Looking at her reflection, she feels a touch of shame, but pushes it aside, telling herself that she knew it wasn't a relationship and it was just sex, no emotion. Taking a deep breath and fixing a smile on her face she returns to the living room and sits back down on the couch to wait for Nathan to return from wherever he had gone.

Walking back into the living room, Nathan goes over to the couch and reaches for the blonde's hand, helping her to stand. "I'm really sorry to do this, but, I have a lot of work to do, and I don't want any distractions, my driver will take you home." He softens the blow by giving her tight cuddle and gives her another knee trembling kiss, "Plus it wouldn't do for the other staff to see us arrive at work together, with you in the same clothes as today and we don't want them thinking you are getting preferential treatment."

She lets out a giggle, and relaxes, chiding herself for her moment of shame in the toilet, he does want her, he is just busy, and important. "I understand, and my lips are sealed, no one in the office will know about this." She motions with her forefinger between both of them, "Will there be other times together, outside office hours?" She bats her lashes trying for sexy but sounding slightly desperate.

Nathan smiles a knowing smile, she is his to play with and she is desperate to please! "I'm sure we will, at some point. Now on you go, my driver's waiting on you." He gives her another quick kiss, physically turns her by the shoulders pats her on the backside.

She turns her head back and wiggles her fingers as a goodbye before she walks out of the large front door.

Nathan gives her a salute back then turns and walks to his office, shaking his head, mumbling to himself, "Thank God she's away, thought she was getting attached for a bit there, no shit that happening." A shiver runs down his spine at the thought of the blonde being more than a casual lay. Pushing the thought away, he sits behind his desk and dials thug one's number to get his update.

****

Jack brings the drinks over to the table in the alcove. Irn Bru for him and Neil and a Brandy for Ava.

Neil starts, "I think you need to contact that policewoman, what was her name? Young? Aye WPC Young," Ava looks at Neil her expression worried and scared.

Jack adds his thoughts gently, "Aye, I think Neil's right honey, you need to contact her again. She did say to contact her if he tried anything or there was any more abuse towards you, so—"

Jack shrugs, but Ava just stares at him with those wide blue eyes full of fear. A second later she speaks, her voice quiet but desperate, "No, I don't think that a good idea, it will only make him worse and I don't want that, I will do what Jack suggested and start a diary, I will put everything in that has happened up until today. Then maybe I'll phone her, but nothing official, I can't do official, not yet."

Neil squeezes his eyes shut and counts to ten before opening them again, when he does open them Ava is staring at him, her eyes wide and glistening with unshed tears and fear. Trying to keep his voice calm, he asks, "Why can't you make it official? If you report him then we might be able to get him detained, then you might relax, instead of panicking every time the phone goes. We could also get a restraining order if he doesn't get detained and that way he can't come near you or contact you."

Ava puts her head in her hands, when she lifts her head she is shaking it, "It won't matter, he hasn't come near me or contacted me as it is, he just sends his thugs. A piece of paper won't stop him, he is master of his own universe nobody tells him what he can or can't do. I will write everything down that he has done to me over the years, including the phone calls to you and the visit from his thug today, and if anything else happens to any of us. This way when we do go to the authorities then we have better proof, just now it's my word against his."

Jack nods, reluctantly, "That's the problem isn't it, and the sneaky fucker knows it too!"

Neil can't argue with Jack on that, and he knows what Ava is saying is true, he knows that domestic abuse can be hard to prove, especially when you are as smooth as Nathan and have as many friends as him. Sighing Neil gives in, "Fine, but from now on you are never on your own, at any time…except when you need to pee."

Jack snorts, glad that Neil had brought some humour into the conversation to ease Ava and her nerves. "Are you pair going or do any of you want another drink?"

Neil looks at Ava, "It's up to you." Ava drains her glass and hands it to Jack, "Thanks Jack, I think I will have another, see if we can't get the shakes to stop."

Jack smiles at her and nods, looking at Neil who shakes his head. Jack pours Ava her drink then brings it over to her, giving her a kiss on her forehead, "Keep your chin up honey it will all work out."

Ava smiles up at her new friend, realising that she was looking at the man that would be the big brother she never had. "Thanks Jack, for everything."

Jack says his goodbyes to Neil then heads toward the office. Ava turns to Neil, "I'm sorry, I know you want me to go to the police, but I can't, not yet, I'm not ready for that yet. They will want proof and statements and everything, plus, I don't know if the police are trustworthy."

Neil's eyebrows shoot up at this statement.

"He has so many people in his pocket and on the books that I don't know who I can trust."

Neil takes her hand and lets his shoulders sag, he knows

he had been coming on too strong with the police, he just wanted her safe. "No, I'm sorry, you don't need to apologise, I should have realised that he might have some of the police on the payroll. I just didn't think." He had been making small circles on the back of Ava's hands, she smiles at him, amazed at how considerate he is being over her reluctance to go to the authorities.

"That's okay, we mere mortals don't live in the same world as people like Nathan, but I am sorry that I have dragged you into this mess."

Neil shakes his head, "You didn't drag me into anything, I chose to be here for you, I chose to help you, if I didn't want to be here with you then I wouldn't be here, okay?"

Ava nods ever so slightly.

"Good, now you ready to go home?"

Ava looks up at him confusion in her eyes, "Home?"

"Yes, home, where we stay. You and me, not together, well we do stay together but not together…much, you know what I mean. I want you to think of my house as your home." Embarrassment is mingled with desire in his eyes as he tries to explain his meaning,

Ava smiles shyly, she can't believe that Neil has accepted her into his home and made her feel welcome, Nathan never referred to his house as theirs, always his. "Yes, I'm ready to go home." She lifts her glass and drains the last of the amber liquid in it, as Neil stands and holds out his hand for her to take. She takes it but doesn't stand,

"Neil, thank you for helping me and making me feel at home."

Neil just smiles and gives her hand a pull to get her up from her seat, "Any time Sweet."

Ava can feel Neil's breath on her cheek when he speaks,

they are within kissing distance and Neil takes a leap of faith and quickly kisses her cheek. He turns and walks towards the front doors, never letting go of Ava's hand.

During the drive home, Ava notices that Neil has taken a different route with some odd turns. She assumes he is just driving about, as he had told her that his BMW is his life line, his pride and joy, the reason he managed to get through his dark days and just driving it can help make him feel better, clear his head and help him think. Leaning back into the soft leather seat Ava closes her eyes, feeling the warmth of the brandy take over and doesn't think too much of the longer drive home.

Neil looks in his rear-view mirror again, the old, but very well cared for 1970 gold Mark 2 1600 Ford Cortina was still behind them. He had seen it as they left the car park near the club, so took a few different turns to check if they were being followed, or if he was being paranoid after the conversation about Nathan and his 'friends'. After five turns and three different streets Neil concluded that yes they were being followed. Glancing at Ava, his stomach knotted, she looked so peaceful sitting there her eyes closed and a hint of a smile on her lips, but he had to tell her what was happening,

"Ava, Sweet, you awake?"

"Hmm, yeah just resting, guessed you decided to go for a drive"

Something in Neil's tone didn't sit right with Ava, "Why?"

"Don't panic, but, I think we might be being followed."

Her eyes flew open, spinning in her seat so she is facing Neil, "What do you mean we're being followed?" Panic soaring through her veins and flashing through her eyes.

"The Cortina behind us has been tailing me since we left the club, that's why I was taking all those different turns.

What do you want to do? I could drive to the police station, go back to the club, or pull over see what they do then?"

Panic had started to overtake Ava, her breathing was fast and shallow, seeing that she was going into another panic attack Neil knew he had to pull over, whatever the Cortina did he would deal with, but right now he had to get Ava breathing normally before she passed out. He calmly told Ava what he was doing, not sure if she could hear him or not, but continued talking as he pulled over to the kerb and killed the engine, undoing his seatbelt and Ava's so he could turn her to face him. The Cortina never stopped and he never looked for it, his main priority being Ava. Taking her hands in his and keeping his voice calm and soft he spoke to her, "Ava, look at me Sweet, we're going to breathe together okay? You breathe with me, just like before okay?"

Ava locks eyes with Neil, the Cortina forgotten as she concentrates on his voice and her breathing, "That's it, in and out, in and out." Refusing to break eye contact both of them breathe in unison for what seems like hours, but is really only minutes until Ava's breathing is back to normal and her panic is under control again.

"Okay?" Neil asks, still holding her hands,

"Yes, thanks, I'm sorry I – where's the car?" Ava turns her head to see out the back window but there is no other car in the street.

"I think they drove past when I pulled over. Are you sure you're okay now?"

Ava nods then lowers her head, she is fighting the tears that are threating, "I'm sorry I fall apart all the time, I'm rubbish."

Neil lifts her head to look into her eyes, wiping the tears that disobeyed her plea for them to stay away with his thumbs, "Sweet, you have nothing to be sorry for, you have had a hell of a life, a hell of a day, and a hell of a battle in front of you. If he isn't going to give up harassing you, he had you at your lowest, but not anymore, you are away from him, never to return, the only way you can go now is up, and I'm here to give you all the help you need. Now I'm going to drive home, but take the back roads just in case they are waiting on the motorway for us.

Ava nods and pulls her seatbelt back over, Neil does the same then drives off, they manage to get home without any more incidents.

Once they are home Neil goes to his office, brings out some paper and a pen and hands them to Ava, "Here, we can start writing on this until we can get a notebook."

Ava takes the paper and pen from him and sits at the breakfast bar. Looking at the blank piece of paper in front of her a wave of nausea passes over her. The thought of writing down every detail of her life with Nathan, every attack, every punch, every insult, everything he ever put her through, makes her feel sick and stupid. She should not have let it happen, should not have let him control her like he did, but she did.

Neil walks into the kitchen with another brandy for Ava and a whisky for him, placing it in front of her Neil looks at the piece of paper, "Struggling?"

Ava looks up at the first man to show her kindness in years, "I let him use me as a punch bag; I was too stupid to see I was in an abusive relationship."

Neil sits down next to her and sighs, "You didn't let him do it, he controlled you, shut you off from everyone you knew, friends and family, until you had no one but him, and nothing unless he gave you it. It was not your fault; none of it was your fault. You have to believe that he took your choices away from you. I just gave you an opportunity to get your choices back. I know it will be hard to put down what he did to you, but remember that that is all in the past and he won't be able to control you anymore."

Knowing Neil is right, Ava takes a sip of her brandy and starts to write. Whilst she is writing, Neil gives Jack a phone at the club to warn him about the tail and to watch out for anyone suspicious.

CHAPTER FIFTEEN

Nine am and Nathan is sitting in the back of his Daimler, the traffic on the M74 is heavy, so Nathan takes the time to phone thug one to get an update on last night's events.

"Ah, Mr Low, how ir ye doin this fine mornin?" The nasal sound of the idiot's voice grates on Nathan, he gives an inward groan, he really despises these two, but needs must.

"Anything else happen last night?" Desperate to keep the conversation on track, and get off the phone as quickly as possible.

"Well, I spoke to the burd in the club—"

Nathan explodes, "Her name is Ava, I don't ever want to hear you call her the 'burd' again!" He may have had to keep her in line with a few slaps here and there, but he did have manners and called her by her given name, at least when she hadn't pushed his buttons!

"Oh okay, raw nerve there, Mr Low, anyway as I was saying, I told AVA, to get her ar...to get back to you or she would be in more trouble than it was worth. Him and AVA, got into his car later an we followed him but I think he got suspicious, he was pure takin weird turns an that so I backed aff a bit, then he pulled ower so I jist left them. I went passed his hoose later and the lights wir oan and his poncy M3 wis in the drive. We're bout to get back oot in bout five minutes, an that."

Nathan was happy at the fact that Ava and the idiot that thinks he is her knight in shining armour know that he is not happy and that he is doing something about the situation they caused.

"Right, keep an eye on anything they do today, but don't make any more contact until I say so, okay?"

"Aye right, whatever you say boss." The thug humphs, he was looking forward to making pretty little Ava panic again, he had so enjoyed it last night.

Nathan disconnects the call and steps out of the car into the crisp autumn morning. Getting to his office only takes a couple of minutes, stepping off the lift into the plush, cream corridor Nathan spots the blonde. She is grinning at him like the proverbial Cheshire cat, he walks up to her desk and gives her his knowing smile, "So, Miss, do I have any mail?"

His voice is low and husky, and his eyes never leave hers, making her flustered as she thinks of last night and everything they did. "Y,yes, Sir, eh Mr Low, here's your, eh, your mail and there has been no calls this morning, Sir, sorry." She stumbles through the sentence.

Nathan can see the effect he has on her and it makes him smile, he loves getting woman to fall at his feet and lose their minds, "Thank you Miss." He winks at her and walks past her desk and into his office, mail in hand. He closes his office door and places the letters on his desk to remove his suit jacket. Sitting in the oversized leather chair he picks up the letters, flicking through them trying to find one from the planning department, he is becoming desperate for the planning to come through for this latest lot of apartments he has started building, but it's not there. Throwing the letters onto the desk in a fit of rage, he dials his estate agent.

"What do you mean there is a problem, the foundations

have been started, so where is my fucking planning permission?" Nathan is trying his hardest not to shout at the agent on the other end of the phone, but it is a losing battle. He listens for a bit the roars again, "Who isn't taking the money, what's the fucker's name, does he have a problem with my money? On seconds thought I don't want to know, just get him told, now what is the problem with the land?" He listens for another second then butts in, "Just get the permission." He slams the phone down, "Fuckin moron!" he growls under his breath, then lifts his phone again to phone the builders, hoping against hope that everything is going well on that side of the development. The builders are getting antsy about the permission but Nathan promises him everything is in hand and they can continue with building the apartments that are going to make him his next million or two.

His intercom buzzes and the blonde's voice creaks through the speaker asking him if he wishes to put in a lunch order, checking the clock he realises that it's one o'clock, not sure where the morning had went to he orders his usual chicken pasta salad and sparkling water. Hearing his phone beep to say a text message has come through he lifts it expecting it to be thug one, as he hadn't heard anything since the phone call that morning. It wasn't either of them so Nathan ignores it and decides he doesn't like not knowing what's happening so sends a text to thug one.

What is happening?

He stares at his phone for a second, willing it to ring or beep, then drops it onto his desk, he shouldn't be this worked up over this, although this shouldn't be happening as Ava should know better than to leave him. He had thought he had made that point abundantly clear the last time she mentioned him not treating her right. She was lucky he managed to control himself or she would've be in hospital that night, as it was they had to cancel a dinner arrangement as her neck was still slightly swollen almost a week later. Hearing the beep of the text Nathan snatches his phone up, chiding himself for the desperation in his movement.

No much, they no left the hoose, let you know if they dae

Nathan lets a growl out at his phone. If they are staying in HIS house all morning, does that mean they are staying in his bed all morning? The thought that Ava would have sex with anyone else other than him, twists in his gut; he was the person to take her virginity so he should be the only person allowed to go there with her. His earlier anger returns with a vengeance and he tries to rein it in as the blonde buzzes the intercom to let him know that lunch has arrived.

"Thank you Miss, could you bring it in for me, thanks." His voice is low and husky, aiming for charming and sexy, grinning to himself, Nathan decides the best way to release his pent up anger is by having the blonde in his office. She shimmies in to the huge office with her boss's lunch, the autumn sun is streaming in the full-length windows behind the desk, Nathan looks up from the paperwork he is skimming over, though not really taking anything in as he thinks about everything he wants to do to his receptionist, and smiles his full, charming, sexy smile.

"There you are, come in and close the door behind you please." She obeys, then walks over to place Nathan's lunch on his desk. "Come here." His voice is saying everything he wants to convey to her and, like the good girl she is, she walks up to him, before she can place her hands on his chest Nathan has taken her mouth and more. When she pressed the intercom to tell her boss that his lunch had arrived, never once had she imagined that she would be getting a quicky against his desk, fantasied at night about it maybe but never imagined it would happen. The reality however was very different to her fantasy, he was rough, and gave her little to no pleasure, taking only what he wanted (last night was very different). Once he was finished, Nathan pulled her from his desk and righted his clothes, as she wiggled her skirt back down and picked up her strewn underwear. Sitting back down at his desk Nathan picks up his lunch and opens it, he looks up at his receptionist as if he just remembered she was there,

"Thanks for lunch, it was just what I needed!" He grins at her and then gets back to his paperwork and lunch, not even bothering to dismiss her.

Disappointment flashes over her face as her boss thanks her, but she manages to cover it up with a dazzling smile, "Anytime Mr Low." She goes for sultry, but she isn't feeling it, she walks from the office back to her desk, knowing full well that she has been used for her bosses own pleasure and she also acknowledges that she has been dismissed twice after sex. It hurts to think that he thinks so little of her, but the naïve, hopeful side of her buries these feelings in order to believe that they do have something. It is her he comes to when he is needing things, it is special, she will be his and she will be a better girlfriend than the mouse of a woman that has just left him. Getting on with her work, the blonde fantasises about their wedding and the honeymoon.

After a lazy morning watching TV, Ava goes upstairs for a hot shower. Feeling the hot spray relax her, she washes her hair and then goes about washing the rest of her body. Knowing she shouldn't really, she lifts Neil's razor and gives her legs and underarms a quick going over, mentally reminding herself she needs to get things like razors and more clothes but not having the money to get them is the problem. Not wanting to bring her mood down she pushes the thought of her money situation out of her mind and gets out the shower. She dries off and pulls on her underwear and one of Neil's T-shirts that she has been wearing as a nightdress and sits down to dry her hair, she gives herself a weird well done for remembering her hairdryer, straighteners and makeup, but chastises herself for not bringing a lot of her clothes or any of her pyjamas! Once her hair is done she sets about doing her makeup, nothing heavy, very natural work makeup, then goes downstairs to eat her lunch in front of the daytime TV that she was never allowed to watch when Nathan was in, but sneaked a few episodes when he was out at work.

Knowing her and Neil weren't going into the club until three, she had set out to enjoy her morning by relaxing and trying to get last night out of her head. Flashes of the scruffy guy threatening her. Neil, Jack and the club, then the car being followed when they were returning home, her freak out and subsequent panic attack interrupted her sleep for most of the night, making her swither on her promise not to go back to Nathan, but knowing what that would do to Neil and the fact that both him and Jack have promised her they would keep her safe. She doesn't have it in her to hurt either of them, especially Neil. However, the will to get away from Nathan seems to be growing in her as her strength and confidence grow, so holding onto that thought Ava had eventually fallen into a dreamless sleep.

Thinking about last night, Ava marvels at how kind and patient Neil was. They were talking again about going to the police or at the very least going to see WPC Young when Ava started to have another panic attack, but because of Neil noticing the signs and acting fast the attack wasn't anywhere near as big as the one in the car. Just getting pulled into his chest and held until she felt better made all the difference, she had taken a few attacks when she had been with Nathan but all he had done was tell her get a grip then leave her to deal with it herself, or slap her to 'shock her out of it'. Again, it makes her realise just how wrong her relationship with Nathan was, every day he made her feel small and weak, caused her pain and embarrassment, telling her she was stupid and useless, even the thought of him brings fear and panic to her chest. Now she is out of the relationship she is having a hard time remembering why she stayed so long with Nathan, why she believed him when he made her believe that it was natural for a man to lose his temper when they were angry, why she believed that it would get better. Looking back she probably did know that it was wrong, but her confidence was so low she thought she wasn't worth anything better. Now she had met Neil he had shown her kindness and patience, made her feel worthy of being, and sometimes he has even made her feel beautiful just by looking at her. Every now and again she catches a look in his eyes, something she thinks, maybe even hopes, is desire, but she can't really be sure, so she doesn't look too deeply, but it boosts her mood so whatever it is she likes it. However, she is sure that never again will she let herself be a punch bag, for anyone.

Neil walks back into the living room interrupting Ava's musings, he had went for a shower after lunch and was now dressed in his usual attire of black jeans, though he was minus a T-shirt at the moment. He was walking towards the swinging doors that led to the kitchen to make another coffee, "You want a top up?" He motions towards Ava's cup,

"No, thanks I'm okay just now, thanks."

Ava tries not to stare at how his jeans hug his butt and his bare muscles, Ava notices that he is in good shape though he had never mentioned going to the gym or training, but she knew his job required lots of heavy lifting, so she assumes it is due to that.

On the other side of the kitchen door, Neil is trying to focus on making his coffee, but his hands don't seem to work properly. Seeing Ava sitting on his couch, totally relaxed and in a T-shirt of his is more than he can handle especially after holding her last night during her panic attack and then holding on some more, God, he just couldn't bring himself to let her go. He knows he has to get the thought of him and Ava being anything more than friends out of his head, but he can't help himself from getting more and more attached and he knows he is falling deeper and harder every day. He desperately wants to take care of her, make sure she is safe and loved exactly how she deserves, he wants to see her flourish, see her confidence grow in and out of the work place, see her love herself and hopefully him, but he is also very aware of not smothering her, of giving her space to grow. She has just came out of a violent, demanding, and extremely unhealthy relationship, so he understands that the last thing on her mind will be getting into another relationship. However, he still hopes that once all the crap with Nathan has calmed down and she has had time to heal that she will see him as a friend, a lover and more.

Pushing the thought of them together from his mind and trying to think of anything else to ease the bulge in his trousers, he walks back into the living room, coffee in hand. "How you feeling?" he asks as he sits next to Ava on the couch, her feet are tucked up underneath her and, without thinking, he places his hand on her bare knee, not the best idea considering the thoughts he was having in the kitchen and the effect that they had on him.

Ava looks round at him and smiles, enjoying the feeling of his touch; surprised that she had that thought she swallows before she answers, "Yeah, thanks."

Neil starts to remove his hand, but Ava places hers on top to stop him, "Neil." She is looking straight into his hazel eyes, "Thank you for last night, for em, for not judging me and just...well just holding me." She breaks eye contact, her cheeks red with embarrassment at her admission and lowers her head, she isn't used to being vocal with her emotions, or at least being allowed to vocalise them.

Neil's heart shatters at her words, he knows the effort that it must have taken for Ava to tell him how she is feeling, and that she is probably not used to letting her emotions out for fear of reprisals, but his heart also swells at the knowledge of him making her feel safe, and comfortable enough to tell him. "Anytime Sweet, anytime." He pauses desperate to take her into his arms and hold her again, but knows that it would be a selfish move, so makes do with squeezing her hand. "You okay for going in soon, 'bout an hour?"

She smiles again, loving how relaxed everything between them, how relaxed she is. "Yeah, just need to pull clothes on and that's me."

"Cool, me too!" Neil cringes at his words; he really needs to get his adult vocabulary back and soon. Neither of them breaking their hand contact, they both start to watch the rest of the crappy daytime TV show until it's time to get ready to leave.

CHAPTER SIXTEEN

They arrive at the Daydream just after three, Neil had taken a different route from his usual one, just to be on the safe side, he couldn't see the car that had followed them last night but wasn't one hundred percent sure that they hadn't been followed, or that someone was watching them.

Jack comes out of the office when he sees the couple walk into the club, "Awright, how's things today then?"

Ava smiles and gives Jack a peck on the cheek, "Hey Jack, things are good today thank you." She walks towards the staff area to hang up her coat then walks behind the bar to start work, there is a girl already serving and the bar is quiet so she starts to clean and rotate the fridges.

Neil and Jack go back into the office to discuss business and so Neil can fill Jack in on the car following them.

"Is Ava keeping a diary like I suggested? She really doesn't want to go to the police?" Jack asks before Neil can say anything.

"She thinks she not strong enough to go through the process of going to the police and everything that comes with that, but saying that she did start the diary of everything that excuse for a man did to her, right up to yesterday when that guy came in to threaten her and the car following us last night."

Jack had noticed Neil worrying a piece of paper that had

been sitting on the desk, "You gonna stop messing with that bit of paper?" He takes it from Neil and looks at it,

"It's an invoice that needs paying and then filed."

Looking down at his now empty hands Neil puffs out the breath he didn't know he was holding,

"Sorry, I didn't realise it was an invoice." looking around the desk he spots a pen, lifts it and starts to fiddle with that instead.

"You want to tell me what's eaten at you? It seems to be more than Ava and Nathan."

Neil smirks, he never can hide anything from his best friend, he always knows when there is something wrong, although his fidgeting probably gave him away too. "Ach, that pish wa that guy coming in here threating Ava, not knowing what's best for her to help her move on and believe in herself, not helping you out here as much as I normally do and crazy Julie hasn't been in touch again about being pregnant or not, so I'm not sure where I stand with her either." He continues to click the pen in and out until Jack removes that from his hand also.

"Why don't you text the crazy one?"

"Aye maybe," Neil is looking at Jack with uncertainty in his eyes, "Though not sure if that a good idea or not, you know with the crazy side of things!"

Jack waves aside Neil's worry of his crazy ex, "And you don't need to worry about this place, that's why you pay me, and if Nathan does anything else to us, this place or Ava then we will deal with it, right?"

Neil sighs some of the stress out of his body, he knows Jack's right and he should calm down. "Ah, cheers man, you always know how to sort me out. Right, next thing, can I swap cars with you?"

Jack's smile spreads out over his face, he loves driving Neil's BMW but he is rarely allowed to even turn the ignition on never mind drive it. "Hell yes!" Jack's excitement palpable.

Neil growls at him, knowing that Jack is desperate to get behind the wheel of his car, and that he is going to enjoy the swap more than Neil will. He does like Jack's Mazda, but it's just not the same as driving his M3, mostly because of the blood, sweat, tears and love he has put into making the car perfect and that the car got him through dark times in life and kept him from prison.

"Cheers, and remember that car is my life so look after it or you're dead to me, understand!" Jack laughs at his best friend knowing he is joking, partially.

"Right I'm going to see how Ava's doing." Neil stands and walks towards the office door,

"Cool, I'll come with you, see how busy we are." Both men walk from the office and notice that the club is quiet, again, but know that it is early yet and there were no parties booked for that night, and that was something that Neil had wanted to get more of in the future.

They walked over to the bar and the other staff member asks Jack if she could speak to him. Jack agrees and he and the girl go to a table at the back of the club. Neil goes behind the bar to speak to Ava, she had stood up from the fridge she had been cleaning when she heard the other girl say Jack's name and now she is watching Jack and the girl walk away with a worried look on her face.

"Hey Sweet, you okay, what you doing?"

Ava brings her attention back to Neil, "Yeah, I'm okay, she is worried about her job," Ava nods towards the table Jack is sitting at with the girl, "I didn't want it to look like I was coming in to take over so I just got on with the cleaning rota." Her cheeks blush slightly at her admission. Neil shakes his head but smiles at how considerate she is,

"Hey Sweet, you don't need to worry about the other staff in here, you aren't taking anybody's job, and thank you for doing some cleaning, I'm not sure any other sod in here bothers about the rota. You are so kind and considerate you know that?" Ava blushes again as she lets out a giggle, she really does love how relaxed she has been feeling lately, especially around Neil, and Jack, but mostly Neil. He is the one that really makes her feel worthy of being more, worth more than material things and a punch, like Nathan did, and she is coming to terms with the fact that she could do a hell of lot better than Nathan. It amazes her how breaking away from one person has completely changed her anxiety levels and her view of the world and herself.

"That's okay, it was quiet enough, so best get things done instead of standing about."

Their conversation is interrupted by customers coming up to the bar and Neil turning around to serve them. They were asking about booking the club for their engagement party, Neil asks them to take a seat at one of the tables as he gets the booking diary from the office and the leaflets they had printed up. Walking back over to the couple Neil grabs Ava's attention, "You want to come over with me and do the booking?"

Ava grins at the thought of learning more of the business so agrees readily, "Yes please that would be great." They both join the couple at the table and go through all of the options open to the couple, Ava added in ideas of her own and the couple really warmed to her, agreeing with her suggestions and seemingly eager to book.

The meeting was concluded by eight with the couple booking their party and leaving with lots of ideas and the price lists. Jack came over to the table where they were still sitting, they filled him in on the booking, and they went through some of the order lists for the next week. Neil looks over at Ava and sees her stifling a yawn, he notices how tired looking she is, but also how happy she is at getting the booking. Neil knows she doesn't sleep very well as he hears her padding about the house, up and down the stairs at all times during the night.

"You needing home Sweet?"

Ava is in the middle of stifling another yawn when she nods her head, "If that's okay."

"Course it is, Sweet, whatever you need." Neil's voice is soft and full of compassion.

Ava looks over to Jack, "You sure? We keep leaving you here to look after the place." Jack shakes his head at her, the cold feeling he had had about going up against Nathan had thawed due to being around Ava and seeing all the good he and Neil were doing for her. Seeing Neil with her was reassuring too, getting him to take time away from the club and the car was good for him and being with Ava seemed to bring him some happiness, and if anybody deserved happiness, it was Neil, and Ava.

"Yes, it's fine, I'm paid to be here and close up so it all good."

Ava smiles at Jack he really is starting to be the big brother she never had, "Thank you, I'll just grab my coat." She stands and walks towards the staff area where she had hung up her coat earlier.

Neil stands and turns to Jack, "I'll come back about tenish."

"Aye if you want. Oh you got my keys?"

Neil looks at his friend, confused for a second until the penny drops, "Oh aye, eh no, where are they?"

Jack jangles them in his pocket then pulls them out tossing them into Neil's hands. "Cheers, I guess I'd better give you mine then." Neil grudgingly hands over the keys to his beloved BMW and Jack takes them with a sly grin, which evolves into an evil laugh making Neil groan even more. They see Ava walking out from the staff area and walk over to meet her at the cloakroom door. Ava and Jack exchanges pecks on the cheek as they said their goodbyes, much to Neil's annoyance. Neil puts his hand on the small of Ava's back as they leave the Daydream and get out into the frosty night air. Ava turns to walk towards where they left Neil's car, but he grasps her hand, stopping her in her tracks,

"We're not taking my car, we're taking Jack's Mazda."

Ava turns to face Neil, confusion firmly set in her features, then the slow change to realisation, she knows that Neil would never give up his car lightly, and the fact that he is at least swapping it for a night because of her and her problematic ex, amazes and humbles her. Never did she think that anyone would do anything that kind for her, even if it is just a car.

"Ah, because we were followed last night?" Neil nods

"Aye, I thought it best, just to be safe, just in case, though I didn't see anyone this afternoon when we drove here." Neil shrugs, trying to convey that it's no big deal, even though it feels like his left arm is being removed, damn he loves that car!

"Are you sure? I mean you're letting Jack drive your car?"

Neil swallows hard at the thought of anybody driving his car, "If it keeps you safe, Sweet, then yes I'm sure." He kisses the top of her head and takes her hand, but Ava refuses to move, instead she raises herself up onto her tiptoes and gently kisses Neil on the lips,

"Thank you." He hears the emotion in her voice and knows for sure that she understands his feelings about his car, and maybe her. Hand in hand, they both walk to where Jack parked his car that morning.

Thug one has situated himself near the car park that both Neil and Jack usually use, he notices the Mazda leave the car park but doesn't give it much thought, he knows that is the other guy's car. He decides to go for a coffee in the bar across from the club to wait on the girl and her new boyfriend to leave. An hour later the thug looks up from his paper and realises that the 'other guy' is standing outside talking to the bouncers. Jumping up from his seat, he curses,

"Ya bastard," He rushes from the bar and back to the car, jumping in, he awakens his pal who is still sleeping in the passenger seat,

"Whit the fuck's up wa you?" thug two grumbles, annoyed at being woken up.

"The fuckers swapped cars on us."

"Ah, awright," Thug two wriggles back down in his seat to get more shut eye, he hates doing stake out he never gets a proper sleep.

"Whit the fuck you think yir doin? Git oot and go see if the burd is still in the club!" Stretching and yawning Thug two opens his door to get out but stops and turns back,

"How come you never looked before you came back to the car?" Thug one growls, he knows that would have been the more sensible idea but didn't think of double-checking until he was back in the car. Not about to admit his mistake to the younger, less experienced partner he turns the blame on him,

"Thought you might want to do some fucking work for the dosh you'll be wanting, and anyway I've already been in the club so they know ma face, now hurry up!"

Humphing thug two gets out and slams the car door before walking towards the club. Jack is just about to walk back into the club when he notices the thug walk round the corner; he turns back round and stands to face the thug, his arms folded across his chest, his stance solid and unmoveable. Thug two walks up to the front door and tries to walk past Jack, but to no avail as Jack is blocking the doorway,

"Can I help you?" Jack is all sweetness and light and manages to keep his anger under control on the outside, but in his head, he has visualised beating the twerp standing in front of him and sending him back to Nathan with a warning to back off.

"Eh, I'm just goan fir a pint an that." The thug shifts from foot to foot, even though he thinks he is acting completely kosher. Jack continues to look at the thug taking in every detail from his manky trainers to his scruffy unshaved face and wild hair.

"I'm sorry Sir, we have a very strict dress code here and you don't even come near it with those trainers," The thug looks down at his feet at the mention of his footwear,

"I really am sorry, but not tonight, maybe another night." The sarcasm is dripping from every word Jack utters to the thug, then he pauses for a beat before adding, "Then again, probably not!"

The thug goes to push passed Jack regardless and Jack's anger gets the better of him. Grabbing the thug, he smashes him against the open door, his fingers around the guy's windpipe, one sudden squeeze and the windpipe would be crushed. The thug is grappling at his throat to get him off. Jack leans in even closer, until he is crushing the thug's chest with his body weight, so he can speak to the thug without anyone else hearing him threaten the thug's ability to father children in the future if he or his partner in crime ever came near the club or Ava again. As far as Jack was concerned he would be doing humanity a favour by ripping the idiot's balls off, but he is sensible enough to know that a court of law wouldn't see it the same way, unfortunately. He lets go of the thug and gives him a push away for the club, just to make sure he knows what direction he should be walking, as a second thought he shouts after the thug,

"And you can tell that prick Nathan the same!" Satisfied that he won't see either thug again anytime soon, Jack walks back into the Daydream. He stands at the bar looking around at everything that Neil started and both of them have built up, and winces at the thought of Nathan taking it all away, he may have just fanned the flames with the threat to Nathan and his thugs.

****

Nathan is stalking around his home office with his mobile phone on speaker; there is no one else in the house so he is unleashing full fury at thug one who has phoned with that day's information on Ava and Neil. The thug knew it wouldn't go down well when he told Nathan about the car swap and what the business partner had said to thug two, but he didn't expect just quite this amount of fury aimed at him.

"He fuckin said what?" Anger rolling off Nathan and down the phone, so the thug could practically taste it, the thug starts to explain what happened again, but again Nathan explodes,

"I heard you the first fucking time you moron." Nathan is still prowling round his office like a caged animal as he roars at the thug,

"Right it must be time that I go and pay them a visit at the club and just take back what is mine. Leave it for tonight, but get back to his house tomorrow morning and let me know the moment they are all in the club." He cancels the call before the thug can reply, then picks up his brandy glass. He did have six of these very expensive Gleneagles crystal glasses, until all this crap with Ava started and now he is down to five. The bitch has ruined everything he has worked for, and now she needs to pay. He drains his glass and plans his next move to get her back, then turns his attention to his planning permission problems. Upping his bribes hasn't worked so far, so he needs to come up with a different plan, but he doesn't know why this particular lot of apartments planning are being blocked, if it's a problem with the ground, or if it is someone not wanting the apartments built, but whatever it is he needs to find out and get the permission he needs to get his apartments up and more money in his account. Thinking about all his problems and Ava has made his anger bubble up again, so much so that before he knows what he is doing, he hurls the crystal glass in his hand at the wall smashing it.

"Fuck, there goes another one," he growls out loud. He looks at his Rolex watch, wondering if it is too late to get the blonde over to help calm him down. Seeing that it's not, he smiles to himself, the best way he has found to get rid of stress is a good night in the sheets with a sexy partner, and it doesn't cost him any of his good glasses!

CHAPTER SEVENTEEN

Back home and feeling a lot safer, Ava changes into some of the T-shirts and shorts that Neil had given her to wear as jammies. She has been trying to keep up with her washing so she doesn't need to use too many of Neil's things, but every morning she wakes up soaked through with sweat due to the nightmares that she has been having nightly. She really does need to buy herself new clothes, but she doesn't have any of her own money and has only just started working two days ago, so isn't due a wage. She knows that Neil had said he would buy her anything that she needed, and he did buy her some essentials when she first moved in, but she is needing more of just about everything now and she feels uncomfortable asking him, either for money or to buy her anything, so instead she has started to hand wash things for quickness. Lifting some of her underwear, she walks downstairs and into the kitchen through the door in the hall. She starts to fill the sink with hot soapy water and starts to wash her clothes through.

In the middle of rinsing them Neil walks into the kitchen through the swing doors leading to the living room, "There you are, I was wonder what you fancied for dinner, I was think—" he stops mid-sentence as he notices what she is doing,

"Ava, what are you doing? Why are you washing your

knickers in the sink?" Ava's blush starts at her neck and rises until it feels like the top of her head might explode off with the heat of her embarrassment.

"I don't, em, I—" she lowers her eyes, too embarrassed to look Neil in the eyes.

Neil sighs, annoyed at himself for causing her any embarrassment, but tries not to show his annoyance,

"Why didn't you say," he moves beside her, turning her head slowly with his hand cupping her cheeks, "I'm really sorry Sweet, I never even thought, I should have had you out shopping before now.

Ava's eyes dart up to look at Neil's then just as quickly she averts them and looks anywhere but at Neil, she really didn't want to see the look of pity that she expects to be in his eyes.

"It's okay, I can wash as I go, until I get my first wage," she pauses then blushes again at her statement of getting paid, "I mean, if I earn one that is. I can't keep using your things, and I need to stand on my own two feet, so it's no problem to wait honest." She stops and sinks slightly, "It's just, I can't keep taking anymore, I'm sorry, it's just that I—" Ava tries hard not to break down. She has spent so many years having to rely on Nathan and having to jump through hoops for him to agree to buy her what she needed and he always threw it back at her, telling her that he was the one who provided everything for her and that she did nothing for him. Now she needs to rely on Neil, and as much as she knows it's different, and it does feel different, she knows in herself she shouldn't have to ask anybody for anything, she should be able to support herself, but because of Nathan and his over powering ways, and fists, she never had the chance to get a job or have anything of her own. She also knows that it's not Neil's fault she doesn't have much and was too weak to do anything about her situation until she ended up putting him, Jack and the club in the middle all the crap between her and Nathan. The car following them, the threats, the phone calls and Nathan's thugs coming into the club, all of it was her fault, and yet he is still here supporting her, offering her anything she needs. Ava puts her head down and closes her eyes, letting go of all the emotions she had been holding on to and letting them crash through her and break free. She starts to cry silently, not a sound leaving her lips, just the tears flowing from her eyes and her shoulders bobbing up and down slightly as she tries to breathe.

"Hey, Sweet c'm here, shhh," Neil pulls her into his arms, closing her into his chest and holds her tight, "I meant to take you shopping before now, and was going to get you new things for starting work, but I forgot, I'm sorry, I'm crap at this looking after you stuff."

Ava pulls up from his chest slightly so she can look into Neil's eyes, fully expecting to see pity or annoyance, but what she sees shocks her, she sees guilt, he is feeling guilty that he forgot to take her shopping and she has had to wash her things through. Not sure where it comes from and certainly not meaning to, she starts to laugh. Laughing she decides is definitely more cathartic than all the crying she has done over the years. Neil looks at her, complete confusion written all over his face,

"I'm sorry, I shouldn't be laughing, but, I don't know, it's just the relief,"

Neil looks even more confused now, but before he can ask, Ava continues with her explanation, "The relief I felt when I realised you weren't pitying me and you looked almost guilty that I have to wash my knickers in the sink."

Neil smiles shyly, he hadn't thought he was the type of person who let his feelings show on his face, but obviously, he must do sometimes. Looking into Ava's eyes he does see relief, he can feel it too as he holds her and she relaxes into him, her full body pressed into his, leaning on him, almost, her laugh, her full bodied cleansing laugh, he feels himself falling another bit for her. Smiling at her, he realises that the woman in his arms could be the making or the breaking of him and his heart.

Ava continues talking, "It's not your fault, it's all mine."

Neil starts to correct her but she places her finger on his lips to stop him. They are still in an embrace and Ava places her head back onto his chest, the warmth she feels sends a thrill through her, something she hasn't felt in such a long time. Pushing the feeling to the side she continues, "I'm the one who allowed myself to be pulled into an abusive relationship and didn't have the strength to leave, but then again it is all on Nathan."

"Listen Sweet, you didn't allow yourself to be pulled into the abusive relationship, you were lured into, given a false sense of security," Neil takes a deep breath before continuing, feeling his emotions trying to take over, "And I was born into it, but we are both free of them, and please don't apologise for laughing, ever, it is such a great sound."

Neil's hand seems to have taken on a life of its own and has moved to Ava's face, his thumb stroking her cheek bone gently. Both of them looking into each other's eyes, their breathing in sync, the bond between them that is growing stronger daily, palpable in the air. Neil is first to break the contact, not wanting to, but also not wanting to push his luck or Ava. Clearing his throat, hoping it would sound like a man's voice and not the horny schoolboy he thinks it might sound like he continues "Well, first thing tomorrow we will go shopping, okay?"

Ava smiles, "Okay, and thanks again." She looks so sweet and innocent standing at his kitchen sink, Neil can't control the horny teenager within him and leans in kissing Ava's cheek. He gives Ava a shy smile as he lets go and walks towards the fridge to start dinner.

****

"What do you mean you can't come over?" Nathan is ready to explode with anger, the blonde has said no to his request – though he had thought of it as more of an order – to come over and help him relieve his stress. She explains that she has already made plans, but Nathan can't understand what 'plans' she may have that would be more important than him, and is demanding to know what these 'plans' are.

"Dinner with your sister? Really, that is what you are telling me, that you won't come over for a night of passion with me because you are having dinner with your sister? Unbelievable. Right, tomorrow you will have plans with me, I will give you the details in the morning at the office!" Without much of a goodbye he disconnects the call, still seething with anger. Not sure what else he can do to de-stress he heads to his gym to work out.

Two hours later Nathan is back at his desk, plans of actions for both of his problems taking shape in his head. Problem one, Ava – Plan, take the blonde to the Daydream Club after dinner tomorrow, both Ava and Neil should be there as it will be a Friday night. Make sure Ava sees them together, then get her alone for a quiet chat. Problem two, Planning permission – Plan, speak to the old goat Drake try to find out if he has heard of any problems with the land surrounding his, maybe even offer to buy his land.

Happier that he has some form of plans, Nathan pours himself a brandy, fed up of breaking his good crystal he opts for a tall glass from the kitchen, not an appropriate glass to drink brandy from, but he will have to make do.

CHAPTER EIGHTEEN

Friday morning after breakfast, Neil and Ava head out to Glasgow Fort, Neil had said about Ava going on her own if she would rather, but she declined, her confidence still low and her fear of seeing Nathan still high. Neil was thankful that she had declined, he really didn't want her out on her own with the threat of Nathan and his thugs still looming, but he would never demand her to do what he wants or thinks is best for her. Not one to like shopping, Neil wasn't looking forward to the trip, but thankfully, Ava isn't like some of his other ex-girlfriends and doesn't traipse about every shop looking at the same clothes then back to the first shop, no she goes into a shop finds what she likes buys it and leaves, it is a breath of fresh air. Before they leave, they drop into Morrison's supermarket, Neil insisting that Ava gets food that she wants, and not to let him over run the fridge with beer and the cupboards with crisps.

Once home and the shopping put away, Ava offers to make them both lunch, Neil starts to decline her offer, but snaps his mouth closed when he sees the hurt in her gorgeous blue eyes.

Ava looks down before explaining herself, "It's just I used to really enjoy cooking and I haven't managed to do any, well not for anybody else other than me and sometimes Nathan's staff if he was away on business."

Neil sighs, hating what she has been through and still trying to make her feel at home in his house, "Yes, if you wish to make lunch then knock yourself out, but please don't feel you have to."

Ava smiles, she looks like she has been given a present and it warms his heart to see how happy such a simple thing has made her, little does he know just how safe and content she feels in his house – with him.

"No, it's not because I feel I need to, but because I can, I want to, I feel comfortable enough to do it."

Neil's shoulders relax, tension he didn't know he was holding onto seeping away as he comes to terms with what Ava was saying to him. She is comfortable in his house, with him. Now it was his turn to smile like someone had just given him a present. "Well when you put it like that, batter on."

Ava turns towards the fridge with a slight skip in her step to start lunch, as Neil continues to talk.

"I need to go into the club tonight, probably about six, after dinner, and I need to stay till closing, that okay with you?"

Ava turns from the cooker where she is preparing their Spanish omelette, and smiles, "Yeah, anytime, it's not like I can get in there without you." She grins at him with a glint in her eye, "I don't mind what time we go in or leave, I enjoy being there."

Neil manages to control the grin threatening to split his face, "You were really good with that couple the other day, I think the next booking we get in we should let you handle it on your own."

Ava freezes, she has never been allowed responsibility, Nathan always said she was too young and needy to help anybody, even herself.

Neil notices the change in Ava's body language, from swishing about the kitchen free and easy to stiff and cold with panic flowing from her. Ava, are you okay?"

Ava catches herself, and starts to move again, rigidly making lunch. Her stomach going from growling in hunger to a huge knot unable to accept food no matter how delicious it smells. Cursing herself inwardly. Why did she think she was ready to move on, to be able to hold down a job? There was no way she would be able to do the bookings and deal with customers and everything on her own, at least not to the standard that Neil and Jack expect of her.

Neil walks up behind her and puts his hands on her arms, "Ava," his voice gentle and full of concern, "Sweet, breathe, you need to breathe."

It's only after hearing Neil telling her to breathe does she realise that she is hyperventilating, he turns off the cooker and turns her round so she is facing him, he locks eyes with and takes her hands in his,

"Just like the last time Sweet, in the car remember, breath with me,"

She manages the slightest of nods as the panic has risen above her, over her, she can just make out what Neil is saying through the crashing sound of the blood rushing round her body and into her ears,

"Breath, follow me, in and out, in and out." They both continue like this until slowly Ava's panic starts to subside enough for her to control her breathing again, although Neil can still see fear in her eyes, continuing to hold her hands he asks,

"Was it me saying about you doing the bookings on your own?" Ava nods not trusting herself to talk, as she feels the panic rising again at just Neil mentioning her working on her own, Neil also notices her panic rising again,

"Ssshhhh, it's okay, it's okay. I'm guessing Nathan didn't allow you to do anything that involved responsibility?"

She shakes her head, still too frightened to speak,

"Did he tell you that you were too stupid to do anything?" again she nods, tears spilling over her eyelids. Neil is desperate to close his eyes, desperate not to show his anger that has been boiling up inside him, so he takes a deep breath and continues looking deep into her eyes as he reassures her. "Sweet, you are more than capable of doing anything you put your mind to, I believe in you one hundred percent and trust you. It is going to take you time for you to believe in yourself and get your confidence back, but you will get there and I will be supporting you all the way, I promise you, Sweet."

Tears still running down her cheeks, Ava smiles, shyly at first then more confident. "Thank you." her voice cracks on the 'you' and she takes a deep cathartic breath as she realises that not only are they still holding hands, but Neil has never once broken eye contact. The support and confidence she feels from Neil is overwhelming, she silently promises herself that she will pay him back with her own growth and confidence. She wraps her arms around his neck and holds tight for a few seconds before dropping her arms.

"Oh, eh, sorry, for the cuddle, it's just, you, you amaze me." Before Neil can respond or see her embarrassment at being forward, Ava turns back to the cooker and starts again on the lunch. Neil stands stuck to the spot, dumbfounded by Ava's reaction to his words and her words about him.

Ava turns to place the omelette on the breakfast bar and notices Neil still standing in the same spot, "You planning on standing there forever or could you get the plates ready?"

The glint is back in her eye and her voice is strong.

Neil stumbles over his words, because he is loving the cheeky look she is giving him and the playful way she can be around him, when life and Nathan isn't getting in the way.

"Aye, I was just, eh, aye, plates." Neil can feel the heat rise in his face, confused at the fact he is blushing, he silently wonders what she is doing to him as he brings the plates over and they sit to eat.

****

Nathan has made sure he has paid plenty of attention to the blonde all morning, with added guilt just so she will not refuse him again. She is lapping it all up and loving the attention, explaining how she is looking forward to dinner and the night ahead. She is almost begging him to touch her, doing everything in her power to get close to him, then stops short to see if he will close the gap, trying her hardest to show him how sorry she is for going out with her sister last night instead of going to him when he asked. Every now and then, he puts her out of her misery and brushes past her, just enough to keep her wanting more, and with every small brush, a small sound escapes her throat, the thrill and excitement growing. Nathan on the other hand is fed up with the games and just wants her to get on with her job until he is ready for her. Brushing passed her for the last time he places his hand on her bony hips, thinking that women should have meat on their bones, he whispers in her ear some of the things he is planning on doing to her tonight, loving what she is hearing she wiggles her rear into his crotch. There should be some movement down there at this, but there isn't, for some reason it wasn't getting the message, but tonight will be different, there will be no games, just him in control and doing what he wants. He walks into his office trying hard to convince himself that it is just the stress of the apartments and the planning permission, and thinking of the apartments he phones Mr Drake.

After a few rings the older gentleman answers.

"Ah Mr Drake, it's Nathan Low, here, how's things?" Wishing he had never asked, Nathan hmms, and yeahs his way through the next five minutes of listening to the old man talk about his business and family. Finally, Nathan is able to ask the questions he phoned to ask,

"Yes, well I was wondering if you have sent in your agreement for my apartments?" The silence from the other side of the phone is deafening to Nathan.

Eventually Mr Drake answers, "No, Mr Low I didn't write a letter of acceptance for your buildings, I actually entered an objection."

Nathan's anger explodes from him before he can get a hold of it, "You did what? You fucking idiot!"

"Now Mr Low I don't think there is any need for language like that! Now if you would calm down I will explain my reasoning behind my decision, as I would assume that will be your next question. Well I did some research of my own into some of your other apartment buildings and I don't believe they are safely built or the materials you use are of the high standard required of this country. I have also been hearing rumours about the class of people who buy your 'luxury' apartments and I don't think that that is the type of people I want living near me. I live in a very high class area Mr Low and this project of yours is not welcome here."

Stunned by the old man's rant, and the thought that the old man thinks he can out-class him, the only thing that Nathan can think of to ask is what people he meant.

Mr Drake lets out a low chuckle, "Ah, Mr Low, you know who I mean, people who make their money through ill-gotten means, and I won't tolerate that type of business or person in my neighbourhood. Now if you don't mind I have other, legitimate business to attend to."

Before Nathan can retaliate, he hears the click of the line being cut off, leaving him standing in his office, fingers grasping his hair, almost pulling it out by the roots. Stunned, he sits down behind his desk, seeing his very perfect life unravelling in front of his eyes, and he can't control it. This thought doesn't sit well with Nathan and he blames Ava entirely. That night in that club when she thought about standing up to him, he had had to put her in her place in public, people would have noticed, important people, people who understand that you have to keep your house in order, but not in public, never out in the open.

"Fuckin' Ava!" he screams as he throws his mobile phone against the wall next to the door, smashing it to a million pieces. He puts his head in his hands and slumps onto his desk. A second later, the blonde rushes into the office, wondering what all the shouting and smashing was all about. She stops at the door, her eyes darting about to find the remains of whatever got smashed, and her eyes find the remnants of the mobile phone on the floor next to where she is standing. She starts towards the desk to comfort her boss who is still slumped on his desk, looking dejected, but stops short when she hears the strange muffled laughing sound coming from Nathan's lowered head. The manic sound of the laugh sends a shiver up her spine and she unconsciously takes a step back. The laugh increases and expands and grows until it is a full belly, hearty laugh, and Nathan has raised his head to the ceiling, unnerved at the sight in front of her, the blonde just stands there, rooted to the spot, unsure of what to do, what has made her boss so hysterical, verging on unhinged even. Nathan's laughing stops as quickly as it started, he straightens up and fixing his cuffs and tie, like bringing back the face of control, he looks up at the blonde, registering the look of shock etched onto her face.

"Ah, sorry about that I'm okay, just a slight hiccup in life." Clearing his throat, he continues, "Well I seem to have broken my phone, could you organise a new one for me please, before finishing time, please." He dismisses her with a flick of his hand, as was his usual practise, showing that he was back to normal.

"Yes Sir, right away." She backs away out of the office, not really wanting to turn her back on her boss even though he seems to be back in control of himself.

"Oh, and Miss, we will be finishing at four this afternoon, for dinner at six." Yes, he feels back in control, just what he likes and apparently, his manhood agrees with this, as it starts to perk up.

"Yes, Sir, as you wish." She closes the door as Nathan smiles, he loves being in control especially when it involves women. He really is looking forward to tonight, being able to control two women, the stupid blonde in his bed and Ava so she returns to him, to his bed where she belongs. Then and only then will everything be in order and he will be able to sort out the mess that is these apartments.

CHAPTER NINETEEN

Ava and Neil arrive at the club. They had made sure that they weren't followed from the house, but as they were walking from the car park, Neil spotted the Cortina sitting on the road near the club. He makes a note of the time and opens an app on his phone that he has been using as a diary, he knows that Ava has started her diary too, but him keeping a backup one won't hurt.

A small party has been booked in for the top half of the club, they call it the top but in reality, it is only up three stairs at the back end of the club. There is a second bar there that gets opened when there are parties and it can also be partitioned off if the party desires some privacy.

Neil had asked Ava to work the bar at the party for the night, with other staff, but to make sure that everyone is happy and everything runs smoothly. Her nerves and fear are clawing at her as she walks to the top level to make sure everything is in place before the party arrives, but she refuses to let either of them get the better of her, Neil has talked her through everything and his belief in her is starting to rub off. Neil is standing at the main bar on the lower level talking to Jack.

"What did the guy say, exactly?" Neil is getting Jack to relate the incident from the night before for the third time.

"I've told you," Jack tells him exasperated, "And I've told

you what I said and what I did."

"I know, I know. I just don't like it, the idea of someone watching her, it's just wrong!"

Jack knows that his friend has feelings for Ava and that the thought of anyone hurting her is just gut wrenching for him, Jack puts his hand on his best friends shoulder, in a comforting bloke way. "I know bud, but look at her now, look how great she is doing. She is mixing with others, God she is actually talking to other people, this time a fortnight ago she couldn't do that, mostly because that prick wouldn't let her, but also she just couldn't, didn't have the confidence to do it, but, thanks to you she can now and is managing to get her life back. Don't let two wee dickheads get to you."

Neil nods in agreement, not taking his eyes off Ava, watching her getting on with the job in hand, musing about how good she looks, so good she is absolutely glowing. She turns and catches Neil's eye, giving him a smile before turning back and carrying on working the party. Jack watches the exchange, hoping that they really can get through this and his friend can find the happiness he deserves.

"Right you, back to work before I need to sack you."

Neil breaks his attention away from Ava and back to Jack, "Yes boss." Giving him, a small laugh and salute as he walks round behind the bar.

Neil's phone buzzes in his pocket taking it out he sees it is a text message from Julie, groaning he opens up the message.

*See told you! *

Seconds later another message comes through, this time it is a picture of a pregnancy test saying positive. Neil's shoulders sag as he considers this new information, with a deep breath he responds,

* Okay, come into The Daydream and we'll talk *

He scrubs his hands down his face, and when he opens his eyes, there is one of the new members of staff standing in front of him, "What?" he growls at the newbie.

"How come you get to show up for the shift whenever you feel like it and have your phone on you and use it?"

Neil closes his eyes again, hoping that when he opens them the newbie will be gone, but he is still standing there looking at Neil, "Because I'm special, now get back to work and out ma face." Neil walks away leaving the newbie and his ruffled feathers to get back to work.

An hour later Julie enters the club, Neil and Jack see her at the same time. Jack walks over to her to get her to leave, but Neil shouts on him and lets him know that it's okay. Julie gives Jack a look that could kill, then turns her attention to Neil as he talks to her,

"Julie take a seat, can I get you a drink?" She bats her eyelashes and pouts at Neil, trying to look sexy but failing quite brilliantly at it. "Yes please, I'll have a dry white."

Neil's eyebrows shoot up at her order, but before he can voice his concern, she retaliates, "I'm allowed one!" with a deep sigh he resigns himself to pouring her drink.

"Fine, whatever." Jack has decided to stay out of the way and has went to see Ava.

Neil sits down and puts the drink in front of his crazy ex-girlfriend,

"Right so," he starts, "you are still banging on about being pregnant and that the baby is mine?"

Julie actually manages to look hurt at his question and that makes Neil feel like an arsehole,

"Well you wanted proof and I gave you proof. So what are you going to do about it?"

Neil bites the inside of his cheek trying not to get angry or laugh. "Well, no, you sent me a picture of a positive pregnancy test, that's not exactly unequivocal proof now, is it?"

Julie blanches at his words, "Well, I have an appointment next week with the midwife, you can come to that." She is looking everywhere but at Neil.

"Okay, let me know when and where. Enjoy your drink." He stands and walks away to the top floor where the party is going on; he looks over and finds Ava. Watching her work for a bit before he walks over, desperate to talk to someone he actually likes and who doesn't want anything from him. Normally when he feels like this he would seek out Jack to talk to, but Ava is prettier to look at in his opinion and he enjoys being in her company.

"Hey Sweet, you look like you're enjoying yourself."

Ava is collecting glasses but stops when she hears Neil's voice, "I am actually. I didn't think I would, you know after my episode, and the thought of talking to strangers and people asking me for things, but I am. Thank you, again for the opportunity." She stretches up and gives Neil a quick peck on the cheek and then blushes.

Neil can also feel heat in his own face and other places of his anatomy, "You are more than welcome, Sweet, you know that, now why don't you go and have a quick break."

She smiles at him and starts to walk towards the break room, Neil loves to see her smile, and loves the thought that it was something he has said or did to put it on her lips, Ava stops in her tracks and turns back round to look at Neil,

"Who was that girl you were talking to? I don't mean to pry, it's just Jack really does not like her."

Neil is a bit stunned at the question but ends up snorting a laugh out while trying to cover it badly with a cough, "She is my ex-girlfriend, Julie, and no Jack doesn't like her, in fact he has never liked her, and he was right about her. I wish I had listened to him the first twenty times he told me she was crazy."

Ava nods slightly before turning and walking away. Frowning to herself at the emotion she felt seeing Neil with another woman, and then the relief that washed over her when he described her as an ex and crazy. She's not sure where the feelings came from, nor is she sure of what to do with them, so for now she will just leave them alone and not dig too deep into them.

As Ava is walking up to the table Julie is sitting at, she starts to overhear the girl talking on her mobile phone, it's not very hard to overhear what the conversation is about as she is not being very quiet. Not liking the way the conversation was going during the small snippet she heard Ava sits down at the table behind to listen in.

"He wants to go to an appointment with me, how the hell am I meant to get round that?" Silence for a second as the person on the other end talks,

"I thought the test would be enough, but he said that wisnay enough proof, I just panicked and said I hid an appointment. I mean I just want some money, know to 'get it fixed' or even just so he doesnay need to see me again! But naw, the arse actually wants to do the right thing, what fuckin guy does that?" More silence,

"I know, I'm gonna need to get a better plan, or buy a cushion to shove up my jumper!" The ex cackles down the phone at her 'joke'.

Ava is incensed at the callousness of the woman in front of her, how dare she concoct a story about a pregnancy for money, does she have no self-respect. Ava stands and walks from the table she is sitting at and sits down in front of Julie. The ex, snaps her head up with a look of confusion on her face.

"Eh, whit d'ye think you're doin hen?"

Ava sits back in her chair slightly at the tone of Julie's voice, wondering to herself what Neil ever saw in such a crass person. Taking a deep breath, Ava leans in again, keeping her voice low, "I couldn't help but overhear your conversation." Julie goes to speak, but Ava holds her hand up to stop her then continues speaking herself, "You really are one of the lowest excuses for a female I have ever met." Julie gasps, trying to look indignant at Ava's words but fails miserably, Ava on the other hand just gives Julie a look that shuts her up where she sat. "Using a fake pregnancy to obtain money from an innocent man is disgusting. Even if I hadn't overheard your sick little plan, Neil is intelligent enough to be able to have worked out your scam, and just so you are clear on the situation, Neil would never have taken you back, pregnant or not, so you would never and will never receive a penny from him, so may I suggest you leave and never return to this club, or contact Neil again."

Julie starts to laugh, "Aye hen, really, the thing is I know who really owns this pub and I know how to contact his da, so, he WILL give me ma money or he will be getting a visit from his da and he will need to give it to him!" Smugness flowing out of her every pore, Julie really believes that she has won.

Ava clears her throat and leans forward in her seat, she is

so close to Julie she can smell the wine on her breath and in a low growl, she snorts her derision, "Listen to me, Neil's dad has no claim on this club. Yes I know who owns it, but I also know he has covered every eventuality where his dad and money is concerned, so that bastard will never get anything from Neil, ever!"

Julie blanches again, knowing she has nothing but bravado left, but not one to give up she tries another tack. "And who the fuck are you to know all this pish, eh?"

Ava starts to stand, placing both her hands on the table in front of her, leaning even closer to Julie so she right at the ex's ear. "I am the woman who gets to make him happy and gives him his hearts desires, *'hen'*, I'm his girlfriend!" Standing up straight, she taps Julies hand then walks away, her head held high and feeling like a million dollars for standing up to a bully, maybe not her bully, but a bully none the less.

Julie scrapes the seat, letting it fall behind her as she pushes it away to get out from the table, looking over to the bar she notices Jack staring back at her, a slight smile on his lips and his eyes dancing with mirth, her anger getting the better of her, she starts shouting at him, poking at Jack,

"Well you can tell Neil, I'll let him off wa being a faither, an you kin tell him that I hope him an his strumpet will be very happy the gither!" She turns on her heels, cursing and grumbling all the way out if the club.

Jack is still standing where he was when Julie came over to him, although now he is more stunned than amused, he stays there for another second or two before walking over to the break room where Ava had taken herself after her showdown.

Ava is sitting in one of the overstuffed black leather

couches with a coffee, still smiling to herself, Jack pours himself a coffee and sits down next to her, looking at her, puzzlement written all over his face. Feeling his stare, Ava turns to look at him, "What?" she asks innocently.

"I saw you talking to crazy Julie, and then she comes over to me foaming at the mouth, ranting about Neil and his strumpet being happy together and that she will let him off with being a father.'"

Ava explodes with laughter, "She said what? Wow, she really is bat shit crazy!" This time it is Jack's turn to laugh. Ava calms herself enough to explain the conversation that really happened with crazy Julie.

Once she is finished, Jack is silent for a second before he lets his thoughts out, "So, she is full of shit, she is not up the duff?"

Ava is shaking her head, "Nope she has made the pregnancy up to get money from Neil, if that didn't work her next plan was blackmailing Neil with his dad."

"Fuckin bitch!" Jack hisses, and Ava agrees.

"I told her she was on to plums either way and that I knew this because I'm his girlfriend." Ava looks down embarrassed at what she has just admitted to Jack, as he explodes with laughter again,

"You told her that you are Neil's girlfriend? Ah so you're the strumpet then." Jack laughs, now he understands everything that Julie was talking about. Ava starts to frown, a look of panic starting in her eyes,

"Do you think Neil will be angry at what I said to her? You know about me being his girlfriend."

Jack smiles at Ava with a knowing smile and a glint in his eye, "No honey, he won't be mad, he is going to be thrilled that you managed to stand up to crazy Julie and that you found out the truth, and he isn't going to be a dad!"

She lets out the breath she had been holding on to and relaxes into a smile, Jack pulls her into a cuddle, "I am really proud of you too hun, you have come a really long way in such a short space of time, you are doing great." He gives her a squeeze and kisses the top of her head.

Ava sniffles, trying to fight back the tears in her eyes but failing as they spill over her lashes and run down her face. "Thanks Jack, you and Neil have both been great." Ava stands and walks over to the oval mirror hanging on the wall next to the door of the break room and starts to wipe at the tears with her fingers, just as Neil walks through the door. He takes one look at Ava wiping away tears and panics,

"Ava, what's wrong, are you crying, what happened?" Ava winces at the questions; she didn't want Neil to see her crying again!

"I am Neil, but honest, I'm happy." Neil looks deep into her eyes searching for something that tells him that she is okay , but he is still not convinced, so he looks over at Jack for the answers,

"You owe our girl a huge favour my friend."

Neil's expression has gone from panic and worry to confusion. As he is still standing just in the doorway Neil steps into the room and closes the door behind him, but remains standing. "What are you slabbering on about?"

Ava giggles as she moves Neil away from the door, "I'll go back out and let Jack explain, but really I'm fine." giving Neil a kiss on the cheek, Ava smiles as she walks back out to the bar.

Neil looks to Jack total confusion still clear on his face, "Spill!"

"Okay, but first get yourself a coffee and a seat; you're

going to need it."

Neil does as Jack suggests and opts to sit on the rocking chair across from Jack and settles in to listen to the story.

CHAPTER TWENTY

Nathan has taken the blonde to 29 Glasgow, the private club that he is a member of, to apologise for his behaviour towards her. He manages to turn up the charm and sexual tension between them and makes sure she feels like the only woman in the world. She has been like putty in his hand since he told her where they were going, which played into Nathan's idea that all women were easy to manipulate.

The restaurant in the club is a very high end one and always fully booked, but, as usual, Nathan knows how to get his own way and so manages to get a table at short notice, because of this he is sure that all the problems with his business and Ava will go the same way, which will be his way.

About nine o'clock, Nathan is paying the bill, which was an extortionate amount for two people, but worth it for the night of control and passion he is expecting. He helps the blonde into her faux fur coat, then with his hand on the small of her back, he glides her out of the restaurant and heads towards Buchanan Street where the Daydream is located. The air is crisp with the plummeting temperature of the October night, and the street furniture is starting to glitter with the oncoming frost, Nathan pulls the blonde under his arm more, trying to keep himself warm as much as her, as he quickens the pace towards the club. Their breaths are puffing out in white as they make small talk on the way from Royal Exchange Square; well the blonde is doing most of the talking while Nathan nods his head and occasionally makes a grunting sound. His goal in sight, Nathan steps up the pace yet again, but is stopped short when the woman on his arm notices that the Argyle Arcade is straight across for the Daydream, her excitement apparent in her high pitched voice,

"Oh Nathan look, The Arcade, that's where everyone goes to buy jewellery and things, like their engagement rings isn't it?" The hint for diamonds or more is obvious, and Nathan is not the buying type so he gives her a non-committal grunt and a slight push towards the front door of the club. The bouncer growls at Nathan as they pass, but nothing more, and Nathan lets out the breath he didn't quite understand why he was holding in. At the cloakroom, Nathan helps the blonde from her coat and removes his own, as he passes them over he gives a small snort at the thought that this is exactly where all his problems started, and here is where he will end them all. The blonde looks up at him at hearing the sound coming from her boss, with a confused worried look covering her features, images of his earlier anger flashing through her mind and again the thought he may be losing the plot following close after them.

"Are you all right Sir?"

Nathan looks at her, trying to cover his disdain for the club, and his disgust that his woman, Ava, left him to work here in this shit hole and mess about with another man, the man who had the tenacity to come to his house and take her from him, no he was not all right, but after tonight he will be.

"I'm fine!" he growls, then he spots Neil, he recognises him from the night of the auction. Spite, anger, jealously, and hatred all burn at the back of his throat, he swallows it down, and gives his head a shake giving the blonde a reassuring smile he adds,

"Yes, I'm fine, Miss, thank you, now, will we get to a table?" Putting his arm out for her to take, Nathan pulls himself from his musings and walks over to table three. Sitting her down he tells her he will go to the bar for their drinks and leaves without asking her what she would like to drink. Looking over at the table he smirks, yes he put her at table three, the same table as that night, and yes he did on purpose, he wants Ava to see him, he wants her to notice him with his 'New Woman' and them sitting there at that table.

Walking out of the office Ava passes table three, noticing the blonde woman sitting there as she passes, she knows she recognises her, but can't work out from where, so doesn't think much else of the woman as she walks on into the private party. Nathan is standing at the bar waiting on his drinks when he catches sight of Ava in the mirrors that cover the length of the gantry behind the bar, as she walks behind him, he turns to see her walk into the reserved area. Taking his drinks, Nathan sits down with the blonde, making sure he can see into the private party from where he is sitting, just so he can keep an eye on Ava if possible. The blonde is blabbering away about anything and everything, she knows that her boss is looking for the mouse that he was dating before her, she had seen her pass by five minutes ago, all swishing hair, and swaying hips, what Nathan had seen in her, she will never understand. Nathan watches as the blonde looks into the private party, scowling as she looks for Ava. He knows that he needs to show her some attention, keep her interested so he gives her a smile, tucking a lock of hair behind her ear that has come free then stroking her jaw line as he takes his hand away. He can feel her shiver under his touch,

"I'm going to use the facilities and then I will be back with another drink for us both okay?"

The blonde nods at him, batting her eyelashes and licking her lips at him, he has managed to convince her that he is here with her. "Okay, but don't be long." she pouts at him. Nathan walks towards the toilets, groaning to himself about how desperate she is, but at the last second, he takes a detour to the reserved area looking for Ava.

****

Neil is doubled over laughing at the story Jack is telling him, tears physically running down his cheeks calming himself just enough to talk,

"She actually faced Julie up and told her where to go?" Neil can't get the smile from his face,

"Yip, she also said she was your girlfriend!"

Jack wiggles his eyebrows in a knowing way at Neil, who stops laughing, but still has a huge grin on his face, and his eyes glinting with hope. "She really said that?"

"Aye." Jack smirks as he watches his friend's emotions pass fleetingly across his face as he paces around the room,

"Do you think that means, maybe, she might, no, well maybe, do you think I should ask? No, she won't, I don't want to get my hopes up, she was just saying that, really she, ah sod it I don't know! What do you think?" Neil sinks in to the nearest seat and looks at his friend expectantly.

Jack feels for his friend, but also finds it funny; he has never seen Neil like this over anyone. "What part of that verbal diarrhoea do you want me to answer, exactly?"

Neil laughs, "Aye I know, I know, cheers man." Neil

loves that his best friend can answer him without actually answering him, the years of friendship and support between them always strong.

"Right I'm going back out, see how the party is going." Jack nods at him and then shakes his head in amusement, Neil really is head over heels for Ava, Jack is amazed that he knows his arse from his elbow at the moment.

Neil walks out of the break room and heads towards the party, which is in full flow. Not long after getting to the reserved area Neil is stopped by another member of staff asking questions, he listens to the staff member but all the time he is searching the party for Ava, he spots her talking to one of the partygoers and relaxes, bringing his attention back to the conversation he is supposedly a part of.

****

Nathan manages to get through to the reserved area and makes a bee-line for Ava, just as he is about to approach her he notices she is talking to a lady, so holds back, proving that he can have manners. After a few minutes the female eventually walks away, leaving Ava on her own, Nathan takes his opportunity and steps in front of her, blocking her way to leave.

"Hello, Ava." He keeps his voice low and menacing, not wanting anybody else to overhear what he is saying. Ava gasps, her hand flying to her mouth, all the air leaving her lungs, she starts to shake. One hour ago, she was full of confidence; standing up to Neil's crazy ex-girlfriend and now Nathan has turned up, blowing all her good work out the water.

"Miss me?" he sneers as he takes a step closer to her.

Instinctively Ava takes a step back, but as was usual when it came to Nathan, she was blocked; there was a chair at her back. Nathan grins, knowing he has her where he wants her, frightened and cornered, just like old times.

Setting her jaw, Ava draws on any of her bravado that she has left from the encounter with Julie, "What do you want?" her voice sounding stronger than she feels, helping boost her bravado to carry on, knowing that Neil and Jack are within shouting distance if she needs them, also helps.

"I want you, Ava, you know you're mine. Now you've had your fun with that idiot, it's time for you to come home, where you belong, with me." Nathan takes another step forward. He is within touching distance and Ava can feel his presence with her every breath.

"I am not going anywhere with you, Nathan, I am not getting back with you, it's over, and Neil is not an idiot, he is a gentleman, unlike you!" Ava swallows, amazed at herself at for being able to say all of that to Nathan. Nathan looks at her astounded at her confidence, then the anger at her insolence overrides it,

"Who the fuck do you think you are a talking to you little slut, now get over here." Nathan grabs her arm and yanks her towards him.

Ava yelps at the vice-like grip on her arm trying to wrench it from its socket. "NO, Nathan, I am not going anywhere with you, I don't even want to talk to you, I am an adult and can make my own decisions, and I am NOT yours!"

Neil hears Ava shouting and looks up. He sees her backed up against a chair, with a guy pulling on her arm. His brain starts making sense of the events unfolding in front of him and he realises it not just any guy, it's him, it's Nathan, he is sure he heard Ava say *that* name, that arsehole is back in his club trying to get Ava back, no way that's happening. He looks at the member of staff, who is continuing to talk at him, "Ssshh," Neil shuts the staff member up, "Go and get Jack, tell him Nathan is here and then tell the bouncers to get their arses up here."

The staff member stands staring at Neil like he has just grown another head.

"Go, now!" Neil growls, then starts to walk to Ava.

"You are mine you silly cow and you know it. You know you are the only woman for me," Nathan smiles, trying to look loving.

Ava smirks, "So, why do you have your receptionist with you?"

Nathan smirks at her, "Jealous are we?"

Ava takes her chance to smirk again, "Of her? Not a chance." then she laughs, "I'm done Nathan," she tries again to remove her arm from his grasp, but he keeps his grip and pulls her back into him, grabbing her hair in the process with his other hand. Dropping her arm to free up one of his Nathan raises his free arm and brings the back of his hand down hard against her cheekbone.

As the tears spring to her eyes all Ava can think is 'no, not again' as Nathan growls in her ear, "Don't be so fuckin' stupid Ava, you don't get to laugh at me or leave me." He goes to punch her again when he feels his arm being pulled backwards, Nathan twists to see who has his arm, but never lets go of Ava's hair. The entire pub is staring at the commotion in the party, as Neil holds onto Nathan's arm, stopping the punch that he was just about to throw at Ava. Jack is running towards them and the bouncers are hot on his heels.

Nathan wrenches him arm from Neil's grip, "You coming to save her again, eh?" his tone taunting, as he looks over at Ava, his eyes dancing with disgust, "Well, save yourself the energy, I can tell you she's not fucking worth saving now she's used goods." With his words dripping with hatred, Nathan pushes Ava, hard. She falls into the table and chairs behind her, breaking one of the chairs as she collides with it. Neil lunges grabbing out trying to save Ava from falling, but to no avail as she crashes to the floor.

Anger floods Neil's senses, "You bastard!" he yells as he punches Nathan, bursting his nose then grabbing his arm he has it up his back and him on his knees before Nathan has time to breath, or comprehend what has happened. Neil may not train much in a gym, but he does know his martial arts and self-defence – something he will be teaching Ava as soon as possible. Neil is desperate to continue beating the ever living crap out of the scumbag he has bleeding on the floor in front of him, but the bouncers manage to get to him before he has the chance. Knowing that it is for the best he drops Nathan roughly to the ground, leaving him free to go to Ava.

The blonde has been standing at the edge of the reserved area watching everything unfold, she knew her boss had a nasty streak in him, but watching him in action with his ex-girlfriend has made her sick to her stomach and opened her eyes. Thanking her lucky stars that she didn't get as involved as she had once hoped she might be, she turns on her heels and runs, leaving the club and not looking back.

Ava is lying on her side where she fell with Neil trying to get her to open her eyes and talk to them,

"Ava are you okay?" Jack and Neil are kneeling beside her, Jack is on the phone to the emergency services, and Neil is cradling Ava's side. He feels a hot slickness on his hand.

His stomach free falls as he removes his hand from underneath her and sees the dark red liquid of Ava's blood covering his hand. Moving Ava onto her side, he takes a better look.

Bile rises in his throat at the sight of a part of the broken chair skewered into Ava's ribs. Neil turns to say to Jack, but realises he has noticed at the same time and is already shouting for an ambulance to the poor call centre worker on the other side of the phone. Kissing Ava on the forehead and whispering in her ear that he will be back, Neil stands and walks over to Nathan, the bouncers still have him on his knees; lifting his foot, he makes contact with Nathans' side, making him buckle to the floor.

"You fuckin' bastard, you won't be happy 'till you fuckin' kill her!" He goes to kick him again only to be stopped by the bouncers, again. He knows the bouncer is right, but the need to beat the ever-living shit out the prick comes back with a vengeance. Through the haze of anger, Neil hears the sirens of the emergency services, using all his will power he walks away from Nathan and kneels back down next to Ava.

The police arrive and get to work asking questions and trying to make sense out of the chaos that confronts them. Within another couple of seconds, the paramedics have arrived and made their way through to Ava.

The officers have asked to speak to Neil, who stands and goes over to them, answering their questions as best he can, all the time keeping an eye on Ava and the paramedics, he will be going in the ambulance with her no matter what.

After questioning the relevant staff, the police detain Nathan and arrest him for assault to endangerment of life, they bundle him into the back of the police car and take him to Stewart Street Police Station in the Cowcaddens area of the City. During all of this, the paramedics have been working on Ava; they haven't removed the piece of wood, but have managed to pack round it to stem most of the bleeding. Ava has come round and has started to panic, making it even harder for her to breath. The paramedics are constantly talking to her trying to calm her down and keep her conscious. Neil can hear them talking to her, while he continues to answer the police's questions, he is itching to get to her side to let her know everything is going to be all right, Nathan is in custody and she will pull through whatever injuries he has inflicted on her. As soon as the police finish with their questions for him he is by her side again talking to her, reassuring her, being strong for her.

Time seems to change constantly, it's not passing in the normal manner, one minute everything is happening at warp speed, then it slows, every second seemingly taking forever to pass, Neil can't get a hold on his emotions either, fear, anger, worry, panic and most of all love, are all crashing through him at an alarming rate.

The paramedics have Ava up onto a stretcher and are moving to the ambulance,

"Can I be with her?" he asks one of the paramedics, his words coming out more like a plea than a question.

The paramedics look at each other then turn back to Neil and nod, "Aye," one of them answers then carries on out the doors of the club and in to the waiting ambulance, Neil hot on their heels climbing in behind the stretcher.

Jack rushes over to the ambulance, "You going?"

Neil nods, "Aye, I'm not leaving her side, ever again! Can you finish up with the police and then close up. Tell the engagement party we will contact them as soon as we can to organise compensation of some sort and that we are sorry for this." Neil gestures to the carnage that is his club at that moment. Jack says he will sort everything and then he will be at the hospital. The back doors of the ambulance close and they take off at speed, lights pulsing and sirens blaring all the way to The Royal Infirmary hospital.

On route to the hospital, Neil watches on as the paramedic continues to monitor Ava, making her as comfortable as possible, feeling completely helpless as he hears her moan, not knowing if she is trying to say something coherent or not.

Getting out of the ambulance, Neil looks at the hospital in front of him, it is an old sandstone building. It looks and feels ancient, decrepit even, a foreboding feeling crosses Neil, but he pushes it away, refusing to let himself think the worst. He goes inside the casualty department, hearing the paramedics talking to the doctors about Ava and her situation, not really understanding everything that is being said, but realising that there is one word that keeps being said, and it scares the life out of Neil. Pneumothorax. Not sure what it is, Neil knows that it must have something to do with the lungs, and that is serious. A nurse stops him from going any further than the waiting room, asking him if he could give them some of the information needed to book Ava in. Pulling his hands through his hair he walks over to the receptionist answering as many questions as he can, which isn't a great deal considering the length of time they have known each other. Neil walks over to one of the hard plastic chairs and slumps into it. The nurses have promised to let him know the minute they have any news on Ava's situation. He texts Jack to let him know what hospital to go to. Putting his phone away, Neil puts his head in his hands and letting the tears that he has been holding back fall silently down his cheeks and onto the scarred vinyl floor.

He had promised to keep her safe, and he failed, he allowed the one person he promised to keep away from her get near her, close enough to harm her, and now she is in casualty with part of a wooden chair sticking out of her ribs (one of his chairs!).What an idiot he is, thinking he could save her, he could hardly save himself when it came to his father. He sits there berating himself until Jack arrives.

CHAPTER TWENTY-ONE

Two hours later and Neil is about to explode with frustration. Normally when he feels like this, he turns to his car, tuning and tweaking until he has relaxed, or at least come to terms with whatever has happened. Neither option viable at that moment, he has resorted to pacing the whole reception area, at least until another patient demands him to stop. They were feeling dizzy from their concussion as it is, and Neil's pacing is making it ten times worse, so he sits down, but to no avail, as soon as he sits he starts bouncing his legs and biting his fingernails. Jack has watched his friend slowly lose his mind, but the nail biting is the last straw, he turns to Neil and growls at him. Even the receptionist feels his frustration, he has asked her for any updates at least five times since Jack arrived, now when they make eye contact she just shakes her head, silently telling him there has been no news – so don't ask.

The fluorescent strip lights are stinging his eyes and the hard plastic chairs are making his backside numb and his back ache, desperate to move again, he stands; ready to punch something or someone, maybe even Jack. Thankfully, before he is able to do either of those things a doctor walks through and speaks to the receptionist, who then points over to Neil.

The doctor hasn't moved, but Neil is at his side and Jack

not far behind. Can I see her? What was the Pneumoti. thing they were talking about? Please God let her be oka. Neil knows he is losing it, but until he sees Ava for himsei. there isn't much he can do about it. Jack is standing next to him and puts a hand on his shoulder to calm him down, but he knows it could also be to stop him from putting his hands on the doctor, not in a violent way, but just out of pure frustration. The doctor however had seen it all before and had put his hands up as to ask for calm, he waits until Neil has finished firing his questions at him before he starts to answer them.

"Miss Connell will be just fine; the pneumothorax that you heard us talk about is a collapsed lung." Neil starts to talk and panic, again, but the doctor again puts his hands up to stop him talking, Neil obeys.

"The piece of wood that impaled Miss Connell's side punctured her lung. We have put in a chest drain; this will remove the air from where it shouldn't be, her chest cavity. We have given her some pain management and she is stable and awake at the moment, though she may be a bit groggy as the hour goes on. The drain will be in for most of the night, which we will monitor throughout. We are going to be moving her to a ward, as she will be staying in for a few days once the drain is out, just for observation." Neil has managed to keep his mouth shut whilst the doctor explains Ava's situation, but loses his patience when the doctor stops talking slightly,

"Can I see her?" Jack winces at Neil's' tone, but understands, as does the doctor, thankfully, and he smiles kindly at Neil.

"Yes, you can go and see Miss Connell." Neil sighs, relief washing over him, as Jack pats his shoulder, partly in support but also in relief with him.

"Is it okay if I go in too Doc?" Jack asks. Neil's attention snaps back to Jack, looking at him as if for the first time, he has been so caught up in his own hell and pain worrying about Ava he never stopped to think about Jack and how he will be feeling. Ava has gotten under Jacks skin too, but unlike Neil, it is more of a brother/sister relationship, the sister he's never had. The doctor nods and then motions for them to follow him.

They arrive at the cubicle where Ava has been dozing; the doctor opens the curtains then excuses himself claiming to give them some privacy. Neil snorts inwardly at the thought of this cubicle being private; the only thing between them and the rest of the world is a rather thin set of green and blue Paisley pattern curtains. They both enter the cubicle and look at Ava lying in the hospital bed. Neil's heart breaks at the sight of her, she looks so small and fragile lying there.

Ava looks up when she hears the voices coming through the curtains, she holds her breath, knowing who she thinks belongs to the voices, but panicking that it might not be, then relaxes when she sees that it is Neil and Jack coming in to see her. For some reason this makes her feel better, makes her feel that she is worth worrying about, she is used to being told she isn't worth anything, so for two other human beings to be here for her is more than she can comprehend, but is enough to trigger something in her to believe in herself.

Neil walks over to the side of her bed, opposite to the drain, and takes her hand. Jack stands at the foot of the bed and places his hands on her feet in a brotherly gesture, a strange place for a comforting touch, but comforting all the same. Ava can feel the stress of the night coming from both of them, the worry for her, and the anger at Nathan. She can also see the guilt Neil is feeling about it all in his eyes, but underneath all of it, pushing through all of the emotion, she can feel their strength, the strength that will get them all through this and her away from Nathan for good.

"Hey you," Ava starts to speak to Neil but winces at the pain in her chest. Neil squeezes her hand, making shooshing noises,

"Sshh Sweet, it's okay, we're fine, worried, slightly pissed off at Nathan, but okay." Neil is rubbing his thumb over her knuckles gently, soothing her, reassuring her before she says it is all her fault, or worse, she apologises for what happened, he will not let her take the blame for any of it.

"Thank you." Ava whispers with a smile, the feeling of support coming from both men is so reassuring for her, but the way Neil is looking at her, like she is the only person in the world, his touch is so gentle, her heart and stomach are doing flips and the butterflies are back. Not wanting to get her hopes up, Ava puts the fuzzy feelings she is experiencing down to the strong painkillers the nurses gave her, but there is still a part of her that wonders if this is how men are meant to treat women, and not the beatings and hell that Nathan put her through.

At the thought of Nathan, Ava starts to panic again, Neil tries to get her to take deep breaths like before, but the pain in her chest returns, grimacing she clenches her teeth, breathing through the pain. Once the pain has subsided slightly and her breathing returns to normal, well as normal as it can be with the chest drain Ava turns to Neil, "Nathan? What happened? Where is he?" Neil can see the fear tingeing her eyes, so he continues to hold her hand, rubbing her knuckles, soothing her fear away, or at least he hoped he was. The muscles in his jaw were twitching as he consciously worked at keeping his anger towards Nathan under control; Jack can see every twitch, so answers Ava's questions so Neil doesn't lose what little control he has on his emotions.

"He was taken to the police station, and is being detained there, so he is out of the equation for now." He gives Ava a smile and squeezes her feet again to reassure her, all the while trying his hardest to look and sound calm and relaxed, although he isn't very sure he managed to pull it off. Neil has managed to calm his anger, so starts trying to relax and reassure Ava more,

"It's okay Sweet, there is nothing to worry about, he can't get to you, especially in here, and you are going to be here for the next few days, so everything is going to be fine."

Ava nods, hearing that Nathan is in custody is enough to make her relax, which then in turn makes her eyes heavy as her tiredness catches up with her and the medication she was given really starts to take effect. Try as she might, Ava can hardly keep her eyes open, tiredness washing over her in waves, the last thing she hears before she slips into the darkness of sleep is Neil telling her to sleep and that he will be with her when she wakes.

****

Nathan is processed into the system, then thrust into a cell to wait on his lawyer. His nose had stopped bleeding but the throbbing is like someone squeezing then releasing his head with a clamp at regular intervals. Pacing the small cell ramps up his anger another notch, not quite at nuclear level yet, but he sure as hell isn't that far off it. Going to the club was meant to get Ava back where she belongs, with him, to make her realise what she's left, make her jealous enough to remember she loves him. It wasn't meant to make her turn on him, deny him. She shouldn't be able live without him, manage without him, but she is. His plan backfired, it all went horribly wrong, she pushed all his buttons again, making him angry and, making him get violent. Damn that woman, if she only listened to him and didn't think she could live without him none of this would have happened, she wouldn't be in hospital and he, more importantly, wouldn't be in this stinking cell. The clanging of the cell window being opened manages to pull Nathan from his angry musings, then a gruff male voice demands that he stands in the middle of the cell where the officer can see him. With an audible huff, Nathan does as he is told and the window is snapped shut again, as the cell door is unlocked and pulled open. The police officer steps into the doorway,

"Your brief's arrived, 'moan." The officer motions with his head for Nathan to follow him. They arrive at a tiny room that has an 'Interview One' plaque on the door; his lawyer is already sitting inside. Nathan walks in and looks around at the depressing little room, it is badly needing a fresh coat of paint (whoever painted it the last time made a hash of it), the Formica table was chipped and scratched from years of abuse and still sporting cigarette burns and nicotine stains from the years when you were allowed to smoke indoors. The plastic chairs didn't fare much better either, matching fag burns and badly spelled graffiti of all those who has passed through before now. Nathan's lawyer stands as he walks into the room, then asks the officers for some privacy. The officer nods and closes the door behind him then stands in situ, like a guard on duty. WPC Young walks down the corridor and stops to speak to him,

"Who you got in there?"

"Nathan Low!" Sian's eyebrows shoot up in surprise at hearing that name,

"Nathan Low? Really, what on?"

"Assault on a woman." Flashes of the broken woman at the front desk flood her mind, she can hear her saying Nathan, the name of the guy who had been beating her, the same guy Sian had been trying to looking into.

"Okay, who's the arresting officer? I think I have some information on Mr Low that will be pertinent to this case." The gruff officer tells her the information she had asked for, she thanks him then continues down the corridor looking for the arresting officer to fill him in on the events of the semi-complaint she had taken about Nathan Low.

In the interview room, Nathan and his lawyer are in deep discussion. Nathan explains his version of events and that he wants Neil arrested for assault. His lawyer assures him that he will organise Nathans' bail then put a complaint in about Neil, once they have finished their conversation, the layer goes over to the door and opens it, informing the gruff police officer that they have finished their mediation. The officer grunts that he will let the Senior Investigating Officer know and he will be with them as soon as he can, the lawyer thanks him, then turns back to Nathan.

"You need to talk to them, tell then what happened, so you need to keep your head level, and your anger in check then we will be able to get you out of here!" Nathan glowers at his lawyer, hating the way he thinks he can talk to Nathan like he's a child.

CHAPTER TWENTY-TWO

"You canny stay here." Jack states, completely exasperated with his friend, he understands Neil's need to stay with Ava, but he thinks it best that Neil gets some sleep, the cold feeling in his stomach refuses to leave, he is sure that this will not be the last they hear of Nathan, and it might even get worse, hence why Neil should be alert. He can also see his friend fall even deeper in love with Ava with every passing day, and, as much as he is happy for him and Ava, he is frightened that it will all go wrong, and he will need to pull Neil back from the brink of oblivion again. He really hopes he is wrong though, they will be great together, if they get the chance.

"I can and I am." Neil lets out a breath, "I know you're worried about me getting too involved too quickly, but , well it's probably too late for that and I don't want to change that, so I am staying with her, if you want to stay, then that's cool, if you want go home, then that's cool too. In fact it might be best if you go and get some sleep, the club will still need to open tomorrow." Neil scrubs his hand over his face, he loves his best friend, but right this minute he really needs him to leave and let Neil have the mini break down that is descending upon him, in private.

Jack thinks for a second then sighs, "Okay, okay, I'll go just now, but I will come back later to let you go and get some sleep. You're not going to be any use to man nor beast if you don't rest. The police said they would need to talk to both of us again and they still need to talk to Ava. You will need to have a clear head to help her."

"I know, you're right," Neil admits. Every moment of the night and every emotion he has felt, is bearing down on him, threatening to break him, something he doesn't want to happen especially when his friend is standing there. He takes a deep, controlling breath, just as the doctor comes back into the cubicle,

"The ward is ready, so we are going to move Miss Connell." Both men look at the doctor like he has just spoken a foreign language,

"Okay." They both say in unison. Jack goes over to Ava, the sister he always wanted and gives her a kiss on her forehead and whispers his goodbyes. Turning to his friend, he assures him everything will be fine and he will see him in a few hours, then he leaves the cubicle. Neil stands to let the hospital porters in to move Ava to the ward, then he quietly follows behind them.

****

Nathan walks away from the police station after being freed on police bail, pending an investigation, and with the conditions not to go near the Daydream Club, Ava, Neil, Jack or anybody else connected to them. He was also made aware that he must make himself available for questioning at any given moment, and he is not allowed to leave the country, plus let the station know if he needs to leave Glasgow for any pressing business he may have. Knowing he had to play the game he agrees to the conditions, he would have agreed to much more if it meant leaving that stinking cell. A well-educated, important businessman like him shouldn't be exposed to such depravity!

The lawyer had phoned his driver to collect him from the police station, so when Nathan emerged from the front door he could step straight into his Daimler. Seconds after settling in to the plush, black leather seats, Nathan has his phone out. First, he phones Mark to find out where Ava was taken by the ambulance, if Neil is with her and if Mark had managed to contact the father. He is informed that Ava had been taken to the Royal Infirmary Hospital, Neil was with her and that they hadn't managed to make contact with Neil's father, in fact he was nowhere to be found. Next, he phones his contact at the planning department, time was up for them, he wanted the information on who was blocking him, and he wanted it now. Unfortunately, there was no answer, so he left a message on his contact's voicemail urging the contact to phone him back immediately. Once all the phone calls were finished with, Nathan put his head in his hands and started to massage his temples where he felt the worst of the pounding. He didn't understand why it felt like his life was unravelling in front of him, it was never meant to happen like this, he was Nathan Low for goodness sake, he has enough money to make everything go his way, so why was nothing going his way just now?

The Daimler pulls up outside the mansion, the driver gets out and holds open the door for Nathan to get out. Heading through the front door he goes straight upstairs to his room and collapses onto his bed, desperate to get some sleep before he heads out to the hospital to pay Ava a visit – again!

****

Ava has been moved to a single room; she managed to sleep through the move and is continuing to sleep. The nurses have tried to get Neil to go home for some rest, but he is completely refusing to move away from her bedside, he promised Ava he would be with her when she woke up, so here he will be.

It's about five in the morning and Neil has been up for nearly twenty-two hours, his eyes are stinging, his head is thumping and his heart is heavy with fear and guilt, but at least Ava is safe, at the moment, so because of the relief he is also feeling at seeing her sleep peacefully he puts his head on the side of the bed and falls asleep almost instantly.

Three hours later Ava opens her eyes, looking about at her surroundings, confused at where she is, she doesn't recognise the room, or the bed she is in. She tries to push herself up the strange bed, so she can see the room better but pain explodes through her ribs, making her scream out. The feeling that someone has just knifed her in the ribs rips through her whole body, and that is when her screams become sobs, the memories of the night before flooding her mind. Nathan coming into the club with his blonde receptionist, him telling her she needed to return to him, the argument and fight that ensued from his statement. Nathan's spiteful words about her to Neil, then the pain in her side when Nathan pushed her away, discarding her like a piece of trash. The last memory she has is of Neil lunging at Nathan throwing his fist. Panic rises in her throat as the worry for Neil sets in. Questions flying through her mind, questions like where is Neil, what happened to him, did Nathan hurt him? Then Ava hears Neil's voice, soft and soothing, trying to calm her, trying to take her pain away. He is saying her name over and over again, she turns to look at him, drinking in every detail of his pinched, tired, worried face. She lets out her worried breath in relief at seeing him beside her safe, then her thoughts turn to Neil's appearance, when did he become so tired looking? Has she made him this way? Surely she can't be worth all of this tiredness and worry and attention? But then again, would Neil be here if he didn't want to be, or thought she wasn't worth it? She wasn't sure, but thought she knew.

"Sweet, it's okay, I'm here, I'm here, ssshhh it's okay." Neil has got to his feet, leaning over her, cupping her face gently in his hands, rubbing her tears away with his thumbs. "Sssh, it's okay you're safe, I'm here sssh."

"Neil—" Ava manages to choke out before the emotion of everything takes over, and she dissolves into more tears.

"I'm...sor...rr... y, I – I"

"Hey, shh, you have nothing to be sorry for, none of this is your fault." Neil is struggling to keep the emotion from his voice, in fact, he is utterly failing to do it, he is also failing at stopping his own tears from streaming down his face and landing on Ava's heaving chest. It is completely breaking his heart to see her so upset and blaming herself, when she was the one who was attacked. He brings her head onto his shoulder and holds her tight, stroking her hair and holding her until her sobs started to subside and she was calming down.

Pulling away from Neil, Ava looks up at him, sadness in her eyes as she tells him her fear. "I'm breaking you." Neil opens his mouth to say something, but nothing comes out so he closes it and then tries again, but again no sound comes out. Ava continues, "If you hadn't met, or spoke to me then—" She leaves the rest of the sentence unsaid.

Neil shakes his head, "If I hadn't met you I wouldn't be in

lo— happy." Neil coughs to try and cover up his slip, before continuing, "Sweet, I'm not going anywhere. I want you safe and happy."

Ava drops her head, tears threatening again as Neil continues to talk, "And before you even think it, you are worth it, worth the worry and the sitting here all night, you are worth all of that and more, trust me." Ava's head snaps back up, shocked that Neil basically knew what she was thinking,

"How did you know?"

Neil smirks, "Because I have been where you are, and we may not have known each other for a long time, but I know you." He leans in and kisses the side of her mouth, Ava closes her eyes again enjoying the feeling of peace settling within her at having Neil with her and knowing that he really does know her, and understands how she is feeling. The thought that this is how it should feel when you care for someone fleets through her head, and her heart answers with a resounding yes!

Neil stayed with Ava until lunchtime when Jack came back to the hospital. They had spent all morning talking, covering every subject known to man, from their school days to their first kisses. They both actively avoided the subject of Nathan and the incident, neither of them wanting to break the happy atmosphere. There was a knock at the door and a nurse comes in. The nurse is ages with Ava, petite, short dark hair, and kind dark eyes; she introduces herself as Eveline Masterson and explains that she was in to check Ava's chest drain. She looks over at Neil sitting in the chair next to the bed, he still has the haggard look of a man who has worried himself to near death all night and slept for an hour in a chair, but with a smile on his face – all of which is true.

Nurse Masterson smiles kindly at him, having seen that look many times,

"Could we have a minute please?"

Neil realises she is talking to him, so takes the hint and gets up from the chair, he leans over and gives Ava a chaste kiss on the lips, "I'll just be outside, okay." Ava nods and smiles and squeezes his hand,

"Thank you, again." Is all Ava can muster before she feels her tears spring back to life again.

Leaving Nurse Masterson and Ava, Neil closes the door behind him as he walks into the corridor, meeting Jack who is walking towards him.

In the room Nurse Masterson is busy checking all of Ava's vitals and the chest drain that they hadn't managed to get taken out during the night as they had thought would happen, although everything was looking good now.

"How long have you two been together?" The shock and blush that pass over Ava's features tells the nurse more than words, they aren't together, but they both want to be. Ava tries to explain the situation, but she ends up talking herself into a knot, she stops talking and takes a painfully deep breath before starting again,

"Can I ask you something Nurse Masterson?" The nurse stops what she is doing and perches on the edge of the bed, she knows this is normally against the rules, but she recognises that this patient needs a wee bit more than just nursed back to health.

"Of course you can, and please call me Eveline."

Ava smiles at how kind the nurse is. "How do you know it's okay to give someone your heart? That they won't break it, or you?" Tears are coursing down her cheeks now. Eveline sits quietly on the edge of the bed, she knew Ava had been assaulted and she thought that maybe the question was about that, or how long she would be in hospital, never did she think it would be such a heart wrenching question, but as she looked at the poor soul in front of her, she knew that she had been through, or was still going through a rough patch in her life, her eyes were full of fear and confusion.

Taking a deep sigh Eveline answers the best she can, "To be honest, I don't think you ever do know for sure, not until it happens, and I think a lot of things have happened to you, and not nice things by the looks of things, but I don't think it was by the guy who has stayed by your side all night, but by someone else, someone who should have loved you, am I right?"

Ava nods, barely moving her head.

"Does it feel differently when you are around him," Eveline points towards the door to motion who she is talking about.

"Neil," Ava offers his name,

"Neil, does he treat you differently, better?"

Ava nods, "Very much so. I never knew I could feel so safe and be myself with a guy. My ex-boyfriend isn't a very nice person and let me know how useless I was, very often. I managed to leave him with Neil's help, and then he put me in here, his way of trying to get me back!"

Eveline is shaking her head, hating what Ava had been put through. "Some men can be complete bastards, and some men will worship the ground you walk on. It can be tricky finding out who's who, but personally I think Neil is in the latter group, and he would never do anything to hurt you and I think you may have his heart already." Eveline stands and straightens the bedding where she was sitting,

"Right I'm going to get another nurse and we can get this

drain out." She turns and walks to the door.

"Eveline?" The nurse stops with her hand resting on the handle and turns when she hears her name, she can see that the talk has helped immensely as Ava has calmed and looks almost peaceful now.

"Thank you." Ava smiles at the nurse, glad she asked her the question.

Eveline smiles back, "All part of the bedside manner honey." She winks, then walks out the room. Silence descends on the room; all the machines have been turned off giving Ava time to think.

Outside the door, Neil and Jack are talking about the incident whether or not to open the club to the public that night or not. There is a private party due in, so they decide just to open it for everyone.

"Get in extra security and show them Nathan's picture, he is not allowed anywhere near the place ever again! Tell them to keep an eye out for the Cortina too." The more Neil talks about Nathan and the situation, the more venom laces his voice. Jack readily agrees.

"How's our girl doing?" Neil eyes Jack due to his choice of words, he isn't sure why it grates on him that Jack refers to Ava as their girl, he knows Jack doesn't see her in a romantic light. Jack sees the look Neil gives him and smiles at his friend,

"She's my friend too remember, in fact I see her as my sister, so stop it with the evil eye. I know how you feel about her, and I think she might just feel the same."

Neil lets out the breath he hadn't known he was holding onto, "Sorry, I know that's how you see her, and I don't know why I feel like no-one else in the world should ever be near her, it's stupid, I know. I'm just being over protective, especially after what I saw on the first night I met them and then how she was when she phoned me to get her out of there and of course after what happened in the club."

Jack nods in agreement, "I suppose being protective is normal after witnessing all of that." Jack takes a pause then smiles a sly grin, "You're still a wee dick though."

Neil lets out a small laugh, only Jack can make him relax and take stock by calling him a dick,

"Now tell me, how's she holding up?"

****

Nathan has slept solidly for seven hours by the time he awakes just before midday. His head and nose is still throbbing. Gingerly he sits up and with a groan, touches his nose, wincing at the pain shooting through his face. He gets out of bed and goes through to the en-suite, looking in the mirror he doesn't recognise the mess of the man that is looking back at him. Stripping he gets into the shower, standing stock still as the hot water cascades down on to his muscled back. Using the time in the shower, Nathan plans his next move on Ava, Neil and the Daydream.

In the police station, WPC Sian Young is talking to the senior investigating officer in charge of the investigation into Nathan, about the incident with Ava in the foyer of the station and how she suspects him to have beaten Ava whilst they were in a relationship together. She also tells him everything she has found out about him from her own musings into him. His businesses, his deals, how he somehow manages to get planning permission for sites that have previously been refused. There also a speeding charge that seems to have conveniently been dropped. She smells something off about him and lets the other officer know her gut feeling. The officer promises to keep her up to date and maybe even use her in the investigation.

CHAPTER TWENTY-THREE

Jack eventually convinces Neil he needs to go home for a shower and a change of clothes, promising that he will stay at the hospital with Ava. On his way out, Neil spots the nurse who was in with Ava earlier, Nurse Masterson. He walks over to her.

She sees him and greets him with a warm smile, "You okay sir, can I help you with anything?"

Neil warms to the nurse immediately, she has warm eyes and an infectious smile, plus, after she left the room, Ava was somewhat calmer.

"I was wondering, will you be here all day?"

Eveline looks at him quizzically, "Em, yeah, well most of the day anyway, I finish about sixish. Why?"

"I need to ask if you could stop this man if he comes in to visit Ava?" He shows her a picture he has of Nathan on his phone. "This is the guy who...attacked her." Neil's voice breaks on the end of his sentence, he clears his throat and starts again, "He is her ex-boyfriend, he beat and abused her when they were together, which is why she left. I don't want him here." He points towards Ava's room.

Eveline nods knowingly, "I'll keep my eye out for him and turn him the other way if he tries to enter. I will also let the other staff members know."

Neil relaxes visibly and puts his hand on the nurse's arm gently. "Thank you. I just need to know that she is going to be safe." Eveline nods again and they say their goodbyes. Neil leaves the hospital, but is already desperate to get back to her.

Once home Neil showers, shaves, and pulls on a pair of clean, black jeans and a Daydream T-shirt they have the staff wear as a uniform. Walking around the house as he gets ready, Neil keeps coming across somethings of Ava's, every time he sees something belonging to her, the house feels that wee bit more empty, he hadn't noticed how she had brought life into his house, someone to talk to, smiles. His heart aches more with every passing second. The guilt of letting Nathan get close to Ava is bad, but the guilt of letting Nathan close enough to hurt her to the point that she has been put in hospital is unbearable. It is pushing down on him to the point he is finding it hard to breathe. He sits down on the stairs and puts his head between his legs, taking deep breaths, in and out, just like he tells Ava when she is going into a panic attack. Ten minutes later he feels his breathing return to its normal pattern, and has managed to push his guilt down deep inside, out of the road for a bit. He collects some clean underwear and jammies putting them into a bag beside the toiletries he has already organised, then locks up the house and walks over to his BMW, putting the bag in the foot well of the passenger side. As he closes the passenger door, he notices the Cortina sitting across the road from his house. Neil's anger rockets from nearly nothing to nuclear in a millisecond. He stalks over to the car, every muscle in his body clenched, counting to ten and then back again, trying to get a hold on the anger that seems to be taking over his every thought. Reaching the car, he wrenches open the passenger door, then rips the passenger sitting there from his seat, and pushing him against the car.

"What the fuck do you think you're doing?" He is screaming into thug two's face. Thug one rushes round the car to pull Neil from his pal. Neil sees him coming and, letting go of the thug, he grabs the other one, slamming him up against the car, next to his partner in crime who has yet to say anything, both of them shocked at Neil's presence at the car and the anger coming from him.

"Get the fuck away from me and don't let me ever see you near my house, Ava, or the club ever again, or, so God help me, I will not control myself, and you can tell your boss to stay the fuck away too!" He lets them go and for a split second, it looks like he is going to walk away, but he turns and punches thug one on the side of his jaw, hard enough that his head swings sideways and rattles off his friends head next to him. Satisfied that they aren't going to retaliate, he turns on his heels and walks away, getting into his car he pulls out of his driveway and heads towards the hospital.

****

Thug one phones Nathan, trying to explain the incident with Neil. His nasal drawl whining through the phone.

"This job wis meant to be just following some bint and her boyfriend about for a bit, now's she's in the Royal an the boyfriend has just had a hawd ae the pair ae us, screaming in oor faces an I get a punch. So whit the fuck's happenin? I mean if we need ta get violent, then that gonna cost you mare, an that."

Thug one is livid at the turn of events. He has never backed out of a fight in his life, never mind let some wee dick get the better of him, but, he also never takes on anybody else's fight without proper payment, and he hasn't had a proper payment. The look in that guy's eyes, his speed, strength and agility, was as unexpected as the attack was. The guy is fighting for something or someone that is close to his heart, that in itself means he would be hard to beat in a fair fight.

"I don't want you to get into a physical fight with him," Nathan growls down the phone, "If anybody is going to hit him it will be me."

Thug one smiles to himself at the naivety of the rich idiot on the other end of the phone.

"Anyway you can stop following them, I know he was the one to help her get away, and I know she isn't going anywhere anytime soon, so thanks for all your help and Mark has your last payment." Then without even a goodbye, Nathan ends the call. Musing to himself, he realises he needs to get Neil away from Ava, so she will eventually come to her senses and return to him. Thinking out the situation, he heads to the gym. Working on the treadmill always helps him think.

During his workout, his phone buzzes at him from its holder on the treadmill. The number of his informant in the planning department flashes up, so Nathan slows down and stops as he answers the call.

"Low," he growls, as his usual greeting when he answers calls.

"Aye, eh, Mr Low, I em, thought I should maybe give you heads up." Nathan is walking out of his gym, drying off the sweat with his towel as he heads upstairs to his en-suite.

He desperately wants to put his hands down the phone and choke the words from the informant, as all the stuttering and stammering is making his bad mood worse, instead he grits his teeth and growls, "Yes, well, what is it?" Nathan hears a very audible gulp, making him think that he isn't going to like the information he is about hear,

"Right, aye, well you see—"

Nathan's, resolve snaps entirely, "Fucking spit it out, for fucks sake!" He sits in the middle of the staircase, waiting.

"Okay, okay, You're not getting the planning permission you need." There is silence on the line, the informant fully expecting and explosion of anger and hatred from Nathan holds the phone away from his ear. Nathan also expects the same from himself, but instead there is just dismay, dismay and emptiness. Nathan can see his entire life fall apart around him, and he blames Ava entirely. If he wasn't so caught up in trying to get her back and getting back at the idiot she has shacked up with he wouldn't have taken his eyes off the ball in his business deals or the planning permission, and so he wouldn't be in this mess, or having this conversation.

"Mr Low are you there?" There had been so much silence the informant had thought Nathan hadn't heard him, "Did you hear—"

Nathan snaps back, "Yes I heard you, now tell me what you are doing about it?"

The informant starts to splutter, "Well, there is nothing I can do Mr Low, this has gone way above my head, it's above my managers head, in fact I think I heard something about a police investigation being mentioned."

Nathan drops his head into his hands, his teeth clenched and his jaw twitching with the pressure. "Fine!" is all he can growl out through his teeth before he disconnects the call.

"FUCK!" Shouting at the top of his lungs to his empty house, Nathan gets up from his seat on the stairs and stomps his way to the shower, phoning the builder as he goes, telling them they need to stop building for the moment, coming up with an excuse of financial problems, other people's not his obviously. Getting into the shower, Nathan scrubs every inch of his skin until it feels raw, then gets out, dries and dresses casual in blue jeans and a powder-blue shirt. He calls his driver and lets him know that he is going to the hospital.

The driver is outside the door within five minutes. Nathan locks up and climbs into the back of the Daimler, revelling in the soft black leather of the seats. Nathan always loves taking in a deep breath when he gets into his Daimler, he loves the smell of the leather, and he loved driving it, but that was something he hadn't had the time to do in so very long, as life kept getting in the way. Thinking about the last time he drove it he realises that it could've been a year or more since he was last behind the wheel, perturbed by this thought he decides it is well past time he took his car out for a run on his own, maybe tomorrow, or maybe even tonight.

****

Neil texts Jack to ask how Ava has been since he left. Jack lets him know that she has been fine, little sore but the medication seems to be keeping the worst of it a bay, and that she is sleeping at the moment. He then asks if Jack could stay for another bit as he was going to head to the club to catch up on some paperwork and get some ordering done, that way when Ava comes out of hospital he can take some time off to help her get back on her feet, again. Jack agrees, nothing is a problem when it comes to helping out his best friend and the only person he has ever counted as family. He may have been the one who helped get Neil away from his abusive father, but Neil was the one who kept him on the straight and narrow, kept him out of jail by giving him a chance, something to work for and be proud of and responsibility when he gifted him his job and part of the club. Both men would do anything for each other; they are all each other have for family, except, hopefully, now Ava will be a part of their wee unconventional family. Jack smiles at Ava sleeping soundly, and decides now would be a good time to go get some coffee and stretch his legs before he ends up falling asleep in the chair. Closing the door softly behind him, Jack walks over to the nurse's station, he wants to let them know where he is going in case Ava wakes up and thinks everyone has abandoned her. The nurses assure him they will let her know where he is should she wake. Thanking them, he walks from the ward, and notices Nurse Masterson a step or two in front. Quickening his pace to catch her he asks,

"Break time?" Eveline looks round at the sound of his voice and smiles, slowing so he can catch up,

"Aye, quickest hour of the day!" Jack grunts a laugh,

"Aye, it is that." They continue to walk along the corridor, "You headed home?"

"No, just for coffee, Ava's sleeping, and I was thinking that I might end up the same if I didn't move, so thought I would get myself a pick me up."

Eveline nods in understanding, "If you fancy some company you can come down to the staff canteen with me. That is if you want." Her face flushes, as she babbles, not normally one for getting in a flap, she wonders why this tall handsome man has her flustered, but then again his good looks would have anyone flustered.

"That would be great, Eveline, I could do with some conversation, lead on." Jack winks at the nurse, as they both continue to walk in step with each other with their conversation flowing easily.

CHAPTER TWENTY-FOUR

Nathan's Daimler pulls up at the front of the hospital, he tells his driver to park and he would let him know when he was finished and ready to go home. Just as he steps from the car the heavens open and the rain starts beating down, one of those downpours that come out of nowhere, seemingly, and is of biblical proportions. Dashing from the car to the entrance was only about five steps, but he still got soaked through,

"Typical," he growls under his breath, life just isn't going his way at the moment. Brushing off most of the raindrops, he walks to the information desk, putting on his best, charming smile he ask what ward Ava is in.

The girl behind the desk was putty in his hand as he turns on the charm, and flirts shamelessly, making sure the girl feels like she is the only person in the world who could help him. Within a couple of minutes he has managed to get all the relevant information he needs from her, and her phone number, although that found its way into the nearest bin! Nathan heads for the nearest bank of elevators and pushes the call button, annoyed at the amount of time it is taking for the elevator to arrive.

Jack is having coffee whilst Eveline has her lunch, he thought he shouldn't wait the whole hour with her, not that he doesn't want to spend the time with her, but because he doesn't want Ava waking up on her own. He checks his watch, then his coffee cup and decides he will stay five more minutes then head back up to the ward.

****

Neil is in his office in the Daydream going through the takings for the nights since the attack and also checking any bookings that have been taken or that are due in. He didn't like not knowing what was happening in his club and hated having time off, but having Ava around meant he had let go slightly. Something he thought he would never do, or enjoy doing, but with Ava being such a beautiful distraction, he wasn't minding as much as he thought he might. Looking at the bookings diary he notices that there has been a few viewings pencilled in, and at least one booking, with deposit paid in full, all in Ava's handwriting. Seeing this made him glad he had followed his gut and given her the chance at running the private party side of the business, he knew she would be a natural at getting people to love his club as much as he did. He also loved the fact that even though she had had her doubts in herself, she had managed to overcome them and get the job done, God he loved her. The thought shocked him; did he really just admit that to himself? Before he could analyse his thoughts any further his phone buzzed in his pocket. Looking at it, he did not recognise the number, but thought he should answer anyway.

"Neil Alexander."

"Mr Alexander, this is WPC Young."

There was a brief silence as Neil remembered the name, "Oh hi, is everything okay?" Realising who was phoning him, panic started to rise in his throat, his thoughts going immediately to Ava and then to Nathan.

"Yes Sir, everything is okay, I have been asked by the SIO to give you a call as we want to talk to Miss Connell. I don't have a number for her, and I thought it might be best if you were present, due to her reaction when she came into the station the last time." Neil let out a breath, he didn't know he had been holding onto, he hadn't been sure what the WPC was going to say, but was relieved she had realised how Nathan could affect Ava.

"Yes, thanks, that's much appreciated that you thought like that. I'm not at the hospital at the moment, but I will be heading back in about an hour, probably about twoish."

"That great Mr Alexander, is it okay to meet you there?"

"Aye, no problem."

They both agreed to meet in the ward before going into Ava's room. Saying their goodbyes, they both disconnected the call. Neil felt better about the whole investigation now he knew that WPC Young was one of the officers involved. Between the very quick meeting in the station foyer and the phone call he just had, he thought the WPC came across as a kind, empathetic and caring officer, just exactly what Ava needs to get her through what will be very difficult questions. Neil spends the rest of the hour working on orders, then leaves the club and heads to the hospital.

****

Nathan walks into Ava's room without any problem, the nurses weren't at their station as they were busy with other patients. Ava is lying there, her eyes closed, Nathan's heart constricts slightly at the sight of her. Pale, bruised, and vulnerable, a wave of what he thought was guilt passes over him, guilt that it was him that put her here, in this hospital bed. Giving himself a mental shake at such thoughts and emotions, he pushes them all away, after all, it wasn't his fault, she shouldn't have left him, he had told her never to leave him or there would be consequences, but she went against him and so here she is, living the consequences. Anyway, he didn't mean for her to fall against the chair, how was he to know it would splinter, that bit was all that idiot Neil's fault for having crap furniture in his club. Ava stirs and starts to open her eyes, she knows there is someone in the room with her, she is fully expecting it to be Neil or maybe Jack so she smiles at the figure before she can fully focus on him. The smile slides off her face as the shock of seeing Nathan standing there at the foot of her bed hits her and steals her voice before she has a chance to say anything let alone scream.

Nathan smirks at her reaction, liking the fact he can still get a reaction from her. "Hello Ava."

Ava continues to stare him, her eyes wide and her voice non-existent, not sure she was even awake, and really hoping she isn't and this is just a really bad dream, her mind playing tricks on her. "How are you feeling?" Again, Nathan sneers at her, and Ava needs to admit to herself that it isn't a dream and somehow Nathan has gotten into her room, somewhere she is sure he isn't allowed to be. Ava opens her mouth to tell him to leave, but closes it, then repeats the action. Fighting to get her brain and voice to work in synchronisation with each other as she tries for a third time.

"Nathan, what—" she manages to croak out. Taking a proper look at Nathan for the first time for a while, she notices that somethings aren't quite right about him, apart from his nose that had been burst open during the incident. He is still dressed as sharply, his smile is still as charming, but his hair isn't quite as sleek or groomed to perfection as it normally is, plus his eyes, there was something off about his eyes. They didn't have the same glint as she remembered, they weren't dull, or lifeless, but darting about furtively, with a definite touch of wildness looking out of them.

"What am I doing here?" his tone mocking her for being unable to finish her question. "Well isn't it obvious, to get you back." Nathan starts pulling a chair over to the side of her bed, and eases himself into it, he would look at ease sitting there if it wasn't for his jaw clenching and unclenching.

Ava takes as deep a breath as possible before speaking again. "I've told you Nathan, I'm not coming back to you." She manages to get the whole sentence out, and it sounded firm and final, at least a lot firmer than she was actually feeling at that moment. Nathan starts laughing,

"Ah Ava, don't be silly, of course you'll come back to me, where else will you go?" Ava looks a Nathan confused at his statement, but before she has a chance to ask him what he means, he explains in very choice words that she is nothing without him. His words don't make her feel anything but anger (unlike in the past when she would believe him and feel shame at being so useless), she remembers everything that Neil has done for her, always building her up, complimenting her, believing in her. It is at that moment she really realises that the way Neil is with her is the way someone who cares for you should treat you, and that Nathan is just evil and manipulative and wrong. Spurred on by this thought, and her newfound belief in herself, she pushes herself up the bed, trying to hold in the grimace of pain. She clears her throat, fixes a stare that is so solid and sure on him, Nathan can see the change in her and shifts in the hard plastic chair suddenly uneasy about his hold on Ava.

"Listen Nathan, I do not need you, not for anything. I have a job, somewhere to stay and friends, I will never need you ever again, now get out." Nathan lets out another laugh, although this time he's not as sure of himself and Ava knows it.

****

Jack and Eveline are walking back into the ward, Eveline decided to come back from her break early to keep the conversation going with Jack. Both of them walk towards Ava's room, Eveline going in to take her temperature and blood pressure, and Jack going back to take up residence in the hard plastic chair again. Both of them notice the extra head in the room. Eveline stops walking,

"Is Neil due back?" Jack stops walking just a step in front of Eveline,

"Not sure, he hasn't texted me to say when he'll be back, but I don't think that's him in there." They both look at each other and then rush towards the room, Jack getting there just in front of Eveline, bursting through the door,

"Ava who's in—" Jack starts to ask, but stops short, not needing to finish his question, as Nathan turns to glare at him for interrupting them.

He stands, "If you don't mind, this is a private conversation." Nathan sneers.

Jack's anger takes over before he can contain it. Lunging at Nathan, Jack grabs him by the front of his shirt,

"What the fuck are doing here? You're not allowed anywhere near her you arsehole."

Eveline steps up to Jack, gently putting her hand on his

arm, using a strong stern voice, she asks Jack to let go. "I'll deal with him, you go to Ava, go!"

Nathan smirks at Jack, and Jack growls back as he lets go roughly, then moves over to Ava. Nathan swings a roundhouse punch, but Jack sees it coming and blocks the attack swiftly, it is second nature for him to retaliate after a block, but he controls his anger and stops the punch millimetres from Nathans already swollen nose. Nathan flinches, it's Jacks turn to smirk as he turns and walks away, taking Ava into his arms as she breaks down and sobs.

Eveline turns to Nathan, and as sweetly as possible she addresses him, "Sir, I need to ask you to leave my ward, please. You know you are not allowed in here." Nathan looks at the nurse and tries to turn on the charm, although he doesn't quite manage it.

"I am so sorry, nurse; I only wanted to check on my beloved girlfriend."

At his words, Ava screams at him, "I AM NOT YOUR GIRLFRIEND, I LEFT YOU! YOU ARE AN ABUSER AND I HATE YOU!"

Nathan clenches his jaw as it ticks with his barely contained anger. Eveline tries again, this time her tone is sterner, "Sir, I think you need to leave now! Miss Connell has expressed that she doesn't want you here." She touches his elbow gently.

He jerks away, "She has been brainwashed, I am not leaving!"

Eveline rolls her eyes, there is something about Nathan that doesn't feel right to her, to the point she inwardly muses to herself about his grip on the situation he created. "Sir, leave now or I will contact the police." This time her body language, tone and determination was leaving no choice.

Nathan turns, looking at her as if seeing her for the first time. His shoulders sag imperceptibly, but straightens before anyone notices, "Fine, I'll go, for now, but I will be back to collect my girlfriend when she is due to be released, so I can take her home and care for her." He knows he really is chancing his arm with this statement, but he has to let them know that he will win and she will be going home with him.

"Aaarrrggh, Fuck off Nathan!" Ava has stopped crying, her resolve to stay free of Nathan and strong, growing with his every word. Jack can't stop the chuckle that leaves his throat, he is so proud his new friend, she has come so far in such a short space of time.

Suppressing her smile Eveline takes the lead again, "Ava has made her feelings perfectly clear, Sir, now you need to leave, immediately!" Motioning to the door so he is under no illusion where he needs to go, but he doesn't move, instead he stares at Ava, hate, confusion and betrayal flash across his features.

"How can you say things like that – to me? I have given you everything; you would be nothing if it wasn't for me." He had started off hurt, but as he spoke his voice gained strength and his tone more menacing, again.

"You owe me!"

To everybody's shock, Ava laughs. She is feeling all of the strength Neil and Jack has given her, everything they have said how Nathan has manipulated her and abused her, and none of it being her fault. She fixes Nathan with a very strong, but cold stare, and when she starts to talk her voice is even, calm and resolute.

"I owe you nothing Nathan, not now not ever. If it wasn't for you I would have had a job, I would have had friends, I would have confidence. I wouldn't have broken ribs and lying in this hospital bed, or have had it drummed into me every single day that I am useless and ugly and stupid." A smile starts to spread on Ava's lips as she continues, "But then again and more importantly, Nathan, if it wasn't for you I wouldn't have met Neil. He makes me feel amazing about myself; he has shown me how men are meant to treat the women in their life. He has shown me that I can feel more than fear. So much so that I think I might be falling for him."

There is silence in the room, Jack and Eveline smiling at Ava. Pride bursting from Jacks eyes. It is a different story with Nathan, the shock evident on his face is only rivalled by the shock Ava is feeling at openly admitting her feelings for Neil, and not only to herself, but to Jack and Nathan. She knew the feelings were there, she was just too frightened to admit them, even to herself.

The roar of Nathan's voice brought Ava sharply from the musings of her feelings. Looking at Nathan, she sees him staring up at the ceiling, screaming. He stops his roar and looks at Ava, his entire being has changed, his look, his stance, even the atmosphere around him, it now seems wild. He rushes towards Ava's side. Jack sees what is happening and lunges over the bed to protect Ava, Eveline grabs out at Nathan, trying to stop him getting at Ava.

The door to the room swings open with a bang, from its position of sitting ajar and starts to bounce back from the wall it hit, but the two burly police office charging into the already crowded hospital room stop it from slamming shut. Eveline manages to get herself out of the way of the officers to let them through, saying a silent prayer for her staff, their training and using their common sense by phoning the police.

The officers restrain Nathan, placing him under arrest for breach of the peace. They remove Nathan from the room and frogmarch him down the corridor at the same time as Neil starts walking up it. He stops walking and looks with disbelief at the scene in front of him

"You have got to be kidding me, what the, why are you here?" Realisation falls over his face when he actually takes in the police escort and that Nathan's hands are behind his back handcuffed,

"What did you do to her?" Neil starts forward, but one of the officers puts his hand up to stop him, before he got any closer.

"Sir, please, if we could get passed. Miss Connell is fine and with the nursing staff, and another gentleman." Neil stops and sucks in the need to punch Nathan, he steps to the side, letting the officers pass, holding on to his self-control. Once they pass Neil rushes to Ava's room, looking about at the people there, worry etched on his face. Ava is still in bed and Jack is just getting straightened up and standing, Eveline is brushing down her uniform. Neil's eyes are still roving the room, from one person to the next and back again, then his gaze eventually settles on Ava, the fear leaving his heart now that he has seen her, only to be replaced by anger that he desperately trying to swallow down.

"What the hell happened in here? I've just seen Nathan getting frogmarched away, how did he get in here?" By the time Neil has asked his last question his glare is on Jack accusing him of letting Nathan in. Jack puts his hands up in his defence, trying to convey his innocence.

"I went for a coffee, Ava was sleeping, and I was nearly sleeping, I said to the nurses that no one was with her."

Eveline added, "I held Jack back, we got talking and my staff were probably busy with other patients, he must have slipped in." Neil smiles at the nurse, and tells her that it's okay, then turns back to Jack and starts shouting some more. Jack opens his mouth to defend himself when they are both stopped abruptly by the sound of a female voice.

The emotional, but strong voice of Ava cutting through Neil's rant, "Boys, I am not a child. I do not need to be babysat, everything is fine, I'm fine. HE doesn't affect me anymore, he can't control me anymore."

Both men turn to look at Ava, she is smiling and more relaxed looking than they have ever seen her. Neil moves to her side, taking her hand in his, "Did he hurt you? Are you sure you're okay?" Ava squeezes his hand,

"No, he didn't hurt me, I'm good, in fact I'm better than good, except from my ribs I mean, I'm good because I'm no longer frightened of Nathan, and that is the best feeling in the world, knowing that that is it, he is never going to have control over me again, it's freeing, it's amazing!" There are tears running down her cheeks, but her smile has only gotten bigger.

Neil holds her head in his hands, sweeping away her tears with his thumbs. "I'm so sorry he got near you again—"

Ava shakes her head, taking his hands from her face and into hers, then pulling them into her lap. Taking a deep breath Ava starts talking again, "I'm not. If he hadn't come here, for me, again I wouldn't have been able to tell him once and for all that I'm not going back to him, that I am not his."

Neil squeezes her hand as she takes a shuddering breath before carrying on, "I couldn't have told him that I know I'm not useless, and that I know how I should have been treated, and that it wasn't as the punch bag that he used me for, and I definitely couldn't have done any of that if it wasn't for you."

Ava and Neil are staring at each other, both of them oblivious to the other two people in the small room, until

Jack gives a small cough. "Eh, excuse me, what about me?" There is a glint in Jacks eye and a cheeky tone to his voice.

Ava looks up and laughs, "Yes, Jack, you too."

Smiling like she has never smiled before. Eveline bumps him with her hip, teasing, then nods to the door, signalling that they should give them some space.

Jack smiles at the nurse, "Aye right, moan then." he grins "I'll wait outside."

Neil turns towards his best friend, remembering that not five minutes ago he was shouting at him ready to blame him for Nathan getting at Ava again, he felt awful, "Thanks, and I'm, sor—" his voice breaks with emotion, and Jack lets him off the hook with his apology,

"It's cool, I know you're a wee dick, you don't need to tell me."

Neil smiles and shakes his head, thankful that Jack knows him so well and knows how to deal with his emotions. Eveline stares between the two men, then Jack ushers her out, explaining what just happened between him and Neil and why he calls Neil that, closing the door behind them.

CHAPTER TWENTY-FIVE

Back in the same holding cell as before, Nathan is going crazy, screaming at the closed metal door that he is going to sue every police officer that has ever laid their hands on him. Demanding to see his lawyer and that nobody with his standing in the community or class of life should be subjected to this type of treatment, being treated like an animal or worse a common criminal. The police officer on duty at the cells was trying to ignore him, and had done for as long as he considered humanly possible, but after two hours of it, he had had enough. The officer walks down the corridor, stops at Nathans cell and yanks down the small hatch,

"Will you shut the feck up, I've got paperwork to do."

Nathan stares through the hatch, astounded at the officer's words. "You can't talk to me like that, I know my rights, and I want to see my lawyer, now!" Nathans face is puce with rage and his tone is full of indignance.

The police officer lets out a chuckle, "Aye, you know your rights. Problem is you've forgot wan ae the important wans, the right to remain silent, so ssshhhhhs! Oh, an yir lawyer is oan his way. I canny make him git here any faster, so will you please shut up until he gits here! Thank you Sir." The hatch slams shut and the officer walks back down the hallway to his desk, revelling in the very pleasant sound of silence (well at least as silent as the cells could get when populated)

One hour later and Nathan's lawyer arrives at the station, stress and sweat bouncing out of him, as he walks up to the front desk. "I am here to see Mr Nathan Low, and I would like to see him in private please, I have a lot to discuss with him."

He is shown to one of the interview rooms and told that Nathan will be with him shortly, which he was.

Nathan walks into the interview room with a smile and holds his hand out to shake his lawyer's hand, but he quickly drops it, his smile falling from his face just as fast when he sees his lawyers scowl. "What the hell did you think you were doing you idiot?"

The lawyer manages to at least wait until the door has been shut before he starts shouting, but that was of little consolation to Nathan as he slams his hands onto the scarred Formica table. "And who the hell do you think you're talking to?" He spat back,

"In case you've forgotten, you work for me, I pay you!"

The lawyer slams his briefcase down inches from Nathan's hands, refusing to back down to his idiot of a client, "Exactly, you pay me to keep you out of jail, but I can't do that if you are going around doing stupid things like breaking your bail conditions and getting yourself arrested again. I mean are you losing your mind, is that why your decisions are so off just now?"

Nathan starts to talk and has managed to calm his voice. "No I am not losing it, she has lost it. Do you know she actually said she didn't need me, I mean really, can you imagine that." He laughs again, spite screaming out of his features and tone.

The lawyer shakes his head, not entirely sure what is going on in his clients head. "Well, I can't get you out this time, so you are in 'till Monday morning when you'll go to custody court. We also need to talk about the phone calls I'm getting about there being an investigation into you and your business." Nathan stills, looking at his lawyer like it was the first time he had noticed him standing there.

"What do you mean you can't get me out until Monday?"

****

In Ava's hospital room, Neil is sitting on her bed, although they have dropped hands. Ava has calmed down from her rage at Nathan and the emotion of her confession about Neil; all in all she is feeling relaxed and even at ease with life, like a weight has been lifted from her shoulders, even though she is still in pain. Neil is looking at her, his expression going from worry to amazement, to admiration and back again. His eyes have been searching her face, but eventually settles on hers and then his expression settles also, but this time it is an expression full of love and desire. Seeing him looking at her that way brings back what she told Nathan, that Neil had shown her what a relationship should be, gets her thinking, is that what she wants, a relationship with Neil? Could it be that she is just thinking this way because he was the one who has been there for her, saved her, held her? She decides she needs to think about her feelings first before she lets them out to Neil, and hopes that Eveline and Jack don't let the cat out of the bag first.

"I am so proud of you Ava." Ava blushes at the softness of Neil's voice as much as the compliment, she starts to look down but Neil lifts her chin, not letting her look away from him, from the compliment, keeping a hold of her gaze, he continues, "I hear you put Julie in her place at the club. You kinda saved my skin there."

Ava smiles at him, "I would never let anyone use you, and she was planning on telling you lies and playing you, all for money, it was just horrible, plus you have been so good to me and for me." She shrugs not able to find the words to finish her thoughts. Pausing for a second she remembers what she had said to Julie about being Neil's girlfriend and blushes profusely, her cheeks burning and her eyes dropping in embarrassment,

"I'm sorry for what I said to her, about, being your girlfriend, I just—"

Neil smiles, then laughs, stopping Ava in her apology, "There is nothing to be sorry for, as I said, I'm proud of you."

Ava raises her eyes again, looking straight at Neil, taking in his features, his short dark hair, normally he has it styled with a slight quiff, always neat, but not today, today it looks like he has dragged his hands through it in every direction possible. His deep hazel brown eyes rimmed red with worry and the blue shadows under them due to his lack of sleep; it gave her heart a tug to see him so dishevelled because of her.

"When was the last time you slept?" Her voice wobbled a bit with worry for him. Neil drags his hands through his dishevelled hair, again, and down his face.

"I slept a bit here last night." He pointed vaguely at the hard plastic chair next to the bed. Ava's eyebrows shot up,

"You slept here, all night?"

"Aye, I wasn't about to leave you, you had been hurt and I didn't want you waking up alone, thinking I'd left you."

The kindness of his words and his actions were her undoing, as she felt her tears running down her cheeks.

"Hey Sweet, why are you crying?" With a smile on her lips,

Ava shakes her head, "You, that's why."

Neil cocks his head to the side like a confused puppy. "Everything you have done for me, being here all night," she gives a small laugh, "You have done more for me in the short space of time we have known each other than he has in all the years we were together. Thank you."

Neil smiles and brushes the flowing tears with his thumbs with a smile, then winks, "Anytime, Sweet, anytime." he lets out a huge yawn, which brings another smile to Ava's lips and worry to her eyes.

"I think you should go home and get a proper night's sleep." Neil starts shaking his head, refusing to leave. Ava puts her hand up and softly holds his cheek,

"Nathan has been arrested, he cannot get to me. So please, on you go, you look awful."

Neil fakes a shocked look, "Well thanks very much," he giggles, "Okay, I'll go, just now, but I'll be back later."

Ava smiles and nods, happier that he is going to rest. Neil stands from his seated position on the bed and leans over, placing his lips on her forehead; he kisses her, holding his lips there for a few seconds longer that would be thought of as normal. Pulling back, he winks at her then leaves.

CHAPTER TWENTY-SIX

When Sunday afternoon rolls around it is bright and crisp. Neil was in the Daydream, but it was quiet. Jack wasn't in yet as he had had a date the night before with Eveline, although he insisted that it wasn't a 'date' they were just meeting up for some drinks. Neil didn't push his friend any further on the matter, he was just happy that Jack had found someone to take out, even if it wasn't a date.

He was going in to see Ava later on in the evening, when Jack arrived at the club. He had phoned her earlier to check on how she was feeling that morning. She had been chirpy and talkative, bored he had thought. Hopefully, he would get her home tomorrow. His thoughts turned to Nathan, he would be called to custody court tomorrow, and Neil could only hope that he would be put away on remand, but quickly reminded himself that Nathan's lawyer was one of the best in the business and his money had a very long reach. Pushing that thought to the side, he walks out of the office and into the main area of the club, only to be assaulted by the sight of Julie sitting at table three; Neil drops his head and mutters under his breath about table three being jinxed, before taking a deep breath and walking over.

"What do you want?" he asks as he sits opposite her.

"I came to ask why you are cheating on me."

Neil shakes his head, "Go away Julie, you know I'm not cheating on you as we are not together. I know you're not pregnant, and you are most certainly a little bit crazy! So please, leave."

She looks at him with sad puppy dog eyes, "Is it true, are you seeing that new lassie'?"

"Ava?" Julie winces at the name.

"Is that her name? Bit fancy for you is she no?"

Neil rolls his eyes. "No, I'm not seeing her, yet, but hopefully soon. She realised your wee game and said that to get you to back off. To convince you that we are definitely over, and have been for about two months, so please, go away and leave me alone."

He is still feeling tired from his night on a plastic chair and the worry of the past few days, so can't really be bothered fighting with someone he doesn't want in his club, never mind his life. That is until she drops her bombshell, "I hear on the grapevine that your da's been in touch with some of his old mates. Someone's been asking around about him, trying to contact him, 'bout you."

Neil tries to stay as still and unaffected as possible even though his heart starts to beat against his chest in a very quick and unhealthy beat. Refusing to show his feelings outwards, especially to the excuse of a human sitting in front of him, he asks, "And this concerns me how?" His voice is steadier than he thought it might be. He refuses to show her that the mention of his dad may still have affect him.

"Thought you might want to know. You know forewarned is forearmed and that, you know, give you a chance to avoid yet another beating from your old man!" Malice sticking to every word, she stands and starts to walk away, turning back to add, "And don't worry, I won't be back. I'm glad I'm not pregnant, I wouldn't want any kid of mine bred by a wimp."

Neil shakes his head at her back as she leaves his club and

his life for good.

He is still sitting in the same spot he was in when he was talking to Julie, an hour after she left, when Jack walks in. He notices his friend sitting at table three completely still, not blinking, maybe not even breathing. Jack gasps in a breath at the thought of his friend not breathing, but manages to let it out when he sees Neil raise his head slightly. Walking over to the table Jack throws a look to the girl behind the bar, catching her eye he motions with his head towards Neil, silently asking what happened to his friend to have him sitting there. The girl shrugs and gets on with her work,

Jack takes out the chair that Julie had sat in and straddles it. "You alright man?" Jack looks at Neil and his stomach falls from him, at the look he sees on his friends face. The last time he seen that look on Neil's face it was due to his dad's involvement in his life.

Neil sighs, "Eh, no really. I just found out that my dad is back in contact with his old cronies, asking about me." His tone sounds almost defeated.

"Ah," is about all Jack can say to the information he has just heard.

"Why? Why now, why is he crawling out of the woodwork? And why do I have an awful feeling that it is connected to Nathan."

"Ah, again." Jack scrubs his face, before thinking of what he was saying, "What do you want to do, and how do you know about all of this?"

Neil gives Jack a derisive snort, "Julie came in, asking why I was cheating on her with Ava."

Jack barks out a laugh, Neil gives him a look before continuing, "I know, I know, I told her where to go, then when she was leaving she told me about my dad."

Jack looks confused, "Why would she do that?" Jack asks as Neil puts his head down again,

"So I didn't get another beating." Jack winces for his friend, that was a low blow, even for Julie. "She also added that she is glad she isn't pregnant with my kid, as she wouldn't want a kid with a wimp."

"Bitch" Jack wouldn't normally speak about women like that, but his anger level went through the roof and hitting the moon with the information he had just heard. He knows what Neil went through during his childhood and into adulthood with the bully that is his father.

"Hey, listen she is punching low because she got caught out in her scam and you're not giving her what she wants. She is pissed that you finished with her and that you want Ava and not her."

Neil nods, "I know all of that, but, there must be some truth to it all, I am still affected by my dad."

Jack starts to protest, but Neil puts his hand up to stop him, "No listen just listen to me, I mean, take this place, everyone thinks you own it, 'cause I'm still hiding from my dad. People who know me, namely Julie, and now Nathan know that all they have to do is mention my dad and they can break me. I'm still letting him rule my life through fear."

Jack continues to sit in silence, not sure what to say, but knows that there is some truth to what his friend is saying. Eventually the silence is too much and Jack feels the need to say something, "So, what do you want to do?"

Neil shrugs, "I think I want to straighten things out. Get it out in the open that I'm the owner of this place." Neil motions round the quiet club as Jack nods solemnly,

"It won't change the way you, we, run this place, if fact I'm thinking of expanding."

This piques Jack's interest, and he sits up in his chair, "What you planning?"

"The function side of things needs a shake up, but let's get through everything with Ava and Nathan first." He pauses, knowing the next part of the conversation is going to be hard,

"If my dad does re-emerge I'm going to need you, again."

Jack takes a deep breath, then puts his hand on his friends shoulder, "Hey, I've never left before and I'm not going anywhere now, especially if your old man is coming to town. So, there is nothing to worry about, well nothing with me, and if you want to tell everyone who owns this place, then that's cool, no skin of my nose. Except I won't get to shout at you for not working hard enough anymore." Jack smiles as Neil starts to laugh,

"Aye right, I'm sure you'll still do that."

Jack makes a face as if he is deep in thought, "Aye, you're right, ya wee dick, so bugger off and go see that woman of yours...even though she's not actually yours yet."

Both men stand, and Neil grabs his friend into a hug, a manly back-slapping hug.

"Cheers pal; you always know just what to say. I'll see you later." Walking out of his club Neil feels ten stone lighter than how he was feeling sitting at that table, and for the first time in days, he feels that life is going to be good.

****

Ava is sitting up in bed, wearing her new pyjamas and reading the book Neil brought in for her, normally when Nathan bought her things she would be made feel indebted to him, but Neil has never made her feel anything like that, and she is working hard at not letting herself feel like that either.

Yes, he has done more for her than she will ever be able to thank him for, but she thinks she will be able to repay him eventually, as she is sure this isn't the end of their relationship, so she should have time. The word relationship keeps popping into her head when she thinks about Neil, which is nearly twenty-four-seven, she has been trying to ignore it, but is finding it increasingly hard so she decides to close her eyes, relax and study the feelings she is having for him.

First, she starts by asking herself simple questions, 'Do I find him attractive?' She snorts out loud at that thought and then smiles at her answer, 'Hell yes', then she asks herself, 'If the circumstances were different would she still be attracted to him?' Again, her answer is a resounding yes. She had found him attractive that first night at the club, but didn't fully acknowledge the attraction due to being there with Nathan. So putting aside everything he has done for her, she thinks yes, he is a guy I would be attracted to, not flash, not arrogant, doesn't think the world starts and ends with him and has a genuinely lovely heart. Now adding everything he has done for her, not just saving her from the abusive relationship, but giving her a job (and his best friend part of his club), believing in her, encouraging her, talking to her, listening to her, and holding her for no reason other than she needed to be held. Ava thinks this information through, slowly, thinking if they were in a different situation would things be different? Would she feel different towards him? After thinking and listening to her heart for what felt like an eternity, Ava smiles to herself, coming to her conclusion, her heart swelling at the thoughts in her head. She realises that for the first time in a long time she feels like the twenty-four-year-old she is instead of the downtrodden woman she had become.

Nurse Masterson walks into the room and is faced with Ava and the biggest smile she has ever seen on a person's lips. "Wow, you're looking great, and very happy. Did something happen?"

Ava lets out the girlish giggle that has been bubbling up inside. "Yes, well no, kinda."

Eveline looks at her with a bemused smile, then goes about her business of checking Ava over, wound, blood pressure, pulse amongst other things.

Ava continues to talk excitedly, "I know I'm babbling, but I've just realised how far I've come, since I walked away from Nathan, and what I really feel for Neil."

Eveline stops what she is doing and her eyebrows shoot up in expectation of what she is about to hear.

"And, don't keep a girl in suspense."

Ava lets out another giggle, "Well, I've thought about it all day, and if this situation wasn't happening, then I realised that yes I would still like him, I would still find him attractive. What has happened between him and me, and Nathan, just proves that he is a really nice guy and that I will be able to trust him, that I'm not making the same mistakes that I made with Nathan." Her features and her eyes turn to steel, determination straightening her spine and squaring her shoulders.

"I refuse to be another statistic; again, I won't jump from one abusive relationship into another. I will never be the victim again!" as soon as she finishes her statement Ava's eyes soften and her bottom lip trembles.

"And it's all thanks to Neil and Jack. So, I know I don't have romantic feelings towards Neil out of guilt or some sort of hero worship, because I don't feel like that about Jack, he is like my brother, and he has helped just as much." Ava relaxes again, taking deep breaths trying to keep her emotions at bay.

"Thank God for that, 'cause that man's mine!"

Ava bursts out laughing at the impromptu confession from the nurse and Eveline is laughing also, but with a touch of embarrassment of being so open about her feelings with Jack's friend.

"I'm sorry, I didn't mean for that to come out. I mean, I shouldn't be saying things like that."

Ava smiles, and puts her hand out, taking Eveline's in hers, "That's okay, my lips are sealed, but just so the playing field is even, I think he is hoping the same." Ava winks, and from that moment, both women know they will be firm friends in the coming years.

Eveline smiles at Ava, her eyes gleaming with hope, "Right," her voice is too high with emotion, so she clears her throat, "Well, everything looks good; your wound is healing better than expected. Doctor will be round later today and he has mentioned that with assurances from you of bed rest and nothing else, you could get home tomorrow."

Ava, who is still smiling, claps her hands in glee and tries to bounce on the bed, but winces with a yelp, holding her ribs,

Eveline looks at her with a withering look, "Aye see, there will be none of that!" her admonishment is stern, but friendly. Ava tried to look contrite at the telling off, but the pain in her ribs had taken away her breath.

"I'm sure the boys will see to my rest, I've got a feeling that Neil is going to be like a mother hen when I get home."

Eveline is nodding in agreement and it hits Ava again at how settled in her life she has become, how calling Neil and

Jack 'The Boys' is now second nature to her and saying, 'home' when referring to Neil's house, instead of picturing some looming, imposing prison. She really has come into her own self and she is so happy about it. Eveline can see the confidant, happy woman that Ava is becoming and gives her hand a squeeze before leaving Ava with her thoughts and dreams for her future.

CHAPTER TWENTY-SEVEN

It's late Sunday afternoon and Nathan is still pacing his cell, the thought that there could be another two people placed in beside him is even more absurd than him being in there on his own. Again he thinks to himself that there is no way they should be holding him, he has done nothing wrong, he is no criminal, they should be out there catching real criminals, murderers, rapists and the like, not him, he was only there to get his woman back.

A police officer opens the hatch in the cell door, bringing him from his musings, "Low," his voice is husky from years of smoking.

Nathan stops pacing and stands in the middle of the cell where the officer can see him. He feels completely gross, unshaved, unwashed, and still in the same suit from Friday night, and it didn't pass him by that he knew where to stand when the hatch got opened!

"Your lawyers here."

Nathan sighs, "About fuckin' time!"

"Tut tut, Mr Low, now mind your language, and get your erse out here."

Nathan rolls his eyes as the officer opens his cell door, then walks out of his cell, and follows the officer down the tired looking, grubby, magnolia coloured corridors to the tired looking, grubby magnolia coloured interview room where his lawyer is sitting looking annoyed. The lawyer looks up when Nathan and the officer arrive, the lawyer nods at the officer and he leaves them closing the door for privacy. Nathan scrapes out the orange plastic chair and sits down at the chipped Formica table that is bolted to the floor.

"Well," his lawyer starts, "what can I do for you?" The lawyer is annoyed at being brought out into the screaming weather on his day off, but Mr.Low pays very handsomely for his time, so one hour won't be that bad.

"I need to get out of here."

The lawyer pinches the bridge of his nose, pushing his glasses up then plopping them back down when he removes his hand. "I've told you Nathan I can't get you out 'till tomorrow, until you've been to custody court. You know this already Nathan. There had better be a good reason for bringing me down here in the pouring rain, other than answering questions that you already know the answer to, so spill." The lawyer is trying to keep his cool and not show his anger, but he knows he's not doing a very good job of it and his tone is bitchy at best.

Nathan tries to stamp his usual authority on the matter of bringing him out in the wet and wild weather, but it falls flat due to his circumstances, and his appearance, but he continues anyway, clearing his throat before talking, "I need to write a letter to Mark."

His lawyer eyes him suspiciously, "Mark?"

"Yes, Mark, he is my head of security."

The lawyer swallows the need to laugh and say 'aye right', but he knows he needs to keep his scepticism under wraps to get paid. "Okay," he pulls open his briefcase and takes out a pad of paper and his pen. "So, what do you want me to write?"

Nathan chuckles, a derisive laugh. "No, no, not you, you're not writing it, I'm writing it and sealing it, then you are going to deliver it."

"Oh no, no way, I'm not getting roped into one of your schemes, which is no doubt illegal."

"All you are doing is delivering a letter, there is nothing illegal about that, so hand over the paper and let me get writing."

Letting out a humph, the lawyer slides over his pen and paper. Sitting back in his plastic chair he looks up at the grimy ceiling, still yellow from all the cigarettes smoked in the room over the years before the ban was enforced, he sighs, knowing very well that this is not a good idea and maybe even the start of the end of his career.

Nathan writes his letter and asks for an envelope, he places it inside and seals it, then hands it over to his lawyer.

"I want that delivered immediately, and I'll see you tomorrow. Oh one more question, I will get the chance to make myself presentable before I go before the Sheriff, won't I?"

The lawyer nods, "Aye you will." His tone is dejected, wondering if working for Nathan is worth the hassle, he stands and places everything back into his briefcase and goes towards the door. "I'll see you tomorrow." He walks from the room with his head hung low, grumbling a thanks to the officer who is entering the room to take Nathan back to the cells.

****

Neil despises having his car out in the gales and rainstorms of the winter, but as he is going to visit Ava, he isn't minding as much as he normally would. Parking at the Royal Infirmary is, as usual, a nightmare and he is parked half way down Wishart Street, meaning he needs to trudge back up the hill in the lashing rain, but at least it's Sunday and there is no parking charge. Stepping out of the car, Neil pulls up his collar, cursing himself for forgetting his golf umbrella, he starts up the hill. Noticing that there is now a space a lot closer to the hospital, typically, but he doesn't let it get to him, he is going to see Ava and tell her his plans about the club.

Neil gets into the elevator and presses the relevant floor. Getting out of the elevator, Neil gives all the nursing staff a cheery hello, and enters Ava's room, stopping dead at the foot of the bed. She is wearing the new jammies he bought her and she is reading the new Stewart McBride book. She is so engrossed in the book that she hasn't heard him come into the room. He stands watching her, her dark hair pulled up into a messy bun, her facial features relaxed, but moving in response to whatever is happening in the book, then all of a sudden she explodes in laughter. Knowing she is relaxed enough to laugh so easily makes his life feel complete. He surprises himself with the thought so shakes his head trying to remove it, he needs to remind himself he still might not get the girl, but not wanting to contemplate that thought either, he clears his throat, announcing his arrival, and walks further into the room, sitting in the chair beside the bed. He places the bag of clean clothes and toiletries on the floor, almost under the bed,

"How long have you been standing there?" Ava's stomach flips and the butterflies start their dance as she looks at Neil, desperate not to let anything change between them, the easiness and the comfort they have between them, she swallows the butterflies, and tries not to think of the decision she made earlier.

"Long enough to know that that must be a good book." Neil is grinning like a schoolboy, enjoying just looking at her, no pressure, nothing from Nathan hanging over them, just them.

"Yeah, McBride always knows how to get a laugh in a gruesome scene. What's in the bag?"

Neil lifts the bag to show her what he has brought in, "I brought clothes for you to go home in tomorrow and some clean jammies too, just in case. You're looking great by the way."

Ava's cheeks flush at the compliment, "Thanks. I think everything is still okay for me getting out tomorrow, as long as I promise to behave and rest."

Neil smiles, "Well that won't be a problem, you've got me to wait on you hand and foot, and Jack, I mean, both of us."

Ava starts laughing.

"What?" Neil looks puzzled at the sudden outburst of humour.

"I knew that was what you would say, that is exactly what I said to Eveline."

This time it is Neil's cheeks that flush, "Sorry, am I being too pushy? I don't mean to it's just I want you to get better."

Ava takes his hand in hers, "No, you aren't being too pushy and I know you want me to get better, I understand, kinda, I mean I'm not used to being pampered and looked after, so maybe I might be a bad patient."

Neil smiles and squeezes her hand, "I don't see that happening, but we will wait and see what happens, and if there are any problems we will sort them out." They smile at each other, both of their hearts battering in their respective cages, but neither of them saying anything for what seems like an eternity. Neil is the first to break eye contact, if he didn't he was going to kiss her until neither of them could breath, which probably wouldn't be a good idea with Ava's lung being damaged.

"Right, eh, so how's the book?" the intense moment over and the easiness returns as their conversation flows.

CHAPTER TWENTY-EIGHT

Late Monday morning and Nathan is walking free from court. A decision that shocked everyone, including his lawyer, but not Nathan. Slapping his lawyer on the back as he shakes his hand vigorously outside Glasgow Sheriff Court, Nathan winks at him, "I always knew you would come through for me, never a doubt in my mind!"

The lawyer rolls his eyes. Yes, he called in every favour he has been owed to try and secure the release of Nathan, but he still wasn't sure it would work, so when the Sheriff gave Nathan his warnings and let him go he had sent up a prayer of thanks to every God he could think of. "Well thanks, but remember you need to behave this time and do exactly what the Sheriff has told you to do, or not to do as is the case." The lawyer starts to count off Nathans conditions on his fingers, "Stay away from the Daydream, stay away from Neil Alexander, and stay the hell away from Ava!" He is stabbing is finger into Nathan's chest.

Nathan puts his hands up trying to calm his lawyer down from his rant, "I know, I know, I've learned my lesson. I'm going into the office for a bit and then home."

The lawyer eyes him sceptically, and Nathan can see it, "Honest, scouts honour." Nathan tries to look sincere and even manages to have the correct three-fingered salute of the scouts.

The lawyer shakes his head; still not one hundred percent convinced, but says his goodbyes, glad to be away from Nathan and the court.

Nathan's Daimler is there and he climbs into the back of it, pulling out his phone once he is buckled up. His mood changes the instant the car door closes and he goes from the elation of being a free man again to the serious businessman with problems. His first call is to his guy in the planning department. Things still haven't been moving in his favour and he needs to find out why, and what he needs to do to get them moving. He had put the builders back to work, so for a week now they had been at work without proper permission, which normally wouldn't worry him, but this time he didn't need any surprise inspections before the planning has been passed, if his business was getting investigated, he needed everything above board, for once. The phone is ringing out, which doesn't help his mood, so he hangs up and places his second call to the builders, this time the call is picked up quickly, the builders' voice is low and gruff,

"I wondered when you would crawl out of whatever rock you've been under."

Nathan is shocked at the disgust in the builder's voice, but refuses to let it come through in the conversation. "Excuse me? Who do you think you're talking to?" Nathan goes to continue with his rant but the builder interjects,

"I'm talking to the dick who fucked off for a full weekend. The same weekend your building site was visited by the planning department and got shut the fuck down." The builder has warmed to his cause and has stopped minding his Ps and Qs and is shouting down the phone as he continues his rant,

"I'm talking to the arsehole who left his phone switched

off all fucking weekend and so doesn't know that all the men on his site have been told to down tools and are losing money daily and have all been interviewed by the polis!"

After hearing what the builder had to say and the way he spoke to him, Nathan's anger has returned with a vengeance. Never in his life has anyone screamed down a phone at him the way the builder just did. The sun had been shining when he left the court, but now, the heavens had opened and the sky was as black as his mood. Trying to keep his voice even and calm, he starts to ask questions, "What do you mean the planning inspector visited, and the police were there?"

The builder humphed into the phone "Are you stupid? I knew there was something not right about this job, you were too shifty. The job's over, and if I get through this with my business and some reputation intact I swear I will never build as much as a dolls house for you."

Before Nathan gets any answers or can reply to the builder's comment the line goes dead, the call has been terminated. He strikes out; punching the headrest of the driver's seat, then sits and stews until the car pulls up at his office. Not waiting for the driver to open the door, Nathan flies out the car and into his building, barking at the blonde to get people on the phone, as he storms into his office and slams the door. There is no answer or noise from the reception area after a second or two, so Nathan stops pacing and opens his office door, looking at the empty desk and chair. Confusion enters his mind as he talks out loud to the empty room, "Well where the hell is she?" He smashes back into his office like a bull seeing red and sits at his desk. He notices the envelope with his name written on it, all in the blonde's loopy handwriting. Nathan opens it up and takes out the letter. He has to read and re-read it three times, taking in the words written on the company stationary before it hits him that yes his life is definitely starting to crumble around him. The blonde has left him and her job. Her plan is to go to the police with all the evidence of his dodgy deals and backhanders. She apparently made her mind up when she witnessed him attack his ex-girlfriend and hospitalised her.

Nathan sees red, standing up he swipes everything from his desk top, like a man possessed he continues to throw and smash everything and anything he can get his hands on including punching walls until his entire office has been wrecked, his arms are too heavy to lift and his lungs are burning with exertion. He slides down the wall, sitting in a pile of broken bits, his head stooped between his knees, his eyes closed and his breathing hard and fast.

After ten minutes, once his breathing has returned to a semi normal pattern he fishes his phone from his pocket and calls Mark. "Yeah I got out, but now I'm doing it. Find out where they are and what's happening, I'll work the rest out. Probably best you don't know all the details." He cancels the call, stands, brushes himself down and walks from the office. Going through the building and back outside to climb into the Daimler, growling at the driver to take him home.

****

"Right Ok I'll tell her, – no, no – Aye I'll keep my eyes open. I know but seriously, how the fuck did he get out? – Aye I suppose, right nae bother, cheers." Neil puts his phone back into his pocket, sitting at his breakfast bar he puts his head in his hands, still trying to get his head around the fact that Nathan managed to wriggle out of going to jail and got released on bail, again. He snorts a derisive laugh, it's amazing what money and power can do. Retrieving his phone back from his pocket her texts Jack,

Prick got out

Within seconds, his phone rings, as he knew it would. He answers it with a sigh, knowing the rant that was about to ensue, "What the fuck, are you serious?"

Neil could feel Jacks anger and exasperation, it was the exact same as his, "Aye, I know——" Neil holds the phone from his ear, he doesn't need the phone to hear Jack or his rant. Once the shouting has calmed to a dull roar Neil puts the phone back to his ear.

"So what're we going to do then?" Neil asks, looking for some moral support,

"Well we need to tell her——" Worry evident in Jack's voice,

"Aye I know."

"She's getting out today?"

"Aye, she's going to phone me when she's ready. I'm not sure whether to tell her before we leave the hospital or wait until we get home, what d'you think?" Neil's tone is almost tetchy at the thought of having to tell Ava the bad news. Ten minutes ago he was on top of the world. Nathan was behind bars and the girl he is falling in love with is coming home from the hospital, so he can look after her, and he is putting things in motion for him to come out of his business closet once and for all. But now, now he was back on edge, having to check every car that passes him by. Worrying about Ava and her safety, her emotional wellbeing, and his sanity when he is trying to keep her safe. He has never felt this deeply or strongly for any girl ever. In fact, he has never felt this protective about anybody other than Jack. He has fallen hard for Ava and he still isn't sure if he will ever get the girl in the end. But for the moment, he needs to put his feelings to one side to get her through everything that is about to happen with Nathan, to get Ava well again, and then, let her get on with her life, whatever that may bring.

Jack brings Neil out of his thought, "I think you should wait and tell her when you get home, she'll feel safer there and so will you."

Neil muses this over for a second before answering, "Aye, I was thinking the same. You in the club?"

"Not yet, I'm just going in, you wanting to come in and tell her here, or you want me to come to yours?"

"To be honest, I'm not sure; I think I'll play it by ear."

"No bother. Right I'm heading so I can get to the club, but you know where I am if you need me, oh and don't forget to give our girl a hug from me."

Neil gives a small growl down the phone, but says nothing, he knows Jack's feelings towards Ava are purely brotherly, and he is saying it to get a rise from him. Jack on the other side of the phone chuckles at the growl. Both men say their goodbyes and end the call.

Within an hour of ending the call with Jack, Ava phones to say she has her prescription and is ready to come home. Neil tries to sound upbeat and not let his exasperation come through in his tone of voice. He drives to the hospital, checking constantly for the Cortina or any other car following him, taking some extra turns and doubling back on himself, just to be on the safe side, erring on the side of caution. Parking his BMW as close to the hospital door as possible without risking a parking ticket, he sits for a second, checking all around him for anybody watching him, or lingering about longer than he would deem necessary. He hadn't seen the Cortina or anything else suspicious, so letting out a sigh of relief he steps out of the car, glad to be going to pick up his girl and take her home.

Mark steps from his shadowy place against the hospital wall and smiles. He knew all the pains that Neil would have gone through making sure he wasn't followed, taking different routes, adding turns into his journey and probably double-backing, but to no avail, as Mark had been waiting here all the time and Neil didn't have a clue. Patience was one of his superpowers when he was working, but not when he was dealing with clients who didn't pay their dues or were asking for too much for not enough money, and Mr Low was on the verge of pushing his patience to it's very limit on both points. Mark has decided to continue and to see the job out to the end, as he has a gut feeling that he will get his money and more at the end of this.

CHAPTER TWENTY-NINE

Ava is sitting on her hospital bed desperate to get out, but every time she thinks about Neil and going home, her stomach flips and the butterflies get set loose again. She has come to terms with her feelings for Neil, but is still unsure what to do about them. If she tells him how she feels and he doesn't reciprocate them, then there is the chance that she will lose not only his friendship but Jack's too, although there is a part of her, deep down, that believes she will always have them in her life, she hopes.

She hears the door to her room open and looks up, seeing Neil walking into her room makes her stomach flip again, and again the butterflies get loose and go crazy. He's smiling at her as he enters the room, but it doesn't reach his eyes, and it doesn't have the same sparkle to it, Ava's stomach drops and a cold shiver runs up her spin. She knows there is something wrong, but can't bring herself to ask what it is, in case he says he doesn't want her to go back home with him, so instead she smiles back and asks how Neil was. She notices the hesitation and the deep swallow he takes before answering.

"I'm good Sweet, I'm glad to be getting you home again. I know you've only been in the house a week or two, but it feels empty without you."

Ava's eyes widen at Neil's confession, which makes the

butterflies in her stomach to start moving again and a glimmer of hope spark up in her heart. Neil's eyes also widen at his confession, he had promised himself he wouldn't say anything to Ava about the house feeling empty or his feelings in general, but obviously his mouth wasn't listening to what his brain was saying and was concentrating on his heart and other parts of his anatomy!

"Oh I'm glad that's all," Ava starts. Neil looks at her with a puzzled look on his face at her comment. So, she continues to try and clarify what she is meaning, "When you came in I thought there was something wrong, maybe you didn't want me to come home to yours or something." She lowers her head, unable to look at him after being so honest to him about her feelings, but also wasn't willing to take back the words.

Neil let out a small sigh which made Ava look up, seeing the pained look in his eyes as he crosses the small room to be by her side, taking her hand in his. "Of course I want you home, I wouldn't leave you out in the streets before, so why would I do it now? No, never, I want you to stay forever...I mean, if you need to stay, no matter how long, okay?" Ava nods,

"But," Neil continues, "there is something I need to talk to you about, but I don't want to have that conversation here, I would rather do it when we are home, is that okay?"

Ava stares into his eyes intently before answering him, "Is it about Nathan?"

Neil closes his eyes at the sound of the guy's name on her lips; he really doesn't want to get into any conversation about him here, but refuses to lie to her, so he nods, "I'll explain in the car. You ready?"

Ava nods mechanically, the cold icy feeling of fear she knows well has crept back up her spine, she gives up a silent prayer that Nathan didn't get out of jail today, but even as the thoughts leave her head she knows deep down in her gut that he did get out, he has the money, the power and the knowledge to do it.

"Yes, I'm ready, my bags are there." She points just behind the door,

"Did you get the chocolates for the nursing staff?"

Neil retrieves her bags from the floor, "Aye, they're in that bag on the bed."

Ava picks up the gift bag Neil had brought in with him and walks from the room, handing the chocolate to the first nurse she sees asking him to thank the rest of the staff and in particular Eveline who is on nightshift, and continues to walk down the corridor. She had said her goodbyes to Eveline the night before and they had exchanged numbers and promised to stay in touch, her first friend made without Nathan's approval first.

Walking from the hospital, Ava felt cold and vulnerable. Without thinking Ava grasps Neil's hand, entwining their fingers together and getting closer to him – it occurred to Ava that when she didn't think too hard about her feelings for Neil, everything she did around him, like taking his hand and feeling strong around him, came naturally, she hoped he felt as natural around her.

Neil's heart is beating so hard he is sure that it is trying to escape, he takes a peek at Ava and sees the tinge of fear and vulnerability in her eyes, he gives her a smile and her hand a squeeze. "You're going to be okay, Sweet, you're with me now, okay."

She smiles her thanks at him and sends up another prayer thanking God that she now has Neil in her life, even though she doesn't fully believe his statement, not because she doesn't think Neil wouldn't do anything to save her, but she knew how long Nathan's reach could be.

Mark is leaning against the hospital wall near the top of the hill on Wishart Street, at the bus stop waiting on the couple to pass him on their way back to the car. He is smoking a cigarette and pretending to be looking at something on his phone, headphones on, just like anybody else waiting on the bus. He looks up the hill and spots them turning the corner and start to walk down the hill towards him, he goes back to looking at his phone and they walk right past him, not even glancing his way. They get into Neil's car and drive off. Mark smiles at how well he knows human nature and at the fact that they don't even realise they have made a huge mistake walking past him, then he phones Nathan.

"Aye, they've just left." He informs Nathan when the call is connected,

"Right tell me when they get back to his and then leave it for tonight. I don't think they will do much for the rest of the week with her injury, and I'm wanting to put some distance between us, you know, 'cause the police will be watching."

Mark makes a sound of agreeance. "I can do it for you if you want?" Mark knows Nathan wants to do it himself, but if he does it then that means more money. Nathan ponders Marks proposition for a moment. He knows that it would probably be safer for him if Mark carried out his plan, but where would the joy in that be for him. No the cow had left him, and because of that his life was shattering all around him, so he wanted to make sure her life was left shattered too. He will make sure she will never find happiness unless it is with him, so he will do it all himself and make life fair and right again.

"No, thanks, but no, I need to do this for me."

Mark rolls his eyes, he never understood why people got emotionally involved, it only causes problems, but Nathan was the one paying him so the way Mark sees it Nathan could do whatever he wanted, regardless of what Mark thought.

"Aye okay, I'll go to the house, to make sure they went back there, then go back on Friday, how does that sound?"

"Yes, that's grand, thanks." Nathan cuts of the call. Sitting in his living room, Nathan takes a sip of his brandy; he can't bring himself to think about what is going on with his business and his life. Four weeks ago, he was on top of the world, he had Ava, his apartments were highly sought after and he could get anything he wanted, and now, now, he was nearly at rock bottom. Arrested – twice – his business getting investigated for breach of planning permission, his informants in the department investigated for taking bribes, and probably going to be sued at some point when it all goes public and people realise their homes might not be everything they thought they should be. He always knew what he was doing was wrong and illegal, but in his view, rules were there to be broken, and it wasn't his fault that people are greedy enough to accept his money when he asks them to do things, legal or otherwise. As he thinks about it more, Nathan comes to the conclusion that it is merely a fact of life, survival of the fittest so to speak, and that is exactly what he is, the fittest!

Knowing there wasn't much he could do for his business at that moment, he turns his attention to taking down the Daydream and Neil's father. Lifting his phone, he dials the number he was given, it should be a direct number to the man who fathered his rival and hopefully the man's downfall. After a few rings, a deep, broad Glasgow accented man answers,

"Aye."

Nathan for the first time in his life is unsure of what to say, if he was honest he didn't think the guy would answer. "Yes, is this Mr Alexander, father of a Neil Alexander?" Nathan is using his best business voice, the one that commands people to listen to him.

"Aye, and?" Neil's father isn't one for small talk or posh people who think they are better than everyone else. Nathan on the other hand rolls his eyes as he hates talking to people whom he deems to have limited vocabulary, who couldn't hold a proper conversation if they tried, who spoke like they came from the gutter, people like the man on the other end of the phone, who he unfortunately needed at this moment in time.

"I was wondering if you could help me out in a little matter concerning your son?" Charisma oozing over his every word, Nathan holds his breath waiting on the reply.

"He is no son of mine! An who the fuck ur you anyways?" The barking cough and rasp to the man's voice gives away his years of smoking,

"I'm sorry?" Nathan smarms, "I should have introduced myself, I am Nathan Low, I am interested in the club he works in, the Daydream, although I've heard through the grapevine that he may actually own it. I was wondering if you could shed any further light on the subject for me?"

There is a sharp intake of breath, then a very long coughing fit from the older man as he hears the news about his son's business. Once the coughing has subsided, Nathan hears the man clear his throat and then spit. He is absolutely disgusted at the sound and lack of manners that the man has, but decides to continue with the conversation.

"Aye, well I thought that he had got rid ye it. Selt it tae that pal ae his, so I couldnay git tae any the money. Well you know whit, fuck him, I dinnay need him or his money, ungrateful wee cunt that he is, I managed tae git ma oan money, so, tae answer yir question, Mr Low, naw I willnae help you wae onything, I'm no dain anything that could fuck up whit I have noo. Goodbye." Neil's father cancels the call.

The hatred and venom in the man's tone when he was speaking about his son was so palpable through the phone, Nathan could almost see it, but still he didn't want to help Nathan bring him down. Closing his stinging eyes Nathan starts to take deep breaths, trying to clear his thoughts, trying to regain control of the panic that is rising in his throat. Panic that everything he is trying to do to fix his life was of no use at all or only making things worse. He stood leaving his brandy with only a sip out of it, next to his phone, he needed to go to his gym and just not think of anything for at least an hour or more. Once he had a clear head everything would feel better...he hoped.

CHAPTER THIRTY

All week, Ava had stayed in the house, doing nothing more than moving from her bed to the couch and to the shower when her pain wasn't too much. Her ribs were still sore, but she could definitely feel improvement as her breathing was almost back to normal and there was very little pain when she took a deep breath. The first few days home from the hospital, walking up the stairs felt like climbing a mountain, puffing and panting all the way up and then having to stand at the top for a few minutes until she got her breath back to some semblance of normal, but now she was managing to get up the stairs with only slight breathlessness, so the doctor was happy with her progress.

All week Neil had fussed over her, as she thought he might, making her food whenever she was hungry, regardless of the time. Every hard puff of breath, cough or yelp of pain she gave, he came running, panic in his eyes, asking if she was all right and if she needed anything. One day he was getting ready upstairs when Ava, who was lying on the couch downstairs, sneezed violently causing her to let a roar rip from her throat as pain coursed through her ribs and lungs. Neil dashed downstairs in a panic thinking she had done more damage to her ribs; he was in such a hurry he had missed the last stair and landed in heap at the front door with an oomph. Ignoring her own pain Ava got up from the couch and dashed into the hall to see what had happened, what the noise was. When she laid eyes on Neil lying there, she started to laugh, and continued to laugh until she was in so much pain she ended up in a heap next to Neil. From then on Neil had promised to calm down on the panicking, and even managed to go out on the Thursday for longer than his usual one hour, leaving Ava in the house on her own. Over most of the week they had spoken many times about Nathan getting freed, Neil's decision about the Daydream, and what he would do if the rumour about his dad was true and he was about to make another visit into Neil's life. Ava assured Neil that no matter what decision he made, she would support him, just like he was supporting her. Even though neither of them had been brave enough to start the conversation about their feelings for each other, there had been no awkwardness, they had both slipped back into the easy way they were with each other, learning about each other, getting know everything about each other, and enjoying every minute of it.

On the Friday morning, Neil asks if Ava would be okay if he went in to the club for a few hours. He hadn't been near the place since the day Ava left hospital and even though Jack had been keeping him up to date and bringing some paperwork over, he was still starting to feel guilty at leaving everything to Jack. Ava agrees, and assures Neil that everything will be fine. He should go and not worry, and she will even have dinner ready for him coming back in, then they could relax on the couch with a film later. Sitting at the breakfast bar, as was their usual routine in the morning, Neil reaches over and squeezes her hand and smiles, before standing. He lifts his coffee cup and puts it in the sink to rinse it. On his way out of the kitchen, he passes Ava and stops, stooping slightly, kissing her cheek,

"I'll see you tonight." he says as he walks out of the kitchen. He is amazed at his actions, he didn't know he was going to kiss her until he did it, then realised how natural it all felt, like a couple in love, talking over breakfast about their day ahead. Therefore, with a smile on his face and his heart swelling with an emotion he daren't name he sat on the bottom stair and pulled on his Doc Martins.

Ava was sitting at the breakfast bar, her coffee cup half way to her mouth, the same position she was in when Neil kissed her. She brought her hand up and touched where Neil's lips had touched her cheek, her heart doing somersaults, and her butterflies going crazy. Smiling to herself, Ava allows herself to enjoy the thought of Neil's kiss and what it may mean and where it could lead, if only she had the confidence to let him know how she feels. After a few minutes more dreaming, Ava stands, clearing up all the dishes and then heads for the shower.

****

Neil drives to the club, totally unaware that he is being followed by Mark. He parks his car in the car park and walks to the club, saying his hellos as he walks to the office and settles behind his desk. He pulls out all the paperwork sitting on the desk and starts to go through everything he had missed whilst he had been off, then he starts to go over the diary for party bookings. Ten minutes later Jack walks into the office, pleasantly surprised to see Neil sitting there.

"Eh who are you and why're you in my office?" Jack jokes, Neil looks up at his friend and smirks,

"I think you'll find I'm the boss, the big boss!" he quips back.

Jack lets out a laugh, "Aye, right, so you are, ya wee dick!" The two friends laugh together, then get down to business, discussing what has been happening in the club. When they get to the party side of the business, Neil points out that the amount of party bookings has increased and that it's the same member of staff advising on parties and booking the parties. Jack's eyes sparkle, and his smile is one of sheer pride,

"Aye, our girl, she's a natural. Neil feels the familiar growl come up his throat when Jack calls Ava 'our girl' he swallows it back down, he knows it's stupid to be jealous and he knows Jack doesn't see Ava in a romantic way, he also remembers talking to Jack about it and being an arse, but it still annoys him.

Jack, however, sniggers at his friends reaction and then continues, "Any way, when the bookings were being taken, I made sure that everyone was asked who they first spoke to about booking a party and they all said Ava, and most of them were spoken to on the night of the attack." Neil feels his heart explode with pride as Jack explains how fantastic Ava was in the club before she was attacked,

"I was thinking, how would you feel about assigning one person to deal with the parties and bookings?" Jack asks.

Neil looks over to his friend, studying his face to see if there was any hint of who Jack had in mind to give the job to, and to see if it was the same person he was thinking of.

"I was thinking about it, especially if it gets more bookings in and gets the appointments more organised. You have someone in mind?" Jack smiles,

"Why do you?"

Neil smiles, nodding his head. "Aye, and I hope it's the same as you. Ava."

Jack starts nodding his head in agreement of Neil's choice, "Yip, that who I'm thinking of. I think she'll be fantastic at it."

Neil agrees again. "Fantastic, I'll tell her tonight, she's making dinner for us."

Jacks eyebrows shoot up, "Hmmm, happy families."

Neil blushes at the thought, then tries to hide it, he doesn't understand why he is being so transparent about his feelings,

"I kissed her cheek this morning when I said goodbye, telling her I'd see her when I got home." Neil can't believe he has confessed this to his friend, and Jack's eyebrows are even higher now with the confession.

"And what did Ava do?"

Neil's smile grows even wider at the memory, "She smiled and said, "Okay?"

This time Jack wiggles his eyebrows, "Think you might be in there!"

Neil rolls his eyes. "Shut it!" Neil's tone is friendly and joking, but Jack knows there is a warning there also so drops that part of the conversation and both of them continue going through paperwork and the re-organisation of the workload to include Ava in her new position of Bookings Manager.

Neil stays in the office for most of the day catching up with the club; Jack had been in and out and even took the opportunity, since Neil was there, to go for lunch with Eveline Masterson. Both Neil and Jack had relaxed slightly about the Nathan situation, as they knew there was nothing they can do about it until either he does something, which would be suicide on his part, or the police get in contact again. They had been to the hospital to question Ava, and the staff there, and to the club to question Neil, Jack and their staff, so for now they watched their backs and waited on any information regarding any court case that might, or at least should, be happening.

Feeling satisfied that he has caught up with his paperwork, and has made decisions about the business, Neil calls it a day, looking at his watch he realises it is past four, he wonders what Ava has been doing whilst he has been at work. Desperate to get back to her, he walks from the office on the lookout for Jack. In his haste to find Jack, he bumps into a customer.

"Sorry Sir, I didn't see you there." Neil glances at the customer and takes in his appearance. Scruffy, with dark hair and dark eyes,

"That's okay." The customer gruffs out,

"Let me get you a drink on the house, I seem to have spilled yours." He walks the man over to the bar and grabs the barmaid's attention, asking her to get the man a refill when he has finished his pint.

He turns to the man again, "I am sorry Mr..." He waits for the man to give him his name.

The man eyes him, then smiles slyly, "Mark, just Mark."

Neil feels a shiver slither up his spine, but isn't sure why so pushes it to the side, but not quite forgetting about it completely, "Well Mark, just let the barmaid here know when you're ready for your next drink."

"That's very kind of you, thanks Neil." Neil stills at hearing his name coming from the stranger's mouth, he knows he never gave the man his name, but doesn't show his unease.

"No problem Mark, it's my mistake, I wasn't looking where I was going, so please enjoy. Now if you could excuse me." He shakes Marks' hand and walks away to find Jack.

Finding him, Neil explains his encounter with Mark and

his uneasiness about never telling Mark his name, but he knew it and used it. Jack eyes the bar to see who Neil is talking about and then assures him he will keep an eye on the stranger, suggesting that Neil point him out to the bouncers on his way out. Neil agrees. They then organise the opening and closing of the club for the upcoming weekend. Neil telling Jack to take the morning off, that he will open up. Jack is grateful that Neil is back at work.

CHAPTER THIRTY-ONE

Mark finishes his pint, feeling pleased that he has managed to see Neil and get a feel for the club, just in case Nathan's plan didn't work out. Mark had always thought it best to be prepared for any eventuality, and since Nathan might call upon Mark to make up a plan B to finish this problem, he wanted to be ready.

Walking away from the club and back to his car Mark pulls his mobile from his pocket and places a call to Nathan.

"Low." As usual, Nathan answers with a growl,

"Aye, it's Mark, he went to work today."

There was a short silence as Nathan takes in this piece information, "Where was Ava?"

"Don't know, but she wasn't there, so I'd guess she was still at his house. However, I did manage to see Neil and his pal talking, and he is going to be opening the club tomorrow on his own, giving the other one most of the day off."

Nathan smiles at this piece of information, "Hmm, interesting. Cheers Mark, that's great work. I think that should be all. I will let you know if I need you again."

There is silence on the other end of the phone, all Nathan can hear is the white noise of silence, he is actually starting to think that Mark has dropped the phone or worse, when he hears him take a deep breath. Mark, on the other hand, is waiting on Nathan to mention payment, it sounds like the end of the contract so, he shouldn't have to ask, and normally he doesn't need to ask Nathan, but for some reason, this time it seems to have slipped Nathans mind, or maybe it's more like his mind has slipped.

"Eh, Nathan, you still owe me my last payment." Mark doesn't want to get angry over this situation, he has known Nathan for a long time but he doesn't do friendships or fools and he hates talking and fighting over money it's crass, so he has no qualms about taking what is rightfully his and if that means having to hurt Nathan to get it, then that is what he will do.

"Yes, I know, I will get it all to you once I know that this is finished with, which should be no later than Monday."

Mark looks skywards, he doesn't like the way the answer sounds, so he takes a deep breath before he answers, "You know that is not how I work Nathan, but I will do you a favour and wait 'till Monday, just in case you need me again, but no later than noon Monday, do you understand me?"

The tone of Marks voice leaves Nathan under no illusion that he means business. "Yes, yes, I know. I will have this finished one way or another by Monday, I promise."

"Right, Monday then, bye." Mark disconnects the call, not happy about how things are panning out, but has said he will wait until Monday so that is what he will do, and with that, he drives away.

Nathan has a slight panic, the last thing he needs at the moment is the wrath of Mark coming down on him. He does have the money, he just doesn't want to tempt fate by letting him and his services go just yet, he wants a back-up plan and that is exactly what Mark is.

****

Ava is pottering about the house, doing bits of housework, then sitting down to regain her energy and breath, she is trying to get her strength back, but knows that she also needs to rest, she hates the thought of not being able to do things. She has been there and done that, been the kept woman, not being allowed to put anything into the house, not even housework or making dinners. Nathan had staff, Jean, to do all of that. He had always said that he wouldn't have any woman of his degrading herself by doing such menial things. Ava had always felt guilty when she seen or spoke to Jean about not helping out, she hated that it must have looked that she was just sitting there all Lady of the manor when she really wasn't. She didn't like having nothing to do. At one point she took up a cooking course, Nathan knew nothing of it, he was at work. She had excelled in the class and found she really relaxed when she was working in the kitchen. Thankfully, the classes were paying off now, she was making Cullen skink, a smoked haddock soup, followed by homemade steak pie with baby potatoes and turnip, then for dessert she was trying her hand at Cranachan – a Scottish dessert with cream, porridge oats and whisky. She wasn't sure why she had decided on an all-Scottish menu, she just wanted to make something that was all hers. By the time most of her meal was ready, apart from the stew, Ava felt one hundred percent better, and on top of the world. She opened a bottle of red from Neil's wine rack. Reading the label she realises it is a Borolo and takes a small panic, but then she realises that it is not the most expensive bottle there, that was the bottle of 2005 Chateau Petrus. Ava knew enough about wine to know that was a £4,000 bottle, and that Neil is something of a connoisseur.

Going upstairs with her glass of wine, to changed, Ava realises that she has major butterflies dancing and bouncing about her stomach. She goes for a shower and takes her time getting dressed in her black jeans – a la Neil – and a butterfly chiffon top (the irony wasn't lost on her, but probably would be to Neil). Putting on her make-up, Ava looks at herself in the mirror, her skin was glowing, her deep blue eyes had a sparkle back in them that she hadn't seen there since her teens, her smile didn't look forced, it wasn't forced. It was natural, real, she was happy, at ease with herself and her surroundings, not a bunched up bundle of nerves like she normally was, in fact, she realises that she hasn't felt this relaxed since before she'd met Nathan.

He hadn't been domineering and abusive to start with, but she was nervous of the new relationship, he was the perfect gentleman and the fact that she was young and naïve went against her. Then, after six months, once she started to relax into the relationship Nathan asked her to move in with him to his mansion, the house she never called home. It was then, once she was under his roof that the overpowering, dominant, abusive Nathan raised his ugly head, but by then she'd loved him, or at least she had thought that that was what love was meant to be like. She had thought about leaving him, but every time she did, it was like he could read her mind and he 'gently' reminded her that she couldn't leave, she was his, and there was nothing she could do that would stop them being together, he 'owned' her. These gentle reminders usually came with a punch or six and a few kicks when she was on the ground, but never to the face.

Ava didn't realise she was crying at the memories until she felt the tears dripping onto her hands that she had in her lap. She shook her head as if to rid the memories from her mind and then wipes the tears away, looking again into the mirror she smiles, she knows now for certain that she is out, she is away from that relationship and that the person she was back then is history, never to return.

She has become a different person in such a short space of time, a stronger person, and now, thankfully, a person who knows what love isn't and is now learning what it should be. After her thoughts of the past, Ava's thoughts turn to Neil and how he makes her feel. Even the thought of him makes Ava's smile increase tenfold; he really has taught her the truth about how she should be treated, how even something as simple as a friendship should be, and that it is everything that Nathan wasn't. Thinking about the difference between Neil and Nathan, Ava realised that whenever she sees Neil walk through the door the butterflies start their dance and then a sense of peace comes over her, the feeling of being safe and strong and loved. It was this strength that Ava had tapped into that night in the club when Nathan came in demanding she leave with him, the more she said no to him the better she felt, the stronger she felt, until she felt almost superhuman. She is so thankful to Neil, and Jack, but mostly Neil, for showing her strength, the strength she used to stand up to Nathan, for helping her feel worthy again, something Nathan never made her feel.

Being in hospital had given Ava masses of time to think about her relationship with Neil and analyse, or actually over analyse, her feelings for him. At first, she was worried that her feelings were connected to his helping her get away from the abusive relationship, but every time he walked into her hospital room, her heart lifted and proceeded to dance about her rib cage, so much so she was certain that it was visible through her pyjama top, but then when it was time for him to go she felt her heart break a little. The pain from her injury on her side would wake her up in the middle of the night and her thoughts would turn to Neil, wondering if he was still working or had gone to bed at a proper time, wondering if he had thought about her, or even better dreamt about her. The thought of her being in his thoughts or dreams excited her in more ways than just her heartbeat, it was then she realised that her feelings were more than hero-worshiping. The thought of being with Neil in a romantic way brings another smile to her lips, as she walks down the staircase. Neil's house is nowhere near as grand as Nathan's mansion, but is absolutely perfect, Ava feels at home, relaxed and comfortable there.

Neil walks through the door whistling to himself, he looks up and stops dead in his tracks, he sees Ava walk down the stairs radiating beauty. Her brown hair was down, styled so it sat just on her shoulders, the black jeans she was wearing clung to her curves perfectly and the butterflies on her top looked like they were floating and dancing as she walked, exactly the way they were in his stomach. Ava could feel him looking at her, but she didn't feel like she was being inspected, the way Nathan did, no she felt admired and beautiful. When she reached the bottom of the stairs they smiled at each other, both noticing how they were looking at each other, their eyes dancing, just like their butterflies.

"You look fantastic," Neil eventually said, they were standing toe to toe, Neil put his hands on her hips and pulled her in, desperate to kiss her, but not wanting to push his luck by kissing her lips, so placed his lips gently to her forehead and kissed, lingering just that little bit longer than necessary,

"And whatever you're cooking smells amazing."

Ava was taken back by the intimacy that Neil was

showing, which made her lost for words momentarily and she could feel the blush creeping up her cheeks. She managed to recover enough to form words that an adult would use and not the hormonal teenager that she felt she was at that moment. "Thank you, it's nothing fancy, just Cullen skink and then homemade steak pie, potatoes and veg."

Neil has let go of Ava and they are walking up the hall into the kitchen, "I've not had homemade steak pie since I left my mum's. She used to make it every Monday. My father had to have certain meals on certain days or there was trouble." Neil shakes his head at the memory.

"Well I hope it's as good as your mum's then." Ava turns to the cooker and stirs the bubbling pot, then takes a fork and tastes a small piece of the meat making sure it's tender enough.

"Mmm, won't be long, where do you want to eat?" Ava asks as she hands him a glass of wine. Neil takes a sip before answering,

"The breakfast bar is fine. I do have a room that I guess was meant to be a dining room, but I use it as my office and junk room, sorry."

Ava tilts her head and looks bemused at Neil's apology, "Why are you sorry, it's your house, you can use the rooms for whatever purpose you want."

Neil's insecurities about his house and bank account have been trying to surface, but he has been managing to push them to the back of his mind and ignoring them due to everything else that has been happening. Neil shrugs, takes another sip of his wine and changes the subject, not wanting to talk about what he doesn't have.

"Ah, Borolo, good choice." He smacks his lips together in appreciation of the wine.

Now it was Ava's turn for insecurities to raise their head. "I hope you don't mind I opened a wine, I made sure you had other bottles of that one, I thought that would make it safe to open. I'm sorry if I've crossed a line." She turns back to the cooker, trying not to let Neil see the panic in her eyes, stirring the stew like there is no tomorrow. She hears Neil put his glass down with a clink on the marble of the breakfast bar, then she feels his arms snake around her waist and his breath on the sensitive skin behind her ear and on her neck,

"There are no apologies needed, and no lines have been crossed, whatever is in this house is yours to use as well as mine. I know I said you could stay here to until you were on your feet, but I really hope that doesn't happen too quickly, I like having you here."

Ava turns in his arms, loving the way she feels encased in his warmth and looks him in the eye. All she can see there is truth and hope. Ava smiles and lets out the breath she was holding on to, her blue eyes sparkling, "Me too."

She goes up on to her tiptoes and softly kisses Neil on the lips. Desire rushes Neil like a runaway steam train, but he manages to hold himself back, and instead of deepening the kiss like he is desperate to do he pulls Ava into his chest and holds her tight, whispering 'good' into her ear. They stay like that for a minute, then Neil pulls back and clears his throat from emotion.

"Right, well, I'm going to get scrubbed for dinner." Ava smiles, she knows that what just happened may be the turning point in their relationship.

"Okay, I'll set out the bar, but don't be long as the soup will be out in five minutes."

"Yes, Miss!" Neil winks and then places another soft kiss on Ava's lips before turning and leaving the kitchen to get washed and changed for dinner. Ava stands in the same spot, holding her fingers to her lips, amazed at herself for being so forward and kissing him, but it all just felt so right she couldn't help herself.

Pulling herself from her trance she gets on with setting the bar for dinner and getting the soup on the table.

One hour later and they have both finished dinner. Neil clears away all the rest of the dishes into the dishwasher. They both go into the living room and cuddle on the couch in front of the TV both relaxed and happy. They talk through the night, until they both fall asleep in each other's arms.

CHAPTER THIRTY-TWO

Nathan's night was not as peaceful. He has had numerous builders on the phone shouting abuse at him about the lack of planning permission, about being out of work now the site has been closed down, and telling him they will still be expecting the full wages they are due, plus the wages they would've been paid had the build continued. They all left Nathan with no uncertainty of what would happen if their reputation was tarnished and they couldn't get other contracts. It would certainly be unpleasant and include nail guns, claw hammers, and Stihl saws. After the last phone call, Nathan gave up on drinking the wine he had opened and poured himself a very large dram of Glenlivet. Sitting in his office, he starts to go through some paperwork and mail that he has been neglecting. He notices that everything he looks at is about the apartment build that is meant to be happening at that moment, but has come to an abrupt stop due to the investigation. Separating the invoices into piles of money due out and money due in, Nathan realises that there seems to be more money due out than due in. He knows that during a big project that would normally be the case, until the apartments are sold at the extortionate price of quarter of a million each, then he had the funds to pay off the debts with plenty left over to line his own pocket. With this build being put on hold, he realises he might need to dip into his own funds to pay off the builders and anything else that might crop up.

Nathan knows he isn't a nice person, and he also knows he is only handy with his fists when it comes to Ava, so he won't be stupid when it comes to the builders, he would pay them. He knows they will keep their promises of violence, and he knows he is no match for them, even in a fair fight, so what else could he do but what he always does to get himself out of a tricky situation, throw money at it until it goes away. The house phone starts to ring and Jean answers it, she taps at the office door and waits until Nathan says she is permitted to enter, she explains that it is his lawyer on the phone. Nathan groans inwardly, this was going to be a phone call he probably didn't want to take, but knew he had to, so with a sense of dread he takes the phone and dismisses Jean with the demeaning flick of his hand as was his usual way. Jean turns and walks away, rolling her eyes at her boss.

Taking a deep breath Nathan put the phone to his ear, "Low!" He wasn't even going to try to be pleasant.

"Nathan, I have just had one of your coppers on the phone, they wanted to give you a heads up." The lawyer was pissed, as much as Nathan was an important client, he was still a pain in the arse and is making him work for his money.

Nathan could feel the dread running deeper through his veins, he only has two coppers on his payroll and he very rarely needed to use them, they usually only gave him a heads up if the newest local thug thought about trying his hand at getting Nathan's business, or if there was someone they thought would be beneficial to him.

Then the thought that there might be 'new evidence' that has come to light in his assault charge, makes a flicker of hope pass over him. Trying to still sound in control Nathan asks the question he isn't sure he wants to hear the answer to.

"About what exactly?"

"The CID want to talk to you, and the building inspectors have been in touch."

Nathan closes his eyes, the hope of earlier dissipating, "What did they want?"

"I'm not sure, exactly, the cop had only heard snippets, they said to just keep your head down they will get back to me as soon as they know anything for definite."

Nathans' anger starts bubbling again, "Fine, let me know if you hear from them again!" He ends the call and sits, stunned, not moving, letting his anger take over. As usual, his thoughts turn to Ava, and how everything in his life is crumbling around him because she left him, if only she remembered her place and stayed none of this would be happening. His anger takes control of him as he screams Ava's name and hurls yet another glass at the wall, sounding like an animal in pain. It then occurs to him that not only has he smashed two of his crystal brandy glasses, he has now just smashed one of his Gleneagles crystal whisky tumblers, and again it is all because of Ava. Letting her name and every expletive known to man rip from his throat, Nathan goes round his office throwing things, ripping his photographs off the wall and throwing them to the ground. Smashing anything he can get his hands on, until his desk is cleared and the only thing not broken is his office chair, looking at it he picks it up and hurls it through the window. Breathing heavy after all his exertion, Nathan calms himself before turning round and walking from the office, leaving the destruction and going to his gym.

Jean hears the commotion coming from the office and knows it would be more than a glass that was getting smashed this time, but when she walks into the office, her jaw drops. Never in her life has she seen such a mess, books strewn everywhere, glass shards over every surface, and the office chair hanging half in, half out of the broken sash window. She knew Nathan paid her handsomely and she knew that there were things going on that had him tense and stressed all day every day, but there is a snowballs chance in hell that she is going to clean this room. After standing by for years while he beat Ava and turning a blind eye to his every flaw, Jean decides that enough is enough, she grabs her handbag from the kitchen, walks out the house and never looks back.

****

Waking up on the couch, Neil realises that Ava is in his arms, he smiles despite the stiffness in his neck and arm, and leans over giving Ava a gentle kiss on her head. He lies there for a minute, enjoying holding Ava, letting his mind wander.

Once Nathan is out of their way, hopefully Ava would see him in the same light he sees her. After the kiss last night and the conversation about how long she would be staying, Neil dared to hope that it may be possible Ava was starting to feel something for him. Ava stirs in his arms, and Neil pauses his thoughts, and panics at the movement in his trousers, praying that Ava didn't feel it move, or maybe there was a bit of him that did want her to feel the movement. Ava opens her eyes and smiles at Neil before something akin to panic flash over them, dulling the sparkle that was evident when she smiled, Neil's heart begins to sink, maybe she isn't feeling what he is feeling,

"I'm sorry," Ava stutters out, she is embarrassed that she is cuddled up to Neil and has been all night, she tries to move but her leg goes into cramp due to being in the same position for the full night, making her yelp in pain and grasp out to reach her calf.

Neil jumps, panicking that he has hurt her ribs, "What's wrong? What'd I do?"

Ava is writhing on the couch trying to massage her calf, part of her is laughing at Neil's reaction, he is sitting on the couch pleading his innocence that he didn't mean to hurt her. Ava shakes her head, trying to tell her he would never hurt her,

"No, my leg, cramp," she manages to get out through gritted teeth. Neil lets out a sigh of relief that he hasn't hurt her then slides down the couch so he is sitting on the arm of the chair, straightening out Ava's leg, telling her to relax as he massages the muscle in her leg. After a couple of minutes, her muscle has relaxed and Ava has managed to stop screeching and writhing. Neil was loath to stop rubbing her leg but he knew he had to, so lowers her leg on to the couch, remaining to sit on the arm,

"That better?"

"Yes, thank you, and I'm sorry—"

Neil waves away her apology, "You don't need to apologise for taking a cramp, if anything I should apologise for falling asleep on you." Neil could feel his cheeks turn pink with his blush, which he was trying to fight but knew he was losing.

Ava smiles and blushes too, "That's okay I didn't mind." She lowers her eyes to hide her feelings,

"Are you not meant to be opening the club today?" Ava looks up the sunburst clock above the fireplace, Neil looks up too, realising that it's ten o'clock, the staff arrive at eleven to set up and normally he's been in for an hour or more.

"Aye, but I don't normally need to be in until eleven," he lies slightly not wanting to worry Ava that he was late.

Ava eyes Neil, knowing that he is stretching the truth for her sake, she smiles, she loves how Neil always thinks of her feelings, "Aye right!" She calls him out in lie.

Neil laughs, "You're right, I'm normally in for about nineish, but I'm not worried, I know the boss." Neil winks at Ava as he gets up from the arm of the couch, "I'm going to get ready."

Ava nods, taking a deep breath she asks, "Okay, could I maybe come in later, I mean to work?"

Neil stopped at the swinging door that leads into the kitchen, "You don't need to." He sees Ava's face fall at his words, "I mean, yes you can, but don't push yourself into anything too quickly, take all the time you need. I don't want you to worry about not working, or money or staying here or anything else." He knew he was rambling, but his mouth just wouldn't stop, "You're not here just so I get cheap labour."

Ava moves from the couch and walks over to Neil, circling her arms around his waist she gives Neil a squeeze, in a silent thanks, "I know, but I need to get back in the saddle, as they say, and I think I need to do it sooner rather than later, I don't want to leave it too long and then take a freak out when I get to the club."

Neil understands what she means, she doesn't want the attack, or Nathan to get into her head and mess up all the hard work she has done by getting away from him, so with that in mind he agrees,

"Okay, I'll go in just now and you can get ready, then I'll come back about fourish when Jack arrives. How does that sound?"

Ava nods,

"Well that will be the perfect time for me and Jack to talk to you. We were wanting to talk to you about your job when you decided to come back." Excitement danced in Neil's eyes that made Ava's panic lessen.

She gives his waist another squeeze before talking, "Sounds interesting." She smiles before continuing, "You go and get ready and I'll fix us some coffee."

Neil gazes down at her, taking in the sparkle in her eyes, the porcelain texture of her skin, then he takes her face in his hands and kisses her, softly to start.

Ava didn't realise what was happening until the warmth of Neil's mouth was on hers, she smiles into the kiss. She can't believe he has feelings for her, and since she has admitted to herself that she has feelings for him, she allows herself to kiss him back, amazed at how right it feels. After a few seconds Neil uses all of his self-control to break the kiss, he doesn't want to push his luck, he knows stopping the kiss before he goes too far is for the best, but he doesn't want to break the intimacy so he places his forehead on her and smiles,

"Thank you." He is trying hard not to pant as he talks.

Ava squints at him in confusion, "For what?"

"For being you." He softly kisses her forehead before walking past her and out into the hall, smiling like the proverbial Cheshire cat all the way upstairs to his bedroom.

In the kitchen Ava is smiling too, she can't remember a time in her life when such a simple kiss could make her heart feel so light and full all at the same time. Thinking about the kiss and the surprise Neil and Jack had in store for her Ava continues making their coffee and tidying up the kitchen while dancing away to herself, all the time she is oblivious to the fact that Nathan is sitting outside in his 2015 blue

Mercedes Benz, SLK Coupe. He rarely drove this car during the week, opting for his Daimler and his driver, as he would normally have paperwork to go over or phone calls to make as he is travelling, plus parking near his office is a nightmare, but at the weekends, he liked getting the Merc out to stretch her legs. Part of him knew that Neil hadn't seen this car and knew that it would be an odds on bet that Ava is too stupid to recognise the car. He sits watching the house, seething, his anger turning murderous. He is now blaming both Ava and Neil for his downfall, the last straw being the realisation that Jean had left last night, he would never have lost everything if it wasn't for them.

Last night after working out for an hour, Nathan had felt his anger dissipate slightly, enough at least that he could breath, so he went for a shower, relaxing under the steaming jets of scalding hot water. Whilst standing there Nathan continued to plan the demise of Ava and Neil, then he started planning how to get his business back on track. With both plans fixed in his head, he stepped from the shower, dried and dressed in his grey loungewear trousers and a plain grey T-shirt, walking back to his office as he shouted at Jean to make him something to eat. Getting to the office, he realises that nothing has been tidied up, it still looked like a mad man had trashed it! Storming into the grand hallway, Nathan roared on Jean, when there was no answer he then went storming in to the kitchen to find it empty. A feeling of déjà vu ran through his body, even though he knew she was away, Nathan still searched the mansion, and the outcome was as he suspected, he was alone, his housemaid of ten years eventually had had enough and walked out.

As Neil walks from the house and into his BMW M3 Nathan is shaken from his stupor of anger. He watches Neil pull away in his car, leaving it a few seconds before following him. Guessing that Neil is going to the Daydream means Nathan can hang back a bit, letting three cars get in between them. He knows he won't get parked near the club so he opts for the NCP car park that way he can walk through Mitchell Lane, which will bring him out onto Buchanan Street.

As he walks up towards the club his phone bursts to life, he pulls it from his pocket and sighs when he sees that it's his lawyer phoning. Knowing that whatever his lawyer is going to say will probably make him angry, he answers with more of a growl than normal, "LOW!"

"Nathan, I have had the building inspectors on the phone, they want to interview you and they want to do it today."

Nathan smirks, so much for the police getting involved, this is much better. One building inspector he can handle, everyone has a price. "Not today, sorry, I'm busy all day, arrange it for a different day, maybe tomorrow, at my office." Quickly remembering his office isn't in the best shape due to his temper the last time he was there, he changes his mind, "No, actually, we will be better off having it in your office, tell them to be there about one o'clock." The lawyer starts to protest, but Nathan cuts him off, "It is that or nothing, it's their choice." He growls his goodbye and then cuts the call, placing his phone on silent before putting it back into the inside pocket of his suit jacket. Walking past the Daydream he notices that the shutter on the door is halfway up, meaning Neil must be in. He walks across the street to the Costa Coffee and orders a large latte, then sits at the window to watch.

CHAPTER THIRTY-THREE

Neil is busy in the office setting up for the day ahead, thinking about the kiss he shared with Ava. Noticing in the diary that there was a christening booked in for the next day, he smiles to himself, today is a good day for Ava to come back to work, that gives her time to find out about the new job and get things organised for tomorrow's party.

At eleven, Neil hears the staff bell at the front door, and goes to let the first of the staff members in. One by one they all clock in, comment on how happy Neil is and ask where Jack is. Neil explains that Jack is having the morning off and that he will be in later. He leaves them all to set up and retreats back to the office, making a mental note to organise a staff meeting to tell everyone the truth. He continues preparing paperwork and finishing off his idea for the management changes.

At twelve on the dot, Nathan notices the shutters on the clubs windows going up and the doors opening, he drains the last of his coffee and walks into the cold crisp sunshine. He walks over to the club and peers in. No sign of Neil or his idiot friend and definite no sign of Ava. Wandering about the street wasn't really an option, so he finds a bench to sit on and gets as comfy as is humanly possible on a cold bench in the middle of Glasgow city centre on an autumn afternoon. Knowing he was going to be there for the long haul, Nathan has brought a paper to read, although he very much doubted that he would read very much of it. After an hour of waiting, watching and seeing nothing, Nathan pulls out his phone. He has twenty-five missed calls and fifteen texts. The first text he looks at is from his lawyer telling him to answer his phone. There are twelve more of the same, only with increasing angry and obscene language. One is from Jean telling him she will not be back and she wants severance pay or she will sue him for constructive dismissal, and the last one is from Mark, which is the most worrying one. He was one of the missed calls and has assumed the silence was Nathan ignoring him, and therefore non-payment. The text was not a good sign. Nathan double-checks the missed calls just to be sure, twenty-four are from his lawyer and one from Mark. Nathan tries to relax and tells himself that Mark knows he will get paid, the text is just a warning, may be not quite a friendly one, but just a warning all the same.

He phones his lawyer back, Nathan is not a man to be hounded, he likes to deal with business head on, in his own time and when he can gives it his full attention.

"Where the fuck are you, and why are you ignoring me?" His lawyer shouts down the phone.

Nathan smirks, for some reason hearing his lawyer foam at the mouth with anger has put Nathan back into a jovial mood. "And hello to you too." his tone dripping with sarcasm,

"Fuck the niceties Nathan, I've got the inspectors breathing down my neck, threatening to get the police here to arrest you, if you don't get your arse over here and meet them today!"

Nathan rolls his eyes; his lawyer wasn't normally as easily wound up. Nathan sighs, "Well when do they want to meet? I mean, I have plans you know."

"PLANS?" The lawyer screams down the phone at him.

The night before, Nathan's lawyer had done a lot of thinking about all his time representing Nathan, and he came to the conclusion that he had never felt this much heat in any of the previous years. Nathan never lets anything get out of control, he is always on top of business, especially any problems that arise, but not this time, this time he is acting as if either the business doesn't matter to him, or he doesn't understand what the implications of being investigated are, not to mention the fact that he has been arrested twice in as many weeks. Holding his head in his hands the lawyer decides he would be bemused, maybe even amused, if he wasn't so worried about all the information he knew personally.

"Are you taking the piss Nathan? The inspectors have found out near enough everything you have been up to over the years, they are gathering evidence for the police. They are also trying to give you a chance to come in to my office and come clean, make life easier for you." The lawyer pauses for a second before continuing his rant, "Do you not understand you idiot, you are facing jail time, and so is everyone connected to you!"

Nathan is silent, all he can hear is the lawyer breathing hard down the other end of the phone. After about thirty seconds of thinking, Nathan decides to answer, "Don't be daft, I haven't done anything that bad. I mean it's only a few bungs here and there, and a few buildings started before permission was given. Stop getting your knickers in a twist!" His tone proving just how smug and arrogant he really is.

"If that is what you think, then you are more out of touch with reality than I thought. Things are going wrong with one of your apartments, and the building control guys are going in to investigate."

Nathan is silent again, pausing to collect his thoughts before answering, "Not really my problem is it?" Again, his tone of voice is relaxed and smug, "I mean surely that's the builder's. I really wish you would calm down, you're going to give yourself a heart attack." Nathan can hear his lawyer laugh on the other end of the line. An incredulous, bemused laugh of someone who knows his reputation is going straight to hell in a handcart!

"Wow, Nathan, you really do think you're made of Teflon, don't you?" The lawyers' anger has started to grow again, "Listen to me, get your slimy arse up to my office now or there will be a warrant out for your arrest, on bribery and corruption charges, do you understand me!" The lawyer is out of breath due to his anger and utter contempt for the man he only yesterday thought of as a gentleman and friend – almost.

Nathan chuckles down the line, "Of course I understand, I will come down to your office as soon as I'm finished what I'm doing. Now will you calm the fuck down please?" Nathan cancels the call with a chuckle. He has no intention of going in to meet with the inspectors today or any day. He comes to the conclusion that they have nothing on him, they are just on a fishing expedition, if they did they would just arrest him. His lawyer has just went into full panic mode, in fact Nathan is starting to wonder if he hadn't started to have a breakdown with the stress. Nathan chuckles again, shaking his head at the thought.

Looking at his watch, Nathan realises that it's three thirty, he gets up and takes a stroll up and down the street outside the club, straining to see if he could spot Neil or Jack inside.

He notices Neil standing at the bar and smiles, feeling his adrenaline levels spike at the thought of his plan. On the last lap of his stroll he sits back down on the bench attempting to get comfy, again when Jack walks down Buchanan Street towards the Daydream, Nathan lifts his newspaper slightly to obscure his face and chuckles at the thought of him looking like a bad private detective from an eighties movie.

****

Jack walks into the club, a huge smile on his face, feeling well rested – even though he was up most of the night – and happy with life. Neil sees him walk through the door and nods his hello, then continues talking to the member of staff he was talking with. Jack nods back then enters the office, taking his jacket off and sitting behind the desk. He starts his day's work by looking at the paperwork that is sitting there and then at the diary that Neil has left open. A few minutes later, the office door opens and Neil walks in,

"You're looking awfy happy the day. You get lucky last night?" Neil's' eyes are glinting with humour as he ribs his best friend.

Jack looks up from the diary and grins back at his oldest friend, "I will not say. A gentleman never kisses and tells! But what I will say is that I had an amazing date with Nurse Masterson last night and I am very grateful for the late start today, as I may not have had a lot of sleep." He winks at Neil then laughs, his eyes dancing with the memories from the night before.

Neil is happy for his friend, glad that he has found someone that makes him happy, although he will not let the opportunity to wind Jack up pass, "I'm glad last night went well, but mind and not mess this one up eh?"

Jack gives Neil the middle finger then shakes his head, "Not planning on it, ya wee dick, not this time!"

Neil smiles and nods at his friend. Both of them understanding the full meaning of their conversation.

"Anyway," Neil changes the subject, "I have been thinking, since I have decided to 'come out' of the who owns the club closet, I have made some notes about what changes I think that will be needed, and what we are going to tell the staff. Oh and we are going to need a staff meeting too."

Jack nods, then looks at the papers on the desk, "These them then?" He picks them and starts to go through them,

"Aye. You read any of them yet?"

Jack nods his head, "Well skimmed them. I agree with the job for Ava, we've discussed as much and looking at the diary she is going to excel at it, but the bit about me I'm not sure I can agree to that."

Neil's' head snaps up his eyes connecting with Jacks, "Why not? I don't see a problem with it."

Jack shakes his head and drops his eyes, "I know you don't, and that there is the problem. You don't need to—"

Neil puts his hand up to stop his friend from talking, "I know I don't, that's not why I'm doing it, I'm doing it because I want to, and you have more than earned it. You do more work than your fair share in the business, so I'm increasing your share of the business. It's as simple as that, and there is no argument, and anyway it's not by much, another five percent. Call it a thank you for everything."

Jack is still shaking his head, but knows better than to argue with his friend when his mind is made up, anyway he doesn't want to ruin his good mood. "We'll see, anyway, when you going home?"

Neil moves from the spot he is standing in at the desk and lifts his jacket from the coat stand, "Right now, but, Ava wants to come in for a bit, a get back in the saddled kinda thing, so we'll be in later, probably after we've had dinner."

Jack nods, "Okay, I'm looking forward to seeing her back at work, it seems like there is something missing, even though she was only here a few times. She slotted in perfectly."

Neil nods in agreement, "Right I'm going to noise the staff up about not working enough, so I'll see you later."

As Jack walks towards the door he slaps Neil on the back, smiles then leaves. Neil lifts his car keys and follows, waving his goodbyes to the staff as he leaves."

CHAPTER THIRTY-FOUR

Ava is ready and waiting to go to work. She has been ready since about twelve, but has also changed her outfit three times, not sure whether to go for casual or business. In the end she decided for smart casual, a pair of black jeans and a red shirt, paired with her black heeled ankle boots, as she is just going in for a bit, to find her feet again.

She is sitting in the living room with her book, another Stewart McBride one, when Neil walks in.

Coming into the living room, he drapes his jacket over the chair nearest the door, "Hello Sweet, how's you?"

Ava looks up and sees Neil's smile, then notices his eyes and how his excitement seems to be dancing in them, with kindness and desire as an undercurrent. Ava feels her stomach flip and her heart beat harder in her chest. He really is gorgeous inside and out, she thinks to herself as she smiles back at him, loving how he calls her 'Sweet'. "I'm good, looking forward to going into the club, though I'm a bit anxious as well," she tells him truthfully.

Neil flops onto the couch next to her, placing his hand on her knee, he notices that she doesn't flinch or pull away, both of them feeling the touch as natural. There has been a kiss or two between them so Neil puts it down to that, "That's understandable Sweet, Jack's there and I'm right by your side so there is nothing to worry about, but if you've changed your mind and don't feel like going in that's fine."

Ava places her hand on top of his, which he has started to move in slow circles rubbing her knee. He stops rubbing when she touches his hand, but doesn't move as she is squeezing it, reassuringly. "No, no, I still want to go in, I need to do it. I refuse to let Nathan ruin my first job, or my life anymore, and anyway, I'm looking forward to seeing Jack."

Neil rolls his eyes, praying that it comes across comically, "What is it with youse two? He said the same when I told him you were coming in today." Neil tries to feign being grumpy about the conversation, but he knows he has managed to come across as a bit pissed off, maybe even a bit jealous.

Ava smiles, her eyes dancing in the light coming in the bay window, she is amused at Neil and his annoyance at her wanting to see Jack, it makes her dare to believe even more that it's due to him having feelings for her, the same feelings she has for him, then she feels guilty at being happy at his annoyance, so she gives his hand another squeeze,

"He is a friend...well I hope he's a friend," Neil relaxes at her words, but still catches the hint of doubt in her eyes. She still has confidence issues with herself, something that pains him, but he swears inwardly that he will help her rectify that. "Of course he is, and so am I." Neil says softly, and catches Ava's eye before she has the chance to drop them, trying to gauge her reaction and her feelings.

Ava holds his gaze, warring with herself about the comments, feeling happy that Neil has told her Jack was her friend, but also she is tinged with sadness that he has referred to himself as a friend also. She had thought that maybe they could be more than friends, and had only minutes ago thought that was possible, but now she decides she was mistaken. Not wanting to show her hurt to Neil, she smiles, trying to make it go to her eyes, but fails, "Friends," she says in a whisper.

Neil sees the pain and disappointment in her eyes as she says the word 'friends' and his heart, and other parts of his anatomy soar, which he knows is wrong, he is sure now that she does feel the same and the prospect of them being more is definitely on the cards.

"Ava, I—" Neil starts to say that he wants to be with her, romantically, to be more than friends, when the timer on the oven goes, cutting him off. Ava stands dropping his hand, she apologies for interrupting him and explains that dinner is ready, her voice strained as she rushes towards the kitchen. The swing doors to the kitchen slow to a close before Neil puts his head in his hands, cursing himself inside and out, desperate, now, to tell her how he feels, but not sure how to go about it.

****

Nathan had seen Neil leave the club and walk up Buchanan Street towards The Royal Concert Hall. Guessing he was going to get his car, Nathan turns towards Mitchel Lane so he can cut back through to retrieve his Merc from the NCP car park. After paying his fees, Nathan wheel-spins off in the direction of the M8 motorway, to go to Neil's house. Once there, he parks up so he can see the house, but not so close that it is obvious he is watching the house. Nathan checks his phone again, and decides that it might be a good idea to text Mark, let him know what is going on and explain that he is not ignoring him.

*Sorry I missed your call phone on silent. Got things in hand, will let you know when things finished. *

Satisfied that the text has explained all, and that all will be sorted out soon, Nathan sits back and relaxes, waiting on Neil's arrival. Nathan wasn't sitting long when Neil pulls up and parks in the driveway, he eyes Neil's car with disgust. As much as the M3 is in fantastic condition for its age, it is old and Nathan doesn't do old, not with anything, especially cars or women. In fact the only things Nathan sometimes uses that could be classed as old (his liquor aside) is the building materials he buys for the apartments. He chuckles to himself at this thought, his lawyer's words of doom about one of the apartments flitting through his mind, maybe, that is what his lawyer meant. Although as far as Nathan is concerned the builders knew where the materials came from, so he could have refused to use them, after all he is the professional builder not Nathan!

Through all his musings, Nathan watches Neil walk from his car and into the house, he can't see into the living room window from his car so decides another wee stroll might be needed, just to see what was happening inside.

After another half hour of waiting, Nathan decides to do just that, he gets out of his car and pulls his collar up to partially conceal his identity, then goes for a walk, crossing the street to look from a distance first, then crossing back over to pass by the other way. On his second pass, Nathan notices a mirror above the fireplace and realises that if he stands in a particular spot he can see what is happening on the couch through it. He then notices both Neil and Ava sitting there, together, his hand on her knee, her hand on top of his. Both of them gazing at each other, laughing and looking happy, together. Looking at Ava more, Nathan can see how relaxed she looks, and free of pain, she never looked that relaxed or happy when she was with him, in fact, she doesn't look as if she is missing Nathan at all, it looks like she is actually managing to live without him. The thought hits him hard, full on the chest, she is doing exactly what he had always told her she would never manage, she is getting on with her life without him. Nathan sneers, the anger bubbling up once again, overtaking everything in him, making him see red. Growling under his breath, he asks himself,

"But will she manage to live without him?" With the thought of taking Neil away from her and being there to pick up the pieces, Nathan returns to his car to wait again, Neil is going to need to leave at some point, so Nathan will wait to put his plan into action.

****

In the house, Ava has started serving dinner, annoyed at herself for getting so upset about being friends only with Neil. She should be thankful that he is in her life regardless of her feelings, she shouldn't be looking for anything more, but she can't help how she feels, or how she thought Neil felt. Pulling herself together enough, she places the plates full of mince and potatoes on the breakfast bar, walking to the swing door; she steadies herself before going to talk to Neil, praying that there won't be any emotion in her voice before pushing it open.

When she does push the door open Ava goes to speak, but stops at the sight before her. Neil is still sitting on the couch, hitting his head off the palms of his hands, whilst growling the word stupid to himself over and over.

Ava clears her throat to let him know she's there before she talks, "I've put dinner out, it's mince and tatties, I hope that's okay. You said that it was one of your childhood favourites."

Neil lowers his hands and looks up at Ava, he loves looking at her, could do it all day, he would love to tell her that and every other feeling he has for her, but doesn't want to scare her off, so instead of his confessing undying love for her, he opts for dinner, "Aye, I love mince and tatties, it's good honest food. I've not had it made for me for years, it smells great." He stands and walks towards the door, stopping in front of Ava, taking her hand and motioning towards the kitchen, desperate to get away from the disaster that he made of their conversation. "Come on, we'll have dinner then we can get into the club. How does that sound?"

Ava nods, then sits down to start eating.

Conversation through dinner is strained, both of them talking about anything but what they want to and should be talking about – them. When they have finished, Neil clears up the dishes, putting them into the dishwasher as Ava touches up her lipstick, and gets her shoes and jacket on, then waits on Neil. Once they are both ready, Neil opens the door and lets Ava walk out first. As she passes Neil, he smells her perfume, Ghost Night, the smell reminds him of the first time he saw her, his immediate reaction to her, his body, his feelings, his heart, everything comes flooding back. Without thinking he reaches out and grasps her wrist, Ava spins round, her eyes wide with surprise, and a flash of fear with the gesture of the grab. Neil sees the fear and hates that he put it there, but knows that it's not really aimed at him, more a memory of Nathan.

"Ava I need to ask you something." Ava stands still, not sure what to say or do, "Earlier, when we were talking, you didn't look happy at the word friends, and for the past few days we've, – I mean, what I'm trying to say is that ever since I met you that first night I, you,"

Neil knows he is making a mess of things; his words are falling out of his mouth before his brain can put them in a sensible order to explain how he feels. Deciding to try a different way of explaining things, Neil pulls her in, placing one hand on the small of her back and the other he slides into her hair pulling her forward the last millimetres until their lips touch. He waits a heartbeat to see if she pulls away. When she doesn't, Neil claims her mouth, trying to put everything he feels for her into the kiss.

Ava is shocked, one minute Neil is talking about their conversation earlier and making very little sense, then he is kissing her like his life depended on it, slowly she realises that this is his way of talking about feelings, so she relaxes into his embrace, into the kiss, and deepens it, opening her mouth, letting Neil's tongue in.

Knowing what Neil is trying to say with his kiss, Ava matches his emotion with hers, taking his mouth with her tongue, both of them coming together, holding each other so tight that not even light could get between them, the intensity, emotion and Neil's erection growing with every passing second the kiss continues. When they break apart, both of them are breathing hard, and smiling, they both continue stealing chaste kisses until they can catch their breath back.

Ava is first to talk, "So, you want to be more than friends then?"

Neil laughs, then puts his forehead on hers, "Yes, Sweet, I do, very much so."

Ava lets out the breath she had been holding on to, she had never asked such a forward question, she never thought she would be brave enough to ask it, but is so glad she did.

Neil takes both Ava's hands in his, "We'll talk more tonight after work, but yes I want more, I want you, I always have from the first second I set eyes on you, but I promised myself that I wouldn't act on my feelings. I didn't think it would be fair on you after everything you've been through," he pauses, trying to steady his heart, "but, seeing your reaction when I said I was a friend made me think that maybe I had a chance of more, and with that kiss I guess we both know now that there is something else there."

Ava nods, not trusting her voice to stay level, or her tears not to pour from her eyes, at how gentle and thoughtful Neil is being.

"Right, I guess we better get to the club then." Neil clears his throat, but all Ava can do is nod her head again. Dropping one of her hands Neil closes and locks his front door. They walk over to the car where Neil places another kiss on Ava's lips, trying his damndest not to let his emotions overpower him, they would never get to the club if that happened.

Ava climbs into the passenger seat, and touches her lips with her fingertips, loving the slightly swollen, tingly feeling left by Neil's kiss. Neil walks round to the driver's side and climbs in, smiling, knowing that he and Ava are feeling the exact same at that very moment.

They drive away in blissful, silent contentment. Both of them oblivious to the Mercedes Benz parked across the road or Nathan sitting in the driver's seat seething with anger at what he has just witnessed. It took all if his willpower to stay in his car, to not get out and rip them apart. He wanted to jump up and down on Neil's face until Ava promised to come back to him, until she saw sense and realised that she is his, she belongs to him, and she is better off with him, Nathan, the leader of his own empire! Shaking his head to get rid of the red mist that has descended over his eyes, Nathan drives off, not sure whether to head back to the club or to his lawyers office, he remembers that there is a pub across the street from the club, so he decides to go there, he could be doing with a drink after what he has just seen.

CHAPTER THIRTY-FIVE

Walking from the car park to the Daydream, Ava starts to wonder if she is doing the right thing, going back to work so quickly after the attack. Sitting in the house wanting to go back, feeling ready to go back is one thing, actually walking into the club and working is another. The closer they get to the front doors the more her chest tightens and her stomach turns. She grabs Neil's hand, and squeezes her eyes shut for a second.

Neil recognises Ava's behaviour from the other times she has had panic attacks. He squeezes her hand in reassurance and smiles at her, "It's okay Sweet, I'm here." He can hear her breathing quicken and then stall with every step she takes. Once they are within two steps of the clubs' entrance Ava's breathing is rapid, she can feel the sweat running down her back, she stops dead in her tracks, turning to Neil, panic written all over her face. Neil knows he has to get her to calm down or she will get to the point where she could lose consciousness. Neil turns to Ava, and just like the times before, he holds onto both of her hands looking straight into her eyes he starts to talk to her.

"Sweet, look at me, keep your eyes on me."

She does as Neil asks, feeling his strength, she manages a nod, she knows the drill, knows what Neil does for her, and knowing all of this, it gives her a strength she never used to feel,

"Right breathe with me Sweet," Neil continues, "In and out, in and out, that's it, same as me." He keeps his voice soft and steady.

After a few seconds Ava's breathing has started to return to normal and she manages a smile. "Thank you, again," Ava manages to pant out.

Neil smiles back, "Anytime Sweet, but this time I think, most of that was you, I saw a determination in your eyes that I haven't seen there before when you were having an attack."

She nods, "I felt it too. I've came to realise that I can't let them control me."

Neil pulls her into his chest in an embrace, "That's my girl!" He gives her a quick kiss, "You still wanting to do this?" Neil asks, as he nods towards the club.

Ava looks over Neil's shoulder and manages to take a deep breath, then nods, "If I have you by my side, I can do anything." She winks at Neil, who is standing with his mouth hanging open. He smiles at her then they both turn and walk into the club.

*****

Jack notices Neil and Ava standing outside the club and goes to meet them at the door when he realises that Ava is having another panic attack. Watching his best friend talk the woman he loves through it as he has done before, is something Jack is in awe at, it amazes him the way Neil can get her through it. Then he notices that it is over, Ava has managed to calm down and get her breathing under control a lot quicker than any other time. He smiles to himself at how far she has come in such a short period of time, even though there are still things happening to her. It is then that he notices them kissing and Jack smiles again, happy that they were getting together, they both deserved happiness, and were perfect for each other.

Neil and Ava walk into the club still holding hands, neither of them wanting to lose the contact for two reasons, firstly they have just admitted their feelings for each other, and secondly they both knowing the contact is moral support.

Jack smiles at them when they reach him, "Hello you," Jack stretches his arms out, and moves towards Ava, bringing her into them giving her a squeeze,

"Hello." Ava snuggles into his embrace, feeling like she is getting a hug from her big brother,

"Ah, Ava, I am so happy to see you, welcome back, I've missed you."

Ava squeezes again, "Jack, I'm glad to be back, and I missed you too. Did you cope without me?" Ava jokes,

"I tried very hard, but it's just not the same when you're not here."

Ava loves the banter between her and Jack, it still amazes how easily she slips into not only Neil's life, but Jack's life too. Thinking about it, Ava realises that this is where she belongs, with Neil, having Jack as a friend and here in the club. She looks up at Jack and then over to Neil before squeezing Jack in a rib crushing hug.

Neil clears his throat, not enamoured with the scene playing out in front of him, "Eh, just whenever you two are finished could we get on with some work?"

Jack and Ava look at each other before laughing; they both heard the tinge of jealousy in Neil's tone. Jack breaks the embrace, but takes Ava's hand in his, knowing it is winding his friend up and starts to walk towards the office with Ava, looking over his shoulder at Neil, "Moan then," Jack sees the daggers that Neil is throwing his way, and sniggers.

Once they are all in the office, they discuss what has been happening with the assault case against Nathan, which isn't much so far, then they go on to discuss the shock of him getting out on bail after the last hearing.

Ava smiles sadly when they discuss this part, before commenting, "Shows you how money works."

Neil and Jack shrug at her statement. They both had some money, they are by no means poor, but they don't have the millions that Nathan has.

Without thinking, Ava adds, "Money really is the root of all evil. I would rather have no money than have so much that it corrupts!"

This time the men nod in agreement, but there is still a part of Neil that worries that what he has will not be enough. Pushing the thought from his head, and knowing deep down that it couldn't be true, Neil changes the subject to work."

"Right, enough of talking about him. Sweet, you need to look at the diary. You have managed to get at least three bookings for private parties on the Friday you worked."

Ava looks at the diary and then looks up shock written all over her face, not really believing she could do such things. She reads through the diary again just to make sure, flipping the pages back and forth taking in the information that's written there, her head snaps up when Jack starts to talk, "We have been talking," he motions between himself and Neil, "We want you to take over the functions side of the business. You seem to have a knack for it."

Ava stares at both men, going between one, then the other, and back again, not sure what to make of the situation, so she reverts back to type and starts disbelieving in herself again, "I...I...but I can't, I'll mess everything up." She shakes her head vigorously at the way the conversation is going.

Neil steps towards her, taking her hands in his, "Sshh, you can do this, we know you can, if we didn't believe you could make a success of it we wouldn't be giving you this part of the business. You will start believing in yourself more once you start doing the job. It's not like we are going to abandon you, we'll still be here if you need help, plus I still need to know what's going on, as will Jack, but we think it's best that you do the front of house stuff and paperwork, things like that. Believe me, you'll be fine, you're a natural at it Sweet."

Ava smiles shyly, putting her head down, Neil puts his fingers under her chin and gently pushes it up so she needs to look at him, "So is that a yes then?"

Ava nods imperceptibly then smiles again, and just like that, she is the Function Manager of the Daydream Club.

****

Nathan is sitting outside the pub across from the club; the weather is changing to suit his mood again. It is turning overcast and there is a spit or two of rain starting, but he continues to sit there, watching. He sees the two lovebirds walking down Buchanan Street looking very cosy together. The red mist that had descended earlier was starting to come down again. The closer they got to the club, the slower Ava walked until she stopped altogether, almost in front of where Nathan is sitting, thinking he had been spotted. Nathan sits perfectly still, hardly breathing, trying to work out what to do, where to go if he needed to move quickly, when he realises that they didn't see him at all, there is something else going on. Nathan watches as Neil turns to Ava and holds her hands, talking to her, looking concerned, he sees every smile between them when whatever had happened was finishing, and then they kiss again, not as passionately as the last one, no this one is more loving, intimate. It is more than Nathan can cope with, Ava is his and only his. He was the one that plucked her from nothing and gave her everything, and as far as he was concerned if she wanted to go back to nothing he was more than happy to help. Annoyed at what he seen, Nathan stands and heads back inside to get himself another pint. The rain has started coming down heavier than just a spit by the time Nathan has his drink, so he decides to sit inside, choosing a table near the window so he can continue to keep an eye on the coming and goings of the club.

CHAPTER THIRTY-SIX

Two hours later and Ava has been through everything that she needs do to prepare for the next day, and her first party as the Functions Manager. She keeps thinking about the new job and smiling to herself, she can't believe how her life has turned around in such a short space of time.

It amazes her that, in that time, she has found the courage to leave her abusive boyfriend, made friends of her own who care for her simply because she is her. She has stood up to a bully who was trying to hurt her friend, she has a job, and been promoted, she even has someone to – dare she think it – love, and that someone may end up loving her back, properly with all his heart and not his fists, regardless of her flaws.

Yes this is how life should and will be from now on, she now knows that she can do it, she can live without Nathan she can be free, free to live her own life how she wants, and she feels great!

She notices Neil walking over to the function area of the club where she is working and her heart lifts. She looks at her watch and realises that it is nearly nine at night, she closes the notebook she has been writing in when Neil sits across from her at the table she has been using. "How's it going?" Neil is smiling at her, his eyes glinting with the pleasure of seeing Ava relaxed and happy.

"It's going good actually, you?"

"Yeah, all's good, I just need to pop out before Jack finishes up for the night. I need to go and collect a part for my car that I bought."

Ava looks at her watch again, giving Neil a questioning look about the time, "It's from a private seller, collection only." He gives a shrug of his shoulders as if saying 'sorry, but this is what I do'.

Ava smiles and shakes her head at him, her way of saying she understands, "That's okay, I'm nearly done preparing for tomorrow, so once I'm finished I'll go help behind the bar."

Neil smiles again, this time it is so wide it is verging on a giddy schoolboy grin. He cups her face in his hands and leans over the table, moving his lips closer to hers. He grazes her lips with his, a small gasp comes from her at the intimacy between them and a short streak of panic rushes through her as they are in public, know the other staff will see them kissing.

As if reading her mind Neil whispers against her lips, "I don't care who sees us, or who knows I have feelings for you, and I refuse to hide them anymore." With that, he closes the gap and kisses her so sweetly and gently it almost brings tears to Ava's eyes. Neil pulls back, "I won't be long, one hour max, then if we're quiet we can talk in the office, okay?" Ava nods again, and again, the butterflies in her stomach start taking flight.

****

Nathan is half way through his fourth pint of lager when he sees Neil leave the club. A subconscious growl leaves his throat as he watches Neil walk back up Buchanan Street towards the Royal Concert Hall, obviously going towards his car which is parked at the bus station car park. Downing the last half of his pint, Nathan lifts his jacket from the back of his chair and leaves the pub. He is starting to feel the effects of the four pints, but dismisses the feeling, telling himself he stood up too quickly, as he hurries to his Merc. He had also left his car at the bus station, but not in the car park, he left it in the drop off zone, and by the time he returns to it, it has an angry letter stuck to the windscreen alongside a parking ticket. Ripping both of them from the windscreen, Nathan throws them onto the passenger seat then climbs in. He starts his car and races out of the station, tyres squealing on the rain-soaked tarmac and narrowly missing a couple of bus drivers walking over the tarmac towards their buses, he sees them in his rear-view mirror as they shout obscenities at the tail of the car, but Nathan can't hear them and doesn't really care what they are saying anyway.

The rain has been on and off for most of the day, but has been pouring for the past hour, and it seems to be getting heavier by the sound of it battering off the car. The window wipers are going constant as Nathan peers through the traffic, trying to find Neil's M3 coming from the car park. Within minutes, the BMW pulls out from the car park and turns towards the motorway. Nathan is done with hiding and watching, he needs to put his plan into action, and that plan, at the moment, is to get right behind Neil and let him know that it is him, Nathan, following and he won't be leaving them alone.

Neil is on a high, he has found the woman he wants to spend forever with; his club is growing and doing great things, and he is going to stop hiding from his father. He is going to be free from him, for the first time in his entire life; he will be free from his father and his threats. He really is completely happy with life, so, with Green Day blaring, he pulls onto the motorway, then changes lanes until he is in the fast lane, he sits back and eases his M3 through what little traffic there is. After looking in his rear-view mirror a few times he notices the Mercedes pull in behind him, then pull up closer and closer to him, until the other car is nearly touching his bumper. Shaking his head at the stupidity of the other driver, Neil moves into the middle lane taking his speed down to sixty, to let the idiot pass him, but to his shock the driver pulls in behind him again. A cold shiver runs through Neil as the thought of Nathan flashes in his mind, but he pushes it away, as he changes lanes again, into the outside lane and pushes the accelerator until he is hitting eighty. Taking a glance in his mirror again, he sees the Merc doing the exact same. Neil takes his foot from the accelerator, peering into the rear-view mirror to see if he could recognise the Mercs' driver, but due to the bad weather, he can't get a good enough look.

The Merc pulls closer again, then pulls over back into the middle lane, bringing the car level with Neil's BMW. The cold feeling that Neil was feeling turns to ice, freezing the blood in his veins as he eventually gets a look at the crazy driver beside him, Nathan.

****

Nathan pulls up beside Neil and glares in the window at him. A look of pure satisfaction covering his face, his eyes sparkling with unrestrained mirth as he draws his finger across his throat in the universal sign of 'you're dead' then he starts to laugh, a manic laugh of a mad man, knowing he has Neil exactly where he wants him, riled, on edge and driving in bad weather. Putting his foot on the brakes, Nathan slows enough to get back into the outside lane, behind Neil, he manages to control the car as the tail end kicks out on the rain slicked road, then pushes the speedo up and up again pushing Neil to do over ninety just to stop Nathan from ramming into him. Every time Neil snatches a look in the mirror Nathan grins, he can see panic starting to cover Neil's face, fear tinging his eyes. Nathan knows he is pushing things too far, but he doesn't care, as far as he is concerned the bastard deserves all the fear, pain and agony that Nathan is going to bestow on him after he took Ava away from him.

Everything was fine until they met Neil, Nathan muses, then his life went to the dogs, so he has to pay. With that thought making his smile turn into more of a sneer, Nathan pushes again on the accelerator get even closer to the BMW, mere inches or less between them.

Neil sees a break in the traffic and moves again, into the middle lane, the plan being to jump on the brakes and let Nathan fly past. He moves the M3 into the lane, struggling to keep the car from skidding, then presses on the brakes, gently to start with so as not to aquaplane, then with a bit more force until Nathan speeds past. Neil takes a slight sigh of relief, as he gets his speed back to eighty. Punching the voice recognition button on his hands-free Parrot, he shouts into the microphone for it to phone Jack. After a few rings, his friend picks up,

"Whit's up?" Jack asks with his usual cheery voice.

Neil's voice isn't as cheery or steady, "Jack, phone the police, Nathan is up to something, he has been on my tail since I left the car park and has been pushing me on the motorway ever since."

Jack can hear the panic in his friend's voice. "What?

Where is he, where are you?"

"I think I've managed to get out of his sight for now, but I don't think he's finished with me yet."

Jack hears all of this through the screeching of tyres and then the stomach churning sound of metal crashing into metal, whilst his best friend screams, "You fucking bastard, what are you doing Nathan, you are going to kill—" before the line goes dead.

CHAPTER THIRTY-SEVEN

"NEIL, NEIL – WHAT THE FUCK, NEIL!" Jack is standing in the middle of the main area of the club screaming down the phone with nothing but horns blaring back at him. The entire club stops and looks at Jack as Ava runs to him demanding to know what is going on, why he is shouting Neil's name like that. Jack takes one look at her and shakes his head as he cancels the call. He places his hands on Ava's shoulders, to keep himself from falling down as much as to comfort Ava,

"I need to phone the police, something's happened. A crash."

Ava doesn't manage to make a sound from her opened mouth. Jack takes her and sits her down at table three, without realising, then goes to the bar; lifting the phone, they kept behind the bar.

Calmly he phones the emergency services, answering all of their questions as best he can with what little information he has. He gives the phone back to the girl working the bar, then asks her to pour two Highland Park fifteen years with ice, one for him and one for Ava before turning and running towards the gents, just managing to reach the sink before the contents of his stomach leave his body with the force of a jumbo jet taking off.

Once he has finished retching, he rinses the sink out,

splashes cold water on his face and stares into the mirror, sending up silent prayers to every God he can think off, that all will be well and that the sound of the crash would leave his head, although at that moment he very much doubted both. Feeling another wave of nausea washing over him. Jack grips the sink and clenches his jaw as tight as his muscles will allow, without cracking any of his teeth, then takes deep breaths, just like the way he seen Neil teach Ava to do, until it passed. Once he is satisfied that the worse is over, he leaves the bathroom and walks over to sit with Ava. The barmaid has brought over the drinks and has stayed with Ava sitting holding her hand, offering words of comfort until Jack returns.

He smiles a sad, kind, thankful smile at the girl, "Thanks Stace, I'll take it from here,"

The girl nods and squeezes Ava's hand one last time, trying to reassure her with a smile. Jack sits down and takes Ava's hand in his; he notices they are cold even though she has been holding onto the barmaid. Ava lifts her head, and looks at Jack, her eyes bloodshot and glistening with tears that haven't had their chance to run down her cheeks.

She opens her mouth to talk, but nothing comes out at first so she closes it and tries again, this time managing to get words squeaked out around the panic that has lodged itself in her throat. "Jack, where's Neil? What's happened?" The desperate plea in her eyes breaks his heart even more.

"I'm not sure honey, Neil phoned from the car, asking me to phone the police, he said that Nathan was tailing him and that he was trying to do something, I'm guessing that was meaning to make him crash."

Ava is making the silent scream again with her mouth, her head spinning with the words she is hearing from Jack but not quite understanding their full meaning. "What do you mean crash, has Nathan crashed into Neil?" She can feel the panic in her throat starting to move and take over, but she is battling it with everything that Neil has taught her to get it under control, she knows now she can't let it win, she can't let Nathan win.

"I don't know honey, I'm not sure exactly,"

Jack can see Ava control her breathing and is so proud of her at that moment and doesn't want to undo all her hard work by explaining what he heard on the phone, but both he and Neil had agreed at the start that they would never lie to each other and he doesn't want to start doing it with Ava, so he decides to tell her what he knows but in as a delicately way as possible,

"I'm not sure what has happened, but yes there has been a crash." Jack closes his eyes against the sound of the crash going through his head.

Ava notices the pain etched on his face, "And you heard it?" Jack nods, not trusting himself to speak.

Ava moves forward, grabbing Jack to her, talking into his ear, "I'm so sorry you had to hear that."

Again Jack can only nod, tears running from his eyes, they both sit there, for what seems like hours, but is only minutes, just holding each, both using each other's strength to hold each other up.

****

Nathan comes back to consciousness with the sound of sirens coming to the scene; a satisfied smile crosses his face as he remembers the crash.

Seeing Neil pull over and hit the brakes was the last straw

for Nathan's cat and mouse game, he wasn't going to let Neil get the better of him, or even think he could get the better of him. He drove on about a mile down the motorway, where there were no cars (a stroke of luck for Nathan) and came to a complete stop in the middle lane, where he sat and waited. When he saw Neil's' BMW make the slight bend, Nathan put the car into reverse. Hitting the accelerator, he lurched backwards and pushed the speedometer until he was hitting fifty and swerving dangerously. Neil noticed what was happening and tried to brake, but between his speed, the rain slicked tarmac and Nathan's speed he had no chance. The car hit a puddle on the road and aquaplaned, making him go into a skid, going round in a full 360 turn until he came to a crashing stop into the back of Nathan's Merc, crushing the passenger side as he went.

The police are the first of the emergency services to arrive on the scene of the crash. Immediately they close the motorway at the exit before the crash and re-route all other traffic through the city centre and back up on to the motorway at the next slip road. As soon as they arrive, they are on their radios asking for back up and an extra ambulance.

When the first ambulance crew arrives the paramedics jump out, one running over to Neil in the BMW and the other to Nathan in his Merc. When the paramedic reaches Nathan he asks him his name, making sure he is conscious, he continues to ask questions about where is sore and if he remembers what happened, Nathan answers all the questions, but is getting more annoyed at the paramedic, as he wants to know one thing and one thing only, so he asks,

"Is he dead? The guy in the Beemer, is he dead?" The paramedic takes the question to be one of concern and not of hope as it was intended, "I'm not sure Sir, I'm sure my colleague is doing everything he can, but let's get you sorted then we can worry about the other guy eh? Now do you have pain anywhere else?"

Nathan closes his eyes blocking the thought that he may have failed at taking the one person Ava wants in her life from her. He tries again, only with more force, "I need to know is he dead?"

The paramedic stills, "Nathan, I am not sure, but right this minute I need to know if you are in any pain."

Nathan groans, both at the medic's lack of knowledge and at the pain he is starting to register in his legs. "Yes," he growls, "My legs are sore, but if you could just go and see if he is dead I would be forever grateful."

The paramedic is stunned by the tone and insistence in Nathans voice, so he relents, "I'll go have a look, I really hope it's good news." He pats Nathan's shoulder gently as he stands.

"You and me both. I need that cunt dead!" Nathan growls, thinking the medic is out of hearing distance.

The paramedic however wasn't, and he heard every word of Nathan's growl. Arriving at the other car the medic explains to his partner the conversation he has had with Nathan and what he heard as he was walking away, he then motions for the police officers to join them.

"Problem?" One of the officers asks.

"I think so," the medic starts, "Guy in the Merc was asking if this guy here was dead and quite insistent that I find out, and when he thought I couldn't hear him he said he needed 'that cunt dead'."

The officer nods, "Is he dead?"

The medic working on Neil shakes his head, "No, but

neither is he conscious or in great shape. I can't do much until the fire brigade gets here to cut him out."

The officer nods again, then nods down the motorway, "By the sounds of things the cavalry are arriving. How's that one doing?"

"He seems to be more worried about him, but is saying he has sore legs. He wouldn't let me do anything until I had come to check on things here."

Another nod form the officer,

"Okay, I'll take a note of it and you will need to give a statement down at the station."

The medic nods and walks back to Nathan, not sure if the news he is going to give him is good or not.

****

Both men are taken to Glasgow Royal Infirmary Hospital. Nathan has remained conscious throughout, managing to get out of the crash relatively unscathed, bruises forming on his legs where they were caught against the door, a split on his head, which would led to a concussion and a shirt full of sore bones looming for the morning, but nothing serious. The police have stayed with Nathan asking him questions about the crash, what had happened, what speed was he doing, could he guess what speed the other driver was doing, etcetera, but he continued to tell them he couldn't remember, his memory was lapsing and so couldn't answer any of their questions. They did breathalyse him which came back positive, so they placed him under arrest for drink driving, asked the doctor to take bloods for confirmation of his blood alcohol level, and an officer is stationed on the outside of his cubical.

Neil hasn't been as lucky, he's still unconscious, his right leg broken in so many places it will need to be operated on, his right shoulder is dislocated and put back into place, he has cuts and bruises all over his face and body. All of his injuries are fixable with time and physiotherapy, if he wakes up.

The police ask for bloods to be taken from Neil, also to check his blood alcohol level, but they guessed it would come back negative, as there had been no smell of alcohol on him or in the car. The hospital staff went through Neil's wallet and handed a business card to the police for them to contact someone at the club to inform them of the situation.

CHAPTER THIRTY-EIGHT

Jack and Ava have moved to the office, fed up with the whole club watching as they have their private breakdowns over not knowing anything ,when the phone goes. Jack snaps it up before it can get its third ring out, "The Daydream Club, Jack speaking" He spits the words out automatically and then holds his breath, waiting for the other person to speak,

"Is this where Mr Neil Alexander works?" The voice on the other end comes through and sounds official,

"Yes, well, it's his, I mean he owns the club. Can I ask who's calling, do you know what's happened to him, or where he is?" Jack knows he is babbling but he can't contain his words until his brain sorts them. Ava is on the edge of her seat listening to the one-sided conversation also holding her breath and constantly asking any and all gods listening to let Neil be okay.

"This is P.C. Loughran, can I ask whom I'm talking to?" Jack drags his fingers through his hair, desperate for the guy to answer his questions, but knows he needs to keep his angst under control so he answers,

"I'm his business partner, Jack Bale. Please, I need to know what's happened. The last I heard from Neil, the phone was cut off after what sounded like a car crash!" Ava held onto his hand as his voice rose to a near shout. Thankfully, the officer on the phone wasn't taken aback by his desperateness,

"I understand Sir," Officer Loughran's voice was soft and full of empathy, trying to keep the conversation and Jack calm, "Mr Alexander has been in a car crash, and has been taken to the Royal Infirmary, he is alive but—"

"Can we see him?" Jack squeezes Ava's hand trying to reassure her, but also to help keep himself controlled. Ava on the other hand is trying not to go into full-blown panic mode at not knowing what is being said on the phone.

"Well, as I was saying, Mr Alexander is unconscious and will be going into surgery for his leg. I am phoning to find out who is his next of kin?"

Without a blink of an eye Jack answers, "Me, it's me, he doesn't have any family except me, and his girlfriend Ava, who's here with me."

Ava's sob catches her throat, she doesn't know if Neil has told Jack about their kiss that day or if he was saying that so she would be able to get into see Neil, but either way she was glad that Jack had referred to her as Neil's girlfriend. For some reason, hearing that makes her feel that everything is going to be okay.

She hears Jack continue to talk, "The car crash, is Nathan involved? Neil said something about Nathan following him."

"Sorry Sir I can't comment on who else was involved, but did Mr Alexander contact you after the crash? I didn't think he was conscious."

"No, no during, on his hands free parrot thing, I'm the one who phoned the emergency services

"Okay, Mr Bale, Thank you, we are going to need to interview you at some point."

Jack snorted in a laugh, "Really? Well I'll be at the hospital when you need me." Jack puts the phone down.

Without releasing Ava's hand, he jumps from his seat and rushes to the door, pulling Ava behind him, explaining as they go,

"He's alive, unconscious needing an operation, but alive!" Ava lets out a sigh of relief as she rushes behind him. Jack shouts to one of the staff members what is happening and that he will be back later to lock up, as they rush out the door and into the nearest taxi, urging the driver to get to the Royal as quickly as possible, or even quicker as long as he doesn't get caught.

Rushing into the Accident and Emergency department of the old building, Jack lands his hands on the reception desk, babbling about Neil and the accident and asking where he is.

The woman working behind the desk puts her hands up to stop Jack from talking anymore, "Yer, gonna need to calm doon Sir, I canny make out a word yer sayin, now who is it you're looking fir?"

Jack takes a deep breath, trying hard not to explode at the receptionist, so Ava tugs his arm and stands slightly in front of him before answering the receptionists questions,

"We are looking for Neil Alexander, he was brought in after a car accident. I'm his girlfriend and this is his business partner and next of kin." She points to Jack who has calmed down slightly after hearing the calmness of Ava's voice, which is belying the turmoil going on inside her.

The woman smiles at her, "Right, Hen, let's have a look here." She then turns to Jack and gives him a look worthy of people who she deems to be asking stupid questions, before checking on her computer screen, "Right here he's here. He's in theatre the now, getting his surgery on his leg. Youse have a seat and I'll let youse know more when we know more okay?"

Ava smiles at the woman, "Thank you for your help."

"That okay Hen, just keep blabber mooth there under control." The receptionist nods her head towards Jack, whose jaw has dropped open and is ready to explode at her words again, but Ava manages to pull him away before he has a chance, walking them both towards the waiting area and as far away from the reception as possible. The waiting room lights are garish and most of the seats are taken up by people bleeding, crying in pain, and swearing about how much time they have been waiting,

Jack stage whispers to Ava, "Did that auld boot growl at me? I think she did, and what does she mean blabber mooth, I was only asking where Neil was, seriously."

Ava takes his hand in her own and looks at him, "Calm down, she might just have a thing against men, not just you, but you were blabbering a bit."

Jack relaxes his shoulders for the first time since they entered the hospital, and puts his head down, "I was a bit wasn't I?"

Ava nods, "We're both worried and desperate for information, it's okay, don't worry." Again, the calmness and confidence in her voice belies her real feelings.

An hour later and both Ava and Jack are still flipping through every magazine in the waiting area, not really taking in anything they have seen or read, just going through the motions of wasting time, waiting to hear anything on Neil, when a police officer approaches them.

"Excuse me Sir; are you Mr Beal, the person I spoke to on the phone?" The officer was tall and slim, though looked bigger than he really is due to the stone in weight he is carrying with his stab proof vest, utility belt and all the equipment that goes along with it,

"Yes." Jack jumps to his feet, with Ava not far behind him,

"I'm Jack, his business partner, and this is Ava, his girlfriend. Has something else happened?"

Officer Loughran motions for them to sit back down on the hard plastic chairs that they have just vacated, "No, Mr Alexander is still in surgery as far as I'm aware. I was wondering if I could ask you a few questions about the phone call you were telling me about?"

Jack breaths out, not realising he was holding his breath, "Aye, eh yes, what do you want to know?"

Office Loughran takes out his standard issue black notebook and starts asking his questions.

Jack relives every moment of the telephone conversation he had with Neil as he explains to the officer what was said on the call. Everything including, Nathan following him, that he had thought he had lost him, but had a gut feeling that it wasn't over, that Nathan would be coming back, and then how he heard the awful sounds of the crash, metal crashing and scraping on metal and Neil's screams as he tried to stop the car.

Ava holds on to Jacks hand throughout the questions, but had to stand and leave for the bathroom at hearing the crash, and everything that Jack had had to hear. Coming back out of the bathroom she sits back down and looks at Officer Loughran dead in the eye, "I think it may be helpful if you spoke to WPC Sian Young." Ava explains briefly, she had spoken to her about being in a violent domestic relationship with Nathan and that Neil had helped her get away from him, then Nathan attacking her and that the accident is more than likely connected to that on-going case. Ava stills at the thought that has popped into her head, "Where's Nathan?"

The officer cocks his head, "He's here." Ava stiffens, a chill running down her spine, Jack grabs her hand back, and the officer notices how pale and terrified looking Ava became at that knowledge.

"Ava, he can't get to you here, okay, he isn't going to hurt you again." Ava nods, but doesn't relax at Jack's reassurances.

Officer Loughran, tries, "Mr Low is under arrest for drink driving and suspicion of causing a road traffic accident, at the moment, and has a guard stationed outside his cubical so, Jack is right he won't be able to do anything to you, not even see you, so please don't worry about him. And I will contact WPC Young and liaise with her to see if the incidents are connected as you think.

Ava nods, this time with more belief, her shoulders sag, and her eyes shine with unshed tears, "Was he badly hurt in the accident?"

The officer shakes his head, "Not really, cuts bruises, and he will be very sore in the morning with whiplash."

Ava closes her eyes, controlling her breathing, exactly how Neil had taught her.

"If there is anything else, either of you think of, please contact me at the station, and Jack, I will need you to come to the station and give a formal statement, at your earliest convenience." Officer Loughran stands, as does Jack and the men shake hands,

"Thank you for your help."

The officer nods then leaves. Jack sits back down and holds Ava as the enormity of the situation takes over her and she sobs on his shoulder, mumbling that she could have gotten the man she is falling in love with killed.

****

Two hours later, a nurse comes over to where they are sitting, clearing her throat as they are sitting with their eyes closed,

"Excuse me, are you waiting on news of Mr Alexander?"

At the sound of the nurses voice, both Ava and Jack are on their feet, both asking the same questions.

The nurse puts her hands up to stop them talking, "Mr Alexander is out of theatre and has been moved to ICU."

Ava is first to speak, "Can we see him?"

The nurse nods, but still has a grim look on her face, "Yes, but he still hasn't regained consciousness, the doctor is waiting in the room to speak to you both about the surgery and Mr Alexanders condition."

The both nod, then follow the nurse through the maze of corridors in the ancient hospital, until they arrive at ICU ward, and meet the doctor in charge of Neil's health care.

The doctor explains that Neil is extremely lucky that he came out of the car with his life. His dislocated shoulder and badly broken leg are fixable, but he will need physio.

Jack stares at the doctor like he has just grown another head, then starts to talk. "But he isn't conscious? Is he going to live? What's wrong, why won't he wake up?"

The doctor shakes his head, then nods in understanding, "Neil is stable and breathing on his own, he isn't presenting any life threating symptoms, just sometimes after a major accident like this the body needs time to recover on its own. I think that maybe this is one of those times, that only time will tell. Maybe if you both talk to him it will help."

They both thank the doctor and enter Neil's room. There are monitors for his blood pressure, pulse and heart rate on him, but other than that he just looks like he is sleeping. Ava looks at Neil, her heart breaking at the sight of all the cuts and abrasions on his face, then turns to Jack, "Do you think he can hear us?"

Jack shrugs his shoulders looking almost deflated at the sight of his best friend. "I've never seen him so – still, not doing anything, not fighting. Throughout everything with his dad, every time he beat him he never stopped fighting back, physically fighting his dad, or fighting to get away from him, and start the business up. Then when his dad came back at him for money he fought back again, making sure the dickhead couldn't get to him or the club, but this." Jack points to Neil's prone body lying in the sterile hospital bed.

Ava drags her gaze away from Neil and brings Jack into her chest and holds him, "He will be fighting, we just can't see it. If he wasn't fighting he wouldn't be here. Now grab a chair and we'll sit and tell him to get on with the whole waking up thing."

Jack smiles at the girl holding him, amazed at how far she has come and how she has become the sister he never had, just like Neil is his brother, he gives her a squeeze, hoping she understands how grateful he is to have her.

Ava is the first to speak directly to Neil, "Hey you. You gave us a big scare, I hope you can hear us 'cause I think Jack might be wanting to have some words with you."

Jack smiles as he takes up the conversation, "Aye, you're damn right, I don't want you to just lie there ya wee dick, get up!" Jacks voice breaks on the last of his words.

Ava shakes her head, "Not really what I was meaning, but at least he'll know it's definitely you."

Jack laughs as his tears fall onto his cheeks, "Very true."

Both of them sit with Neil until midnight, talking about anything and everything, trying to include Neil in the conversation as if he was actually answering them. Jack is first to look at his watch, "Shit look at the time, I better get back and lock up the club. Are you coming?"

Ava shakes her head, "No I want to be here in case he wakes up."

Jack walks round the bed and gives her a cuddle,

"You want me to come back?"

"No it's okay, we can take it in shifts if he hasn't woken by tomorrow. Have you phoned Eveline, were you not meant to be seeing her tonight?"

"I texted her, she is meeting me at the club at closing. You need to sleep too remember." Jack looks at her with the look of a concerned big brother.

"I'll try and get some sleep in the chair later, but I—" She stops talking, her words catching in her throat, her face flushing at feeling foolish at what she was about to admit, "I just want to talk to him, tell him things, I want him to answer,"

Jack smiles sweetly at her, "I hear ya," He gives her a kiss on the top of her head, before letting her go, "We'll get him back, I promise."

"I know, I'm just a bit frightened." She shrugs, and gives him a sad smile,

Jack gives her another hug, "I know, me too."

They nod at each other, none of them able to form any more words. Jack turns and leaves the room.

Once the door is closed Ava sits back down next to Neil and takes his hand in hers, "Neil," Her voice stutters and cracks, tears pooling in her eyes, swallowing the lump in her throat she tries to talk again, "I really hope you can hear me, or maybe I don't. I'm not sure to tell you the truth, but regardless here goes nothing."

She takes a deep breath and continues her tears flowing freely, "I know we haven't really admitted to each other how we feel, exactly, but I need to tell you what you mean to me, in case I don't get another chance. Neil I owe you my life, if it wasn't for you I would probably be dead, or at least wish I was. You not only saved me from Nathan and the abuse, but you also saved me from myself. If it wasn't for you, I would never have realised what I am, what I am capable of and just how worthy I actually am. It took you believing in me for me to see that I am worth believing in. So because of you, I know I am beautiful and I am worthy of being loved, and I also know I can be on my own, the only problem is I don't want to be, I want to be with you. I love you."

Ava puts her head on the edge of the bed and she thinks she feels movement from Neil's hand, her head springs back up, to search his face for any sign that he is waking up, but there is nothing. Her heart sinks, shaking her head and put the feeling down to her imagination and hope. She puts her head back down on the bed and sinks into a fitful sleep.

CHAPTER THIRTY-NINE

Early on the Sunday morning a nurse comes into the room and wakes Ava up, explaining that they are just going to check Neil's vitals then she could get back in. Ava takes the time out to text Jack and let him know there is no change. Jack's reply comes back almost instantly, saying he will be at the hospital about nine. The nurse comes back out and smiles kindly at Ava,

"Is he okay?" she asks hopefully,

"Yes dear, he just needs some time."

Ava nods as the nurse walks away. Going back into the room Ava sits on the bed and leans over, stroking Neil's hair she starts talking again. "Morning honey, Jack's coming in about nine, and then I will need to go home to get showered and changed to go to work for the christening that's coming in today. I would really like to stay here with you, but I know you will still need a business when you wake up so, as long as Jack's here, I will go to work, and that I can do that on my own because you have taught me how to believe in myself."

Continuing to stroke his hair and face whilst resting her side on his chest so she can feel the gentle up, down movement of his breathing, she continues, "I would rather you were awake and talking to me, but I'll be patient and wait, just like you have been with me. But anyway, you'll wake up when you are ready." She pauses for a bit, before continuing, "So, I'm actually looking forward to working, well I was, and I wish it was under different circumstances, I wish you were going to be there, but no matter what, I am going to do my best. Jack was meeting Eveline again last night at the club and I think she is going to be coming in with him this morning."

She knows she is talking rubbish, but she doesn't like the silence so she continues to fill it. "I do hope they work out, they seem good together, and Eveline seems to be a really nice person. I mean she was really nice to me when I was in hospital, though that could have been her just doing her job, but—"

Ava stops talking, she thought she felt movement again, but wasn't sure, she is still trying to listen and feel for any movements or changes in Neil's breathing, she is just about to start talking again when she feels another movement underneath her. This time she is sure that it is a definite movement. She raises her head to look at Neil. Looking up she sees Neil's hazel brown eyes blinking back at her.

Jumping up from her lying positions, Ava turns and grabs Neil into a bear hug, shouting his name, "Neil oh my God, Neil you're awake, are you okay? Can I get you anything?"

Neil grimaces at the hug but doesn't say anything, he doesn't want it to stop. Waking up with Ava laying on him and then crushing him in an embrace is the perfect way to wake up, and he wouldn't mind waking up like this every morning, but maybe without the car crash the day before, or the pain. Groaning as the pain gets too much, Neil manages to lift his arm and wrap it around Ava and attempts a squeeze. Ava realises that she is probably hurting him so releases him and sits up, taking her time to look at him.

Neil smiles again. "Hey Sweet." His voice is hoarse from

not being used, but it is like music to her ears.

"I'm going to let the nurse know you've woken up, stay here." Ava pauses at her choice of words, then rushes out the door, her smile splitting her face,

"Nurse, someone, Neil's awake."

The nurse from earlier rushes over and takes Ava's hands, more to calm her down than anything else. "Okay, dear, come and we'll have a look."

They both walk into the room to see Neil trying to push himself up the bed without screaming in pain.

"Whoa there sunshine," the nurse gently chastises, "You need to watch what you're doing, right, sit at peace and I'll get your vitals taken and page the doctor to give you the once over," The nurse starts with Neil's temperature and blood pressure and asks some basic questions as she works, "Do you know your name?"

Neil answers,

"Okay, good, now do you know where you are?"

Neil nods and answers, "Hospital, I'm guessing The Royal."

"Good, now do you know what happened, how you ended up in here?"

Again Neil nods before answering, a flash of thunder passes over his face, and sheer anger to his eyes, "Yes." His voice is low, determined and menacing, "Nathan Low chased me down on the motorway, then he waited on me, stopped in the lane I was driving in, when I turned the corner he started to reverse at me, I tried to stop before I hit him but I skidded right into him."

Ava let out a gasp as she heard first-hand what had happened. She knew there was a car crash and that Nathan was involved, but the fact that he had done it so deliberately shocked her. She excuses herself, needing to get out of the room for a bit, she doesn't want to worry Neil so she tells him she is going to let Jack know that he was back in the land of the living with them.

****

Waking up, Nathan winces when he tries to move his head. It is pounding like some road worker is jackhammering his brain. Opening his eyes his reality hits home, charged with drink driving, arrested under suspicion of attempted murder and dangerous driving. He moves his arm to rub his face when he realises that he has been handcuffed to the side of his bed, groaning he tries his other arm and it moves freely, so he holds the buzzer desperate to get a nurse's attention for some badly needed painkillers.

At the same time as Jack enters the hospital, Nathans' lawyer also enters, dreading even looking at his client, he stops to buy a coffee to take away, trying to waste as much time as possible before going in to see his client. He knew Nathan was losing it after Ava left him and the business started to come under scrutiny. He knew that not everything Nathan did was above board and fully legal, at least not to start with, but the legal side always caught up with the building work, or so he thought, but never in his wildest dreams did he ever think he was capable of attempted murder. Travelling up in the elevator, the lawyer realises that their best chance at getting Nathan the shortest sentence is to plead diminished responsibility, hopefully Nathan will agree to it.

The nurse is giving Nathan some painkillers with his breakfast, telling him that the doctor will be doing his rounds in the next hour, then if all is well he would more than likely get to go home, or at least be discharged from hospital and taken.

Nathan grins at the nurse, trying for thankful, but looking more like someone who is losing his grip on reality. His lawyer walks into his room just as the nurse is leaving, she stops to ask him who he is and why he is there, and it isn't visiting hours, the lawyer explains himself and the nurse draws him a dirty look before flouncing past him, he rolls his eyes then takes a seat at the side of Nathans' bed. Taking his pad from his briefcase he starts to ask Nathan questions, not stopping for niceties or health updates, he just wants to know what his client was thinking or if he was he even thinking?

After an hour of Nathan explaining what he did and why, the lawyer broaches the subject of his plea, knowing it wasn't going to go down well.

"You want me to say I am mad?" Nathan's disbelief is palpable in the air,

"Well." The lawyer is beyond annoyed at his client, and is very close to telling him so,

"You deliberately drank four pints whilst watching the Daydream Club, then followed Mr Alexander onto the motorway. Once there you gave chase and goaded Mr Alexander, he tried to get away from you and slowed down. You then came to a complete stop in the middle lane of the M8 motorway, then proceeded to reverse in the rain knowing that Mr Alexander would crash into your car. How, pray tell, am I meant to spin that so you can get off scot-free? Diminished responsibility is the best plea, you will get a shorter sentence this way believe me."

Nathan has been shaking his head throughout everything his lawyer has been saying and has actually started laughing now. "I'm sorry, but who are you and what have you done with my lawyer?" Sarcasm dripping from his tone, he continues to laugh. "I'm not mad, I am not pleading craziness and I am not pleading guilty either, the dickhead ran into me and YOU are going to get me a not guilty!" Nathan has resorted to jabbing his finger from his only free hand into his lawyers face.

The lawyer lowers his head and shakes it, "Nathan, it doesn't work like that, there must be CCTV—"

Nathan cuts his lawyer off, "I pay you enough to get me off with fuckin' murder, now this isn't even that, this is easier, so I don't understand what you are moaning about, just do your job!"

The lawyer explodes, "Moaning? Moaning? I'm not fucking moaning, I'm telling you the facts you arrogant twat, so if you're not going to listen to my advice then I have to refuse to be your counsel."

Nathan is stunned at his lawyer's outburst, never has anybody dared speak to him like that, but, he refuses to back down. "I'm sorry, but, what?"

"I will not be your lawyer, if you don't listen to my advice. If you want to listen then fine I will continue, but if not then I cannot continue to represent you." He starts to re-pack up his briefcase and get his jacket on,

"Fine, I'll represent myself." Nathan adamantly states,

"What?" The lawyer can't believe what he his hearing, although a part of him wasn't really surprised,

"You heard, I'll represent myself." Nathan reiterates.

The lawyer shakes his head, "You do know what they say about people who represent themselves?"

Nathan is starting to lose his patience with his lawyer and his lack of willing, "Yes, yes, I know they have an ass for a lawyer, but you aren't even going to try, so fuck off an I'll do it myself!"

The lawyer stands, desperate to get away from the car crash that Nathan and his life was becoming. "Fine by me. I will get my secretary to invoice you with my final bill, then that is the last that me and my company will do business with you, your company or anybody associated with you."

He storms away hearing Nathan mutter something about being the worst lawyer anyway as he left the room, not really caring what was being said, he was just very glad to be out of it.

****

Jack rushes into Neil's hospital room, Eveline following behind him, Ava stands up, getting out of his way as he charges in, Ava moves to stand next to Eveline. A feeling comes over Ava like she has come home, she has found the family she didn't have. She knew in her heart that the four of them were going to be firm friends into old age. With that realisation came more emotion and tears.

Eveline turns to look at her with a worried look on her face, "What's wrong? I thought everything was okay with Neil?" Wiping away her tears Ava manages to nod her head, "It is, he is, fine, well as much as he can be after a crash, I'm just being silly."

Eveline smiles at her new friend and brings her in for a cuddle, "No you're not, it's been a very stressful and emotional time, and I bet you've not really slept have you?"

Ava shakes her head,

"Why don't I run you home and you can get a sleep, is the club opening today?"

"Yes, there's a christening in and I'm working it, since two people thought I would make a good Function Manager!"

Neil and Jack have been having a very animated conversation when they both look over at the women, before Neil adds, "Yes you will. Now the christening doesn't start until two, Jack will open up at twelve and then the staff can deal with it. You go and have a sleep."

Ava scrunches her brows at Neil.

"Go, Jack is here just now, and Eveline can come back for him."

Ava still hesitates, after all the excitement of Neil waking up, her adrenaline spiking and then plummeting, tiredness was starting to wash over her in waves. She doesn't want to leave Neil on his own, but she also knows she should be at the christening, she has been given a chance to prove to herself how able she really is.

"Okay, Eveline, if you don't mind running me back to Neil's I'll grab a sleep, work the christening, then come back to the hospital when it's finished, about fiveish."

She turns to speak to Neil, "That means you will be on your own for a few hours, is that okay?"

Neil nods, "Yes, I'll be fine, I'll probably sleep, you need to look after yourself too."

Ava walks over to Neil and takes his face in her hands she puts her forehead on his and closes her eyes for a second, when she opens them they are again glistening with unshed tears, lowering her voice to almost a whisper she speaks to Neil, "I am so glad you came back."

Neil kisses her gently on the nose, "I didn't go anywhere, and I'm not planning on leaving you, ever. If that's okay with you?"

Ava has to swallow the lump of emotion that has lodged

itself in her throat before she can speak again, "More than okay, it's perfect."

Smiling at each other, they both revel in the unspoken words in each other's eyes, until Neil reluctantly breaks the connection with a quick kiss, "Go, get some sleep, keep my business going, and then come back and see me tonight."

"Okay, I'll see you later." Ava kisses him back and straightens up to leave,

Neil puts his hand on hers, "Love you Sweet." Neil draws in a breath, unable to believe he let the words out, and in front of other people.

Ava doesn't flinch, she doesn't miss a beat with her answer, "Ditto."

It was simple, but perfect. Jack and Eveline smile at each other, feeling the emotion in the room affect them too. Jack hands his car keys over to Eveline and gives her a chaste kiss goodbye, as she ushers Ava out of the room. Excited tones echoing from the women back down the hallway at the scene that has just played out.

CHAPTER FORTY

Jack settles back into the comfy chair at the side of the bed, the one that is meant for patients only, and props his feet up on the hard plastic chair that Ava had been sitting in all night.

Neil grins at him, "You know if the nurse comes in she'll have your guts!"

Jack smirks and shrugs, "I'll turn on the charm and it will all be all right."

Neil shakes his head although he has a smile on his face, he knows that is exactly what would happen, it always does with Jack and his cheeky chappy way.

"Anyway," Jack continues, "How are you, are you in pain?"

Neil shrugs, trying to make out that his pain isn't as bad as it really is, but he knows he won't get anything past Jack so he admits it, "Oh aye, when the painkillers start to wear off my leg is agony, throbbing and my shoulder shoots some bolts of pain if I move it certain ways. Doctor says I dislocated my shoulder pretty bad and if the pain doesn't settle or it keeps coming out they will need to operate, but for now it looks okay. Unlike my leg, which apparently looked like a jigsaw puzzle." He tries to move, sending a shooting pain through every part of his body and exhausts him. Jack jumps up to help but Neil waves him off.

"I can't believe you gave Eveline your car keys without

hesitation too!" Neil changes the subject smoothly, not wanting to think too much about his injuries or the crash.

"Aye well, she's different, she's—" Jack shrugs, being male he can't come up with the right words to explain how he feels about her, even to himself.

Neil laughs, a knowing laugh, which spikes his pain again, but he can't stop it. "I know what you mean pal, believe me."

"I guessed that. So you and Ava together then?"

"Well, we were going to talk about it when we were finished work yesterday. We had kinda admitted to each other how we felt and then we kissed...a proper, amazing kiss, but then—" Neil motions to his broken body to emphasise his point.

Jack nods, understanding what he means. "Well from what I heard there, youse could get married tomorrow."

Neil throws his good arm over his eyes and mumbles, "I know, I can't believe I said it like that." Bringing his arm down looking at his friend with a smile, "She never ran away though, she answered me!"

Jack laughs, then agrees "That she did sir, that she did."

Neil's expression falls and Jack notices the very sharp downward turn of his friend's mood, "What is it?" he asks.

Neil looks at the ceiling, as if the answer to is worries will be found there. "What if I can't give her enough? I mean he could give her the best of the best and—"

Jack stops Neil in his tracks trying not to get angry at his friend, "No, no you don't. Don't even fuckin' go there, ya wee dick." Jack knew there was something worrying Neil before the accident and he knows that now he is injured it will compound his feelings, but Jack isn't about to let Neil go down that road, "That prick gave her nothing but anguish, he beat her, he brought her down, made her feel worthless, told her she was worthless and then assaulted her nearly to the end of her life. She has made it crystal clear that money, possessions and fancy shit means nothing to her. She would rather be living in a cardboard box in Bellahouston Park with you than in that mansion she fled from with him. You have given her everything she needed, you've made her realise her own worth."

Neil has been looking at his hands throughout his friends lecture, knowing everything he was saying is true. "I know, I think she said something along those lines when I was coming too."

Jack slaps Neil's arm in a friendly gesture, "Well there you go then."

Neil roars with pain as it was the arm that had been dislocated.

"Sorry, sorry, shit, sorry, I didn't mean that I forgot I'm sorry."

Neil's jaw is clenched as he breaths through the pain, and is waving away his friends apologies. "It's fine, I'm fine, I'll get over it."

Jack scrubs his hands over his face, feeling like hell at hurting his friend, but laughing anyway.

Neil glowers at him, "Well don't laugh it's bloody sore!"

Jack coughs his laugh away, "Hum, yeah, sorry. Anyway what do you mean she sort of said that, could you hear what we were saying?"

"No, not really. I think I heard her talking last night about getting away from the abuse and then I wake up with her talking to me about the club and stuff."

Jack is nodding, "She was so worried last night, she stayed here all night, and mumbled something about nearly getting the guy she was falling in love with killed by her crazy ex-boyfriend."

Neil's heart soars at Jacks words, "She really said that, that she was falling in love with me?"

"Oh aye, but you don't know she said that," Jack is pointing a finger at his friend in a warning, "I don't think I was meant to hear it, even though she was sobbing in my arms."

Neil stiffens, "You had her in your arms?" The jealousy Neil is feeling is unreasonable, and he knows it, but he can't help it.

"Calm down, ya idiot, I've got my own love life and Ava is like my sister!"

"I know, I know, my feelings are just wacked out. I just want to grab her and never let go, but I know she needs to learn to be on her own too, uch I don't know!" Neil yawns, just as Eveline walks back into the room.

"You need your rest young man." She smiles at Neil, the nurse coming out in her, then turns to Jack, "You want to get going and let Neil get his rest?"

Jack stands, putting his jacket on. "Aye, right we'll get off. You get some sleep and I'll come back in tomorrow for a bit. Have they said when you'll get out?"

"No, not yet, the doctor's been round today and he is happy with me, but he wants to hold on to me for a bit, for observations, and crap like that."

Eveline smiles at his choice of words, "Oh I meant to ask, what happened to HIM?"

Jack is first to answer, "As far as I know he's still in the hospital under police supervision, I think the police will be round to talk to you at some point."

Neil nods, too tired to speak, his eye closing falling into a deep sleep before Jack and Eveline close the door behind them.

****

Two CID officers walk into Nathan's hospital room, Nathan looks up at them and huffs, "Can I help you?" His bored tone letting the officers know his feelings about them being there.

"We would like to have a wee chat Mr Low, about the traffic accident you were involved in. Would you like your lawyer present?"

"No," Nathan states with indignation, "I'm representing myself."

The officers try to talk him out of his decision, but he isn't for backing down, so they continue, "We were wondering if you could explain in your own words, the events that led up to the road traffic accident you were involved in yesterday."

Over the next hour, Nathan spouted his own version of the accident, placing the blame firmly on Neil's shoulders and the weather. Nothing to do with him or the four pints of lager he consumed, although he never mentioned them.

The officers take notes throughout, and then excuse themselves to speak to the nurse, finding out when Nathan was due to be discharged so he could be interviewed properly, under caution at the police station.

From there they walk over to the ward where Neil was staying. Making sure with the nurses on duty that Neil was fit enough for visitors, they enter his room. "Mr Alexander, are you okay to talk?"

Neil opens his eyes, he has been sleeping since Jack and Eveline left, but had come to with the police and the nurses talking outside his door,

"Yeah," He pushes himself up the bed trying to get into a sitting position, grimacing and cursing over the pain.

"Are you needing any pain relief?" one of the CID officers ask,

Neil shakes his head, "No they make me feel doped up, and I don't do pills unless in desperate need."

Both officers nod, then pull seats up to the side of his bed, settling in to ask their questions, "Can you tell us in your own words the events leading up to and including the road traffic accident you were involved in, please?"

Neil takes his time explaining everything that he can remember about the accident.

The enormity of the accident sits heavy on his shoulders as he names Nathan as the other driver. Seeing his car stationary in the middle lane of the M8, "He was trying to kill me wasn't he?" It was more of a statement than a question, and the officers mumble all the right things about investigating and looking at CCTV, but Neil can tell by their expressions and their body language that they agree with him. Deciding not to dwell on the thought of someone trying to kill him, Neil asks, "Have you spoken to WPC Young? This is connected to Ava and her relationship with him."

The officers let him know that they have been on touch with WPC Young and they were building a case against Mr Low on many different charges. They thank Neil for his time and ask him to make an appointment to go to the station when he is discharged from hospital to make a formal statement.

****

Ava goes straight to the hospital after the christening,

everything had gone without a hitch and everyone had thanked her for making the day so special and such a success. For one of the first times in her life she really felt worthy of everyone's praise and thanks. She has thrived on being busy, making sure everyone has everything they need and that the party ran as smoothly as possible, boosting the reputation of the function side of the business. She can't wait to tell Neil all about it and how good she is feeling about it all. Walking through corridors of the ancient hospital, Ava feels a chill run down her spine, putting the feeling down to tiredness she continues walking past the coffee shop, round and straight into a G4S guard who is handcuffed to Nathan.

Ava's breath catches in her throat at the shock of seeing Nathan. "Sorry," she mumbles then stops herself, she will not cower anymore, she refuses to be that mousey girl that gets taken advantage of, especially in front of Nathan. She straightens up to her full height, lifting her head and looks directly at the guard and then at Nathan, "Excuse me, I didn't realise there was a common criminal being escorted from the building." Ava's eyes never leave Nathan's as she talks.

The guard looks between them both, not sure what is going on with the lady in front of him, but is pretty sure she knows his prisoner. Nathan winces at being called a common criminal, but the emotion passes quickly, he refuses to show Ava how she has affected him, so instead he turns on his charm, "Ah, my darling Ava, it's lovely to see you too."

Ava takes a step towards Nathan, standing toe to toe with the man she once thought she had loved, still never breaking eye contact, she calmly explains to him her feelings, "Mr Low, I am thankfully no longer yours and if you had had any feelings towards me as to call me darling, you would never have beat me within an inch of my life, so if you'll excuse me I have to go and make sure that the man I love, is recuperating after you tried to kill him!" And with a side step she strides away from the men with her head held high.

Nathan growls as she passes and tries to get away from the guard, but thankfully, the guard had the sense to hold onto him at his elbow as well as being handcuffed to him. Giving Nathan a slight push in the right direction, he growls for him to calm down and move.

Walking into Neil's room Ava can feel herself physically shake from the adrenaline rush after her encounter with Nathan, but is over the moon with herself at how she handled him, and very proud that she managed to stand up to him. Something she never thought she would ever be able to do, but now she is free she can and has.

Neil looks up from the newspaper he is reading and smiles at his visitor. "Hey Sweet, you're looking pleased with yourself, the christening go alright?"

Ava walks over to Neil's bed and leans over him kissing him before answering his question. Enjoying the sensation of Neil's lip on hers, Ava is loath to break the contact, but knows she must so she pulls back from his lips and places her forehead on his, feeling her body heat. After a second, Ava stands and goes for a chair to sit in, once she's seated she manages to answer Neil's question, "Yes, the christening went well, I gave out more business cards so we will hopefully get more bookings from it, but there is more to my smugness than the christening."

Neil listens as Ava explains her meeting with her ex-boyfriend. His smile is beaming with pride, he knew then that giving Ava his business card on that very first night was the best decision he has ever made and that he was going to do everything humanly possible to make her happy.

CHAPTER FORTY-ONE

A week later and Neil is home from the hospital and it has been Ava's turn to be the one fussing. Every time Neil moves or makes a noise, Ava is by his side making sure he is okay. On his first night home, Ava orders in some Chinese food for them and serves it up on the coffee table in the living room so they can pick at everything she ordered; she sorts Neil's plate first then hands it over to him.

"Thanks." He grimaces at the movement of taking the plate,

"You okay?"

Neil smiles at the concern in Ava's voice, he places his plate on the couch and puts his hand on her cheek rubbing his thumb over her soft skin, "I'm fine, Sweet, just still a bit stiff from the whiplash, but it's getting easier, honest."

Ava relaxes slightly and leans her head into his hand ever so slightly, "What about your shoulder and leg?"

"They're okay, I don't have much pain in my shoulder just some stiffness, the hospital said they would send me to physio and my leg still aches a bit, but it's not too bad." He is stretching the truth and Ava knows it,

"Really?" she questions.

Neil knows he has been caught, so blushes, "Yes, it's sore, but nothing I can't handle, just now."

"Okay." Ava is glad he told her the truth, eventually, about the pain, she needs him to be honest with her about everything if they are going to have a relationship. She turns her head and kisses the inside of his palm, then starts to serve herself food.

Throughout dinner, they chat easily about the club, the christening and Jack's new found love with Eveline. After they have both had their full of dinner, Ava clears up and starts the dishwasher, she knows that Neil has to take his painkillers so she takes a can of Irn Bru for each of them back through. As she walks into the living room she sees Neil trying to get up from the couch, she rushes over to him, putting the cans on the coffee table before grabbing him. "What do you think you're doing?"

Neil is breathing heavily from the exertion of trying to move from the couch with one of his legs feeling like a dead weight. Slumping back to where he was, Neil lowers his head feeling embarrassed, "I eh, I…I need the toilet."

Ava stops herself from nagging as the realisation of what is going to be involved with them living together whilst Neil recovers dawns on both of them, Ava is first to move, she comes round the couch so she is standing in front of Neil,

"It might be awkward to start with, and I know this isn't the usual way people start relationships, but if we…" Ava motions between them, "get through this, then we will get through anything."

Neil opens his mouth to speak then closes it before trying again, still to no avail. Ava smiles at him.

Neil tries once again, managing to find his voice on the third try, "So is this a relationship then?" Neil can't believe he is desperate to hear Ava's answer, but is also terrified of the answer, or least of the wrong answer.

Ava lowers her eyes and takes a deep breath, feeling more confident in herself and her feelings for the man in front of her she answers, "Well, I hope so, I mean I would like that and I thought that's where we were headed before the accident, so I don't see why it should change."

Neil lets out the breath he was holding onto, grins and grabs Ava's face, bringing her in for a kiss. Their lips joining and dance in harmony. Pulling back, Neil places his forehead on Ava's and then rubs his nose gently along hers, he looks at her and his heart soars, she really is here with him, no matter what state he is in. "I am over the moon at hearing you say that you want to be with me, and I desperately want to continue that kiss, but—"

Ava takes in a sharp breath as panic flashes through her eyes. Neil takes her hands and squeezes then in reassurance, "I'm also desperate for the toilet, Sweet, and I need help!"

Ava laughs giving Neil a peck on the lips then stands, "Right come on then let's get you to the toilet, as I ain't cleaning up after you." Ava's light and cheeky tone lets Neil know that even that wouldn't be a problem. Ava helps him from the couch and gives him his crutches,

"Thanks, I should be okay from here." There is still some embarrassment in Neil's tone which is to be expected, Ava thinks, nobody likes being reliant on anybody to do the most basic of things.

Once Neil returns and gets comfy on the couch again, he clears his throat and starts the conversation they both knew had to happen. "Right, I guess we need to work out how things are going to work, like up and down stairs and eh, showers."

Ava swallows hard, thinking that the first time she saw Neil naked it would be in a romantic, sensual, sexual situation and not a domestic one. Pushing aside her thoughts, Ava shrugs, "We'll work it out when we need to. I'm here to help in any way I can."

Neil squeezes her hand, "You really are amazing, most girls would have run in the other direction at the thought of this being the start of their relationship."

Ava smiles back at him, "I think we both know I'm not most girls."

Agreeing with her, Neil motions for her to cuddle in. They both settle down and watch TV until they go to bed.

****

Lying in his bunk bed in his Barlinnie prison cell, Nathan tries to take stock of where his life is, where it is going and what went so wrong that he ended up in the situation he now finds himself in. He knew that pleading not guilty to the attempted murder charge was a risk, but he also knows a lot of people and he has a lot of money, so he is quietly confident that he will get the not guilty verdict that he deserves. He has a feeling that he won't get bail at his first hearing and he has to accept that there is a chance that he would need to go to prison for a bit, and even though it is going to make his life harder if he does end up there, (he won't be able to contact the people he needs to help him with his plan to get out of this predicament), he is going to play the game and make it look as if he is keeping his nose clean. Feeling his anger rise, he takes a deep breath, trying to get it under control, losing his mind in the middle of Barlinnie is not a good idea!

During the course of the day, Nathan works on his so-called defence, and manages to talk to Mark, in code, about his plan and asks him to help, again. Mark reminds Nathan that he is still owed money from the last plan he helped him with, and if he is going to help again, then Nathan is going to need to give him a down payment, a substantial down payment. Being in prison means Nathan hasn't got money at his disposal, and since he fired his lawyer he can't instruct him to access his money for him either and he explains this to Mark. Thankfully, for Nathans sake, they come to an arrangement that Mark will be paid in kind from any items Nathan has in his office, and when this nightmare is over Nathan will make sure Mark gets his payment in full and with some interest. Mark agrees, reluctantly, to help Nathan out, stating that this is the last time.

Once the phone call is finished Mark heads over to Nathan's office to clear out whatever crap is there, then on to make some enquiries. He knows he will need to wait until the intermediate diet hearing in Glasgow Sherriff Court before he can put any plans into place. He needs to know who the Sheriff may be and when the trial date would be set for, before being able to plan anything.

Weeks went past until eventually Mark finds himself sitting in the public gallery of Glasgow Sheriff Court, listening to both sides, or least the prosecution and then Nathan, the charges they were bringing against him were, two charges of Serious Assault and Permanent Disfigurement, Dangerous Driving, driving under the Influence of Alcohol and Breach of the Peace . The Sheriff advises Nathan again of his right to counsel but again he refuses, and again pleads not guilty. Mark hangs his head, realising that what Nathan is expecting of him is going to be impossible, but he will try his best, he stupidly gave his word, and his word was his word, he never broke it. Now that

Mark knows the trial date, and the enormity of the work required of him he arranges a visit to Nathan in Barlinnie, to go through what he thinks is Nathan's only chance, he also goes to work watching Neil and Ava again.

****

Over the past few weeks, Neil has improved and is now managing to get about easier. Ava has been covering some of his shifts at the club as well as the function side of things, bringing some of the paperwork home so Neil can stay up to date and involved. On the days that Neil needs to get out of the house before cabin fever sets in, Jack comes and picks him up, taking him to the club or out for lunch, anywhere that isn't the house for a bit, although by the time they arrive back home, Neil is glad to be back. The relationship between him and Ava has evolved into a comfortable routine of Ava helping Neil get ready whenever he needs extra help, which with each passing day is less than the day before. Ava preparing meals and Neil helping out in the house wherever and whenever he can, which is slightly more each day, and either one or both of them going to the club to work. Neither of them discusses their feelings, both of them not sure of where their relationship will be after everything has settled down, but knowing they are together and that is what they both want. Neil knows he is feeling better enough that he wants to take their relationship to the next level and sleep with Ava, but he is unsure how they would get round the lump that is still his leg, so again he puts off the conversation.

Sitting in his office with Jack on a cold Friday night in November, he pours his fears out about his relationship with

Ava to his best friend,

"You think what?" Jack asks,

"We are never gonna move onto the next level, take it to a sexual relationship. It's just gonna continue in this comfy routine, honestly it's like we've been married for forever. I mean we kiss and cuddle as much as we can, but due to this thing," Neil stabs at his leg that is still in the metal brace from the operation, "We really canny get much further."

Jack is desperate not to have this conversation about his friend's sex life, or lack there off as it turns out, but Neil is his only and best friend and it would be Neil he would turn to if the tables were turned, so he answers, saying the only thing he can think of, "So what you're saying is you can't get your leg over?" He snorts at his own joke, but Neil isn't in the mood and glowers at him, a growl coming from his throat to shut Jack up. Jack coughs and clears his throat, apologising, "Well, your bionic leg isn't forever, so once you're back on both feet you can put your foot on the gas on that side of things. Anyway when do you get it off?" Jack tries to change the subject.

"Are you quite finished with the leg and feet digs?" Neil asks sounding pissed at his friend, Jack shrugs, knowing Neil isn't really pissed at him. Neil shakes his head, "I go back to the hospital in three weeks, so hopefully then, but the court case will be getting called soon, so I doubt Ava will be in the mood during that."

As much as Jack didn't want to think about it, he did feel sorry for his friend, just when he finds the girl, life throws a spanner in the works, Jack sighs before answering, "It'll work out, just keep the faith."

The friends talk about the up and coming court case and their business until closing time. Jack goes to get his Mazda from the multi-story car park as Neil cashes up, then locks up. Jack comes back in and helps Neil out to Buchanan Street and into the car on Argyle Street, neither of the men notice the black Audi 4 pulling in behind and following them back to Neil's home.

CHAPTER FORTY-TWO

December comes and so does Neil's appointment to get his leg brace removed, he still feels stiff and it aches if he does too much, but on the whole, he is feeling better and a lot lighter without the cumbersome metal contraption stuck to his leg. Managing to get into the club easier has made his life feel better, even taking the train in more, due to not having a car anymore (he really is missing his baby M3, desperately waiting for the day he can get his hands on another one).

The day he got his brace removed, he had planned on going home to make a start on the romantic side of their relationship, but returning home, Neil finds out that Ava has heard from the Procurator Fiscal's office. The case was about to start and he wanted to go through what would be expected of them, the Procurator Fiscal's office had left a message for Neil to contact him as soon as possible so he could go through the same process with him. Neil had contacted Jack earlier asking him if he would close up the club that night, leaving Neil free to be with Ava.

Ava has been quiet all night, and Neil is trying to give her space, so by being more mobile means he can make a start on dinner. He is hobbling about the kitchen listening to Linkin Park, gathering all the ingredients he needs for the stir fry he is making as Ava walks into the kitchen through the door from the hall. She had been crying earlier after talking to the

Procurator Fiscal's office, but has stopped now, feeling like she is out of tears, so she is trying not to think about everything in front of them anymore. Seeing Neil get about without his leg brace on made her heart soar, the sight gave her hope that everything would be okay, if Neil's leg could mend then so could she, she would eventually be free of Nathan, from her life of abuse at his hands and free to be with Neil completely. The thought of what 'completely' entailed had her heart racing and her breath catching in her throat, a sound that was almost inaudible, but still made Neil turn around,

"Sweet." Neil gasps at seeing Ava looking at him, she is still blotchy looking with swollen red eyes from crying, but he thinks she has never looked so beautiful. She has a shy sexy smile on her lips, and her eyes are boring into him, a devouring look on her face, he pushes aside the thought, knowing she has had a rough day.

"How you holding up?" he asks, trying to break his thoughts and cool the heat in his trousers,

"Not bad, considering, but I can't keep letting him get to me not if we are—" She doesn't finish the sentence, but she doesn't need to, "Anyway, how are you? How's it feel to be walking without crutches?"

Neil hobbles over to her and puts his arms around her, bringing her into his embrace, enjoying how natural it feels to have her in his arms, and loving how she is blocking Nathan from her mind and putting him there instead.

"It feels great, no more clunking about, and I'm even starting to be able to bend my knee, but the best bit is being able to do this." He brings her even closer until there is no daylight between them, slipping his fingers into her hair, angling her head so he can kiss her completely. Tentatively to start with, teasing her lips until she relaxes and opens her mouth deepening the kiss, feeling everything between them grow, knowing there is nothing either of them would rather do at that moment in time other than be together.

Neil breaks away first, breathing heavy suddenly unsure of himself, "I'm sorry Sweet, I shouldn't have pushed." He is trying to regain control of himself, but he is desperate to have her in his arms and in his bed. He is wary of pushing too far too quickly and blow any chance he may have, plus he knows that the near future is going to be an emotional rollercoaster. Through all of this, he is also wary of their relationship becoming 'old married couple' before they even have that conversation, if they ever get to that stage.

Ava is breathing hard too and looking a Neil as if he has grown another head, "Why are you apologising?" Ava is confused, she thought that Neil wanted the kiss but now he is saying sorry, "Sorry for what? What do you mean pushing?" Neil closes his eyes taking a deep breath,

"This, you, us." Neil drops his arms and goes to move away but Ava stops him,

"We were kissing and it was great."

Neil grins at the compliment, "If there is going to be an 'us' then we are going to kiss and hopefully more."

Neil looks at Ava and sees the sparkle there, shocked, but happy he starts to talk, "I know but today must have been hard for you and the next few weeks are probably going to be hell, I just don't want to add to the pressure on you or us."

They are facing each other, holding hands, Ava is fighting to keep the emotions crashing through her in check as she looks at Neil. She can't believe what she is hearing from this amazing guy in front of her, "Kissing me won't make things worse for me, if anything they will make things better. You help make me feel better, you have helped me realise that I am worth more than I used to let myself be worth. The fiscal said today that Nathan will probably try to make me feel worthless and useless all over again during the trial, so knowing that you are with me, emotionally and physically, then he has no chance of getting to me." Ava shrugs, not sure what else to say. With the trial looming Ava was going to need all the confidence and self-worth she could muster, and knowing that things with Neil are going in the right direction could only help.

Feeling empowered with her new self-confidence Ava kisses Neil, all of her emotion and passion pouring out of her and into the kiss. Neil feels every inch of that emotion and passion Ava is giving and pours all of his into it too. Thanking any god that is listening for the kiss that has officially stopped the comfy old married couple routine and sparked awake the new lover's relationship.

****

Throughout the last month, Mark has been watching Ava and Neil but he's never had the opportunity to approach either of them, so the only other option open to him to obtain Nathan the outcome he needs is to get to the jury.

Sitting in court on the Monday morning, Mark makes mental notes of who each juror is and commits names and faces to memory, so by the end of the day, when they are all leaving he knows what ones he is going to lean on.

Amazingly, the trial starts and Mark sits in, listening to the opening statements of both the Procurator Fiscal and Nathan. Again, he is struck by how arrogant Nathan is in his belief of his own innocence and that he, Mark, is the one that has to move Heaven and Earth to get Nathan his freedom. Cursing himself for taking on another job for Nathan, Mark gets to work trying to catch the eye of the youngest female juror and starts his campaign of flattery and seduction.

Once the day is over Mark waits about outside the Sheriff Court until he spots the young juror and purposely walks over to her making sure to bump into her 'saving' her from falling, making her feel that he has protected her and so earns some trust. He strikes up a conversation, careful not to mention the case, the juror is flattered, as he knew she would be, and accepts his offer of a drink.

Over the next few days, Mark smiles and winks at the young juror as he listens to the case. The more he hears the more he realises how much of a disgusting person Nathan actually is. He always knew that Nathan was a bastard and paid his way through life, but he hadn't realised what he was doing to his then girlfriend.

The evidence of abuse against Ava keeps building until it culminates in her leaving him and then his final attack on her and her hospitalisation. Hearing about the attack in the Daydream makes Marks' stomach turn.

He has made a career out of hurting people for money. These people are normally evil people, bad people or people who have stupidly got themselves into debt to the wrong person, but never has he lifted his hand to an innocent person, especially a female he was in a relationship with, that he feels is unforgivable, so with that in mind Mark makes a career changing decision not to continue with this job.

Throughout the trial, Ava has managed to hold herself together. The questioning by the Procurator Fiscal was hard but bearable, she knew Nathan's questions weren't going to be as bearable. He came at her with his questions, statements and lies. He threw everything at her trying to make her out to be an ungrateful spoiled bitch who was out to ruin him. The Sheriff was consistently on at him to get to the point and to move his defence on, losing patience very quickly. Ava closed her eyes and sent up a silent thanks to the Sheriff when he eventually told Nathan to shut up and sit down, letting Ava know she was free to go from the court room as she had given all of her evidence.

Neil was the next witness to give evidence and again Nathan tried to make out that Neil was lying and had poisoned Ava against him, and again he pushed the Sheriff's patience to the point of no return. Turning to Nathan, the Sheriff explains, in no uncertain terms, to sit down.

During Neil's evidence, Nathan notices that Mark was nowhere to be seen in the court. Expecting him to be outside 'talking' to some of the witnesses, he shrugs off the absence.

Mark isn't out talking to any witnesses, having changed his mind about working with Nathan and knowing he would probably not see any more money, Mark is making arrangements for Nathan to meet some new friends whilst he is in prison, people who not only owe Mark some favours, but also hate wife beaters and arrogant millionaires. A win win situation for everyone involved, except Nathan

CHAPTER FORTY-THREE

For the rest of the proceedings, Ava chooses to stay away from the court. Neil has managed to get a courtesy car from the insurance company while they are dealing with his claim, so he manages to get to and from the court on his own, as well as taking Ava to the club, and back home again. She has been running the club whilst Neil and Jack are attending court, all of them thinking that it's best for her if she stays away from the court and Nathan. Neil filled her in every night on the day's events when they were sharing dinner. Ava worries that Neil is doing too much and driving too much, his leg is still healing and she knows it's still sore, even though he tries to hide the pain, she can see him wincing when he tries to get up if he has been sitting too long.

On the nights Ava closes up the club either Neil or Jack drive her home. Once home she gives Neil's leg a massage, trying to ease the tired muscles but also to try and keep the intimacy between them. They have both agreed to hold off on taking the next step until after the trial. Both wanting their first time together to be special and unspoiled by the stress of anything. The sexual tension between them heavy in the air as Ava massages Neil's leg on this cold December night, both of their resolves ready to break. Ava finishes the massage and goes to stand, Neil sits up and grasps her hand. Unlike the first time he grasped her she doesn't flinch and there is no fear in her eyes, instead she sits back down on the stool she had been using.

"What's up, are you in pain?" The concern in her voice touches Neil's heart as she places her hand back on his leg, trying pulling it back into her lap to rub where it is sore, but Neil refuses to let her move his leg, and holds her hand again.

"No, well not really, the massages are helping. I just need to hold you for a bit."

Ava smiles and lets out her breath she was holding, tears springing to her eyes partly in relief that she is helping and he isn't in as much pain, and partly because of the soft loving way he is with her. She moves onto the couch as Neil moves over to let her in, bringing his arms around to hold her into him. Ava settles in his arms, placing her head on his shoulder and breathes in his scent, feeling at home in his arms. She lifts her head and looks into his soft brown eyes.

Neil brings his hand up and caresses her face, making her stomach flutter and the tears that had dissipated spring forward again. "Hey, what's the tears for?"

Ava shrugs and smiles, "Over emotional and desperate for the trial to be over." Her voice is hoarse with emotion and unshed tears.

"Me too Sweet, I want it all over with, I want my days back and my stress levels back to normal, and you in my bed." He adds the last bit with a heat in his voice that Ava has never heard there before, she gasps but it is covered up by Neil's mouth on hers. Neil moves them so Ava is sitting on his lap. She feels him wince in the kiss when he moves them, she tries to pull away to make sure he is okay and she that she isn't hurting him, but he refuses to break their connection, deepening the kiss instead. Plunging his tongue into her mouth then nipping her bottom lip, grinding up into her letting her feel the full extent of his arousal. Neil breaks the kiss, both of them breathing heavily; he moves his kissing down her neck, nipping as he goes. All Ava can do is feel all of the sensations running through her body (sensations she never felt with Nathan as sex usually came after a beating or was rough to the point of pain) and grind her hips into his running her hands up and down his back, making him push his hips up to meet hers. Slipping his hand under the back of her top, he unclips her bra and moves his hands round to her front, taking her breasts in his hands he caresses them gently at first then increasing pressure, nipping and plucking at her nipple until they are stiff buds and Ava is writhing in his lap.

Using all of his self-restraint Neil brings his head back up from her neck, releasing his grip on her nipple, although he leaves his hand there rubbing gentle circles,

"Ava, I'm sorry I—"

Ava stills in his lap and looks into Neil's eyes, panic settling in her heart and eyes, "For what?"

Neil moves his hand back round to her back, but continues to make circles on her skin, "I didn't mean to push too far, I mean we spoke about this and agreed to wait, but—"

Ava cuts him off by placing her finger on his lips in a 'shh' gesture, "Again with the pushing. You are not pushing me. I was enjoying myself, just as much as you were." She grinds herself against him once more to prove her point against his bulge, "I know we agreed to wait and if that is what you want then that's what will happen. I want our first time together to be right, I don't want there to be any guilt or stress and I definitely want both of us to want it, to want each other without any worry."

Neil places his forehead against Ava's his breathing

nearly back to normal. "I'm just frightened I'll hurt you, or that this will be, I don't know." Neil shrugs, placing his hand on her hips, uncertainty rolling off him.

Ava takes his hands in hers and with a certainty that she has never felt before she tells Neil exactly how she feels. "Neil, I have never felt this way before, ever. I am falling for you hard and not because you were there for me when I needed saving from the most awful situation, but because you gave me your hand and never let go, you never treated me like anything other than a normal human being, because of that I now know how to love myself." She takes a deep breath before continuing, "I want this, I want you, but if this, us, is going to work then I need to know that you want me for me and not out of guilt or some hero must get the girl thing, or something that isn't true." As she talked, Ava could feel the sexual tension dissipate between them and the air take on a more serious feel to it. They both knew they needed to have a conversation like this, but they thought it would be after the court case.

Neil sighs, but refuses to let go of her as he too spills his heart out, "Ava, I knew I wanted you the second I set eyes on you, and then when I saw the way that excuse of a human treated you the need to protect you overwhelmed me. The day you phoned me for help seemed like the best day of my life. You decided you were better than how he treated you, better than he let you believe you were. You decided to put your trust in me, to trust me to help you get away. I have watched you grow from a woman who didn't know whether or not it was okay to breath, to this gorgeous, independent, confidant, intelligent woman that is grinding into me," Ava blushes but doesn't say anything,

"And tempting me so absolutely that it would make me

the happiest man in the world if we made love just now."

This time it is Neil's turn to take a deep breath, not believing what he is about to say, "But I think if we wait until after the trial, when you are once and for all free of him and every bit of stress he has placed on you during and since your relationship it will be even more amazing. Then I will be happy for everything to take its course." Neil sighs and brings Ava down so her head is once again on his shoulder.

"I don't want anything else in this world other than to be with you, and I want all of you forever." Ava pauses, she understands why Neil wants to wait until Nathan is no more of a threat to either of them, but that is also why she doesn't want to wait tonight. She is wondering that maybe this is her way of proving to herself and Neil that Nathan is no longer a part of her life, or her emotions.

"I understand, and hopefully the trial should be over by Friday, so we will be free from it all then."

She smiles at Neil a sad but hopeful smile.

"Yeah, maybe even tomorrow, depending on the jury." Neil says this nonchalantly.

Ava stiffens at his words, "You okay? You've just tensed every muscle in your body. You worried about the verdict?"

Ava moves until she is sitting on the couch, keeping hold of Neil's hand, "I thought it was Friday, I have myself geared up for another day before I need to go back to court. I didn't think I was worried, but now that it could be tomorrow, I guess I might be a bit." She shrugs, unsure of how to explain how she is feeling.

Neil looks into her eyes, "Guess I should've kept my mouth shut and we could've been having incredible sex instead of making you worry?"

Ava gives him a lop sided grin, "Incredible eh?"

Neil puffs his chest out, "Oh aye!"

The mood lightened, Ava leans over and kisses him gently, "At least if the trial finishes tomorrow we can do it then." There is a playful tone to Ava's voice and Neil says a silent thank you that the worry didn't last and panic didn't arrive.

"Right, I'm going to bed." He says as he starts to get up from the couch,

"Yeah, me too." They both go through their routine of tidying up and making sure everything is locked, then they both head upstairs, stopping at the top to say their goodnights. Holding Ava to him Neil knows he doesn't want to let her go, ever.

"Ava?" His voice is quiet, almost a whisper,

"Mmm?"

"Would you sleep in beside me tonight?" She looks at him with confusion in her eyes, she had been wanting to ask him to sleep in with her, but she had made a fuss at the start about single rooms, and then the conversation downstairs where he had made a good argument for not making love, but now he was asking for her to be in his bed.

Neil could see her confusion so tried to explain, "I mean I just don't want to stop holding you. I know what I said downstairs, and I still think that is for the best, but we can be in the same bed without things happening, I think."

She smirks at him, "I'm glad you said that, the holding me thing, I wasn't sure if you would want me there if nothing was going to happen."

Neil shook his head, "You mean more to me than just sex, and having you beside me will mean the world to me."

Ava smiles and nods her head, holding hands they both walk into Neil's bedroom and close the door.

The next day Ava goes to the club with the promise from Neil that he would collect her if the trial looked like it was coming to a conclusion. They had both slept wrapped in each other and woke the same way, being touchy feely all morning with big smiles for each other and lingering kisses.

Neil walks into the court and bumps into the Procurator Fiscal both agree that the entire trial has been a sham and the end of it should be by the end of the day. Neil decides to ask something that has been bothering him since the trial began, "I have been wondering, have you heard of Nathan trying anything, like trying to sway the trial in anyway?" The Procurator Fiscal looks about to see if anyone was listening to them before answering,

"No I haven't, and to be honest I'm shocked and still waiting on it. We'll see what happens with the verdict, but I don't think he has, or maybe he's not managed it."

The fiscal excuses himself, leaving Neil standing, musing over what was said when the gruff looking man from the club walks up to him and starts talking to him as if they have been friends forever.

"All right Neil, good to see you healing, I just wanted to say 'Hi'"

Neil stops the man from talking, "Do I know you?" Neil remembers him from the night in the club but doesn't let on that he remembers, the man laughs in a friendly way,

"No, not really, but I know you and Ava,"

Neil stiffens, but the man ignores it and continues talking, "My name's Mark. I wanted you to know that I used to do some things for Nathan and he had asked me to help him get the verdict he needs to get free, but, I've decided that that is something I cannot do. Hearing what he did to Ava was abhorrent, so instead of helping him I have arranged for something else to happen. You see I have some friends inside, and I was telling them all about his silver spoon life and everything he has done throughout it, and as it turns out one of my friends has issues with Nathan's building business and with men who beat their women, so, he is looking forward to meeting him when this trial is over." Mark pauses for a beat before continuing, "So I will take my leave and you can do what you will with that bit of information." Mark slaps Neil on the shoulder and walks away, leaving Neil once again musing over information he has heard. He is still there when the fiscal arrives back again to go into the courtroom to re-start the trial.

"You ready?" he asks Neil.

Neil looks at him wondering what to say, should he tell him what he has just found out or not? After a split second thinking about it, Neil decides not to tell him, not wanting to upset the trial this close to the end, "Aye, sure."

The morning is taken up with the Procurator Fiscal making his closing speech, summing up his case and making sure the jury understand how horrid Nathan had been throughout his relationship with Ava and since. Just before they broke for lunch, it was Nathan's turn to sum up his case, in his closing speech. To everyone's amazement, he was very quick and to the point. Stating blatantly that all the jury had to say was not guilty, as that is exactly what he was, not guilty. The Sheriff put his head in his hands in despair before giving the jury his advice. He explains to the jury that after lunch they would stay in the jury room to discuss the case and, hopefully, reach their decision.

Neil leaves court to grab lunch and collect Ava, texting Jack as he went to let him know that the jury had been sent out.

After lunch, Neil and Ava arrive back at court meeting up with Jack and Eveline. Eveline takes Ava into a cuddle and gives her some words of advice, support and friendship. Both women have bonded and became very close friends since Ava was in hospital, their friendship growing more since Jack and Eveline got together. Jack shakes Neil's hand then gives Ava a hug, kissing the top of her head,

"This is gonna finish today and then you will have the rest of your life to look forward to, okay?"

Ava nods into his chest, her emotions bubbling up again,

"You know you always have us."

She nods again, feeling like the wee sister Jack always said she was.

Neil coughs to get their attention, "Remember me?"

Ava rolls her eyes at him, knowing that he is joking with them, thankfully. "Of course, how could I forget my knight in black jeans?"

Ava wraps herself around Neil and kisses him soundly on the lips. Smiling up at him, feeling like everything she went through brought her to these people and Neil's arms, and feels better for it. They only had an hour to wait after lunch for the jury to announce that they had their verdict. Everyone files back into the courtroom, Neil holding onto Ava's waist tightly, the feeling of his arm giving her the extra strength she needed to get her through the verdict.

Nathan walks into the courtroom and sees Ava sitting with Neil, his anger starts rising. She couldn't face him throughout the case, but she can face him when she thinks he's going to prison, well the joke will be on her, well at least it should be, he thinks, if Mark has done his job correctly the jury should be giving him a 'not guilty' at any moment. He hadn't heard or seen him throughout the trial, except for at the start, but that was probably for the best, no reason to make anyone suspicious of them.

The jury are brought back in and proceedings commence, Ava takes deep breaths trying to calm her racing heart and the panic attack that is threatening, Neil holds her hand in his and wraps his other arm around her shoulder rubbing gently with his thumb. He knows she is desperate to hear a guilty verdict, not for revenge or even justice – although she does want that, along with saving other women from his abuse – no, Ava needs to hear it so she knows she was believed, the jury believed her and not him. She needs to know that his money didn't save him like he always told her it would.

Trying to give her as much strength as possible through his touch Neil leans in and kisses the side of her head, "You okay?" he whispers, Ava can only nod, concentrating on her breathing.

The Session Clerk asks the jury spokesperson to stand. Ava can feel the air heavy as she hears both men talking to each other, the Clerk asking if they had come to a verdict and if it was unanimous. The spokesman answers yes.

The Session Clerk asks the questions that everyone is waiting for. "On the first charge of serious assault to permanent disfigurement how does the jury find the accused?"

Ava holds her breath, wondering if the spokesperson had spoken and she had missed it, then she hears a man's voice, strong and sure, "Guilty."

There are murmurs going round the court as the Session Clerk continues, "On the second charge of serious assault to permanent disfigurement, how does the jury find the accused?"

"Guilty"

"On the charge of dangerous driving, how does the jury find the accused?"

"Guilty."

"On the charge of driving whilst under the influence of alcohol, how does the jury find the accused?"

"Guilty."

"And on the charge of breach of the peace how does the jury find the accused?"

"Guilty."

Ava's head drops as she lets out the breath she had been holding. Neil grabs her into a tight hug kissing her hair and cheeks mumbling that it was over. The fiscal continues to do his job by giving the Sheriff more information, as Nathan just stands behind his table shaking his head as if he wasn't hearing what was being said properly. The Sheriff talks to him, telling him, and everyone in the room, how he is despicable and cowardly, money orientated and toxic, and a sorry excuse for a man, he then goes on to explain that he feels any sentence he could hand down would not be just, so he will be passing the case up to the High Court for sentencing.

Knowing his life has just been ripped apart, Nathan turns to Ava. Seeing her in the arms of another man, being comforted against him, and not just any man, but that man, the one that helped get her away, the one that made her think she could live without him, is too much for him to bear, he rushes towards Ava roaring that she has ruined his life, and that he should have killed them both when he had the chance. The police officers in the courtroom rush over while radioing for back up. More officers rush in helping apprehend Nathan. Neil has stepped in front of Ava to protect her, waiting on Nathan's fist to fly at them, but thankful that the police managed to get to him first.

Once everything has calmed, and Nathan has been taken away, again, Neil turns back to Ava, "You okay?"

She looks up at Neil tears running down her cheeks freely and nods furiously, "I am now he's gone and won't be coming back anytime soon."

She gives him a cuddle and then the four of them leave the court. Standing in the corridor, they thank the Procurator Fiscal for all his hard work and give cuddles all round. Jack is first to suggest that they go back to the club for a celebratory drink. All in agreement, they go back to where it all started, the Daydream Club.

CHAPTER FORTY-FOUR

Nathan gets back to Barlinnie Prison, depressed, dumbfounded, but mostly furious. Furious at Ava and Neil, but more so at Mark. This wasn't meant to happen, not to him, he has money and plenty of it, which should have brought with it power, knowledge on people and contacts. So how did this happen? He refuses to believe that any of it is his fault. Yes he hit Ava, but nothing that she didn't deserve, she pushed his buttons, knew what to do to get his anger up, he can't be blamed for that. If she hadn't left him, then that idiot Neil wouldn't be involved and he wouldn't have went after him, so again her fault, but he is the one in prison.

The sound goes to inform the inmates that it's dinner time and Nathan joins the queue of men slouching their way to the dining area. Getting his dinner, which he thinks might be mince and potatoes, Nathan sits in the far corner keeping his head down. He doesn't fit in here, in prison, and truly believes he is so much better than every other person in there, including the staff and the governor.

Nathan hears the chair being scraped across the floor, a sign that he is about have uninvited company, so without even looking up he demands to be left alone. "Not really in the mood for company, so with all due respect, please leave!"

A gruff Glasgow voice booms back at him, "I don't recall asking permission and I don't really give a fuck about your respect, pal!"

Nathan lifts his head to see what he would call a short man, but what the newcomer lacked in height and hair, he made up for in muscle, tattoos and scars. Nathan has seen this particular inmate around the prison grounds and has tried to avoid him at all costs. He has tried to avoid everyone, but more so this particular man as his reputations precedes him, he was sure he was called Ross something and had been in and out of prison for most of his adult life for robbery, assault, GBH, carrying a deadly weapon, but this time he was in for life after murdering his son-in-law. Killing him with his bare hands after he found out the son-in-law had been beating his daughter every night, plus other things. Nathan has a stomach plunging feeling crawl over him; he puts his head back down, staring at the grey slop that is in his tray.

Ross clears his throat then growls quietly so only Nathan can hear him. "I have it on good authority that you beat the fuck out the woman you used to be with. Well..." Ross carries on not letting Nathan speak, "I canny be doing wa cowardly fuckwits like you. Bet you wouldn't think about lifting your fists to me would you, ya cunt eh? I also heard you don't pay up when someone does work for you and that person just happens to be a friend of mine."

Realisation dawning on Nathan, that not only did Mark not get him his 'not guilty' verdict, or even try to get it apparently, but he has actually involved someone inside to 'pay him a visit', he knew then that he was in trouble.

"So," Ross continues his very hushed tirade, "I am gonna making it my mission in life to make your life as miserable as you made your pretty ladies'. And believe me when I say, your life will be miserable, it will be. Think hell on earth and then sometimes it will be so bad, you will be begging me to kill you, but I won't, no I won't, well not at least until I've decided you have paid enough. Do you understand me?"

Nausea sweeps over Nathan, sweat running down his back just hearing that he is more than likely going to be spending most of his days either being beaten or in hospital recovering from a beating. His brain took that moment to forget how to function, speech and muscle movement vanished until Ross grabs his neck and growls even closer to his ear,

"I asked you a fuckin' question, cunt now fuckin' answer me! Do you understand that I am going to fuck you up at every opportunity I can?"

Nathan's brain kicks back in and he manages a nod, slow to start, then becoming furious, until a sharp blow to the back of his head puts his face in the mince slop. Nathan stays there, face down in his dinner until he hears Ross scraping his chair back again and then the footsteps announcing his departure.

****

The couples arrive at the Daydream and as they walk in, all the staff stop and look at them, anxious to know the outcome of the court case. Jack and Eveline are first to walk in, followed by Neil and Ava close on their heels. Jack nods to everyone and a cheer goes up from all the staff and the regular patrons. Ava stands still, her cheeks burning red with all the whoops and 'go Ava's' getting shouted, amazed at the commotion and outpouring of support for her and Neil.

Feeling overwhelmed she hides her face in Neil's chest. Instinctively he holds her close and squeezes her into a hug. She looks up at him with tears in her eyes and smiles, "They believed me!" Her voice cracks at the end of her statement.

They start to walk towards the VIP area situated in an alcove at the side of the bar.

Neil answers her, "Of course they do, everyone always has, you just didn't believe it because he had your confidence so low you didn't believe you!"

They arrive at the table and Neil takes Ava's jacket from her then collects Jack and Eveline's' taking them into the office, as Jack and Eveline go to the bar to order Champagne. When Neil returns he finds a queue of people at the table congratulating Ava on the verdict and for having the courage to get away from Nathan and go through the case. By the time the crowd has thinned to the last one or two regulars both Neil and Ava have tears streaming down their faces at the outpouring of support. Even Jack is amazed at the support they all received during the trial and also at that very moment.

Once all of the congratulations and emotions have calmed, Jack opens the Champagne and pours one for each of them. Neil stands with his glass in hand, "I would like to say how strong, resilient, caring, gorgeous and sexy my girlfriend is."

Ava blushes at the compliments as Neil continues, "She has more strength than she has ever given herself credit for, until now and now I hope she realises that without her own strength not one of us would be right here right now." Neil turns to look at Ava, "If you didn't have the strength to phone me that night, asking for my help, getting into my car and trusting me enough to stay in my house, then we may not have both ended up in hospital with life threatening injuries."

Jack's eyebrows shoot up at Neil in a silent warning, not sure where he is going with his speech,

"But, because of that Jack and Eveline are now together,

you and me wouldn't be together and that prick would still be out hurting you and other people with his dodgy buildings. So, because of you, there are many safe people tonight, and two very happy relationships, plus a club full of happy patrons. You my gorgeous Sweet are an amazing woman!"

Jack blows out the breath he was holding in, now he realises where Neil was going with his speech and him and Eveline cheer in agreement as Neil bends down kissing Ava on the lips. Ava tries to fan back her tears but to no avail, so she resorts to wiping them away instead.

Neil sits down and they all chink glass in a toast to Ava. Ava takes a sip of her drink and tries to compose herself, before clearing her throat to speak. "I'm not going to stand to say this, as I don't like being centre of attention. I just want to thank all three of you helping me, helping me see my strength and for supporting me to be strong. Do I believe I am strong? Not entirely, but I am getting there. Do I believe I am worth anything? Yes I do. Do I believe I am worth loving? Yes, I do and it is all thanks to all of you. Eveline you got me back to health and then became my friend without judging me. Jack because of your friendship with Neil you never once questioned me and always offered your support, no matter what, which is why I know from now on you will always be my brother. Neil," Ava smiles at him and takes his hand, "you knew I needed help and you reached out to me, and for that I owe you my life. I may have had the strength to do all of those things you said, but I couldn't have done them if you hadn't realised things weren't right with me and gave me your card and then believed in me. You are the sweetest, kindest most generous guy ever, and I hope that you will forever be in my life."

Neil leans over, taking her face in his hands whispering

'forever' then takes her mouth with his, pouring every feeling he has for her into the kiss. They break and they both flush at the stares they are getting from Jack and Eveline.

Jack is first to speak, "Right, enough of the mushy shit, let's celebrate."

They all chink again and the conversation turns to the trial and how ridiculous Nathans defence was, then on to other topics until closing time.

As they climb into a taxi, Jack tells Neil and Ava to take the next day off, that he will sort the club and he will see them on Saturday.

Neil thanks him then closes the taxi door. Sitting in the back of the cab Ava cuddles in to Neil, exhaustion taking over, she closes her eyes.

"You okay Sweet?"

She can only nod, but finds some energy and looks up at him, "Thank you, for everything you've done and said, it really means a lot to me."

Neil pulls her to him again, kissing her head. "Every word was true, Sweet, every word."

Smiling Ava snuggles in closer. Ava wakes, wrapped up in Neil, it feels early so she snuggles back in trying to get back to sleep again. After half an hour of just lying there Ava gives up and tries to slip out of bed without waking Neil, but he is already awake,

"Where do you think you're going?"

Ava stops and cuddles back in, "I didn't want to wake you, sorry."

Neil pushes himself up onto one elbow so he is facing her. Ava is lying on her back. He reaches over and brushes her bed hair behind her ear, out of her eyes, "I was already awake, I was just enjoying holding you."

Ava blushes at Neil's honesty, "You want a coffee?" he asks.

Ava nods then goes to get up, Neil places his hand on her shoulder to stop her. "You stay here, I'll bring it up, do you want food?"

"No thanks, coffee first."

Neil gets out of bed and Ava swallows her gasp as she realises he is naked. Neil pulls shorts on and smiles to himself at hearing the nearly inaudible gasp from Ava. She was obviously totally sound asleep when he lifted her from the taxi and put her to bed. After locking up, Neil joined her, not thinking, he stripped and climbed into bed. He had stripped Ava, but left her underwear on. Ava tried to remember how she got to bed, hazy memories of being in Neil's arms came to her mind, embarrassed when she realises that Neil must have stripped her then put her to bed. Hearing Neil come back up the stairs, she runs her fingers through her hair, trying to fix the craziness that is bed hair. Neil comes in carrying two steaming cups of coffee handing one to Ava and then placing the other on his bedside table before climbing back in.

Ava takes a sip of coffee and closes her eyes in a sigh. "That's good coffee." Her voice is almost a whisper.

Neil chuckles at her,

"What?" Ava asks, looking at Neil, "I've never been brought coffee in bed before."

"Never?" Neil is shocked at her admission, then realises he probably should not be.

"Never, there was no eating or drinking in Nathan's bedroom, or anywhere really, except the kitchen or the dining room."

A silence envelopes them as Ava thinks for a second

before speaking again. "I guess there is going to be a lot of things I do now that I either haven't done before or not been allowed to do."

Neil puts his coffee down, and turns to Ava, "I am going to make it my mission in life to make sure you do it all."

Ava smiles at him, a relaxed beaming smile. "Thank you Neil for everything, I couldn't have done it without you." Neil blushes, "And I am so sorry I fell asleep in the taxi last night, I don't know what came over me."

Neil is shaking his head, "There's nothing to be sorry about, yesterday was an emotional and long day. The end of a long hard journey for you. No wonder you crashed, I wasn't long after you. I hope you don't mind that I took off your clothes, I just thought you would be comfier without them."

Ava blushes as she looks down at her underwear and smiles, "No I don't mind, I just thought the first time you undressed me it would be more romantic and lead to more."

Neil smirks and his eyes glint, "Well they do say practise makes perfect, and we have all day as Jack is taking the club today, so we can have a break, together."

Ava grins, "Well what are we going to do first then?"

Neil shifts in the bed so he is hovering above her, "I'm not really sure, but I have an idea."

"Oh aye?" Ava's tone is light and flirty

"Aye!" Neil's tone is husky and sensual.

Neil leans down and seals his mouth over hers, ambushing her mouth with his tongue and her senses with him running his hands all over her skin. Ava lets out a small groan when she feels Neil's hands move round to her breasts, gently caressing them. Ava runs her fingers through his hair and down his back, not quite brave enough to go further as she is frightened she might do something wrong.

Neil senses her hesitation and pulls back, both of them breathing hard.

"You okay with this Sweet? We don't need to do anything you don't want to do."

Ava continues to rub Neil's back, "Yes, I really want this, I really do. It's just—" She breaths out, hard then continues trying to explain herself, desperate to get over this hurdle, "I never seemed to do anything right, touching or anything, so eventually I just gave up doing anything, I just kinda lay there, which was also wrong."

Anger bit at the back of Neil's throat at the thought of Nathan telling her she was doing anything wrong and the thought of Nathan touching her was just too much. He swallows the anger away, looking at Ava, her brow slightly frowned in worry. He desperately wants to replace that worry with hope and love, and the fact that she is willing to talk to him, to admit things she's not sure of to him, and to trust him, he thinks is a good start.

He takes her mouth again in a quick kiss, "Sweet you do not have to do anything you are not sure of, if you want to touch me but you're not sure I can guide you, or you can just go for it, just as long as you don't try to rip it off."

Ava bursts out laughing, glad that Neil's sense of humour is still there after everything she has just told him and that he is using it to ease her mind and any tension she is feeling,

"I, I don't—",

"Okay, why don't you relax and we will see where it goes, okay?"

Ava nods, bringing Neil's head back towards hers until they are kissing again.

CHAPTER FORTY-FIVE

Friday morning in Barlinnie Prison and Nathan is feeling out of sorts. The thought of spending the next twelve plus years behind bars is making him feel sick. He never thought that this could happen to him, Nathan Low. No, things like being sent to prison didn't happen to people like him, wealthy, respectable businessmen, but here he is waiting to be sentenced, waiting on another trial and a brute watching his every move getting ready to use him as his own personal punch bag.

Hearing the sound for breakfast, Nathan groans, he really doesn't want to leave his cell, but doesn't think the guards will let him stay, so he hauls himself up and out to the grey depressing corridors. Trudging down the stairs and with his fellow inmates, Nathan spots Ross, the 'friend' from yesterday and he instinctively puts his head down until he has collected his porridge. At least he thinks that's what it is, but it may be mince and potatoes from last night as they have the same colouring and consistency, and sits at a table on his own. Within minutes, Ross sits down beside him, not saying a word just looking at him with a strange knowing smile on his face. Nathan tries to eat the gloop but his throat refuses to comply out of fear, so he pushes away his tray to concentrate instead on his lukewarm coffee, Ross sniggers, but continues to remain silent, just watching. Eventually Nathan breaks under the pressure of the stare and shakily asks, "What is it? What do you want?"

Ross sniggers again, lifting his tray he stands still smiling at Nathan, "See you soon." Then starts to laugh as he walks away, leaving Nathan sitting on his own again, not sure what to do or what's happening, so, with a bad feeling in his gut he trudges back to his cell, to where he should be safe.

****

Ava and Neil make love on Friday morning, then lay talking to each other about anything and everything, getting to know each other, their likes and dislikes. As much as Neil is loath to raise the subject of Nathan or Ava's past, he would like to know what happened in her past, and how her family died.

"Ava?" Neil is lying on his back holding Ava cuddled in to him, drawing lazy circles on her back.

Ava was in that relaxed state where she wasn't quite sleeping, but wasn't fully awake either. She found some strength to mumble, "Mmmm,"

"I was wondering if you would mind if I asked about your family?"

Fully awake now Ava pulls herself up so she is looking at Neil directly, "It's not something I normally talk about, not sure I can, as it leads to him."

Neil nods, bringing her closer to him again, kissing the top of her head, letting her know he is still there with her no matter what, "That's okay, you don't need to tell me just now, you can do it in your own time, Sweet."

Ava sighs, thankful he didn't push it, not ready to re-live her parents' death in a house fire and how Nathan used her grief to get her to live with him. But it does get her wondering something herself, "Why do you call me Sweet?"

Neil smiles, "The first time I saw you, you just looked so sweet and innocent, then, I saw how he treated you and I knew then that you were too sweet and innocent for him, so—" Neil shrugs, feeling embarrassed,

"I've always liked it." Ava smiles as she stretches up for a kiss. "I'm hungry," she states.

Neil's eyes sparkle with desire, "Oh aye, what were you thinking of?" Kissing Ava, then moving his kisses to her neck then her collarbone,

"Well I was thinking of food, but now you've got me thinking of other things."

Grinning, Neil continues his onslaught of kissing her all over until she is moaning, "Ava, I love having you in my bed, in my life."

Ava grinds her hips as an agreement. They make love until they both climax. Spent, out of breath but smiling, they cuddle, enjoying the feeling of being with each other.

"Ava I know it's early in our relationship and you're hungry, but, I love you."

Ava's breath catches as tears spring to her eyes, not trusting herself to move or speak, she stays lying on top of him, cuddled in, "Really?" her voice cracks,

"Really, Sweet." Neil moves her off him so they are both sitting up facing each other. "Really. I knew I wanted you in my life when I saw you at the Daydream, and now after everything we have been through you are still here, in my bed, my life and in my heart, I don't ever want to be without you."

Her tears are running freely down her cheeks, she tries to talk but only a squeak comes out so she clears her throat and tries again, "I...I don't know what to say, I mean I never knew what it was like to have someone care for me the way you do and you have shown me how even a friendship should be, never mind a loving relationship. I thought I was in love with Nathan, but now I know that it was nowhere near love, and do you know how I know this?"

Neil shakes his head.

"Because I never felt for him what I feel for you. I love you too Neil, forever."

Neil's heart swells at hearing the words that he never thought he would hear when Ava started to talk. Looking deep into her eyes, seeing them shining blue with love for him he nods his head in agreement,

"Forever."

EPILOGUE

1 Year Later

Ava puts the finishing touches to the wedding dress. Standing back she looks at Eveline, "I can't believe you and Jack are actually getting married today."

Eveline's grin splits her face,

"I know, and it's all thanks to you."

Ava smiles at the nurse who helped her back to health and then became her best friend,

"Well I'm glad my near death experience was worthwhile."

The women laugh together. They both understand without words that a year ago they couldn't have laughed at the situation of Ava being attacked by Nathan and being hospitalised, but now that Nathan was in prison and wouldn't be getting out anytime soon, plus him being due up in court again to face charges against his property company, they could, but only between themselves.

"Yeah, thanks for nearly dying, I am very grateful, but it's not just me and Jack, look at you and Neil, it gave youse the shove you needed."

Ava smiles, she still can't quite believe that her and Neil were still together after everything that had happened, "Well yes, but when he ended up in hospital too I really thought that was it, he wouldn't want any more craziness in his life." Tears threaten to push their boundaries and roll down her cheeks at her admission. She had never told anyone she had felt like that, she had hardly even admitted it to herself. Eveline gives her a hug, she knew how hard that time had been on all of them, but especially Ava. She blamed herself for Neil's car accident and it had taken many months of Neil and everyone else telling her otherwise before she could try to move on and blame Nathan entirely,

"Hey, now that's all done with, we're not going there okay, especially today!"

Ava nods and smiles, "I know, I'm sorry." Clearing her throat, she shakes her head as if to get rid of the images in her head. "Right, you ready? I think it might be time to leave."

Glancing at the clock Eveline nods, "Ready." Both women walk towards the door of the 'brides' room in the Daydream. Ava re-jigged some of the rooms in the club so she could make a spare room for this very reason. Taking a deep breath, they open the door and walk out.

****

Jack is standing on the first of the three steps that Ava had organised with candles the day before, with Neil who is his best man beside him. Neil is trying to calm his best friend down as much as possible, but it doesn't seem to be working, so he has resorted to laughing at him instead.

"Seriously stop sniggering!" Jack growls quietly so none of the other guests can hear him,

"Sorry I am trying, honest, but if you check your watch one more time I will take it from you."

Jack glowers at his friend again, trying to be angry at him, but knowing he can't be. They have been through so much together before Ava came into their lives and since. Now that all the dust has settled, Neil has given Jack a bigger share in the business and told everyone, including his father, that he is the owner of the club, and to everyone's surprise his father never came near, though they knew he had been in contact with Nathan during the weeks of his onslaught of abuse against Neil and Ava, but they have heard that his father had refused to help, if it was due to some guilt on his father's side Neil didn't know or care, both men were out of his life for good.

"You know she's in that wee room that Ava made over for today, so she's not going to stand you up, and her da's right there waiting on them finishing whatever it is they're doing in there. So calm down and enjoy the day."

Knowing his friend was right Jack takes a deep breath and physically drops his shoulders, "Aye I know, but let's see how nervous you are when it's your chance!"

Before Neil can answer his friend, they hear the door behind them open and then the music that Eveline has picked to walk down the aisle to, start.

Jack looks at Neil again, "Thanks for being here mate, wouldn't want anyone else!"

Neil has to swallow round the lump of emotion that has lodged itself in his throat so he can answer, "Anytime Pal." He playfully punches Jack's arm, before both men turn round to see the bride glide down the aisle on her dad's arm and her maid of honour right behind her. Both men glance at each other and smile.

****

Nathan now knows how brutal prison can be when you've messed bad people around on the outside and then you find out they have friends on the inside. For the first month Ross just messed with his mind, smiling at him in his weird knowing smile, staring at him, letting him know what was going to happen to him, Nathan thought he was bluffing to start with, then he would change his mind and think that maybe he wasn't. Nathan was always second-guessing Ross and himself until he thought he was going to lose his mind. Then, when Ross saw that Nathan was jumping at his own shadow, he spent the next month doing nothing, staying away from Nathan, not even looking at him, then the next again month it started again, only this time the looks were followed by a quick dig in the ribs when they passed each other, or if they were standing together in the dinner queue. Sometimes contraband would turn up in his cell at the same time as a cell check. Eventually the beatings started. Nathan had never felt pain like it in his life. He spent two weeks in the infirmary afterwards. Once he was back in his cell it would all start again, the mind games, the contraband, then more beatings. Nathan knew there was nothing he could do about it, and, if anything, it would get worse if he tried. He is also due back at court for the trial against his business, his bribes, his dodgy materials and his lack of planning permission. There was also talk of a civil case against him as a child was badly hurt when one of the kitchens he had 'salvaged' from another property fell on her. Thankfully, there was no lasting physical damage to the child, once her broken bones healed, but her parents were still suing him for damages.

Nathan may have been stubborn and stupid not to have had a lawyer at his first trial, but not this time, this time he was going to keep his mouth shut and his head down, he needed the best outcome possible and the least sentence possible. Sitting in his cell in the dead of night, he thinks back to how his life unravelled in front of his eyes. It still all came back to Ava, but now instead of blaming her, Nathan has come to realise that it was him, all him. Yes Ava left him and yes she started the police investigation, but only because he thought he could get away with anything and everything because of his money, and now he has nothing, no money, no business, no house, no friends, no Ava, nothing. Maybe Ava was right, Nathan thinks to himself, maybe money is the root of all evil, smirking to himself he realises that that is not a problem he has now.

****

The wedding is in full swing and the drinks are flowing freely, Ava pauses for a second looking about her. She knows in herself she is not the same woman that walked through the doors that chilly September night over a year ago and she will never be that woman again. She has grown, gained inner strength, confidence, a voice and some other skills along the way. Never again will a man rule her life, but she knows that is not something she has to worry about with Neil. He was the one who showed her how strong and beautiful she really is. He believed in her when she couldn't believe in herself and he stood by her when others would have walked, or even ran screaming in the other direction, no, Ava knew she would be safe and loved with Neil and if not then her new big brother, Jack, would have something to say about it!

She sees Neil making his way over to her through the packed room, looking every bit the handsome club owner. They had worn kilts for the wedding, but Neil has since changed into his signature black jeans and T-shirt, not very weddingly, but sexy all the same.

Wrapping her in his arms Neil nibbles her neck, "You

okay Sweet? You're looking a bit overwhelmed."

Ava sighs, loving the feelings he is unleashing on her body with his tongue on her neck, "Yeah, just pausing to appreciate life."

"Mmmm, I've been thinking the same. You need to grab what you can from life and enjoy it." Both of them are swaying together as if they had their very own music, neither of them aware of anybody else around them.

"Very true."

They stay swaying together, not talking, in their own world until Neil breaks the silence, "Ava, can we be next?"

She squints at him, not understanding his meaning, "Next for what?"

Neil pulls back so he can look at her, "This wedding stuff, can we be next to do this."

Ava looks shocked, but smiles, "Is that what you call a proposal?"

"Will I try again?"

Ava nods, "Yes, I would!"

Neil smiles, "Okay, Ava, I would be the happiest man ever if you would say yes and marry me?" Neil's heart misses a beat as he waits for her answer.

"Yes, yes and yes. Of course I'll marry you."

Neil lifts Ava up and twirls her around, sliding her down his front, he kisses her deeply. "I love you Sweet, and I will love you forever."

Ava smiles at him, "Forever."